Debbie Dayla

and Other Stories

BY
K GERARD MARTIN

Shouldercat Books

ISBN 978-1-935816-05-8

Published by Shouldercat Books

2015.0510.A

Contents

Introduction

Debbie Dayla and Other Stories is a collection of fictional stories, most of which tie in with the main character and her adventures, Debbie Dayla. Debbie is the daughter of Roger Dayla, the CEO of Dayla Industries which produces all sorts of advanced high-tech products. The company is based in Brunswick, Georgia, which is on the coast of the Atlantic Ocean. Debbie befriends a dusky dolphin named Sparfy, who himself is from a seamount in the South Atlantic. Stories about Debbie focus on her time both in Brunswick, how she meets Sparfy, and the challenges the two face in the South Atlantic.

Most of the stories presented here are the result of mixing dreams from sleep with extraneous thoughts. Some, such as *Trechopagia*, have factual elements buried in them (there really was a storm in Kenosha on June 30, 2011 that knocked down trees). Others have more direct roots from dreams, often influenced themselves by some random bit of new experience the prior day.

The origins for a story about Sparfy and his dusky dolphins go back to May of 2011, when I was thinking about a new story with dolphins. Given my interest in things black and white (or close to black and white), I searched the internet for images of black and white cetaceans. Besides coming across the formidable orca, I also found rather interesting images of dusky dolphins. Researching their habitats, I found reference to several sites around the world in the southern hemisphere, including Australia, New Zealand, South America, South Africa, the Indian Ocean, and the South Atlantic. The next challenge was to pick one of these areas and find a point of interest upon which I could build a story. Looking at the South Atlantic and focusing on Tristan da Cunha and Gough Island, I realized there were a large number of seamounts in the area, and so the idea of dolphins living in seamounts was born. I named the region *Lagenora*.

Debbie Dayla at first was the spoiled, only child of Roger Dayla, but that concept soon split into two daughters—Connie as the spoiled elder child, and Debbie as the shy and follower type. This allowed me to create a secret life about Debbie that her family would not suspect.

These thoughts and concepts built slowly over a year until in July of 2012 I began actively writing her story and related stories. Many of the related stories are completely independent except for an incidental tie-in with Debbie Dayla, which I added for overall continuity.

I had a small setback on April 11, 2012 at 1:41pm when I suffered a head-on collision with another automobile. I had bruises on my hip where the seat belt held me, but with no airbag deployed, my head hit the middle of the steering wheel, and so I suffered a concussion. I felt emotionally flat for six months after that injury, had a loss of analytical ability, and my ability to perceive motion was greatly reduced. My motivation for writing declined.

In September of 2012, I stopped working on the Debbie Dayla stories to focus on a non-fiction book. I researched the field of interest from that time to December of 2012, taking notes along the way, and then worked on the book itself until July of 2013. But I had had many dreams in that time and wanted to get those into stories, and so I set the non-fiction project aside and resumed the Debbie Dayla stories, completing them in May of 2015.

Without further delay, we begin with Debbie Dayla, her family, and her friends in *The Aimless and the Atlantic.*

The Aimless and the Atlantic

Connie's Graduation

It was a warm Saturday morning in Brunswick, Georgia, being May 7, 2011. Debbie Dayla awoke to her first full day as a high-school graduate of Elbart Academy, the school founded by Walter Elbart, the grandfather of Julie Elbart. Debbie had hoped that graduation would finally give some meaning and purpose to her life, but it didn't. She stepped out of bed and stood in front of her full-length vanity mirror.

"Who am I?" she asked herself. "Debra Jo Dayla. But who am I really?"

She had short, reddish-brown hair, a feature she acquired from her father, Roger Dayla. She had an unusually young-looking face for a girl with parents of European descent. It was round and featureless, like a toy doll, and her eyes resembled half-rounded circles.

"Like a sunset," she said, looking at her eyes. "My eyes don't look like Mommy's or Daddy's or Connie's eyes."

Roger Dayla married Julie Elbart, and together they formed a family with girls Connie Dayla, who was 22 years old, and Debbie Dayla, who was 18. Constance Leeann Dayla, or Connie as everyone called her, was Debbie's older sister. While the day before (Friday) was Debbie's special day, today was Connie's, as she was graduating from Varcher University.

"I want to get an early start," Connie's voice echoed through the house. "Debbie, are you ready yet? There's a class breakfast on campus."

"I'm getting dressed," Debbie yelled back.

Debbie normally didn't yell, but she saw something that caught her eye. It was a five-petaled leaf, vaguely resembling a maple leaf, but the petals were narrow and more like claws. Monkshood. A cold shiver bounced up and down her spine, as if she should recognize what the leaf meant.

"I shouldn't touch it, but I should be rid of it," she whispered.

Debbie took the leaf in a tissue, opened her window, and dropped the leaf outside. She closed her window just as Connie opened her bedroom door. Debbie turned around with a start, as if she'd been caught doing something naughty.

"What are you doing by the window again?" Connie asked, seeing Debbie in her night clothes. "I thought you were getting dressed. C'mon, I've got Vicia and Ramona waiting for me, plus my other university classmates. Well? Here, let me help."

Debbie was a passive person when it came to relationships with others, unlike Connie who actively sought new relationships. Connie's best friends were Ramona Beckusa Bronc and Vicia Ixen Sniar. Ramona grew up under the strict and proper home of her father the county sheriff and her mother the principal of Elbart Academy. Vicia, however, grew up under the wealth and depravity of her father who owned and operated Sniar Oilfield Service (a company that exploited the environment on the backs of abused workers), and her mother who was a fashion model, Vegas showgirl, and all-around alcohol-abusing party woman.

But back to Debbie. It was quite the morning routine for Connie to pick Debbie's clothes and help Debbie dress. Debbie wasn't mentally handicapped, at least not according to any doctors of medicine. She simply had no reason to take initiative in any given situation with people in the waking day.

Connie finished dressing Debbie and escorted her downstairs to a waiting Julie and Roger Dayla. Julie patted Debbie on the shoulder while Roger kissed Debbie on her forehead.

"How's my special daughter?" Roger asked Debbie while he escorted her outside to the family BMW X5M automotive sports utility vehicle.

"I want to drive," Connie said to Roger, and Roger handed her the keys.

Connie jumped into the driver's seat while her mother accompanied her in the front passenger seat. Roger, still doting on his younger daughter, sat with Debbie in the back seat.

"Take it easy, Connie, this is a turbo," Julie said as Connie whipped the BMW out of the driveway.

Scared, Debbie pushed her head into her father's shoulder and side-hugged him.

"It's all right," Roger reassured Debbie. "Connie is a very competent driver—when she exercises *discipline* and *restraint*."

But then Roger tapped on Connie's shoulder to tell her to slow down.

"Oh, don't get *snealy* with me," Connie said, using a nonsensical word she picked up from her friendship with Ramona Bronc.

"Snealy," Debbie repeated like a parrot.

"Snealy snonk," Connie said.

"Snealy snonk," Debbie repeated.

"Snonkadiliac," Connie said.

"Snonka...diliac," Debbie repeated, pulling out of her fear.

"Snonka smonna smooth snia sa maui snow smoolavator!" Connie said.

"Smoolavator!" Debbie replied playfully.

Debbie released her clutch of Roger with a smile on her face.

"There, see? All better," Connie said.

Then Debbie repeated made-up words starting with "sn" and "sm" again and again, whispering them quietly as Connie led the family-filled BMW to Varcher University. Debbie still had the silly words floating around in her mind when Ramona Bronc and Vicia Sniar greeted Connie in the university's cafeteria, where the smell of eggs and bacon filled the air.

"And a *smonderful* hello to you, Debbie," Ramona said.

"Smonderful," Debbie said.

"Oh hello, Professor Monfri, how are you?" Julie Dayla asked.

"Puzzled again," the professor said. "More coyotes are turning up poisoned. I know the coyote populate is a problem to humans, but this is—"

"There wouldn't be a coyote problem if everyone put their trash on the curb in a secure Dayla Industries garbage canister," Roger said.

Roger and Julie Dayla walked with Professor Monfri to one side of the galley while Debbie accompanied her sister and her sister's friends.

"So is everything set for tonight?" Connie asked.

"The party? Of course," Vicia said.

"Debbie's coming too," Connie said. "It's time she had a coming out party."

"There'll be a lot of cute guys there," Vicia said. "All the guys from Seaside Student Apartments."

"That's because the party is *at* Seaside Student Apartments," Ramona said. "Everyone there is twenty-one or older, so everything is legal, except for this issue with Debbie's age. Are you sure—"

"For once you should just let loose and get drunk, Ramona," Vicia said.

"I can see the headlines," Connie said. "*Sheriff's Daughter is Drunk.*"

"*Sheriff's Daughter Pulls Drunk Friends off the Pavement*," Ramona replied.

"*Sheriff's Daughter is Smunking Drunk, Smooging All Over Like a Smoiky Smonko Bronc!*" Connie said.

"Smonko Bronc," Debbie repeated, and the others laughed.

"She's going to be a hit at the party," Vicia bragged. "She might even teach you a thing or two, Smonko Bronc."

"Smonko Bronc," Debbie said, and the girls laughed again.

"Has she had beer before?" Vicia asked.

"I don't think so, have you Deb?" Connie said.

"No, never," Debbie replied, but something deep down said she had, even though she was sure she hadn't.

"Well now's the time!" Vicia said. "We'll start with a game of quarters!"

"I can hardly wait," Connie said. "And I bet Deb can beat you both in quarters. She has skills."

"What kind of skills?" Vicia asked.

"Deb?" Connie coached.

"I like to do needlecraft and embroidery," Debbie said.

Vicia and Ramona laughed.

"She has *skills* all right," Ramona chuckled.

"She can acquire new ones," Vicia said. "We'll teach her."

"Teach me what?" Debbie asked.

"Everything you need to know!" Vicia said with a slithering smile.

Debbie's attention drifted. She turned away from the three girls and looked for her parents. They continued speaking with Professor Monfri, who drew figures in the air with his hands. Debbie thought the professor looked familiar somehow, like an uncle or distant elder relative. He had prominent facial features, like that of a king. Debbie wondered if he was from the Middle East, or India, or Latin America, or Greece. Perhaps he had the blood of a pharaoh of the Nile, a sheikh of Arabia, a Native American chief, or an emperor of Rome. She felt she knew him, but she couldn't place where or how.

"Who is he really?" Debbie asked. "And who am I?"

Debbie made motions in the air with her hands and arms, mimicking Professor Monfri. Then a hush fell around her. Debbie looked at the girls, who had been watching Debbie intently, and they suddenly broke out into raucous laughter as they parodied Debbie's hand and arm motions.

"I can fly, I can fly!" Vicia said while flapping her arms as if they were wings.

"Look at me! I'm smoove and smarvey. I can smile and smave all sday and all snight," Ramona said as she motioned her arms.

"All snight is all right!" Debbie said without thinking.

Debbie lost track of time. The morning progressed, and soon Debbie was watching her elder sister and her friends receive their graduation diplomas.

"Ramona Beckusa Bronc," was announced, and Ramona was the first of the three girls to walk across the stage and receive her diploma.

"Constance Leeann Dayla," was called after several students in between, and then a long wait transpired.

And a wait, and a wait.

Debbie fell into daydream. She imagined flying above the trees, circling and looping and looking down on the ground from above. She was an eagle or hawk, she wasn't sure, but she called out to the world, to let all know of her presence and dominance over creatures bound to the ground. And in her beak she held a blue Monkshood flower, a flower destined for something below. She dove for her prey, a prey she would kill but not eat. Something was alarming about this, but she could not stop. Something...

Connie's Birthday Present

A cellphone rang, bringing Debbie back to full awareness. She was seated at a table in a restaurant with her parents, with Connie, and with Ramona. The cellphone belonged to Roger, and he was in nervous discussion with Robert Sniar, Vicia's father.

"We can't afford additional delay," Roger said. "We must extract high-test crude from the seamount before the end of the month." Pause. "Yeah, but the contract with our vendors is coming due."

Roger held silent while a voice on the other end of the cellphone spoke frantically.

"And today's my birthday!" Connie interrupted, despite Roger's tense situation.

Debbie looked at her mouse-decorated watch and realized it was now 12:30 pm. The family of four and Ramona were just finishing up lunch at The Four Leaf Clover, a sophisticated restaurant for the wealthy. Lunch! How did Debbie get from graduation to lunch and eating without being aware of her surroundings? Roger tried motioning Connie to be quiet, but she became outraged at being stifled.

"I SAID IT'S MY BIRTHDAY!!!" she yelled.

"I'll call you back," Roger said, and he ended the call, but before he put the cellphone away, he placed another call and said, "Garwood. The Four Leaf Clover. Immediately!" and he hung up.

Roger motioned to the waiter, and within seconds, a birthday cake was brought forth by a pastry cook. The other waiters and staff lined up, and as the cake was placed at the Dayla table, the staff sang Happy Birthday. In the time it took for the song to complete, Garwood Harvington, the Daylas' butler, arrived by helicopter and entered The Four Leaf Clover, where he took his place by Roger and stood.

"I must leave you briefly, my sweet," Roger said.

"But Daddy! How could you abandon me like this!" Connie cried like a brat.

"I have a special gift for you, but unfortunately I have an emergency to attend," Roger explained. "Garwood will present my gift. I will rejoin you when I can. Congratulations again, and happy birthday!"

Roger exited the restaurant and left by the same helicopter in which Garwood arrived. Connie felt herself burst into a shriek.

"Hey, don't *smarf* the small stuff," Ramona said. "My dad is never around for my birthday. He didn't even show up for my graduation. Something about a pileup on the expressway. Yeah, there's always a pileup somewhere."

"Connie, please," Julie said. "Garwood is here to give you your present. A special present."

"My present?! O gimme-gimme-gimme-gimme-gimme!" Connie said. "Did you bring me the special present? I want to see it. I want to see it now!"

"It was too big to bring with me," Garwood said.

"Oh, Garwood!" Connie exclaimed, and she jumped up and hugged him. "Daddy didn't!"

"Oh, he did," Julie lamented.

"Where is it, Garwood? Where's my gift? I must see! Garwood? Show me!" Connie said.

"Your gift is at the estate," Garwood said. "It was being prepared while you graduated. And so we must return."

"Then let's go. I'll put the pedal to the metal and send the turbos chiming like church bells," Connie said.

"I, uh, ahem," Garwood said, and then he turned to Julie. "Madam, if you please."

Garwood passed a blindfold to Julie.

"First, you must wear this," Julie said, and she placed a blindfold over Connie's eyes.

"I can't drive with this!" Connie said.

"This is a surprise gift," Julie said. "A big surprise, and not just for you. Garwood will drive. Don't you worry."

"Oh, I love surprises!" Connie said as she adjusted both the blindfold and her mood. "This is going to be the best birthday ever. Ramona, you can squeeze in the back of the Bimmer, can't you?"

"I'll just follow in my convertible," Ramona said.

In this way then, Garwood held Connie's arm and led her from the restaurant to the BMW X5M, where he first helped Connie, and then Julie, and finally Debbie into the vehicle. He even offered to help Ramona in her convertible.

"Thank you no, Garwood. My dad says I need to be independent," Ramona said.

"As you wish," Garwood replied, and he returned to the X5M and drove it to the Dayla estate. The BMW arrived, with Ramona in her convertible, and the troop grouped around something in the driveway underneath a tarp. Garwood pulled the tarp away, and all gasped except for Connie, who was still blindfolded.

"Oh, you are so lucky!" Ramona said.

"What, what!!!" Connie said. "I can't see a thing."

"It's shiny," Debbie said.

"Because it's brand new," Julie said.

"If you don't like it, I'll take it!" Ramona said.

"Are you ready?" Julie asked her daughter.

"Yes, yes, yes! I've been ready for too long!" Connie said.

"Are you sure?" Julie asked.

"I'm sure, I'm sure!" she said. "Let me see, let me see...now!"

Connie could not wait for help, and she ripped the blindfold from her eyes.

"It's a...car," Connie said unenthusiastically.

"It's a black, BMW M6 convertible, V10 engine, with 500 horsepower," Garwood said.

"Happy birthday, sugar!" Julie said.

Julie kissed Connie lightly on the cheek. Connie cried.

"I hate it!" she yelled.

"Sugar, no, you don't hate it!" Julie said.

"I hate it, I hate it, I hate it! It's black, it's ugly, and it's a BMW!" she wailed.

"Yes, it's a powerful BMW. You always want powerful things," Garwood said.

"But a BMW?" she protested. "That's what Daddy drives. That's what executives drive!"

"I don't understand," Julie said. "You were pining away to drive the X5M this morning."

"That was different," Connie said. "That was Daddy's! And that's not all. I've always had white things: my white titanium tricycle when I was three, my white Kona Shred when I was five, my white Velo Scorpion when I was ten, my white Yamaha YZ125 when I was thirteen, and my white Jeep Wrangler when I was fifteen—everything white. White, WHITE, WHITE!"

"The official word from your father is as follows: You're a Dayla. It's time you prepare yourself for the business world. And that means driving a BMW," Garwood explained.

"No, no, no, no!" she screamed, and she stomped her feet, and she turned around, and she threw the blindfold at the new BMW. And! she ran into the house.

"Sugar, wait!" Julie called.

Julie ran into the house after her daughter. Garwood pressed a few buttons on his smartphone, and the chauffeur arrived and took the BMW to a garage on a remote part of the estate.

"Sugar maple, please," Julie said as she entered Connie's bedroom.

Connie cried in her pillow.

"He ruined my birthday," she cried without looking back. "And he ruined my graduation. I hate him. I hate him forever."

"Just drive it and see what you think," Julie said. "He can exchange it for another BMW if you don't like this one."

"I don't want a BMW. BMWs are for business people and stuffed shirts. I'm not a stuffed shirt. I'm Connie."

"You can't even drive it around the estate? Not even once?" Julie asked.

But Connie wouldn't reply. She continued sobbing in her pillow.

"Well, I don't know why I try. I told your father this was a bad idea," Julie said. "It seems he spoils you too much with gifts. He's taught you to hate what normal people would kill for."

"What do you mean by *normal people*? We *are* normal people," Connie said. "And I'm *not* spoiled. Vicia Sniar gets anything she wants. And I get a BMW."

"She demands anything she wants without concern for consequences," Julie said. "But your father has a business arrangement with the Sniars, and we cannot ignore that."

"Consequences," Connie sneered. "That's one of those ancient words."

Julie shot Connie a funny expression then turned away and paced a bit back and forth, searching her mind for a solution to the birthday dilemma. Finally, she retrieved her phone, pressed a button, and held it to her ear.

"Garwood. Prepare the gift for return. Yes, immediately," Julie said. "I know he did. This just won't work."

"What are you...what is Garwood going to do?" Connie asked.

"I will have Garwood take the M6 back," Julie said.

"And that's it?" Connie asked. "No apologies, no nothing. Just spit on Connie."

A knock sounded on Connie's door.

"Go away!" Connie yelled.

"Begging your pardon," said Garwood's voice through the door. "I have a message from Mr. Dayla. He, uh, asked about the gift and its reception."

"Yeah? Shove the gift!" Connie yelled through the door. "Shove it!"

"Please, Connie, remember your manners," Julie said, and she opened the door.

"Thank you, ma'am," Garwood said.

"What is the message?" Julie asked.

"I relayed the less than desired appreciation for...for...Miss Connie is to go downstairs. I am to accompany her on a road trip to a car dealership, where she will be provided another vehicle as her gift. No exceptions."

"No!" Connie said defiantly.

"No exceptions," Garwood repeated.

"No!" Connie repeated.

"NO exceptions," Garwood stressed.

"I think you'd better go," Julie said to Connie. "Your father is in one of his moods."

"And what about me? What becomes of Connie? Doesn't anyone care? I'm being dragged into this against my will," Connie said.

"Aren't you the one who majored in Business? The heir to Dayla Industries? Well?" Julie said.

"I can't believe you just said that," Connie said.

"Neither can I. But one way or another, you need to get through this," Julie said.

Julie took a tissue and dried Connie's tears. Connie looked up and took a deep breath.

"Okay. I'll hate it. But I'll go," Connie said.

"Good. And try to pick something you like. Don't pick something you hate to spite your father," Julie said.

"You know me too well," Connie said.

Garwood accompanied Connie downstairs, where the chauffeur had just parked one of the family cars—Roger's BMW 760Li with the 535 horsepower V12 engine purring away.

"I know you too well," Julie said to herself, now alone, "because that's what I would have done in your shoes. And yet, I don't know who's more stubborn or spoiled, you or my husband."

Garwood escorted Connie into the passenger seat, and he nodded to the chauffeur as if to say, "I'll take over."

"You'd better let me ride along," Ramona said. "Looks like Connie needs *smriendly snapport.*"

Garwood opened the back door for Ramona, but she took the door, closed it, opened it, and then climbed inside.

"Independent," she whispered.

Garwood entered the driver's side, closed the door, and engaged the car forward.

"So don't I get a say, Garwood?" Connie asked.

Garwood drove the BMW from the estate and onto public roads without reply. The car's phone rang. Garwood pressed a button, and Roger's voice sounded through the car's audio system.

"Now sugar sweet, I want you to be good and go to the car dealership with Garwood," Roger said.

"Why are you doing this to me, Daddy? Why?" Connie asked.

"I want you to pick your birthday present," Roger said.

"What!?" Connie exclaimed.

"Maybe it was the color. Maybe it was—" Roger started.

"I'm going to pick the real present!" Connie exclaimed. "Oh Father, you made a mistake, but now you're making good. You want me to pick out my own white car, like I did with the Jeep!"

"Well, uh, yes, uh...I just want you to know that I love you, and I want the best for you," Roger said.

"I knew it!" Connie said. "You're the best Daddy in the world!"

Connie blew a kiss into the dashboard. She said her goodbye to Roger, and the phone call ended. Garwood drove onto a highway and then took a left, a right, and another right to a row of car dealerships, one after another, and all competing to sell one more car than the other dealer. The three passed the domestic car lots, then the Asian car lots, and beyond that were the European cars, including BMW.

"Why are we pulling in here?" Connie asked Garwood as he entered the Bnatta BMW parking lot.

"Just for a moment," Garwood said. "I need to sign the papers to return the M6. Then we'll pick your car."

Garwood parked in front of the dealership, and he escorted Connie and Ramona inside.

"Mr. Harvington and Miss Dayla," said the owner of the dealership. "And who is this lovely lady?"

"I'm Ramona Bronc."

"I've heard that name before," Mr. Bnatta said.

"Her father is Sheriff Bronc, Mr. Bnatta," Garwood said.

"Oh," Mr. Bnatta said in disdain, and he lowered his voice and said, "Stone walls and concrete."

"What was that?!" Ramona asked. "You look familiar, Mr. Bnatta."

"No, not me," he perspired.

"Someone sold flooded cruisers to my father's department. And that someone spent a little time staring at stone walls and concrete. Someone selling different models from a different manufacturer, I believe, under the guise of top-quality products," Ramona said.

"I, ah, only sell BMWs," he said.

"I think that's wise," Ramona said.

"How may I be of service?" Mr. Bnatta said quickly to change the subject.

"Yes, well, we are here about the M6," Garwood said.

"I trust the little surprise went well?" Mr. Bnatta asked.

"It did not!" Connie protested.

Mr. Bnatta backed up a step or two in surprise.

"Eh...Miss Dayla has a fondness for white things," Garwood said. "Mr. Dayla sends his apologies. He selected a black M6 for her. She would like a white automobile."

"Of course, we have many white BMWs of all models here at Bnatta BMW," Mr. Bnatta said.

"No, I don't want a BMW," Connie said. "Garwood!"

"Your father's orders, I'm afraid," Garwood replied.

"Daddy tricked me," Connie cringed.

Connie called Roger on her cellphone and complained about his deceit.

"Now please, my sweet sugar maple, you are there after all. Just look around and see what you think," Roger said through her cellphone.

"No. I don't want a BMW. I don't, DON'T, DON'T!" Connie protested, and she threw her cellphone into a glass window, breaking both.

A few customers looked in Connie's direction with angst expressions on their faces. Mr. Bnatta was quick to usher Connie and Garwood outside and into the back lot. Ramona rolled her eyes and then chased after them.

"Perhaps you'd like something sporty and compact," Mr. Bnatta said. "We have a lovely Zee series."

"No," Connie said.

The three and Ramona walked toward the edge of the lot, with Connie saying, "No," to everything suggested.

"What if I have Mr. Bnatta remove all BMW logos and place whatever logo you like on the automobile of your choice?" Garwood asked Connie.

"Humph. Like that'll ever happen," Connie said.

"How much work is that, Mr. Bnatta?" Garwood asked.

Mr. Bnatta and Garwood conversed back and forth on the various ways of making subtle changes to a BMW to hide the fact it was a BMW. Mr. Bnatta argued that a BMW could not be hidden—even changing emblems could not alter the indigenous BMW style. Garwood suggested that Roger would offer great sums of money to convert, reshape—anything to find a way to convince his daughter to drive a BMW.

But Connie wasn't interested. She stood at the edge of the lot with her back to Garwood and Mr. Bnatta. She stared at the neighboring lot.

"Alpine Audi," she whispered to herself as she read the main sign. "What kind of white cars might they have?"

"Sm—All kinds," Ramona said, now joining her.

Connie did not realize it, but Garwood and Mr. Bnatta had become so engrossed in discussion with each other—pointing at this car or that car— that their positions now drifted from Connie's and Ramona's, and in time they were far enough down the lot that they could not and did not notice what the girls were doing.

"We do have white cars," said a young woman standing in the Audi lot.

"I...do I know you? You sound familiar," Connie said.

Ramona was about to speak, but she bit her lip and suppressed a smile.

The woman had a big hairdo with curls flying every which way and into her face, with only parts of large sunglasses peering through the hair. She wore a blazer and skirt combination that was fit for an executive office environment, and she wore white fancy gloves.

"Over here," the woman said as she motioned her hand to Connie.

Ramona followed as Connie stepped over the low chain connecting one post to another, separating the BMW lot from the Audi lot. She looked back at Garwood, but he was still engrossed in conversation with Mr. Bnatta.

"I'm Miss Vetch," the young woman said.

"I'm Connie Dayla," Connie said. "And that's my butler over there with Mr. Bnatta."

"You're Connie Dayla of Dayla Industries," Miss Vetch said.

"Yeah, that's me," Connie said. "Today's my birthday, and Daddy was supposed to get me a white car, but he got me a black BMW. I hate BMW!"

"Happy birthday! We have lots of white Audis here," Miss Vetch said. "Do you have a preference?"

"A convertible," Connie said. "With lots of power. But I don't want it looking like a guy car or something from a race track."

"I know just the car for you," Miss Vetch said. "This way."

Ramona again followed as Miss Vetch led Connie to the middle of the lot, where at the center of a grassy circle rested the most beautiful car Connie had ever seen.

"Official Pace Car," Connie said. "Does that mean—"

"Yes," Miss Vetch said. "This car was driven once—as the pace car in last week's Brunswick 500. It's an Audi S5 convertible, as you can see, but what you don't see is the engine, which was taken from an Audi R8, a 4.2 litre, supercharged V8 with 550 horsepower."

"That's more than the V10," Connie said.

Miss Vetch looked at Connie funny.

"Sorry, the BMW M6. That was the car Daddy wanted to give me as a birthday present this morning," Connie said.

"Well, you can tell him you like this car," Miss Vetch said. "Would you like to test drive it?"

"Would I? Yeah! Yes! I do, I do, I do! Gimme the key!" Connie said in anticipation.

Miss Vetch disappeared for a moment into the Audi dealership building.

"Ironic that you don't want a car from a racetrack, yet this pace car—" Ramona started, but without warning, Miss Vetch ran out, holding a key fob.

"How did you—" Ramona started to say, but Miss Vetch shushed her.

"You like exciting cars?" Miss Vetch said as she approached Connie.

"Yeah," Connie said.

"Then you drive. And hurry!" Miss Vetch replied as she threw the key fob to Connie and jumped into the front passenger seat.

Connie caught the key fob and jumped into the driver's seat. She pushed the fob into the dash, held it briefly, and the car's engine came to life.

"It makes a beautiful sound," Connie said as she revved the engine in neutral. She then turned toward Ramona and said, "C'mon, get in!"

"Connie, there's something you should know. This—" Ramona started.

"Don't waste time," Miss Vetch said. "Let's go on that test drive."

Miss Vetch pulled Ramona into the back seat, turned back around to Connie, and said, "Now!"

"You have less patience than I do," Connie giggled. "Okay."

Connie engaged the transmission, and the Audi leapt forward.

"Wow, it *does* have a lot of power!" Connie said.

"Hurry onto the road," Miss Vetch said.

Connie did just that. She drove through Alpine Audi's parking lot quickly and reached the entrance to the highway. Several people ran from the dealership building toward the three, yelling all the way.

"Are they yelling at us?" Connie asked.

"Uh...they're cheering you on," Miss Vetch said. "Show me what you can do in this Audi."

"All right," Connie said.

Connie hit the gas and entered the highway quickly. The all-wheel drive car gripped the road willingly and gracefully, leaving Connie little room to play with fishtailing as she might have in a rear-wheel drive car of older make. All wheels, all acceleration, and the nimblest steering of any vehicle Connie had ever experienced.

"Wow, this is fun!" Connie said.

"Get on the expressway right there," Miss Vetch said. "Show me what you've got."

"Hold onto your hairdo," Connie said, and she hit the gas and sent the Audi up to a hundred miles per hour with no effort, and beyond.

"I'm going too fast," Connie said at a hundred and twenty.

"And it's windy back here," Ramona said.

"Nah. Push her, she can handle it," Miss Vetch said, who was indeed holding onto her hair and sunglasses.

"The wind is pulling my face apart," Ramona said from the back. "And my hair. I'll go bald at this rate!"

"Go faster," Miss Vetch said, but as she did, a Georgia State Patrol officer appeared distantly in the rear mirror with its lights strobing.

"Uh oh," Connie said. "There's a *smokey* behind us."

"You can lose him," Miss Vetch said. "Quick—get off at this exit."

Connie did, but the patrol followed behind, so she reentered the interstate, but in doing so, she attracted the attention of another Georgia State Patrol officer.

"Two smokeys behind us!" Connie said. "I should pull over."

"Don't *feed the bears*!" Miss Vetch said, meaning that they should not submit to paying for a ticket.

"I'll just tell them this is your car," Connie said.

"When are you going to tell her the truth?" Ramona asked Miss Vetch.

"Ramona!" Miss Vetch slipped.

"How did you know her name?" Connie asked Miss Vetch.

In that moment, the wind pulled the wig and sunglasses from Miss Vetch's head, revealing another person.

"Vicia Sniar!" Connie exclaimed, and she nearly lost control of the Audi in the excitement.

"Connie Dayla!" Vicia said.

"You...you...you tricked me!" Connie said.

"I know. It's great, ain't it?" Vicia smirked. "It was all I could do to keep Ramona from spoiling it."

"And that meant a lot of tongue biting," Ramona said.

"When did you know, Ramona?" Connie asked.

"Instantly," Ramona said. "But Viss...how did you get the key fob to this car?"

Vicia smirked again.

"You stole it? Oh no!" Ramona said, and as she did so, two additional patrols slowed from ahead and attempted to box in the Audi. "Why me? Why?"

"You're in so much trouble for stealing this car," Connie said.

"No, *you* stole this car. *You* are in trouble!" Vicia sneered.

"I should push you out of this car right now!" Connie said.

"Then do it! You and your dad can't get your butt out of this one!" Vicia mocked.

Connie exited the interstate and returned to the highway where Alpine Audi and Bnatta BMW were located, only Connie was several miles north of both dealerships. She headed south anyway.

"Maybe I can return the car without anyone noticing," Connie said.

"They've noticed already," Vicia said. "They were yelling at you to stop."

"You said they were cheering me on," Connie said. "Another lie?"

Vicia smiled and said, "I thought you knew."

"I can't believe I fell for that. You lie about everything!" Connie yelled.

Then it happened. A local law-enforcement officer had set up a spike strip on the side of the road. He allowed innocent drivers to pass, but when the three girls approached, he pulled on his rope and thus dragged the spike strip into the road. The Audi hit the strip full force with all four tires.

"You hit a spike strip," Vicia said. "It won't be long now before you're caught."

"You'll be caught too!" Connie said.

"We all will!" Ramona yelled.

The tires ripped to shreds and flew off, leaving the Audi to navigate on its magnesium rims.

"Pull over so I can get out," Vicia said.

"No way!" Connie said. "I'm not taking all the blame."

"You can't drive on these rims!" Vicia said. "They'll...they'll..."

"We're on fire!" Ramona exclaimed.

It was true. The magnesium wheels heated and burned, sending a shower of hot sparks around the Audi. Steering the Audi was already difficult, but this was too much for Connie. She panicked and drove the Audi toward an outdoor holding tank full of ocean creatures—crabs, lobster, clams, and other things—on the business grounds of Brunswick Crab Co-op. Vicia and Ramona dove out of the Audi just before the collision, but Connie did not, and she stayed in the Audi as it landed full force into the holding tank.

The magnesium wheels caused a flashover flame around the Audi followed by a massive mushroom cloud of steam. The flames singed Connie's hair and eyebrows, but otherwise Connie was more in shock than she was injured. Spent airbags deflated and allowed her to exit the vehicle, which she did. Soaked and covered in organic ocean debris, Connie made her way through the flotsam and clear of the holding tank, stinking of ocean life.

"*Vicia* did it. *Vicia* did it!" Connie said.

But Vicia Sniar was nowhere to be found. State patrols and Brunswick police converged on Connie and arrested her. Garwood, Mr. Bnatta, and Mr. Alpine ran up to the scene, as Brunswick Crab Co-op adjoined Alpine Audi.

"Miss Connie!" Garwood said. "How unbecoming! And where is Miss Ramona Bronc?"

But Connie, who was speechless, didn't have to answer. Mr. Bnatta yelled from a short ways away. He was beside a collapsed retaining wall— collapsed on Ramona that is, who was trapped, unconscious, and bleeding. Patrols rushed to free Ramona, and they did.

"Sheriff!" one of the patrols yelled. "It's your daughter!"

Sheriff Bronc rushed over, picked up Ramona, cradled her, and carried her to his cruiser, where he rushed her off to a nearby hospital. Connie was taken away in another cruiser. Garwood followed in Roger's BMW, leaving others behind to make sense of the mess.

County Hospital

Connie was booked on a number of charges including theft, speeding, evading officers of the law, destruction of private property, and so on—all in the same day. She was taken to a "jail". Well, it wasn't quite a jail.

"It's more like a retreat," Sheriff Bronc said to his daughter, Ramona, who had just awakened from a brief coma and was recovering from a concussion in County Hospital early that same evening. "All rich children who break the law are sent there. Most kids are detoxing from booze or other drugs."

"What about Vicia? She was with us," Ramona said.

"She was with you?" Sheriff Bronc asked.

"Yes. She acquired a key fob to the Audi," Ramona said. "I don't know how the Audi dealer gave her the fob."

"I *do* know. She stole it," Sheriff Bronc said. "We'll have to pick her up. I'll put out an APB for her."

"Wait, you won't find her if you do that," Ramona said. "Somehow she knows when people are looking for her, and she evades the search."

"What do you suggest?" Sheriff Bronc asked.

"There's a party tonight," Ramona said, and she tried sitting up. "Ow!"

"Easy there," he said.

"I need to get up and move around," Ramona said, "so I can go to the party tonight."

"You're in no condition for a party," Sheriff Bronc said.

"Well if I don't go, you won't find her. Then again, maybe I shouldn't go. I'm torn between protecting my friend and...and..."

"I understand," Sheriff Bronc said.

"She doesn't mean to cause trouble. Things go too far with her. If I could smack some sense into her, she wouldn't be so sneaky," Ramona said. "So what will you do after you pick her up?"

"After a brief interview, I'll take her to the judge," he said.

"And she'll be sent to the reformatory, right?" Ramona asked.

"Most likely," Sheriff Bronc said.

"Well, she'll probably hate me forever, but then again, she's probably always had a little hatred for me," Ramona said.

"Why do you say that?"

"Because she can't fool me the way she can with her father or with Connie," Ramona explained.

Sheriff Bronc laughed.

"That's a knowing laugh," Ramona laughed back. "You're proud I am your daughter."

"You're right," Sheriff Bronc said. "But what about your injuries? They would have killed a grown man, or any ordinary person. And yet you believe you can attend a party in your condition."

"It's all because I'm not ordinary. I'm the sheriff's daughter," Ramona said.

Sheriff Bronc laughed again.

"You are," he said, and he kissed her on the forehead. "You're also a good friend to Connie and Vicia. But you are young, and young people have patience when it comes to friendship."

"What does that mean?" Ramona asked.

"Rich kids are hopeless," the sheriff said. "You can't break their obsession with entitlement. When you're young, time is limitless, but when you hit about forty, you realize time is running out. And so is patience with people."

"I know. You've told me," Ramona said. "But my friends are my friends, and they need my help."

"So you think you can reform your friends?" the sheriff asked.

"I like to think so," Ramona said.

"Just like that?" the sheriff said.

"Maybe not all at once. But they are young, as you might say. And the young are impressionable."

"You are young too," the sheriff said. "But you have the maturity of a responsible adult, much older, perhaps even—"

"A sheriff?" Ramona smiled.

Sheriff Bronc returned the smile.

"Well I'm not a rich kid," Ramona said. "I've worked for everything I have."

"Almost everything," the sheriff said. "I give you my love freely."

"Of course you do," she said, and she hugged her father.

"So do you have a plan for the party?" the sheriff asked.

"Yes. The first thing I need to do is ease Vicia's fears," Ramona said.

"And how do you plan to do that?" he asked.

"With the band."

Saturday Evening

"Debbie," Julie said in the Dayla home, "I'm going to take some things to your sister at Jekyll Island Reformatory. The—"

But Julie was interrupted by Garwood, who had just entered the room.

"Excuse me, ma'am, but Mr. Dayla states he will be leaving immediately from the office for the oil rig in the Atlantic and will be unable to return home for at least three weeks."

Julie stood there in shock for several seconds, and then she spoke:

"When...he did? But how...I mean, did he say why?" Julie asked. "I must call him and see what's going on."

"He also requests that you not call him, as he will be on a secret plane flight and will be unable to answer," Garwood said.

A wall of frustration built up in Julie, and she clenched her fists. Debbie, seeing her mother, imitated this action and clenched her own fists. Seeing Debbie imitating her actions, Julie put on her best smile and dropped all outward appearances of anger.

"Well, if you do hear from him, tell him I love him," Julie said.

"Me too," Debbie said.

"Debbie, would you go downstairs and get me some coffee?" Julie asked.

"I'll be happy to—" Garwood started, but Julie waved him off.

"Okay," Debbie said.

Once Debbie left the room, Julie spoke.

"After I drop off Connie's things, I need to run another errand," Julie said, "and I won't be back until late. Very late."

"I understand. Miss Debbie will be in very good hands. I'll have the maid look in on her from time to time," Garwood said.

"Thank you."

Debbie returned with coffee. Julie took several sips, and she spoke:

"Thank you, Debbie. Well, I must be going now."

"Tell Connie I love her," Debbie said.

"I will. I will."

Julie left the Dayla property with Connie's things and visited Connie at Jekyll Island Reformatory, but only long enough to drop off her things.

"Mom," Connie said. "I...I'm sorry. Where's Dad?"

"On a secret plane to the oil rig in the Atlantic," Julie said with sadness.

"Oh, I'm sorry," Connie said. "He'll be gone for weeks."

"Or longer," Julie said.

"Get me out of here, and we'll go bar hopping tonight. Just me and you," Connie suggested.

Julie smiled.

"A woman in my position doesn't bar hop," Julie said. "But I appreciate the offer, even if you are in no position to make it. No, Connie, a woman in my position meets with society people, and we sit around and play cards or discuss other things and do things."

"What things do you do?" Connie asked.

"Well, you'll find out when you are my age," Julie said.

Connie wasn't sure if she liked that, but she had a suspicion her mother, when in the stressful moments Roger was away, would participate in parties hosted by Mrs. Sniar and her plentiful supply of alcohol. Why? There were some mornings in the past when Julie returned home in time for breakfast, smelling like wine and having bloodshot eyes.

"Don't do those things. Please?" Connie begged.

But Julie just smiled and left.

Party of Deception

Debbie sat by her bedroom window while reading a book. A stone hit the outside of the window with a *plink*. Debbie looked out the window but saw nothing. She returned to her book. Again, a stone hit the window.

"Plink," Debbie said.

Another stone, and Debbie said plink again. Then Debbie's cellphone rang, and she answered it by saying, "Plink!"

"Open your window," said a voice on the other end of the cellphone.

Debbie ended the phone call and opened her window. Down below, the voice spoke.

"Debbie, it's me—Vicia."

"Vicia," Debbie said. "Let me see."

Debbie climbed out the window, down a tree, and landed on the ground next to an awaiting Vicia Sniar.

"Where have you been? The party has already started," Vicia said.

"The party?" Debbie asked.

"Yeah. Did you forget already?" Vicia asked.

"I don't know if I should go," Debbie said.

"You're not afraid, are you?"

"No, but my parents, they...well..." Debbie stumbled.

"Your old man is off on his secret plane," Vicia said.

"How did you know?"

"Because *my* old man asked him to, that's how I know," Vicia said. "And your mother is with *my* mother at a party of their own, and they'll be out all night. Garwood has fallen asleep, and your maid is watching a movie that she's obsessed with. So you're in the clear. No one will know you've been gone."

Debbie paused and then said, "No one will know I've been gone."

"That's right," Vicia said. "My car's right over there. Let's go!"

Vicia drove the two to a fraternity house not associated with any specific college or university. It had a secure lobby, requiring an access card to allow the front door to unlock. Vicia had such a card, borrowed from one of the residents already inside, and she swiped it across the reader. The door opened. Debbie, who walked behind Vicia, drew her fingers across the scanner. She sensed its circuitry, and she became aware of what electromagnetic code would unlock the door.

"Is this Seaside Apartments?" Debbie asked.

"The party got moved," Vicia replied. "But just by one building. Seaside Apartments is next door."

"Vicia, woo-hoo!" the young men hollered.

"Bring your friend over here," said one of the young men. "The band is just arriving, and we are going to have a big party!"

Debbie followed Vicia into a lounge area filled with sofas, chairs, ice coolers, and several television screens displaying various sporting events from around the world.

"Have a beer or two," said the young man, and he gave a can of beer to Vicia and another to Debbie.

Vicia snapped open the beer can, took several gulps, and exhaled with satisfaction. Debbie struggled to open her beer can, but she did, and she attempted to gulp her beer like Vicia, but she coughed on the taste.

"Never had beer before?" the young man asked.

"Looks like not," Vicia said.

"Hold on, I have something better," he grinned, and he returned shortly with a cold bottle, which he opened in Debbie's presence. "Try this. It's a wine cooler."

Debbie took several sips and enjoyed the taste.

"Fruity," she said.

"Fruity, yeah!" he said. "My name is Evan. Over here is Josh, Bill, Rick, and—"

"Jayvogg Hochenstock," Debbie said. "Super model and spokesman for Royal Yacht Clothing. Star quarterback and punter for the Brunswick Ogres. Set a single-season record for passing yards, completions, games with seven touchdowns or more, yards punted, yards—"

"Well, well!" Jayvogg said as he walked toward Debbie. "I have a fan, I see."

"Pleased to meet you," Debbie said with a curtsey.

"I am pleased," he replied.

"Hi," the other boys called.

Seeing his moment evaporating, Evan quickly escorted his prize to the back end of the lounge, where an empty stage echoed excitement that a band was soon on the way.

"They just arrived," Evan said. "The band that is. I know the band leader and her friends. She's got the funniest way of talking, too. She calls it *snonky* talk. She's a riot!"

"Snonky, like Ramona Bronc," Debbie said.

"You know her?" Evan asked.

"Hi, Evan. Hi, Debbie," Ramona said with equipment in both hands and leading her group in, also carrying equipment. "Excuse us. We're setting up. Snickety-quick s'like, s'lemme introduce Brian Kukovich on bass guitar, Nick Fye on keyboard, and Sassi Bryer on drums. And I'm on lead guitar."

The introductions were short-lived, because within a few moments, lights were flashing and moving in sync with Ramona's band as they played their first song.

"I didn't know you know Ramona," Evan said.

"I didn't know you know her too," Debbie said.

"Well, I guess there's a lot we don't know about each other," Evan said. "I'd like to change that. Wow, you finished your drink quickly. Another?"

"Another," Debbie repeated and replied.

Debbie looked at Sassi Bryer's drums and read, "Ramona and the Smackadeliacs."

"Here," Evan said out of breath, fearful that his "date" would be stolen from him.

"I'm here," Debbie laughed.

Evan laughed too. Ramona sang smooth vocals as she and her group played a form of music with happy, melodic tones. Evan asked Debbie to dance. She agreed, and Evan placed her drink on a side table and escorted her to the dance floor, an area close to the stage clear of any furniture. In the brief moment Debbie held Evan's hand, she sensed he was majoring in microbiology and would someday unlock the key to genetic conditions and then formulate treatments, making him a wealthy yet responsible man, one who would invest his money wisely in furthering genetic research. But Evan had to get through three more years of undergraduate school, and that meant surviving the social aspect as well. He had never had a girlfriend before, not even in high school. He had been a bit of a geek and nerd in those days, but in his first year of his university education, he came out of his closet a bit, so to speak, and he decided to socialize more.

Ramona, playing with the band, scanned the area with her eyes casually so as not to attract attention. She looked for Vicia but could not see her. As it turned out, Vicia was just around the corner from the lounge and out of view, as she was with Josh, Rick, and Jayvogg.

"You're as beautiful as ever, Vicia my sweet," Josh said, and he kissed her hand. He fell to a knee and joked, "Marry me!"

Vicia laughed from the flattery.

"Quit kidding, Josh," Rick said. "You ain't got no chance with a rich girl."

"Oh, Rick, you're so jealous," Vicia flirted. "There's enough of me for all of you."

"At a price," Jayvogg said with a knowing look. "I know you, Vicia the snake!"

Vicia hissed back.

"What's wrong, Jayvogg? Don't you know luxury when you see it?" Vicia asked.

"You forget who you're talking to," Jayvogg said. "I can take whatever I want, whenever I want. Like you. Only I don't engage in prevarication like some."

"Yeah, but you throw away every girl you ever date. How many have been found the next day in a dumpster?" Vicia blurted.

Jayvogg put one hand over her mouth, grabbed her arm with his other, and shoved her down the hallway away from all people until the two reached the end, where he slammed the back of her head against the cinder-block wall.

"Don't you ever say that about me, do you hear? Or *you'll* be in a dumpster the next day!" Jayvogg threatened.

"You're hurting me!" Vicia said. "You...you were adopted!"

"That doesn't bother me," Jayvogg said. "The Hochenstocks are very successful. Doctor Hochenstock is a well-known and beloved geologist, finding all sorts of new oil reserves around the world. Your dad would be nothing without mine."

"You...you...were pooped out in a railroad car and abandoned," Vicia managed to say.

"That *does* bother me!" Jayvogg snarled directly in front of Vicia's face.

Jayvogg, despite having an attractive appearance, had a metabolic inability to process certain proteins, resulting in a number of problems, including bad breath. Vicia struggled to turn away in hopes of avoiding the foul stench.

"I'm sorry. I'm sorry," Vicia said.

"It's too late for sorry," Jayvogg said. "You'll have to pay."

"Whatever. How much do you want?" Vicia asked.

"O no, my little beggar. Your money has no value to me. No, you must pay with something more dear," Jayvogg said.

"Okay, I'll submit to you," she said.

Jayvogg laughed.

"No, the little harlot in you would probably enjoy it."

"With that bad breath? It's a sacrifice," Vicia said.

"That's where you're wrong!" he said. "I can get anyone I want. And I will. But you must pay with something more dear than yourself. Your friend. Curtsey girl."

"No!" Vicia protested. "She's just a girl, Jayvogg."

"Those are the best kind," Jayvogg said.

"She's Debbie Dayla. Of Dayla Industries. They're proper, Jayvogg."

"Dayla Industries, the dependent child of Sniar Oilfield Service. And Sniar Oilfield Service is a dependent child of Hochenstock Geology International. I guess that makes Curtsey girl my granddaughter. Time to acquaint her."

Jayvogg tossed Vicia to the side. She fell to the floor with a grunt. Jayvogg proceeded quickly to the lounge, and it was all Vicia could do to pull herself to her feet.

"I...must...find...Debbie," Vicia said. "For once I...must stop...something awful from happening. Ugh!"

Vicia struggled to get her breath and strength back. She reentered the lounge and looked. Jayvogg was speaking with Rick and Josh, and Jayvogg pointed toward the dance floor, where Debbie was dancing with Evan. Rick and Josh each approached Debbie slowly from different flanks. Seeing this, Vicia burst through the crowd in the middle and made her way to Debbie before Rick and Josh.

"Debbie, Debbie! Please come with me! We have to go! Hurry!" Vicia pleaded while tugging on Debbie's arm.

While Debbie, Evan, and Vicia were distracted, Josh slipped a drug into Debbie's drink, which was still on the side table. Rick meanwhile snuck past the dance floor and into a small closet next to the stage, where he manipulated the lounge's audio system.

"Something's wrong with the audio," Ramona said to her band.

The band's music, which had been channeled through the lounge's audio system, was now interrupted.

"There's Vicia," Ramona said to a small device hidden under her shirt sleeve, taking the opportunity to report. "She's on the dance floor."

"Should we move in?" said a voice to an earpiece in Ramona's ear.

"Not yet. Wait for my signal," Ramona replied.

Then an audio of Vicia's voice sounded through the lounge speakers.

"Hey everyone, it's Vicia Sniar!" Josh yelled.

The people laughed. The audio was that of Vicia in a compromising moment, or so it seemed.

"I love the smell of men's dirty underwear," the voice of Vicia said. "It smells like black tea."

The people laughed and pointed at Vicia.

"That's not me!" protested Vicia. "They faked my voice."

"Stand by," Ramona said in her sleeve. "She'll deliver herself to you very soon. Right out the front door."

"I like to put men's dirty underwear in a teapot and bring it to a boil. It's a great way to start the day!" the voice of Vicia said over the speakers.

"It's not me!" Vicia yelled, but her pleas were drowned by raucous laughter.

Vicia fled the lounge and burst through the front door. Engulfed in her embarrassment, she forgot about Debbie and went for her car, where three of Sheriff Bronc's deputies awaited her.

"Good evening, Miss Sniar," said one of them.

Vicia looked up, and she knew it was time to go to the station. Ramona had stepped off the stage and into a side room where through a window she saw the deputies take Vicia away.

"Don't tell her I had anything to do with her arrest," Ramona said.

"She'll never suspect a thing," Sheriff Bronc replied.

"Good. I'll take Debbie home now," Ramona said, and she returned to the lounge area.

"Sassi found the problem," Brian said to Ramona. "Rick intercepted the signal and played that fake tape. We're ready to start the next number."

"You go on without me," Ramona said, looking around for Debbie. "I need to take Debbie home. But where is she? Debbie?"

"Debbie?" Brian asked.

"Debbie Dayla," Ramona said. "She was just here on the dance floor. Look, there's Evan."

"Oh, the girl with Evan? She went toward the lobby," Brian said.

Ramona walked over to Evan and asked him for Debbie's whereabouts.

"She said she didn't feel well, and she went to the bathroom. She'll be back in a minute," Evan said.

"Let me check," Ramona said.

Meanwhile, Debbie walked in a haze from the drug now filling her mind. It was the date amnesia drug, dropped into her drink by Josh a moment ago, and unknowingly ingested when she took a gulp of her wine cooler. Jayvogg was now leading her through the fraternity's unwatched back door, where the two walked a short ways down an alley to Seaside Apartments.

"Shhh," he said. "This will be our little secret."

Jayvogg led Debbie to the back door of the apartment building, and he prepared to unlock the door with his magnetized card. But Debbie dragged her fingers across the electromagnetic scanner, and the door unlocked.

"Heh, heh, heh," Jayvogg chuckled. "You're my kind of woman. Remind me to take you along to other buildings I know. There are several gold watches I'd like to swipe. And some nice diamonds for you. You'd like diamonds."

"Diamonds," Debbie repeated.

As the two walked upstairs, Debbie sensed images through Jayvogg's hand. She saw another woman who had traveled up the same steps, was drunk, and was out of her senses. The woman passed out at the top of the steps, and Jayvogg took her to his apartment, where he took advantage of her. The images disturbed Debbie, and she tried to cry out, but the date amnesia drug in her system prevented such a cry. Then she saw images of a woman who had also unknowingly consumed a date amnesia drug. She too was compromised, but the drug wore off quicker than Jayvogg had anticipated, and she put up a struggle. Jayvogg smashed a lamp across her skull and knocked her out. He injected a fatal dose of heroin into her veins and had Rick and Josh dump her body into a dumpster two hundred miles to the west.

"We are here," Jayvogg said as the two reached his apartment door.

Jayvogg knocked twice on the door. Rick opened the door and allowed the two in.

"Make sure we are undisturbed," Jayvogg said. "This will be a night to remember."

Rick stood guard outside the apartment door in the hallway.

"And this is Josh. You remember him, don't you?" Jayvogg said.

Josh nodded hello. He stood by the balcony window and watched outside.

Jayvogg turned on the stereo, and a low but steady drumbeat filled the room.

"I want to know you," he said.

Images flooded through Debbie's mind. Images of Jayvogg torturing a cat and setting it afire. Images of Jayvogg running over an elderly pedestrian with his truck. Images of more assaults and murders. The images would not abate, and they repeated and overlapped and flapped in front of Debbie's eyes like a hoard of bats and birds fighting for air.

Jayvogg led Debbie into the bedroom, and he sat her down on the bed. Now new images added to the cacophony in her mind, images of more vile crime and filth committed on that bed against innocent victims. And there were other images too. When Jayvogg was not at home, Josh and Rick double-teamed against a single female victim, who was drugged out of her senses much like the others.

Violations and assaults—they were too much for Debbie. Just as Jayvogg locked the bedroom door behind him, Debbie let out a call, like a wolf or crow, with tones sounding like:

"Oh, you *are* the wild animal," Jayvogg said with new excitement. "And I as your master shall tame you!"

Jayvogg produced a whip and cracked it several inches in front of Debbie's face, but Debbie did not flinch. She called out again, but her tone was a little subdued:

"So, you *can* be subdued," Jayvogg cackled. "On your knees."

Jayvogg cracked the whip in front of Debbie again, but she did not move.

"I said, on your knees!" he ordered.

But Debbie didn't move. Jayvogg cracked the whip and caught her arm. He tried pulling her, but he couldn't. Shocked, he loosened the whip and whipped her again, this time catching her leg, her side, even around her back. The whip met her flesh in violent and audible fashion, enough that Josh rushed in out of semi-concern.

"Are you crazy!?" Josh said. "People will hear!"

"Not yet!" Jayvogg said. "Watch!"

Jayvogg cracked the whip upon Debbie's flesh again. Her skin sounded as if it were tearing apart, and her clothing was becoming shredded. She now gave out a new call.

"It's time," Jayvogg said. "Get on out, Josh. I'm tying her down now."

Jayvogg went for some rope and attempted to secure Debbie to the bed, but he couldn't budge her. Annoyed, he punched her in the jaw to subdue her. A new song coursed through her mind, one of pitched drums from a faraway place and time, drums of action starting like:

Jayvogg grabbed Debbie's arm, and she grabbed his free arm. He squeezed to crush her and cause pain, but she reverberated the force and caused pain on his free arm.

"Ow!" he said. "What kind of psycho trash are you?!"

"I'll get her!" Josh said.

Josh reached from behind and began choking Debbie. Foam frothed from Debbie's mouth, a tingly, sparkly goo that steamed from its caustic nature. It traveled around her neck and onto Josh's arm. The goo burned into Josh's flesh, causing a fierce necrosis that ran rampant through his bloodstream until it filled his chest and brain and caused his whole body to turn black. He wrenched in pain and jumped spasmodically like a bug dancing its death in a microwave oven.

"What have you done?!" Jayvogg yelled.

Rick rushed in and threw a punch at Debbie, but she caught his fist and crushed it like eggshells. Blood burst forth, and now Rick cried in pain.

"Throw a blanket over her!" Jayvogg commanded.

With Rick's other hand, he helped Jayvogg throw a blanket over Debbie. But Debbie waved her arms and sent air and wind into currents and updrafts, giving life to the blanket. It twirled into a heavy rope and whipped and cracked like Jayvogg's whip before. It slashed Jayvogg's hair from his scalp, making him bald. It ripped into Rick's neck and decapitated him. Jayvogg ran for the closet to retrieve a pistol. He managed to open the closet door, grab the pistol, and rack the slide, but the blanket now unfolded, opened up, and enveloped him. The blanket forced the pistol to expend its rounds. Bullets exited the pistol but did not exit the blanket. Instead, the blanket manipulated air and matter and funneled the bullets around Jayvogg's body, searing and tearing his outer skin layers to plant the seeds of scar and memory. But they did not kill, and Jayvogg did not die, though he wished it.

"Stop this insanity!" Jayvogg screamed like a filly.

He attempted to rear up like the immature horse that he was, but the blanket yanked him back down, rolled him along the ground, and bowled him out the window and to the ground with a silent crash. Jayvogg lay there, unconscious and in critical condition, but alive. Josh was dead. So was Rick.

Debbie had murdered both. She called out her first call again, but in a quieter volume:

And Debbie blacked out.

When Debbie regained her senses, she was seated at Seaside Sushi in Brunswick. She had finished plate after plate of assorted sushi dishes, and she was just now being delivered the bill—for $305.42. She looked at her clothes—they were not what she wore at the party. Instead, she wore a color-ful Japanese outfit. Her skin showed no signs of injury, not on her hands nor arms nor neck nor anywhere else.

"What...where am I?" she asked herself.

"Thank you again, Miss Dayla," the owner said. "Charge to the Dayla account?"

"Ah...I...yes, charge to Dayla," Debbie said.

Debbie looked around to regain her orientation and to recompose herself.

"Act normal," she said to herself.

The bill was paid, and Debbie made her way toward the exit, but her eye caught a television broadcast behind the cashier's desk. Debbie recognized the two photos displayed as part of a newscast, one of her sister and another of Vicia Sniar. Debbie listened, and she heard the anchorwoman speak:

"...high-profile daughter of Roger Dayla, and rival station WBU's own Vicia Sniar, are being held at Jekyll Island Reformatory."

"Two men are dead and one in critical condition in what police are call-ing the most gruesome attack they have ever seen," another anchorwoman said. "Joshua Jones and Rick Lefter were immediately pronounced dead on arrival at County Hospital. The third victim, Jayvogg Hochenstock, is in crit-ical but stable condition, and County Hospital officials will not speculate on Mr. Hochenstock's chances for survival. Police suspect foul play and are ask-ing that any tips be called in at 999-ANY-TIPS."

The newscast switched to video of a police press conference.

"Any idea who the killer is?" a journalist asked.

"At this time, we do not know what killed the two men. It's too early to speculate what carried out this attack," the officer said.

"Is that a *who* or a *what*? Did an animal attack them?" a reporter shouted.

"Were there claw marks? Bite marks? Any animal fur left behind?" others shouted.

"This is an ongoing investigation, and everything is fluid. We cannot give out details at this time," the officer said.

"What protection does Brunswick have against future attacks?" a reporter asked.

"We have officers patrolling the streets and going door-to-door in search of leads. In addition, the State of Georgia is making additional resources available to us in this investigation."

"Then this is a state-wide emergency?" a reporter blurted.

"No. And no more questions," the officer said.

"They say it was a body builder on PCP," said a customer watching nearby.

"I heard it was roid-rage," said another customer.

"Do you think that I could have..." Debbie said as she suddenly turned around to the customers.

They laughed. A waitress led those customers, still laughing and looking back at Debbie, to a table in the eating area.

"It's late, Miss Dayla," said Miss Chi, owner of the sushi restaurant. "Why don't you let me take you home? Your parents must be worried."

"My parents aren't home," Debbie confessed.

"What about your butler? Garwood?" Miss Chi asked.

Debbie looked down sheepishly.

"Oh, I see," said Miss Chi. "Well, this can be our little secret. Come. I have a new car that I want to show you. It has the most elegant floral design both outside and in."

Debbie agreed, and it took only a few minutes for Miss Chi to bring Debbie home. In fact, Debbie might have walked home otherwise, and Miss Chi knew this, but Miss Chi didn't like the idea of a rich man's daughter roaming the streets in the middle of the night.

"Is this good enough?" Miss Chi asked after parking a few houses down from the Dayla home.

"Yes. Thank you," Debbie said.

Debbie walked the remaining distance until she arrived home. She climbed into her bedroom through a window, avoiding detection by Garwood. She knew her mother wasn't home yet, as the dawn had yet to break.

"Another hour," Debbie said. "I guess I'll get some sleep."

The Following Saturday

Where did the time go? Debbie had all but forgotten the prior weekend. Connie and Vicia were released on Friday, after serving only a week of time at the reformatory.

"But they demonstrated excellent behavior," Garwood explained to Debbie. "It's such a breath of fresh air when the Dayla family is together and at peace."

"But Daddy isn't home," Debbie said. "He's away on business."

"Oh, but he will be here later today. Come, Miss Debbie. Have lunch downstairs," Garwood said.

Debbie finished making her bed and walked downstairs. Garwood had made lunch, and the dining table was already occupied by Connie and Debbie's mother.

"Good morning, Debbie," Julie said.

"Good morning, Debbie," Connie said.

"Good morning, Mommy," Debbie said. "Good morning, Connie."

"It's such a wonderful Saturday, isn't it? The blistering heat has let up, I have my two daughters with me, and your father is coming home today," Julie said.

"Vicia got her job back at the TV station," Connie said.

"Good for her!" Julie said.

"And...she's supposed to be on the twelve o'clock news," Connie added.

"Let's watch," Julie said. "Garwood, would you wheel the portable television in here?"

Garwood wheeled a seventy-five inch widescreen television into the dining room.

"Oh, that's the small one," Julie said.

"I'm sorry. The regular portable is out for repairs," Garwood said.

"Well, this will have to do," Julie said. "Garwood, Channel 48 please."

Garwood turned on the television, and the twelve o'clock news was already in progress. Weather was being reported, followed by sports.

"She's on probation," Connie said.

"What does that mean?" Debbie asked.

"It means she only gets to speak for thirty seconds, and at the end of the show," Connie replied. "They cut out everything except *Rumormill*. Oh look, there she is. Shhh!"

"Vicia Sniar here with *Today's Snitchline* on the Bu, WBU Channel 48," Vicia said on the broadcast. "A certain senator and secretary were seen dining together last night in a famous nightclub. The secretary was wearing a short black skirt and white blouse and had her hair over to the side. She ordered three daiquiris and a margarita. The senator had a Tom Collins and three martinis, and the secretary ate every olive from the senator's martinis! The secretary was seen leaving the nightclub with the senator in his new convertible. I'm Vicia Sniar, and that's *Today's Snitchline*."

The news broadcast ended, and an old black-and-white movie began.

"Looks like *Rumormill* is gone," Connie said. "Now it's *Today's Snitchline*. I wonder who decided that."

"Something is different," Debbie said. "She really knows what she's talking about."

Julie and Connie looked at Debbie in surprise. Debbie was normally quiet and voiced no opinions. This was a first.

"Oh, well uh, she's still good old Vicia. She can make up a story on the spot and have ten cents in change," Connie said. "I didn't think you really watched her on TV anyway."

"Vicia did look different," Julie said.

"Oh come on, Mom," Connie said. "Not you too."

"No, I mean it. She seems...serious," Julie added.

"Yes. She's very serious, because there really is a senator and secretary with a secret affair," Debbie said.

Connie laughed.

"It's more like her boss yelled at her for something," Connie said. "Like driving his car."

"That reminds me, did I tell you that your driving privileges—"

"Have been suspended for two months," Connie said at the same time as her mother. "Yeah, you told me a million times."

"Well, a refresher can't hurt. Now if you were as good as Debbie, there'd be no problems at all," Julie said.

Connie wanted to say something out of anger, but she bit her tongue and let the anger fester such that her hands clenched into fists, and her face turned beet red.

"I...am...trying...to do better," Connie forced from her lips despite clenched jaw muscles.

"I think it was the pendant Vicia was wearing," Debbie said. "It made her smart."

"She did wear an attractive pendant," Julie said. "I've never seen it before."

"We had some Indian dude give us stuff at the reformatory. I got a bracelet, and Vicia got a pendant," Connie said.

"Native American, Connie," Julie corrected. "I didn't know you got a bracelet. Why don't you show us?"

"I'm embarrassed by it," Connie said. "It's made of lizard skin. Yuck. I don't like slithery, slimy things touching my skin."

"But it's Native American craft," Julie said. "There's nothing slimy about it. It ranks up there with modern jewelry, better in fact because of the rarity nowadays."

"Well...okay," Connie agreed.

Connie disappeared and reappeared with the bracelet. The band looked very much like flattened lizard skin, woven in and out such that Connie couldn't tell how many lizards were needed to make such a bracelet.

"Look," Connie said as she pulled two ends. "It's flexible."

"Have you tried it on yet?" Julie asked.

"No. It's a lizard! Yuck!" Connie said.

"May I?" Debbie asked.

"Huh?" Connie replied, shocked at Debbie's initiative.

"May I try on the bracelet?"

"Uh, okay. I didn't know you liked things like that. You don't even have your ears pierced," Connie said.

"I know, but I like the bracelet...there's something about it," Debbie said.

"It's freaky!" Connie said.

"No, something else," Debbie said.

"Nothing else is freakier than freaky. But go ahead. I was going to throw it away. Just touching it is creeping me out," Connie said.

With her right hand, Debbie pulled the bracelet over her left. It stretched just enough to slip over her palm and around her wrist, and then it shrank just enough to be snug but not too much.

"I like it," Debbie said. "Can I keep it?"

"*May* I keep it," Julie corrected.

"Yes. May I keep it, Connie?" Debbie asked.

"Sure, what do I care?" Connie asked.

"Who did you say gave it to you?" Julie asked. "Was it Professor Monfri?"

"No. The dude was his assistant or something," Connie said.

"The *dude* is Chawbree," Julie said. "And yes, Chawbree is Professor Monfri's assistant."

"Whatever. Chawbree said it would bring me luck and keep me out of trouble," Connie said.

But in her mind, Connie could hear Vicia snickering.

"Well, it did, didn't it?" Julie asked. "So far you've been good this week."

"He said I had to wear it, though. And I haven't. It's all superstition anyway," Connie said. "So Debbie, don't take the bracelet too seriously."

But Debbie had withdrawn from the conversation. She stroked the bracelet as if it were fur from a pet bunny rabbit, and she spoke softly to it.

"Debbie?"

"She's in one of her trances," Julie said. "Just leave her alone. It'll wear off by the time your father arrives. Debbie, why don't you go outside and play?"

"Mother, she's not a five-year old," Connie said.

"It'll work. Watch," Julie said.

Debbie nodded her head in agreement, but she was too preoccupied with the bracelet to look up at Julie or Connie. Debbie took a bite from her plate, chased it down with water, and went outside. She was about to take a walk along the beach of the Atlantic Ocean when Ramona drove up in her convertible.

"Well hello, Debbie," Ramona said.

"Hi."

"Is Connie inside?"

"Yeah."

"You know, you had me worried last Saturday when you disappeared like that. There's a killer on the loose, and...well...I guess Brunswick isn't as safe as we thought, at least not until the killer is found," Ramona said. "Don't you go out alone. It's a dangerous world."

"I know," Debbie said.

"You do?"

"Yeah, you know, well, Daddy said that being a Dayla is dangerous because people want to steal from us," Debbie said.

"That's true. But some don't care about money. They just want to kill," Ramona said. "I know you don't run into that kind. But me, well, I'm going to make a career of catching that kind."

"Huh?" Debbie asked.

"I'm going to Forsyth for thirty-one weeks of training," Ramona said. "I've come here to say *goodbye*."

"But you just graduated," Debbie said. "And it's summer vacation."

"Well it's time I put my double-major of Criminal Justice and Public Administration into action," Ramona said. "I'm going to be a Georgia State Patrol officer, that is if I pass training."

"Wow!" Debbie said. "Wow! Wow! Wow!"

Debbie ran inside the house and yelled the news to Julie and Connie, but Debbie's words were jumbled and confused so much that neither Julie nor Connie could make sense of Debbie.

"Slow down, here, sit down," Julie said. "Take a deep breath and...oh hello, Ramona."

"Good afternoon," Ramona replied as she entered the dining room. "I hope I'm not interrupting your lunch."

"No, we just finished," Julie said.

"Did you see Vicia's broadcast?" Connie asked. "Making those wild accusations about—"

"You mean about the senator and secretary? It's all true, you know," Ramona said.

"What!?" Connie said. "Then maybe there *is* magic in that pendant of hers."

Ramona laughed.

"What's so funny?" Connie asked.

"You're so smullible," Ramona said. "I gave Vicia a dime lesson on proper investigative skills. There's no magic there."

Julie laughed at Connie.

"What's so funny?" Connie asked, though with a different tone and now toward her mother.

"Ramona is a true, 21st Century woman," Julie said. "But I sense that's not why she is here."

"It isn't," Ramona said. "But I suppose Debbie already told you."

"She tried, but—" Connie started.

"Forsyth, patrol, she, it, uniform, I..." Debbie said.

"I'm going into thirty-one weeks of training to become a Georgia State Patrol officer," Ramona said.

"I always thought you'd take after your father," Julie said. "But I thought you'd try for a deputy sheriff or a police officer."

"I don't think there's a county big enough for two Broncs in law enforcement," Ramona said. "Don't get me wrong. I love my father, but I have to be independent, as he says. This way, I can visit and still be in my jurisdiction."

"Thirty one weeks is a long time," Connie said. "I was hoping we could hang out this summer."

"Can't wait. I've already spent four years in college instead of going directly into police academy after high school," Ramona explained. "But I wanted to be sure."

"And?" Debbie asked.

Ramona looked at Debbie and smiled.

"I'm sure," Ramona said. "After Rick and Josh were killed, I realized I had to move on to my career as quickly as possible. I want to help fight crime. I can't stand around and do nothing. I'll go crazy."

"We'll certainly miss you," Julie said.

Connie stood up, walked over to Ramona, and gave her a big hug.

"This is the first time we'll really be apart," Connie said with a sadness in her voice. "We've been best friends since kindergarten."

"I'll write," Ramona said. "And I'll call. This isn't like the Old West. But even then they still had mail and the telegraph. Just keep your spirits snickety smoovey, and everything will be smarvey."

And so Ramona Bronc left for Forsyth.

"What am I going to do with myself?" Connie asked an hour after Ramona had left.

But then Julie's cellphone rang.

"Yes? Oh hi, Roger. We're expecting you for dinner. You haven't? That bad? Oh, do problems never cease? Yes, I can do that. This is going to be quite a bit of work. I haven't done this kind of thing in years. But if it brings you back sooner...Yes, I will. Love you too. Bye."

Julie tapped a few buttons on her cellphone then looked up at Connie.

"Why don't you spend time with Vicia?" Julie suggested.

"I can't. She's got community service work as part of her probation," Connie said. "I was lucky. I didn't get *any* community service. Yuck. Who wants to serve the community?"

"Well you'll have to find something to keep you busy. I have another appointment with Mrs. Sniar," Julie said.

"So early in the day?" Connie asked.

"And I'm taking Garwood with me," Julie said. "Mrs. Sniar and I have a lot of work to do."

"Work?! Since when?" Connie asked.

"Things aren't going well on the oil rig," Julie said. "I'll be at your father's office."

"You? Work?" Connie asked. "And Mrs. Sniar. I didn't think she—"

"Mrs. Sniar will act as liaison between the South Atlantic crew and my work. Yes, my work. I *am* a top geologist. And there's real trouble drilling through the seamount, a type of rock never encountered before. Your father is certain he can drill through with the right tools and procedure, but he can't make sense of the rock's conformation. Drill the wrong way, and there's an oil gusher running a slick from Africa to South America."

"I thought Father had a geologist helping him," Connie said.

"He quit. Says he wants no part in drilling into that kind of rock," Julie said, "as do many other geologists."

"Well Father will just have to handle it," Connie said. "But what he really needs to do is get me my driver's license back. I can't go around town with the chauffeur toting me like a box of dog biscuits."

"Well, if you ask nicely enough, *maybe* your sister will drive you around," Julie said. "Actually, that reminds me. Now that we're forced to purchase that Audi you stole—"

"Vicia stole," Connie added.

"You can sit here and wait for it to be delivered, and you two can take *that* car out on the town," Julie said.

"I don't want *that* car," Connie said. "I don't want *any* car. I just want to drive *my* Jeep."

"I don't have time to argue, Connie. I've got to go. Garwood, prepare the helicopter," Julie called.

"Yes, ma'am," Garwood's voice called back as he briefly entered the room.

"I'm not letting anyone drive my Jeep," Connie said.

"Then you're stuck," Julie said. "Because Debbie doesn't have a car. Unless you let her drive the Audi."

"It's not my Audi!" Connie said.

"I'll take the Audi," Debbie said. "I'll take good care of it, like a pony."

"Garwood?" Julie called again.

"Yes, ma'am," Garwood replied, again stepping into the room.

"Register the Audi under Debra Jo Dayla," Julie said.

"Very good, ma'am," Garwood said, and he hurried away before additional requests could be made.

Garwood escorted Julie to the helicopter, and both departed for Dayla Industries. Twenty minutes passed. Twenty minutes of Connie tapping her fingernails on the table. Twenty minutes of determination with nowhere to go. Then, a flatbed truck delivered the Audi S5 convertible.

"There's your car," Connie said to Debbie. "Well? I guess I'm desperate to get out. Give me ten minutes to change and get ready."

Connie had no interest in the car, and Debbie took the moment of solitude to become familiar with her new car. All dents were removed, the pace-car paint scheme had been stripped away and replaced with a solid white finish, and the magnesium wheels were gone and replaced with ordinary-looking wheels. The small and flat headlights were replaced with pairs of large, round headlights, a throwback to sports cars from the 1950s or 1960s. Likewise, the taillights were also simplified into pairs of circles. Overall, the lines on the car were softened to appear less aggressive and instead more fun-loving and free-going. Debbie signed for the car and received the key fob from the delivery man.

"Somehow this Audi looks more like a classic Volkswagen than anything else," Connie said, now returning. "But I must say it does go with your style, Deb. Simple and sweet. Well, let's go. Let's see what's happening in Brunswick today."

Connie sat in the front passenger seat and waited for Debbie to take her place in the driver's seat.

"Adjust the seat. Adjust the mirrors. Adjust the—" Connie said.

"I know how to do this," Debbie said. "Place the key...the key..."

"Place the key fob into this slot on the dashboard and hold it for a second while pushing the brake pedal with your foot," Connie said.

Debbie did just that, and the engine revved to life.

"See? I know how to do it," Debbie said.

"Yes. You know, and if I have to tell the world how to move, I'm going to be hoarse."

Debbie placed the automatic shifter into Drive and began pulling away.

"Maybe I don't have to," Connie said. "Stop. Stop!!!!!"

Debbie hit the brakes, and the car came to an incredibly quick stop, but without a hint of tire squeal.

"What is it?! What happened?!?" Debbie asked in panic.

"Wait here!" Connie said.

Connie disappeared into the Dayla house and reappeared with one hand behind her back. She jumped into the Audi and ordered Debbie to drive.

"But what's in your hand?" Debbie asked.

"Just go already!" Connie insisted, and she pushed Debbie's right knee, sending Debbie's foot across to the right and downward, which released the brake and depressed the accelerator.

The car lurched forward and down the driveway. Both girls screamed, and it was all Debbie could do to prevent the Audi from hitting a tree, stone wall, or shrub. Debbie swerved and spun around, taking out a flower garden and laying tracks across the lawn, but she managed to reduce vehicle speed and regain control before the Audi reached the main road. She stopped just in time to prevent running into Vicia Sniar, who was entering the driveway with her car to visit Connie.

All three girls screamed at the near collision.

"What are you doing?" Connie yelled.

"Me?" Vicia replied. "How did you...the car...is this the car we totaled?"

"Yeah, sorta," Connie said.

"Well I can't believe it," Vicia said. "I should do a news story on the miracle repair job."

"If they would only let you," Connie said.

"Hah, hah, hah," Vicia sneered. "I'm on probation. But I'd do it all over again to see your expression."

"Well maybe we can do it all over again," Connie said. "Anyway, I thought you had community service."

"I did. It's done for today," Vicia said. "And I didn't expect to see you out in a car so soon. Your license is suspended."

"Well if you've noticed, I'm not driving. Deb is. And anyway again, maybe we can do something else," Connie said. "Come with us. We're going cruising!"

Vicia backed up, pulled around, and parked off to the side.

"Don't mind if I do," Vicia said as she hopped into the back seat of Debbie's Audi.

Debbie pulled away, but at a very slow pace.

"Ah, nothing like cruising in a convertible in summer," Vicia said.

"Turn down that way," Connie said.

"What way?" Debbie asked.

"That way," Connie repeated while pointing.

"I can't see which way you are pointing. I'm watching the road," Debbie replied.

"To the right, to the right!" Vicia yelled.

Debbie whipped the Audi to the right, nearly throwing Vicia out the back but scrunching Connie against Debbie.

"Not like that!" Connie said. "Aaag, I'm stuck!"

Debbie whipped the car into a left turn and sent Connie to the right side. Vicia had just steadied herself from the last maneuver when this new one sent her partway out of the right side of the car.

"I guess we should be wearing seat belts!" Vicia said. "I almost fell out!"

Connie and Vicia wasted no time in fastening themselves to the Audi with seat belts. Debbie grinned and giggled.

"You liked that," Vicia said. "I think we're finally getting through to you, Debbie."

"Could it be?" Connie asked. "There's only one way to find out. Let's see what kind of mischief we can get into."

"Go for it!" Vicia said.

"Go for it!" Debbie echoed.

Debbie lightly touched the gas pedal, and the car took off. But Debbie didn't outrun traffic. She kept behind one vehicle, switched lanes, and switched back, without going ahead or dropping behind. The girls yelled and waved playfully as they passed a couple of boys on skateboards. The boys, startled, stopped skating and waved back.

"Pull into that gas station," Connie said.

Debbie did just that.

"Stop by the pump, no wait, stop just *before* the pump," Connie said, and Debbie did just that.

"Hey-ey!" Vicia yelled to several guys driving by in another convertible.

"We need some service here," Connie yelled to the attendant inside, despite all pumps being self service.

A young man rushed out to the Audi.

"We, uh, this is self service, uh, is this your car?" the stuttering man asked.

"It's my sister's car," Connie said.

"Oh, hi sister," the man fumbled.

The girls laughed.

"I have a name. It's Debra Jo Dayla," Debbie said.

"Debra Jo! A Dayla! And you must be Connie Dayla!" the man exclaimed.

"Yeah, I'm a rich girl," Connie said.

"And Debra Jo is rich too?" he asked.

The girls laughed again.

"Of course, silly!" Connie said.

"And you...in the back seat...you're that other rich girl. The oil field girl," he stuttered.

"Vicia Sniar. That's me. I'm a rich girl too. We're like royalty," Vicia said.

"So kneel before us, peasant," Connie said.

The young man kneeled.

"I love you," he said, and he reached for Connie's hand to kiss it.

"Oh, you're too much," Connie giggled. "Now address me as Queen Connie of Dayla."

"Yes, Queen Connie of Dayla. How may I be of service?" he said.

"And I'm Queen Vicia of Sniar," Vicia said. "Address me."

"Oh yes, Queen Vicia. I like you too," he said.

Connie and Debbie laughed, but not Vicia.

"What do you mean by *like*? You *love* Connie!" Vicia snarled.

"Oh, uh, yeah, I *love* you too," the young man said, but he said so in jest more than in sincerity, which made Connie and Debbie laugh all the harder.

"I don't think that's very funny. Off with your head!" Vicia said.

Vicia sliced the empty air as if to behead the young man.

"Pay no attention to her, young peasant," Connie said. "Hear me, now. Go forth young man to the inside of that-eth convenience store-eth and bring forth-eth a cold drink for your Queen. And pronto!"

As the young man ran for the convenience store, Vicia spoke.

"*Forth-eth* isn't a word."

"I know that," Connie said.

"Are we going to wait for him?" Debbie suggested with the most innocent-looking facial expression.

"Why Deb, my sneaky girl, you are becoming like your older sister," Connie said. "What an excellent idea."

"I know just when to drive off," Debbie said, surprised by her own initiative.

"Watch for my cue," Connie said.

"Oh, puhleez!" Vicia said. "You don't expect him to fall for that old routine."

"They always do," Connie said. "Always."

The boy had disappeared inside the convenience store and now reappeared.

"Hurry," Connie called with her right arm extended toward the running boy. "Hurry!"

The boy ran and approached the Audi, but just before he could give the drink to Connie, Debbie pulled the Audi away, leaving the boy to run after the Audi with the drink extended toward Connie.

"Your drink, Queen Connie. Your drink!" he called.

The girls laughed.

"Aw. You forgot to get gasoline," Vicia joked.

"Yeah, *right*," Connie joked back.

"Actually, we really *do* need gasoline," Debbie said.

"Okay," Connie said. "Let's try that again. Go into that next gas station."

Debbie wheeled the Audi into another gas station and pulled alongside a gas pump.

"Fill 'er up!" Connie yelled.

But all pumps were self service. And no one emerged from the convenience store to assist. Seeing this, Connie pulled out the bullhorn and called again.

"WE NEED SERVICE!!" Connie bellowed.

"I guess that means no gullible boys inside," Vicia said. "If only you could call them by another means."

"But I can!" Connie said. "And thanks for the suggestion. I can look up their number in the online phone directory. Yes, there, Save-A-Save Service Station. 999-000-0100. Calling now!"

"They're answering. I can see them," Debbie said.

"You have good eyes," Vicia said. "I can't see through the glare on the window, even with my designer sunglasses."

"Yes, this is Queen Connie of Dayla," Connie started, to which the girls giggled, "and I want to report an Audi in need of full service. Yes, it needs a fill up...No, not me!...I'm rude?! You're the one that's rude!...Hey, I'm going to buy this station and order you to fill up our car. That's right! Goodbye!"

"So what happened?" Debbie asked.

"It was a woman! Can you believe it? Telling me to stop playing my prank," Connie said, and she directed her voice into the bullhorn and yelled at the station attendant, saying, "I'LL SHOW YOU A REAL PRANK! YOU JUST WAIT AND SEE! I'LL GET YOU FIRED IF YOU DON'T SERVICE OUR CAR!!"

Connie dialed a different number on her cellphone and at first tried to speak with the bullhorn.

"GARWOOD?" Connie yelled.

Garwood, having now arrived with Julie at Dayla Industries, was entering the corporate office when he received the call.

"Too loud, Miss Connie!" Garwood said.

"OH, WAIT A MINUTE!" Connie said.

"Put the bullhorn down," Debbie said.

"I AM!" Connie said to Debbie with the bullhorn.

"Ow!" Debbie said, covering her ear.

"OW!" Connie said back through the bullhorn.

"Ow!" Vicia said to be funny.

"OW!" Connie said with the bullhorn to Vicia.

"Miss Connie, Miss Connie, please!" Garwood said in the phone. "I must help your mother. Please be brief!"

"I NEED YOU TO—" Connie started.

"Give me that!" Vicia said, and she pulled the bullhorn away.

"Hey, that's my bullhorn!" Connie said.

"Finders keepers," Vicia said.

"Mine," Connie said, and she pulled on the bullhorn.

"Mine," Vicia said, and she pulled back.

"Miss Connie, please!!!" Garwood said desperately.

"I think Garwood sounds really anxious," Debbie said.

"I didn't think you knew what that meant, anxious that is," Connie said to Debbie, then she turned her attention to Garwood. "Okay. *Garwoot.* Buy the Save-A-Save gas station for me."

"What?! Buy a gas station?" Garwood replied.

"And now! Pronto! Time is ticking! Tick, tick, tick, TICK!" Connie replied.

"Connie, this is your mother," Julie's voice now said over the cellphone. "Garwood and I have important work to do. These pranks will have to wait for another day. When I suggested you go out in the Audi with Debbie, it was so that you would not be imposing on Garwood. I'm ending this phone call."

The connection terminated.

"Hah!" Vicia snapped. "She told *you!*"

"Mother *never* speaks to me like that. Never! Oooooooo, wait until I get home. I'm going to yell at her all night long!"

"You'll lose your voice. And who will be around to use the bullhorn?" Vicia said. "I guess that I, as your best friend, will make the sacrifice and make all bullhorn announcements for you. I might as well start now."

Vicia called to a boy across the street on a bicycle, startled him, and made him fall.

"That's one for me," Vicia said.

"Give me that," Connie said, and she took the bullhorn from Vicia. "Deb, drive on. We're done here."

Debbie drove away and onto the highway.

"You know, it's too bad Garwood had to take my mother to the office," Connie said.

"Yeah, I guess they hit some bad rocks out in the Atlantic," Vicia said. "I've never heard my mother so tense. She's been popping sedative pills all week. My old man is with your old man on the drilling rig."

"It'll pass," Connie said. "It always does."

"I don't know," Vicia said. "Old man Kukovich and your mother are trying to figure out the geology and stuff. Even your boyfriend is helping out."

"Brian?" Connie asked.

"You remember, the one you stole from me? He majored in quantum physics. Well now he's helping his old man out. I thought you knew all that," Vicia said. "Don't you two ever talk? We always talked."

"Yeah, but not about boring stuff like quantum physics. Yuck," Connie said.

"Yuck," echoed Debbie.

"Well, they're talking like he and the old man are going out on the oil rig once they figure out a new type of drill," Vicia said.

"What!?" Connie said in surprise. "Brian? *My* Brian way out in the Atlantic? But he belongs with me."

"Your mother too, if it gets bad enough," Vicia said.

"I don't believe it," Connie said.

"Your mother has a degree and is smart," Vicia said. "My mother is nothing more than a trophy wife. I'm actually jealous of you, Connie. And you too, Debbie."

"Hah!" Connie said. "That's a laugh."

"Which part?" Vicia asked.

"All of it. You're just playing one of your Vicia Sniar jokes on me," Connie said.

"No, not this time. I wish I were," Vicia said.

"Then prove it," Connie said.

"Easy. Drive to Dayla Industries. You'll find your loving boyfriend there who is oh-so honest about everything he does. *He* can explain his plans," Vicia said.

"I think we should. Deb, on to the office!" Connie commanded.

Debbie changed directions and headed for Dayla Industries. Meanwhile, unknown to the girls, a van began following the Audi.

"Is that them?" a deep voice asked from the back of the van.

"Yeah," Jayvogg replied, who sat closer to the front of the van. "Vicia is in back. She's the one who made fun of you, Senator Croius."

"She was very accurate in her telecast," said the deep voice.

"And the girl driving...she...that's the killer! Debbie Dayla!" Jayvogg squealed.

"She's such a petite girl. So innocent and demure. Hardly possible she could hurt a fly," Croius said.

"Oh that's her, all right. Don't underestimate her, Senator Croius. There's something about her voice. It's like she can make the air into a tornado or something."

"Acoustic manipulation. For a human, that is very interesting. We must find out more," Croius said.

"I beg you not," Jayvogg said. "She is dangerous."

"So am I. So are you," Croius said.

"But not like her," Jayvogg said.

"No, not like *her*. I am not like *any* human, am I now?" Croius said.

Croius moved into the light, and his human-shaped head briefly reverted back to its original form—that of an orca. Jayvogg turned pale in fear, as he had never seen the senator like this. Croius's head changed back into human-like form, and Jayvogg breathed again.

"I know you told me what you really are," Jayvogg said. "I didn't believe it."

"Do you now?" Croius asked.

"I...uh...yeah," Jayvogg choked. "Look, whatever you do, don't hurt me. I'm just a person, and we people don't mean harm. I mean, we make mistakes and all, but just let us live, will you?"

Croius let out a deep laugh that jarred Jayvogg to the marrow and paralyzed his chest. With pauses between laughter, Jayvogg could breathe and receive blood from his own heart, but when Croius laughed, Jayvogg became mired in misery.

"You think it's human ingenuity that has brought that oil rig to the R.S.A. Seamount?" Croius asked.

"I know, you dropped a few hints here and there," Jayvogg said.

"I headed up the congressional committee to explore the region," Croius said.

"But why? Why sell out your fish brothers?" Jayvogg asked.

Croius let out a few sonic pulses that hit Jayvogg in the jaw, causing pain.

"FISH!?" Croius bellowed.

"I mean fellow dolphins, or whales, or whatever you call yourselves!" Jayvogg stumbled.

"I'm an orca. *Not* a fish. I chose that seamount for a special purpose — one you will see in time. But not now. You're too stupid to understand. Just say, 'Yes, Croius, my name is Jayvogg, and I'm as stupid as stone.'"

"Please, no, I don't mean —" Jayvogg begged.

"Say it!"

"Yes, Croius, my name is Jayvogg. And...I'm as stupid as stone," Jayvogg said.

Croius laughed again.

"Driver, pull over," Croius said. "The girls are up to something. Let's watch them in action."

"You know, this bullhorn has a remote microphone," Connie said. "Wow, I never knew that. Look. I can remove the microphone part and talk like THIS, and it comes out way OVER HERE FROM THE BULLHORN."

"You know what you have to do now, don't you?" Vicia asked.

"What?"

"Ambush!" Vicia said.

"I love ambush!" Connie said.

"Do you get what I mean?" Vicia asked.

"Um, give me a moment," Connie said.

"Put the bullhorn in a secret spot and scare people when they go by," Debbie said.

Both Vicia and Connie were surprised by Debbie's words.

"Wow!" Connie said. "That's the first original thought I've heard from you that's really good."

"I'm getting lots of new thoughts," Debbie said. "And I don't know why. I feel like something is close-by and giving me strength to speak my mind."

Vicia and Connie exchanged surprised glances, and then they both shrugged their shoulders.

"Just put the bullhorn in that shrub there by the mailbox. That will do," Vicia said. "We can wait around the corner."

The girls did just that, and they awaited their first victim. The shrub was just outside several businesses—a small grocery store, a bank, and an ice cream shop. The girls waited and watched. A young boy walked out of the ice cream shop with his father. He held a cone in one hand and his father's hand in the other. Connie went into action.

"HELLO!" she bellowed remotely.

The boy shrieked, dropped his cone on the sidewalk, and made a mess in his pants. Seeing the girls around the corner and knowing their identities, the father simply whisked his son away.

"That was yucky," Connie said. "Ewww."

"Eww," Debbie repeated.

"That's just a singleton," Vicia said.

"Huh?" Connie replied.

"You went for one person, a kid. That's child's play," Vicia said.

"What are you talking about?" Connie said. "I have the microphone."

"A microphone with a micro brain," Vicia jabbed.

"Phonabrain," Debbie said.

"Give me the mike," Vicia said. "I'll show you how it's done."

Vicia took the microphone and waited.

"There, that one," Connie said.

"No, not yet," Vicia said. "We want a multi fail. Watch and learn."

An elderly woman exited the grocery store with a bag of groceries. A young man rushed toward the bank. Then Vicia made her play, in a low voice resembling a man:

"You got any fresh fruit?"

Shocked, the elderly woman dropped her groceries and began beating the bewildered man with her purse. The girls laughed.

"That's two. What about more?" Connie asked.

"You think you can do better?" Vicia said. "I doubt it. What we really need is—"

"A chain reaction from one person to the next, begun by the bullhorn and finished with falling people," Debbie said.

Connie and Vicia looked at Debbie in surprise.

"Okay, then!" Vicia said as she handed the microphone to Debbie.

Debbie whispered in the microphone. At first, no one noticed. But then Debbie hummed a little. The shrub vibrated then moved as if being blown in the wind, which made for an odd appearance since the air was still and other shrubs did not move.

"There," Croius said. "Do you see?"

"How is she..." Jayvogg said. "No, wait, that's how it started. She makes things move."

"We must capture her and determine the source of this power," Croius said.

"But how?" Jayvogg asked.

"Myoglobin," Croius said. "If my suspicions are correct, she has a high level of myoglobin, like a cetacean. But she may not have learned how to control it."

"What?!?" Jayvogg asked.

"I don't expect you to understand," Croius said. "But when in deep need, one derives oxygen and inspiration from myoglobin. She may not realize how vulnerable she is to suggestion. I will plant the suggestion."

Croius placed a finger on his temple and closed his eyes, drowning himself in thought.

"First, the mailbox," Croius said in a soft voice.

Debbie hummed a different tune, and the mailbox door opened gently and then closed.

"Did you see that?" Vicia said.

"Wow!" Connie said. "Deb...is that you? How did you get the bullhorn... the mailbox...how?"

"Now the concrete around the mailbox," Croius said.

Debbie changed her tune again, and the sidewalk grew cracks around the mailbox.

"Stop," Jayvogg said. "I don't like this."

Croius laughed and said, "That is but a small sample. If only humans were as talented as this girl, I would have used them to overpower Sparfiacus and his seadogs long ago."

"Who? What?" Jayvogg asked.

"Hold your breath," Croius said.

Croius made the suggestive thought to Debbie, but Jayvogg thought he was being spoken to, and he held his own breath.

"It's my turn," Connie said.

"I want the mike back first," Vicia said.

"Let's hold our breath," Debbie said, "and the winner gets the mike."

The three girls held their breaths. Back in the van, Jayvogg looked at his watch, and he burst open his mouth for air after two minutes.

"Two minutes!" he said.

"I didn't mean you!" Croius said.

"Huh?"

"The three girls are holding their breaths as I speak. I predict Debbie will outlast them."

After a minute, Connie gasped for air. Vicia held out for two-and-a-half minutes. But Debbie kept holding her breath.

"Okay, Deb, start breathing," Connie said.

Five minutes passed, and Debbie didn't breathe.

"This isn't funny," Connie said.

"She can't hold her breath forever," Vicia said. "She'll pass out."

Eight minutes passed. Then ten.

"Stop it! Stop it!" Connie pleaded, and she attempted to force Debbie's mouth open. "You win, okay? You win!"

"You're going to kill her!" Jayvogg said. "Stop it, Croius! Stop it!"

"She won't die," Croius said. "But I won't push her too far. Not yet. I don't want her to learn how to resist me. And yet, I can read some of her. I can see that she has allowed herself to become enslaved to monkshood. One should never become a slave to plants. Too late for you, Jayvogg."

Croius handed a small package of drugs to Jayvogg.

"I won't be needing you for a while," Croius said. "Go smoke yourself somewhere."

"I...I want to help. Don't—" Jayvogg started.

But Croius was done with Jayvogg for the moment. He pointed at the door, and Jayvogg reluctantly got out, with the package already tucked in a pocket. He walked into an alley, entered a deserted basement, rolled a few leaves together, and smoked them.

"I have to get out of this. I have to," he said.

Croius then placed a suggestion in Debbie's mind. Without a word to Connie or Vicia, Debbie stood out of the Audi and walked slowly toward the van. And she was still holding her breath.

"Hey! Deb! Where are you going?" Connie said. "Stop! Debra Jo! Stop!"

"I don't like the look in her eyes," Vicia said to Connie. "She looks like a zombie."

"I've never seen her like that," Connie said.

"Is she hypoglycemic?" Vicia said.

"What does that mean?" Connie asked.

"Low sugar level," Vicia said.

"I don't know. I'm scared," Connie said.

"Well? She's your sister. Go get her," Vicia said.

"Okay," Connie said. "She even left the key fob in the dashboard. I hope the Audi will be—"

"Never mind that! I'll watch the Audi. You just go get Debbie," Vicia ordered.

Connie walked after Debbie, but Debbie hastened her stride, and she began to run. She approached the van and stopped, as if expecting something. The van door opened. Connie yelled at Debbie, but Croius pulled Debbie inside the van, and the van drove away just as Connie reached it, with Connie beating on the side. Connie screamed.

"They took her! They took her!" Connie yelled as Vicia drove up in the Audi.

"Jump in!" Vicia ordered, and Connie did just that.

The Audi drove after the van, but the van was surprisingly quick, and it took corners as well as the Audi.

"Floor it!" Connie said.

"I am!" Vicia replied. "That van driver must be on speed or something! And how can that van corner so well!? This is an Audi, after all!"

And so Vicia drove the Audi to its limits, shredding rubber from the tires, barely missing other vehicles, but despite the desperate and wild chase after the van, the van suddenly drove off a pier and submerged into the Atlantic Ocean.

"Debbie!" Connie screamed as Vicia stopped the Audi on the pier just short of its edge.

"She's gone. She's really gone!" Vicia said.

"This is an emergency!" Connie yelled. "What do we do?"

"Call for help!" Vicia replied.

"Help! HELP!" Connie yelled around the pier.

Several people who had witnessed the event came running to help. Vicia called 911 on her cellphone. But then something very odd happened, at least to those who saw. An orca surfaced and appeared to be hurt. It lay on its side, and it moaned in pain. A gash was clearly visible on its side, and blood spewed out.

"What is that?!" Connie said.

"It's a killer whale. And it's hurt," Vicia said.

"Where did it come from?" Connie asked.

But before anyone could answer, the orca swam away. Sheriff Bronc arrived a minute later, along with an ambulance and a scuba-diving team. Just as the diving team prepared to enter the water, Debbie surfaced.

"Debbie!" Connie yelled. "That's my sister! Debbie Dayla!"

"I know," Sheriff Bronc said. "Just try to remain calm, Connie."

One of the scuba divers met Debbie as she swam toward shore and helped her the rest of the way.

"I'm okay," Debbie said as she walked on the beach.

Sheriff Bronc instructed the divers to search the van for others.

"She'll need to be checked out at the hospital," said one of the EMTs.

"One moment if you will," Sheriff Bronc said to the EMT. "Debbie. What happened?"

"I...don't remember. I was in my new Audi. We were parked. And now I'm here."

"Amnesia," said the EMT. "Probably from a concussion. We'll need to take a CT scan and an MRI immediately. We don't want to risk a talk-and-die situation."

Later, at the senator's Brunswick beach house

Senator Croius changed shape from an orca to that of a humanoid just a short ways from the shore of his beach house. He then walked onto shore, but the weight of land versus water dragged on his limbs, plus he was still injured on his side (left). Each step was especially labored, and he limped. He walked into his beach house where his mistress was dusting, and he collapsed on the couch.

"Croius! My dear Croius! What has happened to you?"

"Just had some miscommunication, Arcella," the senator said.

"With what?" Arcella asked. "A great white?"

Arcella began cleaning the wound.

"You're still bleeding," Arcella said.

"It was worse than a great white," Croius said. "And I can handle one easily. Just a quick blunt jab to its underbelly, and it's a log in my fin. But this one, she—"

"She?!" Arcella said, now pulling away from Croius.

"It was nothing like that. Here, put some butterfly bandages on my wound," Croius said.

"Not until you explain what you were doing with a *she*!" Arcella demanded.

"Don't worry, it was just a human," he said.

"I've heard *that* before," Arcella said.

"Maybe you're right. Maybe she's not a true human. I don't know. I can sense a shark or whale or seal from far away. Humans are quite unremarkable. They don't have the ability for sustained presence, except this one. Her name—"

"You know her name?" Arcella asked.

"Debbie Dayla."

"The daughter of Roger Dayla? Of Dayla Industries? They're supposed to destroy Rhynchus for you," Arcella said.

"Not *destroy* Rhynchus. Destroy the *dolphins* in Rhynchus," Croius said. "Oh why do I bother explaining anything to you? You're no smarter than an amoeba. And my side is killing me!"

"Well explain the plan again," Arcella said. "And I'm doing the best I can!"

"The plan. The plan is scrapped," Croius barked. "The Daylas and Sniars can't drill through the seamount. They haven't mastered the art of acoustic wave manipulation. Now Debbie Dayla appears to be a natural, but everyone ignores her."

"Because she kills people?" Arcella asked.

"No one knows she's a killer. Except Jayvogg. But I put a special something in his leaf. He'll forget. And as for Debbie, even she doesn't know," Croius said. "She reacts to what she perceives as evil in her environment."

"And that's how you got your wound? Because you're evil?" Arcella asked.

Croius sighed.

"Yes, I'm *evil*, as you say. But that's just this human altruistic notion of good and evil. In the ocean, it's evil if one ignores one's responsibility as the apex predator. You should know that. You're an orca just as I am. Then again, your name *is* Arcella—an amoeba."

"Stop calling me an amoeba!" Arcella insisted.

"Yes, I should stop calling you that and focus on the problem at hand—drilling into the Rhynchus region while crediting the act to the humans Dayla and Sniar. Since Debbie will not cooperate, I must try other avenues. This Connie Dayla is trusted by Debbie. Unfortunately, she's just a step away from being as stupid as you, Arcella. So while Connie could be influenced, she's not smart enough to relay the information correctly."

"What information?" Arcella asked.

"The sonic manipulation device, of course! What do you think I've been discussing this whole time? Anchovies?" Croius yelled.

"It's all a bunch of psycho-babble to me!" Arcella said. "And speaking of anchovies, why don't you have some? Or even some sardines? Take the edge off your disposition."

"Maybe I will," Croius said.

Arcella brought a plate of fresh anchovies and sardines for the senator and one for herself, and the two began a meal.

"You know, humans like anchovies," Arcella said. "They have something called pizza. Have you tried pizza?"

"Pizza?"

"Yes, surely you've heard of it," Arcella said.

"I've heard of it. But it's junk food, even by human standards," Croius said.

"Well, seems to me you could do a little communication with encoded enzymes placed properly in anchovies that are found in pizza," Arcella said.

"Those who eat the enzymes will receive the message on a subliminal level, and the message will only be received by those capable of processing it," Croius said. "Arcella, you're incredible."

"I thought of it, and you didn't. Now who's the stupid one?" Arcella bragged.

"I'm as stupid as stone," Croius grimaced in defeat.

County Hospital

"We still can't reach your mother," a nurse said to Connie in the waiting room. "But your sister is being wheeled back to her room. You may visit her if you like. And you too, Miss Sniar."

"Yes, please!" Connie said.

"Thank you," Vicia said.

The nurse led the girls down the corridor and into an empty recovery room.

"Well?" Connie demanded. "Where's my sister?"

"Right here," Debbie said as she was wheeled into the room.

"Debbie!" Connie shrieked, and she ran to give her sister a hug.

"We're glad to see you're okay," Vicia said, and she also hugged Debbie.

"Ladies, if you'll step back please," said an orderly who had been wheeling Debbie. "We need to lift Miss Dayla onto the bed."

Debbie was moved from her wheelchair to a bed, and the orderlies left.

"Are you all right? Are you hurt?" Connie asked.

"I'm fine," Debbie said. "The doctor said this is precautionary."

"What about the CT scan? The MRI?" Vicia asked.

"They said they would process the results quickly and let me know. And still they can't reach Mother," Debbie said.

"I'll solve that right now," Connie said.

Connie tried making a call on her cellphone but could not.

"Can't get a signal in here," Connie said.

"Let me try mine," Vicia said.

Vicia experienced the same problem. But before she could speak, Arcella, dressed as a hospital food service worker, arrived with a covered cart.

"Who's hungry?" Arcella said.

"Mmmm," Connie said. "I smell something good."

"Hey! This food is for me!" Debbie said.

"I'm sorry, but this is for patients only," Arcella said.

"Do you realize who we are?" Connie said. "I'm Connie Dayla. Of Dayla Industries."

"And I'm Vicia Sniar, of Sniar Oil!" Vicia said. "We could buy this hospital, if we want."

"So I demand you let us eat that food!" Connie said.

"But the—" Arcella started.

"Leave it! Now!" Connie barked.

"Okay, okay," Arcella said, and she left.

"Open the cart," Debbie said. "I smell pizza."

Connie and Vicia opened the cart, and indeed, there was fresh pizza inside with specially prepared anchovies. The girls ate, drank carbonated beverage, and they felt renewed in spirits.

"You know, Debbie," Vicia said, "you have quite a talent with your voice."

"Aw. You're just saying that," Debbie said.

"No, I mean it," Vicia continued. "I saw what you did with the bullhorn. Remember? With the shrub moving? And the mailbox?"

"Yeah, Deb, and you made the sidewalk break," Connie said. "That *is* a special gift. But what good is it?"

"What good is it?! Don't you see?" Vicia asked. "My dad and your dad are trying to drill into R.S.A. Seamount in the South Atlantic. But they can't."

"And you think my sister can?" Connie asked.

"Not by herself, but if we can amplify her voice and tune it to the rock's structure, then maybe our dads can get through the top layer of rock," Vicia explained.

"It sounds like a good idea," Debbie said. "But...I don't know. Something doesn't feel right."

"She can't go anywhere until she recovers," Connie said. "And what makes you think we can find a way to make Debbie's voice break through that seamount thingy in the ocean?"

"I bet Doctor Kukovich could find a way. Maybe even make a device to mimic Debbie's voice. And you can spend time with Brian," Vicia said.

The nurse walked back in.

"All tests show A-OK. Debbie, you have sustained no injuries. You're free to go."

"If she had no injuries, how come you had her pushed around in a wheelchair?" Connie asked.

"That was precautionary," the nurse said. "Can't take chances. And we never did reach your mother, Debbie, but you are an adult, so you may check yourself out."

"Thank you," Debbie said. "I will."

Dayla Industries

Debbie drove her Audi to the guardhouse, with Connie and Vicia as passengers.

"Miss Dayla, Miss Dayla, and Miss Sniar," the guard said. "The office is closed."

"This is an emergency," Debbie said. "We need to see my mother, Julie Dayla."

"She's not here," the guard said.

"What?!" Connie said.

"She just caught a flight to the South Atlantic," the guard said.

"That's child abandonment!" Connie said.

"We're all of age," Vicia said. "No one was abandoned. But Debbie has a gift that could help the drilling effort. Who else is here?"

"Well, Doctor Kukovich and his son Brian are here," the guard said.

"Perfect," Vicia said.

"But they are in the lab and not to be disturbed. They are working on a super-secret device that—"

"Won't work," Debbie finished.

"How could you know that?" the guard said.

"Because if it worked, they would have sent it to the South Atlantic already," Vicia said. "It's all so easy to understand."

"Guard, we're wasting time with all this explaining," Connie said. "Let us in."

"I'll have to call this in," the guard said.

The guard called upstairs to Doctor Kukovich's office.

"I'm sorry to disturb you, sir. Yes, I know. But there are three girls here who claim...the Daylas and Vicia Sniar. No, I'm not joking. They...I know, sir. Yes. Just a few minutes I would think is all they ask."

As the guard spoke on the phone, Connie leaned over to Debbie's ear and said, "Make that sound again, the one you used to break the sidewalk."

"I...don't remember...what sound?" Debbie asked.

Connie hummed several notes, and bits of Debbie's memory returned. Debbie called out in her musical tones as she had done before. The telephone receiver vibrated, and then it cracked in half. Doctor Kukovich's phone also cracked in half. Shocked, both the guard and the doctor dropped their phones. Doctor Kukovich was the first to pick up his phone, needing both hands to hold it together.

"Hello, hello! Guard? Guard!"

"How...how did you do that?" the guard asked Debbie in shock.

"I told you she has a gift," Vicia said. "Now open the gate and let us in."

"Guard?!" the doctor's voice called from the broken phone. "Send them up right away. Guard?"

The guard opened the gate and let the Audi pass.

"Doctor Kukovich," the guard said into the phone. "The girls are on their way."

Doctor Kukovich's Lab

"Brian, Brian!" Connie called when she was allowed into the lab.

"Connie!" Brian Kukovich called back.

The two ran for each other, met, and hugged.

"I missed you," Brian said.

"I missed you too," Connie said.

"I've been so busy helping with research. It's just crazy in here. And we still can't break through the seamount," Brian said.

"Doctor Kukovich?" Vicia said, now that Connie and Brian were off to the side. "You know Debbie Dayla."

"Yes," Doctor Kukovich said. "I was at your graduation, Debbie."

"Doctor Anton Kukovich. Lead scientist and engineer at Dayla Industries. Inventor of many tools and devices. Winner of the Nobel Prize in—"

"I have an ardent fan," the doctor said. "But you are famous too, I hear."

"Doctor, Debbie here has some amazing abilities with her voice," Vicia said.

"Follow me, please," he said.

The doctor led the two girls to his telephone.

"This is a Dayla Industries telephone, made of a high-tensile strength poly-composite material. Virtually indestructible. And yet here it is, cloven in two," said Doctor Kukovich. "This is exactly the kind of thing we must explore. Debbie, I'd like you to sit in this booth over here. I'd like to conduct some tests with your voice."

"What kind of tests?" Debbie asked as she stepped into the booth, but before she closed the door, she continued her conversation with the doctor.

"See that cylindrical device pointed at that boulder?" the doctor asked.

"Yes."

"The device is called a SOZOD—a SOnic ZOnaton Device," he said. "It emits zonaton particles. These particles are something between electromagnetic and sound waves. The particles are supposed to cause matter to liquefy and harden. Now that boulder is a sample of the rock found in the seamount. We need to find a way to drill through it without causing the boulder to crack or shatter. The boulder must remain sound and sturdy. Just a single, smooth hole is the desired goal."

"What does the device...the SOZOD...what does it do now?" Debbie asked.

"Let me show you," the doctor said.

"Look, Dad is starting up the SOZOD," Brian said to Connie. "Let's go over and watch."

Doctor Kukovich started the SOZOD with the three girls and Brian watching. The device emitted a pencil of light, starting small and diverging until it hit the boulder across its entire surface. The surface shimmered and smoothed, but otherwise it remained unchanged. The doctor turned the SOZOD off.

"Now I'll test the hardness of the boulder. The unaffected area has a variable hardness from six to nine on Mohs scale, but the affected area is dead on ten on Mohs scale. Hard as diamond. But instead of drilling a hole, I've created a new barrier plate that's harder to drill than before."

"Can't you focus the beam or something?" Vicia asked.

"The beam is already attenuated," Debbie said, as if in a trance. "The beam must have been more diffuse at one time. The entire side of the lab looks brand new. Most likely to replace what was damaged by an earlier form of the SOZOD device."

"You're very perceptive, Debbie. That's exactly right," the doctor said. "Right now the hardened surface is a disadvantage. But it can be an advantage if the SOZOD beam can be focused correctly."

"How?" Vicia asked.

"By acting as a support," Debbie said. "A cylindrical hole would be drilled into the boulder, and the melted portion would harden as a cylindrical interior wall, which would support the boulder better than the original, unorganized material."

"Wow!" Connie said. "Is this my sister talking?"

"She does seem to know this stuff pretty well," Vicia said.

"But she couldn't," Brian said. "We've never revealed it to her or any of you until now."

"Like I said, Debbie is very perceptive," the doctor said. "I think we have the missing key to our SOZOD device. I'll start all recording devices when Debbie begins. Debbie, if you will close the door to your booth, please, and watch the panel in your booth for instructions."

Debbie closed her door. The booth walls were of glass, and so Debbie could see out, and the others could see Debbie.

"Do you hear my voice, Debbie?" the doctor asked through a microphone.

"Yes I do," Debbie replied through a microphone of her own.

"Let's start with a few tests. Trill your voice."

Debbie trilled her voice, and the booth glass around her shattered. The others covered their ears to protect against the shock wave.

"Stop, stop!" Doctor Kukovich said.

"That was a glass booth," Brian said. "Perhaps something a bit more flexible would be better."

"Let's try a *polyoplenican* booth," Doctor Kukovich said.

"Poly what?" Connie asked.

"Polyoplenican is a material as flexible as plastic but with a 9.5 hardness on Mohs scale. It's transparent, it does not shrink nor expand with temperature differences, it's UV resistant, it—" Debbie started.

"She *must* have ESP or something," Brian said.

"It's incredible, I know," Doctor Kukovich said. "I think it's time we give the reins to Debbie. Debbie, what do you think? Will a polyoplenican booth hold up to your trilling?"

"Yes, it will," Debbie said.

"Very well," the doctor said. "The booth is just over here, if you please."

Debbie entered the polyoplenican booth.

"Now look at the panel in front of you, it—" the doctor started.

"I know how it works," Debbie said.

Brian and the doctor exchanged glances.

"I'm telling you, it's ESP," Brian said.

"There's no such thing," the doctor replied.

"Then you explain it," Brian said.

"If we have time, and Debbie is willing, we'll investigate," the doctor said. "But the SOZOD is—"

"Is on," Vicia said. "And the beam is different. Look!"

The SOZOD created a tubular zone focusing a rotating group of six, dual-braided zonaton beams. Matter from the boulder became displaced into the desired cylindrical internal wall that Doctor Kukovich desired. The procedure worked so well and with seemingly little effort on Debbie's part that all who watched were in complete amazement. When the hole was finished, Debbie turned off the SOZOD herself, and she spoke:

"You just got *sozzed*, Mr. Boulder."

Doctor Kukovich picked up the telephone and made a call.

"Roger? Anton. The SOZOD is fully functional and ready for use on the seamount. No, no computer control at all. We never advanced that far. Your daughter. No, the other daughter. Yes, Debbie. Just by singing. I think it's some sort of electroaudio feedback. It comes to her naturally. She'll have to operate the SOZOD. Yes. Yes. Connie and Vicia are here and saw the test run. We are all quite impressed. I know you will. Yes. Right away. Goodbye."

"Well?" Connie asked. "What did my father say?"

"Debbie and I are to take a private plane to the drilling rig at the R.S.A. Seamount," Doctor Kukovich said.

"The South Atlantic Ocean?" Connie asked.

"Yes," Brian said.

"I'll need you to assist me, Brian," Doctor Kukovich said. "This SOZOD is very delicate and needs your special touch if we are to install it properly."

"I understand," Brian said.

"You can't just take away the two people I love most in life," Connie said. "I'm coming too."

"I guess I'm left out in the cold," Vicia said. "And it doesn't even snow in Brunswick."

"I forgot about you, Vicia," Connie said.

"Yes, that seems to happen more frequently lately," Vicia said.

"Roger said nothing about sending for you, Miss Sniar," Doctor Kukovich said. "You are, after all, Robert Sniar's daughter."

"I wish he'd send for me. Hey wait, I can ask him to send for me. Give me that phone!" Vicia demanded.

Vicia made a brief phone call and then finished.

"Father is coming here to pick me up!" Vicia said.

"That will take twice as long," Doctor Kukovich said, "to fly from the South Atlantic to here and back."

"You don't understand," Vicia said. "He's at the airport now. Here, in Brunswick."

"Huh?" Connie said.

"He said he lost faith in Doctor Kukovich and came back to speed things up," Vicia said.

"Hah!" Doctor Kukovich uttered. "That is why I work for Roger Dayla and not Robert Sniar. Little does he know...but that is another matter."

"I think he was joking. He didn't say the real reason. Well it doesn't matter. I get to see my father, and we can ride to the South Atlantic together. Hey! Maybe we can all ride together."

"Uh, no," Brian said. "The SOZOD must be loaded specially on the Sara Vossy."

"That's the private plane I mentioned," Doctor Kukovich said. "It will take another few hours to do so. You might as well go ahead and fly with your father, Vicia."

"Yeah, go fly with your father," Brian repeated.

"Hmph!" Vicia said. "I didn't think people could be so rude."

"It's not you, Viss," Connie said.

"Yeah, right!" Vicia said. "Well, I have *plans* with my father at the airport. See you in the South Atlantic, suckers!"

Yakhont Seamount, South Atlantic Ocean

Sparfiacus, a dusky dolphin, swam over to the Yakhont Seamount just west of his home in the R.S.A. Seamount. He passed through a special semipermeable layer which separated the outside ocean from an inside world of air and great stone masonry, a place known as Phocayna, and inhabited by dalli porpoises (Dall's porpoises) in humanoid form. Sparfy took humanoid form himself upon transitioning from water to air.

"Prince Sparfiacus," said a dalli porpoise.

"Prince Metavasi? Is that you?" Sparfy asked.

"Yes. I'm all grown up," said Metavasi. "You're here to see my parents, the king and queen. Aren't you?"

"Yes, yes I am," Sparfy said.

"They are expecting you. This way please," Metavasi said.

"Thank you," Sparfy said.

Sparfy passed through several large chambers with small pools where dalli porpoises were in a variety of phases between porpoise and humanoid shape. Some were cleaning, some were eating, and many were conversing and playing.

"Your citizens are rather casual considering the circumstances," Sparfy said.

"They do not know of what's happening in your realm, Prince Sparfiacus," Metavasi said.

"Your father hasn't said anything?" Sparfy said.

Metavasi shrugged his fins.

"Hmm. This concerns me. Well, I'm glad I came here," Sparfy said.

Metavasi led Sparfy to the great chamber, where King Tugan and Queen Brela reigned.

"The Kingdom of Phocayna welcomes Prince Sparfiacus of the Kingdom of Rhynchus," Metavasi said.

Members of the king's court applauded and welcomed Sparfy.

"Greetings, Prince Sparfiacus of Rhynchus," King Tugan said.

"We are honored by your visit, Prince Sparfiacus. Our dolphin cousins are always welcome," Queen Brela said.

"And I am honored to meet with my porpoise neighbors," Sparfy said. "But I have urgent news that needs our immediate attention."

King Tugan waved for the others to leave. Metavasi stayed behind.

"You too, Metavasi," Queen Brela said.

"But I'm a prince. Sparfy is a prince. Why can't I stay?" Metavasi asked.

"Keep the other porpoises preoccupied," Queen Brela said. "Do some backflips or something in the royal pool."

"Yes, Mother," Metavasi said, and he left.

"It's just us now, Sparfiacus," King Tugan said.

"Tugan, the humans have not abated their assault on our kingdom. They are continuing their attempt to breach Rhynchus Prime," Sparfy said.

"But they will not get through. Your seamount is impenetrable," Tugan said.

"All seamounts in Lagenora are impenetrable," Brela said. "The treaty with the electric rays has guaranteed this."

"I know, yes, the treaty says so. But these humans are very determined. They will continue trying," Sparfy said.

"Let them. They have only their time to waste," Tugan said. "Why do you worry, Sparfiacus?"

"If it were only the humans, then I would ignore them as you suggest. But it isn't. I feel that the orcas south of our kingdom have a flipper in this," Sparfy said.

"The orcas? Of Aiadaka?" Brela asked.

"The same," Sparfy replied.

"But they have no power in Rhynchus," Brela said.

"Not yet, though they desire it badly," Sparfy said.

"It's well known that the orcas of Aiadaka seek to occupy all of Lagenora and oust or eat the rest of us," Tugan said. "But every seamount is protected by a duality of cetacean and electric ray. The rays are not about to break these treaties."

"The orcas are cetaceans too," Sparfy said.

"And they have their own electric rays in Aiadaka," Tugan said.

"Yes, but not as many as they once did," Sparfy said.

"Oh? Did they die? We have heard nothing of this," Brela said.

"It's been kept quiet until we could determine cause," Sparfy said.

"We?" Tugan asked.

"Well, Korlan, myself, and the king and queen of Rhynchus—my parents," Sparfy said. "About two months ago, a group of electric rays sought refugee status in Rhynchus. We granted it, of course. Korlan spoke with them and learned that the orcas have begun farming giant squid inside the lowest seamount of Aiadaka."

"That's Phira, if I remember," Brela said.

"Yes, Phira," Sparfy said.

"But we farm squid too, though not giant squid," Tugan said.

"The refugees claim these new squid are different. They are thorium-based, like us cetaceans and the electric rays," Sparfy said.

"A new thorium life form. There were only us two. Now there are three," Brela said.

"The rays that escaped said these squid draw more power than they generate," Sparfy said. "They are only useful as a food for wild orcas."

"Then wild orcas outside Lagenora can become thorium-based like orcas of Aiadaka," Tugan said. "Now it makes sense."

"The orcas will then need more space because there will be more of them," Brela said.

"Well, there have been no more refugees, and things are strangely quiet with Aiadaka," Sparfy said.

"You mean quiet *in* Aiadaka?" Tugan asked.

"No, not *in*. Because we don't know what's going on inside Aiadaka. In fact, the kingdom has become much closed and very private. Korlan tried to sneak in but was caught and turned away," Sparfy said. "All he could get out of the Aiadaks was that they are in festival."

"Most say they are in festival when they are up to no good," Brela said.

"I agree," Sparfy said.

"So what is their next move?" Tugan asked. "Will they attack another seamount?"

"I don't know," Sparfy said. "I've seen no orca scouts of any kind near Rhynchus. That's why I suspect the humans are somehow involved."

"Are the orcas conspiring with the humans? Humans always think they are at the top of the evolutionary chain, that we cetaceans are little more than animals," Tugan said.

"Again, I don't know about any conspiracy. I tried getting Korlan to help. He is the most advanced Atlantic torpedo ray of his kind, and I know he has an acute sense of changes in electrical charge and so can read brainwaves of all sorts of animals, humans included, but he is still obsessed with Aiadaka itself and the possibility of an orcan attack, and so I can't shake his focus," Sparfy said. "My father, King Acus, is mobilizing our army around the seamount and watching it day and night."

"I hope it's enough," Brela said.

"It might not be," Sparfy said.

"Have you contacted the bottlenose dolphins for aid?" Tugan said. "They have the largest army in Lagenora."

"Not yet," Sparfy said. "Tursiopus is so remote. But Rhynchus and Phocayna are much closer to Aiadaka. I would think the orcas would strike our two regions first. I haven't seen humans attempting any sort of drilling on Phocayna, so I hope that this means they will leave your kingdom alone."

"So do we," said Brela.

"We feel confident that Phocayna is safe," Tugan said. "But for your sake, Prince Sparfiacus, I am tempted to swim up to Tursiopus and ask for the help of our bottlenose cousins."

"But they swim so slowly," Brela said.

"So do I, compared to a dalli," Sparfy said.

"Yes, but at least you are quicker than a bottlenose. I know they are the most popular with humans," Brela said.

"Yes, that's another reason to enlist their help," Tugan said. "If I could convince them to swim around the drilling platform and do backflips and yap and call to the humans, they would be entertained enough to go home."

"I think the days of humans exploring the dolphin enchantments are over," Sparfy said. "Humans are more interested in exploitation than exploration."

"Then there's only one thing to do," Tugan said. "We must assist your father and swim guard over Rhynchus in preparation for attack."

"I hate the thought of attack or being attacked," Sparfy said. "I try to keep an open mind when it comes to other mammals. But this is the reason I came to visit. To ask for your help."

"And we will give it. We will not attack the humans but merely the tools they possess. Humans are helpless without tools," Tugan said. "I will lead an army of dalli porpoises. Metavasi will accompany me, so that he may prepare for the day when he leads his own army."

"And I will also swim guard," Brela said. "There may be many injured cetaceans. And should a human be injured, I will render assistance."

"I'm glad to hear that," Sparfy said. "Above all, we want no loss of life. But we may have orcas to deal with. I foresee that they may begin an attack when the humans escalate theirs."

"I'm not afraid of orcas," Tugan said. "No orca can catch us."

"They may yet catch you in your old age, Tugan," Brela said. "Now Metavasi—"

"Metavasi can swim spirals around them," Tugan said. "I've never seen a cetacean swim so quickly. Sparfiacus, if you are ever interested in racing my son, I'm sure that he would accept the challenge."

"We dusky dolphins are no match for any dalli porpoise," Sparfy laughed. "But I am glad to have you as allies and not enemies."

"There's no need for cetaceans to have enemies within our own," Brela said.

"And there would be none, except for those orcas. Once in a while, they kill dolphins when they should leave well enough alone," Tugan said.

"I know. I wish I had your speed, Tugan and Brela. The orcas have been known to chase down and eat my kind," Sparfy said. "I know you can out-run them or at least keep ahead of them. Perhaps that's why you don't worry so much. But we dusky dolphins aren't so fortunate."

"It's unethical and immoral," Tugan said. "One dolphin hunting another. It's as bad as humans killing their own."

"Well perhaps we can change that," Sparfy said.

"Change what?" Brela asked. "The dolphins or the humans?"

"Maybe a little of both," Sparfy replied.

Sniar Central Airport, Brunswick, Georgia

"Father, father!" Vicia cried as her father stepped off his private, custom jet that resembled a small Concorde.

"Vicia my child!" Robert Sniar said. "I missed you terribly!"

"Me too!" Vicia said. "I'm glad you're here."

"Only for a few minutes," Robert Sniar said. "Just long enough to refuel the plane and exchange the crew. But I have a surprise for you."

"What's the surprise?" Vicia asked. "Is this the real reason you flew back?"

Robert grinned.

"When I mentioned to one of my liaisons in Washington that we were about to make a breakthrough for massive amounts of oil, he agreed to witness the event personally," Robert Sniar said.

"Who? Who, father, who?" Vicia asked.

"Here. He's driving up now," Robert Sniar said.

A limousine drove up. Out stepped the chauffeur, who in turn opened the main limo door. Out stepped Senator Croius with his assistant, Arcella.

"Omigosh!" Vicia said in shock, remembering that this was the man she spoke of during her *Today's Snitchline* show.

"Senator Croius. This is a great honor," Robert Sniar said.

"And may I present my lovely assistant, Arcella," the senator said.

"Mr. Sniar, may I call you Robert?" Arcella said in an overly personal and friendly way.

"I, uh, wow," Robert said. "Did you say this is your assistant?"

"Just an assistant," Senator Croius said, and he gave a hypersonic signal to Arcella that no one else heard, saying, "Gain Sniar's confidence."

"Vicia, this is going to be the best oceanic flight ever, don't you think?" Robert said.

"I'm thrilled to pieces," Vicia said flatly and with disdain. "Oh where did I go wrong?"

"What was that, my dear?" Senator Croius asked.

"I mean, you seem so strong!" Vicia said.

"I have killer strength and animal magnetism," the senator boasted.

"Yuck," Vicia muttered.

"Are you ready to soar?" Arcella asked Robert with tender passion.

"You bet!" Robert replied. "Let's go!"

The plane was refueled, re-provisioned with supplies, and the replacement crew had arrived. The four and crew entered the plane, the hatch was closed, and the plane left Sniar Central Airport for the South Atlantic.

Dayla Industries Hangar, Brunswick, Georgia

"It seems so strange for us to be flying without Mother and Father," Connie said while sitting in a waiting room in the hangar. "But I suppose we should get used to it."

"We'll get used to it," Debbie parroted.

"I feel strange, like this is the last time we'll see this place," Connie said.

"Don't say that!" Debbie said. "Just don't!"

"But it feels so empty here," Connie said. "Don't you feel it?"

"Yes, I do. It feels like...no, I don't want to say it," Debbie said.

"It feels like we're waiting for the limousine to take us to a funeral," Connie said.

"Yeah, it does," Debbie said.

"Maybe this was a bad idea," Connie said. "Oh, what's taking Brian so long? He was supposed to be finished installing that SOZOD on the Sara Vossy or whatever."

"You know, you don't have to go," Debbie said. "I'll be okay."

"That's crazy for you to go alone," Connie said. "Yeah, I know, there's Doctor Kukovich and Father's private crew and even Brian. Brian! I can't let him go down there alone. I must go for his sake—and yours."

The Sara Vossy was wheeled down from a storage area into the main open area of the hangar.

"The space shuttle!" Connie said. "What in the world is that doing here?! But it's been stretched long and thin, and it has extra little fins in back."

"It's the Sara Vossy," Debbie said as if reading a plaque. "It is slightly based on the American space shuttle but made with sleek lines to sustain hypersonic flight. It has a cargo bay and wings and engines like the shuttle, but it also has an ejection capsule. And there's something else about it. It has a very strange way of storing fuel."

"We can't be going to the South Atlantic in *that*!" Connie said. "It's just a glider."

"The space shuttle and Buran were gliders, but this one can take off without external rockets," Debbie said.

"Huh?"

The Sara Vossy stopped. A hatch opened, and steps descended to the hangar floor. Brian appeared in the doorway, walked down the steps, and approached the young women.

"We're ready to go," Brian said.

Connie stared at the Sara Vossy, at Brian, at the plane, and back at Brian.

"Yeah, kind of looks like a space shuttle went through the wringer, doesn't it?" Brian asked.

"It does," Connie said. "And...doesn't."

"No SRBs and no external fuel tank," Brian said.

"It will take off like a conventional airplane," Debbie said, "and land like one. But it can also land vertically, like a Harrier or F-35B."

"Wow! I didn't think anyone knew that. Did your father tell you?" Brian asked.

"No. I sensed it," Debbie said.

"I knew it. ESP again," Brian said.

"That's so old fashioned, and no one believes it anyway," Connie said. "How can you as a science dude believe in such a thing?"

"Because there's no other word in science to describe it," Brian said.

"I can sense subtle voltage differences from a distance," Debbie said. "This lets me learn about things not obvious to others."

"There, you see? ESP!" Brian stated.

"That's *not* ESP!" Connie said.

"Is too," Brian said.

"Is not."

"Is too!"

"Not!"

"Are you two going to argue like this all the way to the R.S.A. Seamount?" Doctor Kukovich said, now walking up to the three.

"I thought you were in the aircraft waiting for us," Brian said.

"I was. And I waited, and waited, and waited some more!" Doctor Kukovich said. "It's time to go. You can argue on the way down."

And so, the four boarded the Sara Vossy. It was towed out of the hangar, and then the tow vehicle unhitched itself. The pilot of the Sara Vossy fired up the engines at very low thrust to propel the craft toward a runway while Doctor Kukovich gave final instructions.

"Stay in your seats with the belts on until we are cruising in the air. We're not going into space, so there's no need to don a space suit. But we will be flying at Mach speed once we are far enough from land, and at a higher altitude than regular aircraft so we can fly quicker."

The Sara Vossy reached the runway. The pilot turned up the thrust on the engines, and the craft blasted down the runway at three Gs of force. It turned toward the Atlantic Ocean, gained altitude quickly, and then accelerated to 3300 miles per hour.

"We will reach our destination in two hours," Doctor Kukovich said.

"You are using a mass compressor," Debbie said. "That's how you can travel such great distances without refueling."

Doctor Kukovich put a hand over his face.

"You're not supposed to know that," Brian said. "That's the biggest secret of Dayla Industries. Only three people know about it—your father, my father, and me."

"And now me and Connie," Debbie said.

"Mass compressor?" Connie asked. "What's that?"

"Shh," Brian said.

"It's a way of compressing matter without causing nuclear fusion," Debbie said. "It works by flattening the electron orbits in atoms. Works best with lighter elements like hydrogen. The lighter the element, the easier to compress."

"You can read all that?" Brian asked.

"Yes," Debbie said.

"I don't ever remember you being like this," Connie said. "Ever."

"Something has happened to me. It's like a radio antenna is suddenly working, and I can receive lots of different radio stations."

"I'll have to investigate to see what your range is," Doctor Kukovich said. "But Debbie, I must warn you. This ability to sense knowledge comes with great caution and responsibility. It can serve you or be made to serve others."

"I will try to remember that. Serve or be served," Debbie said.

"Well, not quite like that. Just be careful. Sometimes quiet knowledge is better than the open truth," the doctor said.

"Quiet knowledge? Like I should be quiet?" Debbie asked.

"Please," Doctor Kukovich said.

"You know, the ocean is so calm and peaceful that it's hard to believe there are seamounts and stuff down there," Connie said. "So where exactly is the R.S.A. Seamount?"

"You don't know?" Doctor Kukovich replied. "I would have thought your father would have told you."

"I know it's in the South Atlantic, but it seems so far away," Connie said.

"There are many other seamounts around it. There's the Zenker Seamount to the south, the McNish Seamount to the southwest, Yakhont Seamount to the west, and many other unnamed seamounts in the vicinity."

"There are also four islands nearby," Brian said.

"Not that near, Brian," Doctor Kukovich said.

"Near considering the speed of the Sara Vossy," Brian said.

"What islands?" Connie asked.

"Tristan da Cunha, Nightingale Island, and Inaccessible Island to the northwest," Brian said.

"And Gough Island to the west. Perhaps it would be easier to explain if I give you a map," Doctor Kukovich said.

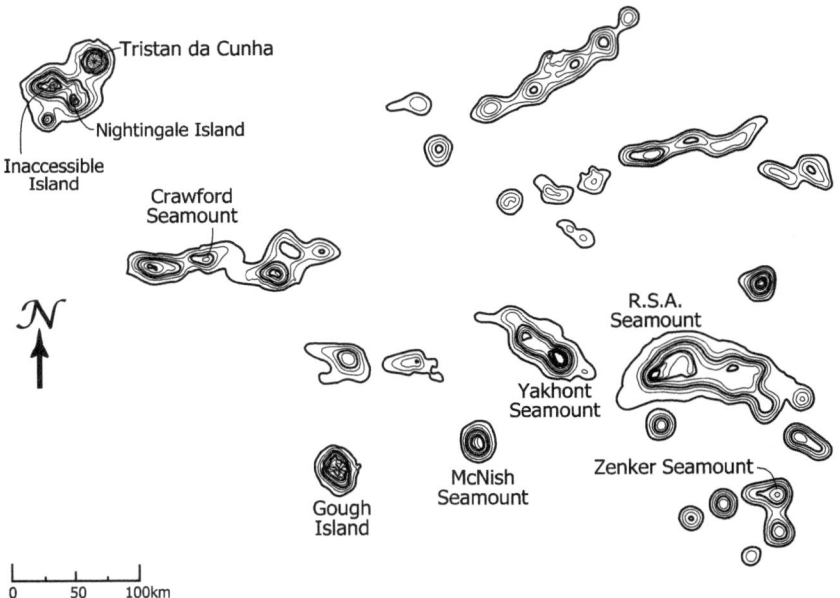

Doctor Kukovich handed a map to Connie.

"Look at all those seamounts," Connie said.

"The R.S.A. Seamount is just the beginning," Doctor Kukovich said. "When this is successful, we will explore all surrounding seamounts for oil and other valuable resources."

Debbie felt a twinge in her neck as if being squished by a crowd of dying people.

"What is it?" Brian asked.

"I...it's nothing," Debbie said. "I just thought...I felt...death."

Debbie shuddered.

"It's just nerves," Doctor Kukovich said. "I'm excited too. It will pass."

But it did not pass. Debbie was agitated and concerned with what she was about to do. She looked at Connie for reassurance, but Connie was too busy staring at the map.

"Try to relax, if you can," Doctor Kukovich said. "Brian and I will finalize adjustments to the SOZOD."

"I'll try," Debbie said.

Debbie tried closing her eyes, but she still felt nervous, and she instead stared out the window at the featureless ocean waves as they passed. Perhaps an hour passed, and without warning, the Sara Vossy stopped, or rather it held a fixed position above the ocean.

"What's happening?" Connie asked. "Why aren't we moving?"

"The SOZOD," Debbie said. "It's ready."

"We need to perform a test," Doctor Kukovich said. "Debbie?"

"I...don't know...if I should," Debbie said.

"It's a harmless test," Doctor Kukovich said. "We will point the SOZOD toward the ocean and see how it performs."

"Okay," Debbie said.

"Will we be safe?" Connie asked.

"We'll take all the necessary precautions," Brian said. "Here, wear these muffs. They will protect your ears from possible injury."

"Huh?" Connie asked. "But that SOZOD thingy wasn't loud in the lab."

"That was at a lower test setting," Brian said. "We've increased its strength from 0.01% to 1%. We need you to wear this headset, Debbie."

Debbie looked at Connie for advice.

"I guess it's okay," Connie said.

"All right," Debbie said.

She took the headset and placed it on her head.

"Power...on," Doctor Kukovich said. "Guidance system...on. Primary target...selected. Voice activation sequence...ready. Debbie? It's all on you now."

Debbie sensed the force of the SOZOD nearby. Her skin tingled like electric ants stinging her every fiber. She hummed softly, and the SOZOD shot out a twirling carousel ring like that in the lab, only larger and more powerful.

Meanwhile, on the Sniar aircraft, Arcella was swept with euphoria as she sensed the SOZOD testing, even from afar.

"My Lord Croius. Doctor Kukovich is testing the SOZOD on the Sara Vossy," Arcella said with gratification in her voice. "The experience of the SOZOD...well...I must say I am overwhelmed with joy. And the test is only a fraction of what we can expect upon Rhynchus. I can barely contain myself!"

"Shh," Croius said. "Do not alert the others. We must contain our celebration until the final moment of victory."

"I know," Arcella said. "But I cannot contain myself. Victory is so close...Rhynchus is ours. Rhynchus is ours!"

Back on the Sara Vossy, Debbie had stepped up her humming into singing, and the SOZOD imparted its destructive energy on the ocean. The water churned and flowed upward and outward, like a giant drill slinging debris up and outward. And then it happened—marine life began churning up from the water. Debbie felt a new course of energy through her body, and she sang outward much like she did against Jayvogg. The sound amplified beyond what Doctor Kukovich expected, and the shock waves bounced back from the ocean surface and into the Sara Vossy, causing the walls to shake and vibrate and nearly break apart.

"Stop it! It's too much! Stop it now!" Connie yelled.

But no one could hear her over the thunderous SOZOD. Doctor Kukovich was mesmerized by the SOZOD, but he caught himself and turned off the device. Debbie fell off her chair, the headset snapped off, and she remained on the floor, prone, and unconscious.

"Debbie!" Connie called out.

"What is that?" Brian said as he looked at the ocean surface.

"I count approximately two hundred dead cetaceans," Doctor Kukovich said. "They appear to be melon-headed whales. Brian, retrieve one for an autopsy. I'll tend to Debbie."

Debbie regained consciousness. Connie and Doctor Kukovich helped her to her chair.

"How do you feel?" Doctor Kukovich asked.

"A little dizzy," Debbie said.

"Here, drink this," Doctor Kukovich said as he passed her a drink.

Debbie took a sip.

"I feel better," Debbie said.

"Good," Doctor Kukovich replied.

"What happened?" Connie asked. "Was there a problem?"

"Instruments showed a powerful feedback loop," Doctor Kukovich said. "The SOZOD nearly destroyed the Sara Vossy. We will need to make several adjustments."

"First autopsy is available," Brian said.

"What?! How did you do that so fast?" Connie asked.

"The SOZOD has an auxiliary mode that scans and analyzes tissue systems," Debbie said. "The autopsy was performed with the cetacean floating on the ocean surface."

"Amazing," Doctor Kukovich said. "Your sensory powers are impressive."

"But she's right," Brian said. "And we are getting more autopsy reports. All two hundred melon-headed whales died from eardrum rupture."

"You...killed them," Connie said. "Oh Debbie, this is all wrong. We can't do this. It kills!"

"It was a bad test, yes," Doctor Kukovich said. "But we can refine the SOZOD so that it minimizes sonic rupture. You must trust us, Connie."

"Is this true, Debbie?" Connie asked.

"I...don't know," Debbie replied.

"I wouldn't have asked you to the South Atlantic otherwise. I'm an engineer, but I'm also a scientist," the doctor said. "I do believe in the preservation of life."

"Do we trust him, Debbie?" Connie asked.

"I...don't know," Debbie replied.

"Tell you what. I'll have the computer scan the surrounding marine life for any sustained injury and have the SOZOD's operation terminated. Will that satisfy you?"

"I...guess," Debbie said.

"If you can promise no more animals will die, then—" Connie said.

"I can," Doctor Kukovich said.

"Then I guess it's okay," Connie said.

"Wonderful," Doctor Kukovich said. "You won't regret this. And your father will be a new man when this is all over."

"It will change his life," Debbie said, unsure of what her words meant.

Inside the R.S.A. Seamount, South Atlantic Ocean

Sparfy returned to his own kingdom of Rhynchus, in the R.S.A. Seamount. As with Phocayna, he passed through a semi-permeable layer, leaving the ocean and entering an air-filled environment. As a dusky dolphin, he reached a pool of water where he changed into humanoid form. He stepped out of the pool and into an alcove, which in turn was connected to a large subterranean city, with shops, homes, and open park areas. There were lots of humanoid dolphins and electric rays busy with shopping, socializing, and overall enjoyment of themselves.

"Prince Sparfiacus," Korlan waved, seeing Sparfy from a distance.

Sparfy walked over to Korlan.

"How did it go? No wait, don't tell me, let me sense your thoughts," Korlan said. "King Tugan and Queen Brela fully support our defensive position. They will send an army over to help. It was a success, then."

"Yes," Sparfy said with dejection in his voice.

"Then why are you unhappy?" Korlan asked.

"I don't welcome what is about to happen. Dolphins and humans will die."

"It might not be so," Korlan said. "The humans have stopped drilling."

"Really?" Sparfy perked up.

"Yes. Perhaps now they realize that they cannot break through the Rhynchus outer wall," Korlan said.

"That is good news. But we cannot celebrate until the humans have withdrawn all equipment and returned to their country. And so we will continue to guard the waters," Sparfy said. "Hmm. This surprises me that the humans have given up. They can be very obsessive. Still, this may give me time to swim up to Tursiopus and secure the help of our bottlenose cousins."

"If you like getting lots of exercise," Korlan said. "The swim may be for nothing."

"Yes. I will go soon. First I must bring word to my father about our alliance with the dalli porpoises," Sparfy said.

"I'm going that way myself," Korlan said. "I also have news for the king."

Sparfy and Korlan walked past the many stores and citizens going about their business without any awareness of the oil rig above. More than once, Sparfy was greeted warmly by young, unmarried countesses and duchesses, with hugs and kisses.

"Sometimes I wish I were a young, unattached dolphin like you," Korlan said. "Look at all the attention you get."

"It's actually tiring," Sparfy said. "Each of them is hoping to form a royal relationship with me, nothing more. It's all a political game. But if it came down to having an honest conversation about real issues, well, that's another matter."

"Does that include Princess Adelfarina of Corleopus?" Korlan asked. "She's here, you know."

"Delfa? Here?" Sparfy asked in excitement. "Where?"

"So you are not as tired of female royalty as you claim," Korlan laughed.

"Well, Delfa is not just another dolphin," Sparfy said. "She's...she's all cetacean wrapped in one. But where did you see her?"

"I didn't," Korlan said. "But I sense she is in the Royal Courtyard, conversing with King Acus and Queen Sparla."

"She's speaking with my parents? Oh no. This can't be good!" Sparfy said, and he quickened his pace toward the Royal Palace.

Korlan laughed, but he had a bit of trouble keeping up with Sparfy, who was practically running.

"I have to wonder, Prince Sparfiacus, which is more urgent—your interest in the humans, or the presence of the princess?"

"Both are matters of great urgency, and I don't appreciate so many questions at once!" Sparfy said.

Korlan chuckled. But Sparfy now went into a full run and left Korlan far behind. Sparfy reached the Royal Palace. The doorman opened the door, and Sparfy entered. He walked from a small lobby-like area into the Royal Courtyard, where Delfa was speaking with Sparla.

"His favorite food is Atlantic mackerel," Sparla said. "But they are so hard to find. They are plentiful up north, but non-existent in these waters. He often sends merchants up north to herd a group to Rhynchus, but so far no merchants have succeeded. Supposedly any dolphin who succeeds in bringing such a school to Rhynchus will win his heart."

"Does that offer extend to other kingdoms, such as Corleopus?" Delfa asked. "What other secrets can you tell me about Sparfy?"

"None," Sparfy said as he approached the two. "I live an ordinary life."

"Hardly," Sparla said. "But welcome back to Rhynchus."

"Thank you, Mother," Sparfy said as he hugged her.

"You remember Princess Adelfarina of Corleopus, don't you?" Sparla asked.

Sparfy looked at Delfa, and she returned a grin.

"I remember," he said. "I take it she came here to see me?"

"Why no," Delfa said.

"No?!" Sparfy wondered.

"She brings news of humans exploring the outer wall of Corleopus," Sparla said. "She was going to ask for our help until—"

"Until I saw an even larger human effort drilling into Rhynchus," Delfa said. "I thought you were over in Phocayna, Sparfy."

"I was. King Tugan and Queen Brela are doing fine. So is Prince Metavasi," Sparfy said.

"I like Metavasi. He's such a fast swimmer. I should visit Phocayna on my way back. Perhaps Metavasi and I can—"

"I'm a fast swimmer too. Quickest of us dusky dolphins," Sparfy said.

Sparla and Delfa laughed.

"I think Acus is calling me," Sparla said as she began walking away.

"I don't hear him," Sparfy said.

"Well *I* do," Sparla said, and she left.

"You're jealous," Delfa said.

"No I'm not. Well, maybe a little," Sparfy said.

"I was just teasing you about Metavasi," Delfa said.

"Then you *did* come here to see me," Sparfy said.

"No, I really did come to give news about my kingdom and the humans," Delfa said. "Don't look so glum. I didn't expect to see you here, as I said. But I'm glad to see you. I know I'm only a striped dolphin and can't compete against the female dusky dolphins in your kingdom, but I'm more aware of our world than they are, I think. Corleopus is not as large as Rhynchus, but we do make the most of our resources. And we are great thinkers and writers!"

"I know you are," said Sparfy. "I only wish our first meeting wasn't so embarrassing."

"It was only embarrassing for Prince Sparfiacus of Rhynchus," Delfa laughed. "There you were, a young dolphin, swimming all the way from Rhynchus to Tursiopus without your parents' permission so you could party with the bottlenose dolphins. But you were too intoxicated to make the trip back. And so you only made it as far as Corleopus. You came in, begged for help, and made a fool of yourself in front of my friends."

"I'm trying to forget. But I have you to thank. You worked things out and managed to keep both your parents and mine from finding out," Sparfy said.

"You would have done the same for me, if ever I were in such a situation. Not that I would. Too risky! Not to mention it's bad for brain cells. And we striped dolphins believe in maximizing our intellectual potential."

"You are as smart as you are beautiful, no doubting that," Sparfy said.

"Thank you," Delfa said.

"I especially like what you've done with your dolphin colors in humanoid form," Sparfy said. "Our people can carry over only the most basic designs, if we have any at all."

"We have the best electric rays in all of Lagenora," Delfa said. "I should lend you a few some time. Or better yet, visit me up in Corleopus soon. I'm sure our top rays can teach you how to shape your colors."

"I will. I wish I could visit with you now," Sparfy said.

"The humans? I know. I worry about them too," Delfa said.

"Fortunately, some of us in Rhynchus are monitoring human activity," said Korlan who had just now caught up with Sparfy.

"Korlan, this is—" Sparfy started.

"Princess Adelfarina of Corleopus," Korlan said. "I'm Korlan, Archray of Rhynchus."

"So you're Korlan," Delfa said. "My archray has spoken much about you."

"All good, I hope?" Korlan said.

"He says you're the smartest electric ray in Lagenora," Delfa said.

Korlan puffed his chest out with pride.

"Outside of Corleopus," Delfa laughed.

Korlan turned red with anger.

"Your archray? Would that be Archray Diplobus?" Korlan said.

"Of course. He says you were a student of his," Delfa said. "And a very good student at that."

"I didn't know you visited Corleopus," Sparfy said to Korlan.

"Korlan is from Corleopus," Delfa said. "Didn't you know?"

Sparfy looked at Korlan in surprise, and Korlan shrank back.

"I thought you were from Aiadaka!" Sparfy said to Korlan.

"I had family in Aiadaka. That doesn't mean I'm from Aiadaka," Korlan said.

"I know lots of things about Korlan and his family when they left Corleopus for Aiadaka," Delfa said.

"That would be something I'd like to hear," Sparfy smirked.

"Perhaps another time," Korlan said. "We must meet with the king and queen about the humans."

Korlan led the way with Sparfy and Delfa following.

"Escort me, please," Delfa said. "This *is* a royal visit. A princess should be escorted by a prince in his domain."

Sparfy held his arm at a right angle, and Delfa placed her hand on his arm. The three then entered the royal Hall of Discussion. King Acus was seated on his throne, and Queen Sparla walked up to and sat on her throne, which was next to Acus's.

"King Acus and Queen Sparla of Rhynchus, I beg that you hear me in the Hall of Discussion," Korlan said.

"You may be heard," King Acus said. "Welcome back, Korlan."

"You...went somewhere?" Sparfy asked.

"One moment, my son," King Acus said. "Korlan, what news from Aiadaka?"

"Aiadaka!" Sparfy said.

"As Your Royalness knows, Aiadaka has closed itself off from the rest of Lagenora. Two months ago, a group of electric rays escaped and became citizens of Rhynchus. Recently, I went to Aiadaka to find out why it has been closed to the outside, especially with the troubling news that the orcas are raising thorium squid. I was turned away in a prior attempt as you may recall, but I decided it was time to try again."

Korlan paused.

"Go on," Acus said.

"Aiadaka is becoming overpopulated with orcas," Korlan said. "Yes, I was able to get inside, with the help of my extended family."

"A secret entrance?" Sparfy asked.

"Something like that," Korlan said.

"What about the squid farming? Is it true?" Sparfy asked.

"Patience, my son," Acus said.

"Well, I only entered Aita, and there was no squid farming there," Korlan said.

"It was in Phira. Did you go to Phira?" Sparfy asked.

"No. That wasn't possible," Korlan said.

"Sparfy, allow Korlan to speak," Sparla said.

"The orcas have definitely begun their plans for expansionism, but so far they have not been successful. Recently, they launched an attack on the pygmy killer whales of Persipi, but the pygmy killer whales fought them off. The orcas were planning a second attempt on Persipi, but now they are putting a hold on that plan and instead planning an attack on Rhynchus. They will do so in an unconventional way."

"How unconventional?" King Acus asked.

"This is the strangest part. The plan assumes there will be a hole in the outer wall. But they don't plan to make that hole. Their plan says the hole will be made by others, after which they will then launch their attack."

"The humans?" Sparfy suggested.

"What makes you say that, my son?" King Acus asked.

"As I told King Tugan of Phocayna, we've seen no orca scouts in our waters. I suspect they will work with the humans to attack us. I'm willing to go so far as to say the recent oil rig above us is a part of the orcan attack plan."

"We've seen humans drill in the ocean before," King Acus said. "They are thirsty for the graveyards of ancient life. But could the oil rig be this unconventional attack you speak of, Korlan?"

"It's possible," Korlan said. "But it would mean that somehow, orcas and humans are communicating with one another. To my knowledge this has not happened."

"It has happened," Delfa said.

King Acus and Queen Sparla spoke in hushed voices with each other. The king called for an aide, spoke something in his ear, and sent him off.

"Please, Princess Adelfarina. Tell us what you know," Queen Sparla said.

"I have news about the orcas," Delfa said. "One of the orcas, Croius of Aita, has taken humanoid form and spent time with the humans."

"Intriguing," King Acus said.

"He joined the United States as a citizen. He ran for and won the office of senator. Arcella of Aita has also become a United States citizen, and she accompanies him wherever he goes," Delfa said.

"So, it has happened," King Acus said.

"I guess it was only a matter of time before one of us fulltrans decided to intermingle with the humans," Korlan said.

"I had hoped that it would have been one of us duskies," King Acus said. "But only when the time was right. I didn't think humans would be ready for another species to live as they do."

"The humans don't know Croius and Arcella are fulltrans," Delfa said.

"They think the two are human?" Queen Sparla asked.

"Yes," Delfa said.

"Then there's only one answer," Korlan said. "Croius and Arcella are deceiving the humans in an effort to manipulate them."

"I agree," Delfa said. "They will manipulate the humans to attack Rhynchus."

"The oil rig?" King Acus asked.

"I did not sense an orca was part of the oil rig above us," Korlan said.

"That's because the orcas have not been a part of the oil rig—yet," Delfa said. "But Croius and Arcella are on their way from the United States to Rhynchus, on an airplane with several humans—a pilot, the crew, and the two Sniar humans."

"Robert Sniar? The owner of Sniar Oil?" Korlan asked.

"Yes. And his daughter, Vicia Sniar," Delfa said.

"He brought his daughter?" Sparla asked.

"To show off what he's about to do," Sparfy said. "It's the only explanation."

"Then this is the imminent attack," Acus said. "Croius will have Sniar use his oil rig to attack Rhynchus."

"But this puzzles me," Korlan said. "They have already tried to attack us and have failed. I cannot envision how Croius and Arcella can make things different."

"We have detected another human aircraft on the way to Rhynchus," Delfa said.

"Who is on that craft?" Queen Sparla asked.

"The lead engineer of Dayla Industries, Doctor Anton Kukovich, among others," Delfa said.

"Dayla Industries," King Acus said. "Korlan, you mentioned something about a Dayla."

"Roger Dayla is the head of Dayla Industries. His company produces all sorts of devices and tools, many of which are used by Robert Sniar's oil rigs to drill," Korlan said.

"The doctor's son, Brian, is on the craft, and so are Roger Dayla's two daughters—Connie and Debbie," Delfa said. "They will meet with Roger's wife, Julie, on the AC Sniar aircraft carrier."

"Indeed," Sparfy said. "Both families will watch the event."

"I don't like the sound of that—*the event*," Queen Sparla said.

"But that is what things have come down to," King Acus said. "It's clear to me this Croius and Arcella of Aiadaka have orchestrated this event."

"They must have a weapon of some sort," Sparfy said.

"Yes, a weapon," Korlan said. "That would explain a lot."

"Nuclear?" Queen Sparla asked.

"No," Korlan said. "They are susceptible to radiation too. The radiation would make working in the area impossible."

"Then some other type of weapon," King Acus said. "A superweapon. Well, it's all very clear what we must do. We must find and destroy this superweapon before it is used against us."

"King Tugan and Queen Brela have sworn aid to us in the form of dalli porpoise guards," Sparfy said. "Delfa, is there a chance your people would be willing to help defend Rhynchus?"

"They would, but there's not enough time," Delfa said. "The human aircraft will be here before my striped dolphin people can swim from Corleopus to Rhynchus."

"Is our time that short?" Queen Sparla asked.

"From what Delfa says, I'd say yes," Korlan said.

"Then this is my decree," King Acus said. "Prince Sparfiacus and Archray Korlan are charged with finding and destroying this human superweapon. I will coordinate the defenses of Rhynchus from here."

"Let me help destroy the superweapon," Delfa said.

"It's too dangerous," Sparfy said. "I cannot let you."

"And I cannot order you without cause in this matter, Princess Adelfarina of Corleopus. But I give you leave to go wherever you wish in my kingdom, to help in any way you can."

"Then I choose to swim with Prince Sparfiacus to destroy the superweapon," Delfa said.

"No," Sparfy said.

"Make it a royal decree, King Acus," Delfa begged. "Permit me the honor."

"There is no honor in death," Sparfy said.

"But there is in life," Delfa said.

King Acus looked at Queen Sparla, and she nodded in affirmation.

"It is so decreed," King Acus said. "Princess Adelfarina shall swim with Prince Sparfiacus and Archray Korlan to find and destroy the human superweapon. The royal Hall of Discussion is closed."

Delfa grinned. The king and queen retired to a side room, and the three left the Hall of Discussion.

"You shouldn't have done that," Sparfy said.

"You need my help," Delfa said. "Besides, you like me."

"Yes, he does," Korlan said.

"Korlan!" Sparfy said.

"And you don't have to play hard-to-get forever," Delfa said. "You're stuck with me, Prince Sparfiacus."

"And he'll enjoy every moment of it," Korlan smirked.

Above the R.S.A. Seamount, South Atlantic Ocean

The Sniar aircraft landed aboard the AC Sniar aircraft carrier, the carrier being within visual sight of the Sniar oil rig. The side door opened, and a set of steps descended from the aircraft. Senator Croius descended first, followed by Robert Sniar with Arcella in hand. Vicia followed disgustingly in third.

"I wish Connie were here," Vicia moaned. "I should have brought her along for company. Well, she'll be here soon enough, and we'll just *have* to plot some revenge."

"Robert, dear, where does a woman go to freshen up after such a journey?" Arcella asked.

"I was going to give you a tour of my castle on the water, the AC Sniar, but I can begin by showing you the powder room. Follow me," Robert said.

The four went below deck to what looked like the inside of a large yacht, with all sorts of amenities for living. Robert pointed to the powder room.

"Father, may I speak with you?" Vicia said after Arcella stepped away.

Once Arcella disappeared around the corner but before she entered the powder room, Croius caught her and spoke.

"Keep close to Robert Sniar," Croius said. "Learn everything about this ship, especially the control room. If for some reason Miss Dayla does not—"

"I understand," Arcella said.

She disappeared into the powder room and re-emerged shortly thereafter, looking more beautiful than before.

"That's my Arcella!" Croius said.

Arcella walked back toward Robert, who was in an argument with Vicia, presumably about Arcella, but the two stopped conversing on Arcella's return.

"This ship...it's magnificent," Arcella said. "A true labor of love. I would like to see more of it."

"Yes, certainly!" Robert beamed. "Let me give you the tour! There's plenty of time!"

Robert whisked Arcella away and into grand tour mode, leaving Croius and Vicia behind. Vicia went back up on the deck, and Croius followed. Vicia stared across the ocean to the oil rig floating above the R.S.A. Seamount.

"The deck is a lonely place for a young woman," Croius said.

"There's plenty to do down below," Vicia said, trying to get rid of Croius.

"I saw your television broadcast about me," Croius said. "I was not pleased with it."

"That's old news," Vicia said. "Besides, it was all true."

"Yes, but no one knew about it, until you made the telecast. Tell me, Vicia, how—"

"It's Miss Sniar," Vicia said.

"Vissssssssia," Croius hissed, and he drew closer to her.

"Gaaaag, you're making me sick!" Vicia said as she shrank away.

"Wouldn't you like to know more about me?" Croius asked.

"No," Vicia said.

"Such as who I know, where I'm from, and what power I wield?" Croius asked.

"My father has real power. He can recover oil from anywhere on the planet. Countries pay well for oil. What do you pay?" Vicia asked.

"I can pay very well, for the right kind of loyalty and service," Croius winked.

"Ick," Vicia remarked. "You remind me of something slimy and slithery under a shaded stone. Like a snail or slug."

"As a matter of fact, I do like slipping through a cool pool in the summer," Croius said. "Perhaps you could join me for a swim. There's a pool on this ship."

"I feel like wearing a coat. Several coats. And huge sweaters," Vicia said, wanting to get away from Croius.

"You'll have to move to a safe spot," said a crewwoman to Vicia and Senator Croius. "The Sara Vossy will be here in five minutes."

"Connie!" Vicia said with glee. "I want to watch her land."

"There's an observation room over here. Follow me," the crewwoman said. "And Senator, there's a private call for you. You may take it in the communications room just over there."

The senator did not look happy, but he took the private call.

"Thank you," Vicia said.

"This observation room is plenty comfortable, but you already know that," the crewwoman said.

"Yeah, I know. I meant to say, thank you for getting rid of the senator for me."

"Oh, it was all by chance. He really does have a private call," the crewwoman said.

"Yeah, but you could have told him about the phone in here. But you didn't. Thank you," Vicia said.

"You're welcome. Enjoy your stay."

Croius became interested in other things for the moment, allowing Vicia the luxury of watching the Sara Vossy make its landing. Vicia ran out to greet Connie and Debbie.

"I'm so glad to see you two," Vicia said to Connie and Debbie. "I had a horrible ride down with that Senator Croius!"

"Senator Croius?!" Connie said. "What's he doing here?"

"I guess my father made a political deal with him or something. Says the senator wants to see the rig drill for oil," Vicia said.

"Well there goes the party!" Connie said.

"There goes the party!" Debbie repeated.

"I only wish Ramona were here," Connie said. "Then we could start our own little party."

"Why don't we anyway?" Vicia asked.

"Ah, ladies, good. You're all here," Croius said after having just finished with his phone call.

"There goes the party," Debbie said.

Brian and Doctor Kukovich exited the Sara Vossy, carrying equipment related to the SOZOD.

"Anton and Brian, I've just received word from Roger Dayla," Croius said. "The new equipment must be installed on the oil rig immediately. A crew here will assist you with the move. Ladies, you are needed down below for a special meeting."

"We aren't going with you anywhere," Vicia said.

"Actually, this meeting is for Connie and Debbie Dayla, Vicia. Their mother is below and would like to speak with them. As their friend, you are invited too. But if you'd rather stay up here with me, I would be more than happy to entertain you, Vissssssia Sssssssssniar."

"Let's go!" Vicia urged, and she rushed Connie and Debbie into a banquet room down below.

"Look at all the food!" Connie said. "Mother!"

Julie Dayla was seated at the end of a long table. A waiter brought her a pot of sweet tea and some appetizers. Connie, Debbie, and Vicia sat down, but not before Vicia noticed her father sitting at the bar with Arcella's arms locked around his shoulders.

"She's got her hooks in him. Hmph!" Vicia sneered.

"Sit down," Julie said. "Oh what am I doing? Give me a hug, all of you!"

First Connie hugged Julie, then Debbie. Vicia still had her attention on Arcella, but Julie broke that stare.

"You too, Vicia," Julie said, and she hugged Vicia. "It's good to see you. I know Connie and Debbie will be happy that you are keeping them company."

"What are friends for?" Vicia said.

"That's right," Julie said. "And you're a very good friend at that. Now the reason I asked you down here is to let you know how things are going to be during our stay. The men will work over on the drilling rig, and the women will remain here in supporting roles where it's safe."

"I thought you'd say something like that," Connie said.

"What's the matter?" Julie asked.

"Why are we always stuck in supporting roles?" Connie asked. "We should be the leaders."

"Okay, go ahead and lead," Julie said. "What's your first order?"

"First thing I want is a party, and plenty of champagne for all!" Connie said.

"And nothing gets done," Julie said. "You're fired."

"Awww," Connie whined.

"Mother wants us to have discipline and a strong work ethic. With that comes confidence and the inspiration to lead," Debbie said.

"Very good, Debbie!" Julie said. "I've been following the reports on the SOZOD. Seems you have mastered the device. Until Doctor Kukovich can program the computer to emulate your technique, it appears you'll be needed to help operate it. The rock structure is very unusual in these parts. It is very hard but brittle, tearing up all of our conventional tool bits. The SO-ZOD, with its ability to drill through and create a reinforcement tube, is the ideal solution, if it works out okay."

"So what happened to all women staying over here? Debbie gets to go over. Is that what I heard you say?" Connie asked.

"Only temporarily," Julie said.

"Everything is disguised as temporary," Vicia said to Connie. "Get over it."

"No, I won't *get over it*. What if this SOZOD thingy doesn't work? Do we *temporarily* go home? Or do we *temporarily* stay here longer?" Connie asked.

"We will continue trying until it does," Debbie said, as if reading Julie's mind.

"That's the right spirit," Julie said.

"It's oil," Vicia said in a resigned sort of way. "The world is fueled by oil. Temporarily. But do we know if there's any oil down there?"

"Nothing definitive," Julie said. "But sonography scans show a hollow section inside the seamount which could be a pocket of natural gas."

"I don't know," Vicia said. "Seems like there are lots of other places in the world to drill. It's going to be very expensive if no oil is found here."

"And then what?" Connie asked.

"We pack up and go home, and Father writes off a big fat loss on the books," Vicia said.

"We haven't gotten that far," Julie said. "Let's think positively."

"The SOZOD can be used to explore other seamounts for oil or other rare minerals," Debbie said.

"It could," Julie said.

"Well why do we all have to be here in the South Atlantic?" Connie said. "Let the little people do the work. We're Daylas! We should be enjoying life, not being slaves to menial work!"

"Connie!" Julie said.

"Mother!"

"Even the wealthy must work from time to time," Julie explained. "With great effort comes great reward."

"But we don't have to be the ones making the effort," Connie said. "Let others do it. We'll just take credit."

"Sometimes that's not enough," Julie said.

"Well it's stupid," Connie said.

Connie was becoming very agitated and annoyed with being displaced from her life in Brunswick. Julie was disappointed in Connie's behavior, and Vicia felt caught in between. Debbie, however, had her attention elsewhere, on the SOZOD device itself, and hummed practice tunes in her mind.

"I had hoped I could talk some sense into you three," Julie said. "Debbie seems to be on board with the plan."

"I'll stay here on the AC Sniar, of course. I can watch instruments or something," Vicia said.

"Good," Julie said.

"So I'm expected to work? Really? You're kidding!" Connie said.

"She can stay with me," Vicia said. "We can watch instruments together."

"Vicia!" Connie said.

"It's not much," Vicia said.

"It will have to do," Julie said.

"You know what I think? The men really want us down here in the South Atlantic to flaunt their egos and showmenship but want us safely out of the way so we won't interfere!" Connie said.

"It's somewhat true," Debbie said. "Though Mother really does have skills in geology that are helpful. And I'm helpful, at least for now."

"For now. Until Doctor Kukovich can replace you by a machine. When do we all get replaced by a machine?" Connie asked.

"Men love their machines first, the power from those machines second, and women third," Vicia said. "That's why we have to be clever and devious. No machine can do that."

"Really, Vicia, that's not necessarily true," Julie said.

"No? Just look at Arcella over there. She's up to something. I don't need a woman's intuition to know that."

"Just one weakness of some men," Julie said.

"One of many," Vicia said. "It's really a game, you see. Find all weaknesses of men and exploit them."

"No, no, no!" Julie said. "Pro-duc-tivity is the name of the game."

"They are young," Debbie said.

Julie looked at Debbie in surprise, since Debbie was younger than Connie and Vicia. She nodded slightly, and then her cellphone rang.

"How are you getting a signal out here?" Connie asked.

"The AC Sniar and oil rig have their own systems," Vicia said.

Julie listened more than spoke, and she was only on the call for a few seconds before ending it.

"Your father is coming over on a boat," Julie said.

"Oh, I should call Brian and see if he'll come over," Connie said.

"Don't bother," Julie said. "He won't come over. He's helping Doctor Kukovich install the SOZOD."

"All work and no play makes everyone dull and annoying!" Connie said. "I'm getting out of here!"

"Wait," Vicia said to Connie, but then she turned to Julie. "Mrs. Dayla, I'll keep Connie company and out of the way. I promise."

Julie paused.

"Okay," Julie said.

"C'mon, Connie, I'll show you around," Vicia said.

Croius stood on the deck of the AC Sniar, and Arcella met him briefly.

"All is going according to plan," Arcella said. "Robert Sniar is monitoring operations from here. The SOZOD is being installed on the drilling rig and will be operational soon. Roger Dayla is on his way over to take Debbie back to the rig, where she will help operate the SOZOD."

"Good," Croius said. "I have received communication from our supreme leader in Aiadaka."

"The mega squid? Aiatethis?" Arcella asked.

"Of course. And never refer to Aiatethis as *the mega squid*," Croius said. "It's disrespectful."

"Sorry," Arcella said. "Sometimes I wish—"

"Wish what?" Croius asked.

"Well...that we had...our own...with a...you know...just orcas," Arcella said.

"Don't even think such thoughts!" Croius said with a stern yet hushed voice. "Aiatethis would have you executed for such treason."

"I apologize. I give full allegiance to Aiatethis, Supreme Leader of Aiadaka," Arcella said.

"That's better," Croius said. "Now pay attention. Aiatethis has put out his tentacles and learned that the Rhynchos suspect the humans have a super-weapon. King Acus has given orders to have the superweapon destroyed."

"They know about the SOZOD then," Arcella said. "Our plans are ruined."

"No they are not!" Croius said. "Despite Prince Sparfiacus and his pathetic seadogs, he is no match for the knowledge and power of Aiatethis. The Rhynchos suspect there is a superweapon, but they do not know it as the SOZOD. They will make an attempt to board the drilling rig and disable whatever drilling device they can find. But they will fail. You will alert Robert about the marine life interfering with the drilling platform, and you will have the humans attack Prince Sparfiacus and his seadogs."

"Yes," Arcella said. "I hope it's enough."

"Enough?"

"Well, I would send a pack of our orcas into the waters and prevent Prince Sparfiacus from his attack," Arcella said.

"Well, you just leave the thinking to Aiatethis," Croius said. "We want the humans blamed for all hostilities. This means controlling them and having them perform work for us. We should not lower ourselves to such menial labor."

"Very well," Arcella said.

"Roger Dayla is nearly here," Croius said. "Go back below and keep Robert occupied."

Arcella descended below, and Roger's boat docked with the AC Sniar.

"Senator Croius," Roger said as he reached the AC Sniar's deck. "Welcome to the South Atlantic."

"This is a special day for the Department of Energy and for all Americans," Croius said.

"We are ready to begin," Roger said. "All preparations have been made. And so now Debbie will accompany me to the drilling rig and activate the SOZOD. You are welcome to join us."

"I appreciate the invitation," Croius said. "However, I will observe from the deck here. I may need to leave quickly to answer the media in the United States."

"I understand," Roger said.

Roger made a call on his cellphone. Julie brought Debbie and Connie to the deck. Roger spoke briefly with Julie, and then he spoke with Debbie and Connie. Connie protested, but Roger spoke directly with her and pointed out that she had to remain on the AC Sniar. Roger then left with Debbie and boated over toward the drilling rig.

"Listen to your father, Connie Dayla," Croius said. "He is highly skilled at his work."

Connie glared at Croius and then stormed off the deck and went below.

Croius laughed. The deck was now empty. Croius placed a hand to his temple, and a holographic image formed on the deck of Aiatethis, a super-mega-giant squid of thorium power who had its tentacles interwoven throughout Aiadaka.

"All is proceeding according to plan, my Supreme Leader," Croius said. "I await any final instructions."

"You are to observe the drilling rig from your position. Be prepared for utter destruction. On my command, you will take the Sara Vossy back to the United States and speak to the media. Take Arcella with you," Aiatethis said.

"Yes, my Supreme Leader," Croius said, and the holographic image dissipated.

Croius called below.

"Have the Sara Vossy refueled and prepared for departure."

Thirty minutes passed. Croius planted a suggestion into Connie's mind. He stood in a discreet location and observed Connie Dayla steal a boat and pilot over to the drilling rig. Then another thirty minutes passed.

"Senator, the Sara Vossy is ready for departure," called a crewman.

"Thank you," Croius said.

"And Roger Dayla says the SOZOD is ready for activation."

"Tell him to proceed," Croius said. "And send Arcella to the deck."

"Yes sir," the crewman said.

Two minutes passed. Arcella stepped onto the deck, and the Sara Vossy rolled into launch position.

"Look to the east, Arcella. Our destiny is unfolding," Croius said.

The SOZOD activated. A bluish-green beam resembling that which formed in Doctor Kukovich's lab shot downward from the drilling platform. At the same time, men on the side of the platform launched depth charges into the water to kill marine life. Explosions of water shot upward where the depth charges dropped. Marine life was hurled upward and then slapped down onto the ocean surface, dead. But that was not all. Sparfy and his seadogs leapt out of the water between depth-charge explosions and cried out, creating an electro-energy acoustic ring that closed in on the drilling rig and caused massive explosions. Metavasi sent a special explosive at the SO-ZOD itself.

"Something went wrong!" Arcella said. "The SOZOD has become deactivated."

"The humans have only partly succeeded," Croius said.

A mental image of Aiatethis formed in Croius's and Arcella's minds and said:

"Return to Aiadaka!"

Croius and Arcella slipped into the Sara Vossy, Croius started the aircraft's engines, and the two took off.

"Emergency, emergency!" called Robert's voice over the public address system.

The AC Sniar moved toward the drilling rig. It was engulfed in a fireball, and the aircraft carrier did what it could to throw ocean water on the blaze. Rescue boats launched from the AC Sniar and began searching desperately for survivors. There were many dead people floating in the ocean, and they were hauled onto the AC Sniar and placed in a make-shift morgue. Among them were Brian Kukovich and Connie, who were together at their deaths. Roger and Debbie were missing. Julie screamed when she saw her dead daughter, and she ran around in hysterics shouting at anyone and everyone to find her other daughter, Debbie, and her husband, Roger. She kept running and yelling, and the search continued. Nightfall came, and the doctor on the AC Sniar, to prevent Julie from giving herself a heart attack, gave her a sedative and put her to bed.

Trechopagia

I'm awake! Shooting pain! Stop, oh please stop torturing me, you demons of pain I cannot see. Let me sleep. Please. Let me sleep.

It's Sunday morning. Early. Very early. I think this is August. Why can't I remember? Ow! I remember pain. Another jolt in my legs. I'm lying on my bed. No, I'm sitting in bed now, with my legs over the side. I'm rubbing them with my left hand while speaking into this microphone with my right. A small tape recorder from my childhood. Do they make these anymore? I don't know. I can hold it in one hand. Portable. Ow!

Why am I in bed? Why am I so sick? Can't think straight. Need to re-member. Need to understand. Look for the answer. Where? I don't know. What's that sound? Music. I hear music through the open window. It's two in the morning, and I hear music. I'll look through the window. Yes, it's the neighbor playing his guitar softly. I could be in the Old West. No, I'm not. It may sound like it, but I'm in Kenosha, Wisconsin on 17th Street, living in a foreclosed house owned by Mockenboose Bank, on their charity (my wife says it's not charity, that by living in the foreclosed house and keeping it up, we prevent vandalism and help the house retain value). I lost my house. No, we lost our house—the wife and me. Her name is Brenda, and I'm Jack.

"John Mark Highbower," the new mother says to the nurse. "My baby's name is to be John Mark Highbower."

The nurse wraps me in a cloth and places me next to my mother.

"He has your eyes," says my grandmother.

"What will I do? Where will I live?" my mother asks.

"You will live with us," my grandmother says.

"I'm so sorry. You were right about Herbert. I should have said no. He was just like Barry, promising the world and all," my mother says. "They're nothing but hot air. Hot air."

"There are worse things," my grandmother says. "But let's say no more. You'll return to work when you're ready. In the meantime, I'll help you with John Mark."

Grandma picks me up and holds me. I don't cry or experience pain of any sort. She is warm and has a country-fresh aroma. Something says "home" when Grandma holds me, though I don't know language at the time.

Pain!

Another lightning jolt in my legs. I must walk the pain off. Forty-four years of age shouldn't give me pain like this. I will walk. Brenda is asleep. I can't sleep next to her while I'm like this. I stir too much, and she's got to get sleep to keep the bills paid. I can't work. I want to, but I can't.

There's an old wooden curtain rod in the corner. It is there temporarily. I'd meant to replace the blinds with curtains, but the pain, my sickness. Yes, I'm sick, I must be sick. Something is causing this pain. It can't be just me.

The curtain rod is long and as tall as me. I need slippers. There. Step out the front door onto the porch. I hear music, but now it is chimes. The houses across the street have hanging lanterns with chimes. They are new. Recharged by solar power in daytime. Now they blink, like fireflies in the night. And they dance on strings. Dance like...like...

It's windy outside, very windy. Mamma can't afford a car, so she can't drive me to school. She won't let me walk alone. Too windy. She's afraid I'll blow away. She sends me in the truck with Grandpa. We're in the mountains, high in the Appalachians on the Allegheny Front in a little town named Coyla. It's so windy. Big rocks are piled on the side of the road. Big rocks. They're edged along the sides, like grating. Grating. Grandpa's truck is big and roomy. I bounce up off the seat over every bump. He has the radio on. What is he listening to? The morning news. President Nixon has resigned. What's a president? I don't know. There's dancing. Traffic lights are dancing on wires from the wind, like happy children playing on a trampoline but not caring how they bump into one another. Twigs are flying about. The light is red, and Grandpa opens a well-worn brown bag to see what's for lunch. He smiles halfway. No, that is a grimace. I thought he smiled, but it pains him seeing the same sandwich day after day.

Pain!

I must move my legs. Been standing on the porch too long. I'll take a walk around back. My back yard adjoins a parking lot on Carthage's main campus. There are sidewalks, a bicycle path, and some inclines, but nothing steep. I'm walking. What is that thing there? Now it moves. Please don't be a skunk. No, it's a rabbit. It runs off in fright. I can't handle another skunk. Two were too many. There's a gate I must open to leave the yard. A gate.

I look out a window and see a gate to the playground. It's almost time for recess. My teacher calls my name to gain my attention. She's showing us a calendar, a big calendar, with each square as big as my palm. No a little bigger. There's a blue-colored transparency over a number eight. She's sliding it to the nine. It is Friday, August 9, 1974. There's a red transparency over the four. She is sliding it over the eleven.

"Bow your heads for morning prayer," the teacher says. "Dear Lord, we thank you for this day and every day. May we be good boys and girls and learn everything we can. Amen."

"Amen," we all reply.

"Welcome to the first day of school. You are now in the first grade," the teacher says.

First grade isn't like kindergarten. We don't sing and run around and sleep on mats. We sit in desks and learn to read. We learn to write. We learn mathematics. We have to learn. It is so much work. Why the work? I get my first headache from the work. Pain.

I want to go through the gate, but if I do, I leave my yard. Someone might see. What's that noise? Carthage students. They're returning from a party. Are they drunk? I can't tell. They are whispering. I thought college students were loud and boisterous. They're whispering like the wind. I can't stand here, but I can't go through the gate yet. They'll see. I'll walk along the fence a little.

I'm walking along the fence during recess. There's smoke. No. My classmates are digging up dirt and dropping it in the air. It's dry. I don't know why. I run to the teacher and cry, "Fire, fire!"

"There's no fire, John Mark," the teacher says.

"But look at the smoke!" I say.

"You can't fool me!" the teacher laughs. "Now you go to your friends and tell them to stop throwing dirt in the air."

She knows. How did she know? I stare at her as if she's a magician or something. Adults know everything. They must, to be adults. How do they get that way?

"I was a student like you at one time," she says. "I tried to fool my teacher, too."

I don't believe her. Adults are always adults. Always were and will be. I want to grow up, but I don't think I ever will. It's taking too long. I walk back along the fence toward my friends. I stop along the way. There's a gate from the playground to the parking lot. Dare I go through? I'm not supposed to. Teacher would say not to.

I open the gate and walk through. There is plenty of light from the Carthage lamp posts. The students have vanished, and that is good. They would laugh at a man using a wooden curtain rod as a walking staff. To think that some blind people use long sticks to get around. Should I try to scan the pavement in front like a blind person? I motion the curtain rod in front to test the pavement. It catches a small rut and sticks. I walk into the curtain rod, poking my abdomen. Ow.

"Ow!" I cry.

"Okay, pull him up," says an older boy.

It's my older brother, Matt. Two of his friends pull me up by my arms. I have fallen onto my bicycle. But it isn't my fault. The handlebars twisted loose, and I lost control of the front wheel.

"How many times have you been told not to leave the yard?" Matt says.

"But I wanted to follow you," I say. "I wanted to see where you're going."

"You're too little," Matt says. "I need to take you home now so Mamma can clean you up."

"No, I wanna stay with you," I say.

"You can't. You're hurt. Now I'll carry you," Matt says as he lifts me piggyback, and then he turns to his friends and says, "Bring his bicycle."

I love Matt. He's my half-brother, but I don't know it at the time. He always looks after me, so naturally I think it's okay to follow him. But Mamma has strict orders: no straying from the yard alone. Matt brings me home, and I feel better. The pain and blood from landing on the bicycle don't hurt as much, and my tears are just about dried out when Mamma wields the metal spatula and takes me across her knee.

Pain!

I sit on a Carthage bench for a moment. My legs jerk again as if being electrocuted. Perhaps they are. They shouldn't do that. My body used to jolt as I'd fall asleep, and I thought it was because my heart had stopped and I was dying. The jolt was to revive me, or so I thought. But this jolt to my legs is wrenching. It is wrong. I should never feel like this, like...old.

"Can I watch Grandpa?" I ask Mamma after she finishes whipping me. "I'll be good, I promise."

Mamma lets me sit near Grandpa. Well, not really. I sit near the fireplace, not quite on the hearth, but close enough. Grandpa moves slowly toward the woodpile near the fireplace. He lifts a log as if it hurts him. He drops it in the fireplace. Orange glowing bits of burning wood leap and dance all about. He takes a poker and tries moving the log just right, but he puts a hand to his back and gives up.

"Someday when I'm a grownup, I'll put the logs in for you, Grandpa," I say.

Grandpa smiles.

"Someday you will," he says. "But I want you to remember something very important. You must do what your mamma tells you. You must be a good boy, eat right, and grow up to be big and strong. Study hard in school. Study very hard, and someday you'll be a man. You'll have your own house and family, and you won't have aches and pains like your grandpa. Promise me you'll do this?"

"I promise," I say.

"Good boy."

A loud pop cracks a burning log, and glowing orange pieces leap out beyond the hearth to the carpet at my feet. One lands on my toe and burns it a little. Grandpa quickly gets up and whisks away the embers with a little broom into a special metal dustpan with a long pole that he keeps next to the fireplace.

"Ow," I say.

The lights fade, and the fireplace goes out. I am still on the bench, and my legs are hurting from not moving. It is time to walk again. The bench is by a sidewalk, and I follow that down a hill until I reach the bike path. I am only able to walk for a few minutes when my path is blocked by a large, fallen tree. Yes, the trees are still here. From the storm.

It's now Thursday, June 30, 2011. It's our first week in the charity house, at least that's what I call it. Brenda works at Mockenboose Bank, and her employer is lending this house to us until we get back on our feet. I lost the farm house. I think I said that. I held out as long as I could, but declining markets and the failure of both Mortgage Bank Brothers and the co-op pulled me under. So yes, we are living in this house. However, as a stipulation, we must pay for all repairs, maintenance, and utilities to the house. There's no free living, and failure comes cheap. Brenda would lose her job and we'd be kicked out of this house should we cause it to lose value.

Brenda is inside enjoying the dinner I cooked for her. I ate already. Wind is picking up. Getting dark out. I go into the front yard. Dark storm clouds are gathering overhead from the lake. Lake Michigan. I can see the lake from my yard. At the end of 17th Street are houses with lakefront property. A block away? Maybe less, maybe more. I'm looking in the sky for rotation. I've never seen a tornado in real life. Will this be the first? Kenosha isn't known for tornadoes. We get straight winds that spin down like the beater bar of a vacuum cleaner.

Branches are flying. They come from very high, dive down, and then swoop over my head. I can't believe how strong the winds are. They won't blow me away, but if I were little...

I'm a small boy again up in the Appalachians. Where is my childhood home? What state? Pennsylvania? West Virginia? I remember coal. Coal and clay. I live in Coyla.

It's very windy. I must be eight years old by now, and I'm with Matt. We're playing in a mountain stream. It's very cold, but it's clean.

"Here, taste it," he says.

"It doesn't taste like anything," I say.

"That's because it's not dirty," Matt says. "I learned in school that the world is full of pollution."

"What's pollution?" I ask.

"That means people go breaking and tearing up things. Then they leave a mess behind. It clogs up the planet," he explains.

"I don't get it," I say.

"Imagine if this water were muddy," he says.

"Icky," I say.

"That's right. Icky and yucky. That's pollution," he says.

"Why do people make pollution if it's icky?" I ask. "That's stupid."

"Because of things they want," Matt says. "They take things and leave trash behind for other people."

"No, people are good," I say. "Like Grandpa, Grandma, Mamma, and you."

"That's what I used to think," Matt says. "Then I found out what the real world is like. When you're older, you'll understand."

I don't understand. I didn't then, and I don't now.

There's a motorcycle driving south on Sheridan Road. In this weather? It could rain any moment. It should rain, but it isn't. Just incredibly powerful wind. Brenda is still eating dinner inside. There's a neighbor standing by the fence. He calls me over.

"Is this what a tornado is like?" he asks.

I walk over.

"Yeah, this is the weather for it," I reply. "But we never get tornadoes here. Just straight winds."

"I'm from Nevada, and we don't get tornadoes, so I've always wondered," he says.

"They get them down south in Texas and Alabama," I say. "People panic up here when it gets like this, but it's no big deal."

Carthage Security is driving along, and he stops to tell us something.

"Better go in your basement. There's a tornado warning," he says.

"Okay," I wave, but I don't take him seriously.

I go back in the house and look out the window. The neighbor goes across the street and says something to someone else standing outside. Warning about the tornado? Being helpful?

"This device will be helpful for the Green Economy," the salesman said in the spring of 2007, a time of past tense and tension.

I was on my farm on Highway L just east of Interstate 94 when he sold me that device. A million dollars, and the size of a school bus, but he said it would revolutionize both farming and America's energy supply. All I had to do was feed any organic material into that device—he called it the Cyclozyme—and methane would come out. The device came with free gas-line hookup to the central methane co-op owned by Mortgage Bank Brothers. The co-op sold the methane back to Wisconsin Energy. Natural gas cars were the wave of the future the salesman claimed. Didn't matter that only Honda sold a natural gas car, the salesman promised that a wave of "green" cars and trucks would flood America, and my purchase would help put Wisconsin on the map.

Brenda didn't like the idea. The farm came from her parents, a marriage gift. I had to take out a loan to buy the Cyclozyme—against the farm. Mortgage Bank Brothers gave me a good deal, or so I thought, at 6.8%.

"This is not the way of farming," Brenda said. "My parents and grandparents saved for everything. How do you think my family got through the Great Depression? Hmm? It wasn't from taking out loans against the farm, and it wasn't from a Psychozyme."

"That's Cyclozyme," I corrected her. "But this is now. We're beyond those old days. Technology today means we have modern conveniences without having to suffer."

"It's the principle. Principles don't change," Brenda said.

"They do if we are to leave the stone ages," I said.

"Are you saying my family came from the Stone Age?" she said.

I didn't reply. Instead, I kept myself busy that spring with planting, and I drooled for the day during harvest when I could convert our entire crop to methane and sell it like free energy. Ironically, our farm equipment was still diesel powered, but the salesman promised that once more farms like mine purchased the Cyclozyme, farm equipment would also convert to methane power.

"I value the land," I would remind Brenda during the summer. "I came from the mountains with fresh water and clean air. That's why I want to farm — to bring back that natural element to people."

"You can't do that with a Psychozyme," Brenda would say. "What will people taste from our farm? Their furnace when they turn on the gas?"

"When more farms convert to produce methane like we do, then we can split the farm. Half the crops we sell direct, the other half we convert to methane," I would say.

"*When*? You mean *if*. And that's an empty *if*."

Harvest season came, and I fed all our crops into the Cyclozyme. I even put grass clippings and the remains of Brenda's flower garden into the Cyclozyme. Nice and tidy. I sold the methane to the co-op and put the money in the bank toward the loan on the Cyclozyme.

"The money we're getting from selling the methane isn't much more than we got for the crops last year," Brenda said. "And after making payments on the Psychozyme, it's almost nothing. This isn't working out."

"It'll get better," I said. "We just need to plant more energy-efficient crops. We'll do better next year."

"I don't know what's better than what we grow. We can't grow sugar cane in Wisconsin. Corn is the best we can do," Brenda said. "Get your money back for the Psychozyme."

"We haven't given it a fair chance," I said. "Besides, we'd only get half our money back. We're better off keeping it and paying off the loan. Think of the money we'd lose."

"I *am* thinking of the money we'd lose. That's why we should return it," Brenda said.

"Just give me another year to show you," I said.

"Are you listening, John Mark?" Matt says to me.

I'm back home with Matt at the mountain stream.

"What?" I say.

"This is mountain moss," he says. "It's very old."

"Older than me?" I ask.

"Older than me and you and Mamma and Grandma and Grandpa," Matt says.

"Nothing's older than Grandpa," I say.

"Well this is. They say this moss was here when the world was first created, maybe back in the time of Adam and Eve. Maybe even before that," Matt says.

"Wow!" I say.

"They say mountain moss remembers everything, like a little history book. It remembers when light and darkness first came, it remembers when rain first came, and it remembers when fish first swam. It remembers when trees came and tried to take over its territory, but the moss still finds places to grow. And it remembers animals, including humans."

"We're not animals," I say. "We're people."

"We're part of the animal kingdom," Matt says. "That makes us animals."

"Nuh-uh," I say.

"Ya-huh," he replies.

"I'm going to ask Mamma, and she'll tell me," I say, and I go running down along the mountain stream, past the pump well, past the huge tree stump, and into the house.

"Mamma, Mamma, Matt says we're animals," I cry.

"Oh that's silly," she replies. "God made people after his own image. God is good, and so are his people."

It's darker here. When the storm blew these trees across the bike path, the trees felled two lampposts. I must be careful. There are deep holes where the trees once stood. I will test the ground with the curtain rod. I will find the edge of the holes. Is that water?

The sun is setting. Days are getting longer. Yesterday's sunset was twenty hours and forty minutes ago. I am in the past, the ancient past.

The Ordovician end. There's warm salt water at my feet and a high mountain range behind me, as high as Mount Everest in modern times. Maybe higher. I turn around and see the first plants take hold from water to land. They look like mosses, but they are much taller. They are soaking in the last of the day's sunlight rays.

I look back in the water and see an occasional trilobite as well as strange squid-like creatures with long conical heads. A long eel scuffs along my feet. I step back onto land. The eel tries to wrap itself over my feet. I look up in the sky and see something bright, a ball glowing whiter than white and burning through the atmosphere with a tail bright blue and green. It's growing larger, which means it's getting closer. It must be a comet or meteorite, but I'm not sure which. It explodes and breaks apart in the sky, with fragments branching out in different directions, growing toward me like an upside-down tree in flight. I shield my eyes and cry out.

It's June 30th in the evening. I am a motorcyclist riding south on Sheridan Road. I ride past 17th Street, proceed past Carthage College on Alford Park Drive, then turn left at the traffic light onto 7th Avenue, go a short ways, and turn left onto Kennedy Drive. The wind is fierce and upends trees to my left. A large one crashes atop me. I fall to the pavement hearing the last sound of my life, that of an ambulance siren in the distance.

It's now July 1, 2011, and a Friday afternoon around five o'clock. The power has been off for an hour. I'm a lucky one. My house had power earlier in the day, so nothing is spoiled in the refrigerator. Brenda will be home soon, so I must decide what to make for dinner. The stove, being powered by gas, still works, and there's meat in the freezer. Should I make stew? Should I make something with pasta? Before I can decide, the power comes back on, but it's too powerful. Light bulbs are very bright for a few seconds then pop. I go out of the house into the back yard for safety. There's hissing and popping from the central air conditioner condenser. I don't have to walk near it to smell something electrical burning. Then it stops. I go in the house, and the air conditioning vents blow warm air on my hand. Broken.

I'm standing next to Grandpa in a coal mine. He's overseeing the coal elevator. Each time miners enter the elevator, he tells them to hit the red button if the elevator won't stop.

A group of four men enter, and he tells them about the button. Grandpa closes the door, the miners press a button, and they descend. The elevator travels quickly, but not too fast. Then it reaches the shaft's bottom. It stops, but before the miners can exit, the elevator begins a rapid ascent, gaining more and more speed. Danger! The miners hit the red button to stop, but the emergency brakes only work when going down, not up. Grandpa hits a brake to stop the machine, but the machine won't stop. Grandpa yells and hits other buttons and pulls at cables, but the elevator won't stop. It accelerates out of control into the overhead and catapults the miners into the top of the elevator car's ceiling, breaking their bones and killing them.

Pain!

My legs ache with it. I can't continue standing next to the upended tree hole by the bike path. I use the curtain rod to steady my descent as I sit on the grass with my legs dangling over the edge into the hole. I feel remaining roots and drainage tiles in the hole. My legs still hurt, so I move them as if pedaling a bicycle.

It is Saturday, July 2nd. I'm walking around these huge fallen trees for the first time in front of Carthage College. This is before my legs become so painful, and so the walk is pleasant. I cannot believe the size of the trees that have fallen nor the size of the holes they've left behind. Soil, sod, and all were pulled up by the tree roots, as if some giant had come along and cut into the soil around the tree. The upended grass is perfectly preserved and shows no effect of injury.

I continue walking south and leave Carthage College behind. I walk up a hill and stop at a parking lot where to the east I see kite surfers in Lake Michigan. Across the road is a wooded park, but many of its trees are now uprooted or snapped. The pavilion, a once-simple no-wall structure with four posts and a gabled roof, now looks like a giant picked up the roof and thrust it upon a snapped tree, skewering it.

"Beep, beep," a man says from the north side of the bike path.

It's old man Martin and his wife riding their tadpole recumbent tricycles past me. Now why don't I get myself one of those? They look very comfortable. Maybe when I get a job, maybe after I buy a new farm to replace the one I lost, maybe...

The vision of sunlight fades quickly. I've returned to sitting at the upended tree hole. I dig the curtain rod into the hole and churn up a bit of dirt. I dig a little more and wonder what secrets are below Earth's surface.

I am below Earth's surface, in a den under a large tree. My name is Nytar, and I'm a skunk. How can I be a skunk? I don't know. Ideas and thoughts of the human sort seem distant and alien, as if from another lifetime. I'm very young and have just developed my coat. I have brothers and sisters, and my mother leads us out of the den into the "wild".

The last rays of daylight are fading quickly. Mother shows us how to dig in the dirt for insects and earthworms. I find an especially long worm, and I eat it. It's juicy and tasty. There's a cricket over there. I trap it and eat it.

Mother leads us to a tree with a hollow area. She motions us to look in the hollow for food. I look in the hollow but jump back as quickly as I can. Bees!

Mother chuckles as well as a skunk can. She sticks her head into the hollow. Bees try to sting her, but they can't get through her fur coat. She pulls herself back out and shows how she's eating bees. I mimic what my mother showed us. As bees come out, I grab and eat them while others try to sting me. But they can't! I show my mother my new skills in foraging for bees, and she nods in approval. My siblings also try their luck with the bees and succeed.

I feel powerful. Nytar the bee slayer. Nytar the invincible. I can conquer any insect, anywhere, anytime.

I'm under another tree, in another den with other young skunks. I have no name, but I am high in the mountains, the Appalachians. It is perhaps 1900, and I hear people yelling in the distance. They are yelling, "Timber!" The ground shakes like an earthquake. Another person yells, and the ground shakes again, only closer.

I peer out of the den's opening and see humans chopping at the base of trees with axes. Others are using two-man crosscut saws against trees. But the results are the same. Huge trees, some as large as California sequoias, come thundering down to the earth. One such tree hits the tree hosting my den. My tree uproots and catapults my family and me into the air and clear of the trees.

"Skunks," I hear men yell, and they shoot their rifles at us.

We run and run, but we are only skunks and cannot run quickly. My mother holds her ground and sprays them. She hits the men, but they get angrier and shoot her dead. I continue running and hide in a mountain crevice, hoping I won't be found.

I hear what sounds like a chainsaw, but it is in fact a motorcycle engine suddenly revving as the back wheel loses contact with the ground from the machine falling. A man yells in fright before a tree kills him. The tree that kills him is the one hosting my den. The tree, in the act of falling, has uprooted and catapulted us skunks into the air, including me, Nytar.

I am a little dazed, but otherwise I'm unhurt. My mother gathers my siblings and me together, and we go looking for shelter. We find temporary places along the Pike River as we head north. We share a den with another mother and her skunks. It's crowded, and my siblings begin fighting with the other mother's children. I don't want them to fight. It was bad enough losing our den, but we skunks should stick together.

One of the other mother's daughters, Herpenda, walks out of the den to avoid being attacked by my older brother. I block my brother from attacking Herpenda. I block him and stop him. He is surprised, but now he and my siblings hiss and growl at me for being a traitor to our family. I realize I can no longer stay with my family. I must leave, and I take Herpenda with me.

We spend the next month living close to Pike River. I show her how to dig for insects like earthworms, how to catch crickets, and how to dig for other grub. She is impressed. She is the runt of her litter and was largely ignored by her mother. Then I show Herpenda my proudest feat. I attack a honeybee nest. At first she fears for my life and warns me away from the bees, but when I re-emerge from the nest with a bee hanging out of my mouth and others trying yet unable to sting me through my coat, her eyes freeze over in amazement. I convince her to make a try at the honeybee nest. She approaches the nest and then backs off. I reassure her that it's safe. She goes in again, grabs two bees, eats them, and stands there, proud that other bees cannot sting her. She then states that she did it, how amazing I am, and that I am her Nytar. And so, I decide it is time to make an announcement to Herpenda.

"Herpenda," I say. "I want you to be my mate. I want to share a den with you."

Herpenda is surprised. We are a bit young for me to make such a proposition, and she hesitates.

"I like living by the river," she says.

"But it will be too cold in winter. I will find us a nice, warm den. Very warm. We'll be cozy all winter and never have to worry about freezing to death," I say.

"I don't like deep holes," she says. "It should be a shallow hole."

"I have an idea," I say. "Trust me."

"I trust you."

In the middle of the night, we follow two chipmunks across Sheridan Road to 17th Street. I can't read, but I know it's 17th Street. Memories from a former life? I am only a skunk, so I cannot be sure. We follow the chipmunks several houses down on the south side of 17th Street where they disappear under a porch.

"I know this porch," I say to Herpenda. "I was here before, though in a different life and as a different animal."

It is my house as Jack Highbower, the one I am borrowing from Mockenboose Bank, but I cannot remember anything more about Jack Highbower the human or an institution named Mockenboose Bank. I am a skunk who has lost his home and family and is looking for a safe place to winter. But I feel I must take chances and live on property owned by others. Will they know Herpenda and I are living below them in the porch?

"Here," I say to Herpenda. "In here."

She follows me through an opening large enough for us to pass through but too small for a full-grown skunk to enter. The chipmunks disappear through openings between the house foundation and the porch's floorboards.

"There," I say. "If a chipmunk can do it, so can we."

Herpenda follows me. We are now below the first floor's floorboards and floor joists. We are standing on insulation which is held up from below by a black tarp-like material that flaps and bounces as we step.

A black and white flag flaps in front of me, carried on a pole by a fellow classmate of Coyla High School. Where's Herpenda? I'm a human?

It's 1984, and I'm in Ithaca, New York. Ithaca High School is hosting the Skunk Bowl, an exhibition game for two high-school football teams who have the same mascot, the skunk. Yes, my high school, Coyla High School, has a skunk as the mascot.

The game is in the second quarter, and already Ithaca is up twenty-four to three. My team isn't so good. We don't have much money or resources back home in the mountains. We are just able to gather enough money for equipment and uniforms. Our uniforms are black with white highlights, same for our cheerleaders, who also wear frilly hair attachments in black and white to give them more of a fancy skunk look. They have short, thick tails, and each time Ithaca scores, our cheerleaders (as part of a cheer) bend a little and pretend to "spray" the opposition with skunk scent. Sometimes I think that cheer helps our opponents beat us more than anything else. No wonder we go winless every year.

I hear talk that this is the last Skunk Bowl we'll play against Ithaca, that they're changing their mascot from a skunk to a bear. I'm glad of it, because it means one less game that we'll lose. As it is, the game plays out like a blur before me, with the cheerleaders cheering to the end. The gun fires, and the game is over. Stadium lights go out.

It is dark, and I prod the upheaved hole with the curtain rod. I suddenly realize that those high school football games aren't about winning at all. They are about comradery and coming together, whether at the player level or the cheering level—all those things are put into memory to give each of us some sanity to hold onto for later. Is this what is happening to me? Am I experiencing these realms in a struggle for sanity?

"Nytar," Herpenda says. "Look, I can see the ground below. It's flat with a mixture of rock and dirt. And there's water over there."

"It's perfect," I say. "And no other animals, except for the chipmunks."

"They won't give us any trouble," Herpenda says. "We're bigger than chipmunks. And you, Nytar the bee slayer, you can teach those chipmunks a thing or two."

I lead Herpenda through a hole to the gravel and dirt ground below. It's the crawlspace to the house above. I give chase to the chipmunks to scare them away, and they scamper across the ground and squeeze through a thin separation between a frame and a trap door to the outside.

Sudden terror strikes my heart. I am too big to follow the chipmunks out. How will Herpenda and I leave the crawlspace when we need to? I dig into the ground for worms or grub, but nothing lives in this earth. Hungry. And thirsty.

"There's water over here," Herpenda says. "I'll take a sip."

"Herpenda, no!" I bark.

I hear a splash. Too late.

"Help, Nytar, help!" Herpenda calls. "I've fallen into a barrel of water, and I can't climb out. Help!"

I rush over to help Herpenda. She's doing what she can to get out, but the sides are too slippery, and she can't climb them. I can't reach down to pull her out, either. If I go in, I'll be trapped too.

I rush all around the crawlspace, looking for something I can use to help her, but there's nothing. In desperation, I begin digging into the gravel under a drainage pipe in hopes of finding a way out so I can summon help. I dig and dig, but the gravel and earth are too hard and won't yield to my claws.

Trapped. Herpenda continues to scream and thrash around. What if the owners hear? They'll come down and do something, maybe even kill us. But I must be ready for that. I must be ready so I can spray them and rush out for help. I wait against the wall by the trap door, out of the way so the owner won't see me immediately. I can barely tolerate hearing Herpenda's screams and splashing. The owner will come down soon, he must. He must.

He never does.

Days have passed. I'm so thirsty. My eyes are glazing over, and Herpenda has long ago stopped splashing and screaming. She must be dead. I'm responsible for her death. The owner must come down and open the trap door. He must.

I hear a fly buzzing over the barrel of water. It's not really a barrel. Something from a long-forgotten prior life tells me Herpenda fell into the well of a sump pump. The fly to animals is like the Grim Reaper to people.

And now, I hear the fly hovering over me, waiting for my end. I spend my last effort peering into the air. The fly passes by a beam of light shining through a screened ventilation window, one I cannot reach. The fly hovers, buzzes, and as I stare at it, she draws near, her image doubling and quadrupling in size before my eyes, becoming hideously large and threatening, threatening to inject hundreds of her kind into me, the destiny of my desire to exploit a higher power's abode.

I am with Grandpa in the funeral home for the miners who died. Mining coal from Mother Earth is very dangerous. Grandpa says that at times it isn't worth it, that the coal belongs to another power, not to men, and it should be left alone. He speaks of leaving coal mining and moving to the other side of Coyla, where he can find work in clay production. He makes good on his plan, and he will refuse to mine for coal ever again.

The miners are not well embalmed, and I can smell death on them. It makes me sick to my stomach, like eating the worst rotten cabbage or spinach in existence. The smell is in my nose, and now everything smells like rotting flesh.

I poke the curtain rod into the upheaved hole one last time and disturb something soft. It is the remains of a dead animal, and judging by the scent just released, a dead skunk. I cannot stay by this hole of death, and so I leave the hole and return home. I want to walk quickly, but pain in my legs prevents me. The curtain rod has the stain of skunk death on it and will not give up its scent despite my dragging of the curtain rod against the bike path. As I cross the bridge over Pike River, I toss the curtain rod over the side and watch it float downstream toward Lake Michigan.

It is August 10, 2011, and a Saturday morning. Brenda has been complaining of a skunk smell all week. I keep hoping the smell will go away. Did a skunk spray the area? Shouldn't it dissipate?

"It smells like it's below the new furnace," she says.

Yes, a new furnace. We paid nearly eight thousand dollars for a new central furnace and air conditioner—all on loan with Mockenboose Bank at 29.9% interest. What is that slogan of theirs? "Stay close to the noose with Mockenboose." Banks prey and profit on the condemned, like the hideous blowfly preparing to inject her scions into the depths of living death where they will branch out in twisted and mangled paths of flesh to become death-mongers of the future despondent.

I open the trap door, and out rushes a heavy air of skunk smell. Skunks in the crawlspace, what will I do? What if they have rabies? What if they spray me? Should I call animal control? Is there such a thing in these parts?

I look around and see the black and white fur next to the wall. Must be sleeping. I touch it with a short board to test it, and there is no movement. In fact, there is very little shape left. Fresh maggots worm through and around what's left of the flesh, and the smell of death combines with skunk smell to leave me choking for fresh air.

I step outside to rejuvenate my lungs and return to the crawlspace with a container, to where I place as much of the dead skunk's remains as I can with the short board.

I place the container in the back yard, go into the house, prepare a mixture of hydrogen peroxide with baking soda, and return to the crawlspace where I douse the affected area in hopes of breaking down the scent.

The scent does fade—from that spot. But while traveling on my knees in the crawlspace, I detect a scent from the sump pump. Another skunk, and more maggots, but this skunk is less decomposed. Most of its flesh remains, though it is all white as are its eyes. The water smells like a sewer, and the fumes are worse than the first skunk. I exit the crawlspace and punch holes in the bottom of a tall plastic container and then slit the container at an angle to make it more or less resemble a dipper or ladle. I return to the sump pump well and scoop the second dead skunk into the plastic container. The fluids leech from the dead skunk through the container's holes and into the sump well, and I hold it there until all fluids have drained. I remove the second skunk from the crawlspace.

I find no other skunks in the crawlspace. The dead ones I take to the bank of Pike River and bury them. I return to the crawlspace with the garden hose and spray fresh water into the sump well for a half hour, doing my best to pump away the bacteria and other micro-pathogens. The spraying of water, however, splashes drops of the microbial goo onto my flesh. I think nothing of it at the time, but as the day progresses, I grow increasingly lethargic and sick as if I'd consumed automotive brake fluid.

The curtain rod is gone. I have nothing with which to help my gait, and so I hobble the remaining distance to the back gate where I collapse and fall into my back yard.

Except it isn't my land.

Stars circle above. They own no man, and no man owns them. Is it the same for all cosmic entities? Yet Earth owns my body at this moment. Its very claws of gravity pin me to the ground. Perhaps then gravity becomes the final master of all things from which nothing can escape.

It is nine billion years since the beginning of our solar system. Earth is quite hot. I look around, but I am no one—not a human nor animal nor anything with eyes. How can I see? I see only through the sense of pressure— pressure from surrounding things, like fellow moss on the last remnants of the Appalachian Mountains, a thin rock formation now worn down below sea level. The oceans are all but evaporated, having been burned off by that scorching, expanding star we once called the sun. The sun is orange and huge in the sky, she has cannibalized her first two children, Mercury and Venus, and she will soon cannibalize her prized child—Earth. But before she does, the Appalachians are to be cannibalized themselves by what was once the Asian continent. I know this history, I know because the DNA memories of life forms from the ages have been preserved in my own DNA. I am what's left of life on Earth, a moss clinging to worn mountain rock, and despite the massive waste of energy on predation and consumption throughout Earth's history, the result is the sum-total DNA of this barbarism stored in me, a lowly moss.

The Rocky Mountains were first. They drifted with the North American plate westward until they met the Mariana Trench. By that time, the trench became volcanic and hot, with rips and tears from Earth's mantle opening up at increasing rates from the sun's expanding gravitational influence.

Now it is my turn. The Appalachians are being consumed by the Mariana Trench. All that's left of water is in that trench, and steam is rising quickly. The water is tempering the fire of the trench. When the water is all evaporated off, what's left of the Appalachians will suddenly slip into the trench, and so will I, the last of life on Earth.

The last.

"*Ihiyahi*," I hear from afar.

Is that a human voice? With my senses, I detect two walking shapes, like humans, but much more advanced. They are of boron and gold, and their bodies more or less resemble lightweight space suits than they do conventional people.

"*Ihiyahi, kolahi aniha a mika ranitan*," the voice says.

It is a male voice, even I can sense that after so many millions of years since the last humans set foot on Earth. He sounds like a parent or guardian —a father, uncle, or grandfather. Another voice giggles, like a girl. Then the realization sets in, her name is, "Ihiyahi." And I can just make out what the guardian's foreign tongue says. He urges his niece to hurry, that their science field trip is nearly over. Is that what is left of Earth? Nothing but a field trip for others?

"*Oncolo Metavasi, paliha oo iwahano. Palihi?*" the girl says.

She begs her uncle to stay a little longer so she can find some form of life for her project.

I'm here, I'm here! I'm trapped in the DNA of this moss, a mere set of information left over from the Cenozoic Era. Can you hear me? Can you see me?

The rock upon which I cling is precariously close to falling into the volcanic Mariana Trench. I am on a conveyor belt of final de-existence, the last remnant of all efforts made by life on Earth for continuation. I cannot move. I cannot escape the fiery maw.

Please, oh please find me. Take me to your science project. Take me to a life on your planet where things grow and prosper and hope for a new spring. If only you can hear me. If only.

"*Oo, ali apia paliano,*" the girl giggles.

She reaches with her hand toward me in an effort to scoop me up, but her uncle rushes and grabs her before she stumbles over the edge into the Mariana abyss below. He warns her of this peril, and she is sad.

I'm parched. All other plants have long ago dried up. As a moss, I've held on the longest, but even I have limits. The sun grows ever larger toward Earth. It fluctuates with intensity—first bright, then dim, and then bright, like a light bulb flickering out. It sends brilliant solar flares all about, but they too are fading.

The uncle and niece remain motionless, and so it is for me. The last throes of life are silent and still.

It is dark, but a single light flashes about.

"I need water and light to survive," I say.

A hand touches my forehead.

"You have a fever," a voice says.

It is Brenda.

"How long have you been in the back yard?" she asks as she points a flashlight in my face.

I try to sit up, but my legs will not move.

"Jack?" she asks. "Stand up."

"My legs won't move," I say.

And so, Brenda calls an ambulance. The ambulance arrives within minutes and takes me south to Kenosha Medical Center. Inside, I am taken to an examining room where a nurse removes my shoes and pants. My legs and arms have become covered in a rash. Worse, the skin on my feet has become gangrenous. Blood tests are performed quickly. I have Rocky Mountain spotted fever.

I am put on intravenous therapy. Antibiotics and fluids are pumped into me from the IV needle to the vein in my left arm. My arm begins to numb from the inside out. I look around to see who is shaking the bed, but no one is. Brenda holds my right hand, but within a few seconds, I lose feeling of her touch. My vision fades, and I lose my humanity.

I'm the moss again on the last of the Appalachians. This is a dream, isn't it? But did Brenda really find me? No, that is a DNA memory fragment of the past. What I thought was a life as Jack Highbower is merely my internal chemistry reconstructing a stored DNA fragment from a human. So many DNA fragments collected in my cells.

The uncle and niece are still here, standing close to me, but the uncle says something to his niece and points to the sun. She waves goodbye to me. No, you're a scientist. You're supposed to preserve life. Don't you want to know the history of life on this planet? You'll win First Prize on your planet!

The uncle and niece walk toward a spaceship and away from me. No, no, no, noooooooooo!

There's no hope left. The Mariana Trench calls me with a deep, gurgly roar. How can I bear this finality? How can I escape? I'm slipping to the edge. Seconds await the end. Seconds. Is there salvation in solitude? Can life transcend the inevitable? The DNA, the information strands, the most incredible repository ever created, yes, that's where I'll go, I'll relive my final moments in that one human, that one life...

I awake a week later in the Kenosha Medical Center. Brenda is asleep in a chair next to me, and I waken her. Happy to see me conscious, she calls a nurse.

"I'm glad you're awake, Mr. Highbower," the nurse says.

"Me too. For a moment I thought I was a dying piece of moss," I say.

"You were delirious from the Rocky Mountain spotted fever," the nurse says. "We gave you fluids and antibiotics to pull you through."

"And I did," I say.

"You certainly did," Brenda says. "And hopefully your feet did too."

"My feet?" I ask.

I look down at my feet. They are covered in mesh-layered bandages.

"Your legs have become gangrenous," the nurse says. "The antibiotics stopped new tissue death, but the old tissue must be removed."

"I'm scared," I say. "What if there's scarring?"

"There won't be," the nurse says. "We have modern methods to remove only dead tissue while leaving the healthy alone. It's very precise and smooth. You'll be amazed with the results."

"Whew," I say. "I was worried for a moment."

Brenda holds my hand in reassurance.

"You know, I dreamt I was a skunk, and a huge blowfly hovered over me like the Grim Reaper, ready to kill me off by injecting me with her eggs," I say.

"Don't say such things," Brenda says.

"It's true," I say, and yet the nurse gives me a strange smile.

I feel myself sliding off the bed, and I half imagine a fissure opening in the floor beneath me as the nurse removes the final bandages, revealing maggots consuming the last of my dead tissue.

In another place and time, a young girl of boron and gold returns home with a bit of moss she spared from final destruction on a planet named Earth. She places the moss inside the base of a sophisticated device resembling a crystal ball. She activates the device and watches as the device displays images of Earth's life forms interacting amongst themselves, fully reconstructed from the moss's embedded DNA strands. She watches and watches, and when she is satisfied, she writes down what she learns in a little book, which she then reads to her classmates at school for a science class report, and for each animal that she describes, she transforms into that animal to show the class what life was like on Earth.

She earns an A.

The Duchess of Darby

Tick, tick, tick, ring-ba-ling-ca-ting-a-bing, pa-zing!

Allen Dofer had pressed the snooze button too many times. It was ten o'clock, and he was two hours late for his shift at Darby Magazine.

"I'll call in sick," Allen groaned. "That's what I'll do. I'll call in—"

A little thin metal device on the nightstand buzzed and chimed like an old-fashioned telephone as Allen started to drift back asleep. He punched the alarm clock out of habit, but his cellphone continued to ring.

"Hello?" Allen said, barely awake.

"Allen? Where are you?" asked the voice.

"I'm right here, Cathy," Allen said groggily.

"You're still in bed? Get up! Get up and fly like the wind to work. Mr. Barcloff is asking for you, and I'm running out of excuses."

"Oh no, I thought he was on vacation," Allen said.

"That was last week," Cathy said. "This is Monday. Did you forget?"

Allen Dofer looked around his apartment, a smelly goulash of dirty clothes, old grease-stained pizza boxes, empty drink containers, plastic wrappers, magazines, newspapers, books, and if one could pry beneath the upper layers, one would find more.

"Ow!" Allen said.

Allen looked to find several ants biting his legs which happened to be next to the half-eaten donut he'd started eating the night before as he was falling asleep. How did it get down by his feet? He usually placed those treats on the nightstand next to him, or at least on the floor.

"Now, Allen, now!" Cathy said.

"Is that loafer Dofer on the line?" Barcloff barked.

"No, it's—"

"Well tell him that he'd better be covering the story of his life, or Dofer will be done for!" Barcloff barked.

"I'll expect your story by noon," Cathy said in a false tone.

Allen jumped out of bed and did so with a large leap to avoid the highest piles of undesirables. He jumped in the shower and didn't wait for it to warm up as he washed his skin and hair. Another few seconds, and he brushed the foulness from his teeth. He threw on fresh clothes (by walking sideways along the wall to the closet) and slipped into his shoes, and then he grabbed his bag and key chain on the way out the door, halfway down the stairs, then back up to lock the door, back down and outside to his car, threw the bag inside, climbed in, then turned the ignition only to find the starter turning over the engine fruitlessly.

"Come on, start, start already!" Allen begged.

The car wouldn't start.

"It's too late to catch a bus," Allen said. "Bogus! I promised Kakuda I wouldn't borrow his Hayabusa anymore. But I don't have time to beg, and he won't notice it gone, I hope."

Allen retrieved a metal coat hanger from the trunk of his car, slipped it up between the sliding garage door and upper frame, hooked the manual release on the inside track, and pulled until a *click* sounded and released the lock. Allen pulled the big garage door up and admired the Suzuki Hayabusa motorcycle. Painted in racing letters on the side was "Boosbaby".

"Getting into his garage is easy, but where is the key?" Allen mused.

Allen looked inside the tool chests, little storage boxes, and even in the garbage can.

"Nowhere. Think, Allen, think. Where would Kakuda hide it?"

Allen looked around and noticed a corner next to a window with no spider web.

"There are no spider webs here," Allen said as he placed a stepladder in the corner and climbed. "That's because Kakuda climbed up like I am right now, and he placed the key, ugh, reach a little more...there! Right behind a fake panel by the window frame."

Allen jumped down with key in hand, placed his bag in the storage compartment, threw on a helmet, jumped onto the bike, and he exclaimed, "Hayabusa, here I go!"

Allen started the engine. It revved smoothly and readily. Allen eased the bike out of the garage, hit a button on the bike to close the garage door, engaged the clutch, and with light but steady throttle, the motorcycle traveled down the driveway and entered traffic.

"Can't play conservatively. I must get to work quickly," Allen said.

Allen twisted the throttle. Instead of the motorcycle lighting into an uncontrollable wheelie, it instead rocketed Allen forward with only the slightest hint of a wheelie. The bike rode with good balance and control, despite Allen's impulsive desires.

Traffic was heavy. This was why Allen took to the cycle. He rode between cars, swerving in-between, out, and around trucks and buses to gain ground as quickly as possible. He needed to get to the thoroughfare, but this dodging and weaving was taking too long. If only the row of businesses on the right weren't there, then he could ascend the hill behind them and reach the thoroughfare that way.

Why not go that way? All Allen needed to do was...was...

"There!" Allen said.

He wheeled Boosbaby through the open door of a soup kitchen, dodged and pushed through the unemployed and homeless, rode past the soup line, into the back kitchen area, and out the back door, leaving a mess of tossed trays, broken bowls of stew, utensils, and various other bits of food and things on the floor, tables, walls, and even some splatters on the ceiling.

Allen ascended the hill and kept up his speed, where he jumped a small gap and landed on the thoroughfare. There he was able to get his speed up, and what bits of food and liquid the bike picked up from the kitchen were now blowing off, though the liquid did run and smear and leave a sticky residue.

"I'll have to clean the bike later," Allen said to himself, but the high speed and thundering wind muffled his voice, and he could hear nothing. He activated a button on the helmet and said, "Testing. Yes, I'll clean the bike."

He had activated a communication system to hear himself through the helmet's speakers, but what he didn't realize was that this activation gave his intentions away.

"Allen, is that you?" came Kakuda's voice through the helmet's speakers.

"I, uh, yes, it's me," Allen said. "How did you—"

"Where are you?" Kakuda asked. "What are you doing? I hear wind and engine. Are you riding my Hayabusa? I told you—"

"There seems to be a problem," Allen said, and he pressed the button again to power down the communication device.

Kakuda stood in front of a television camerawoman for Darby Magazine, preparing to videograph a news conference of Queen Cythia and Duchess Devanna on the steps of the Royal Palace.

"Allen stole my 'Busa again," Kakuda said to the camerawoman, who was testing her camera.

"Report him to the authorities," said Kiyomi.

Kakuda and Kiyomi heard hooting and hollering from a motorcyclist on the nearby thoroughfare doing a wheelie. Kiyomi focused the camera on the cyclist, zoomed in, read the word "Boosbaby" on the cycle and realized she was videographing Kakuda's bike.

"It's him!" Kiyomi exclaimed.

At that moment, Queen Cythia and Duchess Devanna exited the palace doors and walked toward the podium. Other people of royal blood sat nearby, separated from the crowd. Baroness Vasha looked intently at the cyclist, but the queen paid no attention to the two-wheel wonder. Instead, she focused her attention on maintaining a proper gait and overall composure for the news event.

"Trey. Find out the identity of that young man on the motorcycle," Baroness Vasha said to her servant.

"At once, Baroness," Trey said.

"Good morning," Queen Cythia said, and she paused.

The news crowd hushed and immediately focused its cameras on the queen. Kiyomi also focused her camera in the queen's direction.

"The queen is ready to speak," Kakuda said while standing in front of the camera.

Kakuda moved aside so that Kiyomi could cover the news event.

"Welcome to the Royal Palace of Darby," Queen Cythia said. "For those who are new to our land, I am Queen Cythia, ruler of the Commonwealth of Darby."

"All hail the queen," the people said.

"Thank you," she replied.

Duchess Devanna, the queen's niece, remained seated in a chair behind and to the right of the queen.

"As you know, today is Duchess Devanna's twenty-third birthday," the queen said.

"All hail Duchess Devanna," the people said.

Duchess Devanna stood, smiled, and waved to the people, to which they replied with cheers and applause. She sat, and the queen continued.

"As such, the Royal Family will hold a birthday party for Duchess Devanna this evening at the Eicor Mountain Resort," the queen continued. "Invitations were sent out and have been accepted. The party is not just a celebration of my niece's birthday. It is the beginning of her search for a future husband. Royalty from many parts both in the Commonwealth and from other countries will be attending tonight, and those who are bachelors of eligible pedigree will be in the running for becoming Duchess Devanna's future husband."

Someone asked about the press being able to attend. Another echoed the request, and several others asked the same about television media attendance. The queen hushed them with her arms.

"By the duchess's special request, three invitations are being made available to the press," Queen Cythia said.

The press erupted in excited frenzy.

"This is unprecedented," Kakuda said from the side of the camera. "No reporters have been allowed to cover any royal birthday party before."

"The invitations are conditional," the queen continued. "First, the recipients will be chosen by lottery."

More excited reaction from the press. How will the lottery be run? Who will win?

"Second, coverage must start no sooner than 7 pm and end no later than 10 pm," the queen said.

Many sighs of disappointment.

"This is for your safety," the queen said.

A few chuckled in the crowd.

"We will hold the lottery now," the queen said. "Wilfred, bring the lottery bowl."

Wilfred, the queen's butler, brought a stand with an arm that curved up and over, to which a bowl was suspended. Queen Cythia then motioned to Duchess Devanna. The duchess walked up to the bowl and pulled out a paper.

"The first invitation," Duchess Devanna said, "goes to The Darby Globe."

Applause. Wilfred wrote on an invitation, Queen Cythia placed her royal stamp on it, and she gave the invitation to Duchess Devanna. The duchess took the invitation and walked down a few steps, where she met an excited young man, Drayk Nasher, who had been allowed to cross the retaining ropes and walk up a few steps. He knelt briefly, stood, took the invitation with grace and gratitude, and then he turned around and waved the invitation triumphantly for a few seconds before a palace security guard escorted him back to the retaining rope and to the audience side.

"There are two invitations left," Kakuda said to the camera.

Duchess Devanna walked up the steps to the lottery bowl and retrieved another slip of paper.

"The second invitation goes to The Dallas Sunrise," the duchess said.

"Yee hah!" yelled a man with a large Texas hat, checkered shirt, blue jeans, and boots.

The invitation was authenticated as before, Duchess Devanna walked down the steps, and a suave Texan was allowed past the ropes to accept the invitation.

"You're welcome to visit us in Dallas," the Texan said. "I got a ranch, and I cook a mighty good barbeque steak."

The duchess nodded to him, and the Texan returned to the audience with the invitation.

"Only one invitation left," Kakuda said to the camera. "Will it go to Darby Magazine? Will Darby Magazine get special coverage of the duchess's birthday bash?"

Duchess Devanna returned to the lottery bowl. She reached, swirled her arm around to mix the entries, and then she retrieved a slip of paper.

"The last invitation goes to...are you ready?" she asked the crowd.

"Yes!" several members of the press said.

"This is it," Kakuda said. "The final invitation."

"Darby...TV3," the duchess said.

More clapping and applause, except from Kakuda. The invitation was signed, stamped, and delivered to a young woman representing Darby TV3. The duchess returned up the steps and sat in her chair.

"On behalf of the entire Royal Family, I bid congratulations to the lottery winners. And to the eligible bachelors for tonight, I wish you good luck. Until then," the queen said, and she along with Devanna left the steps and returned to the palace.

The press shouted out questions, but no one answered. The crowd slowly dispersed, and Trey returned to attend the baroness.

"Well?" Baroness Vasha asked.

"His name is Allen Dofer," Trey said, out of breath.

"And his pedigree?" the baroness asked.

"A commoner. He works for Darby Magazine," Trey puffed.

"A journalist," Baroness Vasha said. "But that motorcycle...I've seen it before. He's not the owner, is he?"

"No, the motorcycle is registered to a Kakuda Mori," Trey said.

Baroness Vasha's eyes lit up.

"You have that look, My Baroness," Trey puffed. "You are up to something."

"I'm going to bet that Kakuda also works for Darby Magazine," Baroness Vasha said.

"Yes," Trey said. "He is actually over there, covering the event."

Baroness Vasha stared at Kakuda and changed her facial expression.

"Invite him over for an interview in one hour," Baroness Vasha said.

Meanwhile at Darby Magazine, Allen parked the Hayabusa in the garage and ascended the steps in hopes of avoiding Mr. Barcloff. Slowly, he opened the stairwell door that led to the office. No sign of Barcloff. He opened it a little more. Still no sign, and now he could see Cathy Crepp. She waved her hands at Allen as if swatting a fly, but in fact she was trying to shoo Allen away. Allen could not understand why she was waving him off. Unconcerned, he opened the door forcefully and entered.

"Ow," came a muffled voice with the sound of something crunching.

Cathy cringed. Allen cringed as he stepped into the office and watched as a man who stood behind the door pushed it closed, now holding his nose. It was Mr. Barcloff.

"Mr. Dofer!" he exclaimed.

"I can explain everything," Allen said. "I was covering a human interest story about a boy scout and his survival skills in the woods, and—"

"No more fiction, Dofer," Mr. Barcloff said. "No more survival stories, no more tardiness, no more Allen B. Dofer. You're fi—"

"Mr. Barcloff, Mr. Barcloff!" Cathy called. "Important phone call for you, Mr. Barcloff. It's urgent!"

"Cathy, you've been covering for Allen one too many times," Mr. Barcloff said.

"It's Kakuda with urgent news about the royal birthday party," Cathy said. "Somehow he acquired a fourth invitation."

"What party?" Mr. Barcloff asked.

"The one with only three invitations to the press. The one being covered by The Darby Globe, Darby TV3, and The Dallas Sunrise, but not us," Cathy said. "At least not at first."

"The Dallas Sunrise?" Mr. Barcloff asked.

"But now we are," Cathy said.

"What is an American newspaper doing here in Darby?" Mr. Barcloff asked. "Cathy, you tell...never mind. Give me that phone! Hello! Kakuda? You get a scoop at that birthday party, or you're fired!"

Mr. Barcloff hung up the phone.

"And you're fired," Mr. Barcloff said to Allen.

"Mr. Barcloff," Cathy started.

"And you're fired too if there isn't a story on my desk for tomorrow morning's magazine edition," Mr. Barcloff said. "If no one gets the story, everyone is fired!"

Mr. Barnaby Nith Barcloff left the main office area and closed himself in his private office. Heavy cigar smoke seeped through the crevices between his door and the main office area.

"Well, that's that," Allen said. "I might as well pack my things and go."

"Mr. Barcloff has fired you before, and he's rehired you right back," Cathy said.

"Only because I scooped other papers," Allen said. "But Barcloff is adamant about getting a scoop on the birthday party. And how did Kakuda get it? How am I supposed to get in to save my job?"

"Sneak in," Cathy said.

"With Palace Security?" Allen said. "Now wait. I might be able to burst in with the Hayabusa."

"Oh, about that," Cathy said. "Kakuda wants me to take the keys."

"He told you?" Allen said. "I...uh..."

"It's obvious how you arrived here so quickly," Cathy said. "And Kakuda said he already told you 'no'."

"It doesn't matter," Allen said. "The only place I'll be rushing to is the unemployment line."

Allen gave Cathy the Hayabusa keys. He packed his office things in a box, left the main office area, descended the stairs, and exited the Darby Magazine building.

"I don't dare spend money on a taxicab," Allen said. "Guess it's the bus from now on."

Allen walked to the bus stop and sat on a bench. A blind man approached with his German Shepherd and cane, and he sat next to Allen. The dog sat next to his owner, and Allen reached to pet him.

"Please," the blind man said. "Do not pet my dog. He is working."

"I just want to show him that I'm friendly," Allen said.

"He is working. He cannot be distracted. It would mean my life if he led me astray," the blind man said. "Your eyes work. You can focus on anything and follow it to its conclusion."

"I wish," Allen said. "All my eyes are good for is closing so I can sleep in late. By the time I get up for the day, the world has passed me by."

"Then train your other senses," the blind man said. "Let your mind's eye see through other eyes."

"What? My mind's eyes?" Allen said.

"Close your eyes and listen," the blind man said.

"Okay, I'm listening," Allen said.

"What do you hear?" the blind man said.

"I hear cars," Allen said. "I hear people talking. I hear birds. People walking. Horns. Squeaky brakes. Something like air being let out of something. Something opening and closing. How's that, Mr. Blind man? Well?"

Allen opened his eyes in time to see the bus doors close with the blind man taking the last available seat on the bus, which was very crowded.

"Hey!" Allen yelled, and he ran after the bus, forgetting his box at the bench.

The bus did not heed Allen, and it continued driving away. Allen, out of breath, turned around in time to see a homeless person running off with his box.

"Hey!" Allen yelled as he ran back the other way after the homeless person.

But Allen was out of shape, tired, and disoriented. The homeless person disappeared into a crowd of people, and soon Allen was without his possessions, his bus ride, and his spirits.

"Bogus!" Allen said in frustration.

Just then, a Darby Magazine van drove up to Allen and parked. Kakuda jumped out of the van, and the van drove away.

"Hey Allen. Guess what? I'm on my way to a special interview with Baroness Vasha. She promised me a fourth invitation to the party. Guess she really liked the wheelie you did during the royal announcement. I've come back for my 'Busa."

Cathy Crepp ran outside the building, handed Kakuda his keys, and ran back inside.

"She should interview with me!" Allen said. "I'll take the 'Busa."

"No way! You've got it all wrong!" Kakuda said. "She wants to know about the owner of such a fine machine, not some dude who happened to steal it. That's right, she wants to see *me* and not *you*."

"What about me?" Allen asked.

"Sorry. Catch you later," Kakuda said, and he was gone.

Allen was now all alone. He could go home and spend the day there, but a sudden panic overwhelmed him, a panic of not ever earning a single paycheck again.

"What am I going to do?" he asked himself.

Meanwhile, Kakuda arrived at Baroness Vasha's villa. He knocked on the door, and Trey allowed him in.

"May I take your helmet?" Trey asked.

"Nonsense," Baroness Vasha said. "Let the man keep possession of his helmet."

Kakuda smiled and followed the baroness to a side lounge.

"May I get you anything to drink, Master Kakuda?" Trey asked.

"I..." Kakuda stumbled.

"Trey can provide anything you like. Coffee, tea, sparkling water, wine, champagne, and even rice wi—"

"Rice wine!" Kakuda said. "Absolutely!"

"Bring a bottle of rice wine and two crystal glasses," the baroness said. "No, wait, make that three glasses."

"Very good, baroness," Trey said, and he disappeared.

"Is your butler going to drink with us?" Kakuda asked.

"Oh heavens no!" the baroness said. "You will see in a moment."

Baroness Vasha pressed a button on her bracelet and spoke into it.

"Send my personal assistant," Vasha said.

Within twenty seconds, a young attractive woman with a variety of backgrounds walked into the room. She was part Japanese, part European, and part Asian Indian. A true cosmopolite in Kakuda's eyes. She stood and seemed paralyzed on seeing Kakuda.

"Kakuda...I'm sorry, I didn't catch your last name," the baroness said.

"I'm Kakuda Mori."

"Kakuda Mori, meet Julietta Mercrei, my personal assistant. Julietta, this is Kakuda Mori. He's a journalist for Darby Magazine, and he owns quite a powerful motorcycle."

"How do you do?" Kakuda said.

But all Julietta could say was, "Hi."

"Julietta, please take notes of our interview," the baroness said. "We wouldn't want to impose upon Kakuda to take his own notes."

"Wow, it really pays to be royalty, doesn't it?" Kakuda asked.

But Julietta just stood there and stared at Kakuda.

"Did you get that, Julietta?" the baroness said as she elbowed Julietta.

"Oh, yes," Julietta said with a startle, and she began taking shorthand.

"Now then, Kakuda, you have questions for me, and I have questions for you. Let's begin with your questions," the baroness said.

"How long have you been a baroness?" Kakuda asked.

The baroness laughed.

"You're very clever," the baroness said.

"And cute," Julietta said.

"But you should know better than to ask a woman's age. However, it was a valiant effort. I will simply answer by saying I've been a baroness my entire life," Baroness Vasha said.

"How long has Duchess Devanna been—" Kakuda started.

"A duchess?" the baroness said. "I can see this is going to be, uh, how shall we say, uh—"

"Intriguing," Julietta said with more interest in Kakuda saying anything than in what he was saying.

"Julietta, the shorthand!" Baroness Vasha said.

"Yes, Baroness," Julietta said as she jolted herself back into taking shorthand.

"Now then, let's make a little progress here," the baroness said. "I have in my possession an extra press pass to Duchess Devanna's birthday party."

Baroness Vasha held the pass in the air, and Kakuda leapt from his chair to grab it. But the baroness pulled the pass back quickly.

"Ah, ah, ah! Not so quickly," the baroness said.

"You said you have a pass for me," Kakuda said.

"First, I must have your credentials," the baroness said.

"Here, take a look at my ID," Kakuda said.

"Julietta, the ID," the baroness said.

Julietta walked over and took the ID, but as she did, her finger touched Kakuda's and caressed it lightly. She then looked at Kakuda's photo ID.

"Kakuda Mori, Darby Magazine," Julietta said.

"Any other credentials?" the baroness asked.

"Like what?" Kakuda asked.

"Well, tell me about your background, your family, where they are from, and so on," the baroness said.

"Well, I don't like to talk about my family," he said.

"Why not? Are you ashamed of who you are? You should always be proud of who you are. Build confidence," the baroness said.

"I'm proud of who he is," Julietta said.

"Yes, that is becoming more and more apparent," the baroness said.

"Well, my father worked in a chip factory, and my mother was an office lady," Kakuda said.

"Oh, fish and chips! I love fish and chips!" Julietta said.

"I don't think it was that kind of chip, was it Kakuda?" the baroness asked.

"No, he was an operator in a microprocessor fabrication plant," Kakuda said.

"I suspected as much," the baroness said.

"If you want to go out for fish and chips, I'd love to—" Julietta started.

"Later, Julietta," the baroness said.

"Please don't hold my background against me," Kakuda said. "My family is very hard working."

"That's good, that's good," the baroness said. "Every country needs many hard working people."

"May I have the pass now?" Kakuda asked.

"You're a little presumptuous, Kakuda," the baroness said.

"He didn't mean it," Julietta said, defending him. "But maybe if he learned the real reason he—"

"I'm getting to that, Julietta. Kakuda, I was very impressed with your motorcycle during the royal announcement earlier today. I know it wasn't you riding. But I happen to know that before the birthday party officially starts, the queen and duchess and other royals will be outside watching various entertainers—jugglers, sword swallowers, fire dancers, *et cetera, et cetera*. They have been looking for someone to perform motorcycle tricks, and I have been charged with finding such talent," the baroness explained.

"Well, yeah, I can do motorcycle stuff," Kakuda said.

"Motorcycle stuff, yes. Well then, I need you to audition for me," the baroness said. "Julietta will take notes, I *hope*."

Trey walked in.

"Baroness, another appointment awaits review," he said.

"Kakuda, you will excuse me for a moment. Julietta will show you the back lot where you may begin showing what tricks you can do on your motorcycle. Julietta, take this video camera and record his audition," the baroness said.

Julietta took Kakuda in arm, and the two walked to Kakuda's motorcycle like a newlywed couple, both giggling and laughing and hardly holding a straight line. Kakuda offered to give Julietta a lift to the back lot, she accepted, and so the couple darted off on Kakuda's 'Busa, but instead of dropping her off in the back lot so she could videograph the performance from the side, he performed wheelies and jumps and stood up on the bike and did other tricks while she was holding on. She shrieked in delight and wasn't sure if she was scared, excited, or in love.

Baroness Vasha, on the other hand, had more pressing business.

"I did not wish to say anything in front of the others, but it's Chusacuta," Trey said. "Our captive is—"

"You mean our *guest*," the baroness said. "Don't use that other word again."

"Yes, baroness. Our *guest* has refused to show us how to use the device. Our interrogation...er...interview has revealed the purpose of the device," Trey said.

"And that is?"

"It's a fertility device for cetaceans," Trey said.

"Hmmm. Chusacuta is an Atlantic white-sided dolphin, capable of taking human form," the baroness started.

"Captured while...sorry, *found* while we trolled the Atlantic for a new energy source," Trey said.

"It's a shame we didn't find that energy source," the baroness said. "But we may yet have use for this fertility device. If only we can determine how to use it."

"Chusacuta won't say a word. She simply makes squeaking and popping sounds," Trey said.

"But that's when she's in dolphin form," Baroness Vasha said.

"She refuses to take human form again—not since we put her hands in handcuffs, and she switched back to dolphin form to slip her fins out of the cuffs. She swims around, but we can't convince her to change," Trey said.

"I have an idea. Follow me," the baroness said.

Baroness Vasha and Trey walked into an elevator and went to the floor below, where Chusacuta, the Atlantic white-sided dolphin, swam. Several technicians attended to the dolphin's tank, trying to communicate with it, but to no effect.

"The problem with these methods is that they treat this thing as a dolphin and not a human," Baroness Vasha said.

"But if we could mimic its echolocation methods, we could reason—" Trey said.

"Reason, *shmeason*. I don't have time for reason. I need compliance. Now!" Baroness Vasha said.

The baroness looked around and saw a technician wearing headphones. Baroness Vasha walked over to that technician and ripped the headphones and attached music player from his body.

"Feed this into your communication system," Baroness Vasha said.

"What!?" the lead technician said. "That's...that's..."

"It used to be called rock and roll," Trey said.

"I don't care what it's called. Feed it into the tank," she said.

The lead technician did just that. The low bass vibrated the tank walls and sent water rippling throughout the tank. The dolphin transformed partly into humanoid shape, but she resisted.

"Turn up the volume," Vasha commanded.

The technician did that reluctantly, and the dolphin transformed almost completely, with her torso resembling a woman's body in a skin-tight scuba suit, and she kept her dolphin skin colors.

"You...can't...force...me...into this shape...forever!" Chusacuta said.

"This is just phase one," Vasha said.

The baroness threw spare clothes over the tank wall.

"Step out of the tank and put these clothes on," Vasha said.

"No."

"Do as I say, or I'll increase the volume," Vasha ordered.

Vasha pointed, and the technician increased the volume. Chusacuta put her hands over her head to stop the pain, but it didn't help. Reluctantly, she stepped out of the tank and put on the clothing. The technician turned down the volume.

"That's better," Vasha said. "Trey, give her some junk food."

"What!?"

"Junk food. Hamburgers, fries, candy bars, and pretzels," Vasha said.

"I won't eat your disgusting human food," Chusacuta said.

"You will, or I'll increase the volume again," Vasha said.

Vasha pointed, and the technician threatened to turn up the volume.

"No, no, not the sound," Chusacuta said.

"It's music," said the technician whose headphones had been taken.

Trey returned with the junk food and forced it into Chusacuta's mouth. Chusacuta resisted. Vasha turned up the volume, but Chusacuta was out of the tank, and so the sounds did not affect her as easily.

"Hah!" Chusacuta said, and she slowly began reverting to her dolphin state.

"Trey, set the food down," Vasha said.

Trey set the food down.

"Where are the wireless cardio stimulators?" Vasha asked.

"I don't understand," Trey said.

"I think I do," said the lead technician.

The lead technician pulled two wireless micro cardio stimulators from a cabinet and held them in one hand, while he held a cauterizing tool in the other.

"What are you going to do?" Chusacuta asked.

"That's an excellent idea, Alpha Tech," Vasha said to the lead technician. "Tie her to the chair."

"No, no, NO!!" Chusacuta fought.

Several technicians held Chusacuta to a chair while Trey bound her.

"Don't let her move," Vasha said.

Chusacuta fought to avoid the wireless micro cardio stimulators from Alpha Tech, but it was useless. She uttered squeaks and squawks like a trapped dolphin or penguin or something, and at that moment, Julietta appeared in the doorway to the room.

"My Baroness, I'm sorry for the intrusion, but—" Julietta started.

"What are you doing down here?" Vasha asked. "You're supposed to be watching Kakuda."

Alpha Tech cauterized the first micro cardio stimulator into Chusacuta's forehead. She squealed in pain.

"I sent him home," Julietta said. "You all were so noisy down here that I had to. I didn't want him to ask questions."

"Good. Step over here and watch," Vasha said.

Julietta walked toward Chusacuta and looked into the dolphin's eyes.

"Help me," Chusacuta begged Julietta, and this had the effect of unsettling Julietta's nerves.

"The second micro cardio stimulator," Vasha said. "Now!"

Alpha Tech cauterized the second stimulator into Chusacuta's forehead.

"Good," Vasha said. "Push the music through the cardio transmitter."

Alpha Tech took the small music player that had been used to pump music into the tank and connected it to a hand-held unit, which was now transmitting the music into the micro cardio stimulators implanted in Chusacuta's forehead.

"Everyone, release your hold of the dolphin," Vasha said.

They did, and at first Chusacuta writhed to free herself, but Alpha Tech made adjustments to the transmitter, and Chusacuta now took on a rigid-frame look, as if she were being electrocuted.

"Give me that," Vasha said as she grabbed the transmitter from Alpha Tech. "You're not doing it right. You must send pulses. Otherwise, the body will become acclimated to solid pain, and nothing will be effective."

Vasha made additional adjustments to the transmitter. Chusacuta first was rigid with shock for a few seconds, then she regained her composure and struggled to escape the bonds, but back to a rigid-shock look, then she gave less resistance, and finally she stopped trying to escape and instead used her shock-free moments to rest.

"There's an automatic setting," Alpha Tech explained. "All you need to do is—"

"I know about the automatic setting," Vasha said. "I designed this thing, remember?"

Baroness Vasha made a few additional adjustments, and now the transmitter rewarded Chusacuta by shocking her less for continued minutes of obedience. But periodically, it briefly shocked her as a reminder of its existence.

"Uh, why don't we let the dolphin go?" Julietta said.

The baroness shot Julietta a harsh facial expression.

"That is *not* what I intend to do, at least not *yet*," Baroness Vasha said. "This dolphin will be quite useful to us, now that she is under full control."

Chusacuta's eyes exhibited nervous twitches now and then, indicating she was still fighting underneath but had no power to resist external commands.

"You see this device, Chusacuta," Vasha said.

The baroness showed Chusacuta the dolphin fertility device.

"Yes," Chusacuta said with a grimace.

"How does it work?" Vasha asked.

Chusacuta held silent.

"Press that button for interrogation mode," Alpha Tech said.

"I *know* how this works!" Vasha barked.

And so, Vasha flipped a switch on the transmitter, and the device bombarded Chusacuta with musical compression waves when she did not answer.

"OWWWW!" Chusacuta yelled.

"The longer you resist, the greater the pain," Vasha said.

"Please, don't do this," Julietta said. "Give me a minute with her. Let me talk—"

"We are already talking with her," Vasha said. "Chusacuta—answer!"

"It...it works by extracting an ovum from a dolphin, mixing it with the blood from another, and placing the ovum in a carrier," Chusacuta grunted.

"Now that's what I call a good start," Vasha said.

"What are you going to do?" Julietta asked. "Raise an army of dolphin mutants?"

Baroness Vasha laughed.

"My dear Julietta, my interest in dolphins is only passing. The best in life is on land," the baroness said.

"No army?" Julietta asked.

"Of course not," Vasha said. "Now Chusacuta. This part about mixing blood. How is the blood obtained?"

"The device is placed over the donor's upper abdomen, and the glyph for *flipper* is pressed. The device then extracts blood," Chusacuta said against her will.

"And the ovum? How is it extracted?"

"By placing the device over the donor's lower abdomen and pressing the glyph for *bowl*," Chusacuta said. "The blood must be in the device no longer than one *cynor*, otherwise mixing will fail."

"What does that mean?" Vasha asked. "What is a cynor?"

"A hundred under one day," Chusacuta said. "It's a measure of time. I don't know any other way to explain it."

"Alpha Tech?" Vasha asked.

"I don't know what that means," Alpha Tech said.

"Trey?" Vasha asked.

Trey shrugged his shoulders.

"Anyone? Translate this dolphin time for me," Vasha said.

"What do you have with one hundred under one day?" Julietta asked.

"You can't," Alpha Tech said.

"It's a fraction," Julietta said.

"It must be how they describe time," Alpha Tech said.

"It's a fraction," Julietta repeated.

Chusacuta looked at Julietta and nodded in affirmation.

"I'll try another question," Vasha said. "Explain the length of time before mixing fails."

"One hundred below one day," Chusacuta said.

"That's the same as before," Alpha Tech said.

"It's almost fifteen minutes," Julietta said. "Chusacuta. How many dolphin heartbeats per dive is the mixing time?"

"A hundred and seventy five," Chusacuta said.

"I know about conventional dolphins and how long they can stay underwater," Julietta said. "Doing the math, I get the same result as from the one-hundred-below-one fraction—the maximum time between drawing donor blood and mixing with the ovum is fifteen minutes."

Chusacuta nodded in affirmation again.

"The dolphin seems to agree," Trey said.

"Yes, it does," Vasha said. "It would also seem that Julietta understands Chusacuta a little better than we do. Julietta, take this transmitter box and learn how to use the fertility device."

"I don't understand," Julietta said. "Why?"

"I have a special mission for you. Tonight. At the Eicor Mountain Resort. We are going to discredit Duchess Devanna with an illegitimate child. And what's more, the child's father will be a commoner. The child will be unfit to inherit the crown," Baroness Vasha explained.

The room was silent. All were shocked at the suggestion.

"That's...that's...a felo—" Alpha Tech began to say.

"It's brilliant," Baroness Vasha said. "No one dies. Everyone goes home. And I inherit the crown!"

Allen moped around the outside of the Darby Magazine building.

"Is that Dofer down there?!" Barcloff barked from his office window while looking down.

Cathy Crepp happened to be in his office.

"I, uh, don't know," Cathy said.

"You don't know," Barcloff repeated sarcastically. "Well I *do* know. He's loitering. He should go home, unless he doesn't have a home. Then he's a vagrant. I'm calling the police and having him removed."

"Oh please don't do that," Cathy begged. "I'll speak with him."

"I don't have time for idle talk. We have deadlines around here," Barcloff said.

Barcloff had a special telephone for calling police. It was evident, because within sixty seconds, a squad car arrived in front of the building, and two officers stepped out of the vehicle.

"Allen Dofer?" the sergeant said to Allen.

"Yeah?"

"Come with us please," he said.

"Am I under arrest?" Allen said.

"We have a complaint, Allen. We'd like you to come with us peaceably. You're not under arrest," the sergeant said.

"Then I don't want to go with you," Allen said. "I'm just going to take a walk."

"Then walk," the sergeant said.

Allen began walking east. One sergeant followed on foot, the other returned to the squad car and had it follow Allen by road. Allen looked back and saw the foot sergeant staring at him.

"You're following me?" Allen asked.

But the sergeant didn't reply. Instead, he pointed forward. Allen turned back toward the east and resumed walking. He walked and walked. Traffic had to slow behind the squad car and choose careful moments for driving around. Allen walked block after block, and still the two sergeants followed him. Finally, he had the idea to run through a crosswalk just before the blinking pedestrian signal turned into a solid "DONT WALK".

And that was how it happened. A car (trying to get around the slow squad car and beat the light) collided with an oncoming Kellington Catering Service van turning left in front of it, or at least it tried to turn left. It stopped at the last moment to avoid hitting Allen. CRASH! The van and passing car and squad car were all caught up in the accident. The sergeant in the squad car was dazed. His buddy checked on him and then the people in the car. But Allen saw the van catch fire, and a man was trapped inside. Before the two officers could react, Allen had already run to the van, ripped open the door, and freed the man from the burning wreck. The man had sustained burns from the fire. So did Allen, though he didn't feel the pain.

"You...saved my life," the man said from his dazed state just before he fell unconscious.

Allen stayed with the man and checked for breathing and pulse, which the man had, and then Allen realized why the man passed out—his leg was bleeding. Allen ripped off a strip from his own shirt and used it to minimize the bleeding. It helped. Allen had been checking the man's pulse, and it initially weakened, but now it was holding steady. An ambulance arrived, along with TV3 and The Darby Globe. TV3 stuck its camera in front of Allen and the injured van driver, videographing and announcing the event. Two ambulatory technicians placed the injured van driver on a gurney and loaded him into the ambulance. Just before he was fully loaded in, he awoke briefly, motioned toward Allen, and said, "He saved my life."

The TV3 crew then interviewed Allen excitedly about the event, about being a hero, and all but promoted Allen to godship. Back in the Darby Magazine office, Cathy Crepp watched the TV3 telecast on the big office screen. She changed the station, and that station also covered the accident. She turned it back to TV3. Barcloff happened to walk in, and he saw Allen on TV3. In anger, he took a nearby porcelain object and smashed it on the floor, startling people from their television gaze.

"TV3!? What am I paying you people for? Our competitors are scooping us, and we're playing musical chairs with the telly. Well!? Crepp, go out there and cover the crash!"

"Yes, Mr. Barcloff," Cathy said.

But when Cathy arrived, the action and praise of heroism had largely dissipated. The president of the catering service, Sueann Kellington, drove up and offered her thanks to Allen. When he mentioned that he had lots of time now that he was out of a job, she immediately offered him one with the catering service.

"I don't know anything about catering," Allen said.

"It's easy. We'll teach you everything you need to know. And now that Donovan is in the hospital, we're short a person for the birthday party this evening," Sueann said.

"The royal birthday party?" Allen asked with interest.

"We were already short staffed, and this could put us under. Please. If ever you could be a helpful citizen, I ask you—please work for my catering service," Sueann said.

"The royal birthday party," Allen mused. "You have a deal."

"Thank you. You'll need to come with me, then. We are already short of time and don't have a minute to lose," she said.

And so, Cathy Crepp, before she could ask Allen what happened, was able to watch as he entered a car driven by a female corporate executive.

"Somehow I'm jealous, and I don't know why," Cathy said to herself.

The afternoon passed. Allen was now ready to help cater for the royal birthday party. He rode in a van, and behind was a truck-trailer loaded with supplies. The road to the resort ran along the side of a mountain, and the path was not a simple spiral up. The road went up and over and up and a little down and inside and outside and mostly up, but eventually it led to the top of Eicor Mountain. As the group climbed the mountain, the air cooled. Allen felt lighthearted, and all his old worries about Darby Magazine stayed down in the valley. In fact, he looked over the mountain's edge, and the city seemed so far below, as if Allen were up in an airplane.

"We're approaching the main gate," Sueann said from the front passenger seat to her group in the van.

Allen looked, and the main gate was entirely of stone, carved from the mountain, and the attached walls *were* part of the mountain.

"Catering service for Duchess Devanna's birthday party," said the driver to a guard.

The guard checked the driver's papers, waved him through, and waved the truck-trailer through too. Then Allen was in for a real surprise. He was completely surrounded by architecture carved in the mountain. Buildings, columns, stairs, pillars, statues, benches, tables, flower gardens, fountains, flowing water, little pools, and everywhere he looked, there was some sort of torch atop carved rock. This place seemed more like an ancient worship temple than it did a royal resort. The van and truck-trailer felt badly out of place, but after driving a little farther, Allen and company came across a parking place for fancy vehicles only the rich could afford.

"Why aren't we parking here?" Allen asked as the van drove past the cars.

"Delivery vehicles park in back," the driver said.

The van continued on what seemed like another long path to the back, and yet all along the way there was more stone work, and there were a plenitude of horticultural decorations, with more flower gardens in stone work, miniature trees, shrubs with vibrant colors, even patches of grass in strategic locations. And no matter where Allen was, he saw plenty of places to sit with tables and fountains flowing with water, and torches seemingly burning directly from the stone work.

"I could live here forever," Allen said.

The others in the van laughed.

"If you had to run a country, you couldn't hide out here forever," Sueann said. "Business comes first, and that's conducted in the palace. And only when all the people are satisfied, which is rare and short-lived, then are you able to enjoy a moment of peace in a resort. Or you hire someone else to run the country. Or you—"

But Allen's attention was diverted when the van drove past a back lot where Kakuda was entertaining the royal and rich with his motorcycle tricks.

"That should be me. I should be doing wheelies and stuff," Allen said to himself.

The van and truck-trailer parked out of sight from the others. Allen had no time to enjoy the surroundings. It was go-go-go with catering work. Sueann directed the entire work agenda—setting up tables and chairs and getting the cooking equipment started and cooking food and having it prepared and put together and readied for the guests. All had to be ready by 7 pm—the official beginning of the party and the moment when the news media would arrive.

The catering group progressed well and transported all food and equipment into the royal banquet hall. Sueann's employees took their positions and prepared for the guests when she realized something.

"I forgot whipped cream!" Sueann said.

"No time to go back now," said another. "You are needed here to greet the guests."

"I'll get it," Allen said.

Allen rushed out the banquet hall, into the parking area, and around the back of the truck-trailer. Where was it? There, toward the cab, a large container of pressurized whipped cream. It was heavy, and there wasn't a single hand truck in the trailer.

"The hand trucks are inside, in the prep room," Allen said. "There's no time to go back and get one. I'll just have to carry the container."

Allen hoisted the container onto his right shoulder. It was heavy, perhaps forty kilograms, and Allen struggled to maintain his balance.

"I...must...get this...inside," Allen puffed.

Allen managed to exit the truck-trailer, and he walked very slowly along the parking area. He reached a walkway that led to the back door of the banquet hall, with a railing on the right side to prevent folk from falling over. There wasn't much space to walk, and so Allen could not give himself much cushion room from the railing. A mountain moth fluttered in Allen's face, and when he tried brushing it aside with his free hand, the container's weight shifted and fell toward the railing. Desperate to save the whipped cream, Allen held onto the container and attempted to pull it back toward the walkway. But it was too late. His balance was destroyed, and the container pulled Allen over the railing and into a fountain pool on the terrace below.

"Who is there?" a voice called.

Allen tried keeping quiet, but his movement in the water made noise, and now the container, despite its fall being softened by landing in the water, did manage to catch a stone corner, and this caused a small crack to open. Whipped cream hissed out slowly.

Terrace lights turned on, and a shape stood in the doorway.

"Are you hurt?" she called out.

"No, not hurt," Allen said. "Just a few bruises. But the whipped cream is leaking."

Allen pulled himself out of the fountain and hoisted the container onto the retaining wall.

"Oh, I've ruined everything!" Allen lamented.

Three guards rushed onto the terrace and surrounded Allen.

"We heard the splash, Your Grace," said the lead guard. "What shall we do with him?"

The woman emerged from the doorway and walked onto the terrace.

"I'll deal with this one," she said. "You may leave."

The guards left.

"You're...Duchess Devanna," Allen remarked in surprise. "I...am sorry for the intrusion."

"And you're Allen Dofer. I saw you on the news. You pulled that gentleman from a burning van," Duchess Devanna said.

"Yeah, that's me. Dofer the Loafer," Allen said.

Duchess Devanna looked at Allen with a quizzical expression.

"Well, that's what Mr. Barcloff used to call me," Allen said.

"Darby Magazine," Devanna said. "So you are moonlighting now with Sueann's catering service?"

"No," he said. "Mr. Barcloff fired me. Miss Kellington just hired me today."

"Sorry to hear that and good for you," Devanna said.

"Seems strange to hear the queen be sad and happy for me at the same time," Allen said.

Devanna laughed.

"Well I'm not the queen yet," she said. "I wonder what Queen Cythia would say?"

"I...uh...I...I meant future queen," Allen said. "Tonight is your night of the future."

"I understand," Duchess Devanna said.

She walked over to Allen, dipped a finger into the whipped cream, and tasted it.

"It's very good. A shame it's wasted here in the fountain," the duchess said.

"Your guards seemed very angry at me," Allen said.

"They should be. This is my prized fountain. Contains healing minerals from the mountain. It's a felony for any citizen to touch it, much less contaminate it in the way you have," she said.

"I've committed a crime?"

"Yes," she said. "A felony. You could be hanged."

Allen turned white with fright.

"Don't worry," she said. "I would never have a national hero hanged."

Allen looked back in confusion.

"Oh I know, you haven't been officially decorated yet. That's the Ministry's job. I've submitted the application, of course. But they are slow. Don't expect the decoration for at least a month," Duchess Devanna said.

"And the fountain?" Allen asked.

"It's obvious this is an accident. The water will renew itself in a week. However, that doesn't mean you may get out of this without a punishment," she warned.

"What?" Allen reacted.

The duchess took a handful of whipped cream and dumped it atop Allen's head. She then took another handful and plastered it on his face.

"There," she said. "You've been punished. Now come inside, clean up, and change into something dry. I'll have the maid launder your work clothes."

"You have a maid here? And a washer? And drier?" Allen asked.

The duchess laughed.

"You really don't know much about the royal way, do you?" she asked.

Allen wanted to reply, but he was speechless. Courtesy says that royals have the last word, at least that was what he was taught, and so he said nothing. Duchess Devanna sensed he was now holding back for that reason, and she laughed again. She motioned for him to go inside, and he did. Devanna called the maid and told her what was needed—temporary dry clothes for Allen and to launder his dirty ones once he changed. Allen changed into the dry clothes quickly—using one of several attached bathrooms.

"How do I look?" he asked while wearing the smoking jacket and slacks.

"Like you need a pipe," she laughed. "Here, help me with my tiara."

Allen paused.

"What's the matter?" she asked.

"You...uh...queen...uh..." he stumbled.

"Allen Dofer, you can throw yourself into a burning van to save a life, but you cannot help your duchess with her tiara?" she said. "Don't worry, I won't bite."

"But to touch a royal person," he started. "The penalty...it..."

"You aren't touching me. You're touching my tiara," the duchess said.

Allen walked over to Duchess Devanna, who was looking in the mirror at herself. She held the tiara on the top of her head.

"Not a single hair stylist in the Commonwealth has found a way to make my tiara stay put on my hair. The tiara always slips and falls," Duchess Devanna said. "See if you can think of a way to make the tiara stay attached."

"I...uh..."

"Hurry," she said. "All the guests are seated and must wait for me to enter before they may eat. Actually, I would have been in there by now, but I was delayed."

"I was the delay?" he asked.

"Yes," she giggled.

"Then all of your royal rich expensive guests are..."

"Waiting for you, yes, you are holding up my birthday party and the decision of who will be my future husband. I can then say you are holding up the kingdom," she continued to giggle.

"Oh me, oh my," Allen fretted, and his hands shook nervously.

"You're shaking," she said. "Don't be so tense. That's a royal command."

"Can't help it," he said. "If I were to accidentally touch you, it—"

Then without warning, Duchess Devanna removed the tiara with one hand and grabbed Allen's hand with her other. He reeled back in horror with the knowledge that his hand had now touched royalty.

"What are you doing?" he said in sheer fright.

"There, that wasn't so bad," she laughed. "You are way too tense. You're going to drop my tiara with such anxiety."

"But you're touching me. I'm touching you!" he said in a muffled shriek.

"Oh, the horror, the horror!" she said sarcastically. "All the world will come to an end because Allen Dofer is touching someone else's hand. And he's not just touching any hand, it's a woman's hand, and that of a duchess!"

"I'm going to prison now for sure," he said.

Duchess Devanna broke into hysterical laughter. She had to sit from such laughter. The duchess turned red and even began to cough. She sipped some water to stop her laughing, but she choked. Her laughter turned to panic, and she pointed to her throat.

"You're choking!" he said. "Help! No wait, I'm the help."

Allen put his arms around her and performed the Heimlich maneuver. The water was forced from her lungs, and she began breathing again.

"Oh thank you, thank you," she said in between breaths. "You saved my life. Well, you almost killed me with laughter, but you saved me too."

"But I had to touch you again!" he said.

"And I touched you before with the whipped cream, but you didn't react then, which is why I was laughing so hard," she said.

"That doesn't count. The whipped cream touched me, not you," he said.

"A minor technicality. I think you're afraid of normal human contact. But a crisis, well, that's acceptable, isn't it?" she asked.

Allen didn't know what to say.

"Is Your Grace well?" the maid asked, now showing up in the room with Allen's laundered clothes. "I heard choking, and I—"

"How did you clean those so fast?" he asked.

"We have the best laundry devices," the maid said.

"Thank you, that will be all," Duchess Devanna said to the maid, and the maid left.

"So am I going to be hanged?" Allen asked.

"Only if you don't help me get this tiara on," she said. "There are little combs used for attachments. But my hair is too straight—the combs won't hold. A pity I don't have rope for hair. Then it would be easy."

"Hmm," Allen mused. "Maybe we can turn your hair into rope."

Allen twisted a clump of hair and twisted and twisted, and then he placed two pins to hold the hair in a knot. He repeated this with another clump of hair to form a knot. With two knots of hair, the little combs attached between the knots and the duchess's scalp, and the tiara stayed fast.

"Amazing! You save lives and tiaras! Well, Allen Dofer, change into your work clothes and return to work. I have a birthday party to attend," the duchess said, and she walked out the door, down a short passageway, and into the banquet hall.

Allen went back to the terrace to find the container of whipped cream, but to his surprise, it was gone. The mess was cleaned up, and already the water in the fountain had renewed itself. The terrace showed no evidence of his accidental spill.

"Oh no, it's gone," he lamented.

There was nothing else to do. He climbed steps to the parking area to retrieve the second container of whipped cream, but when he entered the truck-trailer, it was gone.

"How strange," he said to himself, and he sat on the trailer-floor's edge to gather his thoughts.

He was sitting this way for an hour when Sueann came out.

"There you are!" she said. "What happened to you? I had to send Wiley out for the whipped cream. But he only found one canister."

"I lost the first one," he said.

"Well there's no use worrying about it. We'll have to come back and look for it another day. Dinner is over, and it's time to pack up everything and leave Eicor Mountain," Sueann said. "So hop to it!"

Allen helped pack up. He noticed that the banquet hall had been turned into a dance and lounging hall. The bar was open, but Kellington Catering Service didn't have that contract, so there was no need for Sueann's group to stay around. In all the running around and packing and stuff, Allen forgot about Kakuda, until Kakuda stopped by and tapped Allen on the shoulder.

"Hey, look at you!" Kakuda said. "How's the catering business?"

"Kakuda!" Allen said.

"Allen, you won't believe the stories I've been getting. I've got interviews of all the royals, even Duchess Devanna. Too bad the queen isn't here, 'cause I'd get her interview too. Boy, Darby Magazine is going to scoop those other media outlets."

"What makes you think so?" Allen asked.

"Because I'm the best, that's why!" Kakuda said. "In fact, I've been invited to stay beyond the 10 pm limit. That's a super exclusive. I'm going to be treated like royalty myself. Yep. I can stay as long as I want and even stay the night."

"Yuck," Allen said.

"And, Duchess Devanna's limo will take me home tomorrow morning," Kakuda said.

"You're making me sick," Allen said. "It's just not right."

"You just have to know the right people," Kakuda said, and he motioned over to Baroness Vasha and Julietta Mercrei.

"I see," Allen said. "But what about the 'Busa? Your baby?"

"Oh, I forgot about that! And it's supposed to rain tonight!" Kakuda said.

"All that fine leather getting wet. Tsk, tsk, tsk," Allen said.

"Okay, you gotta help me out," Kakuda said.

"I have to help you? How?" Allen said.

"Take it to my home and park it in the garage," he said.

"In exchange for what?" Allen asked.

"Huh? After you stole it from me? You owe me and should do this favor for me as return payment," Kakuda said.

"I have a ride home, and it's leaving in three minutes, so you'd better decide how important it is to keep Baby 'Busa out of the rain," Allen said.

"Okay, okay. What do you want?" Kakuda asked.

"I need time here to do my own interviewing," Allen said.

"Why? You've been fired," Kakuda said. "What good is a story? Are you going to the competition?"

"What does it matter?" Allen said. "Just remember. Baby 'Busa will get busted leather from the rain."

"Okay, already, you win. Here are the keys to the 'Busa. I'll talk to a few people and get you a pass to stay until 10 pm, but that's it. After that, you'll have to leave. And even if I could arrange to have you stay past 10, I won't let you. It's supposed to rain shortly after that," Kakuda said.

"Don't worry about 'Busa Baby," Allen said. "I'll leave by 10."

Kakuda walked over to the baroness and had a few words. Then Julietta spoke with Kakuda, and the two ran off to the dance floor and danced the evening away. The baroness motioned Allen over, and he started to walk over, but Sueann caught him.

"It's time to go," she said.

"I'm staying," Allen said.

"What?"

"Kakuda over there asked me to ride his motorcycle home," Allen said.

"Well, it won't look right if you stay with my catering service logo on your shirt," Sueann said.

"Oh, I didn't think of that," he said.

In this time, the baroness walked over to Allen and Sueann.

"Hello, Baroness Vasha," Sueann said.

"Is there a problem?" the baroness asked. "Mr. Dofer is planning to stay, from what I hear."

"My entire staff must leave, that's the agreement," Sueann said. "We're not to impose on the party. As long as he wears one of my shirts, he—"

"That won't be a problem. Allen, come with me. I'll have Trey supply you with the proper attire," the baroness said.

"Thank you, Baroness Vasha," Allen said.

"Don't thank me now," the baroness said. "Thank me later."

She smiled, like a cat preparing to catch its prey. Allen felt goosebumps, and he was unsettled.

"Are you staying then, Allen?" Sueann asked.

"Yeah. I'll be fine," he said.

"Okay, I'll see you tomorrow," she said.

Sueann left with her catering service. Trey led Allen to a men's lounge with extra shirts, ties, slacks, shoes, irons, belts, combs, shaving cream, shampoo, etc.

"Pick," Trey said.

"Well," Allen said. "This is better than what the duchess offered me."

"You saw her this evening?" Trey asked.

"Yeah," Allen said.

"One moment," Trey said, and he left.

Allen picked a shirt and quickly threw it on. He left the men's lounge and returned to the banquet hall. He saw Trey speaking with Baroness Vasha. Allen looked around. Julietta was still dancing with Kakuda, but now the song ended, and Kakuda went to the bar for two drinks. The baroness motioned for Julietta, and she walked over to the baroness. The three then discussed something very important, but Allen could not determine what.

He decided he had to find out. Inconspicuously, he approached the three without being seen. Before he could get within earshot, the three left the banquet hall and went outside in the back. Allen continued to follow them carefully. He had to hide behind one stone pillar, then another, then another in order to get close enough to listen without being noticed.

"So you remember the plan?" Baroness Vasha asked Julietta.

"Yeah," Julietta said. "First I put rohyp—"

"Not like that," the baroness said. "Speak poetically. There are ears everywhere."

"No one can hear us," Julietta said.

"Poetically, dear," the baroness said.

"When the private party begins with the four royal visitors, the local royal, and me, the tap beer magically contains a new ingredient," Julietta said.

"Good. That's much better," the baroness said.

"Then all get sleepy and fall asleep," Julietta said.

"Yes, also good," the baroness said.

"Then I take *it* and use *it*," Julietta said.

"And the source?" the baroness said.

Julietta hesitated.

"What's the problem?" Baroness Vasha asked.

"Kakuda?" Julietta asked.

"Don't say his name," the baroness said. "But yes, that's the source. We've been through this. He's the only non-royal that will do."

"He won't die, will he?" Julietta asked with worry in her voice.

There was a pause.

"I mean, this has never been used on humans," Julietta said. "How do you know?"

Another pause. Allen's heart filled his ears, and he strained to hear. He couldn't believe what was being said. It sounded like the four royal men and Duchess Devanna were in some sort of danger. He trembled. He tried regaining his composure, but in doing so, his breathing simply got heavier and heavier.

"What's that?" the baroness asked.

"There's someone else here," Julietta said.

"Trey," the baroness said.

Trey looked around quietly with billy club in hand. And then it happened. He found Allen and rapped him on the head, knocking Allen unconscious.

"Put him in the caretaker's quarters," the baroness said. "It's vacant for the next three days. And make sure he sleeps all night and remembers nothing. When you're done, meet me at the car. We're leaving."

"I still don't have *it*," Julietta said.

"And Trey, give *it* to our helper here," the baroness said.

When Allen awoke, the sun was just rising over the horizon. He was surprised to find himself in the caretaker's quarters. The door was wide open, and there was an empty beer bottle next to the bed.

"What happened?" Allen asked. "Did I get drunk and pass out? The last thing I remember is promising Kakuda I'd take 'Busa home. Oh no, Baby 'Busa!"

Allen staggered to his feet and walked to where it was parked. Yes, it had rained during the night, but not as much as Kakuda and Allen had thought. The leather was unaffected, for which Allen was thankful, and he rode home.

"I feel terrible," Allen said.

Allen took two aspirin and went back to bed.

Later in the morning, Allen heard beating on his door.

"Allen, are you in there?" said a woman's voice.

Allen answered the door, and it was Sueann.

"Did you forget something this morning?" she said.

"I feel sick," Allen said. "I couldn't get up."

"Take a shower and put on your work clothes," she said. "I'll give you a lift into work today. There's important news you need to hear."

The mention of news caught Allen's attention. He realized he had nothing he could write as a news article for the prior night's party. Then there was this other news that Sueann had. What could it be? He showered, dressed, and locked up his home.

"Oh, I forgot coffee," he said as he climbed into Sueann's car.

"Here, I brought a vacuum flask for you—full of coffee," she said.

"Oh wow, this is royal treatment," Allen said.

"Funny you should use those words. Apparently, there's a little bit of a minor scandal from last night's party," Sueann said. "Duchess Devanna of Darby, Viscount Darro of Breyton, Marchese Antonio of Gravati, Duke Arthur of Cantaloofa, Count Fenton of Farr, and Kakuda Mori of Darby Magazine were all found sleeping in the same bed with their clothes off."

"Wow!" Allen said.

"They claim they remember nothing about how that all happened," Sueann said. "Good for you that you weren't there. Otherwise I'd have to fire you."

"Yeah," Allen said, happy that he wasn't part of the scandal, but worried that he couldn't remember what had happened to himself at the resort.

"Right about now, Kakuda is being fired at Darby Magazine," Sueann said. "The Viscount, Marchese, Duke, and Count are returning to their respective domains and undergoing a heavy grilling by their own media. And Duchess Devanna is a wreck and in hiding."

"That's terrible," Allen said. "All of it. Just terrible."

The two drove past Darby Magazine and saw Kakuda exiting the building with a cardboard box.

"There's Kakuda," Allen said.

Sueann pulled over, and Allen rolled down his window.

"Kakuda!" Allen said. "What's going on?"

"I guess you heard about last night," Kakuda said. "Well, I got fired."

"I'm sorry to hear that," Allen said. "Say, here are your keys to Baby 'Busa."

"Thanks," Kakuda said. "I'll have to sell her, of course."

"Kakuda!" Allen said.

"Well, a man's gotta eat," Kakuda said.

"You know, Kakuda, I'm putting myself way out on a limb with negative publicity and so on, but I'm sure you could do something for my catering service," Sueann said.

"I can't do that to you," Kakuda said. "You'd lose your contract with the Crown. Then everyone would be out of a job."

"Yeah, I guess you're right," Sueann said. "I'm sorry, Kakuda."

"So am I," Kakuda said. "Well, see you around."

"Yeah. See yah," Allen replied.

A month passed. Allen continued working for Kellington Catering Service and developed a reputation as a solid worker. Sueann promoted him to a lead handler and gave him responsibilities in managing others. The Ministry awarded Allen a medal for heroism in saving the life of another. He had hoped to see Duchess Devanna at the ceremony, but she was a no-show. Queen Cythia was there, however, and commended Allen for his dedication.

Allen spent his free time looking for Kakuda. He found him, maintaining tanks for the combersoni (Commerson's) dolphins at Darby Dolphinarium.

"I still don't know what happened," Kakuda said one Saturday while Allen was visiting the dolphinarium. "I didn't even get an interview with the duchess. I had just finished interviewing Count Fenton of Farr, and the next thing I know, I'm sleeping in a huge bed with him and the other three royal men, and Duchess Devanna."

"Did you do anything with any of them?" Allen asked.

"No, I don't think so. How can I prove my innocence? I was lucky to get this job, but the tabloids have otherwise destroyed my career," Kakuda said.

At that moment, Julietta walked up and kissed Kakuda.

"So does this mean you and Kiyomi are through?" Allen asked.

"She dumped me after the scandal," Kakuda said. "I met Julietta just before the party, but unlike some, she didn't desert me after the scandal."

Allen looked at her closely.

"Have we met?" Allen asked.

"No, I don't think so," she said.

"Strange. I feel like I've seen you before," Allen said.

"You might have seen her at the party when you were catering," Kakuda said.

"Maybe that's it," Allen said.

"Yes, I was at the party," she said nervously. "Kakuda, let's get something to eat when your shift ends."

"Actually, my shift just ended," he said. "Allen, I'll see you later."

"Okay," Allen said.

Kakuda and Julietta left. Allen walked around the dolphinarium and wondered about things. He watched the combersoni dolphins from above, then he went below to watch them through the tank's glass wall. The combersoni tank was actually the smaller part of the dolphinarium. The major attractions were in the bottlenose tank and the orca tank. An announcement came over the public address system for the orca show, and what few people were watching the combersoni dolphins now deserted for the orca show. Allen continued to watch the combersoni dolphins.

"Watching them swim is so relaxing," Allen said quietly. "They're like little dogs running around having fun."

As Allen spoke, he sensed someone was nearby. His voice didn't echo back to him the way it should have when no one was around. He turned suddenly and saw a hooded shape disappear behind a corner.

"My mind is playing tricks with me," he said.

Allen walked a little bit and thought to turn around again, but he knew if he did, he wouldn't see the person. Instead, he walked out of sight, opened a door to the stairs leading above, and closed it. But he didn't go up the stairs. The sound of the door opening and closing was a ruse. Instead, he hid behind a refuse can. He waited five minutes. Then ten. Nothing. He was about to give up and go back upstairs when the hooded figure emerged and stood next to the glass wall.

"What a world we live in where we swim in colors of white and black," the hooded figure said.

Allen immediately recognized the voice as that of Duchess Devanna.

"Your Grace," Allen whispered loudly.

She turned around suddenly and started to run, but Allen jumped up and stopped her by holding her arm.

"Let me go!" she said.

"You've been in hiding for so long, I thought I'd never see you again. I missed you at my medal ceremony."

"You're touching a royal," she said.

"That didn't bother you before," he said. "Are you so afraid now?"

"Things are different," she said. "My reputation is ruined."

Then the color drained from Duchess Devanna's face.

"I feel sick," she said. "I need to find the ladies' room."

Allen saw that she was sincere, and he allowed her to go. There was a ladies' room just around the corner. She went in and came back out a few minutes later, moving her teeth, tongue, and cheeks around as if trying to get some bad taste out of her mouth.

"You look awful," Allen said. "And you don't..."

"I smell as bad, is that what you're going to say?" Devanna asked.

"I didn't want to say it," Allen said.

"You don't have to. This whole scandal has turned my stomach into poison," she said. "And the paparazzi hound me everywhere. I wish I could escape all of this royal stuff and be a nobody, if only for a day."

Allen wanted to offer his help, but then he heard the rapid clicking of SLR cameras.

"They are coming. I can't let them find me!" she said.

Duchess Devanna disappeared into the stairwell. Allen ran after her, but she was too quick. There were several turns and doors and corridors and doors, and Allen lost track of where she went. Within seconds, the paparazzi were upon him, like dogs on a pheasant chase. Seeing only him, they gave up and disappeared in despair.

Five months passed, and Queen Cythia called for a major media announcement. Allen went to the dolphinarium to find Kakuda, but word was that Kakuda had taken the day off to be part of the royal announcement.

"Part of the announcement?" Allen asked. "What does that mean?"

"It means," the supervisor started, "look for him on the balcony with the queen and not in the crowd."

Allen was shocked. What was going on? Would Kakuda be exiled from the Commonwealth? There was only one way to find out. Allen had to attend the announcement. He took a bus to the royal plaza, but others had the same idea. The bus could only get so close, and then Allen had to walk. And walk, and walk. But he arrived. The plaza was filled with people, awaiting the announcement. Media was ecstatic and interviewed anyone who had an opinion on what would be announced. Would the duchess lose her right to the throne? What about the four royal men who were found in scandal in bed with the duchess? And Kakuda?

There wasn't much longer for Allen to wait. Queen Cythia appeared on the balcony and spoke.

"My dear citizens," she said. "As you know, the Duchess of Darby celebrated her twenty-third birthday six months ago. In addition to celebrating her birthday, the duchess was to find a prospective husband. Royal men from many domains were invited, and many attended."

Some clapping from the crowd with chants of, "Long live Duchess Devanna." The queen waved the crowd's chanting down to a murmur, and she continued to speak.

"Unfortunately, events followed the not-so-proper path. I will not hide the fact that the duchess was found in a compromising position with five others," the queen said.

Queen Cythia then motioned toward the palace. Viscount Darro of Breyton, Marchese Antonio of Gravati, Duke Arthur of Cantaloofa, Count Fenton of Farr, and Kakuda walked onto the balcony. The queen introduced each by name, with a disdain for Kakuda.

"Oh boy, there he is!" Allen said. "What mess did you get yourself into, Kakuda?"

"And now, the Duchess of Darby," Queen Cythia announced.

Duchess Devanna entered the balcony wearing a robe with the robe's hood over her face.

"Duchess Devanna, would you remove your robe, please?" Queen Cythia asked.

Duchess Devanna first removed her hood to show who she was, then she removed her robe and showed her new royal maternity outfit. The crowd gasped. Duchess Devanna was pregnant, and her bump was very noticeable.

"In one week, Duchess Devanna will be married to the father of her child," the queen said.

The crowd erupted with shouting, but the single thing shouted most often was, "Who's the father?" Queen Cythia hushed them and spoke.

"The father will be announced at the wedding," she said.

Lots of puzzled reactions, mostly with shouts of how can one have a wedding without the groom knowing who he is.

"The groom will be invited, that is not an issue," she said.

The queen had no more comment. She stood on the balcony and waved to the people. The duchess also waved, along with the viscount, marchese, duke, and count. Kakuda stood there rigid, mortified that he would be married to royalty. He looked around in the crowd for Julietta Mercrei but could not find her.

"So far everything is going according to plan," Baroness Vasha said to Trey and Julietta in a shaded, private balcony off to the side where the three could watch unobserved. "Queen Cythia has determined that Kakuda is the father. She has wisely delayed this announcement until the wedding day itself. Otherwise she couldn't get support to hold the wedding in the first place. But it will all unravel when Kakuda is announced as the father of Duchess Devanna's unborn child. The Commonwealth will never accept a non-Anglo and a commoner. Yes, Queen Cythia the procrastinator. Well, the wedding will be a complete fiasco. It will ruin both the duchess and the queen. Abdication is next in order. Yes, the queen will abdicate, and I will become queen. It's all so natural and proper, don't you think Julietta?"

But Julietta had buried her face in her hands in an effort to hide her tears.

"What are you crying about?" the baroness asked.

"Kakuda," she said.

"What about him?" the baroness asked. "Don't tell me you like him. Well, after he is announced as the father, no wedding will take place. And he'll be free. Then you may spend whatever time you wish with him, if that will cheer you up."

"I'll try to cheer up. I really will," Julietta said.

The wedding day arrived soon enough. It was held in First Darby Cathedral. The Viscount Darro, Marchese Antonio, Duke Arthur, Count Fenton, and Kakuda were all groomsmen. Duchess Devanna had many of her friends as bridesmaids. Julietta was a bridesmaid too. Baroness Vasha attended on the side of the bride as did Trey. Relatives from the groomsmen attended on the side of the groom.

"Okay, everyone, this is it," Sueann said to her catering crew in the attached reception hall. "Make sure there's enough food, beverage, and cake. I forgot the cake!"

"I'll get it," Allen said.

"Oh no, not like last time with the whipped cream," Sueann said. "I'll go with you to make sure you don't drop it!"

Sueann led Allen out to the delivery van.

"It's not here," Allen said.

"Of course it's not here. It's supposed to be delivered from Darby Bakery. Did they say when they would arrive?"

"I thought you called them," Allen said.

"No, you were supposed to call them. Oh this is just *great!*" Sueann said.

Sueann called the bakery. They had the cake, but their delivery van was out on another delivery.

"We'll have to rush over there and get it," Sueann said.

"But we'll miss the wedding," Allen said.

"We will if we stand here talking about it. Let's go!" she ordered.

Sueann drove her catering van, and Allen rode in the front passenger seat.

"We'll have to take some shortcuts," she said. "Hang on!"

Sueann navigated the van through alleys, knocking over garbage cans and scaring the feral life.

"Woah!" Allen said.

"We can't take these same shortcuts coming back," Sueann said. "The cake won't stand the abuse."

"Yeah, abuse. What about me?" Allen muttered, but before he could complain any more, his cellphone rang. "Yeah? On no, not that too. Okay, we'll try. Thanks."

Allen ended his phone call.

"What now?" Sueann asked.

"I guess we were supposed to bring the unity candle too?" Allen asked.

"Confound it all!" Sueann uttered.

"Since when is a unity candle considered part of a catering service?" Allen asked.

"Since the royal contract I signed says so," Sueann said. "How could I forget that too? Oh, this is a disaster. I'll lose the contract!"

And with that last word, she took a sharp turn out of the alley and into traffic, cutting off the traffic.

"I want to keep living, please!" Allen shrieked. "This isn't the Darby Grand Prix!"

But Sueann continued to drive like mad. She parked on the sidewalk in front of Darby Bakery and rushed through the front door.

"Where's the cake?" she barked.

"There in the corner," said the attendant.

"Allen, the cake, quick!" she said.

Allen and Sueann hurriedly loaded the cake into the van.

"Hey, what about the—" Allen started to say to Sueann.

"The unity candle!" she barked.

"Over here on a shelf," the attendant said.

"Grab it, Allen!" Sueann said.

Allen grabbed the unity candle, and before he could ask why a baker had a unity candle, the two were out the door, in the van, and racing back to the cathedral.

"Keep the cake from falling over," Sueann said. "I may have to take more shortcuts."

"What!?" Allen quacked. "I thought the shortcuts were over."

"That was before I realized we needed the unity candle," she said. "The cake can wait until the reception. But the unity candle is needed now!"

And so, Sueann drove on sidewalks, cut through lawns, even drove through a small pond! Allen struggled to keep the cake from being thrown in all directions, and just when he thought Sueann would let up, she threw the van into another turn.

"This is worse than being in a jon boat during a hurricane!" he said.

Allen's cellphone rang. He struggled to answer it, but more jostling inside the van threw the cellphone toward the back and out of reach.

"That's probably one of ours at the cathedral," Allen said. "To tell us—"

"To tell us we're too late, and Duchess Devanna has just married Duke Arthur or Count Fenton or whichever groomsman the queen has decided is the father," Sueann said. "Well I say we make it there just in time for the vows."

The van arrived at First Darby Cathedral a few moments after Sueann made her prediction. She waved workers to help with the cake, and Allen rushed the unity candle to a side room from where the groomsmen entered the main church.

"Allen, Allen!" one of the workers said. "They are calling for you."

"Huh?" Allen asked.

"Special request," the worker said. "I tried calling you to let you know."

"Yeah, I lost my phone on the cake ride," Allen said.

"Well stop wasting time. They're all waiting for you," the worker said.

The worker pushed Allen through the doorway. He held the unity candle in hand, which was really three candles in a holder. All in the church stared at him with dead silence. There was no music, no speaking—nothing. Duchess Devanna stood next to her bridesmaids, and the groomsmen still held their positions, but the groom had yet to be announced. She walked over to a table next to the Paschal candle, and she motioned for Allen to bring the unity candle to that table.

Allen took slow steps toward the table. The minister gazed down on Allen, as if Allen were rudely disrupting the ceremony and needed to leave immediately. Scorn and impatience came from all directions, most especially from the groomsmen, except for Kakuda, who was looking up and tapping his fingers together nervously.

The duchess was beautifully dressed in a flowing, white wedding dress, and her tiara twinkled in the light. Again she motioned for Allen to place the unity candle onto the table. He did. Next, she took one of the side candles from the unity candle and lit it from the Paschal candle. She held this lit candle in her left hand.

Allen turned to return to the side room, but without warning, the duchess took his hand with her right hand and guided it to the other side candle on the unity candle holder. Allen was shocked at this development, much as he had been shocked by her when she touched him at the resort. Not knowing what to do, he simply stood there. She had him grasp the unlit candle, light it from the Paschal candle, and then stand in front of the unity candle.

There was whispering and murmuring among the people. The duchess waited no longer. She held her candle to the central unity candle and guided Allen's candle to the unity candle such that both lit the candle at the same time. She placed her side candle back to its holder and guided Allen's candle to its holder. But she kept hold of his hand and led him back to her spot and his new spot to be married.

"It's Allen Dofer!" Kakuda called. "He's the father."

Allen's daze wore off, and he looked around like a caught animal. The people erupted in loud discussion. Folk ran around to speak with others, the minister looked bewildered, and the four royal groomsmen ran over to the queen to voice their complaints.

"What's happening, what's happening?" Allen asked.

"I'll tell you what's happening," Kakuda said, now joining Allen's and Devanna's company. "You're getting married!"

"I am!?" Allen asked.

"Yes you are, my future king," Duchess Devanna said.

"WHAT?!?" Allen said in shock.

"I don't get it. You weren't anywhere near the...I mean...just us groomsmen were part of the..." Kakuda stumbled.

"There must be a mistake," Allen said. "I've never been with you, Your Grace."

"There is no mistake. You are the father of my child," Devanna said. "And you will be my husband."

Baroness Vasha was also in shock. She sat in back and spoke with Trey.

"Queen Cythia is up to something. She has purposely chosen this nobody as the purported father," Baroness Vasha said. "Trey—ask around and find out what her game is. I must think of a counterattack. Hurry, Trey."

"Where shall I go, Baroness?" Trey asked.

"Ask her chauffeur, her guards, anyone. Just go out and start asking. I'll deal with things in here," the baroness said.

The people got noisier and noisier until the queen took her scepter and cracked it down hard on her bench.

"Everyone, please! Return to your positions," Queen Cythia said. "I have the final royal announcement to make."

"I am to be the one," Viscount Darro said.

"No, I am," said Duke Arthur.

"It is I," said Count Fenton.

"No, I," said Marchese Antonio.

"Please don't let it be me," Kakuda said more quietly.

"It is none of you," Queen Cythia said. "I apologize for the delay, but we had to be certain. DNA testing has excluded all five of you from the birthday party...ahem...sleepover. In fact, we weren't sure where to go for the paternal DNA. I commissioned the Director of Science and Medicine to search all medical banks for the matching DNA. It turns out the father made a blood donation a year ago, and a sample remains filed away. By royal decree, the father of Duchess Devanna's child is Sir Allen Beacon Dofer, 13th Knight of Barley."

"13th Knight of Barley?" asked someone.

"Where's Barley?" said another.

"It's a component of beer," said a third.

"This is a fraud," said a fourth.

"Allen Beacon Dofer, 13th Knight of Barley, comes from the Norwegian royal family of Drojiap," Queen Cythia said. "We have contacted his royal heritage, and they have sent his royal uniform with coat of arms. Sir Dofer, if you please."

An assistant brought dress slacks, shirt, coat, shoes, and tie. Allen stepped back into the side room, threw the clothes on, and re-emerged looking like a prince himself.

"I don't believe this," Allen said quietly to Devanna.

"Do you love me?" she asked him.

"Yes. I do," he said.

"And I love you too. That's all that matters," she said.

The wedding was about to resume, but Baroness Vasha grew furious. She tried to keep quiet, but she insisted that Julietta answer.

"What happened that night?" the baroness asked Julietta repeatedly. "Did you use the device on Kakuda or not? Well?"

"I...I..."

"I want to know what happened, Julietta. I want to know now!" Baroness Vasha yelled, and her voice carried throughout the cathedral.

All turned and stared at her.

"You have something to confess, Baroness Vasha?" Queen Cythia asked.

"I only ask that you recheck the DNA tests," Baroness Vasha said. "Just to be safe."

"The DNA tests have been run six times," Queen Cythia said. "All by different agencies. There is no mistake. But it would appear that you yourself have made a mistake."

"I do not make mistakes," Baroness Vasha said.

"That remains to be seen," said Tugan, king of Phocayna of the dalli porpoises.

Tugan wore a special tuxedo, also with color patterns similar to his natural ones.

"Who are you?" Allen asked.

"I am King Tugan," he said. "And I have someone who can explain what has happened."

Queen Brela entered. She wore a black and white dress with color patterns similar to her natural porpoise colors. And with her was Chusacuta, the Atlantic white-sided dolphin.

"Julietta!" Baroness Vasha said.

"I had to let Chusacuta go," Julietta said. "It wasn't right to keep her captive."

"Chusacuta swam all the way to Phocayna for our help," Queen Brela said. "She explained how the dolphin fertility device was stolen."

"The what?" Allen asked. "Fertility what?"

"Listen and learn," Duchess Devanna said.

"The device is only meant for dolphin use," Queen Brela said. "But instead, it was used on two humans."

"The two humans were going to be Kakuda and Duchess Devanna," Chusacuta said. "But something changed. It was used on Sir Allen instead."

"Julietta!" Baroness Vasha repeated.

"I...couldn't use it on my Kakuda!" she wailed. "But I didn't want to fail you. And I didn't fail you. I used it on a commoner. He was a commoner then. He still should be."

"Baroness, do you have anything to say in your defense?" Queen Cythia said.

"This is all very circumstantial," Baroness Vasha said. "I'll have Trey get in touch with you."

At that moment, a royal police officer walked in with Trey. Trey held up his hands to show they had been handcuffed.

"Baroness, this way please," said the royal police officer.

The baroness stood up and smiled.

"Come along, Julietta, this won't take long," Baroness Vasha said.

"Julietta stays here," Queen Cythia said. "She is getting married."

"To whom?" Kakuda protested.

"You, Kakuda Mori," the queen said.

"A double wedding?" the baroness asked.

"Yes!" Julietta exclaimed.

"Officer, take them away," the queen said. "We have two couples getting married."

"This isn't the end, Queen Cythia. The world will beg my return!" the baroness said as she and Trey were hauled out of the cathedral.

Sir Allen Beacon Dofer, 13th Knight of Barley, stood next to Duchess Devanna of Darby and held her hand. Kakuda Mori stood by Julietta Mercrei and held her hand. King Tugan, Queen Brela, and Chusacuta took seats on the bride side and watched. The minister resumed the wedding, but now he included Kakuda and Julietta. He took turns having each couple say vows. And they did. The minister pronounced the couples married.

The people applauded. The two couples walked down the aisleway to the front of the cathedral and greeted people as they exited. King Tugan, Queen Brela, and Chusacuta were nearly the last to leave.

"Congratulations, young man," King Tugan said. "There's a whole world about you that you have yet to explore. Your Norwegian family will be arriving soon to tell you all about them—and you."

"I guess I should return this," Julietta said, and she removed the device from her purse and gave it to Chusacuta. "I was wrong to use it. I could blame Baroness Vasha. But I should have just said 'no'."

"It was fate," Queen Brela said. "You were chosen to do this, just as Sir Allen was chosen to be the 13th Knight of Barley."

"And chosen to be my husband," Duchess Devanna said while hugging Allen.

"I still can't believe it," Kakuda said. "I thought I was going to be married to you, Your Grace. Nothing personal...I mean...you're great...but...I...couldn't give you what you should...I mean..."

Devanna laughed.

"I understand," she said. "You're forgiven."

"Thank you."

"We haven't heard much from you, Sir Allen," Queen Brela said.

"I just want to say, that from the first moment I saw Duchess Devanna, I have always loved her. She is my special dear person. I have been fond of her from afar, and I used to dream of this day. I never thought it would come to pass. But I am glad it has. I hope it never ends."

"It won't," Duchess Devanna laughed. "Now help me with my tiara. The hairdresser can't make my hair into a knot like you can. And when you're finished, we have work to do at the palace. Paperwork and duties and thank-you letters, and—"

"I think I know why I'm the 13th Knight of Barley," Allen said.

"Why is that, Sir Allen?" Queen Brela asked.

"Any royal man will eventually succumb to a soothing mug of beer," Allen replied.

There was a pause for a moment. Then King Tugan laughed. And Kakuda laughed. Julietta laughed and so did Chusacuta. Queen Brela hit Tugan over the head for laughing, and Duchess Devanna pinched Sir Allen in the arm. But Sir Allen and Duchess Devanna exchanged an affectionate kiss, and all those around applauded.

The Blinners of Gathona

Chusacuta, after a traumatic experience as Baroness Vasha's prisoner, said goodbye to Duchess Devanna, Sir Allen Dofer, Kakuda Mori, and Julietta Mercrei Mori. King Tugan and Queen Brela escorted her back to Phocayna, where she visited a while.

"These implants won't come out," Queen Brela said. "It is beyond my skill to heal. How do you feel?"

"I have a headache," Chusacuta said.

"Residual effects of the implants. We need to visit Persipi and see if—" Brela started.

"Uh, I have this great fear of killer whales," Chusacuta said.

"They aren't orcas," Brela said.

"I know, but they frighten me just as much."

"Hmm. I had hoped that if Queen Pyamara could examine you, she—"

"Well maybe if Queen Pyamara would travel here to Phocayna," Chusacuta said. "I just don't think I could visit her in Persipi with all those other pygmy killer whales staring at me like I'm their next lunch."

"Perhaps we are rushing her," Tugan said.

"I just need to rest," Chusacuta said.

At that moment, Prince Metavasi walked in.

"I know just the thing," Metavasi said. "Let's do some flips in the royal pool. And we can race. I can swim so fast that—"

"Metavasi," Tugan said.

"...that I can jump back over my own wake. I can show you how to—" Metavasi continued.

"Metavasi!" Brela interrupted. "We swam all the way from the Commonwealth of Darby."

"So?" Metavasi said.

"So, Chusacuta is tired. As in exhausted. No crazy swimming tricks for her," Brela said.

"I can't swim as fast as you anyway, Prince Metavasi. But thank you for the invitation. Maybe when I can get rid of this headache...maybe then... well...I'll let you know."

"Metavasi, who was that nice young dolphin you brought over for the evening social a month ago?" Brela asked.

"Litivito?" Metavasi asked.

"No, not the one who wouldn't stop talking. The quiet one," Brela said.

"Oh, you must mean Circigi, the hourglass dolphin," Metavasi said. "I think he went back home. To Kmina."

"Oh, Kmina," Chusacuta said with dismay. "I can't escape my home—"

"He is very quiet. Boring as the deep. Wears glasses. He might be still around. Who knows? But we should find Litivito. He's really fun. No glasses needed. You'll like him, Chusacuta. He—"

"Please see if Circigi is still in Phocayna. If not, please send for him," Brela said.

"What?! But Litivito is—" Metavasi protested.

"Litivito is the wrong cetacean at the wrong time," Brela said. "Go find Circigi."

"Ma!" Metavasi continued to protest.

"That's a royal command, Son," Tugan said.

Metavasi left in disappointment. Brela thought he said, "Some porpoises don't understand," and she was about to go after him and reprimand him, but she decided against it.

"I'm sorry to be a burden. I wish I could go out with Metavasi and Litivito. But this stabbing headache is giving me the blahs," Chusacuta said.

"No need to apologize," Brela said. "Spend some time with Circigi. In the meantime, I'll visit Queen Pyamara in Persipi to discuss your implants. Hopefully we'll have a plan upon my return."

"What can you warn me about Circigi?" Chusacuta said.

"Warn? There is nothing to warn. He likes to travel," Brela said. "Don't worry, he's not out for racing. But he does visit Gathona."

"Cetacea of the Dead," Chusacuta said. "Most would be afraid to visit Gathona."

"You are not?" Brela asked.

"I am not. I've never been there, but somehow I don't fear it. Perhaps this is because I know I won't have to worry about dolphins or porpoises or whales distracting me."

"There are other animals there," Tugan said. "Birds, seals, and humans for starters."

"Birds are fine. And I like seals," Chusacuta said.

"But humans," Brela said. "Baroness Vasha—"

"Is a human," Chusacuta said. "I guess we'll assume humanoid shape and pretend we are visiting if we see any. But I don't think there will be many, if any, humans."

"You speak as if you are going there," Tugan said. "What about your headaches?"

"You are staying here to rest, remember?" Brela said.

"Strange. For a moment I thought I was going to Gathona," Chusacuta said. "I don't know what came over me."

Metavasi returned with Circigi.

"That was fast," Chusacuta said.

"I'm always fast," Metavasi said, "even if others aren't. I would have been back sooner, but Circigi is so slow."

"That will do, Metavasi. You may go now," Tugan said.

"Just one trick for Chusacuta," Metavasi begged. "Please?"

"No, no tricks. Go entertain the young female dallis or something," Tugan said. "What about Dalliana and Fellanina? You've been raving about them all year. Or that new porpoise, Zellapuvia?"

"Zellapuvia! Yeah! And I just saw her too! I'll show her my new flip. It's out of this seamount! Chusacuta, oh I'm sorry. You *should* see it, but Zellapuvia is...yeah, I'll show her now!" Metavasi said with such unbridled energy that he could hardly contain himself. "But I hate to leave Chusacuta all alone. She could come with me. I could—"

"Go, Metavasi," Brela said. "Now."

"Oh, I defer," he said reluctantly, and he left.

"Queen Brela says you've been to Gathona," Chusacuta said.

"Many times," Circigi said. "It's part work, part hobby."

"What work?" Chusacuta asked.

"I'm obituary recorder for Central Records in Kmina," Circigi said.

"You mean at the library?" Chusacuta asked.

"Well, library sounds so pedestrian. We prefer Central Records," he said.

"I thought you looked familiar. I've seen you there. You don't remember me, do you?" she asked.

Circigi looked at Chusacuta closely.

"No," he said. "Wait. Natural sciences? Dolphin fertility section?"

"Yes. I do all my research at the lib...Central Records for my study of dolphin fertility," Chusacuta said. "So you *do* remember me. A pity."

"That didn't sound very nice," Circigi said. He looked closer and said, "Your hair is shorter than I remember."

"Baroness Vasha," Chusacuta said. "She cut my hair for starters."

"Who is Baroness Vasha?" he asked.

"I can see you two have a lot to discuss," Brela said. "Why don't you both take a walk around the Royal Palace? I need to prepare for my journey to Persipi, and then I will leave in four *cynors*."

A *cynor* is a unit of time equal to 14.4 minutes. There are one hundred cynors in a day. Not mentioned is the *ploca*, which is a hundredth of a cynor, or 8.64 seconds. And the *neesp* is a hundredth of a ploca, or 0.0864 seconds.

"We should go with you," Chusacuta said.

King Tugan, Queen Brela, and Circigi stared at Chusacuta briefly then looked at one another. Brela walked up to Chusacuta and stared intently at her forehead for indications of what the implants were doing to Chusacuta.

"Not necessary," Brela said. "I will travel with my guards."

"I mean for our protection," Chusacuta said. "Persipi is practically on the way to Gathona. There are more orcas on the Phocayna side of Persipi than the Gathona side."

"I don't understand," Circigi said.

"Chusacuta," Brela said, "the implants are distorting your perceptions. I will not command you, but I implore that you dive deep inside for strength to resist these urges to travel. I feel confident that a little rest here in Phocayna will do you good."

"I...am not sure what to think. A dark voice says I should stay inside a tank and remain a prisoner to Baroness Vasha. Another voice says I must be out swimming free in the ocean to escape her grasp," Chusacuta said. "And no matter what I do or think, these headaches keep me in agony. I feel like death."

"I want to help," Circigi said. "But what could I do or say? I know about our cetacean ancestors and their burial chambers in Gathona."

"I wish to go to Gathona. I wish to walk among the dead and leave everyone behind," Chusacuta said.

Circigi looked to Brela for guidance. Brela shrugged.

"It may be better, or it may be worse. Who can say? Perhaps Chusacuta is right. *Some* swimming with *some* touring of Gathona *might* be beneficial. But everything must be done in moderation," Brela said. "And you will not go alone. You may leave *some* behind, but not *everyone* behind."

"Then we should prepare for the journey," Chusacuta said. "We might as well pack and leave with Queen Brela."

"You have mixed feelings, Chusacuta. At one moment you fear the pygmy killer whales, the next moment you are ready to visit them with me. You show displeasure with your own seamount and those from it, like Circigi.

Above all, you seek escape. I agree then that you should accompany me to Persipi. It will give you a chance to rest instead of exhausting yourself by swimming directly to Gathona. I'm sure I can convince the pygmy killer whales to provide you a place to rest for the night," Queen Brela said.

"I'm ready," Chusacuta said.

Each of the three entered respective thorium enhancement pools. These were filled with thorium-based sponges and helped rejuvenate and recalibrate the thorium-based energy in the three's bodies. After an hour, they were ready for the swim. The three and several royal guards left Phocayna and swam to Persipi. Along the way, Chusacuta explained to Circigi everything that happened to her in the Commonwealth of Darby. The two communicated by modifying their echolocation squeals into understandable language—understandable to dolphin, that is.

"Some humans are like that," Circigi squealed. "But not all. Some are very interested in our welfare and wish to protect us, well, at least the voitrans. We fulltrans usually need very little protection. What I don't understand is how Baroness Vasha caught you to begin with."

Chusacuta paused and then said, "I was swimming...swimming..."

But Chusacuta could not finish her sentence. Her implants caused pain, and she cringed. Chusacuta blinked and blinked.

"What is it?" Circigi asked.

Her timbre changed, and she communicated in more mechanical fashion.

"I tried to help a combersoni dolphin couple conceive at the dolphinarium. It was late at night, and the dolphinarium was closed. I was about to use the device on the male, but the female suddenly got jealous and attacked me. She knocked half my brain unconscious and the other half dazed, and that reverted me back to my natural dolphin form. I was barely able to protect myself, and I tried to get my full wits back, but time passed, the dolphinarium opened, and I was found. They tested me and found me radioactive, and they also found the device. Well, *they* being Baroness Vasha, because she owns that particular tank and decided I had some use alive instead of being dissected and sold as food. And that's how I was caught."

Circigi looked at Chusacuta in disbelief. She shook her head and stared back at him in a mixed emotional state of shock, fright, and embarrassment. Circigi realized her distress and pressed no farther. The two were quiet for the journey's remainder.

The group arrived in Persipi, and Queen Pyamara was so polite and inviting that Chusacuta was immediately charmed and decided to spend the night. Queen Pyamara particularly praised Chusacuta's bravery in surviving the ordeal in the Commonwealth of Darby and thanked Chusacuta for her efforts in developing the fertility device.

"Fulltrans are very long lived," Queen Pyamara said. "Unfortunately, the price is high. We cannot produce children as easily as the voitrans. The thorium assimilation has rendered conventional reproductive systems inert. Before you invented the fertility device, a couple had to spend a full year in a thorium-sponge tank and hope the thorium-sponge performed the genetic transfer. And those cases produced a pregnancy in only one percent of attempts. One percent. So you see, Chusacuta, all of us in Lagenora are in your debt. Do not fear us. We are not like the orcas."

"Thank you, Your Highness," Chusacuta said.

"You know, Brela, we really should give Chusacuta a title. Perhaps make her a countess or assign her a little seamount and make her a duchess," Queen Pyamara said.

"We owe much to Chusacuta and her work," Brela said. "In fact, Chusacuta is so valuable to us that I had thought it too dangerous for her to wander alone. I've assigned Circigi to accompany her."

"A very good idea," Pyamara said. "But even that may not be enough. Perhaps restriction to Lagenora or a seamount itself should be in order."

"Yes, restriction to a seamount. Or a pool. A tank," Chusacuta said.

"Chusacuta?" Circigi asked, realizing she was speaking strangely again.

"Only then will my value be proven," Chusacuta continued in a trancelike state.

"Please, begging Your Royalnesses' permission," Circigi intervened. "Confining Chusacuta would be the ultimate torture. She must get out and swim in the open Atlantic to keep her sanity."

Chusacuta shook her head and tried to regain her composure.

"Yes, swim the ocean. No, not safe. The Atlantic...a tank...the Atlantic..."

Realizing something was wrong, Queen Pyamara called for the court musicians, and they played. Chusacuta regained her composure, but Queen Pyamara knew additional therapy was required. She led them to the auditorium to watch a play about several dolphins traveling west to settle in a new, undeveloped seamount only to be ambushed and captured by humans in their fishing net and sold to a human aquarium park. Then Superpyco, the superhero of the pygmy killer whales, came to the rescue and freed the imprisoned dolphins. The play came to a happy ending.

"Very good," Brela said. "Our superhero is a dalli porpoise and is named Superdaco."

"We have one too," Chusacuta said. "His name is Genory the Great. He also defends us from orcas and mega sharks. I wish he were real, though."

"It's theoretically possible. If we could adjust the thorium resonance frequency to increase the hardness of the dolphin and porpoise tissues without giving this same advantage to the orcas, then it could work," Circigi started.

"You work with thorium frequencies?" Chusacuta asked. "I use thorium frequencies in the fertility device. What devices have you developed? What papers have you published? Well?"

"Uh, nothing. I just read a lot," Circigi said.

"As I suspected," Chusacuta nodded.

The two queens laughed.

The evening's remainder was uneventful. Chusacuta and Circigi were each provided places to rest while Queens Brela and Pyamara held a private conversation.

"I noticed how you inconspicuously evaluated Chusacuta's condition," Brela said.

"The sign of a great queen is her ability to detect while remaining undetected," Pyamara said.

Brela laughed.

"But on to more pressing issues. The implants concern me, Brela. One might think Baroness Vasha acted alone. But I sense something more. A presence in Lagenora is influencing these implants," Pyamara said.

"But Baroness Vasha is in Darby. That is many *cynalli* north of here," Brela said.

A *cynalla* (plural *cynalli*) is the distance a dalli porpoise can swim in one cynor, this distance equivalent to 13.2 kilometers (8.16 miles). Other units of measure include the *plocalla* (plural *plocalli*), the distance a dalli porpoise can swim in one ploca, about 132 meters, and the *nialla* (plural *nialli*), the distance a dalli porpoise can swim in one neesp, about 132 centimeters.

"Nonetheless, the presence is real. It has reached out from Lagenora into northern Atlantic waters and has influenced people of Darby such as Baroness Vasha. I must conclude then that this presence extends to other human colonies. Brela, I did not wish to say this in front of the others, but the removal of those implants is paramount. If we cannot, Chusacuta must be—"

"We *will* find a way," Brela said. "I had hoped you could provide counsel on their removal, not dark unpleasantries."

"I have made a brief inspection, and their removal is beyond my power as well. But dark unpleasantries await us all if the darkness of one is not dealt with swiftly," Pyamara said. "For the good of Lagenora, she cannot leave Gathona in her present condition."

"Then the talk of giving Chusacuta her own seamount was a ruse?"

"It was sincere," Pyamara said, "provided the implants are removed. I do appreciate her service to Lagenora."

"But not enough to spare her life!" Brela said.

"Brela, the orcas threaten us on many fronts. As dear as Chusacuta is to me, I cannot allow my personal feelings to jeopardize the safety of my kingdom or Lagenora," Pyamara warned.

"I see," Brela said. "I see I made a mistake in asking for your help!"

Pyamara approached Brela, held her arms, looked into her eyes, and spoke softly.

"Do not judge me so harshly, Brela, for I have not given up hope. We shall reach out to Queen Tharia of Corleopus. If anyone can aid Chusacuta, she can. You may wish to reach out to other kingdoms yourself."

Brela nodded her head and smiled.

The following morning was pleasant, with Chusacuta, Circigi, and Queen Brela joining Queen Pyamara for breakfast. They didn't really need to eat anything, since all had thorium-based energy sources in their cells, but the breakfast was more of a custom and a sign of goodwill, consisting of a de-ionizing lozenge that dissolved directly in the mouth. Chusacuta and Circigi said goodbye to Brela and Pyamara, but Brela insisted that one of her guards accompany the two.

"There are fewer orcas on the way to Gathona, but they are out there, nonetheless," Brela said. "Garadon will serve you faithfully, and he has a direct communication link to the royal Phocayna guard network, so if something should happen, the royal Phocayna network will send out guards to aid in your need."

"I hope we will not have need for aid," Chusacuta said.

"I hope so too," Brela said. "Chusacuta?"

"Yes?"

"Give me a hug, my dolphin friend," Brela said.

The two hugged.

"When you return, I swear to you that I will remove those implants no matter what the cost. I cannot bear to see such suffering," Brela said.

"I...will endure," Chusacuta said.

"You cannot be allowed to bear this alone. Regain what strength you can in Gathona. I will reach out to all kingdoms for medical assistance. We will help you through this. I promise!"

And so, it was Chusacuta, Circigi, and Garadon together and on their way to Gathona. Garadon was a dalli porpoise, like all guards for Phocayna, and so he could swim at great speed if need be. The three spent a leisurely day swimming to Gathona, and they arrived on shore in the late afternoon.

"This is Gathona, Cetacea of the Dead, as you pointed out before to Queen Brela," Circigi said.

"You've been speaking about me behind my dorsal fin?" Chusacuta said with disdain.

"You worry us, Chusacuta. You say things that aren't true, like that story about being caught in a dolphinarium tank. The last thing you told our people was that you intended to test your fertility device on captive dolphins in Darby, but Brela says you never made it to Darby safely, that her best dalli porpoises lost contact with you while you were still in the Atlantic. How were you really caught?" Circigi asked.

"Brela betrayed me? You are all conspiring against me!" Chusacuta said with a change in her voice. "Strangulation to you all!"

Chusacuta collapsed on the beach. Garadon and Circigi helped her to her feet.

"Chusacuta? Chusacuta!" Circigi begged.

"It would be wise to speak no more of her fabrications nor anything related to her ordeal in Darby," Garadon said. "She cannot take much more."

"I am sorry, Garadon. You are quite right," Circigi apologized.

Chusacuta opened her eyes.

"Oh, what happened?" she asked.

"You..." Circigi started, but Garadon cautioned Circigi with an eye-glance. "The swim was a bit much, I guess. You passed out briefly."

"Well no harm then. Look at Gathona! It looks like just a simple, beautiful island," Chusacuta said.

"Yes, it is on the surface," Circigi said. "Below are the burial chambers. But the island is worth exploring. There are peaks with snow, fresh-flowing water, and all kinds of natural life not found in other places."

"There don't appear to be any people on the island," Garadon said. "There is a weather station, but it is empty at the moment. If you like, I can patrol the shore or accompany you wherever you walk."

"Please accompany us," Chusacuta said. "I don't want you patrolling all alone."

"I am used to it, as part of my duties," Garadon said.

"I'm sure," Chusacuta said. "Please, it would make me feel better. We cetaceans must stick together."

"I think you mean, we dolphins should stick together," Circigi said.

Garadon and Chusacuta looked at Circigi in surprise then laughed.

"Well, I feel like we're all dolphins," Circigi said.

The three walked onto the beach and then gradually walked around the various parts of the island. Chusacuta walked up to different birds and then spoke with a subantarctic fur seal.

"She's basking in the sun after having a good meal. She's expecting to give birth in a few days, she hopes," Chusacuta said. "She can't transform to humanoid form, but I can communicate with her very well. She says she's never seen a dolphin wear glasses before."

"Well, I, uh, the glasses are, uh," Circigi stumbled.

"She says it looks respectable on you," Chusacuta said.

"Thank you," Circigi replied.

"She also says that just a little ways up the hill is a beautiful waterfall flowing into a pool, and we can swim in the pool if we like," Chusacuta said. "She says the pool has healing properties. She has in fact just come from the pool and has successfully healed from several shark bites."

"That sounds like an excellent idea," Circigi said. "In fact, I think I know that pool."

The three walked on the island from the beach among a rugged terrain of jagged rocks and sheer cliffs. The terrain started with beach grass followed by a number of ferns and then mixed with various mosses. And everywhere, there were more types of birds than one could count.

It was easy to find the pool. There was a steady stream of fresh water flowing into the ocean, and the three simply followed this flowing water until they reached the pool.

"Oh, I must go swimming!" Chusacuta said.

She dove into the pool, and as she entered the water, she transformed from humanoid to dolphin. She swam a bit below the surface, came up for a moment, and communicated through squeals for Circigi to enter. Circigi dove in, and he also changed to dolphin shape and swam around. The two swam and splashed and had a good time.

"Listen to this, Circigi," Chusacuta said.

Chusacuta squealed in long wave. Well, not quite a squeal. More like a rumble.

"Did you hear that?" Chusacuta asked.

"Huh? I felt something nip me," he said.

"I squealed in long wave," Chusacuta said.

"I've never heard of a cetacean doing that," Circigi said.

"Nor has most sea life," Chusacuta said. "I've been experimenting with long wave as a form of communication. I can't say much very quickly, but...well...listen again and see if you can figure out what I'm saying."

Chusacuta squealed in long wave again. Circigi concentrated.

"It sounds like, 'We're the only fish in this pool.' That's not right. We're not fish!" Circigi said.

"Hah! You understood it!" Chusacuta said. "No one else has. I've tried bottlenose dolphins, common, peroni, combersoni, striped, and even other hourglass dolphins. No one can hear the long wave—except you and me."

"Wow! It's like our own secret language," Circigi said.

"Listen near the surface. I have another message for you," Chusacuta said.

Circigi held his head close to the pool's surface. Just at that moment, Chusacuta slapped her flukes on the water's surface and sent a spray of water at Circigi.

"Hah!" Circigi said.

"Did that wake you up?" Chusacuta laughed.

"I'm awake. I'm awake!" Circigi replied.

Garadon remained standing on land while observing this behavior. Chusacuta and Circigi changed back to humanoid form and tread water.

"Come in, Garadon, the water is great," Chusacuta said.

"No thank you," he said. "I should remain here where I can best monitor the environment. Besides, the fresh water will wrinkle my skin."

Chusacuta and Circigi laughed.

"You know, I can't get over how you can change to dolphin and humanoid and have your glasses disappear as a dolphin but reappear as a humanoid?" Chusacuta said.

"The same way our clothing disappears as dolphins but reappears as humanoid. We absorb the garments into our blubber as dolphins and release them from our blubber when we become humanoid," Circigi said.

Chusacuta then splashed water at Circigi with her hands, and he splashed back. She splashed more water his way, then he partially transformed back to dolphin to get his tail going so he could whip more water at Chusacuta.

"Partial transformation. That's cheating," Chusacuta said. "I can do that too. Look."

Chusacuta transformed her arm into a flipper and splashed water back at Circigi.

"But how long can you hold a partial transformation?" Circigi asked.

"It's tough," Chusacuta said. "It's like walking around cross eyed. It hurts after a while."

"Then go back to being a dolphin for a while," he said.

Circigi transformed to a full dolphin, but Chusacuta did not. She went back to full humanoid shape.

"Circigi," she said.

Circigi swam around her, with his dorsal fin above the water.

"Very funny," she said. "Are you pretending to be a shark? Change back to humanoid. I want to ask you something. Circigi? Circigi!"

She finally gave up and changed to dolphin form herself. She chased him around the pool. He dove above water, she dove above after him. He did a back flip, she did a back flip. Then Chusacuta put on extra speed. She caught Circigi, then transformed to humanoid shape, and she held onto Circigi's dolphin body with her humanoid arms.

"You can't escape, Circigi. I'm a dolphin too. I can do without breathing just like you," Chusacuta said.

Circigi swam to the edge of the pool right where Garadon was standing, and he transformed into humanoid shape. Chusacuta landed atop him, and the two were now together and laughing.

"Are you two enjoying yourselves?" Garadon asked. "You must be very young indeed, to be finding joy in a portal to the dead."

"Portal to the dead? What are you talking about, Garadon?" Chusacuta asked.

Garadon looked at Circigi.

"What does he mean, Circigi?"

"He's right, you know. This is a portal," Circigi said.

"At the beach you said you knew this pool," Chusacuta said to Circigi. "Is this because of the portal?"

"Yes," Circigi said. "I have often passed to the great dolphin...er...cetacean burial chamber through the waterfall. There are other ways in, but this is one of the few above-ground portals."

"I didn't realize we were so close to the dead," Chusacuta gasped. "We really do take life for granted sometimes."

"Sometimes. How old are you, Chusacuta?" Circigi asked.

"I'll be a hundred and fourteen next month," she said.

"I'm a hundred and twenty," Circigi said. "We're quite young. How about you, Garadon?"

"Much, much older," he said.

"He does look old. I bet he was around in the Middle Ages," Chusacuta said.

"Older than that," Garadon said. "I'm nine hundred and thirty-eight."

"Not as old as I thought," Chusacuta said. "But it's hard to tell after three hundred. As far as I can tell, there's no limit as to how many years we can live. The thorium cells have slowed our aging to almost nothing."

"But until your recent device, we could not have children, at least not easily," Circigi said. "That was the curse of fusing with the thorium sponge. And so death was especially sad, because it meant our numbers dwindled, with a narrowing future for Lagenora."

"Death is always sad. There's no reason for any of us to...die," Chusacuta said aloud, then she whispered to herself, "but sometimes I wish it for me."

"Most deaths have been because of humans or orcas," Circigi said. "After the humans attacked Rhynchus, I was especially busy with funerals here at Gathona."

"I missed out on that," Chusacuta said. "Baroness Vasha held me prisoner while Rhynchus dolphins died."

"In a way I'm glad you missed it," Circigi said. "It was a mega traumatic experience. Prince Sparfiacus led the charge to disrupt the humans and their device, which is known as a SOZOD."

"I don't even know what that is," Chusacuta said. "And something says I don't want to know."

"Then I won't tell you. He and his seadogs stopped it, but not before many died. A human named Debbie Dayla was involved. There was a trial to determine what to do with her and her father. But she fused with a thorium sponge."

"A human fused with a thorium sponge? Only cetaceans can do that," Chusacuta said.

"And electric rays," Circigi said. "And maybe squid."

"Maybe," Chusacuta said.

"Well, no one knows for sure what's going on in Aiadaka," Circigi said. "Some say a giant squid is there. Or that Aiadaka is—"

"I suggest that place be no longer mentioned," Garadon said.

"He's right," Chusacuta said. "Too much bad in that place. Show me the burial chamber."

"I'll defer to your wishes. Follow me to the waterfall. We must pass through as humanoid," Circigi said. "Garadon, are you coming?"

"No, I will wait on this side and watch for humans. I will enter if your safety is at risk," Garadon said.

"Very well," Circigi said. "Let's go then, Chusacuta."

The two walked along the edge of the pool toward the waterfall.

"If I didn't know about this being a portal to the dead, I would think this would be a place to get married," Chusacuta said.

"Some dolphins have," Circigi said. "Wouldn't you like to get married to a nice dolphin?"

"You can't mean you," Chusacuta said.

"I...uh...oh. I mean, like Prince Metavasi?" Circigi stumbled.

"He is a porpoise! I suppose if I were forced into an arranged marriage, I would bear the burden and duty as his wife," Chusacuta said.

"I've never believed marriage should be about duty," Circigi said. "Two dolphins should love each other."

"Like the way you love me?" Chusacuta asked.

"I, uh, how could you tell?" Circigi said.

"You're easy to read," Chusacuta said. "But I don't feel the same about you. Oh don't pout. It's not easy for me to fall in love. I love my work first, and, well, it's hard to divorce myself from that. But you are a nice dolphin."

"*Nice dolphin*," Circigi said. "No male wants to be just a nice dolphin. He must be a fighter, a protector and all that. I'm none of those. You deserve a dolphin like Metavasi or Litivito."

"They aren't dolphins!" Chusacuta laughed. "They're porpoises! You keeping thinking we are all dolphins."

"Well then Prince Sparfiacus or his kin. You are special, a royal in your own right."

"You put me on a cliff so high that you can never reach me," Chusacuta said.

"Then I have a chance with you?" he perked up.

"Not while I'm on your cliff!" Chusacuta laughed. "But here's the waterfall. Show me the way into the burial chamber."

Circigi led Chusacuta through the waterfall. The rock face permitted the two to pass through, and they were suddenly at the corner edge of a wide underground expanse filled with visible, sealed vaults, elevated to eye level. It was the burial chamber.

"This is the great burial chamber of Lagenora. All of our dead are buried here," Circigi explained. "Well, all who can be buried are buried here."

The two walked past vault after vault, and Circigi explained.

"These are the most ancient burial vaults, going back thousands of years," he said. "The vaults are encased in lead so that radiation from the thorium cells does not disrupt the chamber."

"What would happen to the chamber if it leaked?" Chusacuta asked.

"Probably not much, but some studies say that if several vaults leak, there could be a cascading reaction resulting in a nuclear explosion," he said.

"What you mean to say is we are in the largest chamber bomb on this planet," Chusacuta said.

"Yes, we are," Circigi replied. "You must be scared. Let me hold you."

"No, not scared enough to be held. It'll give you ideas," Chusacuta said.

Circigi re-expressed his offer to hold Chusacuta, but she shrank back. Undeterred, he continued to lead her around.

"Lead is very bad for organisms," Circigi said.

"And yet here it is," Chusacuta said.

"Yes, here it is," Circigi said. "As the years went by, workers who buried the dead began getting lead poisoning. And so there was an initiative to change the vaults so that they contained less lead."

"How much lead?" Chusacuta asked.

"Almost none," Circigi replied. "A new material, plastican, was developed to contain the radiation. It's transparent and contains only a trace amount of lead as a polarizing agent when the plastican is being formed. In fact, we are approaching the first plastican vaults."

The vaults changed from solid to transparent. Chusacuta saw the dead dolphins and porpoises in their states of rest. Each dead cetacean was adorned in natural flowers and fern leaves—perfectly preserved.

"The flowers and ferns haven't decomposed at all," Chusacuta said.

"A side effect of the thorium radiation," Circigi said.

"I would have thought the radiation would have killed the plants," she said.

"Not while in plastican. The plastican acts as a resonance modifier to cancel out the harmful effects of radiation. It's by design, and it protects us out here and things inside the vault."

Chusacuta walked up to one of the vaults and read the inscription.

"King Talenopi, benevolent ruler of Aiadaka."

"He was supposed to be one of the best," Circigi said.

"Why, he's not an orca at all. He's a peroni dolphin," Chusacuta said.

"Humans would call him a southern right whale dolphin," Circigi said.

"He doesn't look like a whale at all. Silly humans," Chusacuta said.

"If we walk around his vault, we will see his wife, Pollyenpa, another peroni dolphin, who had the greatest echolocation range of any dolphin, sorry, cetacean ever," Circigi said. "You will see the *pepona* on her head extends out quite a bit—o, what happened to her vault?"

"It's open! And she's gone!" Chusacuta exclaimed.

"There's a bright light emanating from the tomb. It's not radiation from a deceased dolphin. But it's warm like radiation. Like a heat lamp humans would run from electricity."

"Oh, the talk of humans gives me a headache. And I have a mega headache this very moment."

"We should move away from this damaged vault. I'll report this when we return to one of the seamounts," Circigi said. "Chusacuta, there's a funeral chapel just over there where we can rest."

"I will...I..." she started, but when she tried to walk, she stumbled. "O water of the deep, the pain is incredible! OW! CIRCIGI! MAKE IT STOP!!!"

Her temples glowed red in the two places where her implants were buried. Queen Pollyenpa's vault began to make loud popping and crackling sounds, like a high-voltage electric line in heavy humidity.

"We should leave!" Circigi said. "Chusacuta, I'll carry you."

"No!" she said in agony. "Don't move me! It will make things worse. Don't!"

Chusacuta remained on the ground and would not move. The crackling grew louder and now was deafening. Chusacuta fell unconscious from the pain, and Circigi covered his ears.

"Must get help from Garadon," Circigi struggled to say. "Must..."

But the noise overpowered Circigi as well, and he fell unconscious.

Circigi awoke some undetermined time later, and he was no longer in the chamber. Instead, he was on the island grounds of Gathona, but the island looked different. It was flatter, with fewer slopes, and he was now in the middle of a human town. There was a statue of Queen Pollyenpa next to her now-closed tomb in the center of a fountain. Circigi looked around for Chusacuta, but she was not with him. However, he did see prints on the ground showing where she had been. Chusacuta had run a short ways, jumped, and then run again in haphazard fashion as if evading a predator. Circigi tracked the prints for a bit, but then the prints were gone.

"I must get help from Garadon. But where is he? Where am I? This looks like Gathona, but then it doesn't," Circigi said to himself.

Something else was strange about this place. There were video screens positioned where one might find billboards or signs. And these screens displayed an infinite picture of a camera looking at its output screen which showed progressively smaller screens into a central point of infinity.

"How very odd," Circigi said.

Circigi heard clicking and tapping. He looked around and saw a man approaching him with a cane.

"Hello!" the man called between clicks of his tongue.

"Hello," Circigi called.

"My name is Nolan. Yow are new here, aren't *yow*?" Nolan asked.

"Yes. But where is here?"

"Gough Island," Nolan said.

"But how? I was just on Gough Island, and it looked nothing like this," Circigi said.

"What did it look like?" Nolan asked.

"It looked natural and undeveloped. These buildings and roads and screens weren't here," Circigi said.

"They have all been here for at least five hundred years," Nolan said. "So either yow are a liar or...wait, let me touch yow."

Nolan touched Circigi and noticed his glasses.

"Oh, yow have sight," Nolan said with worry in his voice. "Yow wear glasses to correct yower vision. We need to hide yow."

"What?!" Circigi said. "Wait a moment. Did you happen across another person? Her name is Chusacuta."

"No. Just yow. But we need to hide yow now before *they* find yow," Nolan said.

Nolan whistled several times, and other blind people emerged from a building and approached the two.

"Who are *they*?" Circigi asked.

"Not here," Nolan said, then he spoke to the others. "This man is sighted and needs our protection."

The others surrounded Circigi and scuttled him into the building, down a flight of steps, and into a finished basement.

"Don't worry," Nolan said. "This basement is lined with lead. They'll never detect yow here."

"Who is this, Nolan?" asked one of the helpers.

Nolan looked at Circigi with a quizzical stare.

"Who are yow?" Nolan asked.

"My name is Circigi."

"Strange name for a stranger from a strange place," Nolan said.

"Who is from a strange place," said one of the helpers who approached Circigi and inspected him with what looked like a magnifying glass but had a concave lens instead of convex.

"This is Betty," Nolan said. "She can see a little but only at very close range and only with a special hand-held glass. She has the best vision. The rest of us here are blind. And as for the sighted people in this town, well..."

"Well?" Circigi asked.

"They hide in their homes for fear of—"

Three pulses from an old-style air-raid siren interrupted Nolan. Betty ran over to a small display screen and watched it with her hand-held glass.

"One of the sighted people is having *hoy* life televised," Betty said.

Betty used the word *hoy* as a gender-neutral third-person singular pronoun. This threw Circigi off, as he thought he knew human English, but these people weren't using any accent he had heard. They also used *yow* instead of *you*. Strange. Circigi walked over and looked at the screen. The person was running in the town. She fell and got up. When she paused in front of a store window, her reflection displayed on the screen.

"Chusacuta!" he said. "I must help her!"

"No!" Nolan called.

But it was too late. Circigi ran into the street and saw them—a group of people wearing what looked like headband helmets—helmet-like material around their forehead, temples, descending slightly over the ears and then going around the upper back of their heads, but the top of their heads was open.

"Leave her alone!" Circigi yelled.

One of the helmetband people pulled out a rifle and fired at Circigi's head. A dart meant to inject an implant simply bounced off. The video feed from the dart went up on a large screen, but now it showed dirt, and so the screen switched back to Chusacuta's vision.

"They've done something to you, Chusacuta," Circigi said. "They've reached into your visual system."

"I'm going mad, Circigi. I must kill myself," Chusacuta said.

"No, you won't," a helmetband person said to Chusacuta. "You will come with us."

"You also will come with us," another helmetband person said to Circigi.

These people said *you* instead of *yow*. Circigi didn't think much of it at the time. Instead, he put up a fight by punching the helmetband person, and the helmetband person fell back. But other helmetbanders came after Circigi and attempted to subdue him. In the scuffle, Circigi's glasses were knocked off and stepped on. Circigi squealed to echolocate, but he was angry, and this caused his squeals and clicks to be very loud. The helmetband people were caught off guard and stunned. They gave up interest in Circigi and focused solely on Chusacuta. They rushed her away. Chusacuta was too despondent to fight. And Circigi, without having aid from his glasses, could not see what was going on. He squealed and chirped louder and louder to echolocate the attackers, but they had moved away rapidly. He gave chase, but they scuttled Chusacuta into a vehicle. The vehicle lifted into the air and flew away toward a distant castle on a mountain peak.

"Yow are lucky," Nolan said, who had come outside to aid Circigi.

"No, I'm terribly unlucky. They have Chusacuta, and my glasses are broken. I can echolocate to get around, but otherwise I can't see much of anything," Circigi said.

Circigi picked up what was left of his glasses and placed them in a pocket.

"Please, come back in the basement," Nolan said. "It's for yower safety."

Circigi returned with Nolan to the basement. Betty walked up to Circigi and inspected him with her hand-held glass. She noticed a slight bump on his forehead.

"Nolan, he is like the statue outside. He can echolocate."

"Are yow..." Nolan began to ask.

"A dolphin? Yes, I am," Circigi said.

The others fell into a hush.

"I'll show you."

Circigi placed what was left of the glasses on his face. He transformed into a dolphin and then transformed back. The glasses remained broken. Those who had been touching Circigi to sense the changes were in awe.

"My glasses are still broken. I had hoped I could repair them somehow," Circigi said. "Can any of you repair them? What about that hand-held glass? Do you have another?"

"No and no," Nolan said.

"We scavenge for most things around here," Betty said. "This hand-held glass is the only one we have. I'm sorry we can't repair yower glasses."

"Circigi," Nolan said. "How is it yower glasses and clothing...they disappear when yow transform into a dolphin but reappear when yow transform back?"

"They are stored in my outer skin layers. I can't really change them, I'm afraid. So if I rip my clothes or lose a button, there's no magic repair," Circigi said.

"But yower ability to transform *is* magical," Nolan said.

"I suppose," Circigi said. "But it doesn't repair my eyesight. I'm horribly myopic without glasses. So I'll have to echolocate to get around, at least for now."

"We're all blind here, as yow know, and we've been trying to find a way to see or echolocate just to get around. The best we can do is use canes and make clicking sounds with our tongues," Nolan explained. "But the people who attacked yow and yower friend, they are—"

"Chusacuta!" Circigi said. "Her name is Chusacuta!"

"The people who attacked yow and Chusacuta—they are the blinners," Nolan said. "The blinners attack sighted people with the intent of tapping into their vision and controlling them."

"The blinners tapped into Chusacuta's vision," Circigi said. "But they couldn't with me. The implant they fired just bounced off."

"I saw the implant's camera view on one of our video screens," Betty said. "But then it showed the boring ground after it bounced off yower skin. A blinner doesn't like static views, and hoy doesn't like blurry vision. That's why the blinners leave us alone."

"But...I don't understand. Why are the sighted so afraid?" Circigi asked.

"A sighted person—on realizing hoy's vision is on display for all to see—becomes self-conscious and does anything to avert attention from hoyself. So a video screen often shows the infinite screen display—each sighted person has learned that staring into a screen of hoy's own vision eliminates attention on hoy's life. And so the sighted spend their waking moments staring at their own visual output, bleeding their freedom of thought into oblivion."

The room was quiet for a moment. Circigi was in shock. Betty looked at Circigi's head and saw the point where the dart struck his skull.

"This is where it bounced off," she said. "Above the left temple. If only the sighted had such strength."

"What about the blinners? Do they have implants?" Circigi said.

"No," Nolan replied.

"But you said—"

"All *sighted* people," Nolan said. "The blinners are blind, like us."

"Except they wield power over the sighted, unlike us," Betty said.

"Those helmets they wear," Circigi said. "They—"

"Are echolocation devices," Nolan said.

"At least we think so," Betty said. "But they might do more. The blinners use them to communicate with one another. We can't prove it, but we know that they somehow know what other blinners are thinking without any words spoken or hand signals."

"So they can't see the video screens?" Circigi asked.

"No, they can't. But they can sense emotion with the helmets," Betty said.

"We think they are jealous of sighted people," Nolan said. "We think they want to experience the emotion of sight without having to expend the effort to see. While some sighted folk are doing things and having their lives televised, other sighted folk are watching and reacting, and the blinners tap into those reactions."

"The blinners must be very intelligent then," Circigi said.

"No, not really," Nolan said. "They are no more intelligent than those of us in this basement."

"Huh?" Circigi wondered.

"Let me tell him, Nolan. Circigi, at one time the sighted ran this island, and we who are blind were hidden away, because we could not compete with the sighted. Then the town well went dry, and the sighted had some of the blind dig the well deeper."

"Couldn't you desalinate the ocean?" Circigi asked.

"It's full of sulfuric acid and is poisonous," Betty said.

"How did that happen?" Circigi asked.

"It's always been that way, as long as we can tell," Nolan said.

Circigi looked disappointed.

"Are yow saying otherwise?" Nolan asked.

"I used to swim in the ocean. All over. It was safe to do so," Circigi said.

"Sounds wonderful. I'm sorry it ended," Nolan said.

"So am I," Circigi said. "I guess there's no use dwelling on it. So Betty, the well was dug deeper, and then what?"

"A discovery was made late at night when the sighted had gone to sleep. The blind workers lifted a tomb to the surface and transported it to a barn on the edge of town. Somehow, we think with some magical help from the tomb, they were able to create those helmets and then the injectable implants," Betty explained. "That took only a month or so, and late another night, they went through the town and injected the implants into the sighted."

"What was in the tomb? Was it a dolphin? Was it Queen Pollyenpa?" Circigi asked.

"We don't know what exactly was in the tomb," Nolan said. "Some say a squid was found inside."

"A squid?" Circigi remarked. "And you're not sure? Weren't you there digging it up? You said the blind dug it up."

"We who are not blinners were on another dig for borax," Nolan said.

Circigi paced around.

"If yow are wondering why we don't have implants, Circigi, it's because the blinners skipped us," Betty said. "They knew it would be fruitless to use the implants on us."

"Because you would never be self-conscious of something neither you nor someone else can see," Circigi said.

"Correct," Betty said.

"So how do you fight them?" Circigi asked.

The others fell quiet again.

"You mean you don't fight them?" Circigi asked.

"They have better navigation skills," Nolan said. "We are stuck with canes and clicking. They can sense us much easier than we can them, at least as long as they wear those helmets, and so a simple hand-to-hand fight is an easy victory for them. And there are other weapons. They have sonic stun guns. No, the best we can do is to stay out of their way. They ignore us for the most part, and so we've been able to get by."

"But we'd really like to end their rule," Betty said. "Then perhaps we could investigate those helmets and see if they can provide sight for all blind folk without any other side effects."

"Side effects, like desires to control others?" Circigi asked.

"Yes," Betty said.

Circigi walked around and clicked to echolocate. One of the others rang a bell.

"What's that for?" Circigi asked.

"It's lunch time," Betty said. "Come with us for food."

"But I—"

"Yow must be starved," Nolan said. "Forgive my bad manners. Please, eat with us. Don't worry about Chusacuta. The blinners do not harm their captives. She is safe until yow can rescue her."

"Yes, but food is—"

"This way, Circigi!" Nolan laughed. "Food will do yow good."

Circigi followed Nolan into an adjoining room where several tables were laid out with food and beverage. Farther along were places to sit. Circigi walked through the food line, but he did not grab anything. He sat with Betty and Nolan, and his echolocation was good enough to let him know they disapproved.

"What's wrong?" Nolan asked. "Isn't our food good enough for yow?"

"I don't eat food," Circigi said. "It's been so long since I tried, that my digestive tract is atrophied."

"But how do yow survive?" Betty asked. "What do yow use for nourishment? For energy?"

"My cells have a symbiotic relationship with thorium sponge cells," Circigi said. "I'm self powering. I draw moisture from the air if needed, and I can pull carbon dioxide and other gasses from the air to generate new material for my body, but for the most part, I don't need anything."

The others gasped in awe.

"Chusacuta is the same way," Circigi said.

"Oh, that is very bad news indeed," Betty said. "If they find out—"

"And they will," Nolan said.

"Then the blinners will learn how to change their metabolism to use thorium," Betty said. "Tell me, Circigi, how old are yow?"

"A hundred and twenty," Circigi said. "I'm very young."

"Yower people," Betty started. "How long do they live?"

"Some of us are as old as two thousand years," Circigi said. "But as far as we know, there is no limit, though I think there must be a practical limit. The half-life of our thorium is fourteen billion years, so I would think we would become middle-aged by that point."

"Fourteen billion years to become middle-aged," Betty said. "That is practically forever."

"Immortality is what it is. The blinners will be very motivated to learn that technology," Nolan said.

"I don't know if it can be learned," Circigi said. "We had to merge with thorium sponges to be what we are. But if the oceans are as toxic as you say—"

"They are," Betty said.

"Then the thorium sponges are destroyed. That means Chusacuta and I are the last of our kind," Circigi said. "And the only way for them to become thorium-based is to kill Chusacuta and dissect her."

Nolan and Betty were quiet.

"So she's not safe. She's not!" Circigi said excitedly.

"I'm sorry," Betty said. "We didn't know about the thorium. This is a very serious situation."

"Now it's serious. But before it wasn't?" Circigi pressed.

"Don't judge us harshly," Nolan said.

"I'm sorry," Circigi said. "I'm just so...I was supposed to give Chusacuta a vacation from a bad experience she just had. And now I've thrown her into something worse. It's tearing me apart."

Betty heard a beep from her portable television. She pulled out the television, her hand-held glass, and looked.

"Did her experience look like this?" Betty asked.

Circigi took the television from her and pressed it as close to his eyes as he could. He could almost focus his eyes on the image, but he didn't need much focus. He could tell the images were those of Chusacuta's experience under Baroness Vasha while being tortured.

"The blinners are televising her memory," Betty said.

"It's the implant," Nolan said. "It's called a *visicort*."

"That video on the screen...it was one of the most traumatic things she endured in Darby," Circigi said.

"The blinners like trauma, because it gets the sighted all worked up," Nolan said.

"It's corrupt and evil," Circigi said. "Look, I sensed them flying—"

"We can't *look*, Circigi," Nolan said.

"Sorry, poor choice of words. They flew off with Chusacuta. I didn't see them, but I sensed they flew off to a mountain peak, to some sort of castle," Circigi said.

"That's their main stronghold," Betty said.

"Then who will help me travel to this stronghold and break in? I need to rescue Chusacuta," Circigi said.

Betty whispered something to Nolan, and he whispered something back.

"I have very good ears. You're discussing how I must be crazy," Circigi said.

"We can't help yow," Nolan said. "We'd be stumbling with our canes, not even knowing if we are going in the right direction. What help could we provide?"

"Ideas, I guess. Because other than invading their castle, I have none," Circigi said. "If only I had an army. But I don't. I *should* wait and think this through. But I can't. I must try to rescue her."

Circigi left the basement, despite Nolan's and Betty's cries to wait. He started off in a run toward the mountain peak, and he did not tire. Not needing food or oxygen, he did not get "out of breath". But the mountain peak seemed no closer.

"I'll get there," Circigi told himself. "Just have patience."

But Circigi reached a point where the ground was no longer suitable for running. It ran up steeply, with many jagged points, and so Circigi slowed to a walking climb, and then he descended to all fours to climb, and then even that wasn't good enough. The mountain cliffs were very steep.

"If there were a river that wound around and around up the mountain, I could swim upstream," he said. "If I were a bird, I could fly."

Circigi tried transforming into a bird, and he was successful, except the bird he became was a penguin and not a flying bird. He returned to humanoid shape.

"I wonder," he mused. "These humanoid body shapes...could I jump? Normal humans cannot jump very high, but I...energy...I bet Metavasi could jump quite a bit. Let me try."

Circigi jumped up, and it was only as high as a human. Then he concentrated on releasing extra energy from his thorium cells. While concentrating, he jumped, and his legs sent him seven meters up. He reached a ledge and held onto it with his hands, but his feet had nothing to grasp.

"What can I turn into that will help me?" he asked. "Metavasi can turn into a thousand animal shapes. I hate Metavasi. I wish I could turn into a monkey or something useful."

Circigi fell back down from where his jump started.

"I must jump higher," he said.

He looked up and over and realized there was a spot twenty meters up where he could stand and hold onto a crevice with his hands. But twenty meters was a long way, a very long way, and if he missed, he wouldn't be able to land on the spot where he was standing. He would fall at least a hundred meters onto jagged rocks. Even his thorium legs couldn't stand that kind of fall.

"Oh, this is awful, this is awful. I can't do this. I must do this. No, yes, please, someone, help me decide. Metavasi...oh poison me to the deep! Quit wishing you were Metavasi, Circigi."

Circigi took a deep breath. It was more symbolic than anything, because of course he did not use oxygen and so did not benefit.

"I want to feel like a real human for just a moment, even if this may be my last. Well, here goes."

Circigi jumped with all his thorium-stored energy—up and over, as he planned. But he jumped a little too high. He didn't realize this until he was rapidly ascending beyond his target, and so he struggled to slow down by sticking one hand out like a brake while using the other hand in a gyroscopic fashion to keep his orientation. He still wasn't slowing quickly enough, and so he had to stick his foot out at the last moment to help slow down. He caught his foot on the crevice where his hand was meant to go. He stopped suddenly, and his body's inertia yanked and stretched his frame. He grunted. But then he started to fall, and so he reached with his hand for the crevice on the way down, caught it, and got a foot on the ledge.

But his foot slipped, he lost his balance, and he plunged the hundred meters toward the jagged rocks below. As he fell, he transformed into a penguin and used his flippers to alter his trajectory as best he could, and instead of landing on pointed rocks, he landed on a slope and slid several hundred meters until he collided with a boulder cluster and fell unconscious.

When Circigi awoke, it was nightfall. The last embers of daylight faded, and the stars twinkled into his subconscious. He had reverted to dolphin form, but he couldn't move. He had bad injuries, and pain reverberated through his mangled body. He could do nothing but suffer and stare at the stars as they slowly whirled by. He began breathing heavily, not because he needed oxygen, but because fulltrans breathe to ingest nutrients from the air. And he needed many nutrients to repair the many damaged cells in his body. The thorium organelles in his cells worked hard to provide energy and direction to repair his tissues, and his body put out quite a bit of heat. This caused steam to lift from his tissues, and so his breathing also had to pull in moisture from the air to replenish what he was losing. He couldn't ingest moisture as fast as he was losing it, and so he became dehydrated and delirious.

"I'm dying," Circigi said. "I can feel it. I should be immortal. But...I..."

Circigi looked down in the valley. He saw lights of the town below, where Nolan and Betty and all the other good blind people dwelled.

"They are like stars of the night," he said, "with a little solar system of their own. Their lives and things around them are like planets, until life becomes the sudden brilliance of a supernova before all is quiet. It awaits me. Soon."

The lights began to dance. Then Circigi thought he was somewhere else. He was with Metavasi and Litivito, and they were watching female porpoises dancing on a stage, twirling sticks of glowing jewels. One of the females threw the glowing stick toward Metavasi, and he caught it.

Then Circigi's mind returned to the mountain where he remained. He saw something glowing nearby. It was a shape, about the size of a humanoid, and it walked toward him.

"Circigi," the shape said slowly and drawn out.

"Chusacuta? Is that you?" he replied.

"Cirrrrrciiiiiigiiiiii," she said.

"Are you dead too?" he asked. "Will you take me away?"

"Shhh," she said. "Sleep."

"I'm afraid," he said. "I'm afraid that if I go back to sleep, I'll never wake."

"Let me go, Circigi. Let the mist of the ocean carry you away," she said.

"Help me, Chusacuta. Help me. I'm frightened."

"Go to sleep. Think about when we splashed in the pool. The sun, the clean air. Shh. Go to sleep. Silly Garadon. The friendship of our people. Shh. To sleep. Metavasi and Sparfy. Shh. Sleep. Sleep. Sleep. Shhhhh. Sleep."

Circigi fell half asleep, his brain hemispheres alternating consciousness.

The night passed and dawn followed. Circigi's "fever" broke, and he fully awoke in humanoid form.

"I made it," he said, still breathing hard to pull in moisture.

Circigi rose to his feet—slowly. His muscles ached, but the thorium organelles repaired his injuries, and he could walk.

"Chusacuta. She saved me. At least...I think it was her. Well, maybe it was my imagination. Oh I hope not to go through that again," Circigi said to himself.

He echolocated around and then sensed the slope that took him to that spot. He then touched the rock face where he crashed and sensed the silver blood.

"That was a horrible collision," he said. "And I can't go back up. I can only go back down."

And that's what he did. He descended the mountain and returned to the town, where he found Nolan and Betty and others eating breakfast.

"Hello," Circigi said.

"Circigi!" Nolan said. "How did it go?"

Betty approached and looked at Circigi with her hand-held glass.

"Yow look terrible," she said. "What happened?"

"I fell. A long ways," Circigi said. "I never made it to the castle. I can't ascend the mountain all the way. It's too steep. I wish I could transform into a bird and fly up there, but the only bird I can be is a penguin."

"I don't even know what that is," Nolan said.

"It's probably extinct in your time," Circigi said.

The others were silent.

"There's no way I can reach the castle, is there?" he asked.

"Even if yow did, they would stun yow with their sonic guns. They could really hurt yow or capture yow or worse," Nolan said.

"Then Chusacuta will be dissected. She might even be dead by now. I saw her ghost," Circigi said.

Nolan and the others looked at Circigi strangely.

"Unlikely," Betty said. "The blinners will first drain Chusacuta of her memories before...excuse me for saying...dissecting her."

"I wish I could believe that," Circigi said.

"For one of us, it would only take a few days to perform a memory drain, but since she is much older, I would say she has a bit over a week to live. Maybe nine days at the outside," Betty said.

"Nine days," Circigi said. "Nine days. Perhaps...maybe I can look for help. But where? You said the ocean is poisoned. But how can you be sure?"

"Believe us, Circigi. It is poisoned," Nolan said. "Story is that a sighted person walked in one day, and the ocean dissolved and killed hoy. Yow would be killed too."

"But the thorium might protect me," Circigi said.

"That's just energy," Betty said.

"But I can transform. I have some ability to protect myself," Circigi said.

"That protection didn't help much with yower fall," Betty said.

"How can you tell I fell?" Circigi asked.

"Betty can tell quite a number of things the rest of us cannot," Nolan said.

"Well, it turns out the thorium did help me. Not in the fall itself, but in repairing my broken bones and ripped flesh," Circigi said. "Perhaps I can adapt to the ocean."

"Even if yow could, what good would it do?" Nolan asked.

"I can see what happened to my people," Circigi said. "If there are any of my kind left, maybe they can help me."

Nolan whispered to Betty, and she whispered back.

"I guess it's up to yow," Nolan said. "We won't stop yow. We want Chusacuta back in yower company as badly as yow do. If yow die, then the blinners win for sure."

"And if I don't die in the ocean, I'll surely die of despair either in this basement or wandering aimlessly around the island," Circigi said. "Then that's it. But I should go now."

"I will go with yow," Nolan said.

"So will I," Betty said.

It was decided. The three left the basement. Circigi led the way with his superior echolocation skills. Nolan followed with a cane, and Betty used her hand-held glass and followed closely behind Nolan. She carried a backpack over her shoulder and also had a cane. The three traveled for a bit when Nolan became unsettled.

"This isn't the way to the ocean," Nolan said.

"I know," Circigi said. "Don't worry. I want to visit the waterfall first."

"Waterfall?" Nolan asked.

"He doesn't know," Betty said. "But follow him anyway."

Circigi walked to where he and Chusacuta had played in the pool of fresh water by the waterfall.

"At least there used to be a pool here," he said upon reaching the empty hole. "The waterfall is gone too. And it is full of a soft substance."

"Borax. This is where we dug for borax when the blinners found the tomb. But we stopped after a while," Betty said.

"Why?" Circigi asked.

"Occasionally, a tidal wave of ocean liquid floods in with sulfuric acid. It's unsafe," Betty said. "We should not dwell here."

"I had hoped to find something else here," Circigi said. "I guess not. Well, here's where Garadon stood."

"Who's that?" Nolan asked.

"A guard assigned to protect us. I half expected to see a memorial stone commending his service, but there's nothing."

"Yow believe yow have traveled into yower future?" Nolan asked.

"How else can I explain all this?" Circigi asked. "The island formation, the sulfur deposits, the ocean. How?"

"It's always been like this," Nolan said.

"I know, you said that before," Circigi said. "Sigh. There's nothing here for me. It's time I go to the ocean."

The ferns and flowers that Circigi had seen with Chusacuta were no more. Instead, there were very smooth, shiny plants with thin stems and almost no leaves. Circigi picked one up, but it was too fragile and broke.

"It's the only plant that can survive the surge of sulfuric acid," Betty said. "These plants are largely made of glass."

"We have nothing like them in my world," Circigi said. "But they are so fragile. Any animal running through would destroy them."

"No animals venture this close to the ocean," Nolan said. "And we are now as close as should be. We can hear the waves rolling in."

Nolan and Betty stopped.

"We dare not touch them," Betty said. "Even the ground near the fluid line is damp with sulfuric acid."

The acid ate into the sole of Circigi's shoes and began giving off vapor.

"I must transform into a dolphin now," he said. "I want you both to know that I am thankful for all you have done to help me. I don't know how much longer I can survive in a world like this, either physically or emotionally. There is isolation everywhere, as if people had taken the gift of social plenty and destroyed it out of their own depravity. And so I go into its depths, the outflows from all that mindless recklessness."

"We hope yow return safely," Nolan said.

"Yes," Betty said. "A safe journey, wherever yow go."

Circigi transformed into his natural state, an hourglass dolphin. He flipped his way into the ocean. The sulfuric acid began eating into his skin, though not as violently as it did for a sighted person. He swam near the shore with his dorsal fin above the water. Nolan and Betty expected to hear Circigi's splashing grow farther and farther away, but each time they thought he was leaving, he changed his mind and swam closer to shore. Finally, he emerged from the ocean and transformed into humanoid shape. His clothes were torn to rags, his hair singed as if burned, and his skin red with blisters.

"It's too powerful, too powerful," Circigi said. "My skin is on fire."

"Return with us to the town," Betty said. "We have liniment for yower burns."

Circigi led the way back to town and went to the building where he had visited before. He was about to go into the basement, but he was beckoned back upstairs.

"Don't worry, Circigi. It's safe to be on the main level right now," Nolan said. "But yow should get rid of those old clothes. They have residue on them. There's a fresh set of clothes in the changing room. It isn't much, but it's better than what yow have now. Then I'd like yow to join me for a drink in the lounge. I...oh, yow don't drink."

"I'll be back in a minute," Circigi said.

"A what?" Nolan asked.

"Humans say that, or at least they did. I'll explain in a minute, I mean, never mind."

"I always have a mind," Nolan said.

Circigi simply smiled and went into the changing room. When he exited, he wore something one might wear to a sporting event.

"How do I look?" Circigi asked, but no one could see.

"I think it's good we can't see," Nolan said. "If I remember right, those clothes are not well matched."

"Oh," Circigi said.

"Now it's time for a drink," Nolan said. "I wish yow could enjoy one with me."

"I'll just sit here and inhale deeply," Circigi said. "That will help me restore my tissues."

Betty had gone over to another building, and now she returned with a visitor.

"This is Darlina, the town alchemist," Betty said.

"I brought some liniment," Darlina said. "Yow are the dolphin?"

"Yes," Circigi said.

"Let me apply this to yower wounds. It might help," she said.

"You can see!" Circigi said. "You're sighted!"

"Only for another three hundred heartbeats," Darlina said.

"When Darlina awakes from sleep, she can see like a sighted person for five hundred heartbeats," Betty said. "In fact, she was sleeping just now."

Darlina applied the liniment and spoke.

"If I awake from a nap, I only get a hundred heartbeats of sight," she said. "If I close my eyes for fifty heartbeats, I can see for a heartbeat or two."

"How unusual," Circigi said.

"I'm really one of the lucky ones," Darlina said. "Most of us can never see the things I do. I can eventually see everything if I'm patient enough. Do yow feel any better?"

"A little, but my cells are regenerating by themselves. The liniment isn't helping," Circigi said.

"My vision is fading fast," she said. "But I can still see, and yow are right —yow are healing at the same rate on both treated and untreated spots. I'm sorry I couldn't help, but I'm glad yow are healing."

"I can regenerate my cells, but not quickly enough while I'm in the ocean," Circigi said. "What I need is something to protect my skin long enough to survive a lengthy swim."

"I wish the new clothes would help, but they won't," Nolan said.

"The most resistant substance we have against sulfuric acid is glass," Darlina said.

"So I should swim in a glass bottle?" Circigi asked.

"Can yow really turn into a dolphin?" Darlina asked.

"Yes, he can," Nolan said.

"I'll show you," Circigi said.

"Wait," Darlina said as she closed her eyes. "Let me build up a few more heartbeats of sight."

Circigi waited for Darlina. A few minutes passed, and he waited. In fact, Darlina started to snore.

"Awake, Darlina," Betty said.

Darlina awoke with a start. Circigi then quickly turned into a dolphin.

"Wow!" Darlina said. "It's true. I wish I could adopt yow as a pet."

Circigi laughed as a dolphin in a squeaky way and continued laughing while he turned back to humanoid shape.

"Yower clothing," Darlina said. "It disappears and reappears."

"It becomes part of my skin when I transform to a dolphin," Circigi said.

"What he needs is something made of glass that he can absorb into his skin," Nolan said.

"That would be very difficult," Circigi said. "Clothing is easy—it flexes with my skin. Glasses, when I have a good pair, integrate into my skull. But glass—that won't flex with my skin."

"He needs flexy glass," Nolan said.

"Is there such a thing?" Circigi asked.

"No, there isn't," Darlina said. "And now my vision is gone."

"But yesterday yow were talking about—" Nolan said.

"That was just talk," Darlina said. "I was saying it would be nice if I could make something called flexy glass."

"What about those glass plants?" Circigi asked.

"What glass plants?" Darlina asked.

"Circigi saw the beach grass and calls it glass plants," Betty said.

"Oh, beach grass. Yow are thinking we could make flexy glass out of that? No, too fragile," Darlina said.

"How disappointing," Circigi said. "They are very resistant to the sulfuric acid."

"They are, but how would yow weave them into cloth?" Darlina asked.

"Perhaps they could be hydrated, like thin wheat sticks," Betty said.

"Spaghetti noodles?" Circigi asked.

"We don't know what that is," Nolan said.

"They break easily when dry but are flexible when cooked in water," Circigi said. "I don't eat them, but noodles are another one of those human things, at least the humans I remember."

"Beach grass can be heated and softened that way, but then it cools and hardens," Darlina said.

"I can't maintain that kind of heat for an extended period of time. I'd go into nuclear meltdown," Circigi said.

"It wouldn't help yow anyway. Hot glass is too soft for yower needs," Darlina said.

"Well how does the beach grass grow? It must have some way of either acquiring or making new glass from its environment," Circigi said.

"A good point," Betty said. "In that area, there's the borax pool, the beach grass, and the sulfuric acid. There isn't much else."

"That you know of," Circigi said.

"I guess we haven't explored beyond that," Darlina said. "I've explored the site several times when we dug for borax, even waiting for my vision to work, and I've seen nothing else. Did yow sense anything with...how good is yower vision?"

"I need glasses to see," Circigi said. "But my glasses are broken. And so I must echolocate my way around. But to answer your question, no, I didn't sense anything more than the borax, the beach grass, and the sulfuric acid. But I think it's time I go back and look for something else."

"What?" Darlina asked.

"Something I can use as armor," Circigi said.

"Or something that can help yow use the beach grass as armor," Darlina said.

"Exactly!" Circigi said.

"Now I follow yow," Darlina said. "Tell yow what, I'll keep one eye closed while we go over there. That way, I'll get a little heartbeat time to help look for that something. Betty, are yow with us?"

"I would like to, but I'm late for an appointment with the Anti-blinner League," Betty said. "Nolan, I believe yow are also in that meeting."

"Yes, I am," Nolan said. "Circigi, Darlina knows more about alchemy than any of us. I hope she can help."

"So do I," Darlina said.

Circigi led the way, and Darlina followed.

"Wait," Darlina said.

Circigi stopped.

"No, not that kind of wait," she said, and she now had both eyes closed. "I mean, keep walking. Hold my arm. I'll keep both eyes closed, and then when we arrive, I'll have twice as much seeing time—one eye at a time."

"Oh, good idea," Circigi said.

Circigi took her hand and led her. She held onto him closely as if he were her boyfriend. Circigi squealed and clicked to navigate as he had been since his glasses had broken, but now his sounds were louder for outdoor detection of very distant objects. Even Darlina could hear an echo.

"That's so beautiful," she said. "It's like music from the deep. Do yower kind and humans...do yow think that yow and I..."

"I don't know," Circigi said. "Darlina. You're a nice person. But I have a special place in my heart for Chusacuta."

"Does she love yow?" Darlina asked.

"I love her," he said.

"That's not the same," Darlina said.

"I hope that someday she will love me," he said. "But I need time."

"I could love yow, Circigi. I would do anything for yow," Darlina said. "I'll even change how I speak to be more like you. See? I didn't say *yow*."

"I don't even belong here," he said.

"Do any of us feel that we belong where we are? Look at me—blind and trapped on this island. I dream of a world where I can go as far as the horizon and still keep going."

"I can swim that far. And more," Circigi said. "At least I could in my world. Darlina, I must find Chusacuta and then—"

"And then? What? What will you do? Where will you go?" Darlina asked.

"I don't know. I want to go home to Kmina and bring Chusacuta with me," he said.

"I don't even know where that is," Darlina said.

"It's a seamount to the northeast," he said.

"I just...I've only known you for a little while. You're very special, Circigi. Are all of your people as special as you?" Darlina asked.

"I'm a clumsy dolphin who spends too much time studying," Circigi said. "Most of my kind are like Metavasi—full of energy doing jumps and backflips and playing all the time."

"Meta-who?"

"Prince Metavasi of Phocayna. Oh, you don't know where that is either, do you?"

"He's a prince? You have kings and queens?" Darlina asked.

"Yes. Each seamount is a kingdom in Lagenora, ruled by a respective king and queen. Metavasi is a dalli porpoise. Very fast swimmer," Circigi said.

"Somehow I think I would not be as impressed with him as I am with you," Darlina said. "I like the bookworm type. I have braille books I read at home."

"You can make braille books but can't make glasses?" Circigi asked.

"No, we can't make much of anything. They were excavated, as were all of our books. That's how we know you are a dolphin. We dug up a book on cetaceans. We thought cetaceans were a myth, but here you are."

"Yes, here I am, and here we are at the borax deposit. There was a pool and waterfall here where Chusacuta and I swam, and Garadon our guard watched," Circigi said. "Take a look."

Darlina opened her left eye quickly and closed it.

"You hardly opened an eye," Circigi said.

"One learns to savor vision, even if only for a moment, when one is blind."

"I never really thought of it that way," Circigi said.

"And yet you are blind as we speak," Darlina said.

"I am, technically, but my echolocation forms images in my mind. The colors are different—reds and oranges for near and blues for distance, and lines are not always as crisp, but otherwise I don't feel blind," Circigi said.

"That's fascinating how you use color in echolocation," Darlina said. "I wish I could echolocate like that. Do you think you could teach me?"

"You need a special focal pad on your forehead. Humans call it a *melon*. We call it a *pepona*," Circigi said.

"What about...the way you transform...would I be able..."

"No," Circigi said. "I merged with a thorium sponge to acquire transformation ability. But you are a human. And I don't know if thorium sponges exist in this world."

"Well if they did, maybe I could merge with a thorium sponge and be like you. Then I could transform into a dolphin, and we could swim away from here," Darlina said.

"You don't like it here, do you?" Circigi asked.

"No. It's a trap. It wouldn't be so bad except for the blinners. They keep everyone in constant fear. Even now, I shouldn't be out here for much longer. The blinners could come along and attack me. Or you," Darlina said.

"Then the sooner we figure this out, the better," Circigi said. "How does the beach grass grow?"

"I don't know," Darlina said. "Sometimes the grass grows quickly, other times not at all."

"Ah, that's a clue. When does it grow quickly? What precipitates it? Rain?" Circigi asked.

"No."

"Let's walk to the beach and look at the beach grass. Maybe something will present itself," Circigi said.

"Lead the way," Darlina said.

Circigi led the way to the beach.

"Now take a look. See anything unusual?" Circigi asked.

"No, just beach grass," she said with a brief glance of the beach.

"Tell me about the sulfuric acid in the ocean. There's something about a tidal surge," Circigi said.

"Yes, sometimes the waves get very large and surge onto the beach, over the grass, and up into the borax pit. Conventional plants die, and so do any people in the waves' path," Darlina explained.

"And where does the water go?" Circigi asked.

"You mean the sulfuric acid. Some sinks into the ground, the rest runs back out to sea," Darlina said.

"And the beach grass survives?" Circigi said.

"Yes. Come to think of it, the beach grass grows the most about a week after a tidal surge," Darlina said. "But that doesn't make sense. Sulfuric acid doesn't react with glass—silicon dioxide, that is."

"But the sulfuric acid does react with other things," Circigi said. "The borax—it reacts with the borax. It must."

"Sulfuric acid will mix with boron to create all sorts of boron-based compounds—boric acid and boron trioxide for starters," Darlina said. "Wait."

"I'm waiting," Circigi said.

"The beach grass must feed off of those compounds," Darlina said.

"I'm thinking the same thing," Circigi said. "Their roots would pull in the boron compounds as nourishment."

"Wait again—a compound like boron trioxide could be useful as a flux for glass," Darlina said.

"The time for waiting is over. I'm convinced my protection against sulfuric acid lies at the root of the beach grass," Circigi said.

Circigi walked into the beach grass. Darlina took another peek, and she noticed something.

"The light—Circigi, the way the light falls on the beach grass, there's a rectangular depression right about...here," Darlina said as she walked to the depression.

"That could be important. I'll start digging."

Circigi changed his right arm into a pectoral fin and then elongated it into a shovel. He dug through the beach grass and found a layer of boric acid. Then he dug farther and scooped upon a tomb.

"Found something," he said.

Circigi dug around the tomb, pried it up, and lifted it upon the main beach. Darlina looked and saw that it had been broken open.

"It's empty," she said. "But it has an inscription with strange runes that look like dolphins."

"Deep abyss!" Circigi exclaimed.

"What!?" Darlina asked. "What does it say?"

"It's written in Kminian, my home language. It says, 'Circigi Cento, the last of the fulltran cetaceans.'"

"It can't be. You're here," Darlina said.

"So this is my end. This tomb. Here. I'll never go back," Circigi said. "But all tombs on Gathona are written in Lagenorian Standard. Unless, unless...the tomb floated here from Kmina. Fiery lake of abyss!"

"I don't have an explanation for this," Darlina said. "But that doesn't mean we should quit."

"Then what?"

"Finish what we started," she said.

"I can't. This tomb preys on my mind," Circigi said.

"But you'll notice that it's empty," Darlina said.

"Yes. Yes, it is! An empty tomb doesn't mean anything, does it?"

"No, it doesn't," Darlina said. "Maybe someone in the past made arrangements for your tomb, but that doesn't mean you died or will die. It's just a tomb, nothing more. We should focus on what's around the tomb."

"The tomb—"

"Is a distraction," Darlina said. "Countering obsession means blocking direct vision and expanding peripheral vision."

"But I'm using echolocation," Circigi said.

"Well, then, sing around the tomb," Darlina said.

"I'll try," he said.

Circigi sang the sarcophagus circumference.

"I can focus around the tomb now," Circigi said.

"Good."

"It appears the powder is a little different around this tomb. And I think something or someone has been here before us," Circigi said.

"Another human?"

"No. They dug—"

"*Hoy* dug," Darlina said.

"What?"

"*Hoy*, not *they*. *They* is plural and is grammatically incorrect," Darlina said.

"I know you use *hoy* in these parts, but English-speaking humans in my time didn't have a word like *hoy*. I thought you stopped speaking like that."

"There's no reason you can't use the word. Words don't hurt," Darlina said. "And if you had another word, I'd use it instead of *hoy*."

"Well then. *Hoy* dug like a dolphin," Circigi said. "Could it be Chusacuta was here? But why?"

"If I were a dolphin with your power, I'd use the powder for protection, and then I'd escape into the ocean," Darlina said.

"Without me? That hardly seems possible. But maybe she had the same idea as I—find help," Circigi said.

"Then this powder is the answer," Darlina said, "at least for protecting yourself from the sulfuric acid."

"Cover my body with this powder," he said. "I'll absorb it into my skin."

Darlina did so. Circigi pulled the powder into his skin. He walked to the shoreline, transformed into a dolphin, and swam a bit. But like before, he returned to shore and transformed back to humanoid shape. The sulfuric acid had eaten into his clothes a little and given him a small rash, but otherwise he was less injured than his previous swim.

"Not good enough," he said.

"Perhaps you need a better boron compound," Darlina said. "Heating boric acid in stages leads to several different boron compounds, one being boron trioxide. That has good fluxing properties with glass. But we don't have an oven here."

"I do," Circigi said, walking back to the tomb. "Cover me again."

"Agreed," Darlina said, and she covered Circigi with boric acid powder again.

"Stand back," he said. "You may want to keep an eye open for this."

Darlina opened an eye and watched. Circigi heated his skin by releasing thorium energy. The boric acid heated and turned into boron trioxide, it then became a clear goo around Circigi's body, and it carried light from his glowing skin.

"Now for it!" she yelled.

She realized that he was now covered in a glowing flux, and she needed to get him covered in glass. She ran around madly, picking beach grass and throwing it all over his body, so much so that the beach grass melted and mixed with the liquid boron trioxide. Circigi walked in the beach grass too, and this helped coat his feet. He also picked up beach grass and threw it on his face. Darlina covered his back too, and she was just able to cover the last bit of Circigi—the back of his lower legs—when the visual glow stopped.

"I must stop releasing thorium energy," he said, "or I'll go supercritical."

The glow stopped, and a glistening, crystalline structure completely enveloped his body. Darlina reached to touch him. It was glass, but it flexed a little upon touch, and it was cool and clean.

"Flexy glass," she said. "I finally invented it, but only with your help. And now I want to kiss you, but I can't. The flexy glass is in the way."

The two heard footsteps of many people approaching from over the hill.

"They make no clicks and use no canes," Circigi said.

Darlina switched eyes quickly and saw the group of people.

"The sighted people are coming," Darlina said. "We must hide."

"Too late," Circigi said. "No place to hide."

"We can't let them find you like this. They'll take you to the blinners for the flexy glass. Circigi, you'll have to dive into the ocean," Darlina said.

"What about you?" Circigi said. "Won't they take you to the blinners and make you tell them about the tomb and the boron trioxide?"

"They'll find the tomb anyway. And you're more important," Darlina said.

"I can't leave you here," he said.

"I can't go in the ocean. The sulfuric acid will kill me," Darlina said.

"And the blinners won't?"

"I'll have to make a run for it," she said.

"With no vision left? Hop on my back," Circigi said.

"What!?"

"Hop on my back. Piggyback ride," Circigi said.

"You're crazy!" she said.

"The flexy glass will protect you," he said.

"It will protect you only," she said.

"No, I can extend it. Hurry, they're here!" he said.

Darlina used the last of her sight to see the people approach. She turned back to Circigi, who had dropped to one knee, and she climbed on his back. Circigi extended his flexy glass covering over Darlina, he ran to the beach, and he transformed into a dolphin as he dove in, with Darlina holding onto his dorsal fin and riding on his back. The sighted people had just reached the beach and began throwing lassos toward Circigi and Darlina, but their nooses landed in empty ocean fluid and dissolved. Circigi and Darlina were now under the ocean's surface and speeding away from Gough Island.

"Am I breathing? Will I suffocate?" Darlina asked.

"No," he said. "I can recycle your carbon dioxide into oxygen. It's a primitive function amongst us thorium dolphins. The first dolphins who merged with thorium sponges had only a little help in the form of oxygen being renewed from carbon dioxide in the lungs, along with amino acid re-processing in the liver. Modern dolphins like me no longer need to breathe like that because the thorium sponges in us are more advanced. But we can still reprocess oxygen from carbon dioxide."

"I don't believe I'm doing this," Darlina said. "I'm in the ocean riding a dolphin! And I can breathe! But I don't see any fish. We had heard about fish from the books."

"You can see? Continuously?" he asked.

"Yes, I can," she said. "Strange. I don't know why. And I feel like a pressure has been released from my sinuses. Could it be there's something on the island causing pressure on my optic nerves?"

"If I had to name a cause, I'd blame the blinners," Circigi said. "They seem bent on control for themselves and none for others."

The two continued for a time east, toward Persipi. There was no sign of life. The ocean was somewhat clear but had a yellow tint.

"We're going to Persipi first," Circigi said. "It was inhabited by the pygmy killer whales. Chusacuta and I had met in Phocayna, and then we traveled with Queen Brela to Persipi, where we visited Queen Pyamara. From there we swam to Gathona, what humans call Gough Island."

"What will we find in Persipi?" Darlina asked.

"I'm hoping to find the pygmy killer whales," Circigi said.

"I hear doubt in your voice," Darlina said.

"You hear well," Circigi said. "The truth is, I don't expect to find any cetaceans left in the sea."

The two approached Persipi, and Circigi was shocked. The entire top dome was gone. In its place was an underwater tangle of pipes, valves, rigs, platforms, concrete, and chunks of heavy tar.

"Persipi is gone," Circigi said with a sullen voice.

"I am sorry," Darlina said.

"The pygmy killer whales...their kingdom...everything...it's been...robbershafted," Circigi said.

"What about the other kingdoms?" Darlina asked.

"I'm afraid to look. If they are all like this...waste pit...oh, what has Earth become?" Circigi lamented.

"Don't give up hope. You said something about Phocayna."

"Yes, that would be the next closest seamount. We should check that next," Circigi said.

The two traveled to Phocayna, and Circigi was just as shocked as with Persipi. The seamount dome, like Persipi, had been excavated away long ago, and all that remained were things much like at Persipi—pipes, concrete, tar balls, structures, etc.

"King Tugan, Queen Brela, and Prince Metavasi...this was their kingdom. Gone. But where did they go? They would have lived forever," Circigi said. "Let's go to Rhynchus next. King Acus and Queen Sparla reign there. Maybe we'll see them or even Prince Sparfiacus."

The two traveled to Rhynchus, but along the way, they saw floating debris left over from drilling, and tar balls that sometimes floated, sometimes sank, and sometimes remained stationary.

"The tar balls don't react with sulfuric acid," Darlina said.

"I wish they would," Circigi said, "if nothing else than to get rid of them. They're a painful reminder of how desire drove humans to destroy Lagenora. I don't know if it's worth continuing to Rhynchus. I was foolish to think I would find help out here."

"Let's keep going," Darlina said. "We have nothing else to lose."

"Except a future," he said.

"There's always a future," Darlina replied.

The two arrived in Rhynchus, and amazingly, the seamount was intact.

"I don't understand," Circigi said. "It's still here. Did the Lagenors withdraw to the protection of the dusky dolphins?"

"So this is the kingdom? There's nothing here but an underwater mountain range," Darlina said.

"We must go inside," Circigi said.

"How? I see no passages," Darlina said.

"If things are as before, we'll be able to pass through the wall," Circigi said.

Circigi swam into the side of the seamount, but he bounced off.

"The front portal isn't working," Circigi said. "Let me try a side portal."

The side portal didn't work either.

"I don't understand," Circigi said.

"Maybe there's no way in," Darlina said. "Maybe...maybe...this was the last defense...against...against..."

"Against what?"

"Those who attacked them," Darlina said.

"Well I can't figure out a way to go inside," Circigi said. "So at this point we either go north to Kmina, which is my home kingdom, or south."

"What's south?" Darlina asked.

"The Aiadaka kingdom," Circigi said. "There are several seamounts in that group. Aita is the tallest and the most populated. Eta has almost as much population as Aita. The others—Kita, Luta, and Phira—are deeper and less populated. In my time they were populated by orcas. We ordinary dolphins and porpoises stayed away, and we didn't have good relations with them. They would kill us if they had the chance."

"Then let's go north," Darlina said. "At least it's safer."

"Well I hope so, but these waters are all strange to me, so hard to say what is safe and what isn't," Circigi said.

The two swam northeast to Kmina. They arrived, and the seamount was undisturbed.

"It's like Rhynchus, all in one piece. Let's see if we can enter," Circigi said.

The portals were blocked.

"And just like Rhynchus, the normal portals are closed," Circigi said.

"Are there any abnormal portals?" Darlina asked.

"Uh, well, you know, I think, yes, when I was a young dolphin, there was a conventional portal we would use to sneak in and out of Kmina. I had forgotten about it until now," Circigi said. "It's worth a try—if I can remember where it is."

"Just concentrate. It will all come back to you," Darlina said.

"Wait, I think I know how to find it. I made up a song with squeals and clicks," Circigi said. "Here goes."

Circigi squealed and clicked in a sing-song fashion. Darlina hummed along.

"I've got it," he said. "Follow this rift for seventy-eight lengths, then drop thirty-three lengths to the lower rift, then around three pillars and by four crevices. Then squeal as loud as I can at a pivoting rock."

The two followed those geological formations and then reached a rock.

"The pivoting rock," he said. "We are here."

Circigi squealed, but the rock did not move.

"It should move," he said. "I don't know why."

"What makes it move?" Darlina asked.

"I squeal at a certain frequency, and the resonance causes the door to open," Circigi said. "It's based on size and density of the portal door, and its relationship with the surrounding rock."

"And if the rock changes over the ages?" Darlina asked.

"As time passes, the rock may erode, it may shift, and the surrounding rock might change. That must be the case here. The portal door is just a barrier now. We are locked out."

"Or the frequency has changed. Try another pitch," Darlina said.

Circigi squealed a slightly higher pitch. Then higher, and higher and higher. Nothing. Then he tried a lower pitch. And lower and lower. Still nothing.

"Try oscillating tones. Start them far apart and bring them together," Darlina suggested.

Circigi did just that. He alternated between squealing a low tone and a high tone. He did this quickly and brought the tones together. The portal door moved a little but did not fully open.

"There, did you see that?" Darlina asked.

"It moved, but it did not open," Circigi said.

"Double oscillating tones," Darlina said.

"This is getting complicated," Circigi said.

"You can do it, I know you can. All dolphins can," she said.

"All? Hmm. I'll try," he said.

Circigi oscillated a distant high tone against a distant low tone and then a near high tone against a near low tone. He adjusted the distance between sets of tones and how quickly he switched between the tones and finally, finally, the door began to open.

"It's working, Circigi. Keep making the tones. You almost have the door open," Darlina urged.

Circigi worked the tones, and the door opened. The two swam through the opening, down through a passage, and then the passage went up, which they followed until it reached an access portal pool. Circigi dove over the edge, into the air, and onto a platform, and in landing he released the glass shield around Darlina and transformed into humanoid shape. Darlina dropped to the ground. The platform was in a small room, but there was a corridor that led to the main market square.

"This is Kmina," Circigi said while leading Darlina through the corridor. "I'm rather surprised it's still here given how the other seamounts were destroyed."

But when the two exited the corridor, the marketplace was no longer there. Instead, open area was filled with gravestones.

"What...has...happened?!" Circigi exclaimed. "This was the most vibrant marketplace in all of Lagenora. Everything was traded here. And there were shows. And prizes. And dolphins singing and reciting poetry and families playing. It was full of life. Not this. Not this!"

"I'm sorry," Darlina said. "I can't imagine how beautiful it must have been. It's still awe-inspiring just to be here."

"But not like this!" he said. "I feel like I'm in the great burial chamber of...Gathona. Oh what's happened to all the cetaceans of Lagenora? They can't have all died. Not all!"

But there was no denying the gravestones.

"My people. They're all gone. All of them," Circigi said. "I recognize some of these names, too. Mostly friends of Metavasi, but I know them."

"Is there somewhere else we can go?" Darlina asked.

"Go? What's to do? It's all ended," Circigi said.

"Well for one thing, I'm hungry," Darlina said.

"Hungry? Oh, that's right, you humans must eat. I don't know if there's food here. I know there's death. But food?"

"Didn't anyone in Kmina eat conventional food?" Darlina asked.

"The younger dolphins did as a dare, or sick dolphins did with thorisponitis—that's an infection of the thorium sponge organelles," Circigi said.

"And what did they eat?"

"Anchovies, of course," Circigi replied.

"In a restaurant?"

"No, in the medical dispensary," Circigi said. "Perhaps there are canned anchovies left over from my days here."

The two walked to the medical center.

"This is our main medical center. It's called Kminadoma," Circigi said. "Each seamount kingdom has at least one medical center, many have multiple. The primary one in Rhynchus is named Curatidoma, the one in Phocayna is...or was...well, I guess it doesn't matter what it was called. Let's go inside."

But instead of healing beds and healing pools, there was a large array of video screens, all displaying first-person viewpoints of living things going about their business. Darlina began to panic.

"They're here! They're here! The blinners! We must hide!" she said with anxiety.

"Wait," Circigi said. "You can see those screens, right?"

"Yes."

"And you still see them?"

"Of course. They haven't gone black," she said.

"Neither has your vision. You were mostly blind on Gough Island. You regained your sight in the ocean. And you still have it here in Kmina. I'm convinced your vision was blocked by the blinners. If they were here, don't you think your vision would be impaired?"

"I hope you're right," Darlina said.

"He is right," said a voice.

"Chusacuta?" Circigi called.

The two turned around and saw a humanoid woman of immense age holding a tray of anchovies.

"Care for a snack?" she offered.

"Yes, thank you!" Darlina said as she took some.

"You're not Chusacuta," Circigi said.

"No, I'm not. She's still on Gathona," the elderly woman said.

"How did you know...Who are you?" Circigi asked.

"You don't recognize me, Circigi?" the elderly woman asked.

"You *know* me?" he asked.

"Of course. I've been watching your history," the elderly woman said as she placed the tray on a side table and ate an anchovy herself. "Have one, it's good."

"No thank you, I don't eat," Circigi said.

"Of course not. Fully thorium-sponge assimilated," the elderly woman said, "like your family and all your friends from your era."

"From my *era*? Again I ask, who are you? I can tell you're not a real human. Your black and white cetacean colors are showing," Circigi said. "But you aren't from my *era*, as you say, because the cetaceans from my era, except the orcas and voitrans, don't need to eat. And the orcas only need to eat occasionally, as their thorium-sponge symbionts are able to supply most of their energy needs. But you are too nice to be an orca."

"Thank you, although my kingdom was taken over by orcas," the elderly woman said.

"You're Queen Pollyenpa," Darlina said.

"Very good," the queen said. "But I do not know your name. You are not in any of the dolphin memories stored in Kmina."

"I'm Darlina. I'm from Gough Island," Darlina said.

"That's what the humans call—" Circigi started.

"Gathona," Queen Pollyenpa said. "I was buried in the chamber under Gathona."

"And your tomb was excavated by the blinners," Darlina said.

"I was revitalized and imprisoned by them," the queen said. "They used me to begin their reign of oppression."

"We knew this, but we didn't know the details," Darlina said.

Queen Pollyenpa squealed in Lagenorian to Circigi and asked him why he brought a human to a dolphin kingdom. Circigi replied that Darlina could be trusted. Queen Pollyenpa reminded Circigi of the primary laws for humans—don't trust what humans say, don't trust what humans do, and don't trust humans with tools.

"What are you two doing? Are you echolocating?" Darlina asked.

"You know how it is. Sometimes we tell jokes in our native language that don't translate correctly," Circigi said.

"Yes, many jokes," Queen Pollyenpa said with an odd stare for Darlina.

"Your Highness, I beg of you, how did you escape with the sulfuric acid and all that?" Circigi asked.

"I will tell you," Queen Pollyenpa said. "But first, let me say that all the technology they developed was not my doing. They used me to locate another ocean creature from the past."

"Another cetacean?" Circigi asked.

"No. Something more hideous and evil," the queen said. "Aiatethis."

"What!?" Circigi exclaimed.

"He was the ruler of Aiadaka from your time," the queen said.

"We all thought Aiatethis was a myth from childhood," Circigi said, "that our parents used the stories of Aiatethis to scare us into being good."

"Oh no, he is quite real. Quite alive," Queen Pollyenpa said. "I've spent many long days reviewing memories here. There were some electric rays who lived in Aiadaka—they had to tend to Aiatethis—under constant fear. The dolphins in your time were just realizing the existence of Aiatethis when you and Chusacuta went on your trip to Gathona."

"How are you able to do this? Review memories?" Circigi asked.

"Did you get the device from the blinners?" Darlina asked.

"Yes, Darlina. The visicort was developed by Aiatethis during his reign in Aiadaka to control his subjects and his enemies. Aiatethis also helped the blinners develop those echolocation helmets, the airships, and the mountain fortress," Queen Pollyenpa explained.

"How did you escape?" Circigi asked.

"Yes, please, your escape is most fascinating to hear," Darlina said.

Queen Pollyenpa paused, looked at Darlina, and then looked at Circigi. Darlina pressed closer to hear, and Queen Pollyenpa felt uneasy.

"I sang my way out," the queen said.

"What!?" Circigi said.

"I sang my way out," Queen Pollyenpa repeated, and that was all she would say about that. "Now Circigi, you may wonder why I am not surprised to see you."

"Yeah, you should be surprised. I don't belong here," Circigi said.

"I knew you and Chusacuta had arrived on Gathona. And I knew about her capture," the queen said.

"You used Chusacuta's capture as a diversion to effect your escape," Darlina surmised.

"You are very perceptive," the queen said. "I could not both prevent Chusacuta's capture and make my escape. And I knew you would come this way looking for help. And so I left you a note."

"What note?" Circigi asked.

"She means the inscription on the tomb," Darlina said.

"Incredibly perceptive," the queen said of Darlina. "Almost *too* perceptive."

"Is it true? About the inscription? That was an abysmal prank to play on me," Circigi said.

"I had to get your attention," she said.

"You got it, oh porpoiso-dolpho. You got it!" Circigi said. "Couldn't you have left a simpler note, like 'follow me to Kmina'?"

"Too obvious," the queen said. "As it is, you are here. That's the important thing. And now you need my help to rescue Chusacuta."

"And to get rid of the blinners," Darlina said.

"Helping Chusacuta is the main issue here," Circigi said. "But I had hoped to find an army."

"Well before you do that, you should get your glasses repaired," the queen said.

"Then you can see as well as I can," Darlina said. "Are there facilities here for repairing his glasses? I'd love to see them."

"There were in my time," Circigi said.

"And some still remain," the queen said. "Follow me."

The three walked a short ways into the optometry section of Kminadoma.

"Lovely! Outstanding! I could spend a year here learning about this place!" Darlina said.

"She is fascinated with cetacean technology," the queen squealed to Circigi.

"She *is* a human," he squealed back.

"I don't like her," the queen squealed.

"She's nice enough. Humans take time to befriend," Circigi squealed.

"It's not just that," the queen squealed. "There's something about her personality that does not seem genuine."

"Give it some time," Circigi squealed.

"We may not have much time," the queen squealed. "But I will trust her as much as I can."

"Thank you," Circigi squealed.

"More jokes?" Darlina said. "Or maybe you are talking about me. Like how Circigi finds me *very* attractive."

"You do?" the queen asked in the human language. "That is interspecies. Uncouth."

"Let's see about my glasses," Circigi squirmed. "I look into this device over here, press this button, and my glasses will be produced. There. It's working."

Circigi's actions mirrored his words, and the device produced new glasses. He placed them over his ears and looked.

"Much better!" Circigi said. "Now then, how do we rescue Chusacuta? Could she escape the same way you did?"

"No," the queen said. "Chusacuta has neural implants from Baroness Vasha of Darby. Aiatethis controls her through those implants."

"Then we need to get those implants removed, or block Aiatethis's control," Circigi said.

"It won't be easy to remove the implants," Darlina said. "You'll have to invade the mountain fortress, find her, and remove the implants—all without the blinners noticing. And you already tried once and failed to even reach the fortress. What we need is something to destroy this Aiatethis outright. Now what does a squid hate?"

"A whale," Circigi said.

"Besides that," Darlina said.

"Humans?" Circigi suggested.

"Humans with a bright light," Darlina said.

"But they are actually attracted to bright light," the queen said.

"Yes, but think of this. All we need is a bright light to attract this Aiatethis out of the fortress and into the ocean where the sulfuric acid will destroy him," Darlina said.

"Huh? Really? How?" Circigi asked.

"Interesting idea, Darlina," the queen said.

"Circigi has the energy. I just need a way to use his thorium cells to power a light," Darlina said.

"Huh? I'm the bait?" Circigi asked.

"Just the power source," Darlina said.

"That may not be necessary," the queen said. "Follow me, please."

Darlina and Circigi followed Queen Pollyenpa a short ways into another room. There was a diving pod situated on the floor, just large enough to hold two people.

"This is a deep sea diving pod," the queen said. "It is a leftover from the human exploitation in these parts. During the Last Stand, several dolphins of Kmina captured this pod and modified it to use thorium as a power supply. The pod will navigate in the ocean, on the ocean, and approximately four thousand *nialli* above ground. It has a very powerful light beam to enable vision in the deep. Many dolphins in the Last Stand lost their ability to echolocate due to interference from depth charges dropped by the humans. This pod was used by a lead dolphin scout."

"It could work," Darlina said. "But there is only one. And three of us."

"I won't be going with you," Queen Pollyenpa said.

"But you must!" Darlina said. "We need your help to rescue Chusacuta."

"I thought you wanted...yeah, Chusacuta," Circigi said. "But will you at least swim back to Gathona with us?"

"No, my place is here, at least for now. These video memories are fascinating. Had I known that Kminians were so crafty, I might have imported a few for my court. As it is, I must be getting back to watching these memories," the queen said.

"You're hooked on dolphin memory videos?" Circigi said in shock.

"Come on, Circigi, let's go. We'll come back with Chusacuta and visit. Maybe then we can pry the queen from these video machines."

"I...don't know what to say," Circigi said.

"Go on, Circigi. I'll be here when you return," Queen Pollyenpa said.

"Oh...hmmm...well...oh...I defer. But reluctantly I defer. I'll return as soon as this is all over," Circigi said.

"Good. Let the light be on your dorsal fin," the queen said.

Circigi entered the pod and Darlina followed. The queen pressed a button, and the pod was launched into the ocean. Circigi navigated the pod toward Gathona.

"There's radio communication in this pod," Darlina said.

"Yes, if only there were someone else out there with a radio," Circigi lamented.

"What was the queen talking about, Circigi?"

"Huh?"

"That thing about the light on your dorsal fin," Darlina said.

"I think she mixed up the saying. It's supposed to be, 'Let the waves be on your dorsal fin'," Circigi said. "How could she forget the saying? She's a queen and should know better. Whatever. Let's head straight for Gathona...I mean, Gough Island."

"Sounds good to me," Darlina said.

The two traveled more quickly in the pod than Circigi could swim.

"This pod is making excellent time," Circigi said. "We'll be there before you know it."

"I'm so glad. The sooner this is all over, the better," Darlina said.

"Now what we need is a plan," Circigi said. "Once we reach Gathona, we...ack!"

"We have a leak!" Darlina exclaimed.

Sulfuric acid blasted through a small, pinhole-sized opening in the back of the pod.

"I'll hold my finger over it," Circigi said.

"The pressure is too high. It will—" Darlina started to say.

But Circigi had heated the surrounding metal and caused the hole to seal. The sulfuric acid stopped pouring in.

"You can weld metals too?" Darlina asked.

"For a little while. Not constantly, mind you. My skin is charred. See?" Circigi said as he showed his burned finger to Darlina.

"It will heal, right?"

"Of course," he said, and he took the controls back from Darlina.

"Perhaps when all of this is over, you and I could work together to help the others. Maybe we can find a way to use your skills to heal people," Darlina said.

"It sounds like a nice idea, but I really want to find a way for Chusacuta and me to return to our time," Circigi said.

"I don't know how that is possible," Darlina said. "I mean, do you even know how you came to the future?"

"I just know that Chusacuta and I were standing by Queen Pollyenpa's tomb in the Gathona burial chamber one moment, and the next moment I was in the middle of your town square—and Chusacuta was gone," Circigi explained.

"If you do find a way to go back to your time, would you take me with you?" Darlina asked.

"I don't know if that's possible," Circigi said.

"Please? There's nothing for me here. I know you are fond of Chusacuta, but there must be some room in your heart for me, your sweet Darlina," she said.

"I must focus. I must focus on rescuing Chusacuta," Circigi said. "The plan, remember? We need a plan for luring Aiatethis out of the fortress so he will follow the light in this pod. That means navigating the pod into the fortress and into whatever chamber he resides."

"Easy enough," Darlina said. "I stole a transponder key for opening an auxiliary port. We can fly into the port and through an unguarded passageway to practically the very end. We can then shine the light through the passageway into his chamber. That should be enough to lure him out."

"Amazing! You have this all thought out. But how can you know so much about the fortress? And how did you steal a transponder key?" Circigi asked.

"When Chusacuta was being captured, Pollyenpa wasn't the only one to use the diversion to accomplish things," Darlina winked.

"And all done with limited vision. Truly amazing. Maybe I should bring you back with us to the past, if I can find a way back. We could use your help to bridge the gap between cetaceans and humans," Circigi said.

"I'd be happy to help," she beamed. "Now, what I really need to do is take a nap. Not that I'm tired, though I am a little. But taking a nap will help store up heartbeat time for my vision on Gough Island."

"Good idea," Circigi said.

"If you get tired and need a nap yourself, just wake me, and I'll take control," Darlina offered.

"I don't need to fully sleep," Circigi said. "I can stay half awake."

"I should have guessed," Darlina said.

"Have a good sleep," Circigi said.

"Thank you," she said.

The journey back to Gathona was uneventful and did not take much longer. As the pod approached the island, Circigi awakened Darlina.

"We are here," Circigi said.

"Good," Darlina said. "Let's turn to the right and then hook back left around that cliff face. We want to follow it closely so as not to be seen."

"I hope this pod will fly high enough," Circigi said. "Queen Pollyenpa says it will go up four thousand nialli—that's over fifty-two hundred meters."

"I don't know what a meter is," Darlina said.

"Well, you are nearly two meters tall," he said.

Circigi navigated the pod as Darlina suggested.

"Now stop here," she said.

"I don't understand," Circigi said. "This is just a side of the mountain."

"But watch this, Circigi," Darlina said.

Darlina pulled out a small device from her pocket, pressed several buttons, and a door opened in the cliff face.

"This is it," she said. "We should go inside before we are spotted out here."

"Agreed," Circigi said, and he navigated the pod inside the mountain and through the passage.

"We'll need to turn on the pod's light beam to see the passage," Circigi said.

"That's fine, but do not use full power. We don't want to alert Aiatethis," Darlina said.

The two proceeded along the passage, and it reached an opening.

"This is the opening, right?" Circigi asked. "I should turn on full light beam?"

"No, this is just an intermediate chamber," Darlina said.

"This chamber is empty. I thought you said we would go directly into Aiatethis's chamber," Circigi said.

"The plan has changed," Darlina said.

"What do you mean, *the plan has changed*?" Circigi repeated.

"I mean," Darlina started as she pulled out a sonic blaster and pointed it at Circigi's head, "the plan has changed."

"What's wrong with you? Are you playing a joke? Put that away!" Circigi demanded.

"Land this pod in the center of the chamber, or I'll blast your dolphin skull!" Darlina ordered.

"I don't believe this!" Circigi said.

Circigi complied with her order and landed the pod. Darlina forced him out of the pod and into the open chamber.

"You said you loved me and would do anything for me. Is this part of the bargain?" he asked.

"You have a lot to learn about humans," a lead blinner said as he entered the chamber with a dozen other blinners armed with sonic blasters.

"You didn't say *yow*," Circigi said.

The blinners and Darlina laughed.

"Only the blind and manipulated sighted folk use that word," Darlina said. "Arbreezias, this pod will allow us to leave the island."

"Indeed," the lead blinner (Arbreezias) said.

Darlina walked up to Arbreezias and embraced him. "I have missed you."

"Oh, so this is how it is!" Circigi said. "Well let me show you how it is with me."

Circigi leapt for three blinners to overpower them, but two other blinners threw an electric noose over Circigi, and the extreme voltage arrested his movements.

"Ahg, ack, agh," Circigi writhed from the electric current flowing through his body.

"A controlling noose," Arbreezias said to Circigi. "The more you fight, the higher the voltage."

"Circigi is nuclear powered," Darlina said. "So is Chusacuta."

"Impressive," Arbreezias said. "We will need to dissect them and learn this new biological function."

"And there's more. A third nuclear dolphin named Queen Pollyenpa is in a seamount Circigi calls Kmina. There are many resources to extract, and much technology we can learn. This pod is just the start of the number of transportation vehicles we could build."

"Now the whole world will be at our beck and call," Arbreezias said. "Aiatethis will function as our central master, and you, Darlina, will be at my side as we explore and conquer. Explore and conquer!"

"You're getting ahead of yourself," Circigi said. "There will be nothing out there for you to conquer."

"Ye who have little ambition," Arbreezias said. "How could you pretend to love this *dolphin*, Darlina? He is so repulsive."

"It wasn't easy," Darlina said. "I had to be in my best acting form."

"Me? Repulsive? Acting form? You disappoint me, Darlina. I really thought you wanted to help."

"Wake up to the modern world, Circigi," Darlina said. "Everyone is a user and always will be. Those who aren't are weak and will die!"

"The queen was right. Don't trust what humans say or do," Circigi said. "And now you'll use this pod as a tool to exploit my homeland. Defiled again by humans! Don't trust humans with tools!"

"Take him to prison cell three," Arbreezias said. "We have much work to do."

The blinner guards took Circigi away.

"This is the one," said one of Circigi's guards to the prison warden as Circigi was brought in under control of noose. "He can see, unless we do this."

The guard took Circigi's glasses and stepped on them. The other guards and the warden laughed.

"My glasses!" Circigi exclaimed.

"Now he can't see," said the guard. "Put him in a block until the Master decides."

The warden took control of the noose and forced Circigi into a cell. The warden then released the noose and was about to close the door when Circigi lashed back at the warden to escape. A guard pointed his sonic blaster at Circigi and fired. Circigi fell back into the cell, onto the floor, and the warden closed the cell door with a clang!

When Circigi awoke, he was still in the detainment cell. He pulled himself up from the floor and looked around. There were the standard items one might find in a human detainment cell—a cot, a table with chair, a sink for washing up, and a toilet—which of course he could never use. His vision was still heavily myopic, but he could hear voices far down the corridor.

"His body deflected the implant when we fired on him earlier," said one.

"Perhaps we could absorb his memories into the central tethis, using the high-power cortexicon," the first one said.

"Central tethis," Circigi said to himself. "Oh no. Is this where Aiatethis is found? What do these humans think they are doing?"

A third voice approached the other two.

"Master says to bring the male dolphin," the third voice said.

"I must hide," Circigi said. "But how? If I could transform into something that looks inanimate, like...like...a mattress!"

Circigi transformed into a mattress and plopped onto the cot. He wasn't fully transformed into a mattress, but his outer skin layers and general form made him look like one. Seconds later, the two guards entered the cell.

"He has escaped!" shouted one guard.

"Sound the alarm!" shouted the second guard.

One guard ran off to sound the alarm. An air raid siren blasted in pulses. Several guards ran into the cell, and the first guard explained that Circigi had escaped and to search the entire fortress. The guards left, leaving just the first guard in the cell by himself. Or so he thought. He searched frantically through the cell, as if he would somehow find Circigi. He searched under the mattress, and as he did, Circigi changed back into humanoid shape and clocked the blinner on the back of the neck.

The blinner fell to the ground, unconscious. Circigi then took the blinner's helmet and stun gun.

"The helmet just barely fits," Circigi said.

Circigi stuffed the blinner under the cot and repositioned the cot's sheets to cover the guard. Circigi then transformed into a replica of the guard he had just rendered unconscious. Another guard rushed into the cell.

"There's no use looking in the cell," the other guard said to Circigi. "It's obvious he's not here."

"Right," Circigi said.

The other guard ran out, and Circigi left the cell. With no glasses, he had to squeal to "see", and he squealed ultrasonically so as not to be noticed as unusual. He pretended to run around with the other guards to "look" for himself, but what he was really doing was exploring the fortress in hopes of finding Chusacuta.

"He might be trying to free the other dolphin," one guard yelled.

"Send reinforcements down there," yelled another.

A group of guards ran over to a large elevator. Circigi, still posing as a blinner guard, ran over with them and hopped into the elevator just as the doors closed.

"There seems to be excess radiation," said one blinner. "My echolocator is getting static."

"Get it recalibrated after the emergency is over," said another blinner.

Circigi kept quiet but realized that his cells were exuding a little radiation. Meanwhile, the elevator reached the bottom floor, and the doors opened. Circigi stepped out first and pretended to rush toward something, but he didn't know where to go, and so he allowed the others to rush past him. The elevator doors closed. Circigi followed the pack in back, but when the guards passed a small passageway, he slipped into that passageway and hid. He crept down low and peered around the corner, using a large container as cover. The guards jogged a little farther and assembled around a clear-walled cell filled with water. Chusacuta was inside, and in dolphin form.

"Dim the lights," said a deep voice over a loudspeaker.

One of the blinners dimmed the lights. At that moment, the elevator opened again. Out stepped Arbreezias and Darlina.

"Cancel the alarm," the deep voice said.

"But Master, the other dolphin, Circigi, has yet to be found," Arbreezias said.

"He is here," the deep voice said. "Turn off the lights completely. Good. Now activate the nucleolumino array."

Soft, green, miniature lights lit up around the room, like mini holiday tree lights. The chamber was still very dark, but three things glowed brightly in the dark—Chusacuta, Circigi, and a giant squid in a water cell high and inset into the wall.

"Aiatethis!" Circigi let fly.

"There he is!" Darlina said, and she pointed at Circigi.

The blinner guards swarmed around Circigi and brought him forward.

"Circigi Cento!" Aiatethis said. "I remember you from the early Lagenora era. I was much younger then and had only a small reign in Aiadaka."

"It *is* you," Circigi said. "Your kingdom is much smaller now. Gathona is but one island."

"One island today, the world tomorrow," Aiatethis said.

"So this is the part where you tell me your plans, and all the while a secret rescue party is gathering outside, ready to break in and save the day."

Aiatethis laughed.

"No, Circigi, this is the part where you are tortured and scanned for memories," Arbreezias said. "Then we'll decide if you will be dissected for your thorium energy."

"Very well put, Arbreezias," Aiatethis said.

"Look, this is all a mistake. Chusacuta and I don't belong in your time. Let us go, and we'll find a way back. I promise. And even if we don't, we can leave this island and live in Kmina."

"The pod is on the way to Kmina as we speak," Darlina said. "Queen Pollyenpa's obsession with video memories will soon end when she is brought back here and tortured alongside you and Chusacuta. Then we will extract equipment from Kmina and use it to begin our expansion into the world."

"Get Circigi in a water cell," Aiatethis commanded.

"No, I won't allow it," Circigi said, and he squared off to fight.

But Aiatethis had no patience for Circigi's resistance. The squid emitted a pulsed energy burst at Circigi. Circigi was stunned and offered no resistance. The blinner guards took him and placed him in a tank next to Chusacuta.

"What is your name?" Arbreezias said.

"Circigi Cento."

"To whom do you serve?" Arbreezias asked.

"What!?" Circigi asked.

"Wrong answer," Arbreezias said, and he delivered a high-voltage shock to Circigi.

"OW!" Circigi cried.

"The correct answer is, Master Aiatethis," Arbreezias said. "Now I'll repeat the question. To whom do you serve?"

"No, I won't comply," Circigi said.

Arbreezias sent another electric jolt to Circigi, and his body jerked in pain.

"The more you resist, the worse the pain," Arbreezias said.

"You see, Circigi," Aiatethis said, "my subjects are well trained. I'm quite enjoying your feeble attempts at heroism. I can only imagine what memories you must have. I and my subjects will enjoy your engrams long after your death."

"My death?!" Circigi said. "I won't die. I'm—"

"Thorium-based, and thorium-based life practically lives forever. Well I'm thorium-based, and let me tell you, immortality is infinitely boring. Continue the torture, Arbreezias."

"No, stop!" Chusacuta yelled.

"Your girlfriend speaks," Aiatethis said.

"Darlina is my girlfriend," Circigi said.

"Sorry, Circigi, but she was only acting," Arbreezias said.

"Did she tell you about the intimate moments we had? When she hugged me from behind while I swam as a dolphin from Gathona to Kmina?" Circigi asked.

"It was all part of the act," Arbreezias said. "But your attempts to make me jealous are in vain."

"It was fun, Circigi. Maybe another time," Darlina said.

"What do you mean, it was fun?" Arbreezias asked Darlina.

"A girl takes attention where she can get it," Darlina said.

"I'm the one who gives you attention when it's appropriate," Arbreezias said.

The two argued. Circigi squealed ultrasonically to Chusacuta to communicate privately.

"Are you hurt?" Circigi asked.

"No, not as much as you are about to be," Aiatethis replied. "Yes, I can understand your ultrasonic language. I commanded orcas in my youth, you may remember."

"And you learned nothing. Cetaceans are meant to be as free as the ocean is big," Circigi said.

"That...is a misconception," Aiatethis said. "All life forms need order and structure, or else they degenerate and die. I *am* that structure."

"No!" Circigi rebelled.

"Yes!" Aiatethis countered. "Arbreezias. Degenerate Circigi."

Arbreezias began sending random voltages of differing frequencies and strengths. Circigi was now in random pain and becoming confused and exhausted.

"I...can't think...I...don't know...what...who...I am," Circigi stumbled.

"It's time to share your memories, Circigi," Aiatethis said.

"Activate the cortexicon," Arbreezias said to Darlina.

Darlina walked over to a set of controls at the base of Circigi's tank.

"This will be easier on you in your natural form," Darlina said.

"Do I have a choice? Ow!" Circigi cried as Arbreezias jolted Circigi with another electric shock.

"Just change and be done with it," Darlina said.

Circigi changed into a dolphin.

"Oh, I forgot about your glass covering," Darlina said. "I'll have to adjust the cortexicon for that."

Darlina adjusted the controls, and then Circigi's memories began appearing on a video screen. The first was that of when he was a young dolphin. He had snuck out from Kmina, swam to Phocayna, and then met with Metavasi and Litivito. On a dare, the three swam as far as they could toward Aita of Aiadaka. The one who got closest to Aita before turning around was the winner. The three got closer and closer. Circigi was scared and wanted to turn back, but Litivito urged him on. Finally, five orcas surrounded the three. Metavasi and Litivito leapt out of the water over one of the orcas and swam at top speed toward Phocayna. Circigi did the same, but he could not swim as fast as the two dalli porpoises. The orcas gave chase, and Circigi fell behind. An orca began nipping at Circigi's flukes.

"Metavasi, Litivito, help me!" Circigi squealed.

"Slow down, little hourglass dolphin. I'm having you for dinner," the orca squawked.

Meanwhile, Metavasi and Litivito had swum way ahead of Circigi and the pursuing orcas.

"Where's Circigi?" Metavasi asked.

"Back playing with the orcas," Litivito said.

"You were supposed to protect him," Metavasi said.

"I didn't feel like it. Besides, I got the closest to Aita," Litivito said.

"No you didn't. I did, and I left you with Circigi to watch," Metavasi said.

"So?"

"So!? Litivito! Circigi will be eaten by those orcas!" Metavasi said.

"The thorium will protect him," Litivito said.

"Not against five hungry orcas who have a little thorium of their own!"

"That's my point. These orcas have thorium, like us," Litivito said.

"*These* orcas don't have enough thorium to provide their daily intake of energy, *unlike* us!" Metavasi countered, and he turned back toward Circigi.

"Where are you going?" Litivito asked.

"Where do you think? And you'd better come with me and help me piece Circigi back together," Metavasi ordered.

"Yes, my Prince," Litivito replied, and he followed.

The two dalli porpoises swam back to Circigi and swam circles around him, creating a wavefront of charged water that blocked the orcas. Some orcas attempted to chase the dalli porpoises, but each time the porpoises crossed paths, the dalli being chased had the other dalli fight off the orca with a vonk wave.

"Amazing," Arbreezias said. "I wish I had a thousand of these swimming creatures."

"They are dalli porpoises," Darlina said. "I'm linked in to Circigi's thoughts."

"I remember those five orcas," Aiatethis said. "They were fat and slow."

"What became of them, my Master?" Arbreezias asked.

Aiatethis explained how the five orcas were disciplined several times before they were stripped of their thorium cells and set off to sea to fend for themselves in the wild. Circigi used this moment to communicate with Chusacuta, using the long wave technique she had shown him earlier.

"Chusacuta. Chusacuta, can you hear me?" Circigi squealed.

"Yes, I can hear you," Chusacuta squealed back.

"We need to get out of here," Circigi said.

"But how?" Chusacuta asked.

"I have an idea," Circigi said. "Squawk the most powerful harmonic long waves that you can at me. Keep squawking. I'll use the waves to free us."

"I don't understand," Chusacuta said.

"No time to explain. Ready?" Circigi asked.

"Yes."

"Go!"

Chusacuta squawked the most powerful long waves that she could. To Circigi, it sounded like a purr from the largest, most powerful cat that could possibly exist. No one else heard the long waves, and Circigi watched for reaction to confirm. It was verified—no one noticed. Circigi drifted down to the lowest part of his tank. The long waves built upon the glass and upon the boron trioxide just under Circigi's skin. He then released a surge of thorium energy into the glass and boron. This created the combined effect of a super-hard outer protective layer, and an explosive thrust from his flukes.

Before anyone could react, Circigi blasted through the side wall of his tank and through the side wall of Chusacuta's tank. He sent a return long wave that disrupted the implants in Chusacuta (though the implants remained in her head). Freed from the blinner's controlling directives, she changed to humanoid shape and accompanied Circigi (who had also changed to humanoid shape) in a sprint out of the chamber and up a stairwell.

"After them!" Aiatethis commanded.

The blinners except Arbreezias ran after the two dolphins by going up the same stairwell. Darlina and Arbreezias hesitated.

"Darlina. How is it your calculations did not account for Circigi's escape?" Aiatethis asked.

"I...uh...am not sure how he managed to do that," Darlina said.

"If he is not captured, I'll have your implants reinserted, and you will join the other sighted people in their menial service to me," Aiatethis warned.

"We will catch him," Darlina said.

Arbreezias and Darlina took the elevator to the main floor.

"We will catch them on the way up," Arbreezias said. "What was that outer layer he had? It looked like glass."

"It is glass. I didn't think he could use it against us like that," Darlina said.

"How did he get that glass?" Arbreezias asked.

Darlina paused.

"Well?"

"I helped him get it," Darlina said.

"What?!"

"It was the only way he could survive the sulfuric acid in the ocean," Darlina said. "Without the glass, there would be no ocean travel, no trip to Kmina, and no pod for us to use."

"If he does something else—" Arbreezias started.

"What else can he do? Other than leave the island, nothing. And if he leaves the island, it won't matter. Our blinners are arriving in Kmina as we speak. They will take control, and if Circigi goes there, our blinners will meet him and recapture him."

"Recapture him? With his power to escape?"

"I gathered a great deal of data during his escape just now. I'll relay that data to our blinners in Kmina. That will ensure the last of Circigi's heroic attempts," Darlina said.

"You had better be correct," Arbreezias said. "Aiatethis does not suffer failure."

The elevator doors opened, and the two exited. They walked over to the stairwell and opened the door.

"Wait here," Darlina said. "I'll go down to meet them."

Darlina descended the steps as quickly as she could. She heard multiple footsteps ascending, and she also heard dolphin squeals. Darlina pulled a sonic blaster out of her holster and prepared for the confrontation. She continued running. Suddenly, the dolphin squeals stopped. She heard a new sound—that of ocean waves.

"What is happening?" she asked herself.

Darlina descended several more flights, and she converged on the source of ocean waves—an opening in the stairwell wall. Bright light poured in. Blinners from below converged on Darlina's position as she saw two albatrosses flying away.

"WORTHLESS DOLPHINS!" Darlina yelled in frustration.

Circigi led Chusacuta to the beach grass where he had discovered the boron trioxide. The two landed and converted back to humanoid form.

"I didn't think I could transform into a flighted bird," Circigi said.

"It's the most essential skill we fulltrans must learn," Chusacuta said. "Didn't you pay attention in school?"

"I barely passed Applied Transformation 101—with a D," Circigi said. "I'm good at theory, but when it comes to practical application, I'm all dorsal fins."

"Fortunately, I was around to send you the carrier wave sequence," Chusacuta said. "You'll have to practice when we get home—if we get home."

"We'll get home," Circigi assured her. "But first we must deal with Aiatethis and his blinners."

"How?"

"Cover yourself in this white powder. It's boron trioxide," Circigi explained.

"I don't understand," Chusacuta said.

"It's a fluxing material," Circigi said as he helped throw boron trioxide on Chusacuta. "It will allow you to absorb this beach grass. Oh, and you will need to release some thorium energy to heat up the boron trioxide and beach grass."

Chusacuta was covered in boron trioxide. She heated her skin, and Circigi threw beach grass on her. The glass melded with the boron trioxide and Chusacuta's skin.

"This feels strange, like I'm wrapping myself in gooey tape," Chusacuta said.

"Something else is happening," Circigi said. "The implants—are they coming out?"

It was true. The act of melding with the boron trioxide and glass had given Chusacuta's body the ability to decide what belonged and what was foreign. She sensed the implants were foreign, and her tissue began forcing them out like a splinter. But the process stopped as quickly as it started.

"They won't come out," Chusacuta said.

Circigi threw more boron trioxide on Chusacuta.

"Try again," he said.

Chusacuta tried switching back and forth from humanoid to dolphin, but the implants remained.

"No good," she said.

"There's no time to keep trying. The blinners are approaching by airship. And sighted people are running toward us. We must swim in the ocean."

"And the glass will protect us?" Chusacuta asked.

"Yes, exactly," Circigi said. "Ready? Now!"

Circigi dove into the ocean, and Chusacuta followed. As the two did so, they transformed from humanoid shape to their natural dolphin shapes— Circigi into an hourglass dolphin, and Chusacuta into an Atlantic white-sided dolphin. They kept their glass layers active as a barrier against the sulfuric acid.

"I have another plan," Circigi squealed. "Repeat my squawk but at one hundred and ten degrees out of phase. We'll swim circles around the island."

Circigi began a swim around Gathona in counter-clockwise direction, and he squawked "hoy-yow" as loud as possible. Chusacuta followed Circigi and squawked the same hoy-yow but a hundred and ten degrees out of phase. The result was a wavefront being generated on the sulfuric-acid waves along the shoreline, and these waves reacted with the borax in the soil, creating boron trioxide which mixed with beach grass and formed a crystalline wall that grew vertically.

"We must swim more quickly," Circigi said. "If only Metavasi were here!"

"How will this wall stop the airship?" Chusacuta asked.

"It won't," Circigi said. "We can't porpoise anymore. Dive!"

The two dove, and they continued to swim. The airship fired sonic bursts into the water, but the two were protected by their glass coverings.

"I should really be swimming around Gathona alone," Chusacuta said.

"We're in this together," Circigi said. "Why would you think that?"

"I...always do things alone. That's how I work," Chusacuta said.

"But think of how much more you could accomplish with others. I wouldn't mind helping you."

"No, no NO! I won't have anyone contaminating my work!"

"Is that what this is all about? Is that why you were swimming in the Atlantic by yourself to Darby without escort? Or are you going to stick with that story about being caught in the dolphinarium?" Circigi asked. "Does working alone give you the right to lie to the rest of the world?"

"Yes, it does!"

"Then why bother creating a fertility device? For couples? Why not make one for loners like you?"

"Don't tempt me!" she snapped. "Long have I dreamt of starting my own family—by myself!"

"And start your own dictatorship! One based on lies! You'll have your own seamount, that much has already been decided. But it won't be long before war breaks out. And who will you serve then?"

"I will serve no one! Everyone will serve me!"

"Chusacuta, Supreme Ruler of Lagenora. And yet she won't be alone. All will bow before her and attend to her needs. But you'll tire of us. You'll suppress yet avoid us. Just lonely Chusacuta and her miserable Lagenora. Then the humans will move in and take over. You know the end of the story. Massive cetacean displacement and death. That's how Lagenora became what it is now. You created this!"

"No!"

"Yes!"

"Then I will end my life now and spare our precious Lagenora of my tyranny," Chusacuta said.

"No!" Circigi shouted.

But it was too late. Chusacuta surfaced and made herself vulnerable to the blinner airship. Circigi jumped between her and the airship and prepared to take the brunt of any sonic blast. Then without warning, another airship arrived, but it wasn't operated by the blinners. Twenty dalli porpoises dove from the airship (led by Litivito of older age). The porpoises transformed into eagles and flew over the barrier wall and to the fortress, where they transformed to humanoid shape and invaded the blinners' keep. Another twenty dalli porpoises, led by Metavasi (also of older age), dove from the airship into the water. They grouped in pairs and imitated the hoy-yow call from Circigi and Chusacuta (who set their argument aside to resume hoy-yowing). In this way, many cetaceans swam around the island (Circigi and Chusacuta were often passed by the dalli porpoises), and the wall grew taller. But it was no longer just a wall—it was becoming a dome, and it grew as if it were an igloo being built. And in igloo fashion, a single portal was created and reinforced into a tube.

Queen Pollyenpa navigated the airship from where the dalli porpoises dove. She coaxed the blinner airship into Gathona airspace and then forced the blinner airship to land. She then landed her airship in the ocean near the point where Circigi first absorbed beach grass so as to guard the portal to the island dome.

The porpoises continued swimming at amazing speed. Circigi and Chusacuta realized that they were no longer needed, and they stopped swimming when they reached Queen Pollyenpa's airship. They climbed aboard the ship and changed to humanoid shape.

"Queen Pollyenpa!" Circigi said.

"We're so happy to see you," Chusacuta said. "My name is—"

"Chusacuta," the queen said. "I know you very well."

"I thought you were busy watching videos," Circigi said. "I had—"

"Given up hope?" the queen asked. "Never give up hope. I did not wish to reveal my plans to your human friend."

"She's not my friend anymore," Circigi said.

"Who?" Chusacuta asked.

"Darlina," Circigi said.

"That back stabber?" Chusacuta asked.

"Yes, that backstabber," the queen said. "I gave a two-person pod to Circigi and the backstabber as a diversionary tactic until Metavasi could arrive. I had sent word to him for help, but travel from Bruxima 5 takes time."

"Bruxima 5," Chusacuta said. "What's that?"

"A planet far away from here. It's also the happy haven for Earth's cetacean population," Queen Pollyenpa said.

"I thought the happy haven story was a myth," Circigi said.

"It was myth until it became fact," the queen said. "And here is Metavasi to explain."

Metavasi finished swimming, jumped onto the airship, and changed to humanoid shape. He had a few white lines in his otherwise black patches, indicating he was a little older.

"Circigi. You look so much younger than when I left you on Bruxima 5," Metavasi said.

"I *did* make it to the future," Circigi said.

"And Chusacuta, you are as charming and cute as ever," Metavasi said, and he kissed her on the cheek.

"Thank you," Chusacuta said.

"We did not realize the humans on Gathona had gotten themselves into so much trouble. Apparently their desire to dig a hole wherever they please started this whole thing when they unearthed Queen Pollyenpa's tomb and then dug and found Aiatethis's tomb. It was bad enough that we had to defeat him once," Metavasi said.

"But this Aiatethis is not nearly as powerful," said Litivito, who had just passed from the dome's portal to the queen's airship. "All is secure in the fortress. The echolocating humans—"

"They are called *blinners*," Circigi said.

"The blinners, yes, we have removed the helmets and weapons from the blinners," Litivito said. "We are going to rehabilitate all blind humans on Gathona so that they have sight."

"There are two more in this airship who will need the rehabilitation," Queen Pollyenpa said. "They are still in a pod."

"Yes, we locked them in the pod until we could secure the island. Now all is secure," Metavasi said.

Litivito walked to the back of the airship and returned with the two blinners. He removed and smashed their helmets.

"We're blind!" they whined.

"You'll get over it," Litivito said.

"May I?" Metavasi asked.

"Of course," Litivito said.

Metavasi squawked a long wave onto the sulfuric acid ocean, and a standing wave formed, mixed with the beach, and returned—forming a crystalline bridge from the airship to the shore.

"Don't worry," Litivito said. "Prince Metavasi has given you a walkway so that your little feet won't dissolve in the ocean that your ancestors poisoned."

The two humans cringed in fear, but Litivito forced them along the bridge, through the portal, and into the dome.

"I see Litivito hasn't lost his strange sense of humor," Chusacuta said.

"Which reminds me, I can't see anything beyond my nose. My glasses—"

"Are broken as usual," Metavasi said. "Give them to me."

Circigi handed his broken glasses to Metavasi, who squawked a tune or two, rubbed the glasses between his fingers and thumb, and then changed to a little high-pitched squeal to polish the new lenses that he had just created.

"There. Better than new," Metavasi said.

"Thank you," Circigi said.

The cetaceans heard a sound, and the top of the dome had just been completed. The dalli porpoises exited the ocean, transformed into humanoid form, and stood by the portal.

"I guess this is it," Chusacuta said. "This is where we say farewell."

"What? Where are we going?" Circigi said.

"Chusacuta is right, Circigi. The two of you must return to your time. The space-time fabric will only suffer your existence here for a little while longer," Queen Pollyenpa said.

"What about you?" Circigi asked the queen. "How will the space-time fabric handle your existence?"

"I came here naturally," the queen said. "I had lain in my tomb for years beyond count, until the blinners dug me up."

"So you won't come back with us?" Circigi said.

"She can't," Chusacuta said.

"Chusacuta is right again. I no more belong in your time than you in mine. I will go to Bruxima 5 with Metavasi and his pod when they are done here," the queen said.

"I will miss you," Chusacuta said, "even if I have only known you for a short time."

"All good cetaceans are missed," the queen said, and she hugged Chusacuta.

"Do I get a hug from you, Chusacuta?" Circigi asked.

"No," Chusacuta laughed. "But I would like a hug from Metavasi."

Metavasi and Chusacuta exchanged hugs.

"Metavasi, Metavasi!" Circigi complained. "What about me? Circigi? Why won't someone hug me?"

"I'll hug you, Circigi," Metavasi said, and he did.

"Ugh," Circigi said.

Queen Pollyenpa and Chusacuta laughed. Litivito returned by himself and with more news.

"The queen's tomb in the town square has been reverse energized," Litivito said.

"That means the time portal is ready for your return," the queen said. "Follow me."

The queen led, followed next by Chusacuta, then Circigi, Litivito, and finally with Metavasi. They walked across the bridge Metavasi had just created, through the portal, and along the landscape until they reached the town square. Another set of dalli porpoises were lined up in two rows so that the five had to walk in between. Litivito rushed up to the statue of Queen Pollyenpa. The tomb was open, and inside were two glowing crystals. When Queen Pollyenpa reached the tomb, Litivito stepped aside.

"Come forth, my children," the queen said to Circigi and Chusacuta.

The two approached.

"I could not remove my implants," Chusacuta said. "Can you help me remove them?"

"It may be possible," Queen Pollyenpa said. "You must make a choice."

"What choice?" Chusacuta asked.

"You must look for your choice when the time comes. But now is the time for your return. Circigi, stand with Chusacuta to your left and hold her right hand with your left. Place your right hand on the aqua crystal. Chusacuta, place your left hand on the crimson crystal," the queen said.

Circigi and Chusacuta did as the queen asked.

"Porpoises, please hum very low, 'waiyo, waiyo, waiyo,' and continue humming as I speak," the queen said.

The porpoises hummed as instructed. Circigi and Chusacuta felt as if the earth beneath them was liquid, as it seemed to undulate soft waves of relaxation.

"Since the beginning, when we said goodbye to our hippopotamid brothers, cetaceans have always left one environment behind to explore another," the queen said. "We are great travelers, spanning Earth's oceans in our youth, and now traveling the stars in our mature years. And so, Circigi and Chusacuta, you two must also say goodbye to us, for a cetacean is not a cetacean if confined for any length of time to any one place. There must be the freedom to travel and explore beyond Earth's terrestrial confines. Now travel the ether to the place and time wherefrom you came, hereforth you go. Repeat these words in your own way."

Circigi and Chusacuta repeated the words over and over again, "Wherefrom we came, hereforth we go," while the queen hummed musical notes, practically singing, but there were no words to her notes. All the humming around became like a buzz, and the light from the crystals traveled up Circigi's and Chusacuta's arms, encircling them and radiating outward from them, until all was white light and white noise. Nothing could be seen or echolocated, and yet the two were so at peace that nothing could disturb their repose.

The light, sound, and ground all calmed. Circigi and Chusacuta found themselves next to the waterfall. The seal that Chusacuta had spoken with earlier had now given birth to her pups. Two pups. One pup was larger. It was the fittest and the most like its mother, and so it would grow and continue her line. The other pup was smaller and weaker, and it would not continue the line as is. It was an unexpected extra pup, and in some bird species, this was the spare and would only be fed and cared for to adulthood should the larger sibling die.

"It is the weaker," Chusacuta said. "It will die. The implants are still in my head. I guess I will die too."

But something special happened. Residual light and sound and waves from Circigi's and Chusacuta's journey pulled the two from the seal and pups and instead sent them farther back into time, much farther back than necessary, or so it seemed. Chusacuta and Circigi watched the world swirl about, and the two saw a pod of young dolphins in the ocean, being taught how to use their echolocation by an older dolphin. Class ended, and instead of the student dolphins improving their echolocation skills, they instead played pranks with one another and communicated incessantly about social issues, who the most popular dolphin was in the races, why porpoises were to be hated, and how to sneak out from home after the parents went half asleep. Chusacuta swam away from the pod and honed her echolocation skills — alone.

Another scene showed Chusacuta in Kmina's Central Records, researching ways to condition her melon such that she could echolocate with better precision and distance than even the adult dolphins of Kmina.

The scene changed again, and Chusacuta swam all about Lagenora alone, testing her echolocation and playing a dangerous game of shark and dolphin, where she would detect sharks from afar but gradually move closer to determine at what point the shark could detect her, then swim away quickly from the shark. One time she barely got away, but she went back to Central Records and learned how to stun sharks with her echolocation. She then resumed the game with sharks and used her echolocation to stun them. She became complacent and relied more on her echolocation as a weapon and less for early detection.

The scene changed, and a young Chusacuta tried showing off her skills to her peers, but they made fun of her and called her a freak. It was then she decided to make a fertility device, but only to help couples make worthy dolphins, not arrogant and wasteful dolphins.

"Then the fertility device is dishonest," Circigi said. "You don't want to help couples conceive—you want couples to conceive children in your own image."

"So what?" Chusacuta said.

But then an image of a giant squid surrounded the two, with its tentacles searching and probing for the two. Chusacuta reached out to touch the tentacles, but Circigi stopped her.

"No," Circigi said. "Don't touch the squid. You'll stir it to action."

The tentacles withdrew, and the squid moved above the two and morphed into a ship. Then an image of Chusacuta swimming to Darby appeared before the two.

"Baroness Vasha's ship?" Circigi asked. "Then this is how you were captured."

"No, stop this," Chusacuta said. "Do you hear me Queen Pollyenpa? Stop the image! Send us back as we are. I don't need a choice. I'll live with my implants. Do you hear?"

"The choice is yet to be given," echoed Queen Pollyenpa's voice across the ages.

"No one needs to see what happened. I know what I did. Stop this!"

The scene changed, and now a young Chusacuta was shown watching Croius and a group of orcas use their echolocation to influence the course of a ship to come their way. Then Croius appeared above the waterline in human form and pretended to have fallen off a ship. He was taken aboard the ship, and he used his echolocation to influence the people into believing that he was an American citizen.

"Croius!" Circigi said. "So that is how he started his life as an American. He became a senator after that. And you witnessed that, Chusacuta! Why did you not report it? We never knew in Kmina, and I doubt the other kingdoms in Lagenora learned of this."

The scene changed back to Chusacuta's swim toward Darby. The swimming Chusacuta then turned toward Vasha's ship and sent an echolocation burst.

"Stop," Circigi said.

The scene stopped. Chusacuta was angry that Circigi had somehow stopped the scene yet she could not. She flashed an angry expression toward Circigi.

"You tried to influence this ship, like Croius?" Circigi asked. "But Croius is evil. Everyone knows that. Why become something everyone hates? To get a free ride to Darby? Was swimming that tiring? No, we don't get tired like that. We have thorium cells. What was it? Free power?"

"I need not answer to you nor any cetacean," Chusacuta said.

"But still, you tried and failed," Circigi said. "Is working alone that important to you, that you arbitrarily decide right and wrong?"

"It was right for me," Chusacuta said. "There was no one around to...to..."

"To judge you. You are afraid of being judged then. Working alone has that advantage, doesn't it? You can do whatever you want. Right and wrong mean nothing. But that's why we have pods. Our leaders socialize the pod to teach us right and wrong. But you bypass that socializing when you work alone."

"When will you understand? Socializing gets in the way! Wasteful! It blocks all efforts to accomplish my work. If I had abided by all social standards, I could have never created a fertility device, not even in the half-life of thorium!"

The scene resumed. The swimming Chusacuta continued sending sonic bursts at the ship. The ship sent weak replies, and it changed course toward Chusacuta. But it learned her frequency, and it used it against her by stunning her. A great net lowered and pulled her up, along with many unlucky fish that happened to be in the vicinity. Then an aura surrounded the ship, an aura that transformed into ghostly tentacles, each one swimming with images of human activity that caused a loss to other humans and other life forms, the tentacles of power and misery, the elevation of some by the suppression and destruction of others.

The image of once-swimming Chusacuta-in-the-net vanished, but the image of the ship and its tentacles remained strong. The implants throbbed in Chusacuta's forehead, and a great tentacle reached out from the ship toward her head.

"Destroy the tentacle, Chusacuta!" Circigi begged. "Destroy it with an echolocation blast!"

Chusacuta sent a small blast toward the tentacle, but the tentacle grew stronger and rushed all the more quickly toward Chusacuta.

"You must use all your thorium might to destroy it!" Circigi said.

"I cannot without destroying my own cells!" she screamed.

"Then you must sacrifice your cells to destroy the tentacle! This is the choice spoken by Queen Pollyenpa."

"I'll lose my echolocation! I'll be like the blind! The blind!" she screamed.

"Then I will help you!"

Circigi stood behind Chusacuta, placed his hands on each side of her head, and focused her forehead on the tentacle. He directed all his thorium energy into hers, and both turned back into dolphin shape. Circigi yelled from the strain, Chusacuta screamed, and the energy directed from Circigi thrust from Chusacuta's melon, causing it to blast outward and destroy the image of the reaching tentacle, the other tentacles, and the ship. The image faded, and the two returned to Gathona in modern times. Chusacuta collapsed onto Circigi, and he returned to human shape in time to catch her and tend to the massive injury on her forehead. Her melon was gone, and in its place was a gaping hole.

"Change to humanoid shape," Circigi said. "Please. Humans don't have a pepona. You'll bleed less."

Chusacuta changed to her humanoid form.

"I...the implants...are they gone?"

"Yes, Chusacuta! The implants are gone! You're free of it. You're free!"

"I'm so sorry. I meant to swim all the way to Darby. And I was going to help a dolphin couple conceive. But it was going to be of my own engineering. I could never get away with that in Lagenora. I had to keep the test details a secret, so I could perfect the device such that no one would know how I engineered the child. I was selfish and wrong, Circigi. Vasha had me under control...but she was influenced herself, Circigi. Croius had been there. I wanted to be more powerful than Croius, to have more influence over Vasha and the Darby folk than he. I was foolish, Circigi."

"Shhh. It's all over now. You're going to heal and be as cheerful as ever."

"I...Circigi...I can't echolocate. I'm *apeponic*. I've lost everything. Do you understand? I've lost everything."

"No, no you haven't."

"Yes! I have! How can you understand what it's like?"

"Because I wear glasses! My eyes don't see too well, remember? Yeah, it's not a thing when others are handicapped. But you learn to adapt, Chusacuta. We'll help you. Queen Brela makes a little hat you can wear to aid in echolocation."

"Condemned to wear a hat? I'd rather die, Circigi."

"No."

"I'm giving up. Tell the others I'm sorry. I can't live if I can't live alone," Chusacuta said.

There was still an after-effect aura around the two from their time travel. The mother seal and the older pup had now gone, leaving the younger pup behind. It had been abandoned as it had failed to thrive as it should. It would soon perish.

"Come here, little pup," Circigi said.

Circigi continued to cradle Chusacuta's head while he beckoned the pup over. The pup at first made no effort and was willing to let the world decide its fate. But Circigi urged it over, calling and mimicking a seal's voice. The little pup struggled over, slowly but with what little determination it had left.

"Come on, little pup. You can make it. Come on over," Circigi continued.

The pup did make it, but it collapsed from fatigue. Circigi reached for the pup, picked it up, and placed it on Chusacuta's shoulder.

"Oh what a sorry mess we are," Chusacuta said. "The Misfits Three."

"Just relax, Chusacuta. Make some soft squeaks. Very soft. The vibrations will help heal your forehead."

If ever a violin could sound abrasive, Chusacuta's squeaks did a close approximation. She struggled to bring concordance and harmony to her squeaks, but the dissonance was disheartening. Then the little pup moved and molded itself to Chusacuta's forehead, covering her open wound and absorbing the vibrations from her squeaks. At first Chusacuta's squeaks were muffled, but then they took on new sonic resonance, much as the body of a guitar brings warmth and character to vibrating strings.

A strange energy transferred to the pup. The pup glowed briefly, and then its fins curled and grew in length and curled some more. Chusacuta reached for the pup with her hand. The pup purred like a kitten and uncurled its fins, which now had become quite long. It then extended a fin each to Chusacuta and Circigi, as if to shake hands in friendship, and without warning, it shook its fins as if shaking off a bad day and revealed that its fins were now wings. It was the birth of Chusigi.

"Look!" Chusacuta said.

The pup flapped its wings, lifted itself into the air, and then it flew to the top of the waterfall, where it found food that other seals could not reach.

"I feel like we are the parents of a new species," Chusacuta said.

"Yes, Chusacuta. Bringing new life gives life back to us. I guess that's why couples are so desperate to conceive. In a way you are right—we are the parents of the new pup."

Chusacuta smiled and then fell half asleep.

Chusacuta awoke to distant shouting. She and Circigi stood and turned around. Running from the beach were Metavasi and Litivito, and following at a slower pace were Garadon, Queen Brela, and Queen Pyamara. Circigi and Chusacuta waved and walked toward the group, as they knew they were ready to return home.

"The implants are gone," Chusacuta said.

Brela gave Chusacuta a hug, as did Pyamara and the porpoises.

"There are many therapies available for *apeponisis*," Queen Pyamara said.

"Yes, I will start treatment at once," Queen Brela said.

"Don't use the fertility device yet," Chusacuta said.

The two queens exchanged quizzical expressions.

"There are some adjustments I wish to make," Chusacuta added.

Chusacuta nodded to the two queens, and they nodded back. Chusacuta then looked back on Gathona with her own eyes and spoke:

"Now that I have only eyes with which to see, the island looks so much different. There's a certain beauty to unexpected harmonies. I don't think the island would look as nice if I planned it out. I guess...maybe...maybe echolocation isn't so important as our own eyes after all."

Chusacuta winked at Circigi and smiled. Circigi returned the wink and smile, the two hugged, and the group left Gathona.

Debbie's Trial

Interior of R.S.A. Seamount, South Atlantic Ocean

It was dark but dreary,
Isolating yet cacophonous.
Damp,
Ambiothargic,
Earthquatic,
And frightening for the humans:
A count of two.

Debbie Dayla, the younger daughter of Roger Dayla, stood with her father in the center of an arena.

The arena of dusky dolphins and electric rays.

"Father? Father?!" Debbie called.

"I'm here," Roger said. "You're safe."

"I can't see," Debbie said. "I can hear but not see."

Roger could only see a few feet in front. Distance was denied by a blindingly strong spotlight two body-lengths in diameter restricting the pair's escape.

"I hear strange sounds," Debbie said.

"Strange creatures," Roger said. "I hear squeals like dolphins and gurgling like...like I don't know what. I can't see them with this light."

"I don't see light, Father. I see nothing, unless..." Debbie said as she looked directly at the light above. "Unless I look into the light. It's very dim."

"The explosion...the flash," Roger said. "Now we are here. It happened so quickly. We—"

"*Slappaboom!*" crashed hand and fist into a podium of a humanoid-ish creature with an aura bordering its silhouette.

"As command, all in order. All in order!" the creature called from behind the podium, which was perched upon a high-mounted balcony. "In trial now here."

"The flash from the explosion injured your retina," Roger said. "Don't worry. When we return home, I'll take you to the best—"

"Your attention, humans!" the creature from the high podium said to Roger and Debbie.

"What is this? Who are you?" Roger asked.

From the darkness all about, dolphin-like and electric ray-like creatures responded with squeaky-grating jeers, like echolocation sounds gone awry.

"My title as Supreme Prosecutor of Rhynchus Prime, in the Kingdom of Rhynchus. As command, your address to me as Suproc."

"Suproc. We are friendly people. We bear no ill will—"

"*You bear no ill will*," Suproc mocked.

Jeers faded into squeaky-clicking sounds of disapproval.

"You bore an ill drill that killed and destroyed," Suproc said. "Yes, we can speak as you, human, with your disgusting lust for verbs."

"How was I to know about this, about you and these...these..." Roger trailed.

"Your witness of these human obscenities, citizens of Rhynchus Prime and Lagenors from other kingdoms," said a voice at floor level.

A spotlight shone on the voice, and a humanoid dressed in a white and black uniform, named Vorlac, walked toward Roger and Debbie.

"Respect for Rhynchos and Lagenors humans have not," Vorlac said.

"Vorlac," Suproc said. "Your presence sooner than expected."

"The formalities of my introduction, our need have not," Vorlac said. "To my Rhynchos and Lagenors this understanding—insults from the humans with us as name of 'these', insults toward us as petty, as nothing, as 'these'. Insults toward Lagenors and toward the Kingdom of Rhynchus."

The audience, who had been in the dark, now became visible as new lights shone on them with increasing brightness. Roger could see them. Debbie could not see, but Roger trembled from seeing the humanoids in the lower levels, the half-humanoid/half-dolphins in the middle levels, and full dolphins in upper levels splashing water down from individual tubs. Occasionally there was an electric ray in a tub here and there.

"As this as may, Vorlac. Trial we have, and the start now," Suproc said.

Suproc motioned for Vorlac to return to the side, but Vorlac walked only a few steps away from Roger and Debbie.

"On trial for treason with you," Suproc said to Roger and Debbie. "As fact, in stance before us for review of you, Roger Dayla, and you, Debbie Dayla."

"You know our names?" Roger gasped.

"New knowledge of you with us," Suproc said. "As allegation against the humans, breach through outer kingdom wall. As allegation against the humans, destruction of private property. As allegation..."

Suproc continued listing the charges against Roger and Debbie.

"Father, what's going on?" Debbie whispered. "The way they talk—it's weird."

"We must get out of here," Roger whispered. "Hold my hand. I see a way to escape!"

Roger pulled Debbie's arm as he dashed toward an opening at a corner of the arena. The crowd gasped and screeched, like birds caught in the squeaky hinges of a door. Vorlac projected electrical waves from his hands at the area surrounding the two. Tentacles rose from the ground and grabbed the human legs. Roger and Debbie fell to their knees with the tentacles holding fast. The spotlight followed them during the attempt and remained focused on their position.

"There, a sight by the humans for our judgment," Vorlac said.

Vorlac waved his hands and motioned the tentacles to form restraining chairs, which the tentacles did. Roger and Debbie now sat with arms and legs held tightly. The chairs were like hard rubber but in fact were made of advanced sea sponges that responded to the local citizens' commands.

"As allegation against the humans, murder," Suproc said. "And now the addition of another allegation: an escape attempt from trial. As the father of Debbie, you, Roger Dayla, have responsibility for your plea. As my command for your response, Roger, the plea."

"We are innocent, of course," Roger said.

Boos mixed with chatter, and slapping water echoed from the audience.

"As command," Suproc said. "Exposition of the first evidence."

Vorlac waved his hands in the air. The lights dimmed, the audience disappeared from view, and a holographic image appeared of the AC Sniar in the Atlantic Ocean.

"How did you get this imagery?" Roger asked. "You couldn't have tapped into a spy satellite—this projection is from the side, as if..."

"As if?" Vorlac echoed. "Our citizens with watch on you and yours. Their vision in recording now before us."

The projection had started as a wide-view of the AC Sniar, but now it was zoomed in on Roger, Connie, and Debbie.

"This test marks a significant event in energy exploration," the projection of Roger said to the projection of Connie. "For decades, men have struggled to release the energy stores of the ocean. The high cost and stress of deep drilling, pressure management, and the threat of mega-gallon spills will be a thing of the past."

"Do I get to see the thingy do its thingy?" Connie asked.

"You mean the new drilling apparatus? The SOZOD? No, it's too dangerous. You will remain here," Roger said.

"Aw, c'mon," Connie said. "Debbie gets to go. Please?"

Connie fluttered her eyes, tipped her head to one side, finger-brushed her long curly hair, and then whipped her hair to the other side.

"No, honeycake, not this time," Roger said. "I want you to stay here and keep your mother company. She gets very nervous during these test trials. And you know I would have Debbie stay here if I could. But she is needed to operate the SOZOD."

"But that's no fun," Connie said, now placing a hand on her hip and shifting it to the side in a stance of determination. "I can help with the SOZOD. I watched Debbie operate it in Doctor Kukovich's lab."

"You take after me when it comes to adventure," Roger said. "But it's just too dangerous. Besides, who will operate the camera from the aircraft carrier? You're my favorite camera girl."

"Hmmph," Connie said, and she pouted.

"There now," Roger said. "Tell you what, once the first test is complete, I'll let you take a boat from the carrier to the drilling rig and see the second test. Deal?"

"Deal," Connie said with her fingers crossed behind her back.

The projection stopped, and Vorlac held two crossed fingers in the air.

"Crossed fingers," Vorlac said for all to see. "As fact for humans, with crossed fingers a sign of treachery."

"She should have stayed on the carrier," Roger whispered to Debbie.

"She wanted to be with us, Father," Debbie whispered back.

Vorlac waved his crossed fingers at Roger and Debbie. A puff of wind pulled the air from Roger and Debbie. Unable to speak or breathe, they gasped.

"As command to humans, silence," Vorlac said.

"In continuation, Vorlac," Suproc said.

Vorlac waved his hands. The Daylas breathed, and the projection resumed, but the scene changed. The aircraft carrier AC Sniar was in the distance and the drilling platform was close-by. A small boat, which had originated from the carrier, was now arriving at the drilling platform. This platform was a full drilling rig structure of semi-submersible design, with ballasted water-tight pontoons below the ocean surface and the platform above. Roger and Debbie were shown boarding the platform from the small boat.

"Doctor Dayla and Miss Dayla, welcome," said the drill platform's foreman.

"We are here for the first drilling test," Roger said.

"Yes, sir," the foreman said. "Doctor Kukovich is expecting you. This way, please."

The foreman led the two along the drilling platform. Instead of a derrick, the platform contained a double-walled silo-like structure. The inner silo was topped with a dome while an umbrella-shaped roof covered both silos, with supports elevating the roof above the silos to allow for air to exchange between the outer silo and the outside. Coolant pipes with aluminum fins circled the outside wall of the inner silo yet remained inside the outer silo. Heated air from these fins rose to the top between the silos, hooked over the outer silo's edge, and slipped beyond the underside of the roof until it escaped into the atmosphere.

It was inside this structure to where the foreman led Roger and Debbie. The inner silo, known as the drilling bay, was completely protected from the elements of rain and sun. At the center of the bay was a large, cylindrical tube mounted below double arches. Torsional side supports ran from the tube to the inner silo walls. Thick black, red, and green cables ran from a side generator up one leg of the arches and onto the top end of the cylinder. Written along the cylinder's side in large letters was the acronym "SOZOD". In smaller print below "SOZOD" was "Sonic Zonaton Device".

The projection froze.

"For the record and as fact, the weapon against Rhyncho citizens here now before us," Vorlac said. "With name of SOZOD. SOZOD!"

The audience echoed the name briefly then broke into uncoordinated water splashing, teeth gnashing, and seat bashing.

"As command, composure," Suproc said. "The major crime as yet ahead. Vorlac—the continuation."

The holographic image changed from the SOZOD to Connie having a conversation with Vicia Sniar. Vicia held up a mirror while Connie touched up her makeup.

"Hold the mirror steady," Connie said.

"It's hard to hold the mirror out here with the wind and waves," Vicia said.

"I have to look good," Connie said.

"For what?"

"Brian," Connie said.

"You want to distract him while he's working. I do believe my talents are rubbing off on you," Vicia said.

"If I distract him enough, maybe he'll propose to me," Connie said, still working on her makeup.

"Sneaky," Vicia said.

"It's a good way to protect my investment," Connie said.

"Of course," Vicia said. "But I overheard your father. He said —"

"No one can keep a Dayla down, not even another Dayla," Connie said as she put her makeup away.

"Connie, for once I think maybe you should stay here on the AC Sniar," Vicia said.

"What!? Is this Vicia speaking? Vicia Sniar? The one who manipulated me into stealing that Audi for a joy ride?" Connie remarked.

"Yeah, well, that was on land. This is the ocean. There are sharks out there and other things," Vicia said.

"You make it sound like I'm going for a swim," Connie said. "Well I'm not. I'm disappointed in you, Vicia."

It was no use. Connie ran from Vicia and climbed down into a boat. Vicia looked around as if afraid of being caught then leaned over a railing and watched Connie unhitch the boat and fire up the engine.

"What will I tell your mother?" Vicia called. "And what about operating that camera for your father?"

But Connie did not respond. Instead, she sped over toward the drilling platform.

"Oh, oh, oh!" Vicia said. "Mrs. Dayla will have a fit for sure!"

The projection stopped briefly then resumed with a projection of Connie arriving at the drilling rig.

"Miss Dayla!" said a surprised crewman as Connie turned off the boat's engine.

"Don't just stand there. Help me up!" Connie ordered.

The crewman helped Connie from the boat to the drilling platform, but Connie did not thank him.

"Ack-hem," Connie coughed to the crewman.

She tapped her foot on the deck impatiently.

"Well?" she demanded. "Where are they?"

"Oh, begging your forgiveness, Miss Dayla," the crewman said. "Your father and your sister and the Kukoviches are in the drilling bay. If I could lead the way, I'd be very—"

"No. Just point," Connie said.

"Up the stairs across the catwalk," said the crewman. "There's a door leading inside."

Connie walked up the steps and across the catwalk. She opened the door and entered the outer silo wall. Water now sprayed down on the aluminum fins to cool them, and rising steam was the result. Connie could not see very far up through the steam, but she did see the door to the inner silo.

Connie opened the door and entered the drilling bay. She immediately heard voices from several levels down. The holographic projection showed Connie on a walkway along the inside edge of the cylindrical bay. The projection then panned down the bay across lower walkways (also attached to the inside of the bay) until it focused on Roger, Debbie, Brian, and Doctor Kukovich. Debbie wore a headset with earphones and microphone, while Doctor Kukovich and Brian operated controls and monitored progress.

"The Zonaton beam calibration is complete," Doctor Kukovich said. "We are ready for a surface-water test."

"Excellent," projection Roger said. "Proceed with the test."

The projection stopped.

"For all to see," Vorlac said, "the beginning of the humans' weapon use. As question for Roger, the creation of the SOZOD from you?"

"Yes, the Sonic Zonaton Device is my creation," Roger said.

"Then denial of murderous weapon, you not have," Vorlac said. "Your defense in this trial of little value."

"Perhaps the Daylas should receive representation," said a voice from a corner different from the one Vorlac approached.

"Recognition of voice by me," Vorlac said, "though with no pleasure."

The audience reacted in shock when a spotlight shone on the new voice and revealed its identity.

"Prince Sparfiacus!" yelled several fulltrans in the audience.

"My lord, a formal court in need of formal speech," Vorlac said. "But we in apuzzlement. Your speech as like the humans. Why? And why with you in their defense? As recent fact, your leadership of the seadogs against the humans and their SOZOD. As fact, my brother Korlan as one of your seadogs. As question then, of the other seadogs—Tugan, Brela, and Metavasi—as they in defense of the humans?"

"No," Sparfiacus said. "Just me."

"For a royal Rhyncho citizen..." stumbled Suproc. "...in defense of humans? Prince Sparfiacus, our loyalty and respect for you, for King Acus, and for Queen Sparla we have—for the moment. But this action..."

"As request, a recess," Vorlac said.

"As command, a recess," Suproc said.

Vorlac waved his hands, and the tentacles released Roger and Debbie. Vorlac grabbed Roger's arm while Sparfiacus took Debbie's. Four additional guards approached. Two led the way and two followed up the rear. The group then proceeded from the arena to a holding cell for Roger and Debbie.

The holding cell was very simple. There were two cots, a chair, a small table, an alcove for washing up and waste extrication, and another alcove with a bowl of recirculating fresh water aside a bowl of live anchovy fish in recirculating sea water. The walls, floor, and ceiling bore swirling patterns of fluorescent blue and green and in fact were made of sea sponge as were all walls, floors, and ceilings in the dolphinic habitat. The cell door was made of intermeshing tentacles that receded into the doorway upon command or advanced across the doorway into themselves upon another command.

"As command, by my leave for you," Vorlac said to the four guards.

Vorlac waved a hand, the cell door unmeshed, the guards left, and Vorlac waved his hand again to re-mesh the cell door, leaving Vorlac, Sparfiacus, Roger, and Debbie.

"Highly irregular, and certainly out of order," Vorlac said to Sparfiacus. "And what of King Acus? With he the knowledge of your borderline treason?"

"There is no treason here," Sparfiacus said.

"Agg, your style, the style of humans," Vorlac said.

"We must make them feel comfortable," Sparfiacus said. "Speak as they do, Vorlac."

"The disgust...it...my ethos...how...the words," Vorlac said.

Suproc approached the cell, but the door did not unmesh. Instead, Suproc spoke through a mesh opening.

"My lord," Suproc said.

"Yes, I will let you know when to resume the trial," Sparfiacus said. "Please excuse us."

Suproc cringed at Sparfiacus's use of human-style speech. He shot a quizzical look at Vorlac, but Vorlac threw his hands up as if to say, "I with agreement, I with agreement."

"My service in your hands," Suproc bowed, and he left.

"Thank you," Roger said to Sparfy. "We are in your debt. I didn't think we would find an ally in this place."

"You will find no ally here," Vorlac said to Roger, and then he turned to Sparfiacus. "There, I spoke like the humans. And again. Satisfied?"

"It's a start," Sparfiacus said.

"If you're not an ally, what are you?" Roger asked.

"Not *what*," Vorlac said. "He is a *who*, though I don't expect you or your daughter to understand."

"Are you people like us?" Debbie asked. "Strange. I don't sense anything from you."

"My daughter is temporarily blind," Roger said.

"Temporarily," Debbie echoed.

"The accident—" Roger started.

"It was no accident," Vorlac said. "You attacked the Kingdom of Rhynchus, what you call the R.S.A. Seamount. That is where you are now."

"You mean to say that we are now inside the R.S.A. Seamount?" Roger asked.

"Yes," Sparfy said. "We are holding you here until we decide what to do with you."

"Decide? What do you mean?" Roger asked.

"Your fate was sealed the moment you breached the seamount," Vorlac said. "Death is the customary penalty in these cases."

"No, no, no!" Debbie cried. "How can civilized people do such a thing!"

"They're not real people," Roger said.

"There, you see my lord?" Vorlac said. "When a human says that other life forms aren't people, they speak metaphorically. What they really mean is that the other life forms are not worthy, because humans believe any life form but human is worthy of death by their own hands."

Sparfy stood next to Debbie.

"Touch my face," said Sparfy.

Debbie touched his face.

"You have eyes, a nose, mouth, and ears like a person, but your skin is very smooth, moist, and thick, like wet rubber," Debbie said.

Vorlac walked over to the anchovies, thrust his hand in the bowl, retrieved a fish, and pushed it into his mouth as a snack. Sparfy looked at him in surprise, that Vorlac should eat.

"It must be from the explosion. My thorium cells are damaged," Vorlac said.

"See Queen Brela as soon as possible," Sparfy said.

"She is overloaded by the many injured electric rays, dolphins, and porpoises—including my brother Korlan and your friend Princess Adelfarina," Vorlac said.

"We'll get by," Sparfy said.

"Getting by is not enough!" Vorlac said, getting angry and reverting to his native style. "Their lives as worthy as not! All humans with destruction on their minds, the acts of hate, assault, murder! And we as get by?!? My Prince of Rhynchus with words of the human, words of pacification? Where the words of a king? Of leadership?!"

"Vorlac. Peace and calmness of mind inwith you now," Sparfy said. "So the humans kill. Should we retaliate? That is the implication. But I believe that we as aware life forms should learn to respect other forms of life. We should not kill without good reason, and even then we should mourn the loss of the other life. That is the primary purpose of the seadogs, to preserve and respect life."

"Of course, my lord," Vorlac said as he grabbed another anchovy and tossed it in his mouth. "Respect for other life. But when those other life forms don't respect us, then what? We cannot wait for them to kill us. You yourself led us—"

"Yes, I led my seadogs into battle against the SOZOD," Sparfy said.

"You...you...caused me to go blind?" Debbie asked Sparfy.

"No, my dear, that was my brother's doing," Vorlac said. "The special explosive that destroyed your father's SOZOD was Korlan's creation. Metavasi, being the quickest of the seadogs, deployed the explosive, but it was Korlan's creation."

"But both Metavasi and Korlan acted under my order," Sparfy said. "It was necessary to stop your machine."

"You?" Debbie asked Sparfy.

"Yes, Debbie, yes!" Vorlac said. "He ordered the attack. Do you think you are special? Because you are human? You inhabit a minority portion of Earth. We inhabit the majority, the ocean. We are the significant, you are the lesser. Do you understand how little you are? You are nothing!"

Silence filled the room with the exception of the running fresh and salt water bowls. Debbie welled up in anger, and she could not contain herself.

"I hate you," Debbie said with her voice growing into a strong, harsh yell. "I hate you, Sparfy and your seadogs!"

Debbie blindly swung her arms at Sparfy, but he merely stepped away. Vorlac laughed.

"You have no power here!" Vorlac said.

"I had hoped to offer you counsel and advice for the trial," Sparfy said. "I am not without mercy."

"You have done enough. Leave us alone for a moment, please," said Roger. "Or is that not permitted? If you have mercy, then show it."

"We will leave—but only for a moment. When we return, you will both go back on trial. And despite your hostilities toward me and toward my people, I *will* do my best to defend you," Sparfy said.

Sparfy waved his hand. The cell door opened. Vorlac left first, and Sparfy started to leave, but Roger called him.

"What kind of beings are you? Do you let your prisoners starve?" Roger asked.

"Your cell with supply of fresh water and food!" Vorlac retorted. "Anchovies as a food for us and you, human!"

"Wait," Sparfy said.

Sparfy walked over to the bowl of anchovies. He touched the wall next to it, hummed something, and two plates formed from the sponge wall. Next, Sparfy grabbed several live anchovies from the bowl and placed them on the plates. The fish flapped on the plates. Sparfy held his hands over the plates as if warming his hands over a fire, but in fact his hands (through sonic waves like microwaves) heated the anchovies and thus cooked them. He then hummed something else, and different waves from his hands sloughed off the anchovies' bones and excess salt. He touched the sponge wall again, and two forks were produced. He placed the forks on the plates and touched the sponge wall one last time. Two cups formed, and he dipped those cups in fresh water. He placed the cups and plates on the table and left with Vorlac.

"Thank you," Roger said as Sparfy left earshot.

Debbie did not want to eat. She yelled and screamed, and as she did so, the mesh door expanded until it was completely solid, and the walls formed cones and divots such that the louder Debbie screamed, the more her sound was absorbed (and consumed) by the sponge walls until at maximum level of screaming, Debbie's voice could not be heard.

The shock of not being able to hear herself scream threw Debbie into shock. She stopped screaming and sat in place, motionless. The walls smoothed, and the doorway contracted from solid to a mesh with ample small openings.

"Here, eat some of these," Roger said to Debbie, now that the walls had smoothed enough for her to hear him.

Debbie complied.

Roger ate too, and the two drank fresh water. Then Roger helped Debbie to her side on a cot, and she fell asleep. Roger pulled a blanket over Debbie, and as he did he noticed the cot was also made of sponge, dark blue it was. It molded itself to Debbie's form, and it rocked Debbie back and forth gently as if she were in a hammock on a breezy day.

Roger paced back and forth in the cell. He thought about how to escape. He touched the walls and door, searching for weakness. None. The walls felt like hardened rubber, yet wherever he touched, a slight vibration undulated below the wall's surface, as if something replied to his initial contact. Roger touched various parts of the wall, drawing his fingers along in a single direction until he was practically at the mesh door.

"These walls changed shape when Debbie screamed. Could they be influenced to show us the way out of the seamount? And if they could, would we survive the extreme water pressure as we tried to surface?" Roger asked himself.

"No and no," Sparfy spoke in a low voice through the mesh door.

"It's you!" Roger said in an excited yet low voice. "But...what are you?"

"You still don't know?" Sparfy said while maintaining his hushed voice.

"You can't be human," Roger said.

"We're not," Sparfy said.

"Then what?" Roger asked.

"When you were in the arena, did you notice the many different kinds of citizens of Rhynchus?" Sparfy asked.

"There were dolphins, rays, and humanoids," Roger said. "And this Rhynchus. Is it really the inside of R.S.A. Seamount?"

"Yes. *Rhynchus* is the name of my kingdom, at least my father's kingdom. He is the king, King Acus, and I am his son, the prince."

"And is Vorlac royalty too?" Roger asked.

"Not quite," Sparfiacus said. "He and his brother Korlan are of Clan Zigo, a powerful family with ties to electric rays. So is the Suproc, whose name is Krivat, also of Clan Zigo. Should anything happen to my family, Clan Acus, the Zigos would usurp the throne and rule Rhynchus."

"But Korlan is one of your seadogs? You trust him?" Roger asked.

"Yes, he is a seadog, a knight of the sea," Sparfy said.

"What power can they have?" Roger said.

"Korlan is Archray, so he has power over all the electric rays, including Vorlac and Suproc. Vorlac is Chief Scientist and a leading prosecutor," Sparfy continued. "Tugan is actually King Tugan of Phocayna, what you call the Yakhont Seamount, and Brela is Queen Brela and is Tugan's wife. She is Chief Physician of Phocayna."

"I heard mention before of Metavasi as a seadog," Roger said.

"You have good ears, almost worthy of a cetacean. Metavasi is the son of Tugan and Brela. He has exceptional speed, so much so that no other cetacean in Lagenora can catch him. Other seamounts have offered to make him king, even though his subjects would be dolphins, but his heart is dalli porpoise, and so he remains a prince in Phocayna with his parents and the dalli citizens he loves. You would call him a Dall's porpoise though. I could go on at length. You surprise me, Roger. Most humans have no interest in us."

"I'm still not sure who you are," Roger said. "And I'm confused—you speak of electric rays and porpoises as if they were like us with arms and legs. Are you an electric ray? Or a porpoise? Or what?"

"I and many citizens here are dolphins," Sparfy said.

"Dolphins have flippers and swim. They don't have hands and feet," Roger said.

"We aren't just any kind of dolphin. We are dusky dolphins, at least the descendants of dusky dolphins. Some of us have retained the original ancestral form. Such a citizen is a *voitran*. Some can transform from the ancestral form into a humanoid shape with full arms, hands, legs, and feet, as I am before you. I am a *fulltran*. One who can only transform partway is a *halftran*. But we are not human. We still contain the genetics of a dolphin in my case, or a porpoise in Tugan's case, or an electric ray in Vorlac's case. There are other cetaceans involved. I know some orcas who can transform into humanoid shape—they too are fulltrans. All fulltrans are intelligent and can speak in your language as well as others."

"Prince Sparfiacus," Roger said. "You are very intelligent, and you seem concerned for our well-being. I implore you—let us go. We didn't know about your kind and will leave you alone. I will order a full withdrawal from R.S.A. Seamount. Dayla Industries will—"

"Will drill somewhere else, is that it?" Sparfy said. "Or another human corporation will drill—maybe here, maybe in another seamount—but somewhere."

"What good will it do to make an example of us? I heard Vorlac say that our punishment will be death."

"If the arena so chooses, yes, that will be your punishment, though it will be a blow to my heart, as I regret loss of animal life," Sparfy said.

"We're not animals," said Roger.

Sparfy laughed.

"It may be funny to you, but Debbie and I are in mortal danger," Roger said.

"Yes, you are, which is why I have chosen to defend you. I laugh not at your predicament but how you humans believe that you are not animals. Nonetheless, I will do what I can to secure leniency, but it will be difficult. There's more to this trial than your actions. Political power in Rhynchus rests on how much sway the Zigos can wield over the arena audience."

"Oh. I see. So you're not defending us because of concern for us humans, you simply wish to hold onto your power as Prince of Rhynchus," Roger said.

"Taken to an extreme, maybe. That's not the only reason. Roger, I wish all life could live in harmony on this planet. But the food chain says otherwise. You humans place yourselves atop your food chain, we Rhynchos and all those of Lagenora place ourselves on top of ours. I've even considered befriending humans on a large scale for some future hope of world peace."

"And why don't you?" Roger asked.

"The world of animals doesn't work that way. Look at your society. You have interdependent economies—one country affects the other. Before that, you had wars, or colonization, or some other means of one country overrunning another. Do you believe we could simply befriend your United States, and that would be the end of it? No. There would be desire for trade, and with trade comes desire for resources. Some Lagenors would petition to do what you just tried but in reverse—drill for your resources and trade them back to our kingdom. It follows then that some Lagenors would leave Lagenora and live in your country. Don't underestimate us—we are intelligent and highly adaptable. We would prosper and secure positions of power in your country. Those humans who normally hold those positions would then be pushed downward. Don't you see the impact? It's not unlike colonization, like the Europeans of old who displaced the Native Americans and took their land. We would be taking yours, even if done peacefully."

"So I don't understand," Roger said. "Are you a Rhyncho or a Lagenor?"

"Both," Sparfy said, and he pulled out a map with "Connie" written on it.

"That's Connie's map!" Roger said.

"It was found floating in the wreckage," Sparfy said. "It shows our region with your names. Now I will give you a map with our names."

Sparfy touched the blank side of the map. Lines appeared outlining the region, and once those lines settled, Sparfy passed the map to Roger.

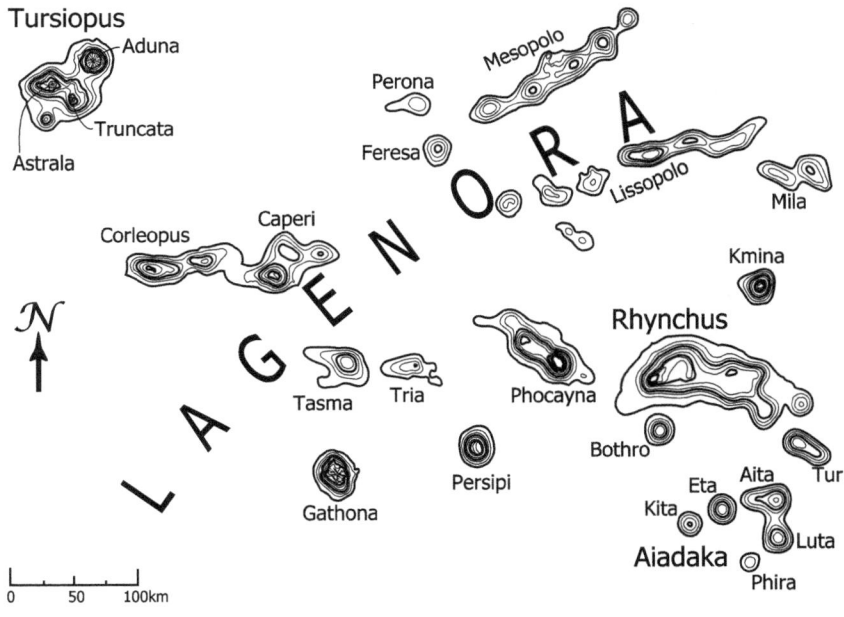

A heavily-built humanoid approached the cell door beside Sparfy.

"My lord," the humanoid said.

"King Tugan," Sparfy said. "This is Roger Dayla, and on the cot is Debbie Dayla."

"Hello," Roger said.

"With regrets," Tugan said to Sparfy.

"What is it?" Sparfy said.

"Vorlac and Krivat, they—" Tugan started.

"Wait," Sparfiacus said.

He closed his eyes, hummed, and touched the spongy wall next to the door frame.

"Yes, there is unrest," Sparfiacus started. "The Zigos are using the delay as a means to create bifurcation and to leverage power over King Acus and myself."

"How?" Roger asked.

"The privacy issue, Sparfy," Tugan said.

"My closest friends call me, 'Sparfy,' to answer your quizzical stare," Sparfy said. "But to the privacy issue, yes, it may interest you to know, Roger, that very little in Lagenora is truly private. Quite literally, these walls have ears. They are living beings, sponges that are cared for by our people, and our people also use them as communication conduits to both send messages and to see what is happening around the kingdom. They are aware of our very conversation."

"Then—" Roger started.

"They believe that if you are not punished by death soon, your corrupt ways will infest our culture, starting with those who have the closest contact with you, meaning myself of course. And so the Zigos will make claim that the royal family is being subverted by outsiders, and that now is the time for strong measures to be taken by a family true to the kingdom, the Zigos, etc. It's nothing that hasn't happened before, but I cannot stand here and chat with you all day and night. I must attend to this disquiet, and that means we must return to trial. Wake your daughter," Sparfy said.

Roger turned from the door and walked to the cot. As if eavesdropping on the conversation, Vorlac arrived in preparation for ensuring the Daylas' return to trial.

"King Tugan here, and why?" Vorlac asked, then with sarcasm he said, "As recommendation, away with you into hunt of mercury-filled tilefish."

Tugan lunged at Vorlac and started to strangle him, but Sparfy intervened.

"Respect for me, King Tugan, respect," Vorlac said.

"I'll show you respect," Tugan said, and he whipped a fist toward Vorlac, but again Sparfy intervened.

"Like humans your speech when madness in you," Vorlac laughed.

"Enough!" Sparfy said.

"But he," Tugan said.

"King Tugan—don't let Vorlac get under your blubber," Sparfy said, and he closed his eyes while touching the wall. "My father sends for you, King Tugan. Please go to him at once."

"I will leave you then," Tugan said, and he left.

"Now then, the girl as prisoner with me," Vorlac said, and he interrupted Roger's attempt to wake Debbie.

"She won't wake up," Roger said. "I removed the blanket, but the cot is sticking to her. It won't let go."

"A simple thing with sticky sponge," Vorlac said.

Vorlac held a hand in the air above the sponge, hummed, and sonic waves traveled from his hand to the sponge. The sponge rippled with colors of bright blue and bright green then returned to dark blue.

"Strangeness before me," Vorlac said.

Vorlac tried again, but the sponge would not yield its grip of Debbie.

"What is it? What's the matter?" Roger panicked.

Roger clawed and beat at the sponge, but it would not let go.

"Your cessation!" Vorlac yelled, and he pointed his palm at Roger.

Sonic waves from Vorlac's palm threw Roger violently across the cell, and just before he landed, Sparfy hummed quickly and pointed to a spot on the floor, where sponge yielded slightly to cushion Roger's fall. Nevertheless, Roger was stunned by the fall.

"No change with humans! Their desire for sponge damage with no end!" Vorlac said.

Vorlac touched the sponge softly and hummed to repair the damage.

"My daughter!" Roger managed to exhale from his impaired position.

"Let me try," Sparfy said.

Sparfy held his palm above the sponge and hummed. Again the sponge glowed bright green and blue, then he held a second palm over the sponge. The sponge loosened ever so slightly but retook hold of Debbie and pulled her a little into the cot. Vorlac tried again with both palms in an effort to help Sparfy, but still the sponge wouldn't quite let go, and again it pulled Debbie a little farther into the cot. Her legs were now completely submerged.

Debbie remained sleeping during this event. In fact, it was as if the sponge kept her asleep. Vorlac whistled and chirped to signal an alarm. Suproc Krivat arrived, realized what was going on, and he too joined the effort to sonically induce the sponge to release its grip of Debbie.

"As prediction from my fears," Vorlac said. "The beginning of the contamination from the humans into the sponge complexus."

"If the contamination with continuation from the complexus to the outer wall," Suproc started, "then doom for us all. Necessary our next action, to her death for our preservation."

"No," Sparfy said. "Fear drives you to speculate the worst outcome. I sense no complexus contamination from this girl."

"Her body into the sponge with increase," Suproc said. "Contamination inevitable."

Debbie had now sunken almost completely into the sponge. Only her face—eyes, nose, and mouth—was exposed to the air.

"This has happened before," Sparfy said.

"But only to our own kind," Suproc said.

"And only to righteous citizens," Vorlac said. "Not to humans."

Other fulltrans arrived and blocked the doorway. Tugan burst in with Brela close behind.

"The alarm into my ears," Tugan said. "My return with best speed."

"Hold off the other fulltrans," Sparfy said. "Do not allow them into this cell."

"Except for me," said a voice.

Brela squirmed past other fulltrans and into the cell, with Tugan allowing only her to enter before he resumed his efforts to keep others out.

"As need, disintegration of the girl, for the good of the sponge complexus, the outer wall, in fact—for the entire sponge domain," Vorlac said. "With her death the sponge purification."

"No," Brela said, and she moved Vorlac aside.

Brela held a hand on Debbie's cheek and hummed with squeaks, clicks, and tremolos. Sparfy realized what she was doing. He too touched Debbie's cheek and also hummed with squeaks, clicks, and tremolos. Suproc Krivat continued working with the sponge, Vorlac watched from behind, and slowly, very slowly, Brela and Sparfy caused a shimmering in Debbie's skin—a sheen and a glow that caused a thin separation with the sponge. As the sponge let go, Sparfy pulled Debbie into his arms, held her, and walked away from the cot while Brela checked on Debbie's vital signs. Vorlac returned to the sponge cot with Suproc, and the two healed the sponge and checked on its health.

Debbie opened her eyes.

"Who...what...where's my father?" Debbie managed to say.

"Over here," Roger said in a weak voice.

Roger had pulled himself up to a chair, and Sparfy placed her in a chair next to Roger. Brela continued checking Debbie's condition by touching Debbie and humming a tremolo.

"Is she okay?" Roger asked.

"Her health into return of normalcy, but—" Brela said.

"You may speak as they do," Sparfy said. "Vorlac and Suproc will simply have to tolerate it."

Vorlac and Suproc Krivat looked irritated.

"How vulgar," Vorlac said.

"There is something," Brela said.

"What?" Roger asked.

Brela lifted and moved Debbie's hair, revealing a thin, sponge strip running from behind Debbie's left ear, up along her scalp, and down along the back of her right ear.

"Like *mittamat*," Sparfiacus said.

"Except the spongiont won't let go," Brela said. "It has fused into her skull."

"The what!?" Roger gasped.

"A sponge symbiont is a spongiont," Brela said. "It is a thinking, living being and is now part of Debbie."

Roger looked briefly at the stuck piece of sponge strip on Debbie's head, and he reacted as one who suddenly sees a monstrous spider on his daughter's face.

"Get it off, get it off!" Roger squirmed as he clawed at the sponge to remove it.

Sparfy held Roger back while Brela held Debbie.

Vorlac, on overhearing the conversation, left Suproc to finish repairing the sponge cot. Vorlac walked over to Debbie to see for himself.

"With witness for all, my warning with truth. The contamination!" Vorlac said, and his voice echoed beyond the meshed door and carried along to the other fulltrans, who repeated his words down a corridor where it echoed and reverberated back.

Suproc finished with the cot and walked over to Vorlac's side.

"Your negligent rule into the result of this disgusting union," Suproc said. "Only holy fulltrans with the right for a spongiont union. But this... this...ugh!"

"Unusual," Brela said loudly for many to hear. "For us the judgment who a sponge for its choice a union? Always the holy fulltran? What about a holy simian? A holy human?"

"From Brela, blasphemy against the Kingdom of Rhynchus!" Suproc said.

"A sponge has no blasphemy and has highest citizen rank. In a sponge bewith a choice, the choice of a uniont," Brela said.

"From Brela the truth," Tugan said from the doorway.

Heated discussion erupted outside the doorway. A sponge chose a human? How? Sponges chose only cetaceans or electric rays. But a simian? A hominid human? How?

"This could change things," Sparfy said.

"The trial with continuation a necessity," Suproc said.

"The trial," echoed the fulltrans in the corridor.

"Prince Sparfiacus," Vorlac said. "Despite what here as seen, an urgent need by the people for the trial's continuation."

"I see no other way," Brela said quietly to Sparfy. "But—"

"Yes?" Sparfy asked.

"Her condition changes by the moment," Brela said. "She is less than what she once was. Perhaps she should be admitted to your Curatidoma."

"This human to the house for cures?" Vorlac said. "Surely the intended destination for the human to Mortidoma instead."

"A living, chosen holy cannot go to Mortidoma," Sparfy said. "That is the death house. Vorlac, the laws of Rhynchus are clear: a union made with a spongiont makes that person a holy and that person must be treated as such. And for now, the best place for Debbie is Curatidoma where Queen Brela can treat her and the spongiont."

"For salvage of the spongiont," Vorlac suggested.

"For both spongiont and the host. Debbie could become a fulltran," Sparfiacus said.

Vorlac cringed.

"Have King Tugan escort you to Curatidoma," Sparfy said to Brela.

"Good idea," Brela said.

Tugan had assistants manage the crowd of fulltrans. Brela led the way to Curatidoma (the Rhynchus main medical center), and Tugan followed with Debbie in his arms. Roger wanted to follow, but Vorlac stopped him.

"But my daughter," Roger said.

"Our people now without patience," Suproc said.

"As command, the trial into continuation," Sparfy announced.

The fulltrans responded with a mixture of cheers supplanted with confused direction, but they returned to the arena. Suproc left for the balcony.

"Now we shall go," Sparfy said.

Vorlac took Roger by the arm while Sparfy followed.

"I would have rather had King Tugan as an escort," Roger said.

"Well, you don't get King Tugan," Vorlac sneered, mocking how humans speak. "This isn't a party. This is trial. You are to be judged."

"Why did you let Vorlac escort my father when you are so much nicer?" Debbie's voice asked Sparfy.

Surprised to hear Debbie's voice, Sparfy turned around (while still walking) to find her, but she was long out of view.

"How are you doing this?" Sparfy said aloud.

"Doing what?" Vorlac asked Sparfy, unaware of Debbie's voice being heard by Sparfy.

"Your trial plan," Sparfy said to recover.

"That as a secret, my lord, even from you," Vorlac said.

"You see?" Debbie's voice said to Sparfy. "Vorlac wants to hurt my father and me."

Sparfy held an arm out and dragged his finger along the corridor's edge as he kept pace with Vorlac and Roger. He probed the sponge complexus for an answer as to Debbie's new-found ability. The complexus replied. Sparfy then sent his thoughts through the sponge complexus and to Debbie.

"You've discovered the technique for thought projection," Sparfy said in thought to Debbie.

"What?" Debbie's voice came back, again without Vorlac or Roger able to hear.

"Only the holies have the ability," Sparfy replied. "The sponge selected you as its host—its partner in union."

"Is that why I feel like there's a megaphone in my sinuses?" Debbie's voice asked Sparfy.

"Yes," Sparfy replied. "Your spongiont gives you that feeling."

"You still didn't answer my question about Vorlac escorting my father. You are the prince, aren't you? You have the power to order Vorlac away," Debbie's voice said.

"I see you have tapped into the news network in the sponge complexus," Sparfy explained. "But I will answer. It's for balance. The kingdom would see the bias if I were to escort your father by myself. My family's position would weaken. All who see this know of this, as do I. And so, my command for the trial is practically automatic, being guided by the forces of this seamount we call Rhynchus. I don't enjoy it, but I keep my responsibilities to the people."

"I sensed what you did back there," Debbie's voice said. "I saw how you kept my father from harm when Vorlac attacked him, and I saw how you saved my life."

"It was the will of the people," Sparfy thought with a quiver in his delivery.

"No, it wasn't. I know you have to say that, but Vorlac and Krivat wanted to dissolve me into nothingness. I could feel it," Debbie said. "Strange. How could I feel it? And when you cushioned my father's fall, I didn't see that with my eyes. I'm blind. But somehow I saw it differently, like a three-dimensional image rotating rapidly in my mind."

"You were seeing with the sponge complexus," Sparfy said.

Debbie rubbed her head and felt the strip of sponge.

"Like hearing with a megaphone in reverse," Debbie's voice said. "Will it ever go away?"

Sparfy paused, removed his touch from the complexus, and thought privately, "Not unless you die."

"But I feel that I will die someday," Debbie said. "I still desire food and drink."

"It is because the spongiont, though able to continue for millions of years itself, has not converted your own cells into using thorium," Sparfy said. "I can sense that through the complexus. You did not fully convert. Perhaps this is because you are a human."

"Is there a way I can complete the conversion?" Debbie asked.

"Unknown," Sparfy said. "And you may not have the time."

"Why not?"

"The trial may decide otherwise."

Mirini and the Aliotrotes

"This is the last shipment," Sheriff Bronc said to Doctor Kukovich. "That's five million pounds of elemental mercury."

"Or the equivalent amount released into the air by humans in a year," Doctor Kukovich said.

"Let's hope this amount won't be released into the atmosphere," Sheriff Bronc said. "I still haven't heard the plan for neutralizing this mercury. Has Roger—"

"Roger Dayla is...away," Doctor Kukovich said.

"It isn't hard to guess that he's avoiding human contact in his tower. That's tough losing a daughter," the sheriff said. "Sorry. I know you lost a son. How is Deb—"

"Good afternoon, Sheriff Bronc," Debbie Dayla said.

Debbie entered the specially protected storage bunker of Dayla Industries where the five millions pounds of mercury were stored.

"It's good to see you, Debbie," the sheriff said.

"Doctor Kukovich is working on a way to split mercury into the safer elements of krypton and ruthenium through nuclear fission," Debbie said. "Unfortunately, the process requires a lot of energy and only transforms a little mercury at a time. We estimate it would take thousands of years to transform this bit of mercury. But we hope that someday we can transform mercury more efficiently. We could then capture emissions from coal-burning power plants, gold mines, and if we stretch our imagination, active volcanoes."

"Very well put, Debbie," Doctor Kukovich said. "In the meantime, we will take extra precautions to ensure this mercury does not escape into the environment, to alleviate your concern, Sheriff Bronc."

"Yes, exactly," Debbie said.

Major Kyler Bohr looked at his tracking screen. The falling satellite was projected to land somewhere on the eastern seaboard.

"Eighteen minutes," blared a voice over the public address system.

Kyler wore a three-channel headset: one channel for chief tracking coordinator, one for the chase planes awaiting visual contact, and one for emergency directives to local governments.

"Scythoc Three will impact eastern Georgia," Kyler relayed through his headset at the request of the coordinator, Haymar.

"Blackbird Five. No visual contact over California," sounded a pilot's voice through Kyler's chase-plane headset.

"No visual contact," Kyler relayed to the coordinator.

"Brunswick emergency crews, stand by," said a voice through the emergency directive channel.

Kyler adjusted the tracking of the falling satellite on his screen, and a precise target emerged—Jekyll Island near Brunswick, Georgia.

"Jekyll Island is the impact site, repeat, Jekyll Island is the impact site," Kyler said.

"Blackbird Five. Visual contact confirmed. Scythoc Three is crossing into California airspace," a pilot radioed through Kyler's headset.

"We have a visual," Kyler said.

A larger screen in Command Center showed a hazy image tumbling through the air.

"There go the solar panels," Kyler said to the coordinator.

"Blackbird Five. Picking up a radiation signature from the bogey," said the pilot.

The Command Center people now stood and looked at one another in nervous confusion.

"That can't be," Haymar said. "Bohr, can you confirm this is Scythoc Three?"

Kyler adjusted his scanners and recalculated using different algorithms.

"It is Scythoc Three. But its mass is unexpectedly greater than expected. Even without the solar panels," Kyler said.

Suddenly, Scythoc Three stopped tumbling and assumed a steady orientation.

"That wasn't me," Kyler said. "There's someone on board."

"Is the satellite altering course?" Haymar asked.

"Yes," Kyler said. "But only slightly. New landing site is downtown Brunswick."

"The President has authorized us to shoot it down if necessary," Haymar said.

"It's over the desert," Kyler said.

"Shoot it down," Haymar said.

"Blackbird Five," Kyler said. "Can you intercept?"

"Negative. Scythoc Three is too fast."

"Can you disable?"

"Negative. Cannot get radar lock. Scythoc Three is too fast," the pilot radioed back. "Blackbird Five losing visual."

The visual image of the satellite faded out.

"This is Blackbird Seven. I have a visual," said a different pilot flying farther inland.

The new visual displayed on the main Command Center screen.

"This is Blackbird Seven. I'm losing visual," called the pilot.

"Blackbird Nine should be in range next," Haymar said to Kyler.

"I have a visual," the Blackbird Nine pilot called.

The satellite now alternated between tumbling and holding a steady orientation. It was as if it tumbled on purpose, using the air drag to alter its course.

"Blackbird Nine, Command Center. Arm an AMRAAM and fire at Scythoc Three," Kyler ordered.

"Fox Three," the pilot said, indicating the missile had been fired.

The main Command Center display now went split-screen. It showed a close-up of the satellite and a tracking map of the satellite versus the missile. The missile exploded before reaching the satellite. The tracking map indicated the missile had self destructed.

"A signal from the satellite caused the missile to self destruct," Kyler said. "Whoever is in there —"

"Whoever is in there certainly knows our codes and is a threat to our national security," Haymar said.

"Visual lost," Blackbird Nine said.

"Blackbird Ten is our last chance," the coordinator said to Kyler.

"Blackbird Ten, Command Center. Arm and ready an AMRAAM missile," Kyler said.

"Authorization code received," the pilot said.

"Fire well ahead of Scythoc Three when she approaches," Kyler said.

"Affirmative," the pilot said. "I have a visual of the satellite."

The satellite now appeared on the Command Center display.

"Fire!" Kyler said.

"Fox Three," the Blackbird Ten pilot said.

Again, the Command Center display was split. One side showed the satellite, another a map of the missile path versus the satellite path. The missile launched well before the satellite, but the satellite moved quickly and appeared as if it would again evade a missile.

"Detonate!" Kyler said.

The Blackbird Ten pilot pressed a button, and the missile detonated. A fiery ball expanded, and the satellite, which appeared able to skirt past the fireball, caught the edge and disappeared from visual contact and tracking display. Kyler pressed several buttons on his panel to reestablish the position of the satellite, but the satellite's position was lost.

"Blackbird Ten, Command Center. Can you track the satellite?" Kyler radioed.

"Visual lost. Radar lost," the pilot said. "No sign of landing in Brunswick."

"Begin a search, immediately," the coordinator said in a headset.

Haymar dropped his headset and walked over to Kyler with a relieved expression on his face.

"That was close," Haymar said.

"Are we sure it was destroyed?" Kyler asked. "It could have landed in the Atlantic."

"Unidentified object crossing into California airspace," said another person tracking the incident.

"Another satellite?" Haymar asked.

"It doesn't read like any of ours," said the other tracker.

"Bohr, plot its course," Haymar said.

"Heading for Jekyll Island," Kyler said. "And it's moving incredibly fast. Too fast for us to stop. Wait. ANG Georgia has a pilot flying over Jekyll Island now."

"Warn that plane off," Haymar said.

"Unidentified object is over Alabama now. Electrical outages being reported," Kyler said. "EMP?"

"Tell the pilot to land immediately," Haymar said. "Ground all aircraft in the area!"

"This is Colonel John Von Brock of the Georgia Air National Guard. My avionics are heavily damaged. Making an emergency landing," called the pilot of the ANG Georgia plane, and his transmission ended.

"Eject," Kyler called to the pilot.

"He can't hear you," Haymar said.

"Impact in twenty seconds, sir," Kyler said.

"Blind and deaf!" the coordinator said.

Twenty seconds passed. Various tracking screens flashed and flickered in quasi-malfunctioning states before returning to normal operation.

"Bohr. Fly down to Brunswick and meet with Debbie Dayla of Dayla Industries. Work with her. Find out what's going on. And take the DF-23."

"The what? Did you say DF-23? I haven't heard of that designation," Kyler said.

"It's an experimental YF-23 aircraft modified by Dayla Industries with updated engines and heavy duty electronics to resist an EMP. It was meant as a trainer jet with room for two, but fly down by yourself. We can't spare anyone else. The DF-23 will get you to Brunswick quicker than anything else we have. We never thought we'd need it over U.S. soil, but here we are. Now suit up and get going. And don't crash the bird!"

"Yes sir," Kyler said.

Kyler left Command Center in South Dakota and flew down to Georgia in the DF-23 jet plane. The first thing he noticed was that this bird had a speedy supercruise mode. Sure, the regular YF-23 could supercruise at Mach 1.6, but these new engines combined with a superior airframe allowed the DF-23 to hold Mach 2.9 with ease.

"It's meant for Mach 2.9," he said to himself.

Kyler was given the okay to fly supersonic provided he kept his altitude high, and of course the aircraft preferred the higher altitude. He'd hardly had time to enjoy this fine craft when he found himself approaching Brunswick.

"Command Center, this is DF-23. No signs of anything unusual," Kyler radioed. "Approaching Interstate 95. Heavy northbound traffic, but no southbound traffic, except for...what is that? There's an F-22 parked in the southbound lanes!"

The avionics in the DF-23 went berserk with all sorts of wild readings. Before Kyler could make sense of the readings, the DF-23 bounced off an atmospheric barrier and became uncontrollable. He ejected, and he was now all alone in the air with his parachute deployed. The aircraft traveled a short ways farther until it plunged into the ocean.

Kyler landed just east of Interstate 95, and now he could see that the cars and trucks were backed up for miles, trying to exit Brunswick. Some had broken through the median and were now traveling the wrong way, but they could do so because no one was driving into the city. Kyler tried to stop a car here and there, but all shouted to get out of the way. He resorted to jumping onto the back of a pickup truck and stealing a motorcycle.

"You're crazy!" the pickup driver yelled back as Kyler rode toward Brunswick.

He managed to ride to the correct side of the road, but he had many wrong-way drivers to dodge. After a few miles it didn't matter. He collided with the same dome that caused his aircraft to crash. The motorcycle stopped running and went out from under him. Kyler slid off the road and into the ditch. He was only slightly dazed. His flight helmet spared him a concussion from the motorcycle fall, but now it was just extra weight, so he removed it, climbed out of the ditch, and struggled southbound along Interstate 95 through a transition layer of the dome.

All vehicles toward the city were stopped. Many had collided with others, but most appeared to be frozen in place, as if time had stopped. People were now jogging as best they could to leave the zone of non-electricity. The wall of people was so dense that many fell to the side, into the ditch, and pushed forward like a massive wave, impeding Kyler's progress. More like stopped it. Kyler wished he had not tossed his helmet aside, because now he was being trampled.

"Stop!" Kyler yelled. "I'm one of you! Stop!"

"Get out of the way!" was all Kyler heard in return.

But the trampling continued. Kyler was getting badly hurt, and he received several concussions. Then someone began yelling with a voice of authority, and the voice charged through the herd of people, swinging a club and bashing people out of the way. The crowd dispersed briefly around Kyler—long enough for a mysterious shape to approach.

"Who...who are you?" Kyler barely managed to say.

"It's unsafe out here, Major Bohr," the man said.

"You know me?" Kyler asked.

"I was told you would fly down. I figured you would end up on the ground like this, so I was sent to find you," the man said. "I'm Colonel John Von Brock, Georgia Air National Guard. We need to get you to Dayla Industries. You're expected."

"I don't see a horse and wagon. That's about all I would expect to see running around under these conditions," Kyler said.

"Follow me. I have an old Dayla Industries pickup truck. Has a diesel engine and heavy duty lights," Von Brock said.

It was true. Hidden behind some brush on the side of the interstate was Von Brock's pickup truck. The two entered, and Von Brock drove away.

"There's no radio, but everything else works," Von Brock said.

"How?" Kyler said. "The EMP—"

"Affects fragile circuits, like those based on silicon. The circuits in this truck are heavy duty and simplified," Von Brock said. "But as for the city, there's no electricity."

"So it would seem. Do we know what is causing all this?" Kyler asked.

"Whatever came down after Scythoc Three is causing this," Von Brock said.

"Interesting choice of words," Kyler said while bandaging his arm. "Do you mean this second satellite came down later than Scythoc Three, or do you mean the second satellite pursued Scythoc Three?"

"Both, and it isn't a satellite. Must be a spaceship of some sort," Von Brock said. "But that's all they told me before they sent me out after you. And that's a *pursuit* after and not a *timewise* after."

"Spaceship? What? No way! And who told you all this?" Kyler asked.

"Doctor Kukovich. Of Dayla Industries. We'll meet him soon enough," the colonel said.

It didn't take long for the two to reach Dayla Industries, but once they were there, the main building was swarming with security people.

"Is this a welcoming party?" Kyler asked.

"They aren't here for us," the colonel said. "And they weren't here when I left."

Von Brock stopped at a checkpoint and rolled down his window.

"Colonel John Von Brock and Major Kyler Bohr to see Doctor Kukovich," the colonel said.

"There's been a new development. Word is that you are to proceed to the corporate side and speak with Miss Dayla," the guard said.

"Excuse me, but what's happening?" Kyler asked.

"Miss Dayla will explain everything," the guard said.

Von Brock drove the pickup a little ways and reached the corporate side of Dayla Industries. He identified himself and Kyler—like before—and was instructed to go into the underground parking. Lights shone in the underground parking area, which surprised Kyler.

"High-powered tritium lights," the colonel said.

The two parked and another guard escorted them into a short hallway, into an elevator, and up to the top floor, where they were then escorted to a receptionist.

"Colonel John Von Brock and Major Kyler Bohr to see Miss Debbie Dayla," the guard said.

"Thank you," the receptionist said. "You may leave."

The guard returned to the elevator. The receptionist pushed a button on an intercom and spoke.

"There's a Colonel Von Brock and a Major Bohr here to see you."

Von Brock laughed. The receptionist apologized, but Kyler wasn't concerned.

"Don't worry. I've heard them all," Kyler said.

"Send them in," Debbie said over the speaker.

The receptionist motioned toward a door, and the two entered the large office of Roger Dayla, except Roger wasn't there.

"I'm Debbie Dayla," the young woman said. "Please, have a seat."

The men sat.

"I hope you don't mind me saying, ma'am, but you're the prettiest CEO I've ever met," Kyler said.

Debbie smiled while she studied a new report on her hand-held computer.

"We're all sorry to hear about your sister," Kyler said. "Wait, is that a computer you are holding? But I thought—"

"Dayla Industries uses diamond as a semiconductor instead of silicon. Makes for very resilient computer circuitry," Von Brock said.

"Diamond computers? Who would have thought if that were possible? I'd like to—" Kyler started.

"We have an ongoing crisis here in Brunswick," Debbie interrupted. "And the situation is critical. First, we tracked two objects from space as they descended through Earth's atmosphere and landed in the Atlantic half a nautical mile east of Jekyll Island. The first object has been identified as the satellite named Scythoc Three. It contained a humanoid that we rescued and are holding here."

"So Scythoc Three *did* land in the Atlantic. And I was right about someone being on board," Kyler said. "Is this alien here? In this building?"

"Yes. We'll see the alien in a moment. But there's more news," Debbie said.

"The second object," Von Brock said. "It's an invasion force, isn't it?"

"Yes," Debbie said.

"How did you know?" Kyler asked.

"It's obvious. The repeating electro-magnetic pulse that's disrupting electronics, the dome barrier preventing aircraft from entering and exiting— it's an invasion. By more aliens, I'd wager. There's something in this city or near this city that they want, at least for starters, and they could expand and take over the earth, given their power over us," Von Brock said.

"That's a good, um, what's the word—assessment," Debbie said. "We believe the second object is a spacecraft with hostile intentions. You are right about the repeating EMP and the failing electronics in the city. Fortunately, Dayla Industries has backup systems that do not use conventional silicon electronics, and these systems are working, but they are only available in this building or with our special vehicles and tools."

"Invasion. I can't believe it. It's like fiction or something," Kyler said. "Now my first question is, who are they? And my second question is, what do they want?"

"Probably the same type of alien that was captured from Scythoc Three," Von Brock said. "And as for what they want, what does any colonizing race want? Land and natural resources."

"We believe the invading aliens are not the same race as the one we have in custody," Debbie said.

Kyler looked at Von Brock in surprise.

"Even a genius can be wrong from time to time," Von Brock said.

"Genius! Hah!" Kyler mocked.

"Gentlemen, please," Debbie said. "They do want our land. But more importantly, they want our mercury."

"The metal?" Kyler asked.

"The same," Debbie replied.

"A species based on mercury instead of carbon. And highly toxic, too. But how have you learned so much about these invaders?" Von Brock asked.

"Colonel Von Brock. While you were out looking for Major Bohr, the alien species from the spacecraft began their first invasion effort. They overpowered our guards and stole our stores of mercury. This was mercury that Doctor Anton Kukovich, our chief engineer, was working to convert into less toxic materials," Debbie said.

"So that's why Doctor Kukovich is not here? But why all the secrecy from the guard?" Kyler asked.

Debbie paused. She stared at Kyler and then at Von Brock.

"He was murdered. Or kidnapped," Von Brock said.

"Kidnapped, we hope," Debbie said. "They took Doctor Kukovich and the five million pounds of mercury."

"You're kidding," Kyler said. "No one has that much mercury."

"Project Krypto Silvo," Von Brock said. "She was just telling us about it."

"She never said anything about a Krypto Silvo. What's Krypto Silvo?" Kyler asked.

"The project to convert mercury into krypton and ruthenium through nuclear fission," Debbie said. "The five million pounds—"

"Represents the anthropogenic contribution to Earth's atmosphere in one year," Von Brock said. "Being able to convert five million pounds is a stepping stone toward installing Krypto-Silvo converters in coal-fired power plants and gold mines, for starters. And if we are ambitious enough, we may even install such converters over active volcanoes."

"Thank you, Doctor Dictionary," Kyler said with sarcasm.

"What about the alien?" Von Brock asked. "Have you learned anything?"

"Maybe the alien can help us," Kyler said.

"The alien already has," Debbie said. "We're standing here, aren't we? The invaders would have completely taken over Dayla Industries had it not been for the alien. And so, the invaders are staying in their spacecraft in the Atlantic, for now, with five million pounds of mercury and Doctor Kukovich. We know they will use the mercury to expand their power, possibly to create more of them or an army or both. And they are probably using Doctor Kukovich to help plan their attack against us."

"He wouldn't help them," Kyler said.

"It's called coercion," Von Brock said. "He won't have a choice."

"But we do," Debbie said.

"And that is?" Kyler asked. "You know there's an entire United States of America out there. I'm supposed to report back to Command Center. And they're supposed to send forces in to help contain the situation."

"They would make things worse by escalating conflict prematurely. Our military is no match for these aliens. Am I right, Miss Dayla?" Von Brock asked.

"You may call me Debbie," she said. "And you are correct. We *will* attack. But in a carefully coordinated manner. We must succeed on the first attempt. Otherwise..."

"Otherwise, the invaders will decimate the human race, possibly even all animal and plant life on Earth," Von Brock said.

"Correct," Debbie said.

"Blast you and your correctness," Kyler said to Von Brock. "What about us? What about the American people? Humans everywhere? Don't you care about that?"

"We won't accomplish anything by expressing sappy feelings in this office," Von Brock said. "We should meet the alien."

"*Meet the alien. Meet the alien.* We should learn more about these invaders by attempting to spy on their spacecraft, perhaps send a single person in on a reconnaissance mission," Kyler said.

"We'll meet the alien," Debbie said.

"But the spy—" Kyler added.

"Would get killed," Von Brock said. "Face it, old man, you just can't keep up with me."

Kyler turned red with irritation, but he restrained himself from punching Von Brock. The three took the elevator down many stories until they reached a sub-sub-basement. The doors opened, and Debbie led the way along a narrow corridor.

"Doctor Von Brock, I need your expertise in analyzing some tissue samples we took earlier," Debbie said.

"*Doctor* Von Brock?" Kyler asked.

"I'm only called by that title when my knowledge in biochemistry is needed," Von Brock said. "Otherwise, I'm just a plain ol' colonel."

"*Plain ol' colonel*," Kyler mocked. "Why am I needed here anyway? I should just return to Command Center."

"You're not, and you should," Von Brock grinned.

"Major Bohr, things are already more than interesting in Brunswick. Any help we receive is appreciated," Debbie said. "While Doctor Von Brock and I review the tissue samples, please make yourself comfortable in the interrogation room. We'll meet with you there shortly."

"And where is that?" Kyler asked.

"Down to the end, a left, another left, and the second door on the right," Von Brock explained.

"*Thanks*," Kyler said, though he didn't mean it.

Debbie and Von Brock disappeared into a lab while Kyler made the walk down the corridor.

"Doctor Von Brock, surgery," Kyler mocked. "Doctor Von Brock, time to have a lobotomy. Doctor Von Brock, report to the garbage chute for evacuation. Doctor Von Brock, you have an appointment to have your teeth pulled and your face rearranged."

Kyler was about to mutter something else when he opened the door to the interrogation room. He closed the door behind him and then noticed that there was a long table with a divider down the middle. But what he didn't expect was to see a young woman sitting on one side of the table. She was attractive with strong facial features, and she had various shades of red in her brown hair. But she was pale and gray, as if she hadn't eaten in days.

"Oh, I'm sorry. I must be in the wrong room," Kyler said.

"Are you...how do I say...here for interrogation?" the young woman asked.

"I, uh, yes. You sound French. And your English is pretty good," Kyler said.

"I learned just a short time ago," she said. "My name is Mirini."

"Major Kyler Huehigh Bohr," Kyler said.

Kyler offered to shake hands, but Mirini looked puzzled.

"Oh, pardon my bad manners. You expect a hug, of course. All you French folk are affectionate," Kyler said.

He hugged Mirini, and she hugged back to mimic his behavior. She sat back down, but then Kyler realized something.

"You're sitting on the wrong side," he said. "See the sign? It says that's the prisoner side."

"I...can't read the sign," she said. "I was told to sit here."

"No, we are the interrogators. We sit on the other side. Please, let me get the chair for you," Kyler said.

Kyler pulled the chair out a little. Mirini looked at him strangely. Kyler pointed to where she should stand. She did, and he pushed the chair under her, which caught her by surprise, and she sat abruptly.

"Sorry," he said. "Tell you what, when this is all over, why don't you and I go get something to eat. That is, if anything is open."

"Open? Like what is open?" she asked.

"Yeah, good point. Let me tell you about a time when I was growing up. There was a power outage. I snuck out to a pub with lit candles and a grill—outside of course—and the pub had beer flowing. It was like going into an old-time saloon before electricity was invented. Had one of the best times of my life. I bet some creative pub owners are doing the same, right now," Kyler said. "All we do is follow our noses to the nearest barbeque grill. The South is supposed to be known for its barbeque beef, pork, and chicken."

"Animal food! Oh, patoosh!"

Kyler sat next to her.

"Oh, sorry again. Vegetarian, huh? Well, I'm sure we could find a soy burger or something. Sorry, that doesn't sound very appetizing," Kyler said.

Mirini laughed.

"You speak strangely. But I like it. You are very fascinating," Mirini said.

"Why thank you," Kyler said.

"Tell me more about things you do where you live," Mirini said.

"Well, I like to fly high-speed aircraft. In fact, I flew here in a DF-23 at Mach 2.9 in supercruise mode. I didn't get much of a chance to test its maneuverability, but let me tell you about the avionics," Kyler started.

"I think you've said enough already," Debbie said, now entering with Von Brock. "You're supposed to wait for us before the interrogation begins, not let the prisoner interrogate you."

"What?!" Kyler remarked.

"Old man! You're breaking security! This is Mirini of Bruxima 4. She is the alien! The Scythoc Three satellite? Remember?" Von Brock said.

Kyler looked dazed. He looked at Debbie, who frowned. He looked at Mirini. She smirked and returned a sheepish wave. He then looked at Von Brock.

"You've been had," Von Brock said. "Well amateur hour is over. Let's get this interrogation going."

Von Brock man-handled Mirini and placed her on the prisoner side.

"Ow!" she said. "You have a strange way to say, 'hello'."

"That's not 'hello', it's 'get back in your place,'" Von Brock said sternly.

"Take it easy, Von Brock, she's just a woman," Kyler said.

"Don't let her appearance fool you," Von Brock said. "That's an alien in disguise."

Debbie and Von Brock sat next to Kyler on the interrogator side. Debbie read notes from her tablet computer and used a magnetic link between her fingertip and the computer to take more notes.

"We've had a brief conversation before," Debbie said. "You are Mirini of Bruxima 4, a planet approximately eighty light years away."

"That's right," Mirini said.

"We were trying to learn more about you when the...what did you call the other aliens?" Debbie asked.

"Aliotrotes. They are aliotrotes," Mirini said.

"When the aliotrotes invaded this building, kidnapped Doctor Anton Kukovich, and stole our five millions pounds of mercury," Debbie said, "the aliotrotes emitted mercury gas and used that to poison those who attempted to stop them. They would have taken over the entire building and more when you, Mirini, used some sort of device to neutralize the gas. They attacked you with methyl-mercury, but you converted that to...wait, one moment, new analysis coming in...you were able to convert their chemical attack to...now this is very interesting...krypton, ruthenium, and methane."

"That sounds like the same process you told us about earlier. About Doctor Kukovich's—" Kyler started.

"Keep a lid on it, old man," Von Brock said.

"The aliotrotes then retreated. It appears they feared for their lives," Debbie said. "Now I'd like you to tell us *why* they feared for their lives."

"I suppose you know the answer to this one," Kyler said to Von Brock.

"Of course I do, but it's better to hear it from the prisoner," Von Brock said.

"How can you call Mirini a prisoner? Look at her. She's the most innocent, helpless, and sweet, dear woman a man would ever meet," Kyler said.

"This *innocent* prisoner just defeated that entire alien invasion force," Von Brock said.

"And we'd like to know how," Debbie said. "And why."

Kyler extended a hand to hold Mirini's. She extended hers back to hold his, but Debbie swatted Kyler's hand, and he withdrew.

"Better mind your manners," Von Brock said. "The boss has spoken."

"The aliotrotes fear me, this is true," Mirini said. "And you saw the device I used. It is here."

Mirini removed a cuff bracelet from her right forearm, no thicker than a table knife, and placed it on the table. It was transparent and iridescent, resembling high-quality crystal drinking glasses.

"Please, look for yourself," she said.

"Is it safe?" Kyler asked.

"It only responds to my command, so yes, it is safe," Mirini said.

Kyler reached for the device, but Debbie swatted his hand again.

"Miss Dayla," Kyler said.

"Call me Debbie."

"Debbie. Is that really necessary?"

"Yes," Debbie said.

Debbie picked up the device and inspected it. She then reached over Kyler and passed it to Von Brock.

"It's as hard as steel but flexible like copper," Von Brock said.

"We call it ferroxicate," Mirini said. "It's a super-hard form of crystallized iron."

"Of course. Iron doesn't mix with mercury," Von Brock said.

"The device projects iron ions and either stores the mercury using atomic contraction, or stores and then splits the mercury atoms," Mirini said. "The aliotrotes fear this because, being made of eighty-percent mercury themselves, the device would destroy them permanently."

"They were chasing you," Kyler said. "You sought refuge in Scythoc Three. They pursued you all the way here to Brunswick."

"No, old man. More like Mirini knew the mercury was here and was sent to stop the aliotrotes from stealing it," Von Brock said. "Am I right?"

"You are right," Mirini said. "But I failed. I did not arrive soon enough to warn you humans, and I was also injured in the landing. I did not anticipate so many difficulties in controlling a human satellite."

"We found you with broken bones and heavy fluid loss," Debbie said. "But I see that you appear to be healthy at the moment."

"We from Bruxima 4 could self repair quickly," Mirini said.

"You mean *can*," Kyler said. "How many of you are there on Bruxima 4?"

Mirini paused.

"She's the last one," Von Brock said. "They killed her people."

"She never said that," Kyler said.

"I could hear it in her voice," Von Brock said. "Don't you pay attention?"

"I'm paying very close attention," Kyler said, "more so than I have with any woman."

"You're paying attention to the wrong things," Von Brock said, "like the way you *landed* your jet. Let me guess—Navy?"

"Marines," Kyler said.

"Figures. No match for Air Force."

Kyler lifted a fist, but Mirini's voice interrupted his action.

"You two are expressing brotherly love?" Mirini asked.

Debbie giggled.

"No, lover boy here is so smitten by you that he's failing to pick out the proper details from this interrogation," Von Brock said.

"What is lover boy?" Mirini asked.

"Moving on," Debbie said before Kyler could lift that fist again. "What happened to the people on your planet? On Bruxima 4?"

"We were invaded by the aliotrotes, of course," Mirini said.

"Told you," Von Brock said to Kyler.

"I tried warning my people that this would happen, but I was ignored," Mirini said. "And so the aliotrotes captured my people and...and...it's almost too painful to discuss. If you would only read my memory cufflet, then you will understand."

"Cufflet? What cufflet?" Kyler asked.

Von Brock touched Mirini's left arm, rolled up the sleeve on her shirt, and revealed a cuff bracelet on her forearm.

"This must be it," Von Brock said.

Von Brock removed it and inspected it closely. It very much resembled the other cuff bracelet, but its form was a mirror opposite of the right cuff bracelet.

"You use the left cuff bracelet to store instructions and procedures, and with those procedures, you are able to control the right cuff bracelet," Von Brock said.

"You can't know that," Kyler said.

"You are very...how do I say...you can understand things with little or no explanation," Mirini said.

"Let me see those," Kyler said.

Kyler took both cuff bracelets and looked at them, turning them over and holding them up to the light.

"I can give you a demonstration of the memory retrieval cufflet," Mirini said.

"What will that entail?" Debbie asked.

"Hey, old man, wake up!" Von Brock said to Kyler.

Kyler looked around. The interrogation room was empty and partially lit. Mirini was gone. So was Debbie. The cuff bracelets were gone, too.

"What happened?" Kyler asked.

"Didn't you Marines learn to stay awake? Now if you were in the Air Force, you'd have to stay awake. Our training programs—"

"I don't care about your training programs. I need some coffee," Kyler said.

"Doctor Von Brock, you are needed in lab 225," a public address system called.

"I'm always needed around here. Go back to the main level. There's a small cafe up there," Von Brock said, and he was gone.

"What was that all about? What am I doing here?" Kyler asked himself. "Better get some coffee and wake up. Then I'll get my orientation back."

Kyler walked to an elevator, entered, pressed a button for the main floor, and the elevator moved upward. But when the elevator doors opened at the main floor, the building was gone. All that was left was the floor. No walls. No ceiling. No upper floors. Rain was everywhere, and Kyler became soaked.

"This is crazy!" Kyler said. "How did this all get destroyed? And there's no evidence of destruction!"

Kyler left the building area and roamed the streets. The rain splashed mud in his face and on his clothes, and he cleared mud out of his eyes to see a tall, sturdily-built man with black hair and a stark widow's peak approaching him. The man wore a rain jacket and waiters.

"You have burns," Kyler said, noticing red blotches and blisters on the man's face and arm. "Where do you live?"

The man pressed three fingers to his temple and looked down for a moment before looking back up and dropping his hand to his side.

"What are you doing here?" the man asked in a stern tone.

"What?!" Kyler asked in surprise. "Do you know me?"

"You're Major Kyler Bohr. Your call sign is *Bleam*."

"How...how did you know my name?" Kyler asked.

"You are ordered to the processing building," the man said.

"What's this all about? Who are you? The Dayla building was just over here. Are you part of FEMA? How did you get here so fast? There's an EMP field that's knocked out electrical devices. How did you—"

"Enough!" the man said, and he grabbed Kyler by the shoulder.

Kyler felt immediate pain, as if he were being electrocuted. He wanted to cry out, but his vocal cords were paralyzed. The best he could do was utter a short groan. Who was this man, and what power did he have? Kyler managed to turn his head a little as the man forced Kyler to walk toward the remains of a main road. The man's hand, which looked normal before, was now split from the connecting skin between the index and ring fingers down to the wrist. The palm was literally split in half. His pinky and ring finger formed one part of a vee shape, and his middle finger with his index finger formed the other part, and this vee formation skewered into Kyler's shoulder like sausage being roasted on a forked stick. Yet Kyler did not bleed.

"Who...are...you?" Kyler struggled to utter.

The man smiled like that of a predator having caught his prey. A silver-colored bus without wheels approached. It was not like a school bus or city bus, but more like a subway car—seemingly devoid of a driver or engine compartment. There was a small gap between the bottom of the bus and the ground, with no visible apparatus elevating the bus above ground.

"You will soon learn about us. Your mind and body will be such that nothing of your insignificant past will remain," the man chuckled as he forced Kyler into the bus.

Kyler endured the electrocution throughout the bus ride. Other people were being held against their wills on the bus in similar fashion.

"You are invaders," Kyler managed to say.

"Yes, we are," the man smiled.

Kyler and the bus reached the doors of an elementary school. Kyler was escorted off the bus first. Then to Kyler's surprise, the man passed through the closed school door yet continued pulling Kyler along. Kyler smashed into the glass and cut his cheek.

"Good, you don't pass through solid objects," the man said.

Kyler was now worried. This man wasn't human. Couldn't be. He had powers from beyond and more. Was this the beginning of the end? Did it finally happen? All those movies and books about aliens from other planets, yet none seemed real, none could be true, and now, now it had happened.

The man opened the door and pulled Kyler into the school building and in so doing led a line of people from the bus into the school. Kyler and the man passed through an archway into the corridor, and to Kyler's amazement, his own clothes were sparkling clean and dry. The man forcing Kyler along no longer wore a rain coat, nor did he wear waiters.

"Devitiation is complete," the man said.

The two entered a gymnasium.

"Kazhak, you found another one," said a tall, thin man with white hair and a less drastic widow's peak.

"Yes, Savien. This is Major Kyler Bohr," Kazhak said. "I found him wandering the city without escort."

Savien placed four fingers on Kyler's forehead. They stung.

"Why were you disobedient?" Savien asked.

"I wasn't," Kyler replied.

Kazhak, with one hand still in Kyler's shoulder, thrust his other hand toward Kyler's chest. The hand split down the palm (like the other hand before it), skewered around Kyler's sternum, and clenched onto Kyler's heart.

Kyler gasped beyond what he thought was possible. With his heart in Kazhak's grip, he sensed immediate doom and death.

"You *will* answer to Savien now or to me later. Which is it?" Kazhak said.

Kyler's face turned white and then green from the strain.

"Wait," Savien said. "Kazhak, release his heart—without Kyler losing blood."

Kazhak retrieved his hand from Kyler's heart, and blood flowed back into Kyler's face. Kyler took several deep breaths. Savien then placed his hand on Kyler's temple, and Savien's hand split down the palm much as Kazhak's hand had done, but Savien's fingers now probed into Kyler's brain. Kyler stopped moving or looking or thinking, as if he were a living zombie.

"He is not part of the original conscription," Savien said. "So you plan to help the survivors, do you? But you didn't expect to find us here. Your misfortune."

Savien removed his fingers from Kyler's brain.

"Take him to processing," Savien said.

"Yes, Savien," Kazhak replied.

Kazhak moved Kyler through the gymnasium and into what used to be a classroom, but two walls to adjoining classrooms had been knocked out and all desks removed. Pairs of glass tubular structures were lined up against the classroom windows, and inside some of the structure pairs were people—an adult human male in the left structure (Kyler's left), and a widow-peaked alien in the right.

"Witness your future, Kyler, as the osmozicon is activated," Kazhak said.

"What's happening? What are you people doing?" Kyler asked frantically, and he tried pulling away, but Kazhak maintained the shoulder snare.

"People? We aren't people. We are *aliotrotes*, from the planet Aliotra," Kazhak said.

Several pumps started up and progressively increased in revolutions per minute. With the human male still inside, his glass tube filled with a semi-transparent silvery fluid to the top. The man writhed and screamed in fear, he pounded on the glass, he knocked his skull all around, but the machines kept increasing in speed and pitch until the machines screamed louder than the man, and suddenly with frightening urgency, the fluid drained, and as the fluid line dropped, so did the man, but all that remained was the outer epidermal layer—the skin—of his body. The last of the fluid was gone, and what looked like a deflated blow-up human remained at the bottom.

The machine chugged and processed the fluid. It even struggled to keep going with the load, but it managed to finish the processing and send the fluid into the alien's glass structure. The alien, who was anemically white, absorbed the now silvery-golden fluid through his skin, and his color darkened to golden bronze.

"You...you...you killed that man!" Kyler exclaimed.

Kazhak laughed.

"We hear you process your live chickens in a similar fashion, only you do so on a mass assembly line, and you lop off the heads as waste. Here, we use the entire body, except for the skin, which we cannot yet osmoze. Your sequenced amino acids are most helpful. Most helpful."

"Thank you," said the aliotrote as he left the osmozicon.

"You won't fade at all for a year," Kazhak said to the aliotrote. "At least that's what our preliminary tests show. Report to Kinnabarics for reassessment of your lifespan."

Kazhak released the shoulder snare on Kyler.

"What are you going to do with me?" Kyler asked. "You're not going to put me in that...that..."

Kazhak waved off an aliotrote managing the line of humans destined for the osmozicon.

"We are not without mercy," Kazhak said. "Instead of making you wait in line with fret and worry, I'll advance you to a quick conversion. Inside the osmozicon you go."

Kazhak forced Kyler into the glass-tube structure and sealed the door. Kyler tried working the door open. No use. An aliotrote entered the adjoining glass-tube structure and awaited his treatment.

"If you kill me, the military will swarm from the sky and nuke you to oblivion!" Kyler yelled. "I will die, but so will you."

"Your insect-like military friends could barely attract our attention with their crude atomic toys," Kazhak said. "But they will be osmozed in time, just as you will be right now."

The pumps started up and whined into high revolutions per minute. A silvery fluid filled Kyler's glass tube from his feet upward.

"Stop!" Kyler said. "Stop this madness! We can talk! We can work something out!"

Kazhak laughed. The fluid reached Kyler's knees, then his waist, and up to his chest. His submerged skin tingled as if a thousand ants were attacking.

"No more, no more!" Kyler yelled.

The silvery fluid reached Kyler's neck and then his forehead. Kyler yelled something, but the silvery fluid muffled his words, and sound-distorted bubbles surfaced.

A loud buzzer razzed, and red lights strobed near Kyler's glass tube. Kazhak hit a big red button, and the silvery fluid stopped filling Kyler's tube, but neither did it drain.

"I'm sorry," Kazhak said to the alien as he exited the tube adjoining Kyler's. "Proceed to the next tube. This one needs reververation."

Kyler tapped on the glass tube. He jumped up as best he could to pull what little air remained in his tube into his mouth and lungs.

"Are...you...going...to...let...me...out?" Kyler asked by jumping and speaking each time his mouth rose above the fluid line.

Kazhak walked about slowly, paced a little, scratched his head, and held three fingers to his temple. Meanwhile, the air in Kyler's tube was growing stale, and Kyler's lungs were filling with an increasing level of carbon dioxide. Finally, Savien walked in.

"I can't decide if I should liquidate him or quarantine him for a day. But we have so many others being quarantined, it hardly seems worth it," Kazhak said to Savien.

"Many more aliotrotes are on the way, and we may have need for Kyler, *if* we can fully devitiate him," Savien said. "The devitiator is not fully functional."

"My apologies, Savien, but our extorticians have been working the problem sunset and sunrise," Kazhak said.

"Very well," Savien said. "Send Kyler to quarantine, and resume processing the fresh human conscription."

"As you command, Savien," Kazhak said.

Kazhak pressed a button, and the silvery fluid drained from Kyler's glass tube. Once gone, a gas blasted from top to bottom and evaporated what was left of the fluid. Kyler choked for a moment, but the gas cleared, and a conventional Earth atmosphere returned to the glass tube. Kazhak opened the tube, and Kyler fell out and onto his knees.

"Get up," Kazhak said. "I would have liquefied you, but Savien has other ideas. You will be quarantined until you are fit for processing."

Kazhak sank his fingers through Kyler's shoulder as before and led him down stairs to the school's basement where other humans were held hostage. A guard lifted a baton and shot electrical bolts through the prison door to push captured humans out of the way. The guard then opened the door, and Kazhak threw Kyler into the cell. The guard closed the door and locked it.

"One day for him," Kazhak said. "If he's still contaminated, liquefy him."

"Yes, my superior one," the guard said.

Kyler sat in the dark with a group of prisoners. His hands went numb, and his brain function clouded over. Every time someone touched him, he shook suddenly as if being electrocuted.

"Get away from me!" Kyler yelled.

"Put a light on him," said one of the prisoners.

Someone painted a portable light on Kyler. Kyler squinted and covered his eyes with his hands. His fingers and palms puffed up, and his skin flaked.

"Move back, move back!" said the prisoner. "He's one of the rejects, but he's been poisoned with mercury."

"We have to kill him," said another.

"Cut him up into pieces," said a third.

"No," said the first prisoner. "If you cause him to bleed, the mercury will contaminate the cell."

Kyler jumped to his feet in full delirium and beat on the door in hopes of escaping.

"Let me out, let me out!"

Despite the pounding, no one let him out. He slumped by the door, exhausted and weak.

"I'm going to die," he said, and he slipped into unconsciousness.

"He can't stay here," said the second prisoner. "We must get rid of him."

"Be kind," said the first.

"We'll all be dead from mercury poisoning if we don't do something," said the third. "I vote we send him through the sewer."

"That's cruel," said the first.

"I second the motion," said the second.

"Are we savages? Do we kick dogs to the street when they become ill? Then show mercy to your fellow person."

The second and third signaled something with their hands, first between themselves, then among the other prisoners, except the first. With a sudden rush, the second prisoner yelled, "Block him," and several prisoners restrained the first. Other prisoners wrapped their hands with plastic bags and carried Kyler over to the room's corner, where two prisoners pulled up a throw rug, pried up a floor board, and revealed an opening to a heavy-flowing sewer system below.

"Don't do this!" said the first prisoner. "This is murder!"

"He's dead already," said the second.

The second and third directed that Kyler be placed through the opening to the sewer below, which the other prisoners did. Kyler, still unconscious (and near death), dropped to the sewage stream and floated away. The prisoners threw a few other bits of garbage into the hole before closing it up and hiding its existence.

Kyler floated downstream face up. He floated and floated, not knowing how much time had passed. He thought he heard fluttery music, like a brass hummingbird treading water in super slow motion. The music was warbled and ominous. The walls swirled and ebbed, and Kyler felt himself floating in clouds at night with stars above him.

"This is the end," Kyler said. "This is my death."

The stars went dark, and a single light shone from above. A wind howled from the light and filled his lungs. Then another wind pushed on his chest, and he exhaled. Trees moved about him—trees that should remain stationary but instead scuttled about. A branch from one such tree touched his arm, and he felt a pinch. Another tilted its leaves, and a fluid entered Kyler's mouth. Kyler coughed.

"There, there," said an elderly man.

Kyler blinked his eyes several times, and he seemed to recognize the old man.

"Father?" Kyler said.

"Father? You are imagining things. My name is Ediom. I am the leader of the resistance."

"What happened? Where am I?" Kyler asked. "How did you get here?"

"Easy there, easy," Ediom said.

Kyler realized he was now on a make-shift cot in a dank concrete room on the side of the sewer stream.

"We found you drowning in the sewage water," Ediom said.

"We? Who else is here?"

"I am here," said a voice.

"Mother!" Kyler said as the sweet, old woman approached.

"He's delirious," Ediom said to the woman, then he spoke to Kyler. "Major Bohr, this is my wife, Mianna."

"We thought you were in South Dakota at Command Center," she said. "How did you end up here in Brunswick?"

"Easy, Mianna, let the boy rest," Ediom said, and then he turned to the darkness and said, "Another chelation ampule, quickly."

"You know me? And where...how do you know so much?" Kyler asked.

A young man brought an ampule and handed it to Ediom.

"This is Raian, our son," Mianna said.

Ediom added the ampule of chelation medication to Kyler's intravenous line.

"We are careful what we say, even down here. The aliotrotes have ways of learning things. They attempted to fill your system with mercury. Fortunately, their attempt failed, and you got away. There. This should help remove more mercury from your system."

"Then it wasn't a dream," Kyler said.

"What wasn't a dream?" Mianna asked.

"I was in a prison cell with other people. Aliens captured us—aliens who called themselves *aliotrotes*," Kyler explained. "You called them that too, just now. You must know about them."

"Unfortunately," Mianna said.

"They put me in a glass tube and filled it with a silvery liquid," Kyler continued. "I thought I would be osmozed. That's what they call it when a person gets deflated into nothing but skin. But they stopped and said I was contaminated or something. I don't remember much more. Hard to think. But they locked me in a prison cell. I felt sick and weak. The other prisoners wanted to kill me. I passed out, and I found myself here."

"That silvery stuff was a solution of mercury compounds," Ediom said. "You're not the first person to be sent into the sewer. We catch people as they come and then treat them. I'm sorry you were caught, but I'm glad you weren't osmozed. For some reason, the aliotrotes don't like certain people, but we're not sure why. And fortunately, they won't venture into the sewers, which gives us this safe haven, though again we don't know why."

"Have you figured out a way to retaliate against the aliotrotes?" Kyler asked.

Raian looked at Ediom, and Ediom returned the gaze.

"We haven't formed a plan yet," Raian said.

"How hard can it be? You know all about these creatures. Don't you have weapons?" Kyler asked.

"We are armed with weapons, but these aliotrotes aren't affected by them, if that's what you mean," Raian said as he pulled out a pistol from behind his back.

"Then why the delay? Let's go!" Kyler said.

"It's not that simple," Ediom said.

"I went on a raid," Raian said. "I fired my weapon against a group of aliotrotes. The bullets went through them. Didn't do a thing. Then I tried a grenade. Most of them were unfazed, but one was hurt and bled. But what he bled wasn't blood, it was a mixture of mercury compounds, and when those compounds hit the ground, they evaporated. The fumes were toxic. I was lucky to get away."

"As you may have guessed, these aliotrote bodies are made up of mercury compounds," Ediom said.

"Each one we kill ends up poisoning a city block or more," Raian said.

"We have to think of another plan," Kyler said.

"You have to rest," Mianna said. "The treatment—"

"Is almost complete," Kyler said.

"What makes you so sure?" Ediom asked.

"I feel better, that's how I can tell," Kyler said. "How long have I been here?"

"About two years. Maybe three," Ediom said. "I lose track of time down here."

"I...don't understand. The invasion only started in the last twenty-four hours," Kyler said.

"The aliotrotes landed here almost three years ago," Mianna said. "You should know that, Kyler."

"There's something strange going on," Kyler said.

"Yes, you've responded unusually well to therapy," Ediom said. "Most people would have died by now, even with treatment. But I gave you an extra-aggressive chelation infusion. There's one thing we don't understand, Kyler. The aliotrotes rejected you. Why?"

Ediom removed the needle from Kyler's vein, and Mianna taped a cotton ball to the wound.

"Press and hold for five minutes," Mianna said.

"We must find a way to defeat the aliotrotes," Kyler said. "If we can't use conventional weapons, we must find a way to weaken them enough to—"

"To do what?" Ediom asked.

"There's time enough to decide on that," Kyler said.

"We thought so too," Mianna said. "But I fear the end is near. Yes, we must learn their weaknesses. Unfortunately, we are limited in what we can do down here. We're fortunate enough to have the medical equipment and supplies that we do, but we have little means of spying on the aliotrotes. Raian does what he can, but there are limits without jeopardizing his and our safety. Even if the aliotrotes don't come down here, they may decide to attack—with gas or some poison, perhaps mercury itself. We can handle detoxing a person, but not the entire environment."

"I'd like to help Kyler investigate," Raian said. "I can show him what I know, the secret tunnels, and other things."

Raian looked to his father for approval, and Ediom nodded in affirmation.

"Good," Raian said. "Let's see what we can find, but I'll lead."

"Be careful," Mianna said.

"And come back healthy," Ediom added.

"We will," Raian said.

Kyler described the dome he had encountered with his aircraft and how he met with Debbie and Von Brock, and then suddenly things all changed.

"Let's start with the...what did you call that?" Raian asked.

"The old Dayla building," Kyler said.

"Okay. Let's prepare to move out," Raian said.

Raian handed a backpack, an ammo belt, a pistol, and a rifle to Kyler, and then Raian selected the same for himself. The two set out through sewage service tunnels. Three blocks straight, turn right, two blocks straight, a left, straight for another three, then right, left, straight, and so on until the service tunnel passed under a bridge and opened up to the sky.

"Stop," Raian (who had been leading) motioned with his hand back to Kyler.

"This doesn't look like the old Dayla building," Kyler said.

"We are two blocks away," Raian said. "I don't see any trotes, but they could be hiding. There's a fountain to the right of the opening. Do you see it?"

Kyler walked slowly to the tunnel's opening, looked, then turned back to Raian.

"Yes, I see it," Kyler said.

"And just beyond the fountain is a lighthouse," Raian said. "It's Old Sturleo Lighthouse, the one that was used before the shoreline was extended. One of us could go in, climb to the top, and look around."

"Yeah, if the trotes aren't in there," Kyler said. "I'll go. If there's a trote inside, I—"

"I doubt anyone's been in there," Raian said. "Loose boards and rocks are blocking the door."

"I'll clear away the junk from the door, plus I know where the Dayla building should be," Kyler said.

Raian nodded in agreement.

"I'll watch from down here," Raian said. "If there are any trotes, I'll try to distract them."

"Okay," Kyler said.

Kyler made his way along the side of the open-top culvert to avoid being seen. He reached a point where the culvert was no longer open to the sky. It descended below a concrete wall that stretched above and perpendicular to the culvert. At this point, Kyler found a ladder and climbed it slowly to street level. He paused near the top, looked, saw it was clear, and kept low to the ground as he scuttled over to the Old Sturleo Lighthouse. He was immediately slowed by gooey, beige mud surrounding the lighthouse. His boots stuck to the goo, but only somewhat, and he was able to reach one wall of the lighthouse and pause. No aliotrotes.

Meanwhile, Raian climbed upon concrete blocks along the side of the open-top culvert, peered over the street's edge, and watched the lighthouse. He saw Kyler place his rifle against the lighthouse wall and work on removing the rocks and boards from the doorway.

"You can do it," Raian whispered.

Kyler reached the door and pushed it, but the goo held it fast. He pushed and pushed and got the door opened a little. He pulled a pry bar from his backpack and pried the door open, and finally the door reached a point where the goo let go and allowed the door to open fully and bang against the lighthouse wall. Not expecting this sudden give of the door, Kyler dropped the pry bar and fell backward. The pry bar hit a rock and made a clash! Kyler landed on rocks and knocked the rifle over. Another clash! Fortunately, the rifle did not go off, but noise had been made, and Kyler stopped moving for fear of being seen by aliotrotes.

Raian held his breath and sank below the street level for a few seconds. Then he lifted his eyes above street level in search of aliotrotes.

"All clear," Raian whispered. "We're lucky this time."

Kyler arighted himself, placed the pry bar in his backpack, and picked up his rifle. He entered the lighthouse. It was dark and smelled like a combination of sewage and underarm antiperspirant. Bits of beige goo had been flung on the steps and railing. Kyler sniffed the goo, and he realized the goo was generating the sewage and antiperspirant smell. He ascended the steps slowly, stopping at the first window, which had been broken open and had goo around its edges.

"This is how the goo got in," Kyler said. "But where did it come from?"

Kyler looked out the window. All was calm. He saw Raian peering over the edge of the open-top culvert. He signaled a thumbs-up, and Raian replied with the same. Kyler ascended the steps again and reached the second window. Again, there was goo on the window edges, but not nearly as much, and Kyler had a better view of the area. Still he saw no aliotrotes, and he signaled as much with a thumbs-up again to Raian below. Raian replied in kind. Kyler now ascended toward the top of the lighthouse. As he neared the top, he felt the lighthouse shake. Earthquake? No, the vibrations were smaller and more subtle, but they grew stronger, as if...

"As if a big machine were getting closer, like the bus that first picked me up," Kyler said.

Kyler peered through a window at the top of the lighthouse. Indeed, an aliotrotic bus stopped at the front of a nearby half-fallen building. Aliotrotes circled the building and held their palms facing toward the building's center. A high-pitched hum vibrated the air, causing walls and material to fall away, revealing three people hiding in a closet. The aliotrotes stormed into what was left of the building (since it was now open to the sky) and forced the people into the bus.

At that moment, Raian climbed from the open-top culvert and onto the street. He ran toward the bus and yelled, "Free the people, free the people!"

An aliotrote held out his hand, and his palm split to the wrist and continued to the elbow. Its newly-split appendages grew in length and whipped through the air in Raian's direction. Raian threw a grenade. The aliotrote caught it with one split appendage, and it exploded, ripping off that appendage at the wrist. But the aliotrote was not maimed beyond function. It lashed back and caught Raian by the neck with its undamaged appendage and pulled Raian toward the bus.

Raian retrieved a blaster gun from his side and fired it into the aliotrote's upper arm, and it released its grip, but by now the fallen appendage from Raian's attack was liquefying and evaporating, creating a toxic cloud (to humans at least) of mercury compounds. The injured aliotrote let forth a brief screech, and along with the other aliotrotes jumped onto the bus. The bus moved away. Raian chased after it and jumped on. Kyler considered firing at the bus, but the toxic fumes wafted up in his direction, and he descended the steps quickly to avoid its haze. The cloud sizzled and popped as it entered the upper lighthouse from one window and exited the upper lighthouse from the opposite-side window.

Kyler waited another minute to be sure. The air was clean. He ascended the steps to the first window and looked out. All was quiet and clear. No sign of anyone, not Raian nor aliotrotes. He ascended to the second window, again no sign of any one or thing. He held his breath and ascended quickly to the top of the lighthouse. No sign of anything. Air was clear. He exhaled, and he slowly inhaled. Yes, he was sure, the air was clear and clean.

"Whew," Kyler sighed. "I survived, but what about Raian?! I must go after him. Where did he go?"

Kyler exhaled loudly. He was about to inhale when he thought he heard an echo of himself exhaling. He inhaled. Yes, a secondary sound of inhaling followed his own. Then he exhaled. Another exhaling sound. Then he inhaled partially, stopped, and held his breath. He heard the sound inhale, but he inhaled the rest of the way and held his breath yet again. The sound exhaled.

Kyler whipped around with his rifle in hand. Someone else was with him. Had to be. Was it an aliotrote? Maybe. And if he shot the alien? Mercury would kill him. But how else was he to defend himself?

"I must warn you, I'm armed and prepared to defend myself," Kyler finally said to break the tension.

A faint voice asked for help. Kyler looked around.

"Who was that?" Kyler asked.

"Help...me...please," said the voice.

Kyler looked around and around. Finally, he looked up and saw a foot hanging down from a broken glass opening at the top of the lighthouse.

"Good god," Kyler said.

He placed his rifle down, unloaded his backpack, and retrieved a rope and body harness. He climbed up to the opening and looked. There situated in an area below the lighthouse's roof but above the inside ceiling was a young woman. She was on her side and unable to move.

"I'm hurt. I'm in pain. I can't climb down," she said.

"Don't worry," Kyler said. "I'll help you down."

"Please be careful," she said. "There's...my legs...I can't move them."

Kyler attached the body harness to the woman, fastened the rope to it, and threw the other end over a steel beam that he used as a pulley point to support her weight. One hand held the rope. The other hand held her hand, and in this way he maneuvered her to the opening and lowered her clear of obstructions. He released her hand and lowered her to the lighthouse's upper floor. Kyler then climbed down and took a look at the woman. It was Mirini! But she looked younger. Her clothing had faded patches, like bleached upholstery left out in the sun too long. Her hands were in good shape, but her feet had fungal infections.

Kyler removed his canteen from his backpack and gave water to her. She gulped the water but coughed from drinking too quickly.

"Take it slowly," he said. "What happened? I thought you were in the Dayla building basement. Now you're up here?"

She drank a little more, but then suddenly without warning, she swatted Kyler's hand (the hand holding the canteen), and it flew across the room and into the wall.

"What did you do that for?" Kyler asked.

"I...don't know," she said. "I'm not myself."

"Maybe you thought I was attacking you," Kyler said. "Don't you remember me? I'm Major Kyler Bohr. Do you remember your name?"

"Mah...mee...I can't remember," she said. "I can't remember anything."

"Concussion," Kyler said. "Try again."

"Wee...ee. Mee...wee...nee," she strained.

"It's Mirini," Kyler said.

"Mir...ini," she repeated. "Mirini?"

She didn't seem sure.

"Mirini," Kyler said. "You need help. And you can't stay here."

"I know. I...don't know...please help me!" she said, and she suddenly hugged Kyler.

"It's okay, it's okay," Kyler said, comforting her. "We must travel a short ways. Not too far is a place where a man and his wife can treat you. He's a doctor, and he's been helping many victims in these parts."

"Okay," Mirini said. "I...can't walk."

"I'll carry you if I must," Kyler said.

"No, please, I must help a little. If I only had a crutch," she said.

Kyler looked around. No crutch, but there was his rifle. He stripped the rifle down to a simple barrel and shoulder stock. He added extensions to the barrel to give it proper length, and he gave it to Mirini.

"Thank you," she said. "It's lighter than I expected."

"It's made of a super-strong alloy that's very light," Kyler said.

Kyler helped Mirini to her feet with the rifle. He placed her right arm around his neck (and above his backpack), and she used her left arm with the crutch, and in this way the two were able to descend the steps, though slowly, and eventually reach the bottom. As she neared the opening, she passed out.

"I'll have to carry her," Kyler said.

Kyler disassembled the rifle such that it could fit in his backpack, which is where he placed it. He then carried Mirini out the door, through the goo, and over to the ladder leading to the bottom of the open-top culvert. Mirini awoke.

"What happened...I...I guess I passed out," Mirini said.

"Don't worry," Kyler said. "You'll receive treatment soon. Can you climb down this ladder?"

"I...I don't know," Mirini said.

Kyler held her upright such that she was on her feet.

"I want you to try taking some steps," Kyler said.

"Okay," Mirini said.

Mirini moved her leg a little.

"I moved it, I moved it!" she said.

"Good," Kyler said. "Try your other leg."

Mirini moved her other leg a little.

"Good, good!" Kyler said. "Now I'm going to let you support your full weight."

"Don't leave me!" Mirini said.

"I won't," Kyler said.

Kyler let go of Mirini and stood a few steps in front of her.

"Walk to me," he said.

Mirini took another little step, and another. Kyler quickly glanced around to make sure aliotrotes weren't in the area, and they weren't, but during that brief moment, Mirini stepped and stumbled.

"Whoa!" Kyler said as he quickly returned his focus on Mirini.

Mirini's stumble threw her head-first toward Kyler, and he caught her before she fell to the ground. Mirini gasped for several breaths but then calmed down.

"I thought I would break my neck, but you caught me," Mirini said. "My legs are still weak. They're improving, but still weak. Thank you."

Kyler pulled Mirini to her feet and held her for a moment. She didn't know what to say or do.

"You...have...very interesting eyes. They are blue with light tinges, like red velvet daylilies," Kyler said in a soft tone. "I've never seen eyes like yours."

"And...you have a strong grip," Mirini said. "I can barely breathe."

"Sorry," Kyler said, and he loosened his grip on Mirini.

Kyler lifted Mirini's left hand and looked at it.

"Your skin is very smooth. I would have expected a fat diamond ring on your ring finger, but you wear no rings," Kyler said.

"Fat diamond?" Mirini asked.

"Yeah, you know. I'd think you'd be married to the richest from your planet," Kyler said.

"What is marriage?" she asked.

"Huh?"

"And you say I should have my finger in a carbon crystal. But my finger is not damaged and needs no splint," Mirini said.

"You're teasing me," Kyler said. "But no one talks like you. What's your game? Where are Debbie and Von Brock?"

"I don't understand your nervous tone," Mirini said. "And I don't know those names. Please, tell me what's wrong. Why must I have carbon crystal on my finger?"

"When was the last time you were kissed?" Kyler asked.

"I don't know about kissed," Mirini said.

"A girl like you would remember being kissed," Kyler said.

"I don't," Mirini said. "What is kissed?"

Kyler drew her close to him, he looked into her daylily eyes, she returned the gaze, and he pressed his lips against hers. He pulled away and spoke.

"That's being kissed," Kyler said.

Mirini tilted her head a little, puzzled.

"I felt something," Mirini said. "Very strange."

"Then you remembered being kissed?" Kyler asked.

"Not exactly," Mirini said. "I sensed that I was not being kissed correctly."

"Correctly?" Kyler said, pulling away in surprise.

"Yeah," Mirini said. "I sense that being kissed should be more like this."

Mirini pulled Kyler close to her, and she pressed her lips to his and kissed him more deeply than he kissed her. She kept kissing him until he closed his eyes. She closed hers, and they kissed more. She felt deep thoughts from Kyler, thoughts of worry about Brunswick, Dayla Industries, the United States, and thoughts of danger from aliotrotes. She pulled away finally and said:

"That's being kissed."

"You said you didn't remember," Kyler said.

"I didn't. I still don't," Mirini said.

"Then how—"

"I read your mind," she said.

Kyler looked at her with a serious expression, and then she burst into laughter.

"Shhh," she said. "I feel like we're being watched."

"Did you read that from my mind too?" he asked.

"No, but look at the water. See how it ripples," she said.

Kyler looked. Vibrations from the street carried into the water and created small ripples—ripples from an approaching aliotrote vehicle.

"We have to leave, now!" he said.

Kyler climbed down the ladder first.

"Come on, I'll catch you in case you fall," Kyler said.

"I see those aliotrotes you talked about," Mirini said. "They're over by—"

"Don't talk now. Hurry on down the ladder!" Kyler urged.

Mirini descended the ladder as best she could, but she lost her footing near the end and fell atop Kyler. Kyler tried catching her, but he could only break her fall to some extent. She rolled away from Kyler and the base of the ladder, along the side ledge, and stopped just as her feet landed in the sewer water toward the center of the open-top culvert.

Mirini screamed. She pulled her feet from the water and writhed in pain. The fungal infection on her feet seethed and foamed as if being ravaged by acid.

"Oh my god," Kyler said.

Mirini grimaced and ground her teeth from the pain. Kyler was beside himself and didn't know what to do.

"We can't go this way," Kyler said. "Something in the water is eating your flesh. It's the fungal infection, isn't it? Everything is all so crazy."

Mirini cried. Kyler ripped his shirt off, tore it in two, and wrapped the halves around Mirini's feet to protect them from further exposure. He tied them firmly, and they held.

"Can't take a chance on you walking on those, no way," Kyler said.

"I heard voices over here," echoed an aliotrote from the street level.

Mirini tried to be quiet, but her feet still hurt. She reached for Kyler, and he moved closer. She put her arms around him and squeezed. Kyler was surprised by her strength, and he found breathing a little difficult, but he held onto Mirini, and the two stayed close to the side wall to avoid being seen from the street level. Mirini's hand reached for Kyler's chest, and she felt stainless-steel dog tags he'd kept from military service. She felt a comfort in holding the tags in her hand, and she relaxed.

"This area is toxic," echoed the aliotrote. "Mark it as highly dangerous with a requirement to wear protective gear."

The aliotrotes left, and Kyler relaxed.

"They're gone," Kyler said.

"May I hold onto your little pieces of metal?" Mirini asked. "I feel safer when I do."

"They're my dog tags," Kyler said. "Here, you may wear them."

Kyler placed the dog tags over Mirini's neck, and she kissed him. Kyler felt warm and tingly inside. He felt he'd known her for quite a while, even if it had only been a short time.

"You're becoming quite special to me," Kyler said.

"I like being in your company too," Mirini said. "And I love your necklace. I can feel the iron in the metal. It's wonderful."

Again, Kyler thought Mirini said something strange, but maybe that was part of the attraction he was having for her, an attraction that grew stronger by the minute.

"I'm afraid we can't take a chance staying here," Kyler said. "And we can't go to where the man and his wife are hiding. I'm sorry to say that I don't know where we can go that's safe. If only we could get to a helicopter or the DF-23, then maybe—"

"The what?" Mirini asked.

"The DF-23. It's an airplane, the one I rode down in, except it crashed. But it has room for two, and maybe I could fly you to another city that hasn't been invaded."

Mirini smiled.

"Your airplane is in the ocean, isn't it?" Mirini asked.

"Yeah, how did you know?" Kyler replied.

"I read your mind," Mirini giggled.

"Hah, hah, hah, a neat parlor trick," Kyler said.

"Kyler," Mirini said. "Why were you in the lighthouse? Did you see me stuck in the top and wished to rescue me?"

"Actually, no. I entered the lighthouse so I could see the area well enough to figure out how to reach the Dayla building."

"Then let's go back to the lighthouse. Climb to the top again, only this time look for where your aircraft crashed," Mirini said.

"I can't leave you down here," Kyler said.

"I'll climb up the ladder with you to the street," Mirini said, "and I'll wait for you."

"Okay, but you can't stand in the open street for all to see. You'll have to come into the lighthouse too, at least to floor level," Kyler said. "No wait, you passed out at floor level. Was it the air?"

"I'll breathe carefully," Mirini said.

"But for how long?" Kyler said.

"That depends on how long it takes you to climb to the top and find a path to your aircraft."

"*And* if I can figure out where it crashed. Okay, but I'll be doubly-quick," Kyler said.

Despite Mirini's foot injuries, she managed to climb the ladder from the open-top culvert to street level. Kyler was quite amazed. She seemed to have picked up strength and confidence. Kyler was about to carry her to the lighthouse, but she walked without issue. He did carry her over the goo, and she breathed carefully as planned. He carried her a few steps up—enough such that she could focus on breathing without passing out.

"There," he said. "This way you won't pass out from any bad fumes."

Mirini smiled.

"Okay," Kyler said. "I'll return soon."

Kyler climbed to the top. He looked out and about for where he thought the DF-23 would have crashed. He saw a pier and the ocean, but no sign of the aircraft.

"It must have completely sunk," Kyler thought. "Or perhaps it broke apart on impact. Either way, it's gone."

Kyler was dejected. He banged his fist against the lighthouse walls and steps all the way down nearly to ground level, but he stopped where he'd left Mirini.

"I can't find my aircraft at all," he said.

Mirini looked at him with concern. Kyler proceeded past her to the lighthouse's ground level, kicking and beating all the way, and he gave an especially hard kick to the floor. When he did, something sounded hollow. He kicked the floor again, and something popped up a little. He pulled a knife from his belt, kicked the floor again, and wedged the knife between what was now a loose square and the rest of the floor. He pried and pulled the loose square up and revealed a set of stairs going a short ways underground.

"What do you know, an underground passage," Kyler said. "But where does it go?"

"It doesn't matter," Mirini said, now joining Kyler by his side.

"You're standing next to me—close to the goo. You're not passing out."

"Somehow, when I'm holding you and wearing your dog tags, the fumes don't bother me so much," Mirini said.

"That's a relief," Kyler said. "Before the magic ends and before the aliotrotes return, let's explore this passage."

"Good idea," Mirini said.

Kyler started to help Mirini down the trap-door's ladder when he heard a voice.

"What is that?" Kyler said.

"An aliotrote," she said.

"The voices are this way," said the aliotrote outside the lighthouse.

"Quick, no time to discuss, or else we will be osmozed. Down you go," Kyler said.

Kyler helped Mirini to the passage below, he followed her down, and he closed the secret trap door above him. A few seconds later, the sound of heavy boots crossed the lighthouse's ground level and one such boot stood on the trap door, but its existence was not discovered, and so Mirini and Kyler were safe—for the moment. Kyler wiped perspiration from his brow in relief.

"I see a light way down the tunnel," Mirini whispered, though Kyler wasn't sure if she had spoken aloud—it was as if she had placed such a message in his mind.

"Let's go then," Kyler whispered.

"Please, hold me," Mirini said, and he did.

The two walked a short ways. The passage was not at all like the sewage tunnels. Instead, the floor was made of railroad ties placed close together, and holes in those ties suggested rails were once attached to the ties. The sides were tiled, smooth, and dry, with support columns every six feet. These columns supported an arched ceiling of finished hardwood. There was just enough ceiling height for the two to walk without having to duck.

Suddenly, the passageway opened up into an area resembling a small town from the 1800s, or the inside of a mall, or both. Store-like booths lined the open area left and right, and at the far side was what looked like a fountain, but it glowed. This then was the source of the light.

"Careful," Kyler said. "It could be radioactive. I'll check with my Geiger counter."

Kyler checked, but as he did, Mirini suddenly sprang to life. She ran to various iron-wrought benches, inside the booths, and swung around columns that resembled lamp posts.

"I feel free," she said. "I feel like I'm finally free."

The Geiger counter registered no radiation, and Kyler returned the device to his backpack.

"Don't you feel it?" she asked.

"Feel what?"

"The air, it's like iron ions everywhere," she said.

"Huh?" Kyler asked.

Mirini dropped to a knee, touched the ground, and touched a black powder from the ground to her nose.

"It's here too," she said.

"Iron?" Kyler asked. "This must be some old underground city where they produced iron."

Mirini ran into a little store and then ran back out with black powder in her hand. She dumped the powder in her mouth and swallowed it.

"I'm alive! I'm full of iron and alive!" she exclaimed.

"You ate that?" Kyler asked.

But Mirini didn't listen. She kicked off the wrapping around her feet, and Kyler was amazed to see that no evidence of her former injury remained.

"How did you heal so quickly?" he asked.

But Mirini wasn't interested. She ran to the fountain, but it turned out to be a pool of very cool water—about five degrees above freezing. Little glowing spheres floated up and down the pool. Mirini took one of the spheres, warmed it in her hand, and tossed it up in the air. The sphere broke open, and a glowing butterfly flew away.

"What the—" Kyler started to say in his shock.

Mirini laughed. Picking up the sphere had left glowing residue on her hand, and she wiped that on her arm, which now had a glowing smear line. Mirini laughed again. She grabbed another glowing sphere from the fountain and drew glowing lines on her body and clothing—along her sides, on her legs, arms, neck, and hair. She painted her face, tossed the sphere in the air, and several fireflies burst from the sphere and hovered about.

"Mirini, don't pick up any more spheres. They could be dangerous," Kyler said.

Mirini drew water from the fountain with her hands and splashed it on the ground in front of her, and the ground glowed. She splashed more water, but now in the air, and it rained glowing drops. Mirini laughed. She ran around the area, found a light and wooden bat, then ran to the fountain with the bat. She dipped it into the fountain and stirred. She then ran with the bat to various metal objects—the lamp post, the bench, an old mail box, and other things, and she slapped glowing water onto them. They vibrated and clunked all on their own, like percussion instruments. At first they were out of sync and made a horrible cacophony, but Mirini clapped her hands in rhythm, and the glowing iron instruments followed her rhythm, and now Mirini had the makings of a beat and rhythm with iron cans providing melody, and the wholeness of the area took on the sound of something between country music and light rock 'n' roll.

Mirini sang, and she sang into the bat as if it were a microphone. She danced and twirled as she sang. Kyler stood in complete shock, but he watched her and listened to her singing:

Night raining light
Light painting life,
Just take a stick and throw
It in the pool so bright.

I was a-lost
On tower tall,
Until ferrum did climb
And rescue me from fall.

Night raining light
Light painting life,
Just take some glowing light
And throw it to the right.

Then down I went
In ditch below,
And up above there came
An enemy oh-no.
Knife wielding blights
Life-stealing wights,
I hoped to hide from them
Completely out of sight.

But trouble came
My feet were maimed,

The water tore and ripped
The flesh and made me lame.

I could not cry
For fear I'd die
I needed ferrum close
And searched with all my might

I touched a plate
An iron nest,
The metal in the plate
Returned me to my best

Night raining light
Light painting life,
Just take some glowing stuff
And ruffle, tussle, fight.

I feel all right
I'm dancing fine
I cannot wait until
The stars come out tonight.

Night raining light
Light painting life,
Just take a scoop of light
And paint the world so bright.

Mirini continued dancing, and the music continued a little more. Her legs carried her about and about until the music slowed and the light faded. She sang one last verse more slowly than the first:

Now comes the end
Of my new song
I had a fine good time
And bid you all goodnight!

"Goodnight!" Mirini yelled.

The glow ceased, the music stopped, and all fell quiet and dark. Kyler scrambled for a flashlight from his backpack, but before he could retrieve it, he saw a gray, glowing outline of a person approach him. The person grew closer, and as she did, it became apparent to Kyler that this was Mirini, but not the Mirini with glowing water smeared on her or the helpless Mirini stuck on a lighthouse. It was a Mirini as if viewed through the green of a night camera, but again—she was grey.

"Do you love me?" she asked as she stood very close to Kyler.

"What!?" Kyler stumbled.

Mirini walked toward Kyler, but suddenly she walked past him. She then began holding a light pole as if it were a human.

"Do you love me?" she asked the iron-wrought light pole.

Mirini then began to kiss the light pole and even nibble it.

"I discovered something about myself, just now," Mirini said. "I'm different from you."

"You are different," Kyler said. "You're a charming woman, like none I've ever known could exist. But you have this infatuation with iron. And you're glowing. Did you swallow some of that glowing water?"

"No," she said, and Kyler became frightened.

"Who...what are you?" he asked.

Mirini released her hold of the light pole, turned to Kyler, and hugged him. She felt just as warm and affectionate as before, but Kyler still shook in nervousness. Then she removed one of the dog tags from around her neck and placed it back over his neck. The metal seemed different to Kyler.

"I want you to wear this again," she said. "It's now more special than before."

Kyler felt fear fall down through his gut, to his legs, and out his feet. He suddenly felt light and burden-free.

"That was weird. I feel completely at ease. There's something about you I find very attractive. I want to say that I love you, but I know that such a thing is impossible when I have only known you for a short time. And yet, I keep feeling I've always known you."

"You must know who I am then," she said. "I want you to walk with me. Hold my hand. Walk with me."

Kyler walked with Mirini toward the fountain. She stopped at the edge. It didn't glow like before, but Mirini continued to do so. The two looked down into the water. Kyler saw their reflections—Mirini's was more of an orange glow than the grey she actually portrayed. Then he looked at his reflection. The dog tag around his neck glowed, just a little bit, but glow it did, and orange, too.

"Are you ready?" she asked.

"Ready for what?" Kyler asked.

"Hold your breath and walk with me," she said.

Kyler did just that, and the two walked through the fountain wall and stood within the fountain without being wet. Mirini touched her fingers to Kyler's forehead, and in this way the two communicated.

"Do not exhale and do not speak out loud. Being inside matter is like being underwater," she said.

"What...what...just happened?" Kyler thought.

"I can pass through matter," she thought. "And when you hold me, you can pass through matter too."

"Then...you...no, it can't be, it can't be!" he thought.

"Yes, it's true," she thought. "I'm totally alien, fearsome and overpowering, and you're attracted to an alien."

Kyler started to pull away, but Mirini held him firmly.

"Do not release my grip! Should you let go just now, you'd surely die when your legs fused with the fountain floor and fountain water," Mirini warned.

Kyler didn't move. Fear started to creep through him again, but Mirini drew close and melted the fear from him.

"I want to know more about you," he thought. "Are...are you an aliotrote?"

Mirini led him from the fountain. Kyler exhaled, and yet he did not feel out of breath. It was as if Mirini had recycled the carbon dioxide in his body back to oxygen. Still puzzled by this phenomenon, he watched Mirini's next move. She let go of Kyler's hand, fashioned her hands around a lamppost, it glowed orange, and she re-formed it into a comfortable iron couch with iron stuffing and a woven iron-cloth covering. She touched Kyler's hand and drew him to the couch, which to his surprise was amazingly soft.

"Is Mirini your real name?" Kyler asked.

"I'm not an aliotrote. Aliotrotes are in love with mercury. But my name is Mirini. Mirini Baliotra. And I'm in love with iron," she said.

"Oh, boy," Kyler said. "Does that mean you're going to bleed the iron out of me? Like the way those aliotrotes...Baliotra...wait a moment...your last name...is it too much a coincidence?"

Mirini looked at him with new concern. She touched several fingers to Kyler's forehead and read his thoughts.

"Yes. Savien, Kazhak, and the other aliotrotes are looking for me," she said.

"Then you are an aliotrote. I don't understand," Kyler said.

"I'm not an aliotrote," Mirini said.

"But you...the things you do," Kyler started.

"The aliotrotes are from Aliotra," Mirini said. "I'm from Bruxima 4."

"Who? What? Where?" Kyler asked.

"Aliotra is a planet about four hundred light years from here. Bruxima 4 is only eighty light years from here," Mirini explained. "We were once as you, a prospering people, and we lived on Bruxima 4. Then the aliotrotes came. They consumed most of my people using that osmozicon. But it was work for the aliotrotes. We had to be devitiated. Heavily."

"I don't know what that means," Kyler said.

"My people were full of iron," Mirini said. "It gave us abilities like passing through walls and such, by altering molecular structure electromagnetically. We didn't need iron to survive, and a good thing too, because iron is incredibly rare on Bruxima 4. But for those who had access to the element, iron helped them do these extra things. The aliotrotes had to remove the iron first before they could consume us."

"I have so many questions. But the thing that keeps coming to mind is — your last name — Baliotra," he said.

"Yes."

"Is there a connection?"

"Yes."

"I mean with the aliotrotes," Kyler said.

"Yes, yes," she said.

Mirini led Kyler back to the fountain.

"Just look into the water," she said. "Don't touch."

Kyler looked. The water became a viewing portal, and Kyler could see much violence.

"This is Bruxima 4, about two hundred years ago. It was filled with war. And what do you suppose we fought over?" Mirini asked.

"Money? Power?" Kyler asked.

"Iron," Mirini said. "Any sort of rare yet valuable resource becomes an issue of violence. And so it was for Bruxima 4. Iron gave a person great strength and power. One could become wealthy with the element that acts as a nuclear fulcrum between the lighter, fusionic elements and the heavier, fissionic elements. And one would need to, because iron is very expensive and rare."

"But iron is plentiful on Earth. Most planets have an iron core. How is it Bruxima 4 doesn't have—" Kyler started.

"Shh. Listen," Mirini continued. "We didn't get the decay of nickel-56 that most solar systems get. And so we have little iron, and for those without that little bit of iron, life is a trap. Because those who had iron then controlled everything and forced those without to work themselves to the bone. All the seeds for an uprising are in play. And indeed, the wealthy were pressured to share their iron, but they hoarded iron even more, creating a vicious spiral that erupted in war."

The pool showed the growing divide and tension between sides, and then the war.

"The rich created machines of control, based on iron, to force the poor people into submission. That only made the people angrier, but they didn't know how to combat the iron machines. Many simply threw themselves against the machines, and the machines crushed them."

Mirini paused. She was practically in tears, and now speech became more difficult. The pool showed one failed suicide attack after another, with the iron machines relentlessly continuing their march.

"A group of rebels sought some way to fight the machines, but without using iron, because none could be had. But there was plenty of mercury available."

"Oh no," Kyler said.

"Oh yes," Mirini said. "One of those rebels was Silano Baliotra—my grandfather."

"A grandfather who lived two hundred years ago?" Kyler asked.

"Yes," Mirini said. "He would still be alive except for the war."

"Incredible," Kyler said.

"I'm eighty years old myself," Mirini said.

"You look twenty," Kyler found himself saying.

"As it were," she continued. "He created the first mercury forms of artificial life. These forms were robotic in nature, needing heavy control circuitry. And so they were called Baliotrotes. The first generation could travel up the iron machines' limbs and disable them. The second generation then broke down the machines into usable supplies of iron. And that would have been the end of the war, except for a revolutionary named Savien Pavanko who decided that more punishment had to be inflicted. He forced Silano under penalty of death to create a third generation that could retrieve iron from people. And so Silano created the third generation, and these mercury-based creatures captured the iron-rich folk and retrieved the iron from their bodies. Unfortunately, the shock killed them."

"Other rebels helped Silano escape from Savien's grip, but it was too late. Savien had learned the technology and now launched a new war to take power on Bruxima 4. Silano worked on a way to reverse the work he had done. Quite often he cursed his *mercury mistake*, as he put it."

"And?" Kyler asked.

"And, Silano engineered new creatures made of boron and gold," Mirini said. "These new creatures captured all the iron back from Savien. Savien was furious and launched a counterattack. Silano knew that this new war would continue to escalate back and forth, so he put a stop to it. He created a spaceship, filled it with all the iron, and led this spaceship with the boron and gold robots away from Bruxima 4. Savien and his mercury robots followed, and as far as we knew, that was the end of it. They spent eternity fighting each other for the iron."

"Perhaps ten years ago, they came back. Not Silano, he was dead. But Savien was somehow preserved and had evolved from the work he had done with his creatures, except his creatures were alive. They had absorbed the DNA from Silano and become true life forms. But now instead of iron, they wanted our DNA, which when broken down binds very well with their mercury compounds. And so that was the new war."

Mirini paused again. The pool showed people on Bruxima 4 dying from being osmozed in the osmozicons.

"Before my parents were osmozed, they created these cufflets for me," Mirini said. "They allow me to convert mercury into krypton and ruthenium. But they require a special kind of iron to make them work. My parents, Ediom and Mianna, gathered what was left of our iron supply to make my cufflets."

"Ediom and Mianna are your parents? Why didn't you say so! They're part of the rebels I met in the sewer. Follow me! We'll see your parents soon enough," Kyler said.

"That's impossible," Mirini said. "My parents are dead. As is my brother, Raian. All that you have witnessed here is a memory."

And when Mirini said "memory," she brushed Kyler's eyes closed. She then touched his arm. He opened his eyes, and he was back in the interrogation room with Mirini, Von Brock, and Debbie Dayla.

"So how will the memory device work?" Von Brock asked.

Kyler looked around, confused.

"It already has," Debbie said.

"What just happened?" Kyler asked.

"What a clever trick!" Von Brock said. "It even fooled me! You must have accelerated the memory retrieval such that Kyler experienced some past event in a few seconds of our time, but perhaps in minutes of his time."

"Hours," Mirini said.

"Wow!" Kyler said. "Then I...was that...where was I?"

"You were on Bruxima 4. At least your character was. The person you portrayed was real, but his name was not Kyler. It was Kieulor, and he was to be my husband," Mirini said. "Your perceptions mixed with the memories from the device, and so you thought my parents were here. But they are not."

"I'm sorry about your parents," Kyler offered.

Mirini looked exhausted.

"Let's take a break for five minutes," Debbie said. "Colonel Von Brock and Major Bohr—this way, please. And we'll take the cuff bracelets with us."

The three left the interrogation room and entered a small office—one of many that Debbie used and had once been used by Roger Dayla. There were many display screens showing a variety of things—weather maps, television news stations, satellite surveillance, sky surveillance, Dayla building surveillance, and statuses on computer servers. Debbie held the cufflets to the light.

"We have already tried analyzing these cuff bracelets to learn how they work, but so far we have been unsuccessful," Debbie said. "Mirini is too weak to use them again."

"How do you know?" Kyler asked.

"It's obvious. The alien is exhausted," Von Brock said.

"Unfortunately, Mirini is the only one who knows how to use them," Debbie said.

"We should ask Mirini for help. She could teach us how to use the cufflets," Kyler said.

"What about the Dayla Adapto-transicon?" Von Brock asked.

"I tried while you were out finding Major Bohr. The cuff bracelets burned out the Adapto-transicon's crystal," Debbie said.

"Let's ask Mirini for help," Kyler repeated.

"Really?" Von Brock asked.

"Yes, let's ask her!" Kyler said.

"Yes, really," Debbie replied to Von Brock. "Complete meltdown. Nothing in this world can do that."

"Hello? Is anyone listening to me?" Kyler asked.

"What about your dolphin friend," Von Brock said.

"He's caught up in a war with the orcas," Debbie said.

"Dolphin? In a war with orcas? An orca *is* a dolphin," Kyler said. "What am I saying, dolphins don't go to war."

"Well what about one of his friends?" Von Brock asked.

"They are all involved in the war," Debbie said. "I wish Sparfy could help, or Metavasi or King Tugan or Queen Brela."

"Who are all these people?" Kyler asked. "Are you speaking in code?"

"If we could get one of them to help, just one, by transforming into one of those mercury aliens and infiltrating their camp, then—" Von Brock said.

"Dolphins hate mercury," Debbie said. "Absolutely hate mercury. Now that I think of it, there's no way one of them would transform and enter the camp. It would be like us crawling through a sewer of radioactive dead skunks and rotting cabbage."

"The girl. Mirini?" Kyler said.

"Then we'll have to tech our way out," Von Brock said. "What if we build a new heavy duty Adapto-transicon crystal to handle these cuff bracelets?"

"We can't, at least not in this environment," Debbie said. "Creating the crystal introduces a slight warble due to Earth's gravity. In most cases, this warble is so minor as not to be an issue. But it's too much for Mirini's cuff bracelets."

"A mission into orbit?" Kyler asked. "With Mirini. Of course. She could teach us from orbit, and she'll be safe, too."

"The vomit comet," Von Brock said.

"Not enough time," Debbie said. "The crystal creation process requires a good thirty minutes to cure. A standard reduced-gravity aircraft would give us only twenty-five seconds of zero g."

"What about the Dayla Malf Machine? It's a more advanced reduced-gravity aircraft," Von Brock said.

"Five minutes—max. Not enough time," Debbie said.

"I keep thinking we're missing something," Von Brock said.

"Yeah, you're ignoring me!" Kyler said.

"Wait, I hear something," Debbie said.

"Finally," Kyler said.

But it wasn't Kyler that Debbie heard. From around the door frame stood Mirini, horribly pale and weak. She held onto the door frame in an effort to stay on her feet, but she couldn't. Before she collapsed and passed out, she spoke:

"Help me."

Kyler rushed to help her.

"Well? Help me!" Kyler said.

Von Brock and Debbie exchanged glances as if to say, "Should we?"

"Let's get her to the mini clinic," Debbie finally said.

Kyler started to lift Mirini, but he struggled with her frame. Von Brock, however, lifted Mirini with ease and carried her down the corridor to the mini clinic, where he placed Mirini on a treatment bed.

"Show off," Kyler muttered.

Kyler stood next to Mirini's left side. Von Brock went to work and looked for a vein to insert an intravenous needle while Debbie attached monitoring sensors.

"I can't find a vein," Von Brock said.

"Well thank god for that," Kyler heard himself say.

Debbie and Von Brock looked at Kyler in surprise.

"I'm trying to save her life!" Von Brock said.

"Oh, what I meant was...never mind," Kyler said.

"Give her oxygen," Von Brock said. "Do it!"

Debbie retrieved the oxygen mask and was about to place it over Mirini's face, but Kyler suddenly felt this was wrong, and he blocked Debbie.

"What are you doing?" Von Brock asked. "Get out of the way, old man."

Von Brock moved Kyler out of the way. Debbie hesitated with the oxygen mask, but Von Brock insisted, so she placed the mask over Mirini's face. Mirini's breathing shallowed, and she became very still.

"You're killing her," Kyler said.

"She's going into cardiac arrest," Von Brock said. "We'll have to give her a shot of epinephrine in her heart."

Debbie opened a package and handed a syringe to Von Brock. Von Brock lifted his hand to stab the syringe into Mirini's heart, but Kyler yelled:

"No!"

He dove in between Von Brock's needle and Mirini, and in so doing he took the full dose of epinephrine. But that wasn't all. Kyler removed the oxygen mask, placed his lips to Mirini, and gave her a form of mouth-to-mouth resuscitation. But as it turned out, Mirini took in carbon dioxide and exhaled oxygen, so in fact Kyler was giving her necessary carbon dioxide that she needed.

"Get out of here!" Von Brock said as he attempted to push Kyler aside.

But the epinephrine took full effect on Kyler's metabolism, and he erupted with fiery anger. Kyler spun around, socked Von Brock in the jaw, and thus knocked him unconscious.

"He needed that," Kyler said.

"You...she...everything is backward. She needed carbon dioxide, not oxygen," Debbie said.

"Yes, I do," Mirini said, now reaching full consciousness. "There's so little carbon dioxide on your planet that at times I become weak."

"Miss Dayla. I have a plan. Mirini and I will go up into Earth's orbit and grow a new crystal for the Adapto-transicon. We'll analyze the cufflets, and we'll study how Mirini uses them. There's an experimental weather laser in geo-sync orbit that we—" Kyler started.

"That weather laser is for seeding clouds to rain, and to cause hurricanes to dump most of their energy in the ocean," Debbie said.

"We will modify the weather laser with the help of Mirini and the cufflets. We then fire a beam directly at the aliens. The beam will go through water, right?" Kyler asked.

"It was designed to do that, yes. It employs a duo-phasic polaric wavelength to minimize unintended dispersion," Debbie said. "But Mirini's health concerns me."

"With luck, we can convert the alien's mercury into krypton and ruthenium," Kyler said.

"There's something you should know," Mirini said. "I thank you for the carbon dioxide, but I must also have iron soon, or else I will die."

"Debbie, Mirini needs iron, and now," Kyler said.

"It must be a special molecular chain of iron," Mirini said. "Elemental iron will not work."

"I suspected as much. Well, I can start a computer analysis to see what she needs. She must remain here then," Debbie said. "We can send you up to grow the crystal and test the cuff bracelets. With luck, the Adapto-transicon will give us the data we need to make this all work from the weather laser."

"Hmmm," Kyler said. "Wait. It will take a little time for us to reach geo-sync orbit, grow the crystal, and modify the weather laser. Could you do the analysis during that time?"

"No, and it's too dangerous anyway," Debbie said. "Even if somehow we determine what she needs, how could you produce it in space? You'd need the right materials, the right fab machine, and a doctor to pull it all together."

"Are you—" Kyler started.

"No she isn't, but of course I am," Von Brock said, now regaining consciousness and standing up. "That was a nasty punch you threw."

"I'm not going up into orbit with Von Brock," Kyler said.

"You're right. Nor is Mirini," Von Brock said. "You go alone. Here."

Von Brock placed the cufflets in a pack and gave the pack to Kyler.

"Wait. I can make this work. I know I can. Just trust me," Kyler said.

Von Brock laughed.

"TRUST—Try Reality, U Stupid Trustaholic," Von Brock said.

"Where did you hear that, in the little boys' room?" Kyler suggested.

"No one with any sense talks trust, old man. Trust is for people who don't know what they're doing," Von Brock said.

"Major Bohr, prepare to launch for Weather-Sat Dayla 105," Debbie said. "Doctor Von Brock, begin analysis for what iron molecule chains Mirini needs. I will—"

But Debbie was interrupted by an alert on her phone.

"How do you get a signal down here?" Kyler asked.

"Shh," Debbie said. "Something's happening with the alien spaceship. I need to return to the main office and coordinate things there. Excuse me, gentlemen."

Debbie stepped out of the room, and Kyler was about to start an argument with Von Brock.

"And gentlemen," Debbie said, poking her head back in the room. "Try to behave?"

Debbie left. Kyler stood over Mirini and looked at her.

"You'd better get going, old ma...I mean, Major," Von Brock said.

"I can't leave her," Kyler said.

"I'll take care of her. Go. Debbie said to behave, remember? We need that crystal," Von Brock said.

"Okay, but if anything changes...if she calls for me...if—" Kyler started.

"Quit if'ing yourself to death and go on," Von Brock said.

"Okay, okay," Kyler said.

Kyler made his way down the corridor to another elevator, which took him first sideways and then up, up, up, until it reached the very top of the Dayla Spacecraft Assembly Building. He exited the elevator, and to his surprise there were technicians running around. Kyler bumped into one.

"Why are you running? What's the rush?" Kyler asked.

"No time to talk. Must get the spaceship ready. Oh wait, this is for you," the technician said as he gave Kyler two things—the Adapto-transicon, and a device for growing a new transicon crystal.

"Thank you," Kyler said.

"They're coming," the technician said, and he left.

"Who's coming?" Kyler asked, but the technician was long gone.

Kyler stepped into the spacecraft and started the pre-flight check, including stowing his pack and transicon equipment into a compartment. He had studied the Dayla Earth High Orbit (DEHO) spacecraft and practiced in simulators, but this was his first time flying a real one. Part of the pre-flight check required that he don a partial pressure suit, and so he began fitting one over his body. He was about to attach the helmet when another technician came running toward him.

"We must accelerate the launch," he said.

"Why?" Kyler said.

"Get inside! We launch in sixty seconds," he said.

"Good god, man, that's not enough time to—" Kyler started.

But he was interrupted when Mirini dashed off the elevator and came running toward him.

"Help me," she said. "Von Brock is going to kill me."

"Get inside now!" the technician said to Kyler.

Von Brock exited a second elevator and came running toward Mirini, presumably to bring her back.

"The spacecraft will launch—with or without you!" the technician warned.

The technician shoved Kyler into the spacecraft, but Kyler grabbed Mirini's arm and pulled her inside with him, and so the technician ended up pushing both in. Kyler then closed the hatch quickly and locked it.

"Stop!" Von Brock yelled. "Open that hatch."

"Too late!" the technician said, and now the two argued while the platform pulled away from the spacecraft.

"Strap in!" Kyler said to Mirini, as he helped strap her into her chair.

Kyler then strapped himself in. The roof had pulled away, and flying creatures now descended into the launch bay and attacked anything and everything in sight. The DEHO launched as Kyler and Mirini watched these creatures devour frantic technicians. Von Brock came under attack too, but he fell out of view, and so Kyler didn't learn of his fate. The DEHO rocket was now at full power, and the craft was blasting through Earth's atmosphere, above the cloud deck, and up, up, up. It was more of a shot up at first, and only well after the blue sky had turned black did it assume any kind of orbit. But the orbit spiraled outward, and so Earth continued to grow smaller and smaller.

"Typically, a satellite launch takes about twelve days to reach geo-sync orbit," Kyler said to Mirini. "But we will be there in two hours. We could be there in one hour, but we would fly right past the weather satellite. We will need that second hour just to slow down and get into proper orbit. In the meantime, let's find out what happened at Dayla Industries."

Kyler manipulated the controls for the radio.

"Dayla Control, this is Major Bohr aboard DEHO 1. Do you read me?" Kyler called through the spacecraft's radio.

No response.

"DAYCON, DEHO 1. Do you copy?" Kyler called again.

But Dayla Central Control wasn't responding. The entire building was under attack from the aliotrotes. They invaded from the sky with their flying army, and they invaded from the ground with their walking army. Kyler was able to tap into a television satellite signal and learn that much. Kyler then switched frequencies and attempted to contact NASA's Mission Control in Houston.

"Houston, this is Major Kyler Bohr of the Dayla Earth High Orbit One spacecraft, do you read?"

"DEHO 1, Houston, we read you," a voice called back.

"I'm on a special mission for Dayla Industries, but I've lost contact with DAYCON," Kyler said.

"Switch to secure channel 103, scramble 207, DEHO 1," Houston said.

"Roger. Channel 103, scramble 207," Kyler said.

Kyler switched his transceiver to a secure channel. But why was this needed?

"Houston, DEHO 1, now transmitting on channel 103, scramble 207," Kyler said.

"DEHO 1, Houston. We've been monitoring the situation there as best we can. There's an electromagnetic dome in Brunswick that's blocking communication."

"The dome!" Kyler said to himself. "I forgot about the dome! But I got through the dome somehow! I'll have to ask Miss Dayla about that another time. But she spoke as if we'd be in constant contact. Unless something else happened."

"Do you copy, DEHO 1?" Houston said.

"I copy," Kyler said.

"Ground units report a battle inside the dome," Houston said. "U.S. forces are attempting to penetrate the dome but are so far unsuccessful."

"But I entered the dome," Kyler said to himself. "And so did Von Brock."

"You two entered when the dome first formed," Mirini said, being able to hear him. "The stolen mercury has given them more power and allowed to fortify the dome. It's a wonder we escaped."

"I think Debbie must have done something special to let us through," Kyler said.

"She did. I could feel it," Mirini said. "Had I remained, either Von Brock would have killed me with his bad medicine, or the aliotrotes would have osmozed me. In my weakened state, I could not resist. You saved my life."

"I wish I could have saved more. Debbie and the others...I..." Kyler lamented.

"Does that include Von Brock?" Mirini asked.

"He is annoying, but I would save him too," Kyler admitted.

"They are safe," Mirini said. "The last bit of my strength tells me so."

"I just wish I could help you," Kyler said. "I may have saved you for now, but for how long? I don't know anything about chains of iron molecules."

"There's something I wish to tell you," Mirini said. "I did not dare tell the others. They would think ill of me."

"Oh?"

"Like a monster, a...what do you call...vampire...or worse," Mirini said.

"What are you talking about?" Kyler asked.

"In your hallucination, when you relived the parts of Kieulor, my future husband, there was one part that was not based on his life," Mirini said.

"I keep listening, but I don't understand a thing you are saying," Kyler said.

"Do you remember when you were in the osmozicon? And the aliotrotes filled it with those mercury compounds?" she asked.

"The memory recall," Kyler said. "Yes, now I understand. What about it?"

"That did not happen to Kieulor. He was taken to an osmozicon, but he was osmozed instantly," she said.

"Then why did I experience things differently?" Kyler asked.

"The memory recall adjusted things for how you would fit in the environment. And it detected that the osmozicon would malfunction when it tried to osmoze you," she said.

"But why?" Kyler said. "Why would it do that?"

"There's something about you that's different," she said. "And though I am weak, I have a suspicion about you that I wish to confirm. Please remove your pants."

"What?!" Kyler said.

"Or roll up your pants leg, so I may see your lower leg," she said.

"I'll have to remove the lower part of my partial pressure suit," he said. "Well, we're far enough away from Earth that it's no good anyway. Okay, I don't know what you'll see, but sure."

Kyler removed his partial pressure suit. He then rolled up a pants leg to show the lower part of his right leg.

"There," she said. "As I thought."

"What?" he asked.

"Look," she said, and she pointed to pigmentation on his skin.

"Those are just some freckles that I picked up when I turned thirty-five," he said.

"It's iron oxide," she said. "You have an excess of iron in your body."

"Vampire?" Kyler said, now beginning to understand.

"Your tissues contain the iron molecular chains that I need," she said. "An aliotrote would just take...but I...cannot...just take."

"Now I understand," he said. "A vampire? So if you drank my blood, would that help?"

Mirini shivered when he asked, and she was afraid to reply in the affirmative.

"You don't have to offer," she said. "It's against our culture to consume animal tissue, much less that of an alien."

"Then how did you survive on your planet? I mean, with the iron stuff?" Kyler asked.

"We had special dispensaries. They were expensive, though. There was also a special plant called ferrosinia that contained the iron molecular chain in the flower and the berry. Ever had ferrosiberry pie?" Mirini asked.

"This is a strange conversation. From vampires to pies," Kyler said.

"I am sorry. I will be quiet," she said.

"No, you don't have to. I'm not annoyed by you. Things just take a little getting used to," Kyler said. "Hmm. Blood will work. Otherwise I suppose you could just cook my leg for supper and eat that."

"It's not like that," Mirini said. "None of my people have consumed animal tissue—ever. The aliotrotes do nothing but consume animal tissue. And they extract many things, but they don't like iron. It doesn't mix with mercury. Understand that if—and I'm speaking about a very big if—I were to consume animal tissue of some sort, I would find it very disgusting and would struggle to keep it in my system."

"I'm almost disappointed," Kyler said.

"I don't understand," she said.

"It's...well...this is going to sound strange...I almost liked the idea of you being a vampire and all that...and biting me on the neck...and we would then...well...never mind," Kyler said. "Stupid human culture making me say stupid human things. Okay, how do we do this? Do I cut a vein or something and let you drink it?"

"Nothing so revolting," she said. "The process more resembles a blood transfusion in your culture. But I need my cufflets."

"Oh," Kyler said. "The cufflets. Yeah, they're in this compartment here."

Kyler reached, opened the compartment, and removed the pack that Von Brock had given him. He opened the pack and removed the cufflets. He stared at them for a moment.

"Beautiful, aren't they?" Mirini asked.

"Yes, they are," Kyler said as he handed the cufflets to Mirini.

"My father made these for me to protect myself from aliotrotes. He sent me away from Bruxima 4 to save me. My craft was damaged, and I was able to transfer to one of your satellites and land. But I had to use the cufflets to make it all happen. Without them, I'm powerless, at least for doing things beyond the normal," Mirini said.

"From what I've seen, you're already beyond normal," Kyler said.

"Thank you. I would explain more, but I really need the iron," she said. "Bruxima 4 is much closer to its star than Earth is to your sun."

"I don't understand," Kyler said.

"I also need starlight to survive," Mirini said. "Aren't you the same? Don't you need starlight?"

"We call it *sunlight*, and we only need it for vitamin D," Kyler said.

"We need it for energy. Um, I suppose your plants are the closest life form on Earth that do what we do," Mirini said.

Mirini attached the cufflets to her left and right forearms. Next, she placed two fingers on Kyler's arm, and she began absorbing blood from Kyler's body.

"This doesn't hurt at all. In fact, I'm beginning to feel better," Kyler said. "I could almost take a nap."

"Try to stay awake," a voice said.

Kyler looked around. He stood in a cube-shaped room with plain, stainless-steel walls. There was a single door, and it was locked. Kyler walked to a far corner and stood.

"I'm bored," he said.

Just then, the door opened, and two Bruxis—a man and a woman—entered. Their complexions and personalities resembled the studious and courteous people from eastern Asia on Earth, but this wasn't Earth. Each carried a manual notebook and a portable table.

"Asmondo Arliaco?" the woman asked.

"My name is Major Kyler Bohr," Kyler said.

"Yes, that's one of your many aliases," the woman said, now writing in her notebook on her portable table.

Her assistant also took notes.

"Let's start. You are a known spy for the aliotrotes," she said. "Do you have anything you wish to say?"

Kyler suddenly felt extremely relaxed and without motivation to offer much of anything.

"Whatever," he said, now falling completely into his new role as spy.

"You can speak...is this true...twenty languages?" she said. "*Hakalo amulipan ikano palukipi ina pali higata!*" which means "You are charged with treason and will hang!"

"So what?" Kyler replied, understanding every word.

"You're very intelligent. Why waste it by helping the aliotrotes?" she asked.

Kyler shrugged his shoulders.

"Don't you care about people? Don't you care about Bruxima 4?" she asked.

"Bruxima 4 bores me," Kyler said, shocked at his words.

The woman conversed quietly with her assistant for a moment. Wanting things to change, Kyler concentrated on an electrical circuit just outside his cell and caused a fire alarm to go off. The woman and man seemed confused at first, but then they ran out of the room to evacuate, leaving their portable tables behind. A guard just outside the room locked the door to keep Kyler in, but it didn't matter. Kyler took a portable table, collapsed it, concentrated, and re-formed it into a super cleaving instrument. With his hands on the legs, he slashed the table through a wall and opened a passage to a corridor. He then walked through the corridor as people ran toward him to stop him, but he concentrated and made them forget who he was.

Kyler took the stairs down a level and walked into a long, narrow room. There was something different about this room.

"This wall is strange," he said, "though it looks like the others."

He tapped on it, and it sounded hollow. He tapped twice, paused, twice, paused, and tapped three times. The wall lifted vertically, revealing a glass wall behind it and a group of elderly people playing cards around a table. They didn't even notice he was there, but after a moment, one did, waved at Kyler, and the wall closed.

"So that's how older people get their peace and quiet," Kyler said. "Well, I may have had my moment of fascination for the day."

Kyler continued out of the room and outside. Bruxis on the street waved to him normally as if he were another Bruxi. He waved back to continue playing the part of an interested Bruxi citizen, but in truth he was not. He wandered around the city for a bit, past the people holding signs begging for help against the aliotrotes, past a woman and her baby, past a man walking his dog, and past a gardener. He walked to the pier and stared at the water. Boring. He walked along a pier and saw a familiar boat, the Mercalli Dream. He climbed into the boat and spoke.

"I'll have another," Kyler said, speaking the code phrase.

The captain undocked and piloted the boat out to sea for a short ways until it reached a small island.

"Thank you," Kyler said.

Kyler exited the boat and walked up to a sheer cliff face. He concentrated for a moment, held his hand up, and walked through the solid rock. He then found a tunnel which led to an office complex. He walked into one such office and spoke to the receptionist.

"Another drink for Asmondo Arliaco," Kyler said.

"One moment, Mr. Arliaco," the receptionist said. She then touched her intercom button and said, "Another drink for Asmondo Arliaco."

"Send him in at once," the man said.

Kyler stepped into the office. A heavy-set man stood up from his desk and immediately offered it to Kyler. Kyler sat in the desk chair and put his feet up.

"Welcome back, Asmondo. It's good to see you," the man said.

"Yeah, I was bored and didn't know what else to do, so I came here," Kyler said.

"You are always welcome here. Always. Boredom is a sickness that can be cured. We are alike, you and I. We are both master artisans, and any endeavor that does not stretch our skills is torture," the man said.

"Yeah, okay. What do you have for me?" Kyler asked.

"Down to the point. I like that," the heavy-set man laughed. He then called in his receptionist, "Rosa, please bring itinerary number one."

Rosa entered the office with a piece of paper and gave it to Kyler. Kyler looked at the paper. It was broken into steps of what to do. Some steps had printed movie tickets and other such things for gaining access to an event. This first step had two photos—one of his alias, and another of his *mark*—the victim.

"Your alias is Scott Braylo," the heavy-set man said.

Kyler waved his hand over his face, and his new appearance now matched that of the photo.

"Excellent work as usual," the heavy-set man said. "Stand up for me, if you please."

Kyler stood up.

"Ah, you need to be a little taller," the heavy-set man said.

Kyler waved his hand again, and he grew a few inches.

"Good," the heavy-set man said. "Now Scott is a bodybuilder."

"That's easy enough," Kyler said, and he increased his muscle mass in all areas.

"Perfect," the heavy-set man said.

"Let's see," Kyler said, looking at the list. "Escort General Grayto's daughter to the State Ball. Her name is Charla Grayto. I will sense what she thinks, say and do those things that will make her fall in love with me, take her to dinner the next day, take her to the theater, show support for her father's efforts in the war—"

"Without actually helping, of course," the heavy-set man said.

"Of course. I'll do my best acting job," Kyler said. "Let's see...take her to a mountain excursion, and then—"

"Make sure the accident is very realistic. There must be witnesses to the accident, so it appears as such, but the body must never be found."

"Because it will be osmozed, of course," Kyler said.

"Of course," the heavy-set man said.

Kyler felt powerless to say otherwise. It was as if he were watching a movie and was unable to change the storyline.

"Any questions?" the heavy-set man asked.

"Why not just kidnap her and have her osmozed more quickly?" Kyler asked.

"We do not wish to arouse the general," the heavy-set man said. "We are not fully entrenched in these parts. Keeping the general from striking back will save us time in establishing our aliotrote friends."

"Okay. Well, I have a suit to purchase for a State Ball. If you'll excuse me," Kyler said.

"You're forgetting the best part. The reward. And that is—all of Charla Grayto's iron, plus ten thousand gold credits," the heavy-set man said.

"I no longer have need for iron. But I can always use the credits," Kyler said.

"I am pleased," the heavy-set man said. "I hope this mission is challenging enough to fight off boredom?"

"It should, at least for a little bit," Kyler said. "Perhaps next time I can date two important women at once. Or five."

The heavy-set man laughed.

"You *are* an incredible man, Asmondo Arliaco," the heavy-set man said.

Kyler folded the paper into his pocket and said his goodbye. He didn't bother to use the door but instead walked through the wall. His vision went dark momentarily, and when his vision returned, he was back in DEHO 1 with Mirini.

"Transfer complete," Mirini said. "I feel much better now."

"Wow!" Kyler said. "I just had another dream or something. I was this guy named Asmondo Arliaco. And I could do all these things."

Mirini shivered briefly in fear.

"Do not say that name again. He was a horrible traitor to all Bruxis. If not for him, I would still be with my people. They would be alive, and we would be winning the war against the aliotrotes. As it is...well...you know I'm the last one," Mirini said.

"And he...this guy who I shouldn't name...he is dead?" Kyler asked.

Mirini paused and looked up. Then she looked down and spoke.

"He could not have survived that nuclear blast. Yes, he must be dead."

Kyler decided it was best not to discuss further this Asmondo Arliaco.

"Your complexion has changed," Kyler said. "You have more red color in your face, like you did when we first met. You look more like a healthy human."

"Good," Mirini said.

"And despite the memory recall, I feel better. My heart feels lighter, and my joints are free of pain," Kyler said.

"You should look into that when we return to Earth. You have too much iron in your system. Donating blood is the easiest way to alleviate your symptoms," Mirini said.

"I never thought I'd donate blood to help me. I always thought it was to help others," Kyler said.

"Now you see it's mutually beneficial to all," she smiled.

Kyler smiled back.

"If you don't mind, I'd like to meditate until we reach your weather satellite," Mirini said.

"I thought...but you're full of energy now," Kyler said.

"Do you sleep better when you are hungry or satisfied?" Mirini asked.

"I see. Okay, good. I'll prepare the Adapto-transicon. We won't be able to grow the crystal until we achieve geo-sync orbit," Kyler said.

But Mirini had fallen into a trance. She kept her left hand on the ship's console, and Kyler realized that she was communicating with DEHO 1's computer.

"That's rest?" Kyler asked himself. "Oh well. I might as well take a cat-nap myself. It's going to get busy when we reach the weather satellite."

Kyler set an alarm for the next thruster burst, and then he closed his eyes. He went into light REM sleep and dreamt he was listening to an old short wave radio, with Amelia Earhart calling for help.

"Keep flying," Kyler muttered.

Kyler opened his eyes with a start. He believed he had been asleep for several hours, but in fact he had only napped for ten minutes.

"Amelia Earhart. Wow," Kyler whispered to himself.

Kyler looked over at Mirini, and she was still meditating and communicating with DEHO 1's computer. She hummed something that was half song, half wind blowing through trees. But now she stirred as if something disturbed her.

"No," she said in her meditative state. "No."

"No what?" Kyler asked.

Mirini opened her eyes, and the radio scanner, which had been searching multiple frequencies, lit up on emergency channel 104.

"DEHO 1, this is DESO 4 on emergency channel 104," said Debbie's voice. "We are on a suborbital flight from Dayla Industries to Command Center. We are being pursued by the aliotrotes. They invaded Dayla Industries just as you launched. They took over the complex and all of Brunswick. Do you read, DEHO 1?"

"We read you," Kyler said, responding to Dayla Earth Sub-Orbit ship 4.

"I don't know if we'll make it. The aliotrotes have a suborbital ship of their own," Debbie said.

"They will intercept us over Iowa," Von Brock's voice said over the radio.

"Debbie and Colonel—don't waste time on the radio. Do whatever you can to escape," Kyler said.

"It's imperative you destroy their base of operations in the Atlantic," Debbie said.

"Debbie, this is Mirini. Take as many iron supplements as you can. It will buy you some time. They won't osmoze you until your iron levels are low."

"Unfortunately, we have none on board," Von Brock said.

"Search your scanners for an iron mine," Mirini said. "Can you divert to Hull-Rust-Mahoning Mine in Hibbing, Minnesota?"

"It's too far," Debbie said. "Listen, don't worry about us. Whatever happens, carry out the mission."

"We will," Kyler said. "When we finish with the aliotrotes in Brunswick, we'll shoot down the one pursuing you."

"It's a pleasant thought. I only wish..." Debbie started to say, but her transmission was cut off.

"DESO 4, do you read? DESO 4?" Kyler called.

Mirini closed her eyes, kept her left hand on the ship's console, and concentrated.

"Her ship has crash landed," Mirini said. "Shot down by an aliotrote interceptor. An Air Force F-22 is attempting to intercept the aliotrote craft. Wait. There's a blast of electromagnetic radiation from the aliotrote craft. That's it. Our long-range Earth sensors are damaged."

"And useless," Kyler lamented. "Well, there's nothing else to do but carry out the mission, as Debbie says."

"Kyler. Your people are very innovative, but I'm afraid your technology is years behind the aliotrotes. I must be honest with you—despite your hopes in the weather satellite, I have little confidence the mission will succeed."

"It's all we've got," Kyler said. "We must try."

"Yes, of course," Mirini said. "I'll do whatever I can to help."

"Thank you," Kyler said.

DEHO 1 continued on its way to the weather satellite. After a time, Mirini spoke.

"I see it."

"How can you? It's no larger than a star," Kyler said.

"I have very good vision," she said. "Interesting. It has two large booms connected to a central pod."

"It does, but...can you really see it from this far away?" he asked.

"Yes," she said. "Now the data is starting to make sense. You know, there might be a chance with this mission after all."

"Well good!" Kyler said. "We'll be there in a number of minutes. Meanwhile, let's get ready. The satellite is not designed for sustaining human life. We'll need to put on spacesuits. Your partial pressure suit will need to come off, and there's a spare suit for you to wear. Here, I'll help."

Kyler first helped Mirini remove her partial pressure suit. He then helped her put on a full spacesuit, and he donned a full spacesuit for himself.

"There's a problem, Kyler," Mirini said. "This suit scrubs carbon dioxide and returns oxygen. But I need carbon dioxide to breathe."

"Wait, how did you manage to survive the landing in Scythoc Three?" Kyler asked.

"I put myself in a low life-level trance," she said.

"Can you do it again?" Kyler asked.

"I could, but then I can't expend any energy on body movements," she said.

"All this fancy technology, and it's all so badly biased toward humans," Kyler said. "But who knew we'd have company from Bruxima 4? Wait, you're breathing okay now, right?"

"Yes, but only because of you. I'm breathing your carbon dioxide," she said.

"Then I'll hook up an umbilical cord between us. We'll keep the carbon scrubbers off, unless levels get too high, of course. This way, you'll get your carbon dioxide, and I'll get oxygen without using the tanks. This could actually be very efficient," Kyler said.

"I'm all for it," she said.

Kyler rigged up an umbilical cord between the two suits.

"Let's test it," he said. "Close your face mask, and I'll close mine."

The two closed their masks.

"How do you feel?" Kyler asked.

"Fine," Mirini said.

"Good."

DEHO 1 approached the weather satellite, and now Kyler could see it growing in the window.

"We'll dock with the central hub, what you call the central pod," Kyler said.

Kyler navigated the ship with ease and brought DEHO 1 ever-so-close until it gently docked with the weather satellite.

"We're docked," Kyler said. "I'm depressurizing the atmosphere in DEHO 1 to match the vacuum in the weather satellite. Are you ready?"

"Ready as I'll ever be," Mirini said.

Kyler depressurized DEHO 1. He then opened the hatch and led the way into the central hub of the weather satellite, carrying his pack. Mirini followed with the cufflets still on her forearms.

"The first thing we must do is build a new transicon crystal," Kyler said.

Kyler retrieved the transicrystal creator device and attached it magnetically to a wall.

"The process has started...now," Kyler said as he pressed a button. "We must be certain we don't make sudden movements. Any jolts to the weather station could cause the crystal to develop a defect."

Mirini stared out the window at one of the weather satellite's arms.

"In my meditation, I learned about this weather satellite," Mirini said. "Each arm is one hundred meters in length."

"Yes, it's a wonder this satellite can maintain orbit. Any slight movement of the arms could throw the satellite into an unrecoverable rotation and render it useless," Kyler said.

Mirini touched her left hand on the console.

"Careful," Kyler said.

"I will be gentle," Mirini said.

"Wait, are you communicating with the weather satellite?" Kyler asked. "But the glove blocks direct contact."

"Even when I touched DEHO 1 without a glove, there was a bit of distance between my fingertips and the electronics. The cufflet uses my hand to focus electromagnetic waves into the desired device. My hand must be in close proximity to the device, yes, but it does not need to *touch* it," Mirini explained. "Hmm. Let me see. At the end of each arm is a phased laser that emits a helical beam. The west arm emits a clockwise beam, and the east arm also emits a clockwise beam. They then converge on a focal point."

"Yeah, a two hundred meter starting distance between the two beams isn't much when Earth is over 22,000 miles away," Kyler said. "This satellite has been more hype than help. Well, at least the crystal is forming correctly. Another twenty-five minutes, and we can begin the cufflet analysis."

"Major Bohr, we—"

"Kyler. Please call me Kyler."

"Kyler. We may be able to save some time. I can try connecting directly to the—"

"Hold that thought. There's an incoming message—on the weather satellite's radio?" Kyler wondered. "Come to think of it, what is a video screen doing in here?"

"It's left over from prelaunch testing," Mirini said. "I'll activate the video screen."

Mirini activated the video by touching her right glove to the console and instructing the weather satellite.

"I'm rerouting the audio to our helmets," Mirini said.

The video screen activated, showing Debbie Dayla, Roger Dayla, and Colonel Von Brock.

"Miss Dayla," Kyler said. "Where are you? What happened? And Mr. Dayla, I hope you are well?"

"Back in Brunswick and all alive—for now," said a voice.

The camera view widened, and Senator Croius was now shown standing next to Debbie and Von Brock.

"Senator Croius!" Kyler said.

"Major Bohr, I want you to stand down and return to Earth," the senator said.

"I don't understand," Kyler said. "The United States is under attack. I must complete my mission."

"Kyler, don't listen to him. He's an orca!" Debbie yelled quickly before Jayvogg entered the view and placed a gag over Debbie's mouth.

"What's going on?" Kyler asked.

"She's right," Mirini said. "He's an orca. And he's working with the aliotrotes."

"I heard that," Croius said. "You're very perceptive, Mirini of Bruxima 4. Too perceptive. But know this, Mirini and Major Kyler Bohr—you have three hours to stand down and return to Earth, or else the Daylas and Colonel Von Brock will die."

"You can't kill them!" Kyler said.

Jayvogg and an aliotrote now wheeled in a cylindrical tube capable of holding a human.

"I trust Mirini recognizes this device?" Croius said.

"It's an osmozicon," Mirini said quietly.

"What was that? I didn't catch that," Croius said.

"You know it's an osmozicon!" Mirini said. "I can't believe a living thing on Earth has conspired with aliotrotes from Aliotra. You're an *Arliaco* if ever I saw one."

"She means you're a traitor," Kyler said.

"He's here, you know. He and I are best of pals," Croius said.

Asmondo Arliaco now entered the view. Mirini screamed.

"I was bored for a long time," Arliaco said. "But no longer."

"Okay, okay. Don't hurt the Daylas. And don't hurt the colonel," Kyler said. "We'll return immediately."

Croius laughed. The transmission ended. Mirini stopped screaming but she now sobbed softly.

"We're too late! It's over!" she sobbed.

"I can't fail now. Not when we're so close," Kyler said. "If only the crystal were ready. If only we could analyze your cufflets with the Adapto-transicon. But there's no time. No time."

Mirini sobbed. Kyler racked his brain for an idea, and then it came to him.

"Mirini," Kyler said. "Before Croius came on the screen, you were about to tell me something—something about connecting directly."

"It won't matter," she said. "Don't you see? I've been through this all before. Everything we do is in vain."

"We must try. We can't quit," Kyler said. "Will you at least try? You were going to connect directly to the weather satellite."

"I already have, to learn about it and to operate the video screen," Mirini said.

"Can you operate the phasic lasers?" Kyler asked.

"I could try, but only in the way it was designed to work. But our mission is—"

"Hold that thought. Okay, watch my lead. When the moment is right, send a short burst to the main aliotrote spacecraft in the Atlantic. Enough to get its attention," Kyler said.

"It's all I can do anyway. I can't do any more—" Mirini started.

"Good. Sorry to interrupt, but time is very, very short! Now open up a communication line to Croius," Kyler said. "Remember, watch my lead!"

Mirini opened up the communication line. The video screen returned a picture of Croius threatening Roger and Debbie with some sort of injury.

"Ahem. Remember me?" Kyler said.

"Our sensors report that you are still at the weather station. For each additional minute that you delay, I shall remove one of Miss Dayla's fingers," Croius said.

"You will not. Release the prisoners, or I will blast the living mercury out of the aliotrotes," Kyler said.

"You're bluffing," Croius said.

Kyler looked over at Mirini, and she activated the phasic lasers. A short burst penetrated the ocean surface, entered the main aliotrote spacecraft, and converted a small amount of stored mercury into krypton and ruthenium. An aliotrote whispered something in Croius's ear, and he nodded his head.

"That's just a small sample of what we can do. Release the prisoners. You have two hours," Kyler said.

Kyler motioned to Mirini, and she closed the communications line.

"Is that what you humans call fighting fire with fire?" Mirini asked.

"An interesting way of putting it," Kyler said. "I've found that the best way to deal with a threat is to pose a counter-threat."

"Except that we really are bluffing," Mirini said. "I could only convert a little mercury. And that was using all my power and knowledge from the cufflets."

"Then we're in big trouble," Kyler said. "Well, the crystal will be done in ten minutes. Maybe the Adapto-transicon can figure out something."

"If you're hoping your Adapto-transicon can figure out some way to make the cufflets powerful enough to convert all aliotrotes into krypton and ruthenium, forget it. The answer is not in the cufflets."

"Then why didn't you tell me?" Kyler asked.

"I just did. Just now. And only because I also just now learned when I fired the weather station lasers. The lasers simply aren't powerful enough. The beams are too close. Like you said, more hype than help."

"More hype than help, that's what I said. I've jinxed us for sure," Kyler said. "This weather satellite was a cross-eyed boondoggle from the beginning. If this were a milling machine, I'd throw in a two-flute and plunge it right down that aliotrote spacecraft."

"Two flute. Plunging? Reconfiguring," Mirini said.

"What did I say? What are you doing?" Kyler asked.

"Shh," she said.

"I'm already getting hushed by her. This can't be good," Kyler said.

"Instead of each laser emitting one helicoil, I can make each emit two interlacing pulses. And, instead of converging directly on the target, I can make the beams start out by diverging—not cross-eyed but walleyed, as you might say—so that they arrive from two flanks. In a sense, they will hold and drill into the target. And, the recalibration to do this...oh, come on, please."

"What? What's wrong?" Kyler asked.

"The lasers won't pivot out more than half a degree each. Are you kidding?" Mirini asked.

"You're picking up our lingo well," Kyler said. "You read our symbols, you know about iron mines. You're getting to be quite the knowledgeable person."

"Except knowledge is no good when I need each laser to pivot out thirty degrees from line of sight," Mirini said.

"Let me try," Kyler said.

Kyler touched some controls.

"No use. There's only one way to change them. An EVA," Kyler said.

"You mean a spacewalk?" Mirini asked.

"Yes. We go out into space. You go to the end of one arm, and I'll go to the other. Then we'll change the angle of the lasers, and—"

"And there's a problem," Mirini said. "The umbilical cord isn't that long."

"Yeah," Kyler said. "Forgot about the umbilical cord. Hmm. The options it would seem are this—either we both go on an EVA, or you wait in DEHO 1 and breathe that air...no, that won't work. You need my carbon dioxide no matter where you are. We have no other source of carbon dioxide."

"That means we do the spacewalk together," Mirini said. "Ready?"

"An EVA is the most dangerous part of going into outer space," Kyler said.

"I know. Imagine how scared I was when transferring from my own spacecraft to your Scythoc Three," Mirini said.

"You went on an EVA?" Kyler said.

"Yes," she said. "And without a protective suit. I was able to endure outer space for a few seconds, but it almost killed me, and without the cufflets to strengthen me, I would be dead."

"Then you understand the dangers—better than I," Kyler said.

Mirini smiled.

"Let's get to it then," Kyler said while grabbing a tool belt. "There's another tool belt over there."

"Got it," Mirini said. "Ready. But I'd better lead the way. I know exactly how much to reposition the laser."

"Ladies first," Kyler said.

Mirini opened a hatch to outer space. She exited the weather satellite and began using her double-tether system to crawl along the east arm.

"Double tethers are a good idea," Mirini said. "I didn't have this luxury with Scythoc Three."

"Let's just keep our wits about us, and everything will be fine," Kyler said.

The two made their way to the end of the east arm.

"I will need to remove these bolts," Mirini said. "Will you hold them? It's very important we don't let them float away."

"I can do that," Kyler said. "Well, the good news is that we don't have to worry about running out of oxygen. As long as we are together, we have respiratory equilibrium."

"I like that," Mirini smiled.

Kyler smiled back.

"I wish things were different. Instead of being perched over 22,000 miles above Earth, I'd rather take you mountain climbing," Kyler said.

"Mountain climbing? Why does a human climb a mountain?" Mirini asked.

"Because it is there," Kyler said.

"For the challenge?"

"Yes."

"I would think something more productive would be a good challenge. Like colonizing other worlds. That's what my people should have done before the aliotrotes attacked," Mirini explained.

"Sometimes there are too many barriers in human society to make such progress," Kyler said. "That's when mountain climbing becomes more attractive. Reaching the summit seems more attainable than convincing the world to work toward colonizing other worlds."

"Okay, the laser is loose. Now I'll just pry this bracket like so, and...oh, too far. I need to pull it back. Umph. Not enough power. I need some help here," Mirini said.

"Hold on," Kyler said. "Let me secure these bolts...there, secured in my pocket. Okay, I'm ready."

"Pull!" Mirini said.

The two pulled, and the laser, which was angled out too far, was now moving closer to Mirini's desired angle of thirty degrees.

"A little more," Mirini said. "Easy...don't pull so much...almost...there, stop. Good. Let's bolt it down."

Kyler passed the bolts to Mirini, and one by one she attached them to the laser and in so doing secured it from moving.

"That's one. Now we must adjust the other laser," Mirini said.

The two reversed direction along the east arm, and so Kyler was now leading with Mirini trailing. Each astronaut's use of two tethers took time, but they managed.

"I'm just so amazed that we don't have to use oxygen or scrubbers or anything to breathe. This is great! We don't have to worry at all about how long we're out here," Kyler said. "You know, that could be a new way of mountain climbing. I always have to carry extra oxygen. What if we go climbing in spacesuits? Wouldn't that space people out!"

"We're almost at the end of the west arm," Mirini said. "I hope this works."

"It will," Kyler said. "I'm confident it will. I'm getting several ideas of what we can do on Earth. Have you ever gone scuba diving? Or played tennis? Skiing, both downhill and water?"

"I've only learned about them a short while ago through the DEHO 1 computer, but no, I never had time for such things on Bruxima 4," Mirini said. "A few more meters, and we'll reach the laser."

"Somehow I find it hard to believe you never had time for recreation," Kyler said. "The memory I had of you was like—"

"DEHO 1, do you read?" Debbie's voice called through their helmet radios.

"Debbie Dayla is still alive," Mirini said.

"Yes, Debbie, we read you," Kyler said. "How are—"

"Listen to me very carefully. Abort, I repeat, abort," Debbie called.

"Tell Croius and his filth that it won't work," Kyler said.

"Something's wrong," Mirini said. "Oh no, it's been almost an hour since your threat, Kyler."

"So?" Kyler said.

"That's the amount of time it would take for—" Mirini started.

"A missile to launch and reach your position," Debbie said. "Croius had it launched. He's going to kill you both. Return to DEHO 1 and get out of there!"

"Debbie, we're on an EVA and are tethered to the west laser on the weather satellite," Kyler said.

"Oh God!" Debbie said, and that was the last transmission from her.

"Let's finish the work," Mirini said.

"And die out here?" Kyler argued.

"We'll never make it back to the ship," Mirini said.

"We're going to have to try. You're too valuable to die on me out here. Come on!"

Kyler untethered both himself and Mirini, and he pulled like mad on the arm's access handles to get the two back to DEHO 1 as soon as possible.

"This won't work," Mirini said. "I can sense the missile. It's locked onto our helmet radios. Wherever we go, the missile goes. I could take off my helmet, but—"

"Don't do that," Kyler said.

"We have two minutes to impact," Mirini said.

"God Almighty, help us!" Kyler said.

"A deity can't help us now. We need something to block the missile. If we had time, I could try to patch into another satellite and have it block the missile's path. Wait, there's another way."

"What?" Kyler asked.

"Back to the west laser," Mirini said, and she pulled on Kyler.

"There's no time to work on that! Mirini, this is crazy!" Kyler said.

"That's not the plan. New plan. Hurry. Trust me. And don't give in to Colonel Von Brock's skepticism," Mirini said.

Kyler followed Mirini to the west laser.

"This is suicide," Kyler said.

"Have faith, as you Earth people say," Mirini said. "Stand right here. I'll secure you to the arm."

"What?!"

"Shh. Good. I'll secure myself too," Mirini said.

"We're sitting ducks—roasted over a fire on a spit called the west arm of a weather satellite!" Kyler said.

Mirini touched her left hand to her right forearm, and suddenly all the spare oxygen from their tanks vented into space. The force was strong and nearly wrenched the two from the west arm. The west arm did move, and this caused the weather satellite to go into rotation with the west arm moving away from Earth, but the spin was excruciatingly slow. Too slow.

"Okay, it was a good idea, but we'll never get the east arm in front quickly enough," Kyler said. "If only we had real rocket power. Hey, what are you doing?"

Mirini tied one of her tether ropes around her right leg.

"Are you trying to kill yourself?" Kyler asked.

"I can see the missile now. Just seconds to go," Mirini said. "I'll create thrust with my reserve iron."

Mirini then spoke strange words and grunted as if straining under great stress. She put her back against the west arm and held on as best she could, and then, a fiery jet blasted out of the bottom of her right foot. They say there is no sound in space, but Kyler was convinced he could hear the roar of the rocket. Mirini screamed as if on a roller coaster ride. The weather satellite now picked up rotational speed, and the east arm was practically between them and Earth.

"Come on! Move!" Mirini shouted. "Move!"

"I can see the missile!" Kyler said.

"RAAAAAWWWWGGGG!!" Mirini shouted.

Stability jets now flared out the side of her foot to keep the main jet steady. The missile closed in with incredible speed. The weather satellite rotated and in fact seemed to strain itself and push back against Mirini.

"Please, God in Heaven, spare us this one moment!" Kyler uttered at the end.

And end it was. The missile impacted the end of the east arm. The warhead detonated, and the blast shattered the east arm off completely leaving a stub sticking out of the central hub. Debris flew in all directions, and much flew toward the two space walkers. But the blast also forced the remaining central hub and west arm into greater rotational speed, along with a twist. The two were now caught on the end of some unbalanced swing, like a laundry machine out of balance. The g-force varied from mild to extreme, and so they were whipped around and suffered from momentary blackouts from the extreme forces. A shard from the east arm plunged through Mirini's upper right leg. She jerked around from the pain. Fluid and air escaped from the puncture point. Her body worked itself loose from the west arm, and thrust was still coming out of her right leg, so her body flung around violently in random directions. Only the umbilical cord kept her from completely detaching from the arm.

"Mirini!" Kyler yelled.

Kyler could sense something else. There was a gradual loss of pressure in his suit, and he realized that the shard's puncture was the culprit.

"Kyler," Mirini said, though with a shaky voice.

"Try to stop the rocket blast out of your foot. Try to stop it!" Kyler said.

"I...can't...the shard...my leg...stuck," she struggled to say. "We're...losing air. Kyler...tie off the line...and...cut it. Cut it, Kyler."

"No!" Kyler said. "You'll tire soon. And then the rocket thrust will stop."

"It will only stop when I die," she said. "I'm stuck. Kyler, your tethers are breaking. You'll die with me."

"Just hold out a little longer. Hold out!" Kyler urged.

"Kyler...goodbye," Mirini said.

She held her right foot just so, and then she both severed and cauterized the umbilical cord. She blasted herself away from the weather satellite with Kyler shouting for her to return.

"Mirini," he said, now shaking and depressed.

Kyler had perspired profusely, and water now filled his suit. But he was powerless. Mirini was out of reach, and the weather satellite continued to whip him around with anger. But the new danger was his air supply. Mirini had vented his oxygen to rotate the weather satellite. And so, he was beginning to choke on his own carbon dioxide. He continued to black out as the weather satellite whipped him around, but with the diminishing oxygen, his blackout durations were longer and his consciousness shorter per rotation.

"This is my end too," he said. "It was all a waste. Complete waste."

Kyler finally blacked out after another rotation and did not wake.

"Kyler, can you hear me? Kyler?" called a voice. "Kyler?"

Kyler opened his eyes. He was inside a spaceship, and Colonel John Von Brock was looking over him.

"Von Brock? Where am I? What happened?" Kyler asked.

"You're aboard DEHO 3. Debbie and I escaped," Von Brock said. "But then Croius flipped out and launched an all-out attack against everyone, including the missile against you and Mirini. Debbie said she was going to warn you by radio."

"She did," Kyler said.

"Did she also tell you that help was on the way? As in me?" Von Brock asked.

"No. She was cut off," Kyler said.

"I wanted to arrive before the missile to help you two. But I couldn't," Von Brock said. "I did find you, and you were barely attached to the weather satellite. Boy, that is a mess, and so is DEHO 1. Completely unusable. But I don't see Mirini anywhere."

"She's adrift in space. We might be able to save her yet," Kyler said. "She told me the cufflets helped her survive in outer space before."

"Definitely. I'll set the scanners to long range," Von Brock said.

Von Brock returned to the pilot's chair. Kyler sat up and looked around. DEHO 3 looked very much like DEHO 1, only Mirini wasn't around. Kyler pulled himself to his feet and staggered to the co-pilot's chair.

"I never thought I'd be happy to see you, Colonel," Kyler said.

"Please, call me John," Von Brock said.

"Okay, John. Whew! I was a dead duck on that weather satellite. A dead duck!"

"Don't sweat it," Von Brock said. "Look, there's an infrared blip on the scanner."

"That's her. Hurry!" Kyler urged.

Von Brock manipulated the controls and sent DEHO 3 toward the blip with great speed.

"We'll be there in no time," he said.

DEHO 3 approached the blip. Kyler looked out the window portal and saw a white dot in the distance. The dot grew larger, and Kyler could now see that the dot was spinning in space. Getting closer still, he could see that the spin was from head to toe, and so it was someone in a spacesuit. The someone wasn't moving, so Kyler couldn't tell if Mirini was alive. Yes, it was Mirini, because now he could see the right foot and leg were dark—remnants from her foot acting as a rocket.

"How much oxygen did she have left?" Von Brock asked. "Do you remember?"

"We used up all oxygen to move the weather satellite's arm," Kyler said.

"So that's how you did it," Von Brock said. "You used one of the arms to intercept the missile."

"Well...yes...it was tricky," Kyler said.

But something seemed odd. Why didn't Von Brock challenge the fact that oxygen tanks were not much thrust for rotating the entire weather satellite? Kyler brushed it off. He was more concerned with Mirini's health. DEHO 3 was now close enough to see details of Mirini's spacesuit.

"What happened to her right leg?" Von Brock asked. "It's been charred. The explosion got her?"

"Something like that," Kyler said.

"Don't sweat it, friend," Von Brock said.

DEHO 3 slowed to prevent overrunning Mirini. A robotic arm extended and caught Mirini. This of course stopped her spinning, too. But the robot arm paused.

"What are you waiting for?" Kyler asked.

"Just taking some readings," Von Brock said. "You know, radiation and all that stuff, friend."

What was it with Von Brock now calling Kyler, "friend"? What happened to "old man"? Kyler didn't know, but he noticed the readout from the scan — no radiation, no heartbeat, and strangely enough, low iron levels. Kyler couldn't wait. He pressed the button to pull Mirini toward DEHO 3 and into the unpressurized bay. Kyler then closed the bay and started pressurization.

"I was just going to do that, friend," Von Brock said.

Kyler was getting annoyed with the "friend" bit, but maybe Von Brock was doing the bit just for that very reason. As it was, Kyler and Von Brock left the pilot and co-pilot chairs to attend to Mirini. They placed her on a treatment bed and removed the helmet and torso section of her spacesuit.

"No pulse," Von Brock said.

"Let's start CPR. I'll breathe into her lungs. You begin compressions," Kyler said.

"We have oxygen," Von Brock said. "Let's give her that."

"Just do what I say," Kyler said.

"Okay," Von Brock replied.

The two started CPR. Why did Von Brock forget that Mirini couldn't use oxygen? And why did he give in so easily? Fortunately, Kyler didn't have much time to dwell on such thoughts. Mirini's heart started, and so did her breathing. She gasped for air.

"She's breathing," Kyler said. "She's alive!"

"Hmm, yes," Von Brock said.

Mirini's vision was blurred at first, and so she looked up toward the ceiling, but then her eyes regained focus, and she saw Kyler. She smiled.

"Major Bohr," she said as she sat up.

"Mirini," Kyler said. "Colonel Von Brock rescued us. Isn't that a lucky thing?"

Mirini looked at Von Brock, and her eyes widened with shock. She then began shouting and screaming in her native language.

"Mirini, what is it?" Kyler asked as he tried to calm her.

Von Brock rushed over and stabbed Mirini in the arm with a syringe. Mirini then became sedated. She was semi-conscious and had weak muscle movement, but not enough to support her weight. Kyler caught her.

"Was that necessary?" Kyler asked.

"She could have done something stupid and killed us all," Von Brock said.

"Don't worry, Mirini, I'll stay with you," Kyler said.

"Kyyyyler," she said.

Her eyes rolled around. She tried to say something else, but she couldn't.

"You won't be needing these," Von Brock said as he took the cufflets.

"Hey, those aren't yours," Kyler said.

"It's all precautionary," Von Brock said. "Do you have the transicon crystal with you?"

"No, I left it in the weather satellite in the central bay," Kyler said.

"That's all been ripped out and destroyed," Von Brock said. "We'll have to make another one here, and then we'll return to Earth."

"There's another weather satellite in roughly the same orbit as the one hit by the missile. If we just change course a little, then—"

"No. We need to return and meet with Debbie soon. Top priority, friend," Von Brock said. "Now then, I must turn off the artificial gravity to make the crystal. So hang on."

Von Brock left the two alone and went into a different room to begin creating the transicon crystal.

"Kyyyyyylerrr," Mirini moaned.

"Shh. You need to rest," Kyler said. "Let's secure you to the wall."

But Mirini didn't want to let go. In fact, she began licking Kyler's arm.

"You are affectionate, aren't you?" Kyler said. "Remind me to keep you away from alcohol. You probably don't have that on Bruxima 4."

She continued licking his arm, and her tongue felt like sandpaper.

"Hey, that hurts a little. You're like a cat!" Kyler said.

Mirini's strength improved, and she could speak a little better.

"So...hungry...need...iron," she said.

"Of course," Kyler said. "You're trying to resupply your body with iron. Well we really need those cufflets, don't we?"

Mirini managed to say, "Yes."

"I'd like to stay and play, but I need to see about getting those cufflets back," Kyler said. "Just wait here."

Kyler pulled away from Mirini, and she didn't want to let go. She stretched her arms out to reach for Kyler, but he was out of reach. Kyler walked into the room where Von Brock had gone. Von Brock had finished setting up the device to make a new crystal, and he pressed the button.

"Another thirty minutes, and we'll return to Earth," Von Brock said.

"Colonel, please give me the cufflets. Mirini needs them," Kyler said.

"Maybe later. I need to prepare them for analysis, friend," Von Brock said.

"Why do you keep calling me that?" Kyler said.

"Aren't you my friend?" Von Brock asked.

"Sure. But you called me something else," Kyler said.

"Major Kyler Bohr. Is that good enough for you, friend?" Von Brock asked.

"Yeah," Kyler said without confidence.

"This mission has made you paranoid," Von Brock said. "Relax."

"And the cufflets?" Kyler asked.

"Not yet," Von Brock said. "You're testing me, aren't you? You don't trust me. Good."

"Is it? What does trust mean? You told me once," Kyler said.

"I've told you many things. But here's one for you. Trust no one," Von Brock said.

"That's not what you told me," Kyler said. "Who are you?"

"You *are* paranoid!" Von Brock said. "Now don't do anything stupid. What do you plan to do, open the airlock and kill us all? Debbie won't like that."

"Let's do a test, shall we?" Kyler said.

"Take an anti-paranoia pill, and you'll feel better," Von Brock said.

"Just follow me into the bay," Kyler said.

"Really! I'm busy growing the transicon crystal," Von Brock said.

"You can't do anything with the crystal until it finishes growing, and that won't be for another twenty-five minutes," Kyler said.

"If I play along with you and do this little test, will you take a sedative and relax?" Von Brock asked.

"Yes," Kyler said.

"Okay then," Von Brock said. "Let's do your silly test."

Kyler led Von Brock into the room with Mirini. Mirini was lightly asleep.

"Put yourself next to Mirini," Kyler whispered.

"That's your test? What will that prove?" Von Brock asked.

"Just do it," Kyler said.

"Okay," Von Brock replied.

Von Brock positioned himself next to Mirini. She was still lightly asleep, but she sniffed the air and moved away from Von Brock as best she could.

"She moved away from you," Kyler said. "Roll up your sleeve and put your arm next to her face."

"To hit her? I won't hit her," Von Brock said.

"Not to hit her. Just hold your bare forearm next to her face," Kyler said.

"Very well," he said.

Von Brock held his unsleeved forearm next to Mirini's face, and she turned her face away.

"I ate onions before I launched from Earth. A natural reaction," Von Brock said as he moved away from Mirini and toward a medical cupboard. "Now, are you ready for your sedative?"

Von Brock prepared a syringe and was ready to stab Kyler.

"One moment," Kyler said.

Kyler placed himself next to Mirini. Mirini moved toward Kyler.

"Obviously she likes you," Von Brock said.

Kyler held his forearm to her face, and she rubbed her chin against it. Von Brock remained motionless and stared hard at Kyler.

"She's desperately hungry for iron," Kyler said. "Humans have iron. You don't. Who are you? Or should I say, what have you done with Colonel Von Brock?"

Von Brock changed shape.

"Asmondo Arliaco! Of course!" Kyler said.

"Let no good deed go to waste. Iron is difficult to devitiate. It will take time to remove it from your body, but Mirini's body can be osmozed immediately, once we return to base," Asmondo said.

Kyler leapt at Asmondo to beat him senseless, but Asmondo simply dephased his matter and allowed Kyler to pass through him.

"You're too boring for me," Asmondo said. "Too bad you can't stay awake and entertain me. But it's sleep time."

Asmondo grabbed Kyler's arm and inflicted massive pain. Kyler writhed and struggled to fight, but Asmondo injected the sedative into Kyler, and Kyler fell unconscious.

When Kyler awoke, he found himself strapped to a chair. Mirini was on an examination table with Asmondo hovering over her. A video screen on the wall behind Asmondo showed Senator Croius, and he was speaking to Asmondo. Kyler was careful to keep his eyes closed as much as possible to feign sleep but open enough to see what was going on.

"The one called Mirini has unusual burn marks and propellant residue on her right foot," Asmondo said.

"What would cause that?" Croius asked.

"I will need to change into her shape to find out," Asmondo said.

Asmondo touched Mirini's foot, changed into her shape, and then turned back after a few seconds, coughing.

"Ugh! She consumes iron! How vulgar!" Asmondo said.

"Our new friends do not like iron," Croius said.

"She is low on iron," Asmondo said. "Osmozication should be easy—if that is still desired."

"What do you mean by *if*?" Croius asked. "Of course she must be osmozed. She was promised."

"She can use iron as a propellant," Asmondo said. "She can fly. I wonder if she could use other metals as a propellant."

"It's irrelevant to the mission," Croius said. "Now the issue with Kyler is relevant. He has too much iron. Our new master wants him ready for osmozication when he lands."

"I will need to kill him, then," Asmondo said.

"Then do so right away," Croius said. "I must attend to other business at the moment. I look forward to your next transmission."

The video of Croius went blank. Asmondo continued inspecting Mirini's right foot. He changed into her shape again but changed back to his own.

"She is the one shape I cannot stand to maintain," Asmondo said. "Irritation, yes, I believe that's what it's called. It's my first emotion. I've never felt it before. What other emotions could Mirini help me feel?"

"None," Kyler said.

"You are awake," Asmondo said. "But you are in no position to make such a statement."

"Why not? Do you really think she'll willingly help bring excitement to your boring life?" Kyler asked.

"My life is boring, yes," Asmondo said. "And your idle talk only adds to my boredom. It's time to end that now. Perhaps I'll enjoy watching you bleed to death after I slit your throat. Not to mention you'll lose a little iron."

Asmondo removed a large knife from a storage compartment and walked toward Kyler.

"Wait," Kyler said.

Asmondo laughed.

"The child always cries *wait* before it receives punishment," Asmondo said. "Don't struggle, and your death will be painless."

"I can help you. I'll show you what life and death are really about. And you'll feel excitement," Kyler said.

Asmondo laughed again.

"You see? You're already being entertained," Kyler said.

"But only briefly. The victim screeches before death. It's all the same."

"Why not make a game of it?" Kyler asked.

"A game?" Asmondo replied.

"We do not have games on Bruxima 4," Mirini said, now reaching consciousness.

"Really?" Kyler asked. "Now I understand. We humans use games to combat boredom. Keeps life interesting and exciting."

"I've learned all about your games," Asmondo said. "Totally boring."

"That's because most games have no significant consequence," Kyler said. "But I can show you a game that does. You against me, with a wager—if I win, you keep us alive."

"And you expect me to honor that?" Asmondo asked.

"That's part of the rules," Kyler said.

"And if I win?" Asmondo asked.

"Then you may kill me now and Mirini later," Kyler replied grudgingly.

"Kyler, no," Mirini said.

"Asmondo wants to see me bleed," Kyler said to Mirini, then he turned to Asmondo and said, "Okay, I will bleed. But so will you. We exchange blood by running a tube from a vein in my arm to a vein in your arm, and another tube from a vein in your other arm to a vein in my other arm. A pump in each tube will move the blood."

"This is your paltry attempt to poison me," Asmondo said.

"Or you would poison me," Kyler said. "Are you afraid to play?"

"I have never experienced fear," Asmondo said. "But my blood is far more complicated than you can imagine. It will kill you instantly."

"Then you will win," Kyler said.

"But why bother playing? Just another boring thing," Asmondo said.

"Or is it? There is risk involved. You could die too," Kyler said.

"Kyler, stop it," Mirini said. "Asmondo, listen. I'll play the blood transfusion game. Let Kyler live. He knows nothing of our planet or our ways."

"Mirini, you don't have to do this," Kyler said. "You should be the one who lives."

"Oh, the boredom of sentimentality," Asmondo groaned.

"Kyler, please. Let me make the sacrifice."

"No, let me," Kyler said.

"I'll put an end to this right now," Asmondo said. "Both of you will play, but I set the rules. The game is Shuffleblood."

Asmondo produced a hydraulic manifold and placed it on a table between Mirini and Kyler.

"One tube from each of us runs to this Shuffleblood manifold," Asmondo said. "The objective is to pump blood into the manifold and overpower the others. There will be no mechanical pumps. All pumping will be done with fist squeezing. The one who dies first wins and may go free."

"The one who dies wins?" Kyler asked. "That's not a win."

"My rules. Play the game or die now," Asmondo said. "Or in your case Mirini, die later."

Kyler looked at Mirini. She looked weak and pale.

"Mirini is too weak to play. Just you and me. That was the original agreement," Kyler said.

"That agreement was too boring. This should be more interesting. Finally, something of interest. I may yet defeat my boredom," Asmondo said.

"If you do, it will be fleeting. Real passion comes from the daily challenge," Kyler said.

"I may try that, Kyler Bohr. I may challenge others to this game—if it doesn't bore me too much. Now, we shall begin."

Asmondo closed all ports on the manifold. Next, he inserted an intravenous line from Mirini and connected it to the Shuffleblood manifold. A small amount of blood flowed from Mirini and into the manifold, which forced air out of the line. Asmondo tapped a button on the manifold, and the air was released. Similarly, he inserted an intravenous line into Kyler, connected it to the manifold, and purged the air in the line. Lastly, Asmondo ran a line from himself into the manifold and purged the air.

"This central button will open all three ports. When we are ready, I shall press it," Asmondo said.

"What's to get ready?" Kyler asked.

"Oh no," Mirini said.

Asmondo changed shape and grew in size to that of eight feet and more.

"You increased your blood pool. That's cheating!" Kyler said.

"You whine like a child with his toy taken away. How boring," Asmondo said. "Now we are ready."

Asmondo held his hand above the button and paused. Kyler readied his hand to make a fist and thus begin squeezing blood. Mirini had great fear in her eyes and appeared ready to go into shock.

"Mirini," Kyler said. "Clench your fist. Clench your fist!"

"Yes, Mirini, clench your fist for the last time!" Asmondo taunted.

Asmondo pressed the button. Kyler clenched and unclenched his fist like mad to pump blood into the manifold, but opposing pressure prevented it. Asmondo barely had to clench his fist to force his blood into the manifold and prevent anyone from pushing back. Mirini tried to pump into the manifold, but overwhelming pressure from Asmondo gradually forced his blood up her tube and toward her vein.

"Pump harder, Mirini. Pump with all your might!" Kyler urged.

"Yes, pump harder, Mirini," Asmondo said. "This is too easy and too boring."

"If you shrank back down to normal size, you'd find this more challenging. I dare you to shrink," Kyler said.

"Oh *now* it's a dare. What's next? Trick or treat? Wheelies and skid marks? I *must* find someone more interesting than you, Major Bohr," Asmondo said.

Asmondo now clenched and unclenched his fist more forcefully. Kyler clenched hard too, and he gritted his teeth with determination. Mirini, trying with her might, was too frail for the effort. Asmondo's blood pushed its way into her arm and filled her tissues. She began to bloat.

"It's over," Mirini said, with speech becoming more difficult from her engorged tissues. "I win. I win."

But her last word trailed. Her body was so incredibly bloated that she appeared to go from a hundred pound woman to an eight-hundred pound woman. Mirini stopped breathing. Kyler struggled to break the straps and help her, but he could not.

"Stop this! The game is over! Stop it now!" Kyler yelled.

"Oh but we need another winner!" Asmondo said.

"I said stop!" Kyler yelled.

But Asmondo simply continued pumping, like a perpetual motion machine. Then Kyler noticed something subtle that Mirini had done. She had wrapped her intravenous line around two fingers. When the game began, there was no real significance to this act. But now that she was fully bloated, the line became pinched between her fingers. All blood flow stopped. Then a light of hope entered Kyler's mind. With the line pinched, the blood could not return to Asmondo. Had Asmondo drained his body of too much blood?

"This is so boring, I feel I must take a nap after this is over," Asmondo said.

This was Kyler's chance. Or was it? Kyler was still pumping with all his might and not making any progress. But Asmondo pumped harder and harder. In fact, he strained. What if Asmondo lost a little more blood? Would he pass out? Was this the secret to defeating Asmondo?

"I'm going to beat you yet," Kyler taunted. "I can pump harder and faster than you."

"Major Bohr-ing, I could pump with my eyes closed. In fact, I think I will. I'm going to take a nap *and* overpower you," Asmondo bragged.

Asmondo closed his eyes and continued to pump, and then Kyler decided to take the greatest risk of his life. He stopped pumping. Completely. Blood rushed into Kyler's arm from the manifold, and his tissues began to bloat, like Mirini's. Asmondo was now snoring, and he continued pumping, like a robot who had not been told to stop. Kyler positioned his limbs so that his bloating tissues pressed hard against the straps. The straps cut deep into Kyler's tissues, and the pain became almost unbearable, but Kyler bit his cheek and suppressed his cries of pain, hoping beyond hope that the straps would break.

They did not. But the chair he was in *did* break. First the back and then the seat. Kyler pushed and rocked, and he managed to stand a little against the broken mess. He jumped up and turned so that he would land the chair on the floor at an awkward angle. The chair broke further. Kyler struggled to step out of the mess of chair parts and straps, but his bloated tissues stiffened his movements and slowed his progress. Despite all this, Asmondo remained asleep. And the pumping continued.

Kyler nearly pulled the button to stop the blood flow from the manifold. But he checked his action and instead ripped his tube from the manifold. Blood poured both from his tube and from the manifold onto the floor. Asmondo continued to pump, but his body began to thin. Kyler's tissues shrank back to normal size, and so his bloating was gone. Kyler pulled the needle from his arm and held his arm high next to his chest to stop further bleeding.

Then he turned toward Mirini. She had turned blue and was still bloated. Kyler ripped her tube from the manifold and worked the line free from her fingers. With his free hand, he pressed against her tissues to reduce the bloating, but the process was slow, as she had filled extensively with Asmondo's blood. Kyler looked at Asmondo, and his body had taken on a skeletal appearance from being so thin, yet Asmondo continued to pump. Asmondo stopped snoring. He had lost consciousness and was near death, yet his obsessed fist continued to pump as if there were no other choice in life. And so it was. Asmondo died.

"Mirini, Mirini!" Kyler cried.

Blood was everywhere on the floor. Kyler tried as best he could to get the excess blood out of her body. But the work was difficult and awkward with one hand. And now, Kyler became tired. Lethargy set in, as if he had been poisoned. In fact, he had. Asmondo's blood was full of lead.

"We...are...poisoned," Mirini struggled to say. "Lead. Lead."

She fell unconscious. Kyler allowed her to bleed until she resumed a somewhat normal shape, but she did not awake, and her pulse was very weak.

"I must get help. I must land this ship," Kyler said.

Kyler fought the desire to slump into lethargy, and he went for the controls of the ship. But the ship was not responding as desired. Asmondo's blood had flooded along the floor into the pilot's area and was causing electrical malfunctions. The ship began descending and spinning out of control. Kyler fought to regain control, but the ship simply spun all the more. The forces were extreme and threw Kyler against the front of the cabin.

"Must...divert...path...from land. Must divert," Kyler struggled.

He pressed several buttons to activate the landing rockets as a means of steadying the craft, which he did to some extent, but still he could not much control where the ship was going. In the end, he lost consciousness just as the ship passed through the cloud deck toward the northern Pacific Ocean.

Kyler regained semi-consciousness. He was dazed and in shock, and all he could do was sit. Where was he? He gazed around, but the world didn't seem to much matter. Try harder, Kyler. Try harder. He was in a life raft in the Pacific Ocean, trying to paddle somewhere, and dorsal fins circled around his raft. Nearby, the spacecraft bobbed up and down. Its parachutes had deployed automatically, but it was damaged and sinking slowly. Mirini was not with him.

"Mirini. Must help...Mirini," Kyler tried to say.

The dorsal fins continued circling. Kyler didn't know how he ended up in the life raft. Did he pull himself out of the spaceship? If so, how? And why didn't he pull Mirini with him? But Kyler felt weak.

"I'm fading," he said.

As he slipped back into unconsciousness, he thought he saw a crystalline wall growing from the top of the water where the dorsal fins circled. Up it seemed to grow and converge toward a central dome peak.

"Trapped," Kyler said, and he lost consciousness.

Kyler awoke, and now he sat up from a bed of soft crystalline structure. It felt very much like a water bed, but instead of water inside the bed, there was a clear, gel-like substance. He looked around the room. The room itself was a dome-like structure, twenty feet high. There was a desk and chair, but they were immensely huge, as if for giants. And there was an assortment of equipment about—again, for giants.

"Medical equipment," he said. "I'm in some strange sort of hospital. Why is everything so huge?"

There was a door to his room. It was closed, and Kyler stood up and planned to open it, but before he could, a giant humanoid creature entered. It had legs and arms and a torso, but instead of a face like a human, it had one of a cetacean creature, specifically a pilot whale, and its skin was very dark, almost black.

"AaaaaaaH!" Kyler yelled, and he jumped back.

"AaaaaaaAH!" yelled the creature, and it left the room, dropping a clipboard behind.

Kyler picked up the clipboard (it too was oversized) and attempted to read it, but the writing was all cryptic and alien. Then a new giant returned along with the first one. Kyler shook in fear and looked for a weapon.

"Relax," one of the giants said. "We mean you no harm. I am Prime Minister Barecki. Welcome to our community, which we call Gaviceti 5."

"I...you're so tall...I did not know that giants lived anywhere," Kyler said.

"You don't want to kill me?" the other giant said.

"Relax, Nurse Yetaria. This is an American," Barecki said. "They don't hunt us."

"I guess you are as frightened of me as I am of you," Kyler said. "My name is Bohr, Major Kyler Bohr. My apologies for startling you, Nurse Yetaria."

"I apologize too," the nurse said.

Nurse Yetaria kneeled and gave Kyler a hug. Her arms were flippers, and her hands had digits like Kyler's, but hers were much longer. She wrapped her flippers around Kyler, and he felt as if he were enwrapped in tractor-trailer inner tubes. She barely made the effort to hug Kyler, but the compression knocked the wind out of his lungs.

"You have a strong hug," Kyler said, now struggling for breath.

"Easy, nurse, these humans are fragile creatures," Barecki said. "Major Kyler Bohr, we—"

"Please, call my Kyler."

"Kyler," Barecki said. "We are what you call *pilot whales*. We are not true whales. We have more in common with our smaller dolphin relatives than actual whales. Our dolphin cousins swim freely in the ocean, but we pilot whales have this special abode on the bottom of the ocean. Well, not the true bottom. We are inside an underwater mountain. We found your spacecraft on the ocean surface and enclosed it in ferrocrystallus so that we could transport you and your friend to Gaviceti 5."

"You found her? Mirini? You must take me to her!" Kyler begged.

"She is very weak, but she is alive," the prime minister said. "Follow me."

Prime Minister Barecki led the way, with Kyler and Nurse Yetaria walking behind. They walked through a corridor filled with other humanoid pilot whales, and each looked at Kyler as if he were an alien from another world, which he was.

"Debbie Dayla was right. Dolphins can talk. But what do you eat down here?" Kyler asked.

The nurse looked toward the prime minister. He looked back and nodded in affirmation.

"Our nearest kin, the non-transforming pilot whales of the ocean, prefer squid," Nurse Yetaria said. "But we who dwell here have no need for such consumption. We consume hydronium. From the ocean water."

"You consume hydronium? As in hydrogen from hydronium? How does that work?" Kyler asked.

"Our cells fuse the hydrogen into heavier elements. Eventually, the process is such that our cells produce iron, and no more fusion can commence. We must then get rid of the excess iron, which we do through our skin. That's why our skin is black. The iron combines with oxygen. We must have daily rubdowns, otherwise our skin gets orange scales and itches to no end," Nurse Yetaria said.

"Iron! And nuclear fusion! Wow! No, I mean really wow!" Kyler said.

Nurse Yetaria looked at the prime minister. He looked back and shrugged his shoulders.

"Americans are a little strange like that, Nurse Yetaria," the prime minister said. "A few more steps...here we are."

The three entered. A humanoid pilot whale was tending to Mirini. A device filled with glowing embers pumped air to a mask covering Mirini's nose and mouth.

"She needs carbon dioxide to breathe," said the attending pilot whale. "Very unusual. Not like any humans we've ever encountered."

"She's not like us," Kyler said, "I mean, not like other humans on Earth. She's from another planet. From Bruxima 4."

"I hope she doesn't hunt whales or dolphins," Nurse Yetaria said.

"She doesn't," Kyler said.

"Major Kyler Bohr, this is Doctor Cephaligi, our top specialist on non-cetacean physiology. I believe you would call him a veterinarian," the prime minister said.

"Why would I call him a veterinarian? Vets are for animals!" Kyler said.

Nurse Yetaria giggled.

"To us, Mirini is an animal. So are you," Prime Minister Barecki said. "Doctor Cephaligi treated you himself."

"Like an animal? I can't believe I was treated by a vet!"

"We do have doctors, but they are for pilot whales," Doctor Cephaligi said. "Which reminds me, Prime Minister, our enclave of doctors was due back here three days ago. Has there been no word?"

"I will speak with you about that in private," the prime minister said. "I do not wish to...well...in private."

"About what?" Kyler asked. "Have they attacked you too?"

"Who?" Nurse Yetaria asked.

"The aliotrotes," Kyler said. "The other aliens. The ones with mercury."

"This is news to us," Barecki said.

"But your doctors...could have been kidnapped...by the aliotrotes. They have already taken over Brunswick...in Georgia," Kyler said.

"United States," Barecki said. "But on the Atlantic coast, right?"

"Yes."

"Hmm. News about the Atlantic is slow or not at all for us in the Pacific. We have other enemies here," Barecki said.

"Oh?"

"We might as well discuss it now," Cephaligi said. "We learned that many of our cousin pilot whales were injured or killed fighting off a fleet of Japanese Research vessels. We sent our doctors to heal them. But those doctors were due back here and are now late. And no word."

"There has been word, but not from the doctors," Barecki said. "Our orcan allies have just sent word that our doctors were captured and taken aboard the Japanese Research vessels."

"You're friendly with killer whales? There's something strange going on," Kyler said. "I thought...Debbie said her dolphin friend was in a war with the orcas."

"Who is Debbie?" Nurse Yetaria asked.

"She is the head of Dayla Industries, in Brunswick, Georgia, United States," said Mirini, who had just regained consciousness and now sat up in bed.

"Mirini!" Kyler exclaimed, and he rushed over and hugged her.

"Kyler. You're here. And so are these lovely people," Mirini said. "The room is filled with love and warm feelings from our new friends."

"But they are friends with orcas! What does that mean?" Kyler asked.

"It means we are your friends," said a new giant humanoid entering the room.

Kyler turned and gasped. The giant humanoid had black and white coloration and the head of an orca.

"This is General Byan," Barecki said.

"My orcan citizens of Gaviceti 2 send their greetings and condolences," Byan said. "Our scouts witnessed your doctors being captured by the Japanese Research vessels. Unfortunately, our scouts were unable to intervene without being captured themselves."

"Do you...also consume hydronium?" Kyler asked.

"Oh yes, but it's not enough. We must have fish from time to time," Byan said. "I haven't tried human yet. I wonder if they are tasty."

Byan laughed as did Nurse Yetaria. And so did Mirini.

"That wasn't funny," Kyler said to Byan, then he turned to Mirini and asked, "Why are you laughing?"

"It's a joke," Mirini said. "It's funny. If they really wanted to eat us, they would have done so. But I imagine humans taste as badly to them as coyote meat does to humans."

"A good analogy," Byan said. "You know much about humans."

"I learned quickly from a computer feed while Kyler and I traveled in space," Mirini said.

"You must tell us about it," Byan said.

"Well, we were at Dayla Industries, and—" Mirini said.

"Wait a minute. Wait a minute!" Kyler said. "Back to this human eating thing. This concerns me. Byan, does this mean you *have* tried human flesh?"

"Don't have to. We can taste your chemical residue in the water. Ick. Mirini, on the other hand, tastes sweet," Byan said as he licked Mirini's hand.

"Back off!" Kyler barked. "Don't even think about attacking Mirini."

Kyler moved himself between Byan and Mirini to protect her.

"I do believe you're over-protective of me," Mirini said. "How cute."

"All joking aside, the situation is serious," Cephaligi said. "We must launch a rescue mission. The doctors of Gaviceti 5 are too important to abandon with the Japanese."

"And how do you propose we launch this rescue mission?" Byan asked.

"You're the soldier. You tell me," Cephaligi said.

"Although we are an apex predator and can defend ourselves against almost any adversary, the *homo sapien* problem continues to elude us," Byan said. "We can ram into their ships, but the ships barely budge. They are more massive. It is these massive machines that make humans such an adversary. By themselves, humans are puny and weak. However, if we could find a human ally, we might prevail."

"General Byan is correct," Barecki said. "We must seek help from humans. The location of the Gaviceti seamounts was purposely chosen close to the North American continent because of how favorably North Americans view cetaceans. It is time we seek outside help. We must ask the North Americans to intervene."

All looked at Kyler.

"I, uh, well. I'd love to help," Kyler said.

"Not you," Mirini said. "They want North American governments to help. But I'm afraid this won't happen."

"Why not?" Cephaligi asked.

"For some reason, that information was not in the computer feed," Mirini said. "But I did sense a bit of apathy."

"You learned a lot from that computer feed," Kyler said.

"Yes, but not enough to help," Cephaligi said.

"There is help. A private organization named Sea Herder roams the seas and disrupts the Japanese where possible," Mirini said. "Unfortunately, the group has limited funds, limited ships, and limited tracking ability."

"Then that is the connection we need," Byan said. "We must work with this Sea Herder group. But we need a powerful weapon. One that will allow us to overpower the Japanese and commandeer their ships."

"What kind of powerful weapon?" Kyler asked.

Byan looked at Cephaligi. Cephaligi looked at Barecki. Barecki looked at Mirini and then at Byan.

"We think Mirini has the answer," Barecki said.

"Yes, there's something about her physiology—something unusual," Cephaligi said.

"You intend to sacrifice Mirini for your needs? No, wait. She almost died up in space, and I won't let you use her as a sacrifice."

"I don't think that's what they mean," Mirini said.

"She's right," Byan said. "Vet Cephaligi tells us that Mirini responds well to metabolized iron."

"She's weak and needs rest. I thank you for your help, but it's best you take us back to North America and let us work on the aliotrote issue. Our need—"

"Can wait," Byan said. "The Japanese come first."

"And if we refuse?" Kyler asked.

"Be a good sport, Kyler," Mirini said. "We'll help the pilot whales and orcas. I'm sure they'll be willing to help us after that."

"Well said, Mirini," Barecki said. "All citizens of the Gaviceti region would be in your debt for the help you would render to stop the Japanese whalers and return our doctors. Not to mention any help you could render to other hunted whales. I don't know what help we could offer against these aliotrotes, whatever they are, but I'm sure if we work together, we can come up with a solution. Now when—"

But Prime Minister Barecki was interrupted by thunderous pounding on the outside wall of the seamount. The inhabitants began running about and yelling, "The sea turtles have returned!"

"You'll excuse me," the prime minister said, and he rushed off.

"Shore up the portals! Ready the cannons!" Byan yelled, and he rushed off as well.

"Nurse Yetaria, prepare for the wounded," Cephaligi said.

"But we are only equipped for animals," Yetaria said.

"We will do the best we can," Cephaligi said.

The nurse also rushed off.

"A fine time for the mutant sea turtles to retaliate," Cephaligi said. "I must ready for the worst."

Cephaligi walked away.

"Wait," Kyler said. "Is Mirini well?"

"Well enough to move about. But please don't get in the way. The mutant sea turtles are a violent race. They could snap your limbs off and spit them out like seaweed," Cephaligi said, and he was gone.

"We should find cover," Kyler said.

"Kyler. I can help. I know I can," Mirini said.

"Please, do as Cephaligi said. Don't interfere," Kyler said. "You've been through enough. Don't risk getting killed."

"Help me remove these things," she said.

Kyler removed the mask and removed a nutrient tube running to her arm. He placed a bandage on her arm to stop the bleeding from the now-removed tube.

"Help me stand," she said.

"You need iron. I'll donate again. Use your cufflets," Kyler said.

Mirini tried pulling iron from Kyler, but to no avail.

"It's not working. Your iron level is too low," Mirini said.

"What about one of the giants? Could they donate?" Kyler asked.

"I thought you were against that," Mirini said.

"I'm against them exploiting you," Kyler said.

"But you're all for me exploiting them," Mirini said.

"It's not like that," Kyler said. "It's..."

But at that moment, mutant snapping turtles smashed through the wall, with their beaks protruding, and water poured in. Kyler rushed Mirini out of the room and closed the door. Several pilot whales rushed up with reinforcement material to hold the door closed, but water seeped from under the door. Mirini touched one of the pilot whales in hopes of drawing iron.

"It doesn't work," Mirini said.

Kyler rushed Mirini down the hallway, but the turtles smashed through a wall in a vacant room, and now water poured into the hallway and toward them. Kyler turned Mirini around, and the two ran the other way.

"It's no use, Kyler. The iron from these pilot whales can't help me," Mirini said.

"There must be an answer. We can't just die like this," Kyler said.

The two continued running. They turned a corner, ran down another hallway amongst running pilot whales, and they sped past several rooms where previously injured pilot whales were struggling to leave their hospital beds. The two passed room after room and were about to turn another corner when Mirini stopped.

"What?!" Kyler called back.

"Look!" Mirini said as she disappeared into the next-to-last room.

"Mirini, this way," Kyler called. "Mirini!"

But Mirini did not heed Kyler's calls. Kyler double backed and entered the same room as Mirini. Inside was a pilot whale lying on a bed, in agony. He was much shorter than the giants that roamed Gaviceti 5, and his skin was brown and scaly.

"Help...me..." the brown pilot whale said.

"Mirini, we really—" Kyler started.

"One moment," Mirini said to Kyler. "His skin is different."

"My name is Ligrino. I have hyperdermaferriosis," the pilot whale said. "The doctors were treating me, but now they are gone. I cannot last much longer."

"Too much iron!" Mirini said. "Ligrino, let me try something."

Mirini placed two fingers on Ligrino's forehead. She hummed something, and immediately the brown scales turned black. Then they began shrinking in size and flattening, until Ligrino's skin became smooth and shiny. He now looked much like the other pilot whales, except he was still much shorter.

"Thank you!" he said. "I haven't felt this way since I was much younger."

Just then, a mutant sea turtle smashed through the wall with its beak exposed. Kyler and Ligrino started for the door, but Mirini held her ground. She yelled something, and a burst of energy leapt from her right arm and repelled the sea turtle. The turtle retreated back to the ocean, but now water poured in through the hole. Without a worry, Mirini chanted, and the surrounding wall melted and re-formed over the exposed hole and sealed it. Kyler and Ligrino looked back in amazement.

"You...you're the foretold prophet," Ligrino said. "You were sent here to save us from the Japanese. O wise and powerful Mirini. Lead us. Lead us!"

"Easy, Ligrino. Mirini is just another person," Kyler said.

"Oh no she isn't. She repelled the mutant turtles and repaired that wall! I saw it. And she restored my health! She's the prophet. She's the prophet," Ligrino proclaimed.

This proclamation echoed throughout the room and down the hallway. Other pilot whales huddled around the doorway to see what was happening.

"Behold the foretold prophet! Mirini!" Ligrino said. "She repelled the turtles and sealed the breach."

"Hurry, she is needed this way!" said one of the pilot whales.

The group of pilot whales rushed Mirini out of the room and back down the way from where Kyler and Mirini first came. Seawater continued flooding in, and now the mutant turtles invaded the hallway. Mirini summoned up her strength and let forth a wall of grated iron that pushed the turtles backward. But the iron did not create a seal against the water, which continued flooding in.

"Help me with the water!" she called.

And the attending pilot whales did just that. They focused their energy on her projected iron grate, and they released ferrocrystallus, which bound to the grate and formed flexible seals. With their help, Mirini was able to push this new wall against the tide of water and force it back out. Steadily, this wall was moved down the hallway, and as new side doorways became available for treatment, Mirini focused side energy into those rooms, forced water out, and sealed them. In this way, Mirini and her company of pilot whales repelled all turtles and sealed all breaches.

"I am tired," Mirini said, who was now pale and fatigued. "I need iron. Where's Ligrino?"

Ligrino approached Mirini, and already his skin had turned brown and scaly. Mirini touched Ligrino's forehead with two fingers. Immediately, his rough, scaly skin became smooth and black. Mirini's complexion and energy level improved. The other pilot whales watched in awe. Barecki and Cephaligi approached.

"So this is the secret to your metabolism," Cephaligi said. "Are there any more like you?"

"No," Mirini said.

"Mirini, on behalf of all pilot whales in Gaviceti 5, I offer our sincerest gratitude and welcome you to stay as long as you like. In fact, if I may be so bold, we would be willing to have you as our queen."

The pilot whales in attendance began a low chant, sounding melodic and royal.

"Mirini, no! I don't want to lose you!" Kyler said.

Just then, Byan returned. He looked around in amazement at how structures were sealed and order restored.

"Let me guess—Mirini," Byan said.

"Queen Mirini," Cephaligi said.

"Really!" Byan said. "Congratulations."

"Thank you," Mirini said.

"You can't have her as your queen," Kyler said. "She...is to be my wife."

Scattered conversations of shock and bewilderment echoed amongst the pilot whales. Kyler dropped to a knee. Mirini placed a hand over her mouth to suppress her complete surprise.

"No, be my wife," Ligrino said, who also dropped to a knee. "I am of royal blood. And we have a special connection. We need each other."

"I have a special connection with Mirini too," Kyler said. "And I need her more than you."

"Then I challenge you for the right of Mirini's hand," Ligrino said.

"I accept," Kyler said.

"There will be no duels today," Byan said as he lifted both to their feet.

"Byan is correct," Barecki said. "The lives of our Gaviceti 5 doctors are in peril."

"I accept your gracious offer to make me your queen," Mirini said. "And as your queen, I ask all Gaviceti citizens to rally with me against the Japanese whalers. We go to war!"

The pilot whales cheered and lifted Mirini upon their shoulders. Kyler looked up in disappointment.

"You see?" Ligrino said to Kyler. "You've lost her already."

Indeed, Kyler did feel he had lost Mirini. She contacted the Sea Herder organization and met with its leader, Pat Wallace. Pat's white hair and beard sparkled in the sunlight aboard his ship, the MS Unapluto, which was already in the area and was able to respond to Mirini's request within an hour. Kyler and Ligrino accompanied Mirini, but the other whales were too large to board the MS Unapluto, as the ship was designed for human-sized folk.

"I'm pleased to meet you, Mirini. I came as soon as I received your message," Pat said. "I heard you were the one aboard the fallen satellite — Scythoc Three."

"Your information network is very good," Kyler said. "I didn't think anyone outside of Dayla Industries knew that."

"We owe a special debt to Dayla Industries for their help," Pat said as he patted his ship.

"You mean the Unapluto?" Kyler asked.

"A special donation from Julie Dayla herself," Mirini said.

"It would appear you also have a good information network," Pat said. "Now I know of you, Mirini, and of course you, Major Kyler Bohr. But I don't know your friend."

"This is Ligrino, a dwarf pilot whale from a seamount his people call Gaviceti 5," Mirini said. "He has a skin condition that creates iron scales. But his skin condition is my great prize. Watch."

Mirini touched Ligrino's forehead with her left hand to absorb the excess iron from his skin. Ligrino's scales diminished, his skin changed from brown to black, and Mirini's eyes fluttered with great excitement.

"Amazing," Pat said.

"I'll need to maintain my link with Ligrino, because my next feat will require a large amount of energy," Mirini said. "Behold."

While pulling massive amounts of iron energy from Ligrino, Mirini projected her right arm at the ocean. Two long walls of water arose from the ocean. They converged at the ends but bowed outward in the middle. As they arose, it became apparent that they were forming a massive cargo ship, so massive that it could swallow up any lesser ship.

"What...are you?!" Pat asked. "I thought you were pulling my leg. You're some sort of alien!"

"I told you, I landed on Earth in Scythoc Three," Mirini said.

"From another place? Another planet?" Pat asked.

"Yes. Now watch this!" Mirini said as she beckoned the mammoth ship toward her.

"You mean to destroy us?" Kyler asked. "Mirini, stop!"

"Don't be afraid!" Mirini said.

The water ship opened up, and it engulfed the MS Unapluto. The water ship then elevated the MS Unapluto completely out of the water.

"Full stop!" Pat ordered his crew.

Then Kyler collapsed and fell unconscious. So did Pat's crew. But Mirini, Ligrino, and Pat remained awake and aware.

"What happened to them?" Pat asked. "Did you...did you kill them?!"

"Do not fear for them. They are only stunned for the moment," Mirini said. "I wanted you to see for yourself how I intend to disrupt the Japanese whalers."

"By capturing their ships and stunning them?" Pat asked.

"Yes," Mirini said.

"But what then? Will you kill them?"

"No. I will transport them back to Japan. But I intend to keep their ships and use them to disrupt more Japanese whalers," Mirini said with an awesomeness to her voice.

"With so much power, why ask for my help? You would merely wave your arm, and all ships could be yours," Pat said.

"Not quite," Mirini said more humbly. "I need your ship and crew to take me to my first Japanese whaler. I cannot simply make multiple massive water ships in any permanent form. If I could, then the task would be easy— I could have my pilot whale friends use these ships to capture the Japanese whalers. But I can't. Just creating one requires as much energy as the ship is massive. So I must use their whaling ships against them. Once captured, I will hold the Japanese as prisoners until I can drop them off in Japan. But I need trustworthy people to pilot the Japanese ships."

"I don't understand why you need us," Pat said. "Can't your pilot whale friends operate the Japanese ships? Your friends like Ligrino here?"

"I am a dwarf among my people," Ligrino said. "While I could help pilot a Japanese ship, my people are too tall for such a task."

"I see," Pat said. "You really do need our help. But historically, we only disrupt Japanese whalers. We do not take their ships. This is a step way beyond what Sea Herder sets out to do."

"I will wake your crew. Discuss it with them. I'll accept your decision," Mirini said.

"Very well," Pat said.

Kyler awoke and stood up, as did the rest of the crew. Pat Wallace summoned his crew below for a meeting.

"What happened?" Kyler asked. "I feel like a man beat me up with a baseball bat."

"Sorry," Mirini said. "I'm still learning how to stun humans with few side effects."

"You stunned me?" Kyler asked. "But why?"

"Please, try to understand. It was important to convince Pat Wallace of my abilities," Mirini said.

"By hurting me?" Kyler asked.

"You are not injured," Mirini said. "Except for your pride."

"My Queen, I would never give complaint as to your wish," Ligrino said. "I would follow you wherever, for I know you would honor our people and keep them in the highest regard. I ask to be your consort and King."

"Cool it, Ligrino," Kyler said. "Mirini is just helping you temporarily. There's still the aliotrote situation to deal with."

"I think Ligrino is cute," Mirini said. "And I haven't decided when or if I will deal with the aliotrotes. I'm becoming quite attached to these pilot whales."

Ligrino smiled.

"Oh brother. I can't believe what I'm hearing," Kyler said. "Mirini—even if you spend time with these...uh...pilot whales, the aliotrotes will venture so far that even you cannot escape them. It's inevitable. We must deal with them now."

"Do not listen to him, my sweet Queen," Ligrino said. "Let's bring our fellow pilot whales back to Gaviceti 5 and assert your sovereign rights upon the throne."

Pat Wallace returned, but he was alone. His crew remained below.

"Where's your crew?" Kyler asked.

"They...are against me," Mirini said, seeming to read Pat's mind.

"I'm afraid so. You shook them up pretty good with that stun," Pat said.

"Then you will not help?" Mirini asked.

"I wish I could," Pat said. "Heck, I left Greenpeace because they weren't active enough in stopping whalers. By all rights I should do everything in my power to help you stop the Japanese. The trouble is...just that—trouble. It's already a challenge keeping my ships registered. I have to hop from one helpful country to another, but courts keep after us, and if I were to be charged with kidnapping and theft, that would just be too much. If I were younger, I might have been more willing. But...heck, I hate saying no. The cards are stacked against me. I can't."

Mirini managed a small smile. She hugged Pat and kissed him on the forehead.

"I understand," she said.

"I wish you all the success in the world. Maybe we can finally put an end to this senseless killing," Pat said.

"But you just said you won't help her," Kyler said.

"That's right," Pat replied.

"I don't understand," Kyler said.

"It means we must launch the rescue mission on our own," Mirini said.

"How? Pat just said no. That means the Unapluto is unavailable. What will you use for a boat?" Kyler said.

"My Queen, I would be honored to provide you with safe passage to the Japanese whalers. And I know many of your loyal subjects would wish to accompany you on this mission. They would lay their lives down for Your Majesty," Ligrino said.

"It can't work. You'll drown or something horrible or—"

"Or what, Kyler?" Mirini asked.

"You'll be missed horribly. I love you! I'm saying this loud and clear. I LOVE YOU!" Kyler shouted.

"You can't. I love Queen Mirini," Ligrino said.

"I've put up with you for the last time. I'm calling you out. Right here on the deck of the Unapluto. Put up your fins," Kyler said as he squared off against Ligrino.

"Kyler, stop it," Mirini said.

"I will put this human in his place," Ligrino said. "No one insults the queen!"

Kyler took a swipe at Ligrino. Ligrino moved his head back, making Kyler miss. Kyler took another swipe. Ligrino caught that fist with one fin and uppercut him with another. The fin caught Kyler squarely on the jaw, snapped his head sideways, and sent Kyler backward, felling him toward the deck, unconscious. Pat caught Kyler and slowed his fall.

"That was a hard hit!" Pat said. "Kyler, are you okay? Kyler?"

"That wasn't necessary," Mirini said to Ligrino.

"I am sorry, Your Majesty, but I did not realize humans are of little strength," Ligrino replied.

Mirini leaned over and touched Kyler. He awoke and was able to listen, but his jaw was now swollen, and so he could not speak.

"Shh," Mirini said. "Don't try to speak. Just rest. I must go, Kyler. I must help the pilot whales. I realize now that you cannot accompany me. I must do this without your help. There would be too much fighting between you and Ligrino, I'm afraid. Captain Wallace, would you please take Kyler back to the United States?"

"I will do that," Pat said.

"Thank you. Kyler, don't give up. I will help deal with the aliotrotes as soon as possible. Remember one thing—they don't like iron! Goodbye, Major Kyler Bohr."

Mirini kissed Kyler on the forehead. Then, she and Ligrino jumped overboard. Ligrino encased Mirini in a ferrocrystallus protective bubble and ferried her away. Kyler watched as she disappeared from sight, and then he fell unconscious.

When Kyler awoke, he was lying on a bed. Captain Pat Wallace had just placed smelling salts under Kyler's nose and now helped Kyler sit up.

"I can speak," Kyler said.

"Yes. Your swelling has gone down," Pat said.

Kyler looked out the porthole and noticed the MS Unapluto was docked.

"We are on Vancouver Island," Pat said.

"I...we were just in the Pacific Ocean. And now we are here. Buildings. I see buildings. A city? What...which..."

"Victoria," Pat said. "The city of the newly wed and the nearly dead."

"And I am neither, though I wish I were the former," Kyler said.

"You were nearly the latter," Pat said.

"How long was—"

"How long were you unconscious?" Pat asked.

Kyler nodded.

"Only four days."

"Only four days," Kyler repeated. "Then she's really gone."

"Yes, I'm afraid so," Pat said. "Look, there's another reason we couldn't help Mirini. Truth is, those aliotrotes you were talking about have spread out all over the United States. And now they're into Canada, too. It's got us worried. I mean really worried. I'm working with my organization to see what we can do to fight them, because if North America falls, the world will descend into chaos. Then there won't be a Sea Herder group—at all."

"Mirini said the secret to defeating the aliotrotes is iron," Kyler said.

"Yes, she did," Pat said. "Look, I know some geographic information experts in the city here. They have the best computer hardware and programmers on the West Coast."

"Even Silicon Valley?" Kyler asked.

"So they claim," Pat said.

"Well, a claim is one thing," Kyler said. "But what can a bunch of cartography number crunchers do about creatures from outer space?"

"People can't deal with this problem. But a computer with the right creative programming can," Pat said. "There's an ace programmer—best I've ever met—her name is Alice Bachproon. She has a way with maps, satellite data, seismic readings—anything about Earth, she can map and predict."

"What do you mean, *predict*?" Kyler asked.

"She's been helping us find the Japanese whalers—using seismic sensor, radar, sonar—anything and everything one could use to map and measure," Pat said.

"I don't believe it," Kyler said.

"How do you think we find the whalers? The Pacific isn't just some little pond you can throw a stone across. It's huge," Pat said.

"And you think mapping will help against the aliotrotes?" Kyler said. "More like a potluck dream."

"If she can't figure out a solution, no one can. In fact, she's already working on the problem, but she says she needs more data. You've had close contact with these aliotrotes. Maybe you can give her some insight," Pat said.

Kyler didn't look convinced.

"Hey, I'm just saying. It's worth a shot. What do you say?" Pat asked.

Kyler paused.

"If the aliotrotes are everywhere, then they are here too. She would then have close contact with them," Kyler said.

"It's not like that. First, they are still heavily based in Brunswick, Georgia. Second, they are spreading by infesting coal power plants for the mercury. They are also getting a taste for coal mines in the Appalachian Mountains. And third, they can't cross over from the main North American continent to Vancouver Island. At least not yet. We don't know why. Alice is working the computers night and day on that problem. But there's a fear they will. There are no coal power plants on Vancouver Island, fortunately, but there *are* coal mines. Kyler...this is it. Are you willing to help?"

"Okay, I'll help," Kyler said.

"Good," Pat replied. "I'll take you there at once."

"Just where is *there*?"

"Farrencamp Digital," Pat said.

The two traveled to the northern edge of Victoria and walked up to a plainly-marked building.

"This is it," Pat said. "Let's go inside."

The two approached a solid door. Pat pressed the intercom button and spoke.

"Hi, this is Pat Wallace with Major Kyler Bohr."

"Yes, Mr. Wallace," said the receptionist. "I'll buzz you in."

A buzzer sounded, and the door unlocked. Pat opened the door and motioned for Kyler to go in. The two entered a small reception area with a locked door to the office area, and a sliding glass window behind which the receptionist sat.

"You're expected," she said. "Please sign the guest book and take these guest badges. You'll be escorted in shortly."

The two did just that and took a seat in the reception area. The door to the main office area opened, and in the door frame stood a tall, thin woman with classy attire and long, straight, blond hair.

"Pat, Mr. Bohr?" the woman asked.

"You must be Alice," Kyler said. "You certainly don't look like the geeky type."

The woman laughed.

"Nice to see you again, Dana," Pat said.

"Dana?" Kyler asked.

"Major Kyler Bohr, meet Dana Farrencamp, owner and CEO of Farrencamp Digital."

"I...uh...oh, nice to meet you," Kyler stumbled.

Farrencamp laughed.

"Follow me," she continued to laugh.

The two followed Dana Farrencamp through a large office area, filled with server after server. Fans blew heat from these servers, and more fans blew cool air from above.

"This is your master computer collection?" Kyler asked.

"Oh no, this is our staging area," Dana said. "New servers are set up here and tested before being moved to the main server room."

"That must be some *room*," Kyler said. "I'd like to see—"

"Perhaps another time," Pat said. "Dana is taking us to the Global Research Analysis Center."

The two left the server room, passed through two sets of locked doors, and walked into a large atrium filled with indoor trees, fountains, and small shops.

"This is like a little city," Kyler said. "But this should be first, not those computers. I don't understand."

Dana laughed again.

"The staging servers act as a front in case someone gets past the receptionist. They think the servers are the main servers for the building. It's a decoy to give security time to deal with them," Pat said.

"Clever," Kyler said.

The three took an elevator to the third floor. They walked past a number of food stores and then past a variety store before entering a clothing store. They walked all the way to the back, into a fitting room, and Dana pulled a wall mirror, revealing it was a door to a secret passage, which traveled only a short ways before reaching an office with many cubicles and laptops and large displays on the wall. Despite all the cubicles and laptops, there was only one person operating them. She stood up and said, "Hello."

"So this must be Alice," Kyler said, impressed by the classy young woman, who had a similar haircut and frame as Dana, only this girl had brown hair instead of blond. But the girl laughed.

"How are things going, Tara?" Dana asked.

"Fine, Mom. Alice stepped out for a—"

"Mom?!" Kyler asked.

"This is Tara Farrencamp," Pat laughed. "Tara, meet Major Kyler Bohr."

Dana and Tara also laughed.

"Oh, my apologies," Kyler said.

"As I was saying," Tara said, "Alice stepped out for a snack. She'll be back."

"Did she set up the neuroanalyzer?" Dana asked.

"Yes, it's ready to go," Tara said.

"Hmm," Dana said.

"It might be a few minutes. She just stepped out," Tara said. "Alice needs to be here to run the analysis part, but I can get Major Bohr started by having him take the chair."

"Good. Gentlemen, I apologize, but I must run off to an offsite meeting. If you need anything, just shout," Dana said. "Thank you, Tara."

"You're welcome, Mom," Tara said.

Tara led Kyler to a special chair, where he now sat. She positioned his head back slightly until it touched a U-shaped headrest. She began securing his head to the headrest when a short, heavy-set woman with wavy-blond hair and pink highlights walked in. She wasn't looking at the chair but instead was busy walking toward her desk with her hands and arms full of food and drink, and so she conversed with Tara as if the two were alone.

"Tara, make sure the neuroanalyzer is preinitialized so we're ready to go for the special guest," the woman said.

"They're here," Tara said.

The woman turned around, still with food and drink in hand, and looked. Her eyes double-blinked, her jaw dropped, and she dropped her food and drink. Confused, she first tried to turn toward her desk, but she also tried walking toward Kyler at the same time. In doing so, she slipped on her food and drink (which were now on the floor).

"Alice!" Tara yelled, then Tara quickly turned to Kyler and said, "Don't get up."

Tara rushed over to help Alice, but Alice pushed Tara away and helped herself up. Her clothing was now wet and dirty from the food and drink, but she was too excited to care.

"This is the special guest? It's Major Kyler Bohr!" Alice exclaimed. "My god!"

"Oh no," Pat said. "Alice...may I speak with you for a moment?"

"No," Alice said, "not until I get the treatment...I mean begin the treatment."

"Alice, what are you doing?" Tara asked.

"Get away, Tara, this one is mine!" Alice said.

Alice was now drooling, and she blushed beet red.

"This setup is all wrong," Alice lied. "Stand up, *Kyler*."

Alice's pronunciation of Kyler had a special sweet slurp to it, which caused Kyler to shudder.

"Turn around," Alice drooled.

Kyler turned around.

"Do you have a girlfriend?" Alice blurted.

"Alice!" Tara said.

Tara escorted Alice out of the room and spoke to her in hurried whispers, to which Alice whispered back just as quickly.

"What was that all about? That Alice Bachproon is acting strangely. You *did* tell her about me, didn't you?" Kyler asked.

"I told Dana to expect you. But that was all," Pat said. "Apparently, Alice did not learn your identity until just now, and she has the hots for you."

"Of all the people...no, this isn't right. Mirini, where are you?" Kyler muttered.

"Off fighting Japanese whalers. So you have a thing for Mirini, do you? I gathered that on the ship when you put up a fight with Ligrino," Pat said.

"This isn't going to work. I can't have this Alice Bachproon person going crazy over me. Yuck," Kyler said.

"What do you suggest? Tara is good, but Alice is the best," Pat said.

"I was afraid you were going to say that," Kyler said.

"You're a trained pilot. You've met danger in the field," Pat said.

"I've never flown with a red-tailed boa," Kyler said, referring to Alice.

Pat laughed.

"I'll speak with Dana," Pat said. "Give me a...oh, what's that?"

Pat's cellphone rang.

"Yes. Yes. Get out of there! Now! No, don't wait! Now!" Pat yelled, and he ended his phone call.

"What happened? You're not leaving me here, are you?" Kyler asked.

"I need to," Pat said. "But I can't return to the MS Unapluto. She's departed. Kyler, there are people who don't agree with my position—people who would do whatever they can to imprison me and impound my ship. Which means I need to find another way back to sea. And fast."

"How?" Kyler asked.

Unexpectedly, Tara entered the room.

"I've distracted Alice for the moment by creating an artificial crisis," Tara said. "I'll start the scan without her."

"Unfortunately, I have a real crisis of my own. The authorities nearly caught the MS Unapluto, and I ordered its departure. Now I need my own safe departure," Pat said.

"I can arrange it," Tara said. "Normally Mom would do this, but she's dealing with other issues."

"Wait," Kyler said to Tara, but she and Pat had now exited the room. "Don't let Alice the maniac return!"

No one heard him. Two minutes later, Alice returned.

"Where's Tara!" Alice asked, but it was a statement of excitement, and a broad smile broke out.

"God no," Kyler said. "Save me."

"I have you to myself, you big hunk of man," Alice drooled.

"Look, I'm here to fight aliotrotes. Pat said you're an ace computer person," Kyler said. "That's all. I want nothing else."

"Yet," Alice said slyly. "Please sit."

"Why don't we wait for Tara to return?" Kyler asked. "I mean, how long can it take to help Pat escape?"

"Escape! Hoh, hoh, hoh!" Alice said. "Escape will take a long time, a very long time. But for *Kyler*, it's time for a little fun."

"Ick," Kyler muttered.

Kyler sat, and Alice attached the probes. She moved unusually close to Kyler and inhaled.

"Ahh," she breathed. "I can inhale you all day."

"The test, please. The test," Kyler said.

Alice pulled a desk on wheels over to Kyler and hit a few keys on the laptop.

"Starting the initial checks, *Kyler*. Probe attachment—okay, neural link—okay. I'm starting the first pass."

"That's already happened," Kyler said, referring to Alice's overtures toward him.

"We'll get together after the test, and then I'll show you a *real* first pass!" Alice promised. "Ah, the first pass is complete. Hmm. Initial results are unclear. I will need to fine tune the focus."

Alice remained close to Kyler and continued to breathe in his aroma. She touched him softly, and Kyler got the shivers again.

"Alice!"

"A girl needs a moment, like a junkie with her ice cream. You are my chocolate sundae," Alice said. "Okay, the results, the results. I'll need to run another pass. Starting the analyzer. Ohhhhhh, look at those axon activity levels and how they dance!"

"Are you learning anything about the aliotrotes?" Kyler asked.

"The what?"

"The aliotrotes!" Kyler repeated. "Isn't that what your sensors are...are..."

"The sensors are recording you!" Alice said. "And I do love what I see!"

The lights flickered, and there was a momentary drop in power. The laptops, having their own built-in batteries, slid over the power drop.

"What was that?" Kyler asked.

One of the wall monitors automatically switched to a Victoria television news station, and it now broadcast video of aliotrotes crossing over from the main continent to Vancouver Island.

"Alice, this is Dana," called Farrencamp from another monitor on the wall. "The unthinkable has happened. Aliotrotes on Vancouver Island. Urgent that you expedite the tests. I'm rushing back to the office. The—"

But her feed was cut short. And so was that of the news station. People ran around in the atrium in near panic.

"Aw, heck," Alice said. "Party is over, Major. Time to transfer the testing to the emergency underground lab."

Alice pressed a button. Several walls shot up and surrounded the two, and then these walls and the floor suddenly dropped, like a fast-moving elevator on the way to the center of the earth. Deep it traveled within a few seconds, and then it stopped as suddenly as it started. Kyler instinctively squeezed his legs to prevent G-LOC, but Alice was caught unaware and blacked out. She stopped breathing, and Kyler instinctively gave her mouth-to-mouth resuscitation, despite his natural repulsion for her. She then awoke.

"I...am flattered...that you share our deep sense of love in this deep place," she said in a deep voice.

Kyler quickly pulled away and said, "You were unconscious. I was only helping you breathe. Nothing else."

"A hero and a gentleman. You saved my life," Alice said. "Oh you are a woman's man, aren't you? But there's work to be done. Play must wait. And I saw some analysis before I hit the emergency button. I think I know how we can stop the aliotrotes."

"We?"

"Yes. You and I. I just need to run multiple scenarios through the computer. Fortunately we are well stocked with Dayla diamond computers down here to survive any kind of attack. Even the electromagnetic discharge of two lovers cannot disrupt these servers."

"Thank god for Dayla Industries," Kyler said.

"Let me just transfer the connection...there," Alice said. "Now we'll run all the scenarios."

"Scenarios?" Kyler asked.

"Yes. All the scenarios where you and I save the world," Alice said.

Kyler laughed.

"Don't underestimate the diamond computer," Alice said. "It's told me a lot so far. Your experience with the aliotrotes, the DF-23—maybe you can take me for a ride—and the weather station, and with...no, not the real John Von Brock...a fake one...it's all being analyzed by the computer. Every enemy has a weakness, and the computer will find one. No, it found two! Do you see on the big monitor?"

"Scenario One has a forty-five percent chance of success. Success of defeating the aliotrotes? How could the computer run—"

"Diamond computers are a girl's best friend," Alice said. "Let's look at the first scenario details."

The details came up on the screen.

"This is a map of the United States and the lower portion of Canada. Brunswick is in the southeast corner, and we are in the northwest corner. Now I'm compromising security policy by telling you this, but...oh...I love you, *Kyler*."

"Huh? How does that violate security?" Kyler asked.

"It...sorry, my train of thought was derailed by your handsomeness. What I'm about to tell you is compromising security policy. Farrencamp Digital has a link with Dayla Industries."

"A digital line? How?" Kyler asked.

"Deep underground diamond twisted fiber," Alice said.

"I've never heard of such a thing," Kyler said.

"No one has. They're not supposed to," Alice said. "But back to Scenario One. You and I must step into a magno-hydraulic suspension tube. We will share neural responses, you and I, while suspended in a stainless steel emulsion with special radioactive elements that I invented. I call it *radiinox*. Then, the deep underground diamond twisted fiber will project our combined essence to Dayla Industries, where we will appear in another magno-hydraulic suspension tube. You and I, Kyler. Joined."

"The computer decided that? Out of billions of people in this world? And all the technology we have?" Kyler asked.

"Yes."

"It considered all of it?"

"Yes."

"Really? All of it? Everywhere? Everyone?" Kyler pressed.

"Yes, yes, yes! Everywhere and everyone! They were all considered. And this is it. This is the plan. This is what we must do," Alice insisted.

"But how can this work?" Kyler said. "How can this—if this can really do what it claims—how can this stop the aliotrotes?"

"It creates a harmonic wave from Victoria to Brunswick and taps into Earth's magnetic core. Aliotrotes are composed of mercury compounds, and iron doesn't mix. Our act will use Earth's iron to contain the aliotrotes."

"And? Then what?"

"They could be thrown back into space," Alice said.

"Bad idea. They'll return," Kyler said.

"They could remain in containment and be sent to the sun. The sun would vaporize them," Alice said.

"Hmm."

"It's the perfect plan," Alice said. "I can't believe the computer concurs with my original assessment that you and I are destined for each other."

"Trust me, I can't believe it either," Kyler said. "But there is a Scenario Two."

"Usually, each scenario after the first has less and less chance of success. But they are provided just in case," Alice said. "Scenario Two probably just has you in the suspension tube, and it will prove how much you really need me to defeat the aliotrotes."

"Don't make me any more sick than I already am," Kyler said. "Forget about Scenario Two."

"Now, now. A good scientist examines all solutions, no matter how bleak," Alice said.

"Then I'll turn away, and you look for yourself. And don't share the details," Kyler said.

"If you're that afraid—"

"It's not fear. More like revulsion."

"Major Bohr! That's no way to conduct yourself. Now shape up. Well?"

"I...I just can't look at Scenario Two," Kyler said.

"Fine! I'll review it privately!" Alice snorted.

Alice removed a small, crystalline disk from a computer panel and began walking toward a side room.

"Now what are you doing?" he asked.

"I'm reviewing the alternative plan!" she shouted, and she slammed a door behind her.

Kyler decided to stand up and stretch. But there were probes and sensors to remove. One by one, he worked to remove them.

"Ow!" he said. "That one hurt. I think next time I'll ask that I get my chest hair shaved before they stick one of these probes on me. I may have lost some skin pulling that one off."

Kyler then pulled another probe off his chest, but before he could say, "Ow," from the pain, he heard a bone-chattering scream.

"What is it?" Kyler yelled back. "Are you hurt?"

Alice stormed into the room, screaming and cursing the most vile of things. She threw the crystalline disk on the floor to break it, but it simply bounced. She took scissors and tried scratching it, but this disk was harder than the scissors. And so with all her might, she bent the disk. Suddenly it broke into shards, and the force of breaking it sent the shards against her hands and forearms, cutting them up badly and causing her to bleed heavily. Unfazed, she smashed the little door to a fire extinguisher, and she used that to bash in the computer panels. The panels shorted and sent showery sparks all over. The room was about ready to go ablaze when Kyler managed to pull off the last sensor and rush over to Alice.

"Stop it! You're going to kill yourself! Is that what you want? Stop this madness now!" Kyler ordered.

Then Alice fell into Kyler's arms and sobbed like a child whose favorite toy had been taken away. But she became mad again and pounded on Kyler's chest.

"It's all your fault!" she screamed.

Kyler tried to contain her, but she fought all the harder, and her increased blood pressure forced her blood out of her veins all the quicker.

"Calm down, Alice! We've got to stop the bleeding! Alice, do you understand? Alice?"

But it didn't matter. Alice now lost too much blood, and she fell unconscious. With her resistance dissipated, Kyler went to work and bandaged her wounds with material he ripped from his shirt. A short while later, an elevator door opened at one side of the room, and Dana Farrencamp arrived with two technicians.

"Alice!" Dana yelled.

Dana pulled out her cellphone and made a call.

"Medical emergency in Deep Lab 3," Dana said.

"She was reviewing a computer analysis, and she just went berserk. She broke a data disk and cut herself," Kyler explained. "I've done what I can, but she needs a transfusion and stitches."

"Hold her steady," Dana said. "Medics are on the way."

"How did you know?" Kyler asked. "You arrived so quickly."

"Our security registered power fluctuations in this area. We thought the aliotrotes somehow invaded this deep. They're everywhere at ground level," Dana said.

A doctor arrived in the elevator with an assistant, who wheeled in a gurney. The two and technicians placed Alice on the gurney, and then the two took Alice away.

"How bad is the damage?" Dana asked.

"Very bad," one technician said. "The main core is destroyed. There's an auxiliary server still working, but it's only powerful enough for communication."

"Communication. What networks?" Dana asked.

"Only one," the technician said. "Dayla Industries."

"Get that link working," Dana said. "And do what you can to get the memory core working in this lab."

Dana then turned to Kyler.

"Major Bohr, Alice was supposed to work on a solution to the aliotrote problem. Did she make any progress?"

"Yes," Kyler said. "The computer completed its analysis. The aliotrotes can be defeated."

The technicians heard this and rumbled with cheer.

"This is good news. Very good news. I knew Alice was gifted, but...Kyler, what happened with her?" Dana asked.

"Alice ran the numbers," Kyler explained. "And rather quickly, too. The computer found two solutions."

"Two!" a technician said with delight.

"Just get that memory core working," Dana said to the technician.

"She showed me the details of the first solution, which had only a forty-five percent chance of success," Kyler explained.

"Hmm," Dana said. "That doesn't sound promising."

"It was a situation where she and I were in a tube filled with a stainless steel emulsion," Kyler explained.

"That sounds like an Alice-engineered solution," Dana said. "Very Alice engineered."

"I think she has some sort of crush on me," Kyler said.

"What was the second solution?" Dana asked.

"I don't know. We had a disagreement about viewing it together, I guess. She went into the other room to view it, and she started screaming. She came out with the disk, and—"

"A memory disk," Dana said to the technicians.

One of the technicians walked over to where Kyler was pointing—a pool of blood.

"It's almost unrecognizable," the technician said. "Covered in blood and in many pieces."

"Can you recover the data?" Dana asked.

"Perhaps some of it. But it will take time," the technician said.

"Then start immediately," Dana said. "Well, it would seem that whatever the second solution was, Alice did not like it. And she's too ill to participate in the first solution, so it would seem we must rediscover the second."

"We have a link with Dayla Industries," a technician said. "It's Miss Debbie Dayla herself."

"Debbie!" Dana called. "How are you?"

"Not as bad as some might think," Debbie said over the videophone. "We're weathering this thing out in our deep-tunnel bunker."

"Debbie. This is Major Bohr," Kyler said. "How on Earth did you escape the aliotrotes?"

"Sparfy and his seadogs," Debbie said.

"But he was at war with the orcas," Kyler said. "How—"

"It's a long story," Debbie said, "but for now we are safe."

"Roger too?" Kyler asked.

"Yes, he is quite safe. But our nation is not. After your launch from here, we launched an attack of our own against the aliotrotes, hoping to buy you some time. It failed. We did not account for Senator Croius and his orcas.

He's worse than a traitor. Fortunately, Sparfy and his dolphins followed him and his orcas to Brunswick and gave them and the aliotrotes enough of a fight to permit our escape, at least temporarily."

"I'm glad to hear that," Kyler said.

"Debbie, Alice Bachproon was running a computer analysis on how to defeat the aliotrotes," Dana said.

"As have we. So far our computers have found nothing," Debbie said.

"Well our computers found two solutions," Dana said.

"Really! I'd love to hear them," Debbie said.

"The first one is unworkable," Dana said. "And the second one is...well, we're trying to recover it. Alice has been working too hard, I fear, and... well...we're trying to recover the second solution."

"If there's anything I can do to help, my computers are at your disposal," Debbie said.

"We can do it," said a technician. "We can link what's left of our core to the Dayla system."

Debbie turned to someone on her side and said something.

"We're ready. Go ahead," Debbie said.

The technician hit a few keys on a keyboard. One and only one monitor on the wall lit up, and it showed a partial spider's web graphic of attempted connections and failures.

"We're getting a feed now," Debbie said. "Yeah, lots of damage on your side. Lots of damage."

"I've cleaned up the memory disk and placed it in the atomic scanner," said one of Dana's technicians.

"We're getting that feed now. We can read sixty percent of the content. That's pretty good," Debbie said.

"Is there a way you can combine the data from the disk with the memory core?" Kyler asked.

"We're doing that now," Debbie said. "Let me help it along."

Debbie began humming softly. Sparfy now walked up to her station and stood next to her, and he too began humming. Then as quickly as Debbie started humming, she stopped.

"Well, we didn't make much progress," Debbie said. "As near as we can tell, the second solution involves your station and our station. But a good forty percent of the data is missing, which means we simply can't guess as to what else is needed to make this work, not to mention what exactly the plan is. We did get a complete picture of the first solution, and, uh, well..."

"You don't have to apologize," Kyler said. "Alice had a crush on me."

"But maybe she wasn't that far off track," Debbie said. "The portion that we can see from the second solution requires two people in a suspension tube each in your station, and two people in a suspension tube each in our station. I can tell you that Sparfy and I are the ones for our station. Major Bohr may or may not be one of the two in your station—that part is on the edge of the data disk. And I cannot determine who the other person should be in your station. It's certainly no one in your room right now."

"Interesting. Maybe it *is* Alice. But then why did she make all the fuss?" Kyler asked.

"Wait one moment," Debbie said. "We're receiving a strange transmission from...I don't believe it. It's coming from the Pacific Ocean."

"Near Vancouver Island?" Dana asked.

"No. Much farther away," Debbie said.

"A few miles?" Dana asked.

"A few thousand miles," Debbie said.

"Mirini!" Kyler exclaimed.

"It's...I don't believe it's...it's..." Debbie started.

"Believe it, believe it!" Kyler cheered.

"It's on long wave. I didn't think it possible. Even Morse code is a challenge at this particularly low wavelength. But there it is," Debbie said.

"Debbie Dayla, do you hear me?" said a distorted voice, but Kyler immediately recognized it as Mirini's.

"Mirini, Mirini, Mirini!" Kyler cheered.

"Kyler?" Mirini called. "Are you in Brunswick?"

"No, he's in Victoria on Vancouver Island, at Farrencamp Digital," Debbie said. "He is with Dana Farrencamp and a few of her technicians. I am accompanied by Prince Sparfiacus."

"I have completed a mission against a Japanese whaler. We have commandeered the ship and are holding the crew as prisoners," Mirini said.

"Who is helping you?" Debbie asked.

"Ligrino, his pilot whales, and an amazing group of harbor porpoises we met are helping me. Ligrino is with me now," Mirini said.

Sparfy squealed in echolocation language. Ligrino squealed back. The two then exchanged excited squeals as if they were long lost brothers catching up on years of lost correspondence.

"Easy, easy, Sparfy!" Debbie said.

"I did not know we had such advanced cetacean kin in the Pacific Ocean," Sparfy said.

"And I did not know the Atlantic had such noble dolphins," Ligrino said. "We must make plans to meet. I would welcome you any time on Gaviceti 5. And I would like to visit you in your realm."

"I would under other circumstances, but we are at war with the orcas in our area," Sparfy said.

"Strange. The orcas are allies in our realm," Ligrino said.

"Really! That's an interesting twist," Sparfy said.

"In fact, just the other day we were—"

"Gentlemen, if you please," Dana said. "It's clear to me now what the missing forty-percent entails."

"Of course," Debbie said. "Why didn't I think of it before? Mirini is part of the missing data. Then she and Ligrino must be a *third* couple."

"That can't be right," Kyler said. "Mirini and I are destined to be a couple."

"There's a story here, and no one has told me," Dana said.

"Apologies, Dana. We *will* explain in time. If only we could get some sort of final calculation on this matter," Debbie said.

Just then, Tara entered the room.

"Pat Wallace is safely in the Pacific. I had one of our boats take him to the MS Unapluto," Tara said. "Hey, what happened here?"

"She's the one!" Debbie said. "I can sense it! Your daughter, Dana. She's the missing link. No question about it!"

"Tara? The missing link? Of course!" Kyler said. "That would explain why Alice was so upset."

"But Alice and Tara are good friends," Dana said.

"Think back to when you were younger," Debbie said. "If you had a crush on a boy, and there was a suggestion that your best friend would take him away, wouldn't you be angry?"

"But I'm not trying to take anyone away," Tara said.

"Debbie, I've tapped into your feed and have read the computer data," Mirini said. "I think I can solve your puzzle, but I need one additional piece of evidence. Could one of you place a sample of Alice's blood in the atomic analyzer?"

"You must have powers indeed if you can read part of the second solution from Alice's blood," Dana said.

"Her thoughts of the moment were preserved in her bloodstream," Mirini said. "Those thoughts are faint but detectable."

Dana motioned to one of the technicians, and he took a sample of blood from the floor and placed it in the atomic analyzer. Mirini breathed in deeply and exhaled.

"I have the solution then," Mirini said. "Debbie, you were on the right track with what you said earlier, before I joined the conversation."

"Your skills are very impressive," Debbie said.

"I must learn more about you, Mirini," Dana said. "I'm sure we could help each other accomplish many things."

"I'll pay you a visit in the near future, Dana Farrencamp. But now it is time to deal with the aliotrotes. I know the second plan, and we must act quickly. Tara and Kyler, you must each enter separate tubes filled with an emulsion of stainless steel and sodium acetate," Mirini said. "Debbie and Sparfy, you do the same. Ligrino and I will use make-shift vats here on the Japanese whaling ship."

"Alice has all the ingredients prepared, but only one tube is ready. I'll get the other ready," Tara said.

"Hurry," Mirini said. "We must link up with four weather satellites. I'm relaying their locations and transponder uplink codes now."

"Got it," Debbie said. "Very clever. This is like the original weather satellite plan. But they don't have enough power to alter mercury on Earth's surface."

"If calculations are correct, they won't have to," Mirini said.

"Okay, Sparfy and I are in our emulsion tubes," Debbie said.

"The mixture is ready for my emulsion tube," Tara said. "Major Bohr, please step into your tube."

"What do I do?" Kyler said. "I didn't get to see the second plan."

"You'll know what to do," Tara said.

Kyler entered the emulsion tube. Tara entered hers, and Dana closed the doors. Debbie and Sparfy were in their tubes, and Mirini and Ligrino were in their vats.

"Tara must begin," Mirini said.

"I think I know what to do," Tara said. "I did something similar before while testing a new satellite calibration program."

"Alice predicted you would remember the calibration program," Mirini said.

"All I did was whistle a musical I heard as a child," Tara said. "I changed a few of the notes to sync up with the satellites, but otherwise it was the musical."

"Start your musical, Tara. Debbie and Sparfy, join in as a round. Ligrino and I will provide harmonics," Mirini said.

"East, north, west, south. East, north, west, south," Tara said. "Kyler repeat the-words with-me. East, north, west, south."

Kyler said the four cardinal directions, and Tara whistled in four-four time for patterns of four measures at a time, with these patterns of four feeling like one traveling along a baseball diamond starting with first base (east), second base (north), third base (west), and home plate (south). Then Debbie hummed in a round such that she was one baseball position/cardinal direction behind Tara. Sparfy added light puffs of squealing. Mirini hummed harmonics and Ligrino provided a percussive thump.

"East, north, west, south," Kyler continued.

Kyler closed his eyes and opened them. He was suddenly in a different place and different time. He was seven years old in the middle of a meadow. Running around him was a brook that forked at a northern point, surrounded Kyler, and rejoined at a southern point. In a way, Kyler was on an island, if a brook could create such a feature. At the edge of the meadow was a grove of trees in a formation such that the meadow itself had a diamond shape. Kyler was not alone. Wearing a simple tunic and covered in a weave of stemmed flowers danced a seven-year old girl, whistling a musical. It was Tara.

"How are we...what is this place?" Kyler asked.

Tara put a finger to her lips to shush Kyler's questions. She briefly chanted, "East, north, west, south," in order to get Kyler chanting the same.

And he did. He then looked, and to the southwest on the other side of the brook stood Mirini and Ligrino on a pedestal. They too were wearing tunics. To the southeast on the other side of the brook stood Debbie and Sparfy —again, wearing simple tunics. And now when Kyler looked to the north at the point where the brook forked, he saw Dana standing on a much taller pedestal, but she was on the island side of the meadow. She wore a long robe, and she appeared much younger with blonder and longer hair.

Then she held out her hands as if giving something to Kyler, but in fact she was not. In her left hand, she held what appeared to be a dynamic model of hydrogen, with the electron orbiting the proton at incredible speed. In her right hand, she held a much more complex atom with many neutrons, protons, and electrons. It was thorium. She brought the two progressively closer, and as she did so, Tara danced and whistled more quickly. The sun, which Kyler did not notice until now, picked up speed across the sky, and it set and then rose in cadence with the whistling for west and east. More quickly it traveled across the sky. More quickly Tara whistled. Kyler could no longer keep up, and a rock formation with blinking lights jutted up from the center of the island. It picked up the whistling where Tara left off, because even Tara could not whistle that quickly. The sun strobed, the whistling degraded from music to a two-tone siren, and just when Kyler thought he would go mad, Dana brought the two atoms together.

A cluster of amber sparks erupted from Dana's hand. Kyler cried out, as he thought the burst had killed her. But now her robe had changed from white to a glowy, silvery, stainless steel. And she wore a crown of stainless and her fingernails were of stainless. A glow emanated from her skin, and she laughed, as one might when one has finished a good meal and is enjoying the comforts of a Broadway musical.

Then Kyler looked up in the sky, and he saw four points of light, faint, and they formed the geometric shape of a diamond and aligned with the four points of the brook. The lights grew larger, and Kyler recognized small outlines to these lights—they were weather satellites. The satellites grew larger in size, and each satellite projected a beam of light. The four beams of light converged, diverged, and danced around one another, creating circles of light around the forked brook and the island, expanding and contracting as if in respiration.

The circles of light crossed the brook and entered the island, and they crossed paths. Then gelatinous flying insects of mercury gray which had been hiding inside flower petals took flight. The light beams caught them and vaporized them into puffs of smoke and shiny glitter—krypton and ruthenium. The insects appeared to grow in number, but in reality they were simply being flushed out, and the circling lights vaporized more and more until there was a shower of ruthenium glitter. The krypton then coalesced into a floating webwork a dozen meters in the air, creating a dancing light display.

Tara danced and ran around in the glowing glitter. The glitter was crunchy and self adherent, and so she took a clump and threw it at seven-year-old Kyler, as if throwing a snowball. Kyler in turn picked up a clump of glitter and threw it back. The two ran and ducked and threw ruthenium glitter balls until the two laughed and laughed and fell onto their backs where each made ruthenium glitter angels—like snow angles. Then the two worked together and built a ruthenium igloo, and they made a ruthenium glitter man—like a snowman. The lights faded, the weather satellites shrank into the heavens, and the sun slowed its path across the sky, until it began to set in a slower time frame. Tara and Kyler crawled into the igloo and started a krypton plasma fire to keep warm. A little smoke from the last of the mercury gelatinous insects escaped through the hole in the top of the igloo. The music died down, and all were quiet. Then Tara took Kyler's hand and sang a soft song in the evening quiet. The two fell asleep.

Kyler opened his eyes slowly. He was still inside a tube, but now the stainless steel emulsion was draining away, and a soapy water mix filled the tube. It swished and swirled, drained away, a rinse filled the tube, it swished and swirled, and the rinse drained away. Columns of hot air rose through the tube and dried Kyler off. Then Tara walked over and opened the tube.

"Welcome back," Tara said.

"Aliotrote activity—zero. Mercury content in North America—zero," Dana said.

"The aliotrote spaceship has been destroyed," Debbie said. "All aliotrotes have been vaporized into krypton and ruthenium. We did it."

Cheer filled the Dayla Industries communication, and the technicians cheered in the Farrencamp lab. Sparfy squealed in delight as did Ligrino. Mirini clapped and offered her congratulations.

"Oh, but Doctor Kukovich!" Kyler exclaimed, suddenly remembering the doctor had been kidnapped.

"He was thrown clear," Debbie said. "A Dayla rescue ship picked him up, and he is safe."

"Whew!" Kyler said. "I'm relieved."

"He distracted the aliotrotes in the end and almost paid with his life. But he survived."

"I'm so glad to hear that, Debbie. And for all of us, that was the finest display of combat against the aliotrotes," Mirini said. "What a team effort. I only wish we had such a team on Bruxima 4."

"Will you go back?" Debbie asked.

"No. The pilot whales have offered me a position as their queen. I have accepted. I will help them fight illegal whaling," Mirini said. "Kyler, please do not think ill of me. This is my place now."

"I don't. I value the time we had together and hope to meet again," Kyler said. "And something says that my life is about to change."

"It is," Tara said, who was facing Kyler this entire time. "We have shared something together. Happiness comes through the play of a child, and we have seen happiness where others have not. I think we have more to explore, Major Kyler Bohr."

"Indeed we do," Kyler said. "Indeed we do."

Between the Lake and Mountain

Morning Mail

Between the lake and mountain, in the far distant future, a humble man named Loran Laculic lived in a comfortable cozy cabin. He farmed waxy wheat, milkweed, woody shrubs, and oysters. Everything that he needed for food and supplies came from his farm. Waxy wheat provided essential amino acids and energy. Detoxified milkweed was spun into thread and made into a variety of liquids such as paint, ink, glue, and medication. Furniture he made from woody shrubs, and planks he made to repair his cabin or boat. The oysters he harvested for special meals when entertaining visitors, and he had a skill for softening the shells so he could mold them into any desired shape and then reharden them.

Loran's specialty was his love for smokehouses. He smoked all sorts of food (even non-food) using a variety of special shrubs to impart taste and preservatives. Only the hardest of shrubs produced the right caramelized mixture of carbonyls and phenols. He had several smokehouses lined up together, looking like missile silos with their cylindrical walls and pointed tops.

Loran lived at the end of a path. This path came from Millfork, a nearby town where farmers brought their goods for processing and exchange. Loran often thought of extending the path, if he could, to open access to a special part of the lake, but he could not—the path was blocked by an outcropping of the mountain.

Breakfast was done. Loran had just finished off a portion of waxy-wheat-leaf bacon, toast with jam made from shrub berries picked a few days ago, scrambled oyster with spices, and mead made from shrub berries and milkweed extract. The day was sunny, the breeze light, and the air pleasant. Loran opened the front door to his cabin (his front door faced the lake), walked onto his porch, stretched, and then walked down the porch steps to another set of steps leading from the ground around his cabin to the lake shore, where his boat was tied to a dock.

"Time for a morning row and a wash," he said.

He paddled his boat a little bit into the lake. The water was clear, very clear, which was unusual for some freshwater bodies, but not this one. There were no waves, no pollution, no water churning, and very little animal life. There were oysters, and they were especially hardy. The water could be consumed without ill effect, and Loran did so frequently. Dissolved minerals from the mountain mixed in with the lake and gave good health to Loran. Loran concluded that those minerals bound themselves to undesired particulates and caused them to sink, resulting in the lake's clarity.

Loran dove into the water. He swam in his clothes, both freestyle and on his back. In this way, he washed both his clothes and his body. He floated for a bit, saying something about feeling like an otter. A few minutes more of relaxation, and that was it. He finished his swim and climbed into his boat, and then he paddled to shore. Loran tied the boat to his dock and went inside his cabin, where he dried off by standing on the main-floor hearth, with a running fire for heat.

As he dried, he thought back to when he was a boy, when his granduncle read him stories about animals of old, before the world had changed. That's how Loran learned of the otter, among other animals.

"I still have that book," Loran said. "I should find it and read about the otter."

Loran finished drying off, and he walked over to a cabinet to retrieve the book when the doorbell rang. Loran answered the door.

"Morning mail," said Hughward.

"Ah, Hughward the Mail Steward. Thank you. Please, come in and make yourself at home," Loran said. "Have something to drink?"

"Thank you, Loran," Hughward said, and he poured himself a glass of mead. "Ah, very refreshing."

"You're welcome to all you can drink, if you like," Loran said. "Hmm. Let's see what's in the mail for today: a package from the Buckner Falls Paleo Fair. The Buckner Fair! That must be the lucky fossil I ordered!"

Loran opened the package and then unwrapped paper from a long, slender bone. Another piece of paper contained writing, and Loran read it aloud:

"To our beloved customer Mr. Loran Laculic: Enclosed please find your lucky cuttlebone for warding off evil spirits and curing all that ails you."

"Superstition, Loran. The Buckner Fair will say anything to make a sale," Hughward said.

"It's the ankle version," Loran said, ignoring Hughward's warning. "I'll put it on now for good luck. Lucky cuttlebone, lucky cuttlebone, bring me good fortune!"

Hughward laughed.

"What would your cousin say if she saw you?" Hughward laughed.

"Cousin Lillianina! She sent a letter finally?" Loran asked.

Hughward's laugh failed.

"Sorry. Not today," Hughward said.

"Let me check!" Loran said, now returning to the rest of his mail. "An advertisement for the local stores, a circular for a town meeting next week, and a letter from the Millfork Fire Department. But nothing from Cousin Lillianina? It's been three months, Hughward. Are there any problems with mail to Sathiakia?"

"I wouldn't know about that," Hughward said.

"Hmm," Loran said, and he paced a little.

Filled with nervous energy, Loran changed his focus to the mail from the Millfork Fire Department.

"Let's see if my application is approved," Loran said. He opened the letter and read it: "*We regret that due to a low score on your physical fitness test, we are unable to accept your application for Fire Deputy.*"

"I'm sorry, sir," Hughward said.

"I can't believe they rejected my application. Are they trying to say I'm unfit?" Loran asked.

"You do look a little pale," Hughward said, trying to be subtle.

"I do, don't I? Well, I can't help that," Loran said. "I try to get a little sun. But my skin burns so easily. I guess a fire wouldn't be so kind either."

"Thank you for the mead, sir," Hughward smiled after a pause.

"You're welcome. Come again, hopefully with a letter from Lillianina," Loran said.

"I hope to," Hughward said, and he left.

"No letters from Lillianina," Loran muttered. "How will I finish the new formula for shellioster? I need her recipes to get the right mixture of oyster, milkweed extract, and shrub sap together. I can figure out the cooking time and stuff, but only if I want to spend another year of trial and error. I don't want to wait a year. I can make all sorts of things with shellioster—thread, cookware, eating utensils, lightweight boats, shoes, and so on. Oh Lillianina, where are your letters?"

Two Intruders

Loran brooded, and this made him forget about finding the book on animals. To get his mind off his problems with shellioster, he walked out the back door (which faced away from the lake and toward the mountain), and he approached several closed canisters sitting in the edge of a mountain stream with lots of little holes in the bottom to let mountain water through.

"Better check the oyster shells to see if they're soft yet," he said.

Loran opened the first canister. It was empty! Shocked, he opened the second and the third. All empty.

"My oyster shells have been stolen!" Loran said.

Loran looked around for evidence of foot prints. There were none but his own.

"There's only one explanation," Loran said. "The picocians have stolen it."

A picocian is a small, human-like creature no taller than a house cat. Picocians live in the mountains and work extensively with stone. They mine tunnels and have cities inside the mountain. Some picocians trade cutting tools and small stonework at the Millfork Trading Mart, but generally speaking, picocians have a bad reputation as thieves, as they have often been caught taking things from farmers and villagers. They also have a reputation for sending their mining waste into the mountain stream (the one running between Loran's cabin and the mountain).

"I must set a trap for these picocians," Loran said to himself. "I will catch them and make them return my oyster shells. Oh, but the stress has made me weak with hunger. I must have a bite of lunch first."

Loran returned to his cabin, opened a door to the cellar, lit an oil lantern, and walked down the steps with lantern in hand.

"Let's see," he mused while looking through his stores. "I have some apple shrub root here, wheat bread, salted oyster meat—o what a delicacy—and breeberry ale."

Loran's stores were wrapped in wax paper, except for the ale, which was bottled. He placed the packaged food in a wicker basket and was about to return upstairs when he noticed several spare candles had been knocked off a storage shelf.

"Now how did those fall down?" Loran asked.

Loran temporarily placed the basket and lantern on a side table. He reached for the fallen candles when he heard a scuffing sound from behind the storage shelf. Suspicious, he slowly crept to the back side of the storage shelf and kept absolutely still. More scuffing, and now a sound of digging. A brick dislodged itself from the cellar wall and swung open, then out climbed a picocian with dark red hair and heavily-freckled skin. The picocian knelt on one of the storage shelves and helped another picocian climb out, who had light red hair and ruddy-red skin.

"Where are we, Myoxi?" the second-to-climb-out picocian asked.

"We seem to have taken a wrong turn, Gliria," the first picocian replied.

Loran reached for a small bottle from a nearby shelf, a bottle labeled, "Ethaloid — For a Good Night's Rest."

"All that digging for nothing," Gliria said. "You promised new wealth and fresh oysters to eat after we find the mine. Well?"

"Maybe there's something here we can—" Myoxi started.

But Myoxi couldn't finish. Loran had removed the Ethaloid bottle's cap, shaken the bottle with his thumb over the top, and angled his thumb up to allow Ethaloid to stream over Myoxi and Gliria. The picocians fell on the shelf, unconscious.

"Lillianina's recipe for Ethaloid works wonders not only for getting to sleep on restless nights, but for capturing picocians, too."

Loran quickly wiped the excess Ethaloid from his thumb so that he would not grow drowsy. He rummaged through his cellar for an old bird cage. It was a family heirloom passed down for many generations as a reminder of the days when birds once covered Earth in swarms. Loran had never seen a bird and wondered why he still kept this bird cage, but now he had good use for it. He placed the two picocians in the birdcage and carried it upstairs, where he placed it on the main dining room table. He then returned to the cellar for his lunch and for the lantern, and then back upstairs with both and placed his lunch on the dining room table and was about to return to the cellar to seal off the removed brick, but the episode wore him out (or perhaps the Ethaloid on his thumb had affected him), and he settled for simply closing the cellar door and returning to the dining room table, with the lantern still lit.

"I need a bit of food to rejuvenate me. These picocians have troubled my stomach," Loran said.

Loran ate through his lunch quickly. The picocians continued to sleep, and Loran, now feeling full and satisfied, wondered if he should take a nap as well.

"No," Loran said. "They might awake and escape. Or friends might come to their rescue. Best I wake them and find out what mischief they're up to."

Loran got up from the dining table, cleaned up from lunch, and opened the cupboard, revealing a collection of spices, tonics, and more medicine jars. He took one labeled, "Daylazine — For Pep and Go." Loran placed three drops of the Daylazine in the cage and returned the bottle to the cupboard. The drops evaporated into a fine, misty cloud that filled the bird cage. The two picocians awoke, and they began to scratch restlessly.

"See here," Loran said. "What do you mean by breaking into my home?"

Loran placed the lantern close to the bird cage. The picocians cowered back and shielded their eyes from the light as best they could while still wiggling and scratching.

"Please, oh please, let us go!" Myoxi begged.

"Not until you explain yourselves," Loran said. "My prized oyster shells were stolen from my soaking canisters, and I find you burrowing into my cellar to steal more things. Well?"

"Please, sir, we stole no oysters and had no plans to steal from you or your cellar," Myoxi said.

"Oh Myoxi, I'm frightened," Gliria said. "And I itch all over."

Gliria held onto Myoxi with all her might.

"Steady there, Gliria, steady," Myoxi said, but it was difficult to steady themselves with their fright and itching.

"And I'm supposed to believe you?" Loran asked.

"We picocians never lie," Myoxi said.

"That in itself is a lie," Loran said.

"Oh please, help us," Gliria said. "Something is wrong, horribly wrong. I've never itched so much in my life."

"That's the Daylazine purging the Ethaloid. You'll feel fine in a moment."

"Daylazine and Ethaloid!?" Myoxi said. "You attacked us with drugs?"

"Please, sir, don't hurt us," Gliria said. "Don't hurt us with drugs."

"Don't call me *sir*. Makes me feel old," Loran said. "Address me by my name. I am Loran Laculic, owner and resident of Laculic Manor between Lake Meadowash and Rainbear Mountain. Please, call me *Loran*."

"Mr. Loran sir, please, we mean no harm," said Myoxi, now scratching less. "We are tunneling for an underground mine with precious metals. We heard there was one in these parts."

"There isn't," Loran said. "Just my cabin and me."

"Rightly so, sir, yes sir," Myoxi said. "It must be a myth, that's for sure. I bought a map from a traveler at the Millfork Trading Mart."

Myoxi produced a map from his pocket. He and Gliria had stopped scratching.

"Let me see that," Loran said.

Myoxi handed the map to Loran.

"I paid three hundred *malooples* for this map," Myoxi continued. "The gentleman said I would find iron, silver, gold, and platinum!"

Loran looked closely at the map.

"This map makes no sense. How are you to know where to start?" Loran asked.

"The gentleman said I could start anywhere, that all I had to do was say three magic words, and the map would show me where to go by pulling me," Myoxi said.

"And just what are those magic words?" Loran asked.

"Ah-hah! I know your trick. You would have the treasure for yourself," Myoxi said.

"There is no treasure. I simply wish you to see the folly of your fantasy," Loran said.

"Oh tell him the magic words!" Gliria cried. "They're no good anyway!"

Myoxi tapped and stamped his foot. He didn't want to give up the three magic words, but he wasn't in much of a position to bargain. Or was he?

"I'll tell you on one condition," Myoxi said.

"Oh forget the condition," Gliria said.

"You have no claim of duty over me," Loran said. "But if it helps you feel better, name your unclaimable condition."

"You help us find the underground mine, and we'll split the claim with you," Myoxi said.

Loran stared at the picocian and then burst into laughter.

"It's not funny!" Myoxi said. "On your honor, do swear an oath!"

"Oh for the love of lollipop," Loran said. "Do you really believe I can take your offer seriously? Pa-fooey!"

"Then I have nothing else to say, ow!" Myoxi said.

Gliria kicked Myoxi in the shin.

"Oh very well," Loran said. "I, Loran Laculic, do swear on this dining table to help Myoxi and Gliria find an underground mine with treasure. There. And if I might add, you two seem like the classic picocian married couple if ever a one did I see."

"Going on eighty-five years now," Gliria said.

"Ahem, yes, well, please don't remind me," Myoxi said, and Gliria kicked him in the shin again. "Ow!"

"The magic words, Myoxi. What are they?" Loran asked.

"*Devie Cede Nim*," Myoxi said.

"Those are magic words?" Loran asked.

"That's what the gentleman told me," Myoxi said.

"And just what is the gentleman's name?" Loran asked.

"*Ekans Egroeg*," Myoxi said.

Loran laughed again.

"Did I say it wrong?" Myoxi said.

"Yes, you did," Loran replied. "You just said *George Snake* backward. And there's a reason his last name is *Snake*. He has a forked tongue that'll split a lie quicker than a pie. And now I will solve your puzzle."

"The mine?" Myoxi said in excitement, not catching on that he'd been duped.

"Let's see. George Snake likes to reverse things. So your magic words are *Min Edec Eived*. In other words, *Mine Deceived*," Loran explained.

Myoxi stood with his tongue hanging from his mouth. Gliria kicked him in the shin, and he bit his tongue in reaction.

"Ow!" Myoxi said.

"I should take you both to Millfork and turn you over to the head sholiff. He'd put you behind bars and hold a trial. That would teach you picocians a thing or three," Loran threatened.

"Oh no, please sir, we are all out of sorts here, my wife Gliria and me, and someday we are going to have a little family. We hope to start with a little boy. Gliria and I have been thinking about names, but now I think we should name him after you. We'll call him *Laculor*."

"He's to be called *Baruben*, after my grandfather," Gliria said.

"Oh no, Gliria, his name will be *Laculor*. It's been decided," Myoxi said.

"You shouldn't try to bribe your way out of situations," Loran said. "And you should take advice from your wife when it comes to family names. I take advice from my cousin all the time when she writes."

"Oh, do tell us about your cousin," Gliria said. "What is her name? Does she like to sing? What is she like?"

"Her name is Lillianina Duben. She is very pretty but shy," Loran said. "She does sing very well, but I haven't seen her in thirty years."

"Oh, you must go visit her. Take us along. We'll help you find the way," Gliria said.

"Gliria, let the man make his own decisions," Myoxi said.

"Unfortunately, I have lost contact with her. I have received no mail from her in three months, and I'm worried. It used to be that not more than a week went by without a letter, even if I didn't write back immediately," Loran explained. "And as for where she lives, I'm not sure. I only know she lives in Sathiakia. I address my letters to Lillianina Duben, in care of Sathiakia General Delivery."

"Sathiakia!" Myoxi and Gliria said in unison with despair.

"You both sound surprised," Loran said.

"Ah, yes, well, what do you know about Sathiakia?" Myoxi asked.

"It's a wild frontier—rare trees growing thicker than tar in the remains of an ancient skyrise city. Concrete and metal buildings and piles of rubble with those trees pushing up to the sky, often carrying parts of the ancient buildings with them. She could be in one of those vaulted buildings or in some wooded area away from that, but I suspect she's near water and milkweed and can make a fire. She's always coming up with new milkweed medicines, and you can't do that without proper water and fire."

"Sathiakia is a place of death," Gliria said. "The Sathiakia Slaughter of eight summers ago is well known."

"What slaughter?" Loran asked. "I would have heard of it."

"You may not have," Myoxi said. "Three hundred picocians were killed in slave camps after one refused to work in protest of abusive conditions."

"I didn't know anything about that," Loran said. "I know there are trees of great size, and stories say there are large flying insects, though I thought all insects were extinct."

"There *are* flying insects, and they are giant dragonflies," Myoxi said.

"So it's true? But how?" Loran asked.

"Some say a woman of many talents has been enslaved and forced to work against her will, breeding these new creatures for an evil master," Myoxi said.

Then a cold wind blew into Loran's cabin. It picked up strength and rattled anything and everything around. Doors opened and closed. Pots clanged. Window curtains flapped. The lantern fell over and went out. The bird cage hopped and scuttled to the table's edge.

"Help, help!" Myoxi and Gliria said.

Loran pulled the bird cage back to the table, then he arighted the lantern and threw a rag over the spilt oil.

"I just had a horrible feeling," Loran said. "What if...what if...Lillianina! I hope not, I hope it isn't true. Tell me, Myoxi or Gliria, what is the name of the enslaved woman?"

The picocians looked at each other.

"No one knows her name," Gliria said at length, "that is, if the stories are true."

"But what other explanation is there?" Loran asked.

"Your cousin may have left Sathiakia and moved elsewhere," Myoxi offered. "She may yet write you once she settles in her new home."

"I don't know what to think or what to say," Loran said.

"I know one thing you can do," Myoxi said. "You can keep your promise and lead us to the mine of treasure."

"Forget the mine, Myoxi. It doesn't exist," Gliria said. "But we would like to be released, if you please Mr. Loran Laculic."

Loran, sitting at the dining table, buried his face in his hands for a moment. Myoxi was about to ask for his freedom and the treasure mine again, but Gliria stopped him. Finally, Loran lifted his head. His face was wet with tears, and shadows grew under his eyes. Slowly and with no care for a future, he opened the bird cage door.

The Journey Begins

Myoxi burst from the cage and started to run, but Gliria did not follow her husband at such speed. Instead, she walked slowly over to Loran, who had reburied his head in his hands, and she touched his face to comfort him.

"Gliria, what are you doing? Run for it!" Myoxi called.

"This man needs our help," Gliria said. "And we should help him."

"There's no time. Run for it, run for it now!" Myoxi said, and he ran for the back door, but Gliria continued to touch Loran's face. One of Loran's tears touched her hand, and she immediately understood Loran's despair.

"Myoxi, come back here. We must help Mr. Laculic. We must help him find his cousin, Lillianina," Gliria said.

"I...what are you saying, my wife?!" Myoxi said. "Help a human? Are you mad?"

"No, I'm sad. I'm sad for Loran and his cousin. We should help, and not just for him, for us too," Gliria said.

"How can helping a human help us?" Myoxi asked, not expecting an answer.

"I can think of three hundred picocian reasons, that's why," Gliria said. "Now do you understand? And think, Myoxi, if there are other picocians enslaved, we could rescue them."

"Or become enslaved as they are," Myoxi said.

"No, we won't, because Loran won't let that happen, will you Loran?" Gliria asked.

Loran looked up at her. He hadn't been listening at all to her discourse, but now suddenly he seemed resolved to go on a journey to find Lillianina and set his mind at ease regarding her safety.

"No, I won't allow harm to come to you Gliria, or you, Myoxi," Loran said. "And I must go. I cannot stay here in my cabin, wondering what has become of my cousin and friend, Lillianina. My fortune in arts and skills is all her doing. I welcome your companionship, Gliria, and yours too, Myoxi. But I'm afraid I have no means of transportation other than my two legs and a walking stick."

"That's all right, we can walk too," Gliria said.

"Oh, if only I were as tall as you, Loran. My legs will tire quickly from such a journey," Myoxi said. "Do you really plan to walk all the way to Sathiakia?"

"Not in one day, but eventually, yes," Loran said. "And you may have to ride in my backpack at certain points. I think humans would take ill to seeing you and would wish to capture you or maim you."

"That sounds awful at best!" Myoxi said. "Maybe this is a bad idea."

"No, it's a good idea, and we'll help you pack your things as best we can, won't we, Myoxi?" Gliria said.

"Yes," Myoxi grimaced. "We shall."

Myoxi and Gliria helped Loran pack a spare set of clothes, preserved food, medicines, a sleeping bag, a lightweight tent, a glowstick, and a small set of tools. These were all placed in the backpack. A collapsible blowgun and set of blowgun darts filled with Ethaloid were also placed in the pack. The backpack, when Loran threw it over his back, was a bit wider than his shoulders but was very long, with one end a bit higher than his head and the other hanging below waist level.

"That's everything," Loran said. "I feel like I'm forgetting something. Ho-hum, what am I forgetting?"

"Our tool bag is back in the cave," Myoxi said. "We should bring that with us."

"Tool bag?" Loran asked.

"For digging through rock, for cooling the tools so they don't overheat, for—"

"Heat! Of course! I'm forgetting the most important thing. Oh, I would fail the Fire Deputy test for sure if I forgot these—my fire piston and tinderbox!" Loran said.

Loran removed the backpack from his back, packed his fire piston and tinderbox, and led Myoxi and Gliria to the cellar, where the two picocians climbed to the shelf and entered the hole in the wall. A minute passed. Then two, then five, and ten.

"They left me anyway," Loran said to himself. "So much for picocian honesty."

"It's alive and well," said Myoxi as he reappeared from the hole in the brick wall, some thirty minutes after he left, and with a backpack of his own on his back.

"I thought you changed your mind and decided to leave me for good," Loran said.

"No, not at all," Gliria said, now appearing from the hole with a backpack of her own. "We went home and gathered up a few things."

"Very good, very good," Loran said. "We're ready then. I'll leave a note on the front door for visitors."

Loran first locked the front door, scribbled a short message on paper, and then he exited his cabin through the back door. Myoxi and Gliria followed him through the back door to the outside, he nailed the paper next to the back door, and he started to lock the back door when a waft of stove-pipe smoke caught his eye. He put a hand to his forehead in disbelief.

"What am I thinking?" Loran said. "I forgot to put out the stove fire. One moment."

Loran reentered his cabin and threw a yellow-white powder from a jar into the wood-burning stove. The stove made a whuff-puff sound, and bits of the powder escaped from seams in the stove. The powder blasted up the stove pipe and into the outside air.

"There, stove fire is out," Loran said.

Loran returned outside, locked the back door, and took two steps along the path toward Millfork when he stopped short and laughed. Myoxi and Gliria were completely covered with the yellow-white powder from Loran's stove, as was much of the plant life and ground around the immediate area.

"There are better ways to put out a stove fire," Myoxi said as Loran helped brush the powder from him.

"Perhaps," Loran laughed, "but this way I can put out the fire and get rid of the weeds around my house at the same time."

"You put poison in the air?" Myoxi asked as he brushed the powder from Gliria.

"Not poison. It's *pelapine*," Loran said. "And it's only poisonous if you're a charlock plant, and there are plenty of those around here."

Gliria sniffed a bit of the powder.

"This *is* pelapine," she said, a bit shocked.

Myoxi and Gliria continued shaking off powder as Loran started them walking down the path.

"Of course it is. I get plenty of stock from Millfork. Several farmers make the stuff from the halfcone pine shrub," Loran said.

"You should use charlock salt instead," Gliria said.

"Pelapine is cheap. Charlock salt is hard to find," Loran said.

"We mine lots of charlock salt," Myoxi said. "We sell plenty on the other side of the mountain, in Buckner Falls."

"I never see any in Millfork," Loran said.

"Because the market is blocked from buying or selling charlock salt," Myoxi said. "No one will let us sell it there."

"Pelapine is bad for river life," Gliria said.

"I've never had a problem," Loran said.

"Maybe not here, but downstream it mixes with things and makes for bad reactions," Gliria said.

"Hah!" Loran retorted. "Pelapine is lean, not mean, and is clean from what I've seen."

"Then your eyes are stale, begging your pardon," Gliria said.

"Gliria, please," Myoxi said.

"Well it's true," Gliria said.

"Loran may not know about the river down south, but that's no reason to insult him," Myoxi said.

Loran was flustered from being told his eyes were stale. He said nothing to the picocians for several hours. In fact, he had half a mind to send them away so he could be alone. But the sun was shining, the day was clear, and the path was fresh and pleasant. After several hours of trying to decide if he should continue stewing or not, he saw something ahead. He stopped.

"My eyes are stale, are they? Hah! My eyes are as good as ever," Loran said. "I can see the first fork in the path up ahead. And the sign says Millfork is to the left, and Wretched Cave is to the right."

"You say that because you know it's there, not because you can see it," Myoxi said.

"No, really," Loran said.

"And you can see the dragonfly, too?" Myoxi asked.

"Dragonfly?"

"The one beating its wings at the Millfork sign," Myoxi said.

"There are no dragonflies in these parts," Loran said. "Look, I'll throw a rock and prove there's nothing on the sign."

Loran picked up a rock and threw it as far as he could. It fell short of the sign by a large margin, but it landed on a boulder, made a sound, and startled the dragonfly which flew a short ways then fell.

"You scared it," Myoxi said.

"And it fell," Gliria said.

The three continued their pace. As they neared, Loran grew steadily out of breath.

"I must be terribly out of shape," Loran said. "I can barely go another step. I can't imagine how I will ever reach Sathiakia."

"There's the sign up ahead," Gliria said.

"Good. Wouldn't it be nice if it said that Sathiakia is just a few more paces?" Loran puffed.

The threesome reached the sign for Millfork and Wretched Cave and stopped. Loran puffed in exhaustion.

"I can't go another step," Loran said, and he collapsed to the ground.

Wretched Cave

"Please Loran, you must get up," Myoxi said.

Loran pulled himself up to his knees and noticed a normal-sized dead dragonfly in front of him. He leaned forward to reach it, but his backpack's bulk toppled him over, and he was on the ground again.

"Help, help," Loran said.

Myoxi helped unstrap the backpack from Loran while Gliria examined the dragonfly.

"There's a bench over here," Myoxi said.

"Yes, good idea," Loran replied.

Myoxi helped Loran to the bench as best as possible without Myoxi being squished or tossed aside by Loran's weight. Loran plopped on the bench and sighed in relief.

"Oh, wouldn't you know it? My lucky cuttlebone is grating against my skin. Myoxi, would you please bring my backpack? I must get this cuttlebone off my ankle and put it away," Loran said.

Myoxi dragged Loran's backpack to the bench. Loran placed the cuttlebone in one of the pack's pockets and then pulled a bottle from another pocket. Loran removed the lid and took a sip.

"Ah, very fresh," Loran said. "I didn't realize how quickly I'd tire from a short walk. Well, maybe not so short. Hughward usually gives me a ride into town. I'm not used to walking, and certainly not with a laden backpack."

"This dragonfly was poisoned," Gliria said with insect in hand as she approached the bench. "Most likely by pelapine or other such extracts. Its wings are coated with it."

Loran shot Gliria a puzzled look when he heard *such extracts*.

"But there are no dragonflies in these parts. Where did it come from?" Loran asked.

"There are silver specs on its body. Which means it comes from a quarry in Sathiakia," Gliria said.

"Sathiakia is a place of hate and death," Myoxi said. "Makes me miserable just thinking about it."

"Let's not speak of it then. I feel wretched myself. I could use a visit to Wretched Cave. It's just the thing I need," Loran said. "Up I go."

Loran stood up and threw the backpack over his back. Gliria placed the dead dragonfly in a folded leaf and placed that in her travel bag.

"So on we go," Loran said, with Myoxi and Gliria following behind closely.

The three traveled for several moments when Myoxi stopped short.

"What was that?" he asked.

"What was what?" Loran asked.

"I heard it too," Gliria said. "Sounded like a demon howling."

"I heard nothing," Loran said.

"We picocians have very good hearing," Myoxi said. "Sounds like trouble ahead."

"In these parts? How can that be?" Loran asked. "I wouldn't worry about a thing. We're almost at Wretched Cave, and soon you two will feel better."

"I hope so," Myoxi said. "These dark woods are creeping on my nerves. I feel as if we are being watched."

"These woods are supposed to be dark. That's part of the Wretched Cave pre-effect," Loran explained.

"This Wretched Cave must be truly wretched," Myoxi said.

"You'll be surprised," Loran said.

The three passed through the dark and gloomy forest until they arrived at an archway flanked by two totem poles. The figures on the poles were sculpted into animal heads, and the heads moved! Groans, growls, hoots, and yelps from the heads vibrated throughout the air and sent shivers down the spines of Myoxi and Gliria.

"Hold me, Myoxi. I'm scared," said Gliria.

"I thought these parts were familiar," Myoxi said. "This is Beguiling Grotto! No picocian who has entered has ever returned. They say it drives us to insanity. Loran—do not go inside."

Loran laughed.

"I've been inside many times. Many times. But if you two are afraid, you may ride along in my backpack," Loran offered.

Myoxi and Gliria returned surprised expressions. Was this the same human who a moment ago was too tired to carry on and needed rest on the bench and help with his backpack?

"I know what you're thinking," Loran said, "but things are different here. The way the wind blows, the way it swirls, it makes me feel light on my feet."

Myoxi and Gliria quickly chatted in their picocian language, and they came to an agreement.

"We'll ride along in your backpack," Myoxi said.

The two climbed into Loran's backpack in spare side pockets.

"Much better," Gliria said.

Loran passed through the archway and into the cave. At first it was pitch black. Myoxi and Gliria were scared silent.

"Hello," Loran said cheerfully.

A low red-orange light built up in the distance, and a dull whoosh of air grew into a thundering roar. Myoxi and Gliria buried themselves inside the spare pockets of Loran's backpack. The light and roar faded into black silence. Myoxi and Gliria peered above their pockets but could see nothing.

Loran chuckled, and a yellow light from a different part of the cave grew in sync with a devilish snickering sound. Myoxi and Gliria cowered again.

"I hate splinters," Loran yelled. "I hate splinters under my fingernails when I'm working my garden without gloves."

Myoxi and Gliria were puzzled by this strange outburst of Loran's.

"Did you hear that?" Myoxi whispered to Gliria.

"He's gone mad," Gliria replied. "Now what do we do?"

Before Myoxi could answer, a strange thing happened. Bluish-white lights shot upward and burst outward like fireworks.

"I hate splinters!" Loran yelled.

Myoxi and Gliria heard music, like that from a harp.

"And thorns!" Loran continued. "Thorns around my neck! They hurt and itch and hurt some more!"

More fireworks lit the cave followed by echoing of more harp music, happy harp music, as if a party had been thrown for the gods. Air swirled around and lifted Loran a meter or so off the ground.

"But nothing is worse than poison ivy!" Loran yelled with increased anger. "Poison ivy causing blisters and unbearable itching! And eating food with poison ivy! I can't scratch inside my stomach!"

The cave transformed into a well-lit outdoors, with Loran now standing on a moving float in a parade. Horses pulled the float along while a marching band played behind. People applauded from both sides of the street, happy to see Loran and his float.

"We're in a parade!" Gliria said.

"How is this possible?" Myoxi said.

"We must climb to the top of the float and see for ourselves!" Gliria said.

"No!" Loran said. "You will become trapped. Stay in the backpack!"

After a few more seconds, the parade faded into the dim cave. Myoxi and Gliria could now see thousands of ear-shaped glowing things, each with a thread-like surface.

"Mushrooms!" Gliria said. "I love mushrooms!"

"No!" Loran yelled. "They are glowing fungi, they are real, and they are poisonous! Don't eat them!"

Gliria had jumped out of the backpack to reach for one, but Loran's shouting triggered the glowing fungus into action. The three now seemed to be on a sunny beach with pleasant waves. Gliria ran into a wave, and another larger wave formed behind it, growing into a tidal wave of massive proportions.

"Splinters, poison ivy, hitting my thumb with a hammer, shutting the door on my hand, falling on stairs!" Loran shouted.

The tidal wave stopped in full form, ready to crash, but Loran's shouting kept it from slamming onto Gliria. Somewhere in the distance, pleasant guitar music played. The happy bark of a dog carried along the beach. It started to snow sugar.

"Go after her!" Loran yelled.

Myoxi ran after Gliria and brought her back to Loran. The tidal wave let go and started to crash atop the three, but before the three got wet, the barking stopped, the guitar music faded, and the beach scene ended, returning the three to the cave where the fungi continued glowing. They fluctuated and flickered before going dark.

"Quickly, jump into my backpack," Loran commanded.

Myoxi and Gliria did just that, and Loran exited the cave. It was darker outside than when they entered. Loran chose a different path that hugged the edges of Rainbear Mountain, and in so doing he led the group from the gloomy forest to a small clearing. The day had progressed further than the three anticipated, and soon the sun would set.

"The day is almost over!" Myoxi said.

"I forgot about that part," Loran said. "Time passes quickly inside the Wretched Cave. If one isn't careful, a week or even a month will pass by."

"Do we know if it's the same day?" Myoxi asked.

"It is," Gliria said. "I can sense it."

"We must hurry then if we are to reach Millfork by dusk. Come along then," Loran urged.

Loran hurried his pace, sending Myoxi and Gliria in a light jog.

"Tell us about the cave," Myoxi said.

"The fungi feed off shouting," Loran said. "In return, they create wonderful illusions. So if you're upset and angry, you can shout your way back to happiness, thanks to these fungi. But the illusion is also a self-defense mechanism for each fungus. If you had managed to touch one, Gliria, that fungus would have tricked you into killing yourself. The Wretched Cave can be pleasant for those who know how to use it, but it can be deadly for those who would harm a fungus."

"I didn't know," Gliria said. "They looked delicious."

"Now I understand why picocians have never exited Beguiling Grotto," Myoxi said. "They were tricked into their own demise."

"I've never heard such told, but I understand how that's possible. I'm sorry for any friends you have lost," Loran said.

After an hour of this rapid pace, Gliria finally gave up and stopped.

"Loran, wait, my wife cannot continue," Myoxi said.

"Hop into my backpack," Loran said. "I'll carry you the rest of the way."

They did and Loran did. Sunlight faded until only the topmost parts of clouds reflected light, and even that light was now golden and fading. Dusk arrived, and in the distance was lit the first lights of Millfork.

Millfork

"We're almost there," Loran said. "I'll be happy to see my brother and sister-in-law."

Loran hurried his pace with such anticipation. At first his feet and backpack felt light, but as he continued barreling along, the steps grew heavier and his breath more strained until without warning, he tripped and fell flat on his face about twenty paces from the town's outer fence. The backpack shook loose, and inertia carried the picocians into the air and onto shrubs.

"Ugh!" Loran groaned, but fortunately a thick carpet of pine shrub needles cushioned his fall.

On hearing the fall, a woman passed through the north Millfork gate and approached Loran with a photograph.

"Have you seen my son?" she asked. "His name is Stephen."

Stunned and flummoxed, Loran didn't know what to say. Here he had made a fool of himself by tripping and falling, and a woman was pushing a photograph in front of his face.

"I, uh, o dear, let me get my things together," Loran said.

"His name is Stephen Royer," she said as Loran arighted. "I'm his mother. Stephen has been missing for a week now. Said he was going south to find his missing friends."

"I'm sorry," Loran said, "but I haven't seen him."

"If you do, let a sholiff know," she said, and she walked inside the north gate back into Millfork.

"Strange," Loran said. "Here I am in obvious pain from falling down, and she didn't notice. Now where are those two picocians?"

"Over here," said Myoxi, who had climbed down a pine shrub and was helping his wife down another pine shrub.

"Thank you, Myoxi," Gliria said.

"Are either of you hurt?" Loran asked.

"I'm fine," Gliria said.

"I'm fine, too," Myoxi said.

"Good," Loran said. "First things first. I'm going to find whatever it was that tripped me and rip it out. That's dangerous. Someone could be badly hurt."

Loran found the offender, a pine shrub root extending above the surface.

"How strange," Loran said. "No matter."

Loran placed his backpack on the ground, removed a hatchet, and chopped into the ground on the shrub side of the root just before the root ascended ground level. Fortunately, this spot was at the edge of the path and posed no real hazard of disturbing the road. After several chops, he broke through. The other side of the root, however, threatened to uplift into the path, causing a greater risk for other passersby.

"I'd better pull the root out. Don't want to chop a hole in the path," Loran said.

Loran pulled and pulled, but the root would not come out.

"Ugh," Loran grunted. "This root won't come up."

"Pardon me, Loran," Myoxi said. "Gliria and I have special tools we can use to help loosen the root without digging a rut in the path."

"Really?" Loran asked. "I don't see how."

"You forget we are expert miners," Gliria said. "A path is very simple compared to mountain rock."

"Very well," Loran said. "Go ahead."

Myoxi and Gliria removed special little hammers, and they tapped on the path where the root first burrowed down. The two followed along a line, making marks on the path's surface on this line. Next, they took a drill with a small diameter bit and positioned it over the first hole. Myoxi drilled while Gliria tapped with the hammer. She called out speeds and angles and depth numbers. Myoxi adjusted to these numbers, and when Gliria called, "done," Myoxi removed the drill from the ground, inserted what looked like a thin straw, and attached it to a hose. They repeated this all along until ten holes were drilled and filled with straws, the straws all being connected to a single hose. Myoxi removed a miniature air pump, attached it to the hose, and pumped.

"The air will separate soil from the root, giving you less resistance," Gliria said. "Try pulling again."

Loran pulled and pulled, and the root came free! He fell on his back from pulling too hard, and the root flew out of his hand and traveled multiple meters through the air until it landed out of view on the other side of the pine shrub. Myoxi went to help Loran as best he could without getting squashed, but Loran shrugged him off.

"That's all right. I am fine," Loran said. "I didn't think the root would give so suddenly. But the path is in good shape and unruptured, thanks to you and...you and..."

"Gliria, where are you?" Myoxi called.

"Over here," Gliria said. "I'm on the other side of the pine shrub."

"Well what are you doing over there?" Loran said.

"I thought I saw something on the end of the root as it flew through the air," she said.

"Let me see," Loran said, and he made for the other side of the pine shrub.

Loran helped Gliria look.

"It was just a clump of dirt," Loran said.

"Oh, that's a relief. I thought it was something else. Never can tell what strange things are in these parts," Gliria said. "Perhaps the odd shape of that root acted like a catapult."

"I would say you are right," Loran said. "In fact, I'll keep this root and place it on my mantelpiece at home. Should make an excellent display. I'll wrap it in *oysterphane* and stow it in my pack."

"May I wrap the root?" Gliria asked. "I have a special talent for wrapping roots of this kind."

"Be my guest," Loran said.

But Myoxi rushed in between Loran and Gliria.

"Is it safe to touch that stuff?" he asked Gliria. "He *did* drug us. Could be a trick. He might wrap us in it!"

Gliria laughed.

"It's no trick, Myoxi. Why are you so skittish?" Gliria asked.

"These human towns always make me skittish," Myoxi said.

"Here, give this to her," Loran said after he pulled a clear, plastic-like transparent sheet known as oysterphane from his pack. "I'll put away your air pump contraption."

"Say 'thank you,' Myoxi," Gliria said.

"Thank you," Myoxi said.

"You are welcome. We should get going before a root trips *you* up, Myoxi," Loran laughed.

Gliria laughed too.

"Hah, hah, hah!" Myoxi said with sarcasm. "Everyone laughs at my expense."

Gliria was about to say something, but someone approached.

"You entering Millfork?" a fire deputy asked.

"Yes," Loran said.

"Then you'd better take this," he said, and he gave Loran a flier.

"What's this?" Loran asked.

"Fire code update. No burning of half-cone pine shrubs in South Millfork," the fire deputy said. "New pollution laws."

"Of course," Loran said. "The improper burning of half-cone pine shrubs causes the blackest, ugliest smoke."

"You can still burn half-cone pine shrubs in Millfork and anywhere east, north, or west," added the deputy. "Just south-side burning is illegal."

The fire deputy looked at Myoxi with distrust and spoke to him, calling him by a slang name.

"Think twice before entering town, *snee-snocs*. No one takes kindly to little thieves," the fire deputy said.

Myoxi didn't like being called a snee-snoc or a little thief. Both references were rude, and his face turned red as he prepared to retaliate, but Gliria pinched him from behind with one hand, and she spoke up.

"We'll make no trouble," she said.

"Good," the fire deputy said.

The deputy returned through the north gate into Millfork and continued making his proclamation while handing out fliers. Gliria straightened up Myoxi and combed his hair, and then Loran led the group through the north gate into Millfork.

"This flier bans the burning of half-cone pine shrubs," Loran said. "Even proper burning of half-cone pine shrubs is outlawed. Seems strange."

"Why?" Myoxi asked.

"Properly burned, a half-cone pine shrub produces no smoke. I wonder why South Millfork is—"

"Have you seen my daughter?" a man asked as he showed a photograph of a young girl to Loran.

"No, no I haven't," Loran said.

"Her name is Claire Stackhart," the man said. "She went south looking for her missing friends. If you see her, please let a sholiff know."

"I will, I will," Loran said.

"She looks to be sixteen years old," Gliria said.

"Two young people missing while looking for other missing young people," Loran said. "What is happening here?"

Loran stood up and walked to the town billboard, where he saw many postings of many missing youths.

"Incredible. It's an epidemic," Loran said. "What bad luck for these young people and their families."

"It may have nothing to do with luck," Gliria said.

"What do you mean, Gliria?" Loran asked.

"Sometimes Gliria says strange things when she's hungry," said Myoxi. "I say we get something to eat."

"It's not that I'm hungry. It's just...it...I..." Gliria stumbled.

"There, you see? Food will do you good," Myoxi said.

"Very well. Laculic Tavern is just down the street here," Loran said. "It's dinner time anyway, and I'm starved."

The three walked to and entered Laculic Tavern.

"Do you own this place?" Myoxi asked.

"No, but my brother does," Loran said. "His name is Braegan Laculic."

"Loran," said a woman's voice.

Loran turned around and saw the hostess.

"Morga," Loran said. "How is my wonderful sister-in-law?"

"Busy!" she replied. "Are you looking for Braegan?"

"Not particularly. Actually, I'm here for a bit to eat," Loran said.

"We're hungry too," Myoxi said.

"Sorry, we don't serve your kind," Morga said.

"Oh, I'm sorry. My manners have deserted me. These picocians are with me. Morga, meet Myoxi and his wife, Gliria," Loran said.

"The honor is ours," Myoxi said.

"Pleased to meet you," Gliria said.

Morga looked at the picocians, then at Loran, around the tavern for Braegan, and then back at Loran.

"If you can vouch for their good behavior and promise you won't let them out of your sight, then I think we can make an allowance," Morga said. "But I'll have to put you in the corner away from the other patrons. I want no trouble."

"What trouble?" Loran asked, but Morga said nothing.

The picocians followed Loran who in turn followed Morga, but as they approached the table in back, a half-clean man (named Captain Friscott) with partly ripped clothes stuck a leg out and tripped Gliria. She fell flat on her face, and the captain motioned to stomp his foot on her body.

"Gliria!" Myoxi cried, and he reached for her quickly and pulled her away just as the captain's boot came stomping to the floor in the spot where she had just lain.

"Get out of here, little thieves," the man said.

"Hey you," Myoxi said defiantly. "I won't have you say that to us."

"Oh no, no no," Loran said, and he ushered Myoxi and Gliria ahead of him. "We won't start anything here."

But the man wasn't finished. He stood, reached around Loran, and threw his beer onto Myoxi and Gliria.

"Don't drown, little worms," the man said.

"That's enough," Loran said. "Leave us alone."

"Or what?" the captain asked.

Loran pushed the captain. He pushed back and then swung at Loran, but the captain's fist bounced off Loran's muscular abdomen. Loran laughed, took two steps back, leaned forward, and launched himself toward the captain. With Loran's strength, he plowed into the captain and slid him across the room. The man fell but stood quickly and reached for a knife.

"Put that away, Captain Friscott," said a booming voice, "or I'll serve you on a platter!"

Loran turned to see a familiar figure standing in the doorway between the kitchen and the dining area. He had broad shoulders, thick arms, and large hands, one of which was wielding a meat cleaver.

"I was only havin' a little fun, Braegan," Captain Friscott said.

"Your fun is over. Get going, now," Braegan said.

"I'm not done with my dinner," Captain Friscott said.

"You're more than done. You're overdone. Show him out, Darmon," Braegan said.

A tall, muscular man standing by the doorway kicked the knife from Captain Friscott's hand, lifted the captain with one hand, carried him across the doorway, and tossed him outside to the ground.

"You'll hear from me again," Captain Friscott said. "You worms are marked."

"Let's leave," Gliria said. "I don't feel so well."

"Everything will be fine," Loran said. "Don't pay attention to that Friscott guy. He's caused trouble before, from what I've heard. Here, sit on the table. Braegan makes good soup, if you don't feel well, and he makes other good things that will tickle your tummy."

Gliria settled for soup, and Myoxi also had soup in support of his wife. Both sat on the table, as Loran had suggested. Loran himself had oyster-ka-bobs on a flaming stick with vegetables and thrice-baked bread.

"Mmmm. Braegan cooks the best oyster-ka-bobs," Loran said.

Loran followed the ka-bobs down with a strong mug of mead. He repositioned himself to the side as if to prepare for sleep when Morga attended the three.

"So what brings you to Millfork with two picocians?" Morga asked.

"I'm on my way to Sathiakia," Loran said.

Morga shot a strange look at Loran, and then she laughed.

"No, really," Loran said. "I want to know what's become of Lillianina."

Morga stopped laughing. She disappeared into the kitchen, and within a moment's time, Braegan exited the kitchen, removed his cooking outfit, and motioned Darmon over. Darmon walked over to Braegan and listened to Braegan's instructions. Darmon nodded in agreement and disappeared into the kitchen. Braegan walked over to Loran's table and sat down.

"Darmon will cover for me in the kitchen," Braegan said.

"Braegan, this is Myoxi and his wife, Gliria. Myoxi and Gliria, my brother, Braegan."

The three exchanged nods in acknowledgment.

"Is it true what Morga tells me, my little brother? Are you really going south to that forsaken place?" Braegan asked.

"Sathiakia? Yes," Loran said.

"Surely you are not going tonight!" Braegan said. "It is many paces away, more than any a person could travel in a day, much less a night."

"Well, no, not tonight," Loran said. "Fact is, we'll be lodging in Millfork for the night."

"Good. I have a room upstairs for the three of you," Braegan said.

"I didn't want to impose on you, Braegan," Loran said.

"Not at all," Braegan said. "I'd feel better if you did, anyway. Do you think any other inn in Millfork will accept picocians? Sorry you two, no insult intended."

"He's right," Gliria said. "Thank you, kind sir, we accept your offer."

"Yes, we accept," Myoxi said.

"I...you do?" Loran said, caught off guard. "And here I thought I was making the decisions. But I suppose you are right, Braegan. We'll stay here tonight."

"And you can stay the night after, a whole week if you like. We'll have conversation and shoot blowdarts like when we were young, and after your visit, you'll be a new man when you return home," Braegan said.

"Uh, no, you forget, I'm going to Sathiakia," Loran said.

"He didn't forget," Gliria said.

"Shh," Braegan said. "You'll spoil everything."

"I know you, Braegan. I did, after all, grow up with you. You'll do anything to keep the family from harm," Loran said.

"It's true. Going to Sathiakia is harm if ever there were any. Stay in Millfork a while. Don't go to Sathiakia," Braegan said. "Why would anyone want to go there anyway?"

"I must find Lillianina," Loran said. "I haven't heard from her in months."

Braegan paused, looked down, and then looked Loran squarely in the eyes.

"Cousin Lillianina made her choice to migrate there when she was twenty," Braegan said. "She turned her back on the family."

"It was the best place for cultivating milkweed," Loran said.

"And other things best not spoken here," Braegan said. "But let me tell you, little brother. Sathiakia, though never a good place, has turned unexpectedly wicked. Did you hear about the young people here? Did you know they are here one day and gone the next?"

"I was approached about two such people," Loran said. "Let me see, they were Stephen Royer and Claire Stackhart."

"The fliers from Mrs. Royer and Mr. Stackhart," Braegan said. "Yes. And there are many more. Rumor is they are turning up in or near Sathiakia and joining cults. Some like Stephen and Claire were top students in their class and come from wealthy families. There's no reason for them to throw away their lives for what they'd become in Sathiakia."

"They'd become?" Loran asked.

"I don't like the sound of this," Gliria said.

"Then close your ears, Gliria," Myoxi said.

"Gliria's concern is warranted," Braegan said. "In fact, most folk are afraid to speak aloud on what's happening in Sathiakia."

"Why?" Loran asked.

Braegan looked around as if being watched.

"They say there are spies everywhere," Braegan said.

"I don't see anyone but town folk," Loran said.

"Not like that, and not even picocian spies," Braegan said.

Myoxi stood in protest.

"It's no lie that some picocians have spied on us for lesser reasons," Braegan said. "But that is no matter."

"Sit, Myoxi," Gliria said.

Myoxi sat down on the table.

"Then who are the spies?" Loran said.

"Not *who*," Braegan said.

"What do you mean?" Loran asked.

"*What* is what I mean," Braegan said. "Some *thing* is spying on us, but you can't see it, or them. They are cleverly hidden in other things, possibly other people. They have people afraid to eat anything. Look around you. What are the patrons eating?"

"Smoked oyster meat," Loran said. "What's so strange about that?"

"No potatoes, no bread, no fruit, no wine, no nothing else but straight meat and mead," Braegan said. "I noticed these things, because it's my business, and even the mead sells less than it did. People only trust meat that's been smoked."

"You're telling me that people eat something, and they disappear?" Loran asked.

"That's the rumor," Braegan said. "They say something in the food grows inside a person and tells a person what to do."

Myoxi stared at his soup and stirred it with a spoon.

"Then that something sprouts from the palms and feet, producing a flower," Braegan said. "The flower has tentacles and can move at will, often manipulating objects, even from a short distance."

Myoxi stared at his palms and scratched them as if digging out a parasite.

"These tentacles give the host amazing abilities to run, jump, swing, and throw things with distance and accuracy, and always against the host's will," Braegan continued. "And there's something in the flowers, something that buzzes and wiggles and squirms all around."

Myoxi grabbed his left hand with his right, and his left came toward his own neck as if to choke himself. Myoxi fought his left hand with his right.

"Help, help!" Myoxi said. "I'm possessed."

Braegan chuckled.

"It's not funny! I'm infected with the tentacle thing," Myoxi said.

"No, you're not," Braegan said. "You've convinced yourself you are infected, but in fact you are not."

"How can you be sure?" Myoxi said, with his left hand pausing before his own neck.

"For one, your fingernails would be concentric circles of red and green," Braegan said.

Myoxi looked intently at the fingernails on his left hand, and they were light pink—normal.

"Oh," Myoxi said, and his left hand went limp.

"Loran, my little brother, I ask that you do not go to Sathiakia. You too would be infected," Braegan said.

"I'm not so sure about that. We Laculics are immune to possession," Loran said as he beat twice on his chest with pride.

Braegan returned a grim expression.

"They say no one is immune, little brother," he said.

"Which is what I fear about Lillianina. She is only half Laculic. I fear the Duben side has placed her in grave danger. I must find her," Loran said.

"Even if you do—even if you find her—what then?" Braegan asked. "Will you bring her back to Millfork? Do you think she'd let you?"

"She *did* leave under unusual circumstances," Loran said.

"She cursed these grounds *and* the Laculic family. Said she was going to find herself, her true Duben roots, in Sathiakia," Braegan explained. "And that was the last we heard from her, except from what you'd tell us when she wrote you, and only you. How she chose my little brother over me for correspondence escapes me."

"Well, if you complimented her on her recipes instead of badgering her to return to Millfork, then maybe—" Loran started.

"I never badgered her," Braegan said.

"Yes you did," Morga said, "and it's about time you return to the kitchen. Darmon is making a mess back there."

"Very well," Braegan said. "Good luck to you, my younger brother. Morga, don't forget the gift."

Braegan returned to the kitchen.

"What gift?" Loran asked.

Morga produced a blue, vial necklace wrapped in ornate gold.

"This is a vial of my best cuttleberry gin," Morga said as she gave the vial necklace to Loran. "It is a mixed derivative of cuttlebone and elderberries."

"Where did you find elderberries? I thought they were a myth!" Loran said.

"Elder trees exist—for those who know where to find them. The tonic will cure any disease, whether from wound or bad food. One drop in a wound is enough to cleanse it, or one drop on a piece of bread may be eaten to purge bad food. Use the tonic sparingly, but do not fear to use it. It is made from fully ripened and refined elder berries, and so it has no cyanide. The cuttlebone is the finest and from Buckner Falls."

"I hope I will have no need to use it, but I accept it just the same," Loran said. "Thank you very much."

The Arsonist

The following morning, Loran and the two picocians finished breakfast and bade farewell to Morga. Myoxi and Gliria followed behind as Loran, with new strength from a good meal, increased his pace in speed and size of stride. The three followed the main road south of Millfork, and as they progressed southward, the three noticed signs posted with increasing frequency.

"*No pine fires,*" Loran said, repeating what a sign read. "*Pine fires banned. Burning of pine shrub illegal. Pine shrubs not to be burned, under penalty of law. Report illegal fires to Head Sholiff Grant, Blackpier.* These signs were never here. What's happening around here? Will they ban fires altogether?"

"Uh, Mr. Loran," Myoxi said. "May we rest a moment? My legs are sore."

"We have been walking for several hours now, haven't we?" Loran asked rhetorically. "Very well. Let's stop here at this boulder. And I need a good smoke."

Loran placed his backpack next to the boulder, sat, and retrieved his pipe and tobacco. Next, he retrieved his fire piston and tinder box, placed some tinder in the fire piston, and engaged it. He removed the piston and placed the burning tinder in his pipe, which then ignited the tobacco.

"Ah," Loran said after several good puffs. "We've made good progress, and soon it will be supper time."

"And after that?" Myoxi asked.

"After that will be dark," Loran said. "Did you want to travel in the dark?"

"No, not at all," Myoxi said.

"Don't worry," Loran said. "I expect us to reach Blackpier for dinner. I'm sure we'll find a place to sleep there. If I remember right, there's an inn next to the Sholiffs' Office. Well, we'll never get there if we stay here. Let's restart the walk."

Loran was about to put his pipe away, but he took a close look at the pipe and tilted his head to the side with indecision.

"I must put the pipe away, or must I?" Loran said.

"What do you mean?" Myoxi asked.

"I've always smoked a pipe while sitting, never standing," Loran said. "To smoke and walk...well...that seems so strange. Yet I do enjoy a good pipe. Why should I deprive myself?"

"Myoxi, my legs are beginning to stiffen," Gliria said.

"Mr. Loran, we must get walking, or else Gliria won't be able to continue," Myoxi said.

"I can debate the issue on the walk," Loran said as he stood and placed the backpack over his shoulder. "And for empirical evidence, I'll need to smoke while I think, while I walk, and while I talk."

For the next three hours, Loran did just that. He so enjoyed his smoke that his pace slowed and his desire to reach Blackpier by late afternoon faded. Six o'clock came and went, and Loran was still three thousand paces from Blackpier.

"O dear," Loran said. "The sun is setting, we are still on the open road, and I'm hungry, very hungry."

"The pipe was good then?" Myoxi asked.

"Too good," Loran replied. "It made me too relaxed, too happy. Slowed me down, it did. But a joy it was for sure. I had a good chance to think about Lillianina, the missing young people, and the ban on fire. And I've decided that...that...Myoxi, Gliria, where are you?"

Loran had looked away during his discourse, but when he turned back toward Myoxi, he was gone. So was Gliria.

"Where are you?" Loran asked.

"Psst," Myoxi said from behind a rock.

"What are you doing over there?" Loran asked. "Come out."

Myoxi held a finger to his mouth to tell Loran to keep quiet.

"What?" Loran asked.

Myoxi again repeated the signal for Loran to be quiet. Gliria motioned Loran over. Loran walked over and stood behind the rock, though his stature rose above the rock's level. Myoxi motioned Loran to sit, and Loran did.

"What is it?" Loran whispered.

"We are being watched," Gliria said.

"I don't see anything," Loran said. "How can you be sure?"

"Gliria has excellent hearing. She knows these sorts of things," Myoxi said.

"I suppose I should put out my pipe," Loran said.

"It won't matter," Gliria said. "He already knows where we are."

"He?" Loran asked. "How can you—"

"Shh," Gliria said. "In the trees above us. No, don't look up. You'll only antagonize him."

Loran took several more puffs from his pipe. The smoke carried up over the rock, and stretched rays from the setting sun gave the smoke a golden vibrancy.

"We can't stay here all night," Loran whispered. "I'm hungry. We need to get to Blackpier for dinner and rest."

"I'll make sure you do," said a stern voice from the other side of the rock. "Now come out of there and identify yourself."

Loran looked at Myoxi and Gliria with a quizzical expression, but both shrugged their shoulders.

"Don't make me come in there after you," continued the voice.

Loran stood with the pipe still in his mouth. On the other side of the rock was a Blackpier sholiff.

"Over here," the sholiff said.

Loran walked around and stopped in front of the officer. Immediately, Loran noticed a tri-point scar on the sholiff's right cheekbone.

"What is your name?" he asked.

"I am Loran Laculic."

"And what are you burning there?" he asked.

"Burning?" Loran asked. "You mean my pipe? I'm smoking tobacco, nothing more."

"We have an ordinance against burning," he said.

"I saw the signs. They said no pine burning," Loran said.

"That's north of here," the sholiff said. "You are now in Blackpier vicinity. That means no burning of any plant matter. That includes tobacco. Therefore, you're under arrest."

"You can't be serious," Loran said. "It's just a pipe with tobacco. What's the harm—"

"The law is the law," the sholiff said as he held Loran's arm.

Two other sholiffs appeared, and both had the same tri-pointed scar on their right cheekbones. One took Loran's pack, and another took Loran to a steam-powered cart and locked Loran in the back compartment. The first sholiff searched behind the rock where Loran had hidden with Myoxi and Gliria, but the two picocians had already fled. This first sholiff then returned to the cart and sat in back with Loran. He motioned for the other two sholiffs to engage the cart forward toward Blackpier.

"Here is the arsonist," the first sholiff said.

"I am Head Sholiff Grant, Mr. Laculic. I can tell by your accent that you're from north of Millfork."

"Yes, I am," Loran said.

"You're a long way from home. What brings you to these parts?" Grant asked.

"I'm on my way to Sathiakia, if you must ask," Loran said.

Grant's eyes glazed over with a fierce determination.

"Are you insane?" Grant said. "I should lock you up for good for making such an attempt."

"Is that what you're going to do with me, lock me up?" Loran asked. "I've done nothing."

"You were caught burning a plant in a no burn-zone," Grant said, "and now you—"

"Take a look at this," a sholiff in the front section said to Grant as the sholiff passed Loran's tinderbox through an opening.

"What do we have here?" Grant asked as he opened the tinder box.

"It's just a tinderbox," said Loran.

"With pine needles?" Grant asked. "And you've been burning these?"

"I—" Loran started.

"Yes, he has," said the sholiff in front while passing Loran's fire piston through the opening to Grant.

"A fire piston," Grant said, and he opened the fire piston and smelled the inside cylinder.

"It's only a—" Loran tried to say before being cut off.

"Only the remains of burned pine needles. That's a felony for sure," Grant said.

"Oh this is preposterous," Loran said.

"What were you going to do? Smuggle pine needle to Sathiakia? Or perhaps even entire pine shrubs? Tell me the truth, Mr. Laculic."

"I...I..." Loran stumbled.

"More evidence," said a sholiff to Sholiff Grant. "Looks like a pine shrub root."

"Give me that, Sholiff Gregg. Hmm," Sholiff Grant said.

"It was in the way," Loran said.

"Oh, hoh, hoh! So it was just *in the way*? How would you like to be just *in the way*? We'll see how long *you* last. But this root is more than just needles. You're hunting big game now, aren't you?" Sholiff Grant said. "Let me guess—as a trophy? For your wall?"

"My mantelpiece," Loran confessed. "But it has such an unusual shape."

"And this," said Sholiff Grant, pulling out a bottle from Loran's pack. "It has writing on it."

"Give that here. You should learn to read, Sholiff Gregg," Grant said. "Hmm. This says, *Ethaloid*."

Grant removed the cap and dropper, and squirted Ethaloid on Gregg. Gregg fell to the ground, unconscious.

"He isn't dead. Only sleeping," Loran said. "That's for—"

"It's a weapon, of course. So now I know your plan. You would render us all unconscious, steal our goods, and set fire to Blackpier," Grant said.

"What are you going to do with me?" Loran asked.

"You cannot stay locked up here in Blackpier," Grant said.

"Then you'll set me free. I'll be on my way, then. I won't trouble you or anyone in Blackpier. I promise," Loran said.

"You're right. You won't trouble us. Because you'll hang at dawn," Grant said. "Lock him up for the night."

The other sholiffs hauled Loran away.

"But you said you wouldn't lock me up!" Loran said.

"You cannot stay locked up. But you can and will hang!" Grant said.

Loran was thrown into a jail cell, and the cell door clanged shut behind him. Locked. The sholiffs left, and Loran was alone. Myoxi and Gliria were not to be found, and Loran had hoped they would appear at the small grated opening to the outside, which provided the only fresh air to Loran's cell. Loran tried calling for help out this grate, but that only drew two guards, who lashed their whips against the cell's bars, which rattled Loran's nerves. Then one guard entered the cell and tapped Loran's skull against the brick wall. Stunned, Loran slumped to the floor and lay in a daze. The guard left the cell and locked the door.

The Vine

The guards dimmed the lights in the cell area. Loran gazed out the opening to the outside and saw stars. How he had enjoyed the starlight from home, sitting on his porch in a padded rocking chair with the crackling sound of his fireplace coming from the window. Now he was lying on a cold floor with foul puddles of water. He struggled to get up, but he had no balance and no sense of orientation.

The stars moved, or at least Loran's perception of them changed. And he heard fluttering, like that of leaves, but the fluttering was strange, more like something between a bird's wings and leaves. He looked and thought that perhaps there was a bird perched on the cell's opening to the outside, but he knew this to be impossible, because all birds were extinct. But something was there. A finger or thing slithered from the opening down the wall. A snake? Those were extinct, too. Loran tried to cry out, but he was still dazed from his concussion, and he remained there, paralyzed. Then another finger-like thing slithered from the opening, and another. Little wings fluttered from the fingers, and these continued down the inside of the cell's wall and covered it.

"It's a plant," Loran realized. "A vine of some sort. It's taking over the cell!"

The vine sent its runners to the bottom of the wall and then across the floor, with the vine's leading tip acting as a feeler and sniffer to sense what it might find advantageous. It sensed Loran.

"No, no! Go away!" Loran whispered.

Loran wanted to shout, but the whisper was all he could manage. Two runners now crawled along Loran's legs—twisting and constricting as they crept. The blood rushed toward Loran's head, and he felt ready to explode. The vines now constricted Loran's torso, and he labored to breathe. Loran fought to free himself, but the vine was too powerful. It then wrapped itself around Loran's head and pressed against it, especially against his right cheekbone, where it sent such great heat against the cheekbone that the skin began to burn.

Loran tried to yell, but the vine pressed too forcefully against his lungs. Then, a single vine with a sundew flower hovered over Loran's chest. It was intent on burrowing the flower into Loran's heart and thus take full control of Loran's body. The vine chewed a hole through Loran's shirt, and then it hit the vial of cuttleberry gin. It chewed through the vial and absorbed the gin en route to Loran's heart, but the vine suddenly stopped.

"Help," Loran managed to say, though quietly.

The vine still constrained Loran, but it was no longer pressing hard against his cheekbone, and he tried moving to free himself. Then without warning, the vine went into convulsions. It jerked and shook as if electrified.

Its grip loosened completely, and Loran backed away and watched as this vine danced like a snake on fire. It caught fire, but instead of burning from a conventional orange flame, it burned with a bluish-green flame—one that produced little smoke but gave off a smell of fresh pine. Loran kept his distance, because the vine whipped its tentacles around and broke various furnishings in the cell (which were few). It tried withdrawing through the opening to the outside, but it became entangled in itself and was too big. Frustrated, the vine pulled at the wall's edge where it met the opening and broke wall fragments away, creating a larger opening.

Loran watched as the vine completely withdrew from the cell. It retreated from the building and into the woods. Deep thuds and digging sounds echoed through the woods as the vine tore up the ground in an effort to purge itself of the cuttleberry gin that tormented it.

"Well...I...I...am I well? Am I well?" Loran gasped as he regained his breath.

He checked for injury and found a little blood on his cheekbone, but that was all. His shirt was torn over his heart, but his chest sustained no injury.

"I must get out of here," Loran said. "I must!"

Loran didn't know if he could escape. The guards and sholiffs were sure to have heard the ruckus. So why didn't they rush to his cell? He didn't know. He walked toward the large opening to the outside and looked around.

"Loran," said a soft voice. "Are you well? Loran?"

From around a boulder peeked a picocian. It was Gliria.

"Gliria?" Loran called back.

"Hurry this way, Loran!" Gliria said. "Don't ask. Just hurry!"

Loran did as she said and rushed over to the boulder as best he could. He was still dazed and struggled to regain his strength, but he felt better that he was no longer in the jail and that his life was no longer threatened.

"Where's Myoxi?" Loran asked.

"He will return shortly," Gliria said. "He...he...your face! You have the mark! You're infected!"

"I what? Infected?" Loran asked.

"You have the same mark everyone else has in Blackpier," Gliria said. "The *sunderag*. It got you. It's only a matter of hours now."

"That's what you call that vine? A sunderag?" Loran asked. "I thought it was a strange sort of pine vine. There must be an antidote, Gliria. There must."

"There isn't, at least not that anyone knows," Gliria said.

"What about Myoxi? Maybe he knows a treatment. Where did he go?" Loran asked.

"He said he had a plan to break you out of jail," Gliria said. "But... but...that vine!"

"So you *did* see the vine? And you saw what it did?" Loran asked. "I thought I half imagined it."

"I saw the vine go into the cell. I didn't know if it was your cell or whose it was," Gliria said. "Then the vine went crazy and broke open the wall. It—"

"Loran?" called Myoxi's voice from the opening in the cell.

"Over here," Loran called back.

Myoxi hurried over to Loran and Gliria as best he could while dragging Loran's backpack. Loran ran toward Myoxi and helped with the pack.

"The guards and sholiffs are all in a room together, communing," Myoxi said as the two returned to Gliria. "I was going to find the Ethaloid they took and...you have the scar on your cheekbone!"

But just then, shouting echoed from the town.

"Let's get moving," Gliria said. "Someone is bound to find us here."

"But Myoxi said they are communing," Loran said.

"The sholiffs are. I don't know about the others," Myoxi said. "Gliria is right. Let's go!"

Loran slung the pack over his back, and the three disappeared into the woods. The shouting grew stronger, and the three hurried their pace, but Loran was still weak, and for once it was the picocians who were able to travel more quickly. They kept urging Loran forward, but Loran tired too much, and he finally collapsed.

"Get up, Loran. Get up!" Gliria urged.

"I'm too tired," Loran said.

Then the three heard men shouting, and the shouting grew louder.

"They'll find us very soon," Gliria said. "Myoxi, do something!"

Myoxi rummaged through Loran's pack and found the bottle of Daylazine. He opened the bottle and placed a drop on Loran's face. Loran awoke immediately, but he was all crabby and strung out.

"Can't get a decent rest around here. What a mistake I made leaving my cozy home, my Laculic Manor," Loran lamented. "This was the worst idea I've ever had."

"Shh," Myoxi said. "Oh, this won't do. Those men will find us for sure. We must get out of these woods."

The three ran toward an opening between two rows of pine shrubs, but the shrubs sent vines toward the three with intent to entangle them.

"No, that's a trap!" Gliria said. "This way."

The three followed Gliria, who now headed for another opening between pine shrubs, but again—the shrubs sent vines to entangle the three.

"Oh this won't do at all!" Loran wailed. "We're trapped for sure!"

The three ended up running in a trench formed by the vine that at first attacked Loran but then retreated and vacated the ground. Myoxi led, followed by Gliria and Loran.

"We're safe from the pine shrubs, but the men are getting closer," Gliria said. "And I'm tired, Myoxi."

"Just a little farther," Myoxi said. "I think this heads to the lake. If we can—"

"I can't. I just can't!" Gliria said with exhaustion.

"She can't make it!" Loran said. "None of us can! We must hide in this trench. Dig!"

Loran stopped, pulled out a shovel from his pack, and dug.

"No, we can't stop!" Myoxi urged.

But Loran was determined to dig. Gliria, tired from the run, stopped and breathed hard.

"I see a light!" Myoxi said. "Could be a house. We could ask for help!"

"There's no help around here!" Loran returned. "I'm sure of it."

Just then, Loran hit a hollow spot.

"There's something down here," Loran said.

Gliria walked over to see.

"Just another shovel or two, and—whoa!" Loran said.

But Myoxi never heard the *whoa*. A deep hole opened up and swallowed Loran and Gliria. Dirt, branches, and leaves caved in atop them. Myoxi realized that something had happened to the two, and he looked all around for them.

"Myoxi! Myoxi!" Loran and Gliria shouted.

Myoxi heard nothing until he reached the part of the trench where the earth was lower. He then crawled along it until he reached a small opening.

"Gliria? Loran?" Myoxi called through the opening.

"We're down here," Gliria said. "But there's a thundering sound."

"We can hear the heavy footsteps," Loran called. "It will cause another cave-in for sure. And we'll be killed. Myoxi! We must get away from the opening! Do you understand?"

"Run, Myoxi, run!" Gliria yelled.

But instead of running, Myoxi jumped down into the opening. It was dark, but the picocians had very good infrared vision. And again, Myoxi led the way.

"There are tunnels down here," Myoxi said. "I think we can go—"

But Myoxi was interrupted by the thundering of men's footsteps. There was another cave-in. The tunnels behind were now completely filled in, and the three were buried in dirt—Gliria and Myoxi completely, and Loran partially, with his mouth just above the dirt line. A rock hit Loran on the head, and he fell unconscious.

Zdannag Hall

Loran awoke hours later. He was disoriented and confused, and he wasn't sure how much time had passed.

"Myoxi?" Loran coughed. "Gliria?"

Loran continued coughing. It was pitch black, and he could see nothing. And somehow in the darkness, he felt as if he could hear less and feel less.

"I feel like I'm in a complete empty nothingness," Loran said. "If I could just light a lamp. Where's my pack?"

But Loran's pack was no longer over his back. It had somehow come off after the second cave-in, and so he was completely without tools.

"Myoxi? Gliria?" Loran called.

Using his hands, Loran dug around frantically, but he might as well have been digging in a desert.

"They'll suffocate. They'll die!" Loran said.

Loran continued to dig with his hands, but there was nothing. He moved around a bit, and his hands found a wall. He followed the wall with his hands, crawling because for some reason, the cave was too short for him, and he couldn't stand. Then his hand hit something. It was a small wooden box, and it was unlocked. He opened it. He could not see its contents because his surroundings were too dark. Should he place his hand inside and touch? No, too dangerous. He closed the box and shook it. He heard small things jostling inside, like lots of short twigs. Loran opened the box again and dumped out its contents. Lots of little twig-like things fell to the ground by his knees. He reached and grabbed and realized these weren't twigs—they were snap peas. He broke one in half, and to his surprise, a bright, amber light came out.

"These aren't ordinary snap peas. They're fluorescent snap peas."

The light continued for several more seconds and then faded out.

"The light is brief, say, a hundred heart-beat's worth and no more," Loran mused.

He snapped another pea open, and it too put out amber light. Loran felt comfortable, as if he were by some sort of fire. The light was steady and did not flicker, and so Loran's nerves were completely soothed. He nearly fell asleep, but the light faded after a minute, and the total darkness reminded him of his picocian friends.

"Myoxi and Gliria. Can you hear me? Hello there!" he called.

He snapped open another pea pod and held it in one hand while he sifted dirt with the other. But there was no sign of the picocians, and the snap pea dimmed out.

"These snap peas don't last long enough. I must find my pack and use my glow stick," Loran said.

Loran picked up several fluorescent snap peas, snapped them one at a time, and headed a bit farther down the tunnel. There were more boxes, many more, piled high and as far as the eye could see. And just past such a collection of boxes was Loran's pack.

"It was thrown clear. And it's here," he said.

He sifted through his pack, found the glow stick, and uncovered it just as the last snap pea dimmed out. Now he placed the pack over his shoulder and used his glow stick for light. He headed back to the area where he first woke up, which was close to the cave-in site.

Then he saw a pile of rubble and had the horrible thought that his friends had been crushed. He set the glow stick aside and removed the rocks, one by one, tiring from the labor but continuing nonetheless. He removed a large pile of them, and still no picocians. Now he had reached dirt and was about to abandon the dig and look for other rocks to remove when he saw the edges of woven material. It was Gliria's pack.

"Gliria!" Loran called.

Loran brushed the dirt from the pack o-so-carefully, and still holding it was Gliria's hand. Loran now brushed the dirt from around her and pulled her out. Her skin was no longer ruddy red but was instead black.

"She's not breathing. She's not breathing!" Loran exclaimed. "I killed her! Oh where is Myoxi? Is he still alive?"

Loran brushed away more dirt from where he had found Gliria. He found another little pack and then found Myoxi, whose skin was also black.

"Myoxi!" Loran said.

But Myoxi was also unconscious. He placed Myoxi next to Gliria and tried tapping them and shaking them, but they would not wake.

"They're dead. Both of them. Shake, wake, breathe!" he pleaded.

Loran sat there and pondered what to do, and as he did, an old rhyme from his childhood sprang to mind:

Shake the sleeping,
Wake the weeping.
Breath, breath, breath!
Beware the death!
Be careful there.
Become aware.
Pneuminair,
Pneuminair.

He rushed to retrieve his medicine box from his pack, then he opened the box and revealed several bottles—Ethaloid, Daylazine, others, and there it was, "Pneuminair — Air of Breath, Nary a Death." He placed a drop each of the liquid in Myoxi's and Gliria's mouths. The picocians began breathing and regained consciousness.

"Gliria! Myoxi! You're alive!" Loran said with glee.

"Of course we are," Myoxi said. "What's that awful taste?"

"It's bitter," Gliria said. "Like *sourfran* weed."

"It's a mixture of sourfran weed and *eckelberry*," Loran said. "And I'm glad it brought you back to life."

"We were never dead," Myoxi said.

"But you weren't breathing," Loran said. "I'm sure of it."

"We picocians can go for days without breathing," Gliria said.

"What?" Loran asked in bewilderment.

"Comes in handy when tunneling," Myoxi said. "We store oxygen in our tissues in the form of iron oxide."

"That's why our skin is brown and red and orange of sorts," Gliria said.

"But your skin isn't red—it's black," Loran said.

"Look," Myoxi said. "It's changing back to red as we breathe."

Myoxi was right. Loran watched as the picocians' skin lightened from black to shades of brown.

"I've never seen such as this," Loran said.

"You can store a little oxygen in your muscles, but only a few minutes' worth," Gliria said. "Loran, tell us—where exactly did you find us?"

"Buried under those rocks," Loran said, pointing to the pile he had moved.

"Then we owe you our thanks," Myoxi said. "And though we weren't dead, we surely would have died without your help. Not immediately, but in the course of a few weeks after our oxygen ran out, we would have."

"Thank you, Loran," Gliria said. "Say, that mark that was on your cheekbone—it's gone."

"She's right," Myoxi said. "Which means you weren't really infected."

"The vine was about to pierce my heart, but it never did," Loran said.

"Then that's how it subdues people," Gliria said. "I'm very glad for you, Loran. You have not succumbed, and we haven't died."

"We still might die, as we are trapped in this tunnel," Loran said.

"But there's light from your glow stick," Gliria said. "That will help us find a way out."

"The tunnel goes on this way," Loran said. "I know, because I found my pack amongst a collection of wooden boxes."

"Show us," Myoxi said.

Loran led the two down the tunnel where he had found his pack.

"These are picocian-made boxes," Gliria said.

"How can you tell?" Loran asked.

"The craftsmanship," Myoxi said. "See how the boards are dovetailed together without nails? Picocians don't use metal to join boards together, especially not iron. We'd eat the iron first before wasting it. Look at the style of joints—that's picocian, all right."

"I'm looking at the joints...no wait, back up. You'd eat iron? *Eat* iron?" Loran asked.

"To store the oxygen," Gliria said. "It's too precious to waste on something like a wooden box."

"This means picocians are nearby," Loran said. "I don't know if that's good or bad."

"Good," Myoxi said.

"Unless the boxes were stolen," Gliria said.

"Then bad," Myoxi added.

"Well we need to find out," Loran said.

"What's this?" Gliria asked as she picked up an unopened snap pea that Loran had previously dumped out.

"Snap it open and see," Loran said.

Gliria snapped the pod, and the peas began to glow with amber light.

"These are *picocioli* peas from the other side of the mountain," Gliria said.

"Stolen," Myoxi said. "I bet there are many stolen picocian things in this tunnel."

"Picocioli? What is that?" Loran asked.

"The picocians found a way to make various vegetables and oils glow in the dark," Gliria said. "Such products are called *picocioli*, after Farmer Picocioli who made the first one."

"We must be careful," Myoxi said. "Whoever has stolen these could be close-by. No telling where this tunnel leads."

"Then I will lead the way," Loran said.

Loran did lead the way, but the tunnel grew increasingly narrow and short. The picocians had been walking aside Loran, but now they followed. Loran himself was forced to crawl on hands and knees.

"This isn't working," Loran said. "I'll be trapped very soon."

But then the three heard distant voices. It seemingly came from behind an oaken door.

"I hear voices," Loran whispered.

"Shh," Myoxi said. "They might hear you."

"Well, I can't go any farther," Loran said. "These boxes and shelves are all in the way."

"We must be very close, Myoxi," Gliria said.

"Loran, hide behind that collection of boxes," Myoxi said.

"I can't. There's not enough space," Loran said.

"Myoxi, we must move the boxes," Gliria said.

"Wait, I can move these boxes up here, and these others can go over here, and—"

But before Loran could finish his sentence, he had knocked over a box. It banged against several boxes and scattered them all over on its way down to the floor. The picocians scuttled into small crevices while Loran backtracked as quickly and as far as possible until he could hide behind a different set of boxes. And just in time. The three heard the eerie hinge-squeal of a door opening.

"Hello?" said a small, female voice.

Myoxi and Gliria immediately recognized the voice as picocian. They began making squeaking sounds, like mice, to communicate.

"What is it?" called a deep, human voice from the distance.

"Mice," the female picocian said. "They knocked over several boxes."

"Well clean it up!" the voice ordered. "And finish dusting the chandeliers!"

"Yes, sir," the picocian replied.

She closed the door almost all the way and ventured into the tunnel. She made squeaking noises back into the dark to communicate with Myoxi and Gliria. The two convinced the picocian to venture deeper into the tunnel until the three met up with Loran. Loran then saw her for the first time, a young picocian woman with silver hair and silver skin. She looked tired and thin, as if she had neither slept nor eaten in weeks. Loran was about to say something to her, but Myoxi hushed him and led them as deeply into the tunnel as possible without chance of being heard by the voice outside the door from where the picocian woman had come.

"My name is Loa'neth," the female picocian said. "I am one of several slaves to Lord Zdannag here at Zdannag Hall."

"Zdannag Hall?" Loran asked. "I've never heard of it. Who is Lord Z—"

"This is Loran Laculic, of Laculic Manor, his home, which is on Lake Meadowash just north of Millfork," Gliria said. "This is my husband, Myoxi. And my name is Gliria. We are picocians of Rainbear Mountain."

"What brings you to these parts? The peoples and lands are changing into darkness. And our people...they..." Loa'neth started.

But Loa'neth fell faint and suddenly collapsed. Loran caught her and held her.

"She's very weak, Loran," Gliria said.

"Yes, her skin and hair are very silvery," Myoxi added. "She is fully oxygen depleted."

"You mean it's not natural for her?" Loran asked.

"Oh no. Her silver skin is like a human having pale-blue skin," Gliria said. "Let me check something."

Gliria took a small crystal from her pack. Like a jeweler's glass. She inspected Loa'neth's skin and sighed.

"She is also iron deficient," Gliria said.

"Really? But the silver," Myoxi said.

"Is not iron. It's a symptom of a disease. She has *hydrargyria*," Gliria said.

"Mercury poisoning," Loran said.

"It's worse than that," Gliria said. "The mercury has completely displaced whatever iron she once had. She will die soon. There is nothing we can do."

"Oh yes there is," Loran said. "I have something for mercury poisoning. It will remove the toxic metal from her body."

"Loran," Myoxi said. "We picocians must have some form of metal in our bodies. Even if you can remove the mercury from Loa'neth, she will die of metal depletion."

"What do you have for removing mercury?" Gliria asked.

Loran removed his medicine box and looked at the various bottles until he found it.

"Sulfaurium — Drown Hydrargyrum with Sulfur and Gold," Loran read from the bottle.

"It contains gold?" Myoxi asked.

"It could work," Gliria said. "But instead of iron, she would have gold. Still, it could kill her. I've never heard of a picocian using gold to store oxygen. Don't you have a medicine bottle for adding iron?"

Loran looked.

"No, I don't," he said. "It's Sulfaurium or nothing."

Myoxi and Gliria exchanged glances. Gliria finally nodded in affirmation.

"It's the best we can do," Gliria said. "Go ahead with the treatment."

Loran placed a drop each of the Sulfaurium on Loa'neth's limbs and her forehead. He then passed his glowstick in circles above her head, and the Sulfaurium seemed to catch fire! Myoxi and Gliria held hands over their mouths to muffle their cries, but the fire they witnessed was not of the ordinary combustible type. Loa'neth's clothing did not burn, neither did her hair nor any other thing on her person. The flame swirled around Loa'neth with colors of yellow and green. And just as quickly as it started, it ended. Loa'neth awoke, and her hair and skin, which had been of color silver, were both now cherry red. Her cheeks had puffed out a little, and she didn't seem quite as thin as before. She stood, and her height had increased.

"I feel so strangely," Loa'neth said. "My limbs feel flexible, light, and warm. Dreariness has left me, and I can hold my breath. Look!"

Loa'neth inhaled deeply and held her breath, puffing out her cherry-red cheeks in the process. After several seconds of such a pose, Loran touched her cheeks, and she suddenly exhaled with a laugh. Her laugh made Loran laugh, and he felt warm and cozy inside.

"You're a completely different person," Myoxi said.

"It's a miracle," Gliria said. "I didn't know humans had such magical medicine."

"Not all of us do," Loran said. "Sulfaurium is a special recipe from Cousin Lillianina."

"Loran is on his way to find his cousin," Gliria said.

"Where does she live?" Loa'neth asked.

"In Sathiakia," Loran answered.

Loa'neth's face changed from cherry red to gray and back to cherry red.

"She is in grave danger, then," Loa'neth said. "I hear of nothing but evil from that place."

Just then, the echo of the door opening carried through the tunnel.

"My Master!" she said in fear.

"He'll discover us for sure," Myoxi said.

"Then I must act," Loran said.

Loran pulled a blow gun from his pack and filled several darts with Ethaloid. He hid his glowstick in his pack so that only a faint light came out, and then he motioned that he was ready. Loa'neth called toward the door.

"Where are you, Loa'neth?" the voice called.

"I found more mice," she called back.

"Never mind about them. Clean the chandeliers. I'll have the porter straighten up in here."

"I...I can't clean now," Loa'neth said.

"Why not!?" the voice said angrily, and it neared.

The voice became a shadow and a shape, and it held a lit lantern in its hand. When it was close enough, Loran blew into the tube, and a dart hit the man. The man reached to remove the dart, but it was too late—the Ethaloid filled his veins and put him to sleep.

"Because I've freed her from your tyranny, that's why!" Loran replied to the sleeping man.

Loran walked up to the man, picked up the lantern, and held it close to the man's face.

"It's George Snake!" Loran said.

"I thought he looked familiar," Myoxi said. "I should kick him good for selling me a fake map."

"No, it's Lord Zdannag," Loa'neth said.

"Apparently, he has more than one name," Gliria said.

"George Snake has always been a deceiver," Loran said. "Well, we can't stay here. Loa'neth, will you help us find my Cousin Lillianina in Sathiakia?"

"Anything is better than being a slave in this House of Lies," she said. "But I must warn you—there are other people here: the maid, cook, porter, butler, chauffeur, gardener, three alchemists, and five guards. There's also one boatman."

"Boatman?" Loran asked with new interest. "George has a boat! We could travel on Lake Meadowash to Sathiakia instead of getting caught again on land. Now Loa'neth, is there a way we can sneak—what's wrong?"

"I'm afraid of water," she said.

"We all are," Myoxi said. "Picocians, while excellent miners and craftsfolk, are terrified of being on water. Wading through a stream is bad enough. But a lake!"

The three picocians shivered.

"If we did manage to acquire possession of a boat and go on Lake Meadowash, what would happen?" Loran asked.

"We would get sea sick," Gliria said. "Then we would get uncontrollable shaking of the limbs."

"That's just the first ten minutes. Shortly after that, we go into convulsions, slip into coma, and die," Myoxi added.

"I didn't realize it was that bad," Loran said.

"I want to escape this place," Loa'neth said. "But I don't know what's worse—dying on the lake or being caught and tortured on land."

"I wouldn't let that happen to you, not either of those choices," Loran said.

"You may not have much power to stop it," Myoxi said. "My senses tell me there are more sholiffs and other men under the influence of these pine vines. Plus there are the pine vines themselves to contend with."

"But they are not on the lake," Loran said.

"No, they are not," Gliria said. "If only we could go with you, the lake would seem to be the best hope."

"Perhaps there is a way you can," Loran said. "Let me look at my medicine box. Let's see. Has anyone here actually been on a lake and experienced these symptoms?"

"I have," Loa'neth said. "Lord Zdannag forced me to tend to his needs while on his boat. I was lucky to survive, but it caused great depletion of my iron reserves. And in its place I absorbed mercury from the many fish I was forced to gut and clean."

"So that's how it happened," Gliria said. "You poor child."

Gliria gave Loa'neth a hug.

"I didn't think any fish survived. I thought all were extinct," Loran said. "How did you survive such an ordeal?"

"There are a few fish left," Loa'neth said, "but only in the deepest parts of the lake and only if one knows where to find them. Most died long ago from mercury poisoning and were swept to the deepest part of the lake, where the remaining fish absorbed the toxin. That's why shallow parts of the lake are clean. But as for me and my own poisoning, I felt...like time and space were ripping apart. My left arm seemed to separate from my shoulder and fall to the ground while my body seemed unmoving. Then my left arm would slam back against my body with an incredible sting, like a brick hitting the side of the mountain. One of my legs felt as if it were on fire, the other was stiff and cold. And the whole time, I felt out of control."

"I think I have something then," Loran said while removing a bottle from his medicine box, and it said: "Enpriosol — For Control of Spirit when Spirits are Many".

"What is it?" Myoxi asked.

"*Enpriosol*," Loran said. "It's used to return one's senses after things like too much ale or other confusion. In this case it should work. However, it has one side effect—it blocks the sense of fear. You must be very careful after receiving a drop. Think actively about consequences to actions instead of relying on fear to keep you from walking into a wall or jumping off a ledge. But first—Loa'neth, how can we get to the boat safely?"

"I know a back way to the boathouse, which will get us past everyone except for one guard and the boatman himself," Loa'neth said.

"I can sedate them both with Ethaloid blowdarts," Loran said, "provided they don't see me first."

"I'll lead the way," Loa'neth said.

"Good," Loran said. "I'd better administer the Enpriosol now. One drop each."

Loran placed a drop of Enpriosol on Gliria, Myoxi, and Loa'neth.

"I don't feel anything," Gliria said.

"I do," Myoxi said. "I don't care what they do to me. Let's burst through those guards and overpower the boatman."

"Myoxi? Remember what I said?" Loran warned.

"But...I feel...my muscles are more powerful. And tough. I could punch my fist through this box, and it would crumble into splinters," Myoxi bragged.

"No, don't!" Gliria warned.

Too late. Myoxi drove his fist into a wooden box and broke through. But in the process, he broke his knuckles. He looked puzzled for a moment, then the pain hit him. Gliria put her hand over his mouth to keep him from crying out and giving away their location.

"Enpriosol does nothing for pain," Loran warned. "I told you to think before acting."

"Oh, it's the same story," Gliria said. "First the map from that George Snake that led us on a wild chase. Then...uh...and now this—he's broken his hand."

"Don't put this adventure to Sathiakia on my shoulders. It was your idea," Myoxi said. "Ow, ow, ow! Loran, can't you give me something for the pain?"

"Normally I could," Loran said. "But the Enpriosol blocks it. It blocks most drugs."

"Most drugs?" Myoxi asked. "What doesn't it negate?"

"Daylazine," Loran said. "If I were to give that to you now, your pain would triple, and no drug could help you then. Not with Daylazine circling your innards. It destroys all drugs—even pain suppressors."

"It's too dangerous," Gliria said. "Loran—give me a moment to wrap Myoxi's hand. He should live with his pain anyway."

"What!?" Myoxi asked.

"As a reminder to be more careful," Gliria lectured.

Myoxi grumbled something.

"What was that, Myoxi?" Loran asked.

"I said, that Enpriosol made Gliria lose her sense of caring," Myoxi said.

"How dare you!" Gliria said, and she punched Myoxi.

"Please, no more," Loa'neth said. "We must leave now, Loran, before anyone else is hurt."

Loa'neth led the way. Loran followed, and the other two picocians completed the foursome. They passed through a large hallway but kept themselves along the right wall. They approached an intersection with another hallway. Loa'neth peered around the corner then quickly withdrew and signaled the others to hide. They did so, and Loran prepared his blow gun. He put the tube to his mouth and so readied his first shot. It was the butler. He entered the intersection, paused, and then walked down the hallway where the four hid. Just as he passed Loa'neth's position, she jumped out and called him.

"Miss Loa'neth," the butler said as he turned around. "What happened to your skin?"

But before the butler could hear the answer, a dart from Loran's gun penetrated the butler's shoulder and sent Ethaloid into his system. The butler fell to his knees, mumbled something, and then fell to the floor, asleep.

"That's one," Loa'neth whispered.

"He wasn't part of the plan," Myoxi said. "Oh why must we linger here? We should just blast a path to the boat."

"Shh," Gliria said.

The four took a right down the hallway from where the butler came and were headed toward the kitchen. The cook had unexpectedly started down the hallway. Loa'neth had them hide again behind statues and hallway cabinets. The cook had nearly walked past them all when Myoxi grumbled:

"This Loa'neth said there'd be only a guard and boatman. And already there are two other people."

Gliria pinched him to stop his speech, but it was too late—the cook heard.

"What are you—hey, intruders!" the cook called.

Loran sent a blowdart into the cook's side. But now shouting echoed from up the hall where the foursome came.

"Guards," Loa'neth said to the three. "We must hurry!"

Loa'neth tried opening a side door.

"This is the back way, but the door is locked!" Loa'neth said.

"Is there another way?" Loran asked.

"Yes, but—" Loa'neth started.

"No time. Let's go," Loran urged.

The four ran toward and into the kitchen, and to their surprise, there were additional cooks.

"Intruders!" the cooks yelled.

"Only one cook?!" Myoxi complained.

"Be quiet!" Gliria replied.

The four then rushed into the dining room, and the reason for the extra cooks became clear—George Snake had invited guests to a dinner party. There were too many people to sedate. Loran tried to follow Loa'neth, but she disappeared under the tables, and he was too big to follow. With there being too little room to run along the floor, he resorted to running atop the tables.

"Little people!" the guests yelled. "Grab them!"

"No, grab the idiot stepping on our plates!" said another.

Loa'neth, Gliria, and Myoxi managed to finish running under the tables and escape the dining room into a side room with steps leading down, but many arms and hands slowed Loran's progress and pulled him down where they held him with his back and pack pressed against a table.

"Let me go, let me go!" Loran demanded.

"Not until the guards deal with you!" said one of the guests.

Loa'neth had started for the boathouse with Myoxi and Gliria following. But she stopped. Myoxi and Gliria continued down the steps past Loa'neth, but Loa'neth doubled back to see what was delaying Loran.

"I must help him," Loa'neth said.

"Loa'neth, be careful," Gliria warned. "Remember what Loran told us? Be aware of your actions. The consequences."

"I know," Loa'neth said.

Loa'neth slipped back into the dining hall and snuck behind a bowl of whipped cream. She took the cream and plastered it over her skin to hide its color. Then she burst onto a small stage used for entertaining the guests. She began telling jokes—jokes about picocians! The guests thought it was all part of dinner and began to laugh. Then she began to sing and invited the guests to sing with her. She had them lifting their hands to form a wave. First one side of the room, then another. And in so doing, she made them loosen their grip on Loran enough where he could reach into his pack —briefly—so that he could find and retrieve...where was it...the canister of *Kelofuge*? He reached and reached and...there it was. He turned the valve, and the gas escaped. Then Loran began to laugh. He couldn't help it. The Kelofuge was designed just for that purpose—to make people laugh. The people around him laughed—uncontrollably. Loa'neth continued her act, and Loran was able to get off the table and walk around the room, dispersing the Kelofuge where he walked. He enjoyed himself too much, he was afraid, and had to cut short his fumigation lest the gas overpower himself and render him unable to walk. He motioned briefly to Loa'neth that he was leaving the dining hall, and she acknowledged his sign with a wink.

Loran turned off the gas, disappeared through the side door where he met up with Myoxi and Gliria (he was still laughing), and then quickly pulled out the Daylazine and placed a drop on his skin.

"Ooo, ow, ack," Loran groaned. "Purging Kelofuge out with Daylazine hurts. Not funny!"

"Another medicine?" Myoxi asked.

"Yes. To effect my escape, although Loa'neth gets much of the credit," Loran said.

"And Loa'neth is here," she said with whipped cream on her face.

"You're a mess," Gliria said.

"I'll clean up later. Let's go," Loa'neth said.

She led the three down the steps, along a narrow, underground passage, and then back up another set of stairs that terminated with a door.

"This is it. The boathouse is just beyond this door," Loa'neth said.

"I'll ready my blow gun," Loran said.

Loa'neth opened the door only a little and looked outside. She then closed the door.

"What's wrong?" Gliria asked.

"There are eight guards out there!" she said.

"I thought you said there would only be one!" Myoxi demanded. "And where did the extra guards come from?"

"I don't know. They...they must have been alerted," Loa'neth said. "I'll distract them. And then—"

"No, you've done enough. It's our turn," Gliria said.

Gliria rushed out with Myoxi and began dancing and singing in front of the guards. Their shadows stretched across the ground from the setting sun, but the guards were not amused by the dancing picocians nor their shadows.

"Get them!" the lead guard said.

Loran got one dart off and felled a guard into sleep, but then six other guards came at Loran. He knew he couldn't hit them all without one of them getting to him, so he opened the valve to the Kelofuge, lit it with his fire piston, and threw it at the men. It exploded in their faces, setting them on fire and forcing them to laugh their way into the lake to extinguish themselves.

"Kelofuge is inflammable," Loran explained to Loa'neth.

That left one guard and the boatman. Loran got off another blowdart and felled the guard while the boatman, fearful of what he had seen, ran off in fright.

"That's all of them. Let's go," Gliria said.

The four ran into the boathouse and readied the boat. Loran had untied the last rope and was preparing to launch when the picocians heard a muffled cry.

"A picocian!" Gliria said.

"And in trouble," Myoxi said.

"Wait, Loran!" Loa'neth said as she jumped out of the boat.

Gliria and Myoxi followed Loa'neth while Loran steadied the boat and tied it back to the dock.

"We must be quick," Loran said. "No doubt there will be more guards."

But it wasn't the guards who echoed from the distance. It was the original pack of men who had pursued Loran from Blackpier.

"Oh, not them again," Loran said.

"Look, Loran. She is chained to this post. We must free her," Loa'neth said.

The four saw a female picocian with silver hair and silver skin, similar to how Loa'neth appeared before treatment.

"It would take too long to pick the lock on her handcuff," Loran said.

"Can you break the chain?" Myoxi asked.

"Or remove the other end from this post," Loa'neth suggested.

"That I can do!" Loran said.

Loran removed a crowbar from his pack and chipped into the wooden post until he could get a good leverage point, and when he did, he pried the large anchor bolt from the post and removed it—straining and grunting the entire time. Loa'neth and Gliria helped the silver picocian to the boat while Myoxi carried the anchor bolt. Loran did not have time to put the crowbar back in his pack, because the men were now too close. Holding it in one hand, he jumped into the boat and prepared to loosen the rope when one of the men was nearly on top of him. Loran threw the crowbar at the man to gain time. The man fell back. Loran then loosened the rope and pushed the boat from the dock with an oar.

The man regained his balance but was no longer within arm's reach of Loran or the boat. Instead, the man readied a bow and fired arrows at Loran and his group. The picocians easily hid in the boat, but Loran was taller and had less cover. An arrow narrowly missed him, and that motivated him to action.

"This won't do at all," Loran said. "We must get out of here quickly."

Loran pulled out another canister of Kelofuge. He tied it to the back of the boat, opened the valve, and lit it. The gas ignited and pushed against the boat, propelling it quickly away from shore. The exhaust also overpowered the man and several others now arriving and set them to a laughing fire. One of the newly arrived men had sent a blowdart just before the flames overpowered him, and that dart hit Loran in the arm. Loran quickly removed the dart to avoid its poison, but it was too late. He slipped into unconsciousness and remembered nothing more.

Sun, Sail, and Oysters

When Loran awoke, it was morning. The lake was calm, the sun was rising, and a light breeze blew through the boat's sail. Loran was on a bed inside the cabin. His boots had been removed, his hair had been cut, washed, and combed, and his wound had been cleaned and bound. Loran looked to his right side and saw another bed on the other side of the cabin. Loa'neth, who was now all cleaned up, was sitting by the silver-skinned picocian female, wiping her face with a soft cloth.

Loran tried sitting up, but he became dizzy and fell back to his bed with a thunk.

"You're awake," Loa'neth said. "Just rest here a moment. You must be hungry."

"I should be hungry, but I'm not. I guess I had a good night's sleep," Loran said.

"You've been asleep for two weeks," Loa'neth said.

"I have?" Loran asked in surprise. "That's impossible. The Daylazine should have kept me awake and not let me sleep more than a few hours, much less than two weeks."

"But you did sleep for two weeks. We escaped the men at Lord Zdannag's house, but you were hit by a poisonous dart. I cleaned and bound the wound as best I could," Loa'neth said. "I was sure you would die."

"Perhaps the Daylazine did its part and purged out much of the poison," Loran said. "Then I was lucky to have taken the Daylazine when I did. I would be dead otherwise."

Loa'neth smiled, but a few tears belied her expression of relief.

"And my boots? And hair?" Loran asked. "You took care of me, didn't you?"

Loa'neth kept her smile, quickly wiped the tears away and said, "I guess I am uninhibited. Must be the Enpriosol. I have a weakness for folk in need."

"And I have a weakness for caring people," Loran said. "And you're a pretty one at that."

Loa'neth blushed, and her already cherry-red skin became a deeper shade.

"But the Enpriosol would have worn off by now," Loran said.

"After a couple of days, we began getting sea sick. Myoxi—I hope you don't mind—went through your pack and gave us more Enpriosol," Loa'neth explained.

"I'm glad he did. I would hate to think what would have happened to me if all of you went crazy with sea sickness. You're quite a pretty lady, as I have said. And you seem to have grown a bit."

"Myoxi and Gliria said the same thing. I'm not very tall for a picocian," Loa'neth explained. "But poor Dara."

"Who?" Loran asked.

"This is Dara," Loa'neth explained, pointing to the silvery picocian female on the bed. "She has the same mercury poisoning I once had...that you cured."

"Oh! We must cure her at once. Why did you wait? You could have used the medicine box," Loran urged.

"I...we were afraid. Of harming her. She is very ill," Loa'neth said.

"It should be very simple. Let me see...where is my pack?" Loran asked while looking around.

"Here it is," Loa'neth said.

"Let's see...things are a little jumbled. There—my medicine box," Loran said.

"Loa'neth?" she said in a weak voice.

"I'm here, Dara," Loa'neth said.

Gliria entered the cabin to give news but was surprised to see Loran awake.

"I just wanted to—oh Loran! Thank the mountains you are awake and well," Gliria said.

"Gliria, hello," Dara said.

Gliria looked at Loa'neth for an update on Dara's health, but Loa'neth shook her head *no*.

"You were going to say something, Gliria," Loran said.

"Only that Myoxi has gone oyster fishing and will soon be back with breakfast," Gliria said.

"What do you think, Dara? Would you like breakfast? The food will do you good," Loa'neth said.

"I will try. I am so weak. I do not know if I can eat. But I will try," Dara said.

"Good. I'll start the grill," Gliria said.

Gliria left the cabin and went up to the deck where she started a fire on a grill.

"You have been such a good bedside companion, telling me stories of you and your family in your redwood homes," Dara said. "I would like to visit your people someday."

"And you will. Loran will give you some medicine to make you better," Loa'neth said.

"I would offer to show you my home, but it is a miserable outcropping of rocks south of Rainbear Mountain. Even Myoxi and Gliria would shudder," Dara said.

"They would not, and we'd be happy to see where you grew up," Loa'neth said. She turned to Loran and said, "You must help her now. She will not last much longer."

"I will do so then," Loran said.

Loran removed the Sulfaurium bottle from his medicine box, removed the cap, and placed a drop of the fluid on Dara's forehead. A yellow and green glow passed over her body and then faded. Her skin briefly changed to red.

"Loa'neth?" Dara said very weakly.

"Shh. You'll feel better soon," Loa'neth said.

"You are like a sister to me. Friend," Dara said.

The red in Dara's skin faded back into silver, and her body went completely limp.

"What's happening?" Loa'neth asked. "She has no breath, and her heart has stopped."

"I don't understand. It should work," Loran said.

"Try again," Loa'neth said. "Try again!"

Loran placed another drop on Dara's forehead. A much fainter yellow and green glow passed over Dara, but there was no change in her silvery skin. Just then, Gliria and Myoxi appeared with breakfast, but they stopped short and waited.

"The whole bottle!" Loa'neth said.

Loa'neth grabbed the bottle of Sulfaurium from Loran and dumped its contents all over Dara's body. There was only the faintest of yellow and green glow.

Dara never recovered and was dead. Loa'neth cried and wailed the loss, and Loran sat there, confused. What else could he try? Daylazine? He took out the bottle and placed a drop on Dara's forehead, but her lifeless body did not change. Loa'neth continued to cry.

With sadness, Gliria led Myoxi back out of the cabin. It was no time for breakfast. Loran stood up to leave too, but Loa'neth grabbed his arm and held him in check. Then she gave Loran a hug and did not stop.

"Don't let me go," she cried. "Don't let me fade away like Dara. Hold on to me. Will you hold onto me?"

"I will do everything in my power to keep you safe. I promise," Loran said.

The two hugged each other like this for several minutes. And again, Loran believed Loa'neth had grown another inch or two—just since he awoke. It was the strangest thing, but already he was warming up to the idea of Loa'neth reaching his height and becoming a lady he could see eye-to-eye. He looked at her ruddy-red hair and wished to see a light breeze flow through that red hair while she picked flowers. However, the moment of solace could not last. Without warning, the two heard Myoxi and Gliria arguing from the deck.

"I should have never come along. And you neither!" Myoxi yelled.

"Oh shut up!" Gliria yelled back.

"We have no place on this lake! And one of our own has died! Are we next?! Curses all! We should go back now and return home. Forget this wretched rescue mission."

"We can't leave now!" Gliria said.

"What are you saying, Gliria?!"

"You know what I'm saying. We're staying put with Loran!"

"Wrong! I'm going back. With or without you!" Myoxi shouted.

"Without, I hope!" Gliria shouted back. "And you might as well move out of my home."

"That's *our* home!" Myoxi said. "And I'm going to sell it!"

"Wrong! That's my grandfather's house. I'm the rich one, and I dug you out of that wretched clay pit you call a house," Gliria said.

"That was ceramic, and it was my mother's!" Myoxi said.

"Then go back to her, you mamma's boy!" Gliria laughed loudly.

"I should throw you overboard right here to shut you up!" Myoxi said.

"And kill me?! Water is death to picocians. No picocian in her right mind would throw another into the water. You cold...blooded...murderer!" Gliria screamed, and she went at Myoxi.

It was Loa'neth who jumped in between the two. She was taller and stronger than them, and she surprised herself at how easily she could break up the fight.

"Stop it, you two! Just stop it now! You love each other!" Loa'neth said.

"Step aside, Loa'neth," Myoxi said. "Gliria needs a lesson."

"Yes, step aside, Loa'neth. Myoxi needs to be kicked back to the clay," Gliria said.

"I'll show you kicking to the clay," Myoxi said while gnashing his teeth.

"You don't know the meaning of the word," Gliria yelled back.

"Stop it, I say! Don't you see what's happening?" Loa'neth said.

Loran went back to his pack to see what medicine he could use in this instance, and then he found the Enpriosol—empty. He returned to the deck with the empty bottle.

"Myoxi!" Loran called.

"What!?" Myoxi snarled.

"How much of this did you use? How much?" Loran asked.

Myoxi held silent.

"Well!? Aren't you going to tell him?" Gliria shouted.

"What of it?!" Myoxi yelled.

"You took most of it. I only had a little more than Loa'neth. And only a very little went to Dara," Gliria said.

"That's it then. Myoxi—you're suffering from Enpriosol overdose," Loran said.

"I haven't overdosed on anything, unless it's too much of *Gleeereeea* and *Gleeereeea's* shrill voice!" Myoxi mocked.

"I can't give him Daylazine," Loran said. "He'll get sea sick."

"Then we will need to return to shore soon," Loa'neth said.

"No, let's leave Myoxi out here so he can play with more oysters. I hear you have an oyster girlfriend down in the lake. Go tell her your woes!" Gliria taunted.

"We can't reach shore in time. For once I am at a loss," Loran said.

"Steer the boat to shore. I have a plan," Loa'neth said. "One thing—do you have any salt?"

"Salt?"

"Yes, plain salt," she said.

"In my pack is a seasoning box with salt," he said.

"Good," she said.

Loran worked the sails and rudder to send the boat back toward shore. Loa'neth tied Myoxi to a post and then took a bucket, filled it with water, and mixed in salt. She then took the bucket to Myoxi, cut him loose, and began dunking his head in the bucket. Myoxi choked on the water.

"Now I want you to repeat after me," Loa'neth started.

"I ain't repeating nothing after no *picosneezey* woman!" Myoxi snorted.

"Bad answer!" Loa'neth said.

She dunked Myoxi's head in water again, waited while he struggled, and then pulled it up.

"That salt is nasty," Myoxi snarled.

"It's to clean out your crabby cranium," Loa'neth said. "Now repeat after me: I love Gliria."

"Good. You marry her," Myoxi snapped.

"Bad answer!" Loa'neth said as she dunked Myoxi into the bucket.

"There's an island up ahead," Loran called.

"Land?" Gliria called.

"Land?!" Myoxi asked as Loa'neth pulled his head out of the bucket.

"Land," Loran replied. "Strange. I don't remember there being an island on Lake Meadowash. But then again, I have no map of the entire lake."

"I once heard Lord Zdannag speak of three islands on this lake," Loa'neth said as she released Myoxi and joined Loran's side. "The first is a smooth mountain with no life of any kind. The other contains a fortified castle."

"This island is none of those. There are shrubs abound. No mountain, and no castle. What did he say about the third one?" Loran asked.

"He said, 'People who leave Stip Worc Island never enter.'"

"And since everything with George Snake is backward, the warning is that people who enter Crow Pits Island never leave, presumably because of more than one pit."

"Then we must be very careful where we step," Loa'neth said.

"So the question now is—do we run this boat all the way onto the beach, or do we anchor out a bit and take a rowboat in?" Loran asked.

"If we run aground, we'll be shipwrecked for sure. Lake Meadowash is too large to be paddling about in a rowboat," Myoxi said.

"We should run aground," Loa'neth said.

"Why!?" Myoxi protested.

"One never knows what things are out in the water, ready to topple our boat or throw it against the rocks," Loa'neth said.

"There are no rocks, and there's nothing to topple us. This is foolish talk, Loa'neth," Myoxi said.

"The only foolish talk is that which is unsaid," Gliria said. "And rather than bite my tongue, I will say it—Loa'neth is right. Anchoring will leave us exposed."

"And running aground won't? Waves crashing against the shore. Rocks on the shore," Myoxi said.

"But the shore is solid and shallow. Out here, some creature could swallow the anchor and pull the boat down," Loa'neth said.

Myoxi laughed.

"There are no creatures. All animal life is extinct, except for picocians and humans," Myoxi said.

"What about oysters?" Loa'neth said. "And the mercury fish?"

"Oysters are animals," Gliria added. "Fish too."

"So a mercury fish will eat the anchor for breakfast. Or a giant oyster will clamp down on the boat and pull it under? Let them try!" Myoxi said.

"There is a solution," Loran said. "We can compromise."

"Compromise? How?" Myoxi asked.

"I will guide the boat close to shore and anchor from the bow—close enough to be in shallow water, but not so close as to completely run aground," Loran said. "You, Gliria, and Loa'neth take a rowboat to shore. I will remain behind and watch the boat. Then we will know if running aground will work."

"That's a horrible plan," Myoxi said. "You sound like Gliria now."

"Oh shut up!" Gliria said.

"If something happens, I'll cut the rope so the boat is neither pulled under nor pulled away," Loran explained. "I alone will take the risk. You three will be protected."

"No, I won't let you do this alone," Loa'neth said. "I'm staying with you."

"We should all stay," Gliria said. "As was mentioned—I won't say by whom—a rowboat out here is not much use. We would not make it back to the mainland."

"Hmmm. Very well. How about this—we set anchor right here out in the deep and wait," Loran said.

"Wait for what?" Gliria asked.

"The giant clam," Loran laughed.

"Everyone is a laugh man," Myoxi said. "But at least you are making sense. I'll set the anchor now."

Myoxi loosened the anchor and its rope.

"Stand clear," he shouted as he prepared to throw the anchor overboard.

"Stop! We cannot idly wait out in the deep. There is something else to be done," Loa'neth said.

"Yes, something else," Gliria added.

"What?" Myoxi added.

"Forgive me. I don't know where my manners are today. What is the custom?" Loran asked.

"Of what do you speak?" Myoxi asked. "There's no custom for setting anchor. Nor is there for waiting, as it stands. If you ask me, we should all go to the island now by rowboat, as I've been saying all along."

"Can we do it by sea?" Loran asked.

"Picocians are mortally afraid of water as it is," Gliria said. "We always perform such ceremonies on land."

"Then we must bring her along," Loran said.

"Oh, that!" Myoxi said.

"She has a name! Dara!" Gliria said.

Loa'neth broke into tears and rushed down into the cabin. Loran went after her.

"Why must you be so insensitive?" Gliria asked Myoxi. "No, don't reply."

"I'll guide the boat in. Let's get Dara ready," Loran said to Loa'neth.

Loran guided the boat as he promised—very close to the shore without running it aground. He turned it around so that the stern faced the shore, and then he had Myoxi throw the anchor from the bow.

"Wait, don't place Dara in the rowboat yet," Loran said. "I want to run a rope from the stern to a tree on shore, and I'll use the rowboat to stay dry."

"There should be no delay, Loran," Loa'neth said. "Dara must reach her destination immediately. Gliria—help me load Dara into the rowboat."

Loran looked at Loa'neth in surprise.

"See? It all starts so innocently," Myoxi said. "Then they take over."

"Shut it," Gliria said.

Loran tied one end of rope to the boat's stern. The others agreed to wait in the main boat, except for Loa'neth, who insisted on going with Loran. He reluctantly agreed at first, but after the rowboat was launched with Loa'neth and himself, he realized this was a two person job anyway—one person to row, and the other to dole out rope. Shore came quickly. Loran took off his boots and socks, and he rolled up his pants. He was about to jump into the shallow water with his bare feet, but Loa'neth stopped him.

"Do not step into the water like that," she said. "This island is dangerous, and things may decide to bite your feet."

Loran smiled and agreed to Loa'neth's request. He touched her chin and was about to say something else, but instead he went about the job. He stepped out of the rowboat with boots back on his feet and pulled the rowboat to shore. Loa'neth stepped onto shore and doled out more rope until she reached the tree Loran had mentioned before. Loran pulled the rowboat a little more onto shore and prepared to help Loa'neth secure the rope to the tree, but without warning, something took hold of the main boat's anchor and began pulling the main boat down the shoreline. This in turn pulled Loa'neth's rope, which caught her off guard and pulled her along the beach and toward the water. The rope had wrapped around her right arm and would not let go.

"Help! Help!" she shouted as she attempted to free herself.

Loran ran with all his speed after Loa'neth and the rope, but it was for naught. The main boat was pulled very quickly, with Myoxi and Gliria fighting to cut the rope to the anchor, and Loa'neth being pulled into and under the water. Loran put forth one last burst of speed, but now the boat and picocians had rounded a distant outcropping of shoreline rocks, and they were gone.

The Island of Clamifores

There Loran stood, leaning over and holding his knees. He gasped for air and was completely exhausted. Worse, he had run too hard, and now his calves and upper legs went into full cramp. He fell to the ground and shouted in pain, beating his leg muscles with his fists as hard as he could to release them from absolute contraction. But his muscles would not let go.

"Am I to remain like this in a living *rigor mortis* until the end?" Loran shouted.

The sky darkened quickly, and it began to rain. Then a clap of thunder shook the ground and sent the remaining muscles of Loran into cramp, and he was paralyzed with the most excruciating pain possible. A lightning bolt struck a tree close to Loran, and a step leader bolt lit upward from the sand below Loran and threw him six meters into the air. The shock ended his cramps, but now his nervous system was overloaded, and he landed with a painless but paralyzed body. Only his hearing and vision still worked.

He was now facing the rowboat. Another bolt hit another tree, and another step leader thrust upward from the sand, but it went through the rowboat and animated Dara. Loran was shocked by what he saw—a dead person in full movement and dance. Dara was dancing as if in some voodoo trance. But she was not alone. Pits opened along the beach where additional step leaders ascended, and with them were other dead humanoid creatures —many in various states of decomposition—and some with multiple heads. They danced along in a line, and the ones fully decomposed (i.e. the raw skeletons) were now clanking their limbs against their rib cages, creating a mixture of quasi-xylophonic music and crowing.

Now a step leader shocked Loran upright, and his muscles were forced into the same dance as the others. It was a haunting music, and a haunting dance, and Loran had lost complete control. His last thoughts were that he would die of exhaustion and heart failure. He tried in vain to break free of the electrical control, but it was useless. And as quickly as the animated dead had arrived, they descended back into their pits. So did Dara. And to Loran's surprise, he did too.

Loran's vision was blackened out. Then he thought he saw flashing. Not like the bolts of lightning or the step leaders, more like a flickering of light from bluish-white to black and back—several times a second. The flickering shrank his entire vision to a narrow, central point until it disappeared altogether.

He coughed. And gagged. The air was heavy and stifling, like breathing into a bag for too long. Loran tried to get air, but the air was bad.

"My pack," he tried to say, but there was no good air with which to speak.

On all fours, he crawled through the dark, looking for his pack, which he knew was with him when he fell but now was no longer on his back. He did find it, fortunately, and he quickly pulled out his glow stick to see. Then he retrieved the Pneuminair and placed a drop in his mouth. His lungs dilated but could only inhale more of the bad air. Loran coughed harder, and his chest was seizing from the strain. He pulled out a small container, opened it, and popped a lozenge in his mouth. Immediately, Loran could breathe.

"I didn't think I would need these," he said, now that his gagging fits had ended. He looked at the container to confirm he had taken the correct lozenge, and the label read: "Lozox – Air Sweets when Air Reeks".

"You are Loran Laculic," said a choir of voices.

"Hello? Who are you?" Loran asked.

The voices laughed.

"There are many here, of many kinds," said the voices.

Loran held his glow stick in the air, and he could see figures at the edge of its light. Many figures. They had encircled him, and so there was no way of escape without going through them.

"Who...who are you?" he asked.

"We are the many," said the voices.

Then lights shone from the eyes of the figures. Now Loran could see that there were hundreds of figures—all about the same height as Loran. A few were shorter.

"Do I frighten you?" the voices asked.

"I? But there are hundreds of you," Loran said.

"There is no proper word in your language for me. Or us," the voices said.

"Me or us? You speak as one but are many. Do you have a name?" Loran asked.

The voices were silent.

"A name. My name is Loran. What is your name?" he asked.

"Meorus," the voices said.

"What?" Loran asked.

"You asked if I had a name. I do not. But now you have given me a name. I accept it," the voices said.

"I did?" Loran asked.

"Yes. Meorus," the voices said.

"I...that was more a question than a name," Loran said.

"But I am a question, or perhaps I am between the question and the answer, for I am between good and bad, light and dark, and I take all that is of help and harm and coalesce such into sentience and thought. Your glow stick is unnecessary. Lights from many shall guide you," the voices said.

Suddenly, giant clam shells lit up the great hall. They were situated in the back—behind the hundreds of humanoid figures—and many were on ledges and shelves such that Loran felt as if he and the figures were on stage for an audience of clams. Their shells were open, and each clam had a light of some color coming out of its "throat". But more interesting was that each clam had a set of "teeth". These were in fact crystalline stalactites and stalagmites. They had a twinkling of light, with lights of many colors and direction pouring out. But generally speaking, the stalactites had colors of red, orange, and yellow while the stalagmites had colors of violet, blue, and green.

Then Loran looked again, and in one particular direction was a single gigantic clam far larger than any of the others. It too had crystalline stalactites and stalagmites for teeth, but Loran looked more intently and wasn't sure, and he thought he could make out images on the "teeth", as if each tooth were a porthole to the action of another time and place. Loran retrieved a spyglass from his pack and looked at the teeth.

Loran was right. Each tooth *did* show moving images from another time and place. Loran looked and saw animals of old—fighting and consuming one another in the most vicious fashion. He also saw humans of old attacking other humans with weapons and tools of their own make. Then he noticed a pattern. The stalactites showed the creatures in a mode of desire and hunt, and the stalagmites showed the creatures in the final moments of action—the killing of foe or consumption of meat or other such moment of satiation.

"Lights from many shall guide me? Guide me to what? Insanity?" Loran asked. "Such hatred and violence. How can a man be guided by that? These... these images...are all of great disgust and despair. Why show them? Why show them at all? You are all safe down here in this place of protection. And you show these images? Why? Do you feed on them? Are you predators too?"

Then a figure approached Loran. It was Dara, and she had grown.

"Dara!" Loran exclaimed. "You're alive! But you are nearly as tall as me."

"I am neither alive nor dead," Dara said in unison with the voices.

"But...I know this person. Her name is Dara. Release her!" Loran said.

"Your name is Loran," Dara said without the other voices speaking.

"Dara! What happened? Why do your eyes glow?"

"I am not Dara," Dara said. "The other voices I have stopped so as to ease your disquiet. But I am all that is in this place."

"Then you...I'm speaking to the keeper of this place, is that right?" Loran asked.

"Keeper? You give me yet another name? I'm Meorus," Dara said. "I am not a keeper. I am this place. All that is here is me, except for you, Loran Laculic."

"You know my last name?" Loran asked.

"Yes. I learned about you when Dara became a part of me. I also read much of your mind during the Conclusion process. You were not absorbed fully, but Dara was, as were the other organisms on the beach at that time," Dara said.

"The other organisms? Oh no! Loa'neth and the other picocians—Gliria and Myoxi! Are they here too? Did you kill them?" Loran asked with agitation in his voice.

"Relax, Loran," Dara said. "How easily you humans change focus. First you call me a predator. Now a killer. Any other accusations?"

"I cannot comprehend all of this. You...this place...all of it...I don't know what to think," Loran said. "I wish I were back in my home smoking a pipe and reading mail from Lillianina, with Loa'neth and Gliria and Myoxi there. Dara too, but that seems impossible now."

"Dara's body cannot leave this place. All that keeps this body from dispersing in the wind is here," Dara said. "I think it is time you experience the salts for yourself."

"Salts? Now you mean to poison me?" Loran asked.

"Rest easy," Dara said. "Look!"

The large clam glowed and acquired an aura which closed in on itself and became a large, glowing cloud. The cloud showed an image of Loran—first calm but then becoming agitated. The image of Loran paced and moved nervously, and it became thin and gnarly like an old oak tree. A fine white dust gathered on its skin, which by now looked more like bark. The image of Loran withdrew a pipe, filled it with tobacco, lit it, and smoked it. The tree-like features disappeared, returning the image of Loran to a settled, relaxed person. Then the white dust fell off the image of Loran and disappeared into the ground.

"That white stuff. What was it?" Loran asked.

"Ethereal salt," Dara said. "When you feel satisfied after a consumptive event, you lose a bit of ethereal salt and a bit of control. Ethereal salt gives you control. The bit you lose travels through the ether until it reaches this place. All such *clamifores* are—"

"*Clamifores*?" Loran asked.

"You call them clams," Dara said. "All such clamifores filter these outside events to retrieve the ethereal salt. New clamifores are made with the salt, but much of the salt is stored. I hope someday to restore order to the world, given enough ethereal salt. Perhaps life will not be so consumptive of one another and will work toward noble gains."

"You filter bad events?" Loran said.

"Yes," Dara said. "If we did not, such events would persist into the future. Think, Loran. When something bad happened to you, it bothered you still after the event. But then you slept on the matter and felt better in the morning."

"That's true," Loran said.

"Because we filter bad events," Dara said.

"Then...I...was wrong about you. I am sorry for what I have said."

"No harm has come to me by your words," Dara said. "And I have lost nothing. But you have. Look!"

The prior image of Loran was replaced by the Loran of here and now, standing next to Dara. It showed him apologizing to Dara and losing a bit of ethereal salt.

"I don't feel like I've lost anything," Loran said.

"That's the insidious part," Dara said. "Control is lost little by little until you are controlled by outside forces."

"Then I shouldn't apologize?"

"Once you felt remorse, it was too late," Dara said. "The ethereal salt had already formed. It would be lost one way or another, whether by your apology or by some force manipulating you to its advantage."

"Manipulation! Now that's something I didn't consider. Wait. Are you sure you are only filtering bad events? You said some of your clams use—"

"Clamifores," Dara corrected.

"Sorry, clamifores. Some of your—" Loran started, but he looked at the screen and noticed he had lost a little more ethereal salt. "Some of...I'm going to run out of ethereal salt at this rate. And you clamifores will grow and grow. Isn't that manipulation?"

"I do not trick life forms into yielding ethereal salt. They do so from other forces," Dara said. "But I *could* arrange such an event, to test your resolve. In fact, it would answer one of your questions."

"Loa'neth!" Loran shouted. "What have you done to her?"

Now Loran wasn't speaking to Dara. He was shouting at the giant clam. The other clams rumbled a bit as if stoking a desire to feed off of Loran's ethereal salt. The humanoids all spoke, including Dara.

"Behold your great downfall," the voices said.

The screen showed Gliria and Myoxi in the boat searching desperately for Loa'neth, calling and navigating the boat about. Then the screen changed view and showed a lifeless, silver-skinned Loa'neth, floating face-down in the water with nothing around.

"Loa'neth!" Loran shouted. "Drowned? But she has oxygen stores. How—"

"A wild clamifore consumed the anchor and dragged the boat around the island," the voices said. "Loa'neth was caught in the rope and dragged through the water. She over-exerted herself to survive and depleted her oxygen, until..."

"Until? Until what? Tell me!" Loran demanded.

The screen now split into two views—that of Loa'neth floating in the water, and that of Loran with ethereal salt dust forming over his skin. The clams rumbled again as if wanting more antagonism thrust upon Loran.

"Until she was dragged into a rock and knocked unconscious," the voices said.

"Then I can still save her! You must let me save her! I demand it! Now!" Loran shouted.

The screen image of Loran showed heavy ethereal salt crystallization forming around his skin. The clams had never experienced such close proximity to ripening ethereal salt and began moving their shells up and down as if readying for consumption. Dara began to wave her hand toward one side of the hall, but she stopped herself. She tried to wave her hand again, but again—she stopped. The screen's view of Loran drifted about the hall and showed various other humanoids, but now it focused on the smaller clams that were closer to Loran and showed that they were becoming covered with excess ethereal salt that had built up on Loran and was floating in the air, landing on their shells and teasing them with the promise of more to come.

Another humanoid stepped toward Loran and Dara—one with three heads and bark-like skin. It then spoke for the group.

"Behold," the creature said.

A lit stairway opened up along one wall of the hall. At the top was an opening to the outside, and sunlight shone inward.

"The stairs lead to the outside, where you will find Loa'neth washing ashore," the creature said.

Loran looked at the stairs. Then he looked at the screen again. Loa'neth was indeed washing up on shore. And Loran was now dripping with ethereal salt.

"You will go to her and try to revive her. If she lives, you will be relieved. If she dies, you will despair. Either way, you will release massive amounts of ethereal salt and feed my clamifores!" the creature said.

Loran started to run for the stairs, but then he stopped himself. He turned back and spoke:

"And what will become of me? Will I lose all control and sanity? Is my quest to save Lillianina also lost? Is it?!" he shouted.

"Save Loa'neth!" the creature commanded.

Then Loran realized that Dara was not reacting in unison with the others. And this creature was the main spokesperson now, not Dara. Loran rushed back to Dara and pleaded with her.

"You have to help me. You're Dara now, aren't you?" Loran asked.

"No, Loran, I am Meorus," Dara said.

"You must help me," he said.

"I cannot. I would need the desire to help you, and such desire would deplete me of ethereal salt. I would perish," Dara said.

"You are not part of them!" Loran said. "You're not!"

"Loa'neth is alive, but only barely," the creature said. "She will surely die if you do nothing."

"I can't let her die," Loran said to Dara. "And it will rob me of ethereal salt."

"And all that you have left, too," Dara said.

"Help me," Loran said.

"I...cannot," Dara said, and she walked away.

Loran's nerves twitched and forced him into the shakes. Clams began moving toward him. He looked at the main screen, and now it was dark. Instead, smaller clams showed that Loran was dripping more ethereal salt. These clams could not wait for Loran's rescue of Loa'neth. They moved toward him to consume what ethereal salt had already fallen.

"I can't stand it anymore. Loa'neth! Hold onto life! I'll be there soon!" Loran shouted.

He ran toward the stairs, up them, and then paused at the top. He heard a great clashing, like that of stone being toppled. He turned around and looked. Clams had converged on his trail to consume dropped ethereal salt, but the clams had not caused the noise. It had come from the giant clam. But all was dark in that direction, and Loa'neth's life was at stake, so Loran left the clams behind, ran into the open air, down to the beach, and to the shore where he found Loa'neth with full human size. The waves had been rolling her along the beach, and her hair and skin were covered in sand. He kneeled, turned her over, and held her head on his lap.

"Loa'neth! I'm here! I'll give you some Pneuminair. It's in my pack right...right..."

But the pack was no longer on Loran. It had not passed with him through the portal from the clam world to the beach. Nor did much of his clothing, which had been reduced to a tank top and shorts with no socks or boots.

"My medicines are gone! Gone! Loa'neth!" Loran shouted.

Then he thought of the vial of cuttleberry gin. He pulled out the necklace from his shirt, but the vial had been broken and emptied by the vine in the Blackpier jail cell, and he sighed upon remembering this fact.

Loran held Loa'neth up higher now—against his heart—and he hugged her, trying to remember an ancient text he had read on how to resuscitate drowning victims.

"Please! Remember!" he pleaded.

He did. He stood up and pulled her up with him. Then he turned her around and performed the Heimlich maneuver to force water out of her lungs. Water came out, but she did not breathe. Now, he had to get her heart and lungs working. He pulled her away from the water and released her to the beach on her back—slowly. Next, he knelt over her and prepared to blow air into her lungs.

"Stop!" yelled a voice now running toward him.

"Dara!" Loran said. "I can't stop! She'll die!"

"And you'll lose all your ethereal salt!" Dara said.

"There's no way to stop it!" Loran said.

"There is!" Dara said. "Are you prepared to die?"

"What?!"

"You must die to avoid losing your ethereal salt!" she said.

"That...can't be true," Loran said.

"If you value all that you know and cherish, you will trust me this one time and do as I say," Dara said. "I can save Loa'neth. But you must be ready to die for her life. Will you give up your life for hers?"

Loran stared at Dara, then at Loa'neth, then at Dara.

"What do I have to do?" Loran asked.

"Kneel toward Loa'neth, and hold her such that she is kneeling toward you," Dara said.

Loran did so.

"Hug her with your soul, but do not desire her to live," Dara said. "Be of mind to give up your life for hers. I must stab you."

"I...I...oh please...I...Dara? Dara? Do it quickly!" Loran said.

Dara pulled a stalagmite from a leg and a stalactite from an arm. With the stalactite in one hand and the stalagmite in the other, she opened her arms wide, stood to the side of the two, spoke strange words to the sky, and then brought her arms together and stabbed Loran in the back with the sta-lagmite and Loa'neth in the back with the stalactite—and thus penetrated both hearts. Loran screamed with pain and lurched to the side, but in doing so he pulled Loa'neth with him—not because of his hold on her with his hands, but because the two were skewered together with the stalagmite and stalactite. It was a ghastly scene, and Dara looked to be nothing more than a cruel murderer.

And so the pair fell to the ground, but Dara was not finished. She pulled another stalagmite from her leg and another stalactite from her arm. She held both up in the air, first far apart and then gradually brought them together. As she did so, the winds picked up, and a dark cloud descended. Then Dara touched the points together, and this produced a single bolt of lightning that started from the cloud toward the ground where the three remained. Two step leaders ascended from the ground to meet it—one through Loran and Loa'neth, and the other through Dara. The step leaders then met the lightning bolt above. Dara touched her stalactite/stalagmite pair onto Loran and Loa'neth, and the two step leaders then joined. The two sets of stalactites and stalagmites glowed and shattered into plasma balls, encircling the three and re-sequencing Loran's and Loa'neth's cells before leaving a cloud of smoke behind and ascending into the heavens with the lightning bolt, leaving Loran, Loa'neth, and Dara behind—all whole, without injury, and with no evidence the stalactites and stalagmites had existed.

Dara collapsed in total exhaustion, as if most of her life force had been drained. She struggled to regain her composure and her form, bringing herself up to her knees.

"I...give myself, my power, and my island to you," Dara said, and she collapsed again.

Myoxi and Gliria saw the lightning bolt.

"They are there," Gliria said.

The two made for the beach where the lightning bolt had struck. It took them an hour to reach the spot, but when they did, they found Loran and Loa'neth singing softly and dancing together around a fire they had built, while Dara—still recovering her strength—sat by the fire and warmed her limbs.

South to Slaffton

"Loa'neth and Dara! They're alive! And Loran too!" Gliria exclaimed.

"We have no anchor. And no rowboat," Myoxi said. "This could be—"

"Then run us aground!" Gliria said.

Gliria yanked the controls from Myoxi and steered the boat toward the beach.

"Stop! We'll be stranded!" Myoxi barked.

But Gliria held fast onto the controls and forced the boat onto the beach, where it plowed into and put out the fire. The bow came very close to Dara, but Loran and Loa'neth pulled her to her feet and moved her out of the way in time—and yet without any special fear or concern. It was simply another thing for them to do.

"You almost hit Dara!" Myoxi added.

"This is an emergency! Look at them!" Gliria said.

Indeed. Loa'neth now had streaks of white in her hair. Loran had a streak of white running along his right side from his ear to his foot. And Dara's skin color had changed into that of a rainbow, with reds high up and violets at her feet. Gliria jumped off the boat and ran first toward Loa'neth.

"I'm well," Loa'neth said.

"Why you're as tall as a human now," Gliria said. "And your hair is different. And Loran has a streak down his side."

"I too am well," Loran replied.

"And...Dara! We thought...but you were...what in mountain's name is happening here?" Gliria asked.

Myoxi now jumped onto land and kissed it.

"Land. Land! How I missed you!" he praised.

"Shut up," Gliria said to him.

"It's a bit of a story," Loran said. "But I think we best get going."

"You no longer have desire in your heart," Dara said.

"No, I don't. Saving Lillianina has passed me by. But there is a great evil growing, both in Sathiakia and nearby, and this evil is fed by great desire. It is noble to end this desire and restore noble pursuits to life," Loran said.

Gliria and Myoxi exchanged confused expressions.

"Loa'neth, what's happened to Loran?" Gliria asked.

"He is right, you know," Loa'neth said. "He and I are now one."

"You're married?" Myoxi said.

"And you didn't invite me?" Gliria asked.

"Loa'neth and Loran have passed on from consumptive animals to beings of noble existence," Dara said. "They will have no need to eat or drink or breathe."

"You I understand least of all, Dara," Gliria said. "You were dead. I was sure of it."

"Dara is still dead. I am not she. Her body lives on but only after going through Conclusion. I who speak from this body am from the ethereal salt community down below. I am Meorus, the chief clamifore," Dara said.

"Meorus? The chief what?" Gliria asked.

"I'll explain it on the boat trip down south," Loran said. "Myoxi—prepare to depart."

"How? We've run aground," Myoxi said.

"His faith is weak," Dara said. "Do you remember what I taught you two?"

"Yes," Loran and Loa'neth said at the same time.

Loran and Loa'neth helped Gliria and Myoxi back aboard the sailboat. Then Loran and Loa'neth looked back at Dara, and she nodded.

"Join hands with us, Gliria and Myoxi," Loa'neth said. "Close your eyes, and clear your minds of all desire."

"This is ridiculous. No amount of tom-foolery will save us," Myoxi muttered.

Gliria kicked him in the shin.

"Ow!" he yelled.

"Or more directly, prepare to give up your life and all its pettiness to be noble," Loran said. "Now hum this tone and hold it."

Loa'neth and Loran hummed a tone and kept humming. Gliria was next to hum, and Myoxi followed. Then Dara hummed as well, but her hum was especially loud. She then took a stalactite from her arm and a stalagmite from her leg, touched both to the bow, and the boat began to move back into the water, slowly at first, but then with increasing speed until it had enough inertia to leave the shore and carry into the water.

"We did it!" Gliria said. "You two really have changed!"

"I feel calm. I thought I would need more Enpriosol, but I don't," Myoxi said.

"We have channeled your ethereal salts back into your bodies to give you peace and control," Loa'neth said.

"You speak strangely," Gliria said. "Like on the island."

Loran explained what had happened to him on the island, how he was powerless to prevent Loa'neth from being dragged into the water, the lightning dance with Dara, the great hall underground, the many creatures speaking with one voice, the clams, the ethereal salt, how Dara became Meorus, and how Loa'neth was brought back to life.

"Incredible!" Gliria said.

"We did everything we could," Myoxi said. "Some creature of the deep dragged this boat around. I kept trying to cut the rope, but the boat threw us around, and I couldn't get a good hold of it."

"We knew Loa'neth was caught in her rope and was being dragged, but for the same reasons, we couldn't help her," Gliria explained.

"Then Loa'neth's rope went taunt and the boat was nearly ripped in two," Myoxi continued. "We almost flew over the bow, but we caught the gunwale and pulled ourselves back into the boat."

"But the sudden jerk must have been too much for the creature of the deep, as it suddenly stopped pulling us," Gliria said.

"I pulled up on the rope to retrieve the anchor, but the rope was short and the anchor was gone," Myoxi said.

"While Myoxi was doing that, I tried pulling Loa'neth back into the boat, but her rope was severed, and so I pulled in nothing," Gliria said.

"We backtracked and looked for Loa'neth, but we couldn't find her," Myoxi said. "I swear, we did everything we could. Then the wind and currents worked against us, and we had a devil of a time getting back. By the time we did, we saw the lightning bolt and followed it to the beach where we found you."

"Your efforts are commendable," Loa'neth said. "Have no more desire to think of it. We purpose southward now."

"Southward? To Sathiakia?" Myoxi asked. "They will see us and capture us."

"We'll be their prisoners," Gliria said.

"We will not go to Sathiakia yet," Loran said.

"We must go to Slaffton first," Loa'neth said.

The boat sailed southward, and night set in.

"I am sorry, but we are tired," Gliria said.

"Have no desire to apologize," Loa'neth said. "Loran and I have no need for sleep and will keep watch."

Gliria and Myoxi fell asleep in their cabin. At one point during the night, Myoxi awoke with a start from a bad dream. To help ease his mind so that he would not return to his nightmare, he exited his cabin and looked out on the deck. There he saw Loa'neth retrieving one of the oyster nets and hauling in a number of oysters. But instead of shucking the oysters for their meat, she simply drew her fingers across the outer shells. She then dipped those fingers into a pail of some fluid. She threw the oysters back in the lake, and Myoxi put a hand over his mouth to muffle a cry of loss. Those oysters would have made a good nighttime snack to settle his stomach. But he maintained an even composure and watched as Loa'neth repeated this process several times. Finally, she dipped her fingers in the pail, threw back the last oyster, and then dipped her fingers in the pail again, only to retrieve a glistening shirt of many hues. She gave this shirt to Loran, he accepted it graciously, and then he put it on. The fit was perfect, and he kissed Loa'neth on the cheek in thanks.

"Gliria, Gliria!" Myoxi said as he slipped back into his cabin. "Wake up!"

"Go back to sleep," Gliria said groggily.

"No, really, you must see this!" he said.

"It's nighttime. There's nothing to see," she said while rolling over.

"Please, Gliria!" he said as he shook her.

"All right then!" she said, now perturbed and awake.

The two exited the cabin and went on deck. But neither Loran nor Loa'neth were to be found.

"They were here a moment ago!" Myoxi said. "You should have seen them. Loa'neth was—"

"This is their first night as a couple!" Gliria said. "Give them some peace!"

Gliria returned to her cabin and went to sleep. Myoxi stood there a moment. He looked for the pail of water, but it was gone. No oysters, and no evidence that they had been retrieved from the water.

"But they were here!" Myoxi said. "They were! And Loa'neth...she...was throwing this net in the water like this. And she pulled the net up like this. And there was...was...no, not this. But what is this?"

Instead of pulling up an oyster in the net, Myoxi pulled up a yellowish seaweed-like goo.

"What is this?" he wondered.

Myoxi touched the goo, and his hand and forearm broke out into a terrible rash, as if he'd touched the most toxic poison ivy in existence. He threw the goo and the net into the lake, and that was the end of it for that evening. He returned to his cabin and searched through his pack for medicine to treat the rash. In doing so, several bottles clacked together.

"What's all that noise you're making?" Gliria asked.

"I'm looking for medicine," Myoxi said.

"Medicine for what?" Gliria asked.

Gliria lit a candle and moved its accompanying holder toward Myoxi to get a look at him. His rash had now become blisters and boils, and he winced in pain.

"What on this planet have you done?" Gliria said as she put the candle holder down.

"Yellow seaweed did this," Myoxi said. "From the lake. I've never touched anything like it."

"Well be sure you never do again. Fortunately I have some sample drops from Loran's medicine box before he lost his pack," Gliria said as she looked through her own pack of small medicine bottles.

She had copied the labels from Loran's medicine bottles, and then she found it, "Soomadeen – When Skin is Green, Make it Clean." Gliria took the bottle and shook drops from it onto Myoxi's arm and hand. Immediately, the blisters and boils shrank into a rash which then dissolved away, restoring Myoxi's skin to its natural tone.

"Good thing you stole those medicines from Loran," Myoxi said.

"Salvaged, Myoxi, salvaged," Gliria said. "Now stay out of that water and go to sleep. Or do I need to give you some Ethaloid?"

"You snitched that too?" Myoxi said.

"Salvaged."

"Salvaged, yes. I'll try to remember that," Myoxi said.

"Good night, Myoxi."

"Good night, Gliria."

The King and Queen Arrive

Myoxi and Gliria awoke the next morning to sunshine pouring into their cabin. They freshened up and then went up to the deck to see about breakfast. To their surprise, Loran's and Loa'neth's attires had changed.

"Loran!" Myoxi said. "You're dressed like a king. With crown and all."

"Loa'neth too!" Gliria said. "She's like a queen. See how her gems sparkle in the sunlight? But where did you get such exquisite jewelry? I wouldn't mind having a bracelet or necklace myself."

"They are sallerites from the lake," Loa'neth said. "And to answer your next question, sallerites are ethereal salts stored in salt crystals. Not sodium chloride salt like you would put on your food—the other ionic salts—such as calcium carbonate found in oyster shells. And there are many others."

"I was right then! See Gliria? They harvested oysters for their precious materials," Myoxi said.

"You saw us in the early stages of our transformation," Loa'neth said. "The water contains many ethereal salts but only a portion have we taken from the oysters. And we have used such to create our noble clothing. See how it glitters?"

"Marvelous!" Gliria said.

"Look in the water! The yellow stuff!" Myoxi shouted.

"Yes, do not touch the water," Loa'neth said. "It is contaminated with parasites of menace."

"I don't remember the water being so filled with such filth," Myoxi said. "The lake has always been clean."

"Much has changed," Loa'neth said. "We have fully passed through the interface where the runoff pollution from the north meets the affected life forms of the south—creating, among other things, deviant plants."

"These deviant plants...it's pelapine, isn't it?" Gliria said. "Did I not warn you? But that was just the river. I didn't know it had entered the lake and created such bad-smelling seaweed."

"It is not seaweed. It is *eldebrecken*," Loa'neth said. "And yes, pelapine is a part of the problem, but eldebrecken feeds on more than that."

"Such a lovely name for a foul plant," Myoxi said.

"It is neither plant nor animal, but a twisted desire of both," Loa'neth said. "Myoxi—your hand and arm. Let me see."

Myoxi showed Loa'neth his arm. It had no evidence of rash or blister from the night, yet Loa'neth could see something.

"I touched that...stuff...what did you call it? Eldebrecken. I pulled some up in a net and touched it last night. Then I broke out in a rash and blisters," Myoxi said. "But I'm over it."

"Whatever you used to treat it did not purge it clear but instead put the parasite to sleep. Allow me to finish," Loa'neth said.

Loa'neth hummed a tune and drew her hand across Myoxi's arm. His arm went from plain and smooth to being peppered with glow spots. Loa'neth then smoothed her hand across those spots, and they moved! Like insects being shown the insecticide, the spots made a mad rush through Myoxi's wrist, into his hand, and out his fingertips. Dragonflies emerged and flew away. Myoxi's hand jerked back as if being shocked, then he relaxed.

"They are purged clear," Loa'neth said. "You used an alkaloid-based medicine on your arm, didn't you?"

"It was Soomadeen," Gliria said. "A leftover."

Loran shot Gliria a funny stare.

"I borrowed some?" Gliria restated.

"What other medicines of mine are *leftover*?" Loran asked.

"Lots!" Myoxi offered, to which Gliria kicked him.

"It is as Meorus warned," Loa'neth said. "The medicines and treatments used by the many have created these menaces to the south. First the sunderag vine, then this eldebrecken. They are known as *pharmapetties*, and they are driven by pharmacological appetite. They will continue to grow, acting as hatcheries for nasty things, until the dumping of such chemicals stops."

"I've never given thought to the consequences of using my medicines," Loran said. "Now I understand. Even with conservation, a pharmapetty will feed from the runoff and come after us for more, in whatever guise it chooses."

"When Loran passed from the clamifore kingdom to the here and now, all that contributed to the appetite of pharmapetties was stripped of him," Loa'neth said. "It is not an accident. He became noble, and so he has no desire nor purpose for such arts."

"Then we should be rid of these," Myoxi said, reaching for Gliria's medicine box.

Gliria resisted and shoved Myoxi back.

"That will do no good," Loran said. "They have already been created. Whether you use them up slowly in application or dump them into the lake now, the pharmapetties will feed on them. And if you *should* dump them into the lake, we would see such an uprising that would overturn our boat and cause us to sink. No, there are more noble arts for such a task. Hold onto them for now, but be aware of their consequential use."

And so, Loran navigated the boat through thickening eldebrecken. The four entered a fog, and so progress was slowed, but then out of the fog appeared floating timbers, planks, and wooden boxes.

"Something broke apart here," Myoxi said. "Could be rocks. We should be cautious."

"Good advice," Loran said.

But the debris became thicker, and the boat's progress slowed. Then Gliria noticed masts standing out of the water, along with sails and ropes.

"The ropes will tangle us if we are not careful," Gliria said.

"I anticipated this," Loa'neth said. "We have reached the ships of abandon. Many sailed down this way under false direction and gave up their boats for other pursuits."

"What other pursuits?" Myoxi asked.

"We should be close to Slaffton," Loa'neth said. "That is where we will find the answer to your question, Myoxi."

"There are too many abandoned boats in the way to reach the main docks," Myoxi said.

"We shall enlist the help of the eldebrecken," Loa'neth said.

Loa'neth opened the right half of her royal blazer and revealed a short scepter hidden along her side. She removed the scepter from a little holster and then pulled the ends to make it longer. It was a telescoping scepter! She dipped the head of the scepter into the water and spoke these words:

Scepter of sallerite
Send crystals near,
Use all your might
And make path clear.

Glowing orange salt crystals dispersed outward from the scepter's head and mixed with the nearby eldebrecken. The eldebrecken glowed and wiggled like snakes and then entangled themselves around the abandoned boats and debris and pulled them aside for Loran's and Loa'neth's boat to pass.

"They really *have* changed, haven't they, Gliria?" Myoxi said. "They have such powers. Think about the things they could do for us!"

"Do not think of such things," Loa'neth said. "You will only lose ethereal salt. And you will need as much as you can spare to get through Slaffton."

"What exactly is the plan for Slaffton?" Myoxi said. "I'm guessing you and Loran are going to portray yourselves as visiting royalty."

"Which places you and Gliria as our royal advisers," Loran said.

"We don't look the part," Myoxi said.

"For once I agree with Myoxi," Gliria said. "It doesn't happen often. But this time, I agree."

Loa'neth walked over to Myoxi and Gliria.

"Now hold hands," Loa'neth said.

The couple held hands in nervous expectation. Loa'neth tapped the scepter on Gliria's head and Myoxi's head and then said:

From head to toe
Be trim and flat
With Gliria a bow
And Myoxi a hat,
Spin clothing fine
From crystal salt
But better than brine
And having no fault.

Gliria's and Myoxi's clothing changed. They now looked like picocians of nobility. Gliria had a blazer much like Loa'neth's, and she opened the right side to reveal a slim and straight trumpet. It could be used for playing music or as a megaphone.

"You shall be the royal herald, to announce our arrival both in music and in speech," Loa'neth said.

"Thank you," Gliria said.

Myoxi placed a hand in his pocket and removed a little laughing skull.

"What is that?" Myoxi asked.

"It's obvious you're the court fool," Gliria laughed.

"Myoxi will be the court jester," Loa'neth said, "to relax those who may feel hateful. Now on your left side you each will find mini scepters, similar to mine. These you may use for making small tools and things."

"They can also be used for self defense," Loran said.

Gliria and Myoxi smiled in amazement as they inspected their mini scepters. Myoxi used his to make a crystalline pocketwatch, while Gliria changed the color of her hair.

"There is only a limited charge in your scepters. Use them wisely," Loa'neth said. "They can be recharged, but only if we are on the lake."

"Also, Dara can recharge them, but I don't think we will see her for quite a while," Loran said.

"So why these uniforms?" Myoxi asked.

"These are just formalities for entering Slaffton," Loran said. "We must play the part of nobility to awe the public."

"And to discover those who seek the greatest amount of power," Loa'neth said.

"They will be drawn to us and seek to acquire our wealth and power," Loran said.

"We must play along with this up to a point," Loa'neth said.

"What point, I wonder?" Gliria asked.

"Until they lead us to the evil forces in Sathiakia," Loran said. "Then we must use all our resources to overpower those forces."

"We sense that the corruption that has been working its way northward is because of these forces," Loa'neth said. "Our sallerite scepters will offer us protection for a while, and they will be used extensively before the end. But follow our lead, whatever may happen."

"We will," Gliria said.

"One last thing," Loa'neth said, and she touched her scepter to the boat and spoke:

> *Scepter of sallerite*
> *Spare crystals not,*
> *Transform this boat*
> *Into royal yacht.*

The four heard creaking and groaning timbers as salt crystals poured from Loa'neth's scepter and reshaped the boat into a yacht. The sails disappeared, and the yacht now gave off steam.

"We will no longer rely on the wind for propulsion," Loran said. "This yacht is self powered."

And so it was. Special salt crystals provided heat, and water drawn from the lake was converted to steam to drive a steam engine, which then drove a propeller. Loran navigated the ship through the path created by the eldebrecken. After a time, a port appeared out of the fog, but the port was filled with dragonflies. Loa'neth held up her scepter, and a shield protected the group from such insects.

"This is it," Loran said. "Slaffton."

The yacht passed by the breakwater wall then entered the marina where the water was protected from waves. Amazingly, the marina had no other boats docked, except for one, which was painted in bright green and labeled.

"Master One," Gliria said, reading the name of the green boat. "We should name our own ship."

"I shall call it, the *Mara Brilla*," Loa'neth said. "To shine in the sea."

"Look, the dock posts are covered in leaves," Gliria said.

"They looked like short trees," Myoxi said.

"I've never seen trees like that. Or shrubs," Gliria said.

The Mara Brilla pulled into one of the docking ports, and to the surprise of the four, one of the "shrubs" walked toward them.

"It's moving!" Gliria said.

"Gliria, please announce our arrival," Loa'neth said.

"To that?" Gliria asked.

Gliria looked closely and saw legs, arms, and eyes on the approaching "shrub". She removed the trumpet from its holster and put it to her lips. Then she played a few notes to call for attention.

"Make way, make way for King Loran and Queen Loa'neth of..." Gliria started, but she realized she didn't know where to say the two were from, and she looked at Loa'neth, Loran, and back at Loa'neth, then she seemed to hear a voice whisper a word, which she repeated as, "Clamiforia."

Instead of hearing the common language in reply, the four heard clicking, popping, and flapping. Myoxi unrolled a red carpet onto the dock, and Gliria played her trumpet. Loran and Loa'neth then stepped onto the red carpet together. Loran waved and Loa'neth nodded. The "shrubs" stood along both sides of the carpet and watched. More "shrubs" rushed from the shore to watch. Myoxi threw out more and more red carpet until there was a continuous path from the dock to shore. Loran and Loa'neth walked the full length amongst much clicking, flapping, and clacking of the "shrubs"—what the foursome considered applause. Gliria continued playing the trumpet, and Myoxi juggled several skulls. Loa'neth's shield continued to protect the group from dragonflies.

When Loran and Loa'neth reached the end of the carpet, they were swarmed by "shrubs" who wished to touch the king and queen in hopes of receiving noble blessings. But then a much taller humanoid shape with fewer leaves and more human-like features approached with several assistants. The humanoid waved a wand of his own, and the dragonflies dispersed.

"I am King Loran, and this is Queen Loa'neth. We wish to see the Master of Slaffton," Loran said.

"I am First Guard of Slaffton. The Master is very busy and sees no one without an appointment," the human-like shape said. "You may wait in Slaffton for a week, and I will see then if he has time for you."

"I could use a week of vacation," Myoxi said. "Land o land—what kinds of places do you have for picocians?"

Myoxi started walking onto shore, but First Guard stopped him.

"Wait! By order of the Master of Slaffton, no one shall enter without an invasive-insect inspection. You could be carrying dragonflies or other such unapproved parasites. Observe."

First Guard pointed to one assistant, who revealed and opened a small box. Inside was an insect that no one in the royal group had seen before. It was long and very flat with many short legs, and it could roll its body longwise and writhe like a worm, or it could fold itself in half and lengthen a few legs to mimic a butterfly. The assistant placed the insect on another assistant. The insect mimicked one of the many green leaves on the second assistant. Then it disappeared from among the leaves and entered the assistant's body. The leaves on his skin wilted and thinned, making the assistant's skin more visible. The invasive insect was then seen burrowing under the assistant's skin, with the occasional leg sticking through the skin like a periscope or snorkel, as if to see where to go to get air.

"Your servants shall be inspected next," First Guard said as he motioned toward his first assistant to put a second insect on Gliria.

"We are here on a mission of peace and wish to speak with the Master of Slaffton," Loa'neth said, blocking the assistant with her scepter. "We are royalty and have our own means."

"To refuse the search is not permitted," First Guard said. "All are searched. It is policy. None may refuse."

"I refuse," Gliria said, and she took her trumpet and blasted the insects into bits of dust.

The "shrubs" gasped.

"You defy the invasive search, and now you have destroyed the sacred inspection beetle. This is high treason!" First Guard said. "You must be arrested and brought before the Master without delay!"

First Guard motioned to his assistants, who in turn drew their spears and pointed them at the noble four.

"That's a sharp point," Myoxi said as a spear poked him in the back.

Gliria played her trumpet to announce the arrest, but then a spear was jabbed in her side to stop her playing. She was about to retaliate when Loa'neth looked at her and said "no" with a facial expression. Then Loran and Loa'neth sent their thoughts to Gliria and Myoxi that this was a quicker way of visiting the Master than waiting a week.

"Oh, so soon? I had hoped to have some young shrub fan me and serve me food and drink," Myoxi lamented.

The four were escorted through the streets of Slaffton. Many of the "shrubs" stopped to look and even bow, but many more continued their errands—tending to the needs of the plants and vine gardens, servicing smokehouses, servicing bathhouses, and providing transportation—all in the name of serving plants and the elite humanoids.

"I think these must be the missing children from Millfork," Gliria said.

"They are," Loa'neth said through thought. "They were enticed by the intoxicating aroma of the plant and enslaved to cultivate the plant and produce harvest for the elite of this town. Their wills have been broken down, and they have no power to resist nor escape."

"Braegan said they went to Sathiakia," Loran said. "Evidently, the reach of Sathiakia has expanded to include Slaffton."

Then the four passed a church with columns made of intertwined shrub vines. A couple had just been married and had exited the church door.

"Look!" Gliria said. "The...I think the groom...is not human!"

"Same-species marriage is illegal in Slaffton," First Guard said. "Only marriage between animal and plant is allowed. It's the natural way of the world since the beginning."

The four continued to walk, and there was (after a few buildings down the way) a building with luring sounds and flashing lights. Myoxi broke away from the guards and rushed into the building, but the guards ran after him and brought him out.

"That is a building of bad desire," First Guard said.

"I...saw...plants...on tables...bending and moving in the air...with fans blowing the air on them to move them in different directions. And humanoids were watching and cheering the plants on. I couldn't believe it."

"We have been trying to shut those venues down for a long time," First Guard said. "But the plants claim the right of freedom of expression, and so they stay open. The plants are always right."

The four continued until they reached a stone building—the only stone building in the town. It was a temple, and it was adorned with statues bearing flowing water or burning oil. The statues, instead of being representations of animals or humanoids, were representations of plants. Stairs led everywhere in the temple, and the four were led up one such flight of stairs until they reached a long, dimly-lit hallway with columns on both sides. At the end of the hallway was a light shining down from the ceiling onto something sparkly.

"It is a long walk through the hallway," First Guard said.

"Then we shall give you comfort," Loa'neth said.

Loa'neth waved her scepter, and a cloud of multicolored salt formed a thin sheet at the entourage's feet and carried them in solid form down the hallway. The group felt they were on a moving sidewalk, and some of First Guard's men sat on the cloud. First Guard himself nearly sat down, but the cloud approached the light at the end of the hallway, and it was now clear what was at the light—the Master of Slaffton in one chair, and a shrub in another. First Guard straightened himself and his men so as to appear in charge, but it was too late for that—the Master of Slaffton saw them float down the hallway, and so he knew this was no ordinary visit.

"Cloud, dissipate!" Loa'neth said as the group arrived at the Master's throne.

"Master of Slaffton and Supreme Queffil Stilillick," First Guard said to Master and his plant wife, "these outlanders have docked their ship and entered our town while refusing to undergo inspection."

"Indeed," Master said while standing. "And who might you be?"

Gliria then announced the group with her trumpet, "Make way for King Loran and Queen Loa'neth of Clamiforia, Myoxi the Jester and me, Gliria the Herald."

"You have defied the laws of our town," Master said. "And you have shown power beyond our ability to understand. Therefore I name you hostile and a threat to our well-being. You must be executed at once."

But the threat was empty. Gliria raised her trumpet to blast the Master, but Loa'neth raised her scepter and requested that Gliria back down (which Gliria did). Loa'neth then whispered softly, and Supreme Queffil Stilillick quivered and waved her branches gently.

"They are up to no good, Master," First Guard said. "They mean to bewitch us. See how they attack Supreme Queffil?"

Supreme Queffil Stilillick bloomed with flowers and cooed with satisfaction. Supreme Queffil then cozied up to Master.

"She is blooming," Master said. "My sweet wife is blooming! Why, this is not an attack. It is a gift. What other gifts do you bring? We must celebrate this good fortune. Come! I shall declare today as Clamiforia Celebration Day! We shall have the finest entertainment, and you shall enjoy all the amenities of Slaffton!"

Loa'neth waved her scepter, and the floating cloud returned and carried the noble four, Master, Supreme Queffil Stilillick, and First Guard with his assistants. They left the temple and proceeded down the main street. The residents all cheered the Master and Supreme Queffil along with Loran and Loa'neth. The group reached a collection of short and slender trees circling a large tar pit.

"Halt," Master said.

Loa'neth dissolved the floating cloud, and the group stood on solid ground.

"People of Slaffton," Master said. "We have before us the most noble folk of Clamiforia—King Loran, Queen Loa'neth, Jester Myoxi, and Herald Gliria."

Clicking and clacking for applause from the residents. The tar pit, which was at first smooth and flat, now undulated with gentle waves as if it were a pond stirred by the wind. Citizens of Slaffton played music and danced around Master and the noble group, and some danced onto the tar pit. They stepped as if the pit were solid and clean, and they were not impeded or slowed by any stickiness, as the pit appeared to have none.

"My Master and Supreme Queffil," First Guard said, "Prime Kylalac of Slaffton has a prize for you."

A pine tree-like creature hobbled forward, leading four other pine tree-like creatures who carried a cage with two young people inside who had not yet been covered with leaves.

"Stephen Royer and Claire Stackhart," Loran said in thought to the others. "From the fliers in Millfork."

"What is a *kylalac*?" Myoxi asked.

All went silent, and a grim expression crossed Master's face.

"Jester Myoxi makes a joke," Loran said. "We are honored to meet your friendly citizens of the city."

Then Loa'neth placed thoughts in Gliria's and Myoxi's minds, that *queffil* was the name for a female plant, and *kylalac* was the name for a male plant, and so a humanoid woman married a kylalac, and a humanoid man married a queffil. The topmost queffil (female plant) in social standing was Supreme Queffil Stilillick, and Prime Kylalac was the topmost male plant.

"And what is Jester Myoxi? A little man with skulls to juggle!" Myoxi said as he performed such a feat.

The silence broke out into laughter, and the singing and dancing resumed. But the four nobles were not celebrating. They knew something horrible was about to happen, and their lives could depend on keeping their composure.

"Two escaped slaves," First Guard said, continuing about the prisoners in the cage. "They were found on our northern borders, attempting to poison the water supply."

"We only wish to find and cure our people," said Stephen. "They have been drugged and changed into these leafy shapes."

"Cure *your* people?" Master asked with a stern voice.

"See here, they have forbidden items in their possession," quivered Supreme Queffil as she sent out runner vines and removed a cuttlefish bone each, oyster powder, and a vial of blue fluid.

"That's medicine!" said Claire.

Then Supreme Queffil threw the items in the tar pit, and they burst into flames and formed the images of clean-shaven, upstanding human men of the highest dignity and class. The citizens of Slaffton clashed their limbs and jeered as best they could.

"Atrocities." "Evil invaders." "Destroyers and thugs from abroad."

These were only a few of the things yelled in the air. Master held his hand up, and the citizens lowered their voices to a strained growl.

"They should be put to death. The charge—biotoxicacity," First Guard said.

The citizens agreed.

Gliria and Myoxi exchanged nervous glances while Loran and Loa'neth held a steady gaze.

"Royals of Clamiforia, what is your opinion?" Master asked.

"Have the full charges been brought forth? Has guilt been determined?" Loa'neth started.

"Both have been, yes," Master said.

"Then punishment must be to undo what is done. Let their desire to change Slaffton be removed," Loa'neth said.

Loran looked at Loa'neth, not sure of what to make of her statement, but hoping it would go over well with Master and would not jeopardize their own position.

"Their weapons of poison have been destroyed," Master said. "And their desire can easily be stopped by execution."

Then Supreme Queffil spoke.

"But our way is love," she said. "And we will end their lives as they are today, but they should continue on as one of our citizens and so be one with us. They must Arrive."

The citizens chanted, "Arrive, arrive!"

"Let it be so then," Master said. "Begin the Arrival."

Prime Kylalac's team used their branches to lift the cage high, like booms carrying a small load, and they swiveled the cage above the pit. The pit now grew excited, as if lots of fish were nibbling at food thrown on the surface.

"We can't let them be converted into plant-like creatures," Loran thought to Loa'neth.

Loa'neth agreed. She raised her scepter and forced the kylalacs to loosen their grips. The cage fell free, but she said something briefly, caught the cage with a beam from her scepter, and began moving it from the tar pit.

"You should not have done that," Master said. "*She* won't like that."

The four nobles thought at first that Master was referring to Supreme Queffil, but then a tree stump emerged from the tar pit, grew two branches, and latched onto the cage, where it attempted to pull the cage back into the tar pit. Loa'neth issued stronger commands like, "Leiolaki," "Appanakahi," and, "Reekaiya, reekaiya," to pull the cage away from the tar pit. Her scepter drained significantly, and she was concerned.

First Guard and his assistants made for Loa'neth to restrain her, but Gliria blew her trumpet and held them at bay. Myoxi waved his mini-scepter to help, and Loran took his own mini-scepter and held it to Master's throat.

"You have no power here," Master said. "*She* is here. *She* will take all that you are and make you one of us, under my control and *hers*."

Then the stump grew larger, into a full tree—an elder tree—and it grew a humanoid head with a woman's face and long hair. She was covered in the tar, and she belched fire when she spoke. Loa'neth managed to pull the cage to the ground next to the noble four, and Myoxi released them, but now the six were completely surrounded by Slaffton citizens, and these citizens had the six backed up against the edge of the tar pit, where this belching creature sent tentacles of tar and flame which the noble four did all they could to deflect.

"Who are you?" Loran yelled.

But she only laughed, as did Master and the citizens.

"King and Queen of Clamiforia, meet our beloved elderhag," Master laughed.

"So you believe you can defeat me?" the elderhag belched.

"Loran!" Loa'neth called.

"All our power to escape!" Loran called back.

The elderhag sent flaming tar strands toward the six to trap them. Loa'neth and Loran exerted all their might to repel the force, but it was not enough. The elderhag's force was creeping in on their position.

"Make a run for it...ready...now!" Loran called.

With Loran and Loa'neth converting the last of their power into a shield, the six ran around the tar pits and headed west of Slaffton. The elderhag continued throwing her tar strands, and First Guard sent his troops after the six. The six managed to get away (barely) but only by entering a desert of salt. The six then ran a bit farther, and the elderhag's attacks along with the Slaffton residents fell far behind.

"That's it. We escaped," Myoxi puffed. "I'm tired. I need to rest here."

"But where is here?" Claire asked.

"We're in the Sabina Salt Desert," Loa'neth said.

"I'm thirsty," Loran said.

Loa'neth looked at him in shock.

"You're not supposed to get thirsty," she said. "But come to think of it, so am I."

"We've lost our power," Loran said.

"The fight must have drained it all from us. Gliria, Myoxi, do you have any power left?" Loa'neth asked.

Myoxi and Gliria checked. Nothing.

"Salt, salt everywhere, and not a crystal to convert," Loran said. "It's all halite. Not a crystal of sallerite."

"What does that mean?" Claire asked.

"It means we can't use the salt in this desert to regenerate our power. It's the wrong kind of salt," Loa'neth said.

"Here, drink our water," Gliria said, removing a canteen from her pack. "Myoxi, your canteen. Offer it."

"There's hardly any water left in it," Myoxi said. "It needs more time to condense moisture out of the air."

Gliria kicked Myoxi, and he produced his canteen. The picocians then shared their water.

"It will be dark soon," Gliria said. "And it will be very cold. We must try to build a shelter."

"Out of this?" Myoxi said, picking up a clump of salt and dropping it to the wind.

"What did Dara tell us?" Loran asked.

"That if we ran out of energy, seek to the underground for help," Loa'neth said.

"I doubt there are any underground oysters here," Loran said.

"We need a communication instrument," Loa'neth said. "Something made of aragonite."

"I lost everything on Crow Pits Island when we...we..." Loran said.

"Yes, I know," Loa'neth said.

"It's a shame, too. I had some aragonite in the form of a cuttlefish bone," Loran continued to say. "If only—"

While Loran spoke, Myoxi returned his canteen to his pack, and out fell a cuttlefish bone in an ankle strap.

"Oops," Myoxi said quietly.

"Oops?!" Gliria exclaimed. "You stole Loran's cuttlebone!"

"Well you stole his drugs!" Myoxi exclaimed back.

The two got into a tussle. Stephen coughed to announce himself.

"Oh, I'm sorry," Loran said. "Stephen Royer and Claire Stackhart. Myoxi, Gliria, and I saw fliers with your photos in Millfork. We are on our way to Sathiakia to find the evil behind all this and the capture of my cousin, Lillianina. And along the way, we met Loa'neth, of whom I've become fondly attached."

"Maybe we can help," Claire said. "We don't have much. The Slaffton folk took almost everything. All we have left is what we're wearing, and then I have this hidden in my shoe."

Claire pulled something oblong and flat from the inside of her shoe.

"Another cuttlebone," Loran said. "Hidden to prevent discovery."

"Claire, with your permission?" Loa'neth asked as she reached for the cuttlebone.

"Sure! Anything to help!" Claire said, handing the cuttlebone to Loa'neth.

"Here's your cuttlefish bone," Gliria said, finally wrestling it from Myoxi and giving it to Loran.

Loa'neth placed Claire's cuttlebone between her (Loa'neth's) teeth, and Loran placed his cuttlebone on his forehead. Loa'neth appeared to blow through the bone, and indeed, there was a barely audible whistle emanating from the cuttlebone. Loran whistled in harmony, and the cuttlebone on his forehead resonated. Then Loa'neth held the cuttlebone to her ear, and she kneeled on the salt flats with her ear and the cuttlebone practically on the ground.

"It's here," Loa'neth said.

"What's here?" Stephen asked.

"Our transportation," Loa'neth replied. "At least I hope so."

Serpent in the Desert

The six stood together, and a circular indentation in the salt moved around them.

"What was that?" Myoxi asked.

"There's something in the salt," Gliria said.

"We'll be eaten alive!" Myoxi said. "We should run for it!"

"No, wait!" Loa'neth commanded. "Be perfectly still. Remain calm. We don't want to startle the creature."

"Then it is an animal," Stephen said.

"We thought all land animals were extinct," Claire said.

"All living land animals, yes," Loa'neth said.

"Clever. You're calling the undead," Loran said.

"Of course," Loa'neth grinned.

"An undead what, though?" Gliria asked.

Just then, a giant snake skull and the upper part of its skeletal body surfaced. It brought its teeth very close to Loran and Loa'neth, and it then exhaled salt dust onto them and the group, who were now all covered in white.

"Anything?" Loa'neth asked Loran.

"No power," Loran said.

"Well, even salt dust from a salt serpent is beyond our grasp," Loa'neth said.

"But you are not beyond my grassssssp," said the salt serpent. "I can drag you all in the ssssssalllt, and dehydrate you to bone, and then eat your remainsssss until you are dussssssst."

The serpent was most menacing. He circled the six clockwise (when looking down from the top) at increasing speed, all the while rattling his bones and chopping his jaw. The six found themselves craning their necks to the right but unable to look back to the left.

"I...can't look ahead," Myoxi said.

"Nor can I," Gliria said.

"Our necks are stuck!" Claire said.

"How do we get out of this?" Stephen asked.

"You don't!" the serpent replied.

The serpent's skeleton chafed on the six, who were now herded together in a tight group, like a dolphin herding fish.

"A dolphin!" Loran said.

Loran again placed the cuttlefish bone to his forehead and whistled out at the serpent, with a warble and variable pitch that resembled a dolphin. Though he'd never seen (or heard) a real-life dolphin, he'd seen pictures of dolphins, and he had purchased some black disks from an archeologist in Buckner Falls which were called phonographs, and those contained dolphin calls.

"Whistle like Loran," Loa'neth said to the others. "We must cover the serpent's entire path."

The other four whistled, and with Loa'neth whistling through her borrowed cuttlefish bone, the combined effort set up a resonant wave in the serpent's skeleton. Loran put full effort into his whistle, and this whistle resonated through his skull and onto the cuttlebone, where it projected and focused on the serpent on each pass. Then something happened. Instead of the serpent changing the six, the six affected the serpent and effected a transformation of the serpent's skeleton into a dolphin skeleton.

"Acquiesce!" Loran shouted.

The dolphin skeleton stopped circling the six and rolled over, as if to indicate its submissive position. The six regained their ability to look forward and to the left. Indeed, Gliria and Myoxi put extra effort into loosening their necks.

"Oh, I don't know if I could ever go through *that* again," Myoxi said. "My neck is in horrible straits."

"It's good and straight now," Gliria said. "Stop complaining. Look. Loa'neth is commanding the creature to aright itself. Everyone is climbing aboard as if the creature were a ship."

"Oh no, not another boat ride. I'm still recovering from the last," Myoxi complained.

"Come along, Myoxi," Gliria said as she started for the dolphin skeleton.

The others had settled into position on the upper part of the dolphin's spine while Loran held the dolphin in check with soft whistles.

"Here, you'd better keep this," Loa'neth said, returning the cuttlebone. "If we become separated, whistle through it and call for another desert creature."

"Perhaps you can teach me how," Claire said.

"Simply hold it between your teeth, stretch your mind across the land, and exhale like this," Loa'neth said as she blew through the cuttlebone.

"Thank you," Claire said.

Loa'neth took the shreds of her blazer and Loran's jacket to fashion a control harness. Shreds, yes. Depleting their power also caused damage to their royal clothing, and now the noble four looked tired and worn.

"How do I get myself into these situations?" Myoxi muttered, and he gave in to Gliria's request and joined her on the back of the giant dolphin skeleton.

"Prepare for departure!" Gliria called through her trumpet, still performing her job as Herald.

Gliria's trumpet no longer had special power to combat things, but she could still use it as a megaphone and to play a tune. With her and Myoxi taking a sitting position close behind Loran and Loa'neth, Gliria played music while Loran and Loa'neth directed the dolphin skeleton to start porpoising through the salt desert.

"Whoo-hoo!" Claire hollered.

Claire stood where the left flipper met the main body. The dolphin traveled rather quickly, yet his porpoising did not take the six too far down into the salt, and so the passengers were able to hold on without salt getting in their faces.

"I think the dolphin is speaking to me," Claire said. "Stephen, you should try this."

"It's an animal, Claire. And a dead one too," Stephen said.

"All I hear are my knees shaking," Myoxi said.

"And the dolphin bones rattling," Gliria said.

"Stephen, do you see?" Claire called. "I'm in the ocean, the Atlantic Ocean! There are millions of other dolphins and sea creatures in it."

"What's wrong with her?" Gliria asked Loa'neth.

"She is tapping into the memories of the dolphin skeleton," Loa'neth said.

"Look, Stephen, I have dolphin colors," Claire said. "My name is Queen Tharia. I can change shape. Look. First I'm a human. Now I'm a dolphin. Now I'm a human again. I have an underwater kingdom. Let's go visit it."

Claire moved toward the edges of the fin, and this caused her to be dragged deeply into the ground, filling her mouth with salt.

"Claire, no!" Stephen called.

Stephen rushed toward Claire to pull her up, but a chunk of salt spray sent him backward and onto the fluke. The fluke then flipped him up, forward, and onto the fin opposite Claire.

"*Skeyabat!*" Loran yelled while Loa'neth pulled back on the reins.

The dolphin skeleton stopped suddenly, with the shift in movement throwing the picocians past Loran and Loa'neth and ahead onto the salt. The dolphin's fins were buried—as were Stephen and Claire.

"Dig quickly," Loa'neth said. "They should not stay submerged for long."

Gliria picked herself up and helped Loa'neth dig up Claire, while Loran went over to dig up Stephen.

"Did everyone forget about me in my distress and discomfort?" Myoxi asked.

"Go over and help Loran!" Gliria barked.

"All this work I'm doing, and not a bit of thanks. I could sure use a hot bath!" Myoxi grumbled.

"Dig!" Gliria barked.

"I'm getting there!" Myoxi barked back.

Myoxi walked to where Stephen had been shoved into the salt. He removed his digging tools from his pack and gave them to Loran. Gliria shared the digging tools from her pack with Loa'neth, and those two dug while Loran dug and Myoxi sat on the ground and rested.

"You got stone in your legs?" Gliria barked.

"I've been through enough salt and adventure for one day," Myoxi said.

"I'll have Mister Royer out in a moment," Loran said. "I may have been rejected as a fire deputy, but I can rescue a man out of trouble in no time flat."

But it was Loa'neth and Gliria who had retrieved Claire out of the sand first.

"What happened?" Claire asked.

"Stay with her," Gliria said. "I'll help Loran."

"I was a dolphin swimming in the Atlantic Ocean," Claire started, "and now I'm here. Where's Stephen?"

Loa'neth pointed. Claire suddenly gained new strength and rushed over to Stephen. She grabbed a shovel from Myoxi (who wasn't using it anyway) and dug furiously into the salt.

"No, Claire," Gliria said, blocking Claire's shovel with her own. "Don't punch into the salt. You'll cut into Stephen. Scoop it gently. Gently!"

And in this way, Gliria, Claire, Loran, and Loa'neth dug up Stephen from the salt. He had been buried much deeper, and he was calling out.

"Croius! Get away! Don't kill me!" Stephen yelled.

"Stephen! It's over! You're here now," Claire said.

Stephen got up and brushed off the extra salt.

"It was terrible! I was caught on an ice flow and surrounded by five, giant, black-and-white dolphins. Orcas they called themselves. One was called Croius. He was on one side of the ice flow and signaled to the other four, who were on the other side, to swim toward me. And those four sent a huge wave at me which pushed me off the ice. Then Croius opened his great jaw as if to consume me. And he would have. But now I'm here. Animals! I hate animals!" Stephen said.

"I don't understand," Claire said. "It wasn't like that at all for me. I was riding in the Atlantic Ocean, and there were other dolphins who could change shape. We had a lot of fun swimming together."

"They sound crazy in the head," Gliria said.

"It is a dangerous thing—experiencing the memory engrams of this giant dolphin skeleton—because one might lose oneself in the memory and not see the immediate dangers of the surroundings."

"But it was incredible," Claire said. "A world with so much water. Dolphins changing shape. And there was this girl named Debbie Dayla who befriended the dolphins. Her father owned Dayla Industries, and she had access to flying machines and motorized carts. She lived in Brunswick."

"I wonder how such a world disappeared?" Loran said. "We have such simpler times now."

"What was that about Brunswick?" Gliria asked.

"A city on the coast," Claire said. "Debbie mentioned it was close-by."

"Then a part of Sathiakia—" Loran started.

"Could be on top of the ancient city of Brunswick," Loa'neth said.

"Debbie Dayla and Dayla Industries," Myoxi whined. "So it's ancient humans to blame as usual. Factories and machines and corporate greed. We learned all about that in the anthropological museums of Buckner Falls."

"Are you suggesting Debbie and her Dayla Industries caused the evil in Sathiakia?" Loran said. "But Lillianina lived and wrote to me from there. There was no evil that she spoke of. Only now is there some treachery afoot."

"Probably something dug up from the past," Myoxi said. "Humans are always obsessed with the past and can't stop digging up their history. Now take us picocians. We don't dig anything. We just—"

But everyone went silent and shot hard stares at Myoxi.

"Never dig at all do you? Just through mountains," Loran said.

"That's not the same," Myoxi said.

"Oh let the humans dig if they want," Gliria said.

"But we don't go digging up picocian history," Myoxi said. "We're always looking to the future."

"I wouldn't mind knowing about our past a bit more," Gliria said. "Seems like we just appeared out of nowhere, and here we are. The museum in Buckner Falls has many ancient animals and ancient humans. But no picocians. Who knows? Maybe we evolved from an animal like the oyster."

"I doubt that," Myoxi said.

"Maybe Myoxi and I could ride on the flippers," Gliria suggested. "We could learn about our past."

"It's too dangerous," Loa'neth said. "I should have never allowed Claire to do so in the first place."

"Besides that, folk here are hungry," Loran said. "It is time they be fed so that we may continue to Sathiakia."

"Then we best get a move on and get out of this salt desert," Loa'neth said. "Climb aboard the dolphin. We have one last run to make. And no flipper riding."

Incandescence

The group traveled a bit farther in the Sabina Salt Desert, toward Sathiakia. They came to a point where a collection of hills appeared in the distance. As the group neared, the hills were visibly human-made, being formed into pyramids. The sun was setting, and its orange flickers reflected off these pyramids, which had a sparkle of glass to them.

"We will need to stop for the night," Loa'neth said.

"Those pyramids could make a good place for shelter," Gliria said. "Myoxi and I have emergency tents in our packs, unless Myoxi you're too lazy to pitch one."

"I can still do *some* things," Myoxi replied.

"Good. You'll need to," Gliria said.

But just at that moment, something squawked in Myoxi's pack.

"You *must* secure everything in your pack before travel!" Gliria said.

"I did, I did!" Myoxi said. "That's the autocanary."

"Then the air is bad," Gliria said. "STOP!"

Loa'neth pulled on the harness, and the giant skeleton came to a stop.

"What's wrong with the air?" Claire asked.

"Seems fine to me," Stephen said.

"Loa'neth?" Loran asked. "Do you smell anything unusual?"

"No," Loa'neth said. "I am a little nervous, however."

"So am I," Loran said.

Myoxi removed the autocanary from his pack and studied the swirling lights on its display.

"There's a mixture of toxic metals in the air," Myoxi said. "Mercury, arsenic, lead, and cadmium."

"MALC," Gliria said in disappointment.

"Lord Zdannag said this area was contaminated with CLAM," Loa'neth said.

"As in clams? Like oysters?" Stephen asked.

"No," Loran said. "Lord Zdannag is George Snake, and he reverses everything. CLAM and MALC are acronyms for the metals Myoxi just mentioned."

"But where are these metals coming from? Those pyramids?" Claire asked. "They don't look silvery or anything like metals. They're all white."

"Well we can't get any closer to them without protection," Myoxi said.

"Camp out here?" Loran asked. "But without food and water, we won't last long."

"We have water," Myoxi said. "Our canteens—"

Gliria checked her canteen.

"Our canteens aren't condensing enough water for all six of us to stay here for much longer," Gliria said. "The air is too dry."

"How much longer?" Loran asked.

"Another six hours. Maybe seven," Gliria replied.

"What kind of food can we find where there is poison?" Claire asked.

"None," Loran said. "But to answer the next question, it's too far to go around by the southwest. We could try going east toward Lake Meadowash, but we risk running back into the people of Slaffton."

"What about protection from the stuff in the air...what was it called?" Claire asked.

"MALC," Gliria said. "Myoxi and I have a protective mask each. We could go a little bit and explore. Maybe we will find something."

"It's better than nothing," Loran said.

Loa'neth agreed.

"Go ahead," Loa'neth said. "If you get into trouble, sound your trumpet. We will do what we can."

"What can you do, I wonder?" Myoxi asked.

"Never mind that now," Gliria said to Myoxi. "Just put on your mask and follow me."

"Your trumpet has a way of guiding you back to my scepter," Loa'neth said. "In this way, when you return and cannot find us, simply blow through the trumpet backward, and it will bend itself toward my scepter."

"Thank you," Gliria said.

The picocians now had their masks in place, waved a last goodbye, and made for the pyramids. As they walked closer, the autocanary squawked with more frequency.

"It's getting stronger," Myoxi said. "It's settling on our clothes."

"Our clothes will protect us, but we must be sure not to expose our skin for any length of time," Gliria said.

"It isn't that strong yet," Myoxi said.

"But it could be," Gliria said.

"The autocanary says the MALC is coming from those pyramids," Myoxi said. "The autocanary also says the pyramids are made of glass."

"I thought so," Gliria said. "And now that the sun has all but set, they seem to have an afterglow."

The autocanary stopped squawking and instead gave out a steady, low growl.

"Too much MALC!" Myoxi said.

"We must dig. Quickly!" Gliria said.

The two dug into the salt, and they created a tunnel as quickly as possible. The salt managed to filter out the bad air enough such that the autocanary went back to a squawk.

"Turn on your mining light and cover up the entrance to the outside air," Gliria said, and Myoxi did so.

Gliria also turned on her mining light, and the two continued to dig. The autocanary lessened and lessened in frequency until after digging farther along in the salt, the autocanary stopped squawking altogether.

"So a tunnel in the salt may be the answer," Myoxi said.

"It's only a short ways to tunnel into the pyramids. Let's see how far we can go," Gliria said.

The two tunneled farther along in the salt, but then they reached a point where the salt changed into sand for a meter or two. The autocanary began to squawk.

"We're out of the salt desert and on the edge of an ancient shore," Gliria said. "Put your mask back on."

Myoxi complied. The two had their masks on, and they dug through the sand several meters with a squawking autocanary until they reached clay, which contained fragments of white-painted glass, speckles of silvery metal, and bits of plastic, and now the autocanary went into solid growl.

"The soil is too badly contaminated with MALC," Gliria said. "We'll have to dig around."

"More digging," Myoxi moaned. "Are we to dig all around the desert?"

"You never used to complain about digging," Gliria said. "This is easy compared to mountain digging."

"But the mountain rock was not so poisonous," Myoxi said. "This MALC makes me crabby."

The two continued digging in the sand, hoping to find a point where the MALC was not so strong, but this was not the case.

"I'm ready to give up. Let's go back to Loran and Loa'neth and tell them it's impossible," Myoxi complained.

"Keep digging," Gliria said.

The two dug more along the sandy line, and then it happened. Myoxi's shovel broke on an unexpected hard metal. The sudden collapse caused Myoxi's arm to be stressed beyond its limit, and he broke his forearm.

"Ow!" he cried in pain. "Ow!"

"Easy there, Myoxi. Let me see," Gliria said. "I'll have to bind it. Let me get the emergency splint."

Gliria removed a collection of connecting rods and rope, and she fashioned it in such a way around Myoxi's arm to prevent it from moving.

"Well there goes all hope of *mining* our way to Sathiakia," Myoxi said with sarcasm.

"Are you blaming me for all this? You're the one who broke his arm!" Gliria said.

"Like I could help it! What's metal doing down here? This is supposed to be salt, sand, or clay! And a hard metal it is, too!" Myoxi said.

"Too hard to be mercury, arsenic, lead, or cadmium," Gliria said. "I would say it is some sort of steel alloy. Let's see what the metlurometer says."

Gliria removed a small, telescoping device from her pack, extended it, and touched the end probe against the hard metal.

"Nonmagnetic, with chromium, iron, molybdenum, and nickel. This is stainless steel," Gliria said. "In fact, just by striking it, I can tell it's very large. Myoxi, help me dig."

"Like this? One handed?" Myoxi complained.

"Help me dig!"

The two dug around the stainless and realized they had reached the top of a structure.

"It's a building! If we dig farther, we may be able to find an entrance!" Gliria said.

"I'll be known as the one-armed miner after this," Myoxi said.

"How can you be glum at a time like this? We're on the verge of a great archeological discovery! I bet the experts in Buckner Falls would be jealous of our find," Gliria bragged. "Keep digging. Keep digging."

"Quit the digs. This is hopeless!" Myoxi said.

"It isn't. See? We've reached a window. Oh, but it's sealed and won't open," Gliria said.

"Like I said. Hopeless," Myoxi said.

"Well if there's a window, there must be a door. We'll simply have to dig for it," Gliria said.

"I can't. I simply can't," Myoxi said. "The strain in using one arm has thrown out my back."

Gliria sighed and kept digging.

"Keep going, you're getting closer," Myoxi teased.

"You're neither straw nor a boss, so stop acting like the two," Gliria said. "Here, I've found a frame. Now, a little more...yes, there's a latch. The door is here, no thanks to you, Myoxi. Now then, are you going to stay up there and look for more straw?"

"I'll climb down," Myoxi said.

The two opened the door and entered the stainless steel building. It was more or less the size of a house, but inside it was set up like an office. They were currently in a hallway, and there were photos of all sorts of devices with the stamp of "Dayla Industries".

"We must look for food," Gliria said.

"Here? In this tomb?" Myoxi asked. "What's in this side room?"

"Not in there. Have you forgotten our methods, Myoxi? Look, I'm using a nargiometer," Gliria said.

Gliria looked at a little device that detected organic material. She followed it to the end of a hallway and into a pantry where she found a sealed cabinet. The two broke a lock on the cabinet and opened it, revealing sealed cans of food.

"There. Canned food," Gliria said.

"I'd forgotten how sensitive the nargiometer is. It can detect food, even through sealed metal," Myoxi said.

"You've forgotten because—never mind," Gliria said.

"Because I've been complaining so much, is that it?" Myoxi asked.

"Yes, but that's not important. We must return to the others and lead them back here," Gliria said.

"Gliria, Gliria, do you hear me?" said Loa'neth's voice through Gliria's trumpet.

"I hear you," Gliria said. "How is this possible?"

"We've heard you two argue for the last few minutes," Loa'neth said. "The trumpet must be near a power source, causing the trumpet to act as a communication device."

"We found food!" Gliria said.

"Yes, we heard," Loa'neth said. "I'm commanding the giant dolphin to burrow through the salt. We should be there in a few heartbeats."

The picocians heard a deep rumbling sound, first from the distance in the north, but very quickly approaching the stainless building until the front bones of the giant dolphin collided with the building.

"They crashed!" Myoxi yelled. "They're all dead!"

"Calm yourself, Myoxi," Gliria said.

The picocians ran to the door and saw that the others had traveled inside the rib cage of the giant dolphin. The dolphin's skull and neck were completely shattered by the collision, but this was the only thing that had been damaged—the occupants were unhurt.

"You're alive!" Myoxi exclaimed.

"Of course," Loran said.

"We followed the signal from your trumpet," Loa'neth said to Gliria. "From what we heard, it was safer to travel below the salt line than above it."

"You heard us for that long?" Myoxi asked.

"Yes, we did," Loran said. "Though I must say the air is a bit stale in here. I wish I had my old pack. I could make the air more breathable."

"The air will be good for half a day, at least according to this oxiometer," Gliria said while looking at a device she had now just pulled out of her pack.

"We'll need to see if we can extend that," Loran said. "Perhaps there are devices in here that can generate more oxygen. Not that our picocian friends need them—they can go for weeks without fresh oxygen."

"Let's show you the food first," Gliria said.

Gliria led them to the end of the hallway to the canned food, and she opened the cans with a tool from her pack, since Myoxi's broken arm limited his ability.

"I've read about these," Loran said while looking at the cans of food. "These are emergency stores for wartime. Designed to last hundreds of years."

"Loran, there may be a way for us to recharge our stores of ethereal salt," Loa'neth said.

"Yes, we must look for a main office or control room," Loran said.

"This magelectrometer detects a faint power source in this direction," Gliria said.

The group followed Gliria into a room with a single, oblong table—something between rectangular and circular. The walls had shelves of multicolored crystalline cubes, and in one corner was a desk with chair, computer keyboard, and computer display screen.

"Let me try a few things," Myoxi said.

Myoxi walked over to the desk, looked underneath, and attempted to turn on the small computer. Nothing.

"There's no power running to that device," Gliria said. "Let me trace the power...hmm."

Gliria followed the magelectrometer to a section of the wall that was not covered by shelving. She tapped in several places and threw one sharp strike at the wall. A hidden door a meter high and a third as wide opened up—too small for a human to walk inside, but large enough for a picocian to enter.

"There's a...oh, what did they call these things? A portable fusion generator," Gliria said. "Very clean. Needs no external fuel and has no exhaust. I'll activate it."

There was a slight hum after she threw a switch, but not from the generator. The room lit up with incandescent bulbs of various sizes and arrangements—some were old-style light bulbs for lamps, some were miniature lights as once appeared on small Christmas trees, and some were actually vacuum tubes as used in old-style radios or amplifiers—and it was these amplifiers from where the hum came.

"Now how does the magelectrometer read?" Loran asked.

"It's buzzing with excitement," Gliria said.

"Here, I have it," Myoxi said, and he powered up the computer. "Oh, look at this. It's going through a self check. A million-core little computer, but only twelve are now working. This machine is heavily damaged. But it's working a little bit. I wonder what this does?"

A line of light now lit the top of the table with a shape proportional to the table itself but only using up the middle third of the table. Back light illuminated the cubes on the shelves.

"I wonder what these do?" Claire asked. "If I toss one in the air, I see little flashing images."

Claire tossed the cube in the air repeatedly to catch glimpses of the little images. She then looked at the table as if tempted by something. She restrained herself.

"Go ahead, Claire. Toss it on the table," Loa'neth said.

Claire tossed the cube on the table. It rolled like a ball for a little ways and then began sliding on one of its edges. And when it did, video projected upward from the cube in the form of holographic display, and audio projected outward. In the course of displaying video and audio, the cube slid gradually toward one side of the table and then to the other and back and forth, but always remaining within the middle third of the table—inside the boundary of line light that lit up when Myoxi started the desk computer.

"This is Debbie Dayla," said the voice in the video.

Indeed, it was Debbie Dayla, but she looked to be in her forties or at least had many years of stress and worry showing on her face.

"The obsession by governments for false environmental gains has reduced energy consumption by poisoning the earth with heavy metals. I have fought to make low-energy Dayla devices more popular in the world, but the technology requires the fabrication of synthetic diamond, gold, and boron, and though I have made our products as cost effective as possible, they are marginally more expensive than the imitation heavy-metal products produced overseas by...by..." Debbie's projection said, but she was too distraught to finish her statement.

The projection ended, and the cube fell on its side.

"It stopped," Stephen said.

Claire picked up the cube and looked at it.

"There are cracks in the cube," Claire said.

Loa'neth walked over to a shelf and held other cubes to the light.

"They all have cracks. They appear to have sustained a massive shock," Loa'neth said.

Myoxi and Gliria looked at several cubes.

"I would say a loud explosion or some other assault on a large scale caused these cracks," Myoxi said.

"There are microscopic cracks in the table as well," Gliria said while looking at the table through a microscope device (pulled from her pack). "Other structures have similar damage. The damage is not visible to the naked eye."

Claire picked up another cube and tossed it on the table. Another projection of Debbie began.

"I buried father today," a slightly younger Debbie said. "His body was in good health, but...well...I think he was tired of living. He said something strange to me before he died, that the age of invention was over, and *exploration* was now a pejorative. I remember as a child when we explored the back woods of Dayla Industries. I used to find such pretty flowers, and moss, and old stones that made me wonder about their history. Now if I made such a walk, everyone would think me crazy. People don't just move about in a peaceful and thoughtful way—everything must be by car and must be a fight to be considered healthy and normal."

The video ended.

"I'd like to try," Stephen said.

"Go ahead," Loa'neth said.

Stephen tossed a cube on the table, and another video displayed. Debbie looked much older now, in her seventies perhaps.

"The heavy metals have built up so gradually in the systems of people that they have not noticed how gradually they have gone from loving, social people to paranoid, caustic people. I can measure high levels in people, but the device I use for such measurements is banned, because it uses a fraction more electricity than market quota. Everything is a quota now, as the quota system is the solution for restricting the heightened bad behavior of people. No one seeks understanding or a solution to the problem, because that exceeds a social quota."

"I have put my entire life into Dayla Industries and how best to help people, but things have spiraled downward beyond even my help. Many of

Sparfy's people are leaving Earth and are resettling on Bruxima 5. I hope humans never settle into outer space, at least not the humans of today. They would only spread more heavy metals around and destroy life on those planets too. I must now decide if I will spend the rest of my days here, or join Sparfy on Bruxima 5, should he decide to leave Earth."

The video faded. The six looked at one another, not sure what to think.

"I had hoped we would find information on restoring our ethereal salt," Loran said.

"We are seeing some sad parts of our history," Loa'neth said. "Perhaps we were meant to see them. Throw a cube, Loran."

Loran took a cube from a shelf and threw it on the table.

"How does this thing work, Father?" an eleven-year old Debbie asked.

"Just say whatever is on your mind," Roger Dayla replied out of view. "Think of it as a visual diary."

"Well, okay. When I grow up, I want to get rid of all disease and bad medical conditions. And I know I can do it. I have the smartest and most loving parents in the world. I know not everyone is as lucky as me. But I believe most problems come from disease or bad workings of the human body, and if we can learn how to fix these things, even at the lowest levels, then I think people will feel right and good and will want to help others, and it will be a great wave of wonderfulness."

The cube stopped. Claire threw another cube from a shelf. Debbie was now back in her seventies.

"All of Sparfy's people, and all the fulltran cetaceans from the Pacific have left Earth for Bruxima 5. Sparfy has stayed behind to help me work on a cellular transmutation device. The goal is to convert food-dependent intracellular processes into self-sufficient processes."

"That's like those underground clams," Loran said.

"As a test," Debbie's projection said, "I have placed a number of mice in a cage and will put the cage in this chamber device, what I call the Mitothoriac."

The video ended.

"Wait!" Claire said. "What happened next?"

"This cube is damaged like the rest," Gliria said, looking at the cube.

"Here, let me try something," Loa'neth said.

Loa'neth took the cube from Gliria and slid the cube along the same edge. The same video as before started up. Loa'neth quickly took the cube and selected another edge. Nothing. Then yet another edge. A different video displayed.

"I have now put six batches of mice through the Mitothoriac. Each batch has survived successively longer than the prior, and I have made adjustments to the Mitothoriac, but something substantial is missing from this conversion procedure."

The video ended.

"I'll try one more edge," Loa'neth said.

Loa'neth slid the cube on another edge.

"I have been experimenting using oyster stem cells in the Mitothoriac to protect the mouse cells from excessive damage, but I find that this provides too much protection, and the mouse cells do not fully convert. I will now add elderberry stem cells to the Mitothoriac. The controlled release of cyanide on the mouse cells will weaken the cellular respiration process sufficiently to allow conversion to a thorium-based process. Here goes."

The video ended. Loa'neth slid the cube on other edges, but nothing new played.

"Is it possible that Debbie's experiments contributed toward creating the clam beings you encountered, Loran?" Myoxi asked.

"Could be," Loran said. "Let's try a few more cubes."

Stephen took a cube and rolled it on the table.

"What do you have there?" said Connie Dayla's voice outside of view.

"It's something Father gave me," Debbie said.

"Let me see," Connie said, and now she appeared on screen. "Hi! My name is Connie, and there's a cute guy I met yesterday, his name is Vance Hall, and he goes to college and is the quarterback. Oh wait, his name isn't Vance Hall, his fraternity is Vance Hall. His real name is...well...what is his name? Sugar Flowers, that's it."

"That's not a real name. You made that up," said Debbie.

"Did not," Connie replied.

"Did too. Give me that cube. I want to talk about my day at school. It was a rough one. The teacher gave a pop quiz on conic sections," Debbie said.

"That's not a rough day. I'll tell you about rough. Sugar Flowers getting hit by a linebacker," Connie said.

The video ended.

"This could take hours going through these," Stephen said.

"Let me see if there's an index for these cubes on the computer," Myoxi said.

Myoxi tapped a few keys, but then the power went out.

"Oh no!" Claire said.

"Let me check the power," Gliria said. "Hmm. It appears the same microfractures are also in the power supply. It has suffered a catastrophic failure. Fortunately everything is self contained, so there is no radiation from the device."

"What's radiation?" Stephen asked.

"Invisible waves emanating from certain materials. It is like energy, but it causes death to living things. I have a detection device for that too. It's important in mining, because one should never go digging up things that will kill," Gliria said.

"Hello, what's this?" Myoxi said.

"What is what?" Loran asked.

"There's something attached to this computer," Myoxi said. "It's a cube. Here."

Gliria took the cube from Myoxi and inspected it.

"This cube is different from the others," Gliria said. "It appears to have its own power source."

Gliria rolled the cube on the table, and without need for external power, it projected video and audio of Debbie Dayla in her seventies.

"This is Debbie Dayla. The new war has fully developed. It is no longer country against country, but human against human. Everyone has a portable fabrication device, capable of creating almost anything—food, drink, clothing, and weapons. The only thing it can't create is wisdom. People are not as domiciled as they once were. They travel freely, more or less, and provoke one another over almost everything. I could go on, but there is little time. The ultimate tool of doom is that people are creating portable nuclear weapons and using these to push individual agenda, no matter how badly misguided. Every day and every night, people fire their weapons, and the air is filling with radiation. I cannot delay any longer. I must step into the Mitothoriac and risk conversion, or else I shall surely perish."

"Are you sure, Debbie?" Sparfy's voice said. "It could kill you."

"I must. Please help me in this, Sparfy," Debbie said.

"Very well," Sparfy replied.

Debbie entered the Mitothoriac chamber with the cube in hand, and Sparfy (who showed no signs of aging) closed the door behind her. Because Debbie carried the cube, the perspective of the video also changed.

"Can you hear me, Sparfy?" Debbie's voice said.

"Yes. Very well," Sparfy replied.

"Good. I am now in the chamber. To my right are elderberry stem cells to be used to agitate my mitochondria. To my left are oyster stem cells to counter that effect once my cells are converted into using thorium."

Debbie took a deep breath.

"This is it. The end of my life as I know it. Throw the switch, Sparfy," Debbie said.

Sparfy did so. The lights glowed, swirled, and hummed, with a shooting-star-like effect that grew in intensity until the inside walls and features of the chamber were no longer recognizable. Debbie's body was now all that was visible, and the stars shot through her body, initiating great pain and causing her to scream until she was hoarse. Claire and Myoxi turned away from the video, but the others looked on and witnessed as Debbie's writhing and foaming body fell to the floor and changed from that of a seventies-plus woman to a twenty-something woman with silver-speckled skin. Sparfy turned off the power and helped Debbie to her feet.

"We must go now," he said.

"Wait," Debbie said. "Let me put this in a prominent place."

Debbie grabbed the cube. The two exited the room, went down a hallway, and entered the very room where the six were now watching. She placed the cube on the computer, typed a few things on the keyboard, and turned off the computer. She then turned off the lights in the room by powering down the portable fusion reactor, and the two exited the room. A short time later, one could hear the sound of a spaceship leaving. The video from the cube ended.

"I think she became immortal," Claire said.

"I would agree with that," Loran said. "It's a tempting thought that a device of immortality is but a few rooms away."

The six looked at one another for a moment. Then Claire, Stephen, Gliria, and Myoxi bolted for the door and ran down the hallway to where they thought the Mitothoriac would be.

"They are not being noble," Loran said.

"No, not at all," Loa'neth said.

"We'd better go after them, in case they attempt to harm themselves," Loran said.

"Yes, for sure," Loa'neth replied.

Loran and Loa'neth walked (but did not run) down the hallway to follow the others. At the end of the hallway was the room where the Mitothoriac would have been, but when Loran and Loa'neth entered that room, they saw two humans and two picocians in total shock and looking frantically for the remains of the device.

"There's just a rough wall where the Mitothoriac would have been," Loa'neth said.

"Maybe there's some part of the device still around," Claire said. "Some part that could make us immortal!"

"Hmm," Loran said.

"There's a cube on this wall," Loa'neth said. "I wonder."

"Could it be it recorded those last moments?" Loran asked.

"Let's find out," Loa'neth said.

Loran and Loa'neth started for the hallway.

"They aren't following us," Loran said.

"They'll be fine," Loa'neth said. "I sense that they won't find what they seek."

Loran and Loa'neth returned to the room of incandescence.

"Hmm, no power," Loran said.

"If you remember, the last cube we played—the one Debbie took into the chamber—was self powered," Loa'neth said.

"Energized by the chamber, is that it?" Loran asked.

Loa'neth nodded.

"Then perhaps this one was also energized, though it was outside instead of in," Loran said.

Loran placed the cube on its edge on the table, but no video displayed.

"Wait," Loa'neth said.

Loa'neth placed the cube on its edge but on top of the cube that was in the Mitothoriac chamber, and now a video displayed. It showed what appeared to be a time-lapse collection of photos, that of clams growing from dots of nothing to large sizes inside the Mitothoriac chamber, moving outside the chamber, and then chewing a tunnel through the wall and away. Then the time-lapse photos showed elder tree-like creatures entwining their roots throughout the Mitothoriac until they consumed the device afterwhich they exited through the tunnel the clams had created, pulling down debris and sealing the hole behind it.

"Oh no," Loran said.

"This device then has created these two creatures," Loa'neth said.

"A twisted elder tree and clams. But those clams could be the ones who settled on Crow Pits Island," Loran said.

"Elder tree," Loa'neth mused. "Loran, it would seem we must next follow the tunnel, if it still exists."

Loa'neth and Loran now walked down the hallway to the room where the others had been looking for the Mitothoriac chamber. But the others were gone! And the rough-looking wall that was once there was now open, and the opening that was revealed in the video was the same opening now shown to Loa'neth and Loran.

"They found it?" Loran asked.

"Or they were captured," Loa'neth said.

At that moment, the two heard a brief scream from the tunnel. The two rushed down the tunnel as quickly as they could, but the tunnel was long, and despite peering down as far as they could, the others were not to be found.

The Tunnel of String and Pearl

"Pearl," Loran said as the two moved forward. "These walls are made entirely of pearl."

"With very ornate designs," Loa'neth said. "No humanoid could have carved these."

"So much beauty. And yet there is something down the way that is dangerous. The tunnel imparts desire to rush after our friends, but we could be captured too," Loran said.

Loa'neth touched the smooth, pearly wall while the two progressed. At first this touch was to brace against possible attack, but then she sensed something else.

"Loran," she said. "Touch the wall."

"Trouble?" he asked.

"No. Not even," she replied.

Loran touched the architecture and symbols on the wall while still walking down the tunnel.

"Ethereal salt," he said.

"Yes," Loa'neth said. "An ancient form of it."

"We could replenish ourselves," Loran said, "just by touching a few symbols like this."

Suddenly, the surroundings began changing in a whirlwind of electrified plasma.

"Hold my hand!" Loran said.

Loa'neth grabbed Loran's hand, and the two were transported to another time and place—ancient Egypt. Slaves pulled obelisks and statues by rope over a series of oversized dowels smoothed from logs. Motivating the slaves were whips, fashioned from the hides of animals. And watching the work from a high platform was a queen adorned in gold and pearls.

"How do we get back?" Loran asked.

"How do we avoid becoming slaves?" Loa'neth asked.

A whip-master noticed the two and pointed in their direction.

"Give them a rope!" he shouted.

"Give us a rope?!" Loran and Loa'neth shouted together.

"Run!" Loa'neth said.

The two ran for quite some time until they reached the Nile. There they came across a woman who tried to escape into the Nile but was caught by two whip-masters, who had her neck wrapped with a whip and were dragging her their way.

"More slaves!" whip-masters from the Nile said, and they converged on Loran and Loa'neth which forced the two between two sets of whip-masters, enabling their capture.

"We are just visitors from another place!" Loran said.

"So am I!" the other captured person said. "My name is Amicolli. I come from the Nile upstream and was washed down from the first cataract in Swenett."

"From upstream on the Nile? Then you are a spy from the Kingdom of Kush," said a whip-master. "All of you now, to the queen you go for judgment!"

A whip-master bound Loran's and Loa'neth's arms with rope, as was done to Amicolli, and now all three were on a single rope and being led to the queen. There was a water inlet from the Nile, and it led into a small building with extravagant stone architecture.

"Bring the spy first," the queen said when the three and whip-masters arrived. "Well? Have you nothing to say?"

"I have only to say that I am not one of you," Amicolli said.

The queen's court laughed.

"You are no citizen of this kingdom. You *are* a spy and admit your guilt. But I will be merciful with you. I will spare your life and give you work as a slave to build my temple," the queen said.

"You cannot make me a slave. For as I said, I am not your kind. You should instead focus your efforts on your neighbors. The Kingdom of Kush plans to conquer you. But I shall not be around for that!" Amicolli said.

Amicolli turned herself into a giant spotted-neck otter, dove into the water, and swam away into the main Nile River, where she was not to be seen again. War drums approached from the distance, like an ominous thunderstorm. Loran and Loa'neth also dove into the water in hopes of escape.

But when they surfaced, they were no longer in ancient Egypt. It was 1811, and they were on the Pacific coast on San Nicolas Island. A sea otter in part humanoid form was meeting with the Nicoleño, a Native American tribe.

"A great curse has fallen upon your people," Lutris, the sea otter said. "The many peoples of this land make deals with the white man. But the white man is using the peoples of this land as beasts of burden and will slay the peoples when they are no more use to him."

"We make no deals with the white man," Black Hawk said.

"It is too late," Lutris said. "The treachery runs far and deep. One such people from the far north are leading the white man here. They come to hunt my people."

"No. We will not permit it," Black Hawk said.

"You cannot stop it. And you too will be hunted to the end. You will either lose your flesh from arrow or black power, or you will lose your spirit from men claiming to convert you to the worship of their white leader in a faraway country. Otter and Nicoleño shall perish."

"We will fight to the bitter end," Black Hawk said.

"I cannot allow you to perish so easily, Lutris," said a woman later known as Juana Maria. "Take this amulet as a gift from my people and wear it always. It comes from a faraway place where people and animals share the waters of Earth."

"Thank you. I hope I never have need for its use," Lutris said. "But fear has taken hold of me."

Lutris looked down, and Juana Maria walked over and kissed him on the forehead.

"Have no fear, Lutris," she said. "Should evil press close, dive deep. Dive deep!"

The scene changed, and now Loran and Loa'neth were on shore watching a group of Russian boats. They formed a line and ran nets in between. A

single Aleut boat moved between the line and the shore, looking for a sea otter for the Russians to trap. Lutris happened to be alone that day, and the
Aleut saw him. The Aleut lifted his paddle in the air to signal the Russian
boats, and the Russian boats formed a circle around Lutris, where they
closed in with their nets to prevent his escape. The Aleut placed an arrow in
his bow and prepared to fire at Lutris. Lutris surfaced one last time, the Aleut
fired, and Lutris dove deep, deep, deep into the ocean floor, where he placed
himself inside a giant, abandoned clam shell, closed the shell, and with the
help of the amulet, put himself into deep hibernation for eons to come.

The two returned to the cave.

"These caves also contain memories of the past," Loa'neth said. "We
must be careful not to touch them too much."

"I think we should hurry down the tunnel," Loran said. "I feel new
strength from the ethereal salt."

The two hurried their pace down the tunnel, but as they progressed, the
pearly walls showed an increasing number of cracks, and now these cracks
were filled with root and vine working the pearly wall and breaking into it
until the walls were part pearl and part root with pearl debris on the ground.
The pearly walls were all but gone, and the two reached a point where root
and vine constricted the tunnel more and more until it was blocked. Vines
then lashed out at the two, but Loran held his cuttlebone to his forehead and
whistled while Loa'neth chanted with scepter in hand, and the vines withdrew.

"This must be where the others were captured," Loa'neth said. "If only
they could have waited for us."

"All this pearl, but it wasn't enough to block these roots and vines. Such
beauty wasted and destroyed by the twisted desire of the plant."

Loran picked up a clump of broken pearly wall, shook it, and threw it at
the roots in disgust.

"They were not at fault," Dara said, her image now appearing before the
two.

"Dara!" Loa'neth said. "We see you!"

"I am still on Crow Pits Island," Dara said. "But I am able to communicate through the pearly walls before you. These walls are the first creation of
the clamifores before they migrated into what was once the Atlantic Ocean.
But land and sea will change over the many years. The land uplifted, the

ocean water receded, and a basin filled with fresh water and became Lake Meadowash."

"The others," Loran said. "You said it wasn't their fault."

"Vines broke through an old wall into Debbie Dayla's lab," Dara said. "These vines then lured the others into the tunnel with sweet whispers of delight. The others did not have to go far before the vines surprised them and dragged them swiftly away. When you first entered the tunnel, the vines had already withdrawn, having their captives, and so you were able to walk much farther down the tunnel before they detected you. Fortunately, you replenished your ethereal salt somewhat and were able to thwart the vines' attempt. I know all this because the pearly walls communicated to us what happened."

"Can you help us find the others?" Loran asked.

"I can only direct you to where they went. You have reached the end of the clam section of the tunnel, and so the clamifore knowledge fails beyond that," Dara said.

"Dara, there's something else," Loa'neth said. "When we touched the pearly walls, we were suddenly somewhere else. First we were in an ancient place with towers and statues, and I believe there was even a pyramid. And we met the strangest creature. She was a woman, but then she changed into a furry animal and dove into the river."

"Then there was the other place," Loran said. "We were on an island, and another furry animal was caught in a circle of boats with nets. But he dove deep and hid—"

"In a giant clam shell," Dara finished.

"Yes!" Loran said. "How did you know?"

"The second animal is a sea otter, and his name is Lutris. The first is a spotted otter and is named Amicolli," Dara said. "Their stories are well known in clamifore legend. They are both feared and revered. Feared because they can subdue the clamifore, but revered because they can also subdue an arch enemy of the clamifore—the starfish."

"I've never heard of a starfish," Loa'neth said.

"I have. I saw a fossilized starfish on display in a Buckner Falls museum," Loran said.

"This is all very interesting, but we must find our friends," Loa'neth said.

"Could Lutris and Amicolli help us?" Loran asked.

"No one knows where they are or if they even survived to this day. Supposedly, Lutris is still hibernating in a clamifore somewhere in the world," Dara said.

"And Amicolli?" Loran asked.

"No one knows. But it is said the two, though they have never met, will one day join forces, take ownership of this world, and aright all that is wrong," Dara said. "But as to the others, it is simple. The tunnel continues on a little farther, and then it ends."

"Ends? As in dead end?" Loran asked.

"Don't speak like that," Dara said. "The tunnel becomes something else. We do not know for sure what. Most likely it reaches the surface and opens up. I give you the best of luck. I will do what I can when I can to help, but do not wait for me. You must use all you have to find your friends and stop the threat in Sathiakia."

The image of Dara ceased.

Meyta Merco

Loran and Loa'neth now forged a path through the tunnel—Loa'neth with her scepter, and Loran with his cuttlebone. The vines and roots responded with violent twitching, but the two managed to continue onward for an exhausting number of hours until the tunnel reached the surface. The pyramids were behind them.

"The scepter says the air is safe, but the ground is still contaminated with MALC," Loa'neth said. "We must be careful."

There was a short path before them that led to a settlement up ahead. But this was no ordinary settlement. Instead of seeing houses or huts on the ground, all buildings and paths were up in the trees. Vines formed tracks between trees, and steam-powered vehicles traveled along the tracks. Loran and Loa'neth approached this settlement with caution.

Just at that moment, the two heard Gliria's trumpet from one of the steam-powered vehicles. The back of the vehicle contained a cage, and inside were Gliria, Myoxi, Claire, and Stephen. As Gliria continued playing her trumpet, the other three yelled for help.

"There they are!" Loran said.

Loran rushed toward the vehicle.

"Wait!" Loa'neth said with concern.

Loa'neth rushed after Loran, more to stop him than help their friends. Their experience at Slaffton was no easy ordeal, and they were still tired from fighting the vines in the tunnel, so she feared this confrontation would be too much. As it turned out, the settlement they entered was called Meyta Merco, and it was just inside the border of Sathiakia. As they entered, they were able to see the residents close-up. Two of them dropped out of the trees and attacked Loran and Loa'neth for their clothes.

"Stay back!" Loran said.

Loa'neth waved her scepter, and the two attackers fled in fear. Then Loran and Loa'neth watched as the attackers changed their focus and attacked two other residents for their clothes.

"It seems these people make nothing for themselves. Did you see their clothing? Hardly a thread on them," Loran said.

"Their bodies are full of MALC," Loa'neth said. "They can no longer think for themselves and be productive. Their single thought is what they can steal."

"And yet there is technology in this settlement," Loran said.

"Not of their own doing," Loa'neth said.

Three people descended from the trees and attacked the two for their clothes. Loa'neth repelled two, and Loran held one by the neck.

"You!" Loran said.

"Give me that shirt! You don't need it!" the squawker said. "Give me half. You owe it to me."

"No he doesn't," Loa'neth said.

"I can do anything I want. Now give me that shirt!" the squawker said. "I saw it first. It's mine now. You've had it too long. Get rid of it and feel better. Give me that shirt!"

"What is this place?" Loran asked.

"It's the place where you give me that shirt," the squawker said.

Then Loa'neth pointed her scepter at the squawker. He became rigid and now spoke in monotone as if being electrocuted.

"I am Sleego," the squawker said. "You are in Meyta Merco. This is the queen's front doorstep. You will be taken captive soon. The queen has learned of your presence. She already has your friends."

"Who built this place? You and your people?" Loran asked.

"The queen provides for all. We are her servants. We dig MALC from the ground and feed her roots and vines," Sleego said.

"There," shouted a voice from the trees. "Those are the invaders."

"Attack!" another voice shouted.

The people in the trees threw all sorts of things down on Loran and Loa'neth.

"Not me! You're hitting me!" Sleego said to the people above.

Loran held the cuttlebone to his forehead and whistled. A shield formed over Loa'neth and himself but not Sleego.

"Protect me too!" he begged.

"No!" Loa'neth said. "Take us to the prisoners."

"I don't know what you're talking about," Sleego lied.

Then Loa'neth pointed the scepter at the objects raining down, and she focused the onslaught on Sleego.

"Ow, ow, ow!!" Sleego wailed. "Okay, okay! I'll take you to the prisoners. Just protect me from the attack. Please! I'm getting hurt!"

Sleego let out a whistle, and a steam-powered vehicle descended a tree and stopped at the ground.

"This way," Sleego said.

Loran and Loa'neth followed Sleego to and into the vehicle. They sat down, and then a gate closed.

"Do you think you can make us your prisoners?" Loa'neth demanded.

"The queen operates these vehicles as she wishes," Sleego said. "It is by her will that we travel through the trees, not mine."

"But you did whistle," Loran said.

"She heard me. She heard me," Sleego said.

Then Gliria's trumpet sounded again.

"I'm taking over this vehicle," Loa'neth said as she pointed her scepter at it.

"Oh please, don't do that. You'll upset the queen," Sleego said.

"I'm a queen in my own right, and I'm plenty upset. And I'd say you'll have more to fear from me than her!" Loa'neth said.

Loa'neth now commanded the vehicle with her scepter. It sped along the viny track through the trees. Other residents of Meyta Merco hung close to the track, and several dropped down onto the vehicle. But Loran held the cuttlebone to his forehead and whistled, and a sonic burst pushed them away. More fell on the vehicle, and they began to damage it. They didn't care about being injured, they just kept falling onto the vehicle. Loran put his shield back up, and that protected the two, but now he was getting tired.

"Hurry, Loa'neth. I cannot hold them off much longer," Loran said.

Just as Loran's strength gave out, the vehicle reached the top of a circle of trees. The vehicle with Gliria, Myoxi, Claire, and Stephen was also at this top, and they were being pulled out of that vehicle and placed onto the platform. Torches surrounded the platform, and at one side was a plank. Many meters below the plank was a cauldron of hot MALC. One by one, the prisoners were being paraded to the plank. Horrified, Loran and Loa'neth jumped out of their vehicle and attacked the Meyta Merco residents. But the residents were strong, and they gave Loran and Loa'neth a good fight. Loran whistled at the vines around the legs of his companions, and the vines fell away.

"Get behind us," Loran said to his companions, and they did.

The Meyta Merco residents continued the fight. Loran held the defensive shield while Loa'neth pointed at various residents with her scepter. Gliria got into the act with her trumpet, and that pushed a few residents away. But more jumped onto the platform and continued the attack. While this was going on, a distant sound of thunder rumbled. Stephen and Claire looked, and they saw a huge tree of fire that was several thousand paces away. Then the thunder turned to laughter.

"ENJOY YOUR MOMENT, LITTLE FLIES IN MY WEB," the voice bellowed.

"Wonga, Wonga!" the residents said as they suddenly stopped attacking and bowed before her in homage.

"Make a break for it!" Loran shouted.

The six now scrambled to the vehicle that Loa'neth commanded. Sleego was inside bowing and praying to Wonga. Stephen pulled him out and threw him aside.

"No, we will take him along as a guide," Loa'neth said.

Stephen seemed puzzled. Loran wasted no time, put his arm around Sleego's neck, and dragged him back into the vehicle. The seven then raced down the trees and sent the vehicle along the ground away from where they had seen Wonga, with Loran driving.

"Good," Myoxi said. "We're leaving this wretched place. This was a bad idea anyway."

"But where are we going?" Gliria asked.

"We're going to get help from Dara," Loa'neth said. "I think we underestimated the power of Wonga. My scepter is almost drained. We'll need to head back to Crow Pits Island."

"There's a road we can take back to Slaffton," Loran said. "From there we'll have to figure out how to reach our boat without being attacked."

"If the boat is still there," Myoxi said.

The vehicle sped on a road along the shore.

"We should be able to avoid the MALC pyramids and the Sabina Salt Desert," Loran said.

"Weee...cannoooot...leeeeave...heeeeere," Sleego said.

"What are you talking about?" Gliria asked.

"Wonga! Wonga wants to meet you!" Sleego said. "You are in her web! You cannot leave!"

Then Sleego removed something the size of a pea shooter, but it shot mini blowdarts. He shot Loran, Gliria, and Myoxi before Loa'neth could get her scepter trained on Sleego. Sleego got one more shot off, and it hit Loa'neth. She shot at Sleego, but it went wide and knocked out the back wall of the vehicle. Loa'neth got another shot off and knocked the blowdart gun out of Sleego's hand. But a drug in the blowdarts affected the four. It sent Loran driving toward a grove of vines. He fought to veer around the vines, but Sleego grabbed the wheel and turned him back in. Loa'neth trained her scepter on Sleego one last time, despite the drug affecting her vision and will. The scepter's blast hit Sleego just as Loran made one last fight to veer the vehicle from the vines. The vehicle hit an outcropping of rocks, ramped into the air, and sailed far above Lake Meadowash. As it did, the blast from Loa'neth's scepter knocked various items out of Sleego's pockets, blasted Sleego himself out the back of the vehicle, but it also knocked Claire and Stephen out with Sleego. The vehicle then dove into the water, where it quickly submerged.

Creature from the Sand

Claire and Stephen swam to the surface, and they then swam to shore. Exhausted, they collapsed on the beach. Claire stared back at the lake, and she glimpsed Sleego slithering away on the shore farther down.

"I hit my head," Claire said. "I'm dizzy."

"Rest here a while," Stephen said. "We're safe."

"What happened? One moment we were in that vehicle, and now we are here," Claire said. "But where are the others?"

Stephen looked around.

"I don't see them," he said. "It was a good swim back to shore. We must have traveled sixty paces or more through the air before we hit the water."

"You'll have to go back and look for them," Claire said.

An expression of great dread fell upon Stephen's face.

"Please," Claire said. "I can't live knowing we just left them there to die."

"I will go," Stephen said.

Stephen swam back out to where he thought the vehicle had landed. This took time, and while he did, Claire ambled over to the very rock outcropping from where the vehicle launched. She sat on the outcropping and rested. Still in shock, she struggled to get back her orientation and her breath.

"I can't believe they're gone," Claire said. "We were all together. We were fine. Everything was fine. Now this. What are Stephen and I going to do? I guess we really do need to go back now. Go back to Millfork and sort things out. Loa'neth wanted Dara's help. Can she help? I don't know."

Stephen reached the point where he thought the vehicle sank into the water, and so he dove down. Claire's heart pounded with such force that it felt as if it would burst through her chest. She counted her heartbeats while Stephen was underwater. Thirty, forty, fifty, eighty, a hundred.

"Come up for air, Stephen. Don't drown too!" she said.

A few moments later, Stephen surfaced. Claire tried to shout to him and ask if he'd found them, but she was too weak. Sensing Claire's question, Stephen yelled back.

"Nothing so far," Stephen yelled. "I'll go down again."

Stephen repeatedly went down and surfaced. The sun sank in the sky, and soon it would be dusk. Realizing the hopelessness of the situation, Claire began to cry. With strong emotions overpowering her, she could no longer stay on the rock outcropping. It was the "scene of the accident," the last known point where all were alive. She wandered along the beach and came across a depression in the sand. She tested the depression, expecting it to give way, but it was surprisingly more firm than the rest of the shore. She sat on the regular sand and placed her feet in the depression. Dusk had arrived, and Stephen yelled that he was swimming back.

"I don't have to ask," Claire said to herself. "I know Stephen didn't find them. Oh I wish the lake would open up and swallow me."

A cold wind came from the lake and chilled Claire. She shivered, and this was how Stephen found her when he swam to shore.

"I tried, Claire. I really did," Stephen said. "And it's too dark to keep looking. Maybe tomorrow we can try again."

"What's the point?" Claire asked.

"Well, maybe they found an air pocket somewhere in the mud."

"In the mud?" Claire shivered.

"Look, you're chilled to the bone," Stephen said. "And I need to dry out these clothes. I'll start a fire. That will help cheer things up."

Stephen gathered wood, twigs, and dried moss. He had no flint or any other special device for starting a fire.

"Oh, this is a bad day indeed. I've lost my flint and iron," Stephen said. "Maybe I can find two special rocks to make a spark. Otherwise, I'll have to make a bow and twirl a stick."

Stephen walked off in search of special stones for striking sparks. Claire searched her pockets and found a metallic cylindrical object about the size of a tube of lipstick. She didn't know it, but the object had flown from Sleego into her pocket when Loa'neth blasted Sleego with her scepter. Claire walked up to the kindling materials, picked up a stray rock, and struck the object against the rock. Several sparks flew onto the dry moss, and the moss caught. She blew on it, and flames grew.

"You got a fire going!" Stephen said, rushing back to the flame. "It's a good fire too. I'll put this kindling in to get it going. There. And this wood now will help. Perfect. Oh, not so perfect. If only we had food to cook. I'm so hungry I could eat a dozen oysters. What about you, Claire?"

"I have no appetite," Claire said. "I can't think about anything but our friends at the bottom of the lake. Oh why did we have to live?"

"Don't talk like that," Stephen said. "It only makes things worse. We should rest here for the night. Let's see. There are two trees behind us. I should be able to make a lean-to for shelter."

Stephen looked for long branches to use for construction of the lean-to. But he realized he had used up the loose supply for the fire. In need of a tool to cut down saplings, Stephen took several rocks and smashed them against other rocks in an effort to get one to split into a usable axe head. The sounds jarred Claire's nerves, and with each smash, she felt as if her friends were being crushed.

"Stop!" she pleaded.

"I need to make an axe," he said.

"I...can't handle the sound of smashing rocks. I feel like we're killing our friends all over again," Claire said.

"I won't smash anymore," Stephen said. "I didn't get exactly what I wanted, but this piece will do, I suppose."

Stephen fashioned his axe, and he chopped down saplings for his lean-to. Each sapling quivered when struck, as if the sapling were playing music or sending a message to some distant place. But Stephen finished the lean-to, and it was close enough to the fire to capture its heat. Stephen fashioned a bed out of leaves and moss.

"Here now, Claire. Try to get some rest," Stephen said.

Claire moved back a bit and reclined on the bed Stephen had made. She was comfortable, but her body was torn between being incredibly exhausted and being tortured with intense sadness that began to set in like a hot iron in her side. Eventually, she compromised by simply staring at the fire as she reclined on her side. Stephen placed a few more heavy logs on the fire to keep it going, and then he found a place in the lean-to and settled in for the night. Soon, Stephen was breathing heavily and snoring. But Claire could not fall asleep. She stared at the fire, watching the flames dance and the sparks float like fireflies. All along, she felt as if she were being watched. Not by humanoid or other animal, but by the trees. They moved in the wind with creaks and groans, and Claire was sure that these trees would uproot themselves, amble over to her, pick her up, and strangle her. She wanted to scream, but her fatigue prevented her, and so she remained motionless, hoping the trees would just stay put.

"Go to sleep," she whispered to the trees. "Go to sleep and let me be."

But the trees *did* uproot themselves. They approached the fire and the lean-to, and they bent over to crowd in on Claire and Stephen. Claire shook Stephen to wake him, but he kept sleeping. Then it happened. A tree stepped into the fire, and instead of being just a tree, the humanoid-tree shape of Wonga appeared. The flames flew up high, but Wonga did not fear them. Rather, Wonga harnessed the flames and sent them all around the lean-to, trapping Claire and Stephen in a wall of fire.

Claire screamed. And still Stephen slept. But Wonga's reign of terror was short-lived. Something in the sandy depression lifted upward with a short thrust as if that something had suddenly let loose. Then as quickly as Wonga arrived, she left, taking the fire with her. And finally, like a child who was kept asleep by the constant sound of a moving locomotive but awakened when the locomotive stopped, Stephen awoke.

"Smells like something nearby was burning," Stephen said. "What happened to the fire? It's gone out."

"It...the fire...Wonga...why didn't you wake up?" Claire asked.

"Wake up for what? There's nothing here," Stephen said. "And that goes for the fire, too. I'd better rebuild it."

Stephen got up and left the area to find more loose wood. While he was gone, the depression lifted again. A bluish-green glow came from the depression, and now the depression was no more. It was a step, and it grew. Claire wanted to cry out, but fear made her speechless, and the step grew higher, with sand falling off the sides of—a large clam shell. The shell opened.

Strangely, curiosity overpowered Claire's fear. She stood up and walked toward the clam shell, and inside was a sea otter. Was it asleep? Was it dead? Claire didn't know. She reached into the shell and touched the otter. It was warm and well preserved.

"What a beautiful animal, and such fine fur," Claire said. "I wonder why there aren't more around?"

"Because we were hunted to near extinction," the sea otter said.

"You're alive!" Claire said.

"My name is Lutris," the sea otter said.

"My name is Claire Stackhart. I'm so glad to see you. Why just a moment ago, Wonga was here, and I thought she was going to strangle me. She—"

"You'll have to forgive my ignorance, Mrs. Stackhart," Lutris said.

"*Miss* Stackhart. I'm not married," Claire giggled. "And you may call me *Claire*."

"Thank you, Claire. The last thing I remember was a group of Russian boats closing in on me in hopes of trapping and killing me," Lutris said.

"Oh. You really don't know about Wonga and what she's doing. And what about picocians, did you have any of those?" Claire asked.

"You speak strangely," Lutris said. "Claire, you have soft hair."

"Aw," Claire said, and she blushed. "It's not as soft as yours."

"I knew humans in my time, but none had hair as soft as yours. Let me touch it. Mmmm," Lutris said.

Just then, Stephen walked back with wood in his arms. The sight of Lutris and Claire shocked him, and he dropped the wood on his foot.

"Ow!" Stephen said. "Who...who...what is that?"

"I am Lutris, sea otter of the east Pacific. Once I was leader of many sea otters. A group of Russian boats tried to murder me, and I escaped," Lutris said. "Thank you for participating in my awakening. You started the fire then?"

"Claire did," Stephen said. "I helped get it going. And it went out. I've never seen the likes of it. That fire should have lasted all night."

"It was Wonga," Claire said. "She's a demon from Sathiakia—part human and part tree. We saw her in Slaffton, Meyta Merco, and now here. But I don't want to see her ever again. Loa'neth and Loran—those are my friends—they were taking us to Crow Pits Island to get help from Dara. But now that won't happen. They are dead at the bottom of the lake."

Claire hugged Lutris, and she snuggled in his fur.

"Claire!" Stephen said. "What are you doing? You're touching an animal? That's disgusting!"

"He's not just an animal," Claire said. "He's Lutris. And I can tell he's very special."

Lutris looked into Claire's eyes, and Claire returned the gaze. It was more than one exchanged by casual friends.

"I've had it," Stephen said. "You're making eyes like that to an...an...animal. It's disgusting. I'm leaving."

"Stephen, wait. Wait!" Claire called.

But Stephen quickened his pace and disappeared into the darkness, shaking his fists in frustration.

"Are you two...is he?" Lutris asked.

"He's my cousin," Claire said. "But he acts more like an over-protective brother."

"I see," Lutris said. "He is angry, but he is a good person and will come to his senses. We will catch up with him in a moment. But first, you have friends in the water?"

"Yes," Claire said, now becoming sad. "But they're dead. Stephen tried to rescue them, but they're dead."

"Listen to me. I want you to stay here. Don't start another fire—it will only draw unfriendlies. But I will dive into the water and look for your friends. I'm an excellent swimmer. If anyone can find them, I can," Lutris said.

"You'd do that for me? And yet you hardly know me," Claire said.

"I feel I know you very well. You have a good heart. I've only known such goodness among Black Hawk and his people. But they are in another place. I must find my way in this place. Wait for me," Lutris said as he stepped toward the water.

"I will," Claire said. "I will."

Lutris dove into Lake Meadowash and disappeared from sight.

"Be careful, Lutris," Claire called.

Lutris was underwater for ten minutes. Claire was worried. Could an animal hold its breath that long? She knew she couldn't. But just as a low scream was about to overtake her, Lutris surfaced. He swam back to shore and rejoined Claire.

"There's nobody down there," Lutris said. "There's some debris, but that could be from anything."

"Then they really are gone," Claire cried.

"Don't cry," Lutris said.

But Claire could not stop. To comfort her and distract her, Lutris picked up Claire and carried her. Surprised, Claire let out a short yelp of excitement.

"You're very strong!" she said, forgetting her sadness.

"We should go find Stephen now," Lutris said.

"I can walk on my feet," Claire said. "Though I rather like being carried. You have such soft, warm arms. But really, I'm fine, I'm..."

But Claire became so comfortable that she fell asleep in Lutris's arms. He shifted her around and placed her on his back, where his thick fur clung to her and in fact completely covered her such that Lutris appeared to simply have a hump. He walked down the path where Stephen had gone. About twenty minutes into the walk, he found Stephen, sitting next to a boulder and fast asleep. Lutris picked up Stephen and carried him.

A Problem for Dara

The sun rose over Lake Meadowash. Stephen and Claire to their surprise awoke in a dugout canoe, which had been pulled onto the shore of an island.

"We're on Crow Pits Island!" Claire said. "That's exactly where Loa'neth and Loran were going to take us!"

"How did we get here?" Stephen said. "I left you and Lutris behind. I know I did. I thought I walked all night."

"And I was with Lutris. Now I'm here with you," Claire said.

"One thing is for sure. I'm hungry," Stephen said. "When was the last time you ate?"

"I don't know," Claire said. "But I *am* hungry. Oh I wish Lutris were here."

"Claire, animals and people...well, we're just not meant to be with them. It's not the way of the world. Don't you understand?" Stephen said.

"No, I don't," Claire said.

"What would your mother say? Or your father? You and Lutris, getting married. Isn't that the most ridiculous thing?"

"Stephen! What kind of crazy talk is that?" Claire asked.

"And do you really think you could have children? What would they be, animal or human?" Stephen asked.

"Quit talking like that!" Claire insisted.

"Think about it, Claire. Think really hard," Stephen said.

"Maybe you should have walked back to Millfork. I thought you were more open-minded than that," Claire said.

"I've learned a lot in the last few weeks," Stephen said. "Look at all our friends. Look at what open-mindedness has done to them. They started by doing all sorts of things with plants—using them as a tonic, eating them, and smoking them. Look where it got them—slaves to the plants like a bad addiction. Now I see you starting the same thing, only with an animal instead of a plant."

"WE'RE ANIMALS TOO!" Claire blurted out, and she ran down the beach. "LEAVE ME ALONE!"

Stephen started after Claire briefly, then in frustration he picked up a rock and threw it as far as he could out in Lake Meadowash.

"Ow," said a voice far out in the water. "You'll need a larger rock to harm me."

Then a furry animal swam to shore with three large oysters and two pebbles. It was Lutris, of course, and he was bringing breakfast.

"Take these pebbles and start a fire," Lutris said. "Two of these oysters are for Claire and you. I will eat mine raw."

"You...are helping us? I didn't think animals helped anyone. They always fight amongst themselves," Stephen said.

"Well, some of us *animals*, as you would say, are helpful. And it was I who brought you two here. To help you," Lutris said while walking up to Stephen.

"You call stranding us here helping us? You kidnapped us!" Stephen said.

"Nonsense. You meant to travel here all along," Lutris said.

"What makes you say that?" Stephen asked.

"Claire told me," Lutris said. "And I sensed the direction through vibrations in the ground. I'm good with such things. Here, I'll start the fire," Lutris said.

Lutris gathered some wood and kindling, and then he struck a claw against one of the pebbles. Sparks from the rock caught the kindling on fire, and it spread to the wood.

"We have no bowls here, so I'll make one," Lutris said.

Lutris used one rock against another, and he fashioned a bowl. Then he placed two oysters in the bowl and the bowl atop the fire.

"Here, hold this for me," Lutris said. "I'll bring Claire back for breakfast."

Lutris gave the third oyster to Stephen and then ran after Claire.

"What am I doing holding this? If he wants to play human, he can eat like a human," Stephen said, and he placed the third oyster in the bowl with the other two so that all three oysters were now cooking.

Meanwhile, Lutris ran down the beach. His speed bothered Stephen, however.

"This is why animals should stay extinct," Stephen said to himself. "They think that just because they are stronger and quicker than us, they are superior. Well there's more to superiority than brute animal ability. Brains, that's what superiority is all about. What brains can an animal have?"

Stephen watched as Lutris ran back toward him. Claire rode piggyback, with Lutris's fur holding her snugly. She had her upper body exposed to the air with her hands holding onto Lutris's coat. She hooted and hollered the whole way, as if riding a horse for the first time.

"Did you make the canoe for us?" Claire asked.

"Yes, I did," Lutris replied.

"I knew you did," Claire said.

"You? An animal? How?" Stephen asked.

"With my teeth and claws," Lutris said. "A beaver once taught me the art of felling trees and shaping them to proper design."

"Proper design," Stephen said. "Hah! I suppose we humans are another part of your *proper design.*"

"Don't mind Stephen," Claire said. "He's jealous."

"Disgusted is more like it," Stephen said.

"Well there's nothing like a good breakfast to cure that. Come now. The oysters are surely cooked," Lutris said. "Oh, you placed my oyster in with the others."

"Yes," Stephen said. "We don't eat raw food. If you were civilized like us, you'd eat cooked food too."

"I don't understand," Claire said. "What happened?"

"Lutris brought three oysters for breakfast and put two into this bowl for cooking. I held onto the third one for him," Stephen said.

"So you put it in with the others, didn't you?" Claire asked. "Why do you have to be so difficult? Lutris was nice enough to find us food."

"He is an animal. Animals eat food raw. They are uncivilized," Stephen said.

"Actually, I don't need to eat at all," Lutris said. "I only choose to eat for a specific purpose. In this case, my purpose is courtesy."

"Courtesy! Hah!" Stephen barked.

"I will eat my oyster cooked, Stephen. For your sake. And my courtesy is real. You'll notice I made the cooking bowl, and I started the fire," Lutris added.

"He likes to brag about things he makes. Already he bragged about the canoe," Stephen said.

"Sour grapes, Stephen. You're all sour grapes," Claire said. "I *am* hungry. But we have no plates or anything."

"I will take care of that," Lutris said.

Lutris walked over to a tree and used his teeth to cut out three plates. He then carved out three forks for the plates, and he carved three cups. He also carved out a ladle for scooping up the oysters from their cooking bowl, and he found three nice stones for breaking the oysters open.

"Here," Lutris said as he handed Claire a wooden plate, fork, cup, and a stone.

"Thank you," Claire said.

"And these are for you," Lutris said, but Stephen resisted.

"Stephen!" Claire said.

"I don't need his help," Stephen said.

"Quit being passive aggressive," Claire said. "Lutris is—"

"Lutris! Is that all you can say? We should be fending for ourselves," Stephen said.

"You have pride," Lutris said. "That's good. My people had pride, as did Black Hawk and his people."

"It's not pride. It's stubbornness," Claire said. "Take your plate, Stephen."

Stephen took the plate, cup, fork, and stone.

"There, that wasn't so bad," Claire said.

But as soon as Lutris turned around, Stephen threw the wooden tools and stone into the lake.

"Stephen!" Claire said.

"He must make his own decisions," Lutris said. "Here, Claire."

Lutris used the ladle to place an oyster on Claire's plate and then another one on his own plate.

"Please hold my plate for a moment," Lutris said, and he walked over to the canoe.

"*Hold my plate. Hold my plate,*" Stephen mocked.

Lutris pulled the canoe toward the fire.

"You may sit in the canoe, if you like. Also, these cups have built-in filters. You can place them in any stream of water—fresh or salt—and only clean water of the highest purity will enter," Lutris said. "And the water won't fall out, except through the top."

"That's impossible," Stephen said.

"I'll demonstrate," Lutris said.

Lutris took Claire's cup, placed it in Lake Meadowash partway, and water filtered into the cup through its walls.

"That's the greatest invention I've ever seen," Claire said.

"If only I could place my plate in the water, and food would magically appear," Stephen joked.

"You can't," Claire said. "You threw your plate away."

"Well maybe I'll get my plate and try!" Stephen said.

Stephen jumped into Lake Meadowash and swam out toward his floating plate. The waves had already carried the plate (and fork and cup) out a bit, so he spent some time swimming. Meanwhile, Lutris and Claire enjoyed a nice breakfast in the canoe.

"He'll get used to you," Claire said.

"There's a very important reason I brought you both to this island," Lutris said. "I sensed something unusual last night, just after you fell asleep, and it came from this island. There's a power here, a special power of good. I also sensed a power of evil at the southern tip of this lake. And I believe I can help. The clams—"

"You see?" Stephen yelled. "No magic food. Just a piece of chewed up wood."

Just at that moment, lightning struck the island. Step leaders rose as before when Loran was on the island.

"Stay close!" Lutris said to Claire. "Stephen! Come out of the water! Hurry!"

But Stephen waved Lutris off. Pits opened up as before, and skeleton creatures ascended from the pits and beat on their chest bones, creating frightening music as before. Several skeleton creatures raced toward Lutris and Claire, but Lutris took Claire and placed her on his back, where his fur coat enveloped and protected her. The skeletons attempted to attack Lutris, but he used his fur as a barrier, and any attempt to strike him bounced off, and any attempt to move Lutris caused a bristling vibration on their bones. But what surprised the skeletons the most was how Lutris began chewing on their bones with his long teeth. Lutris was so incredibly quick with his gnawing that the attacking skeletons fell into a pile of bone fragments within a split second.

But there were other skeletons, and while Lutris had made quick work of the ones attacking Claire and himself, several others had scampered across the lake and had reached Stephen.

"Stephen!" Claire yelled.

"Hold on!" Lutris said.

Lutris dove into the water and swam at top speed, with Claire held on his back, and despite that incredible speed, he was unable to reach the skeletons before they reached Stephen. The skeletons captured Stephen, a hole opened up in the lake, the skeletons dragged Stephen down into the hole, but before the hole closed, Lutris swam into the hole with Claire still on his back. The hole closed, and now Lutris and Claire were chasing the skeletons in a flooded tunnel. Lutris had no need for breathing, and Claire was able to breathe the air trapped in Lutris's fur coat, but Stephen had no such help and was now drowning. Lutris continued the pursuit and followed Stephen and the skeletons into a pool at the corner of an underground chamber—the same underground chamber where Loran had been with Dara and the clamifores.

"Stop!" said a voice as Lutris began gnawing two of the skeletons to bits.

Claire ran to Stephen and gave him the Heimlich maneuver to force water out of his lungs.

"Is that command to the skeletons or to me?" Lutris asked.

"Both!" Dara said.

"I can't get him to breathe," Claire said. "And I can't breathe either. The air here—it's bad. I'm going to pass out."

"The air is bad," Lutris said. "But that is because it is made to be bad. Clams. I shall crack them open until they release their stores of oxygen."

"That won't be necessary," Dara said. "I will give the order."

Dara cupped her hands and clapped them twice. The colors on the clamifores changed, and oxygen was released. Claire caught her breath, Stephen expelled water from his lungs, and he began to breathe.

"What are you doing here?" Dara asked Lutris.

"It was your skeletons that pulled Stephen here. I was merely giving chase. To protect him. You kidnapped—"

"Just like Lutris kidnapped me," Stephen said. "We seem to be in a world of one kind kidnapping another. First there were the folk of Slaffton, and I could almost say that Loran and Loa'neth kidnapped us."

"They did not," Claire interrupted. "They saved us."

"Still, they took us away. Then there were those roots that dragged us to Meyta Merco. Then Loran and Loa'neth again. Then the water, Lutris, these skeletons, and here we are."

"Yes, here you are. And you are not welcome. Clamifores and sea otters are natural enemies," Dara said.

"I happen to be very fond of clams, or clamifores as you say," Lutris said.

"Well they don't like you," Dara said.

"I like you, Lutris," Claire said.

"I know, and I'm fond of you too. In fact, I'm fond of most life forms, except for certain forms of people, but only those who are full of bottomless greed," Lutris said. "But it seems I have entered the middle of a war."

"You're very perceptive, Lutris. Loran and Loa'neth had learned of your past and how you entered hibernation inside a giant clam," Dara said. "And now I see you have emerged from that clam."

"For which I have Stephen and Claire to thank," Lutris said.

"I don't want your gratitude," Stephen said. "And if you ask me, there are too many strange animals in this world. A talking otter, a crazy tree woman, now these sickening clams, and—"

The clams rumbled and shot electrical bursts outward. The air went bad.

"Stop it, stop it!" Lutris said. "Or I shall turn your clamifores into cleansing powder."

Dara motioned to the clamifores, and they returned good air to the chamber.

"That's better," Lutris said. "And Stephen, hold your tongue, or I'll stitch it to your cheek with a shard of clam."

"Lutris, you wouldn't do that, would you?" Claire asked. "You naughty boy, you! Give me a kiss!"

Lutris gave her a brief kiss, and she sighed.

"Lutris, your presence here is a threat to us. Not only because of you, but because of what Claire has in her possession," Dara said.

"What do you have, Claire?" Lutris asked.

Claire pulled the cylindrical object from her pocket, but then Stephen grabbed it quickly.

"Where did you get this?" Stephen asked.

"I...found it in my pocket...it must have come from Sleego," Claire said.

"We should find out how it works. Could be useful," Stephen said.

"Let me see that," Lutris said.

"No way," Stephen said, and he resisted.

"Give it to me!" Lutris insisted, and now he reached for Stephen.

Stephen was no match for Lutris's strength, and though Stephen tried to get away, Lutris grabbed Stephen, held him, and pried the object from

Stephen's hand. Under stress from Lutris's paw, the object suddenly flew out and landed across the chamber in a clamifore's mouth.

"No!" Dara yelled, and she ran for the device.

It was too late. The device sank into the soft tissues of the clamifore and contaminated it. The clamifore turned black with spots of green, and a five-legged creature suddenly emerged and began to constrict the clamifore.

"A starfish!" Lutris said.

A head emerged from the starfish, and Claire gasped.

"Wonga!" Stephen yelled.

The other clamifores surrounded the starfish, and Lutris started for the starfish, but it was Dara who made the first attack. The starfish simply swatted Dara to the side. Dara sat up but remained in a daze.

"It's not really Wonga," Claire said. "It's just her image."

"But her image is attacking that clam," Stephen said.

"More like draining the clam," Lutris said. "I'll put an end to that. I'm particularly fond of starfish."

Lutris reached the starfish and was about to take a nibble, but the image of Wonga spoke.

"Stand back, you heathen of this world," image of Wonga said.

"Are you Wonga?" Stephen said.

"I...*am*...Wonga," the starfish said, with the head of Wonga weaving. "You and all that you know are subject to my domain."

"See here," Lutris said. "Do you know who I am?"

"You are nothing more than an animal of the animal kingdom," Wonga said.

"I am Lutris, king of the east Pacific sea otters," Lutris said.

The image of Wonga laughed.

"I command all things. Behold!" Wonga said.

The image of Wonga belched out a ball of fire, and it held its shape and displayed images of captured people, first the workers of Slaffton, then others in Meyta Merco. A last scene showed Loran, Loa'neth, Gliria, and Myoxi along with many others working in a gold mine. Claire gasped.

"Your friends then?" image of Wonga said. "I am pleased. See how I make use of the weak-minded to perform my labors. I mine gold so that I may melt it and use it to extract mercury from the ground. And meet my master architect, the one person who has made this all possible."

The fireball now showed an image of Lillianina at a control center, but she looked tired and drugged.

"Your kind is one toothful away from being toppled over," Lutris said.

"I doubt that indeed," image of Wonga said. "You would be poisoned by mercury before your teeth finished their first bite. But there is another prize that awaits, Lutris, king of the east Pacific sea otters. Lillianina has performed seismic analysis of the gold mine, and she has found that we are only three days away from up-heaving a sarcophagus with a golden spotted otter inside. I believe you know the name, Dara. Amicolli?"

"That's impossible," Dara said.

The image of Wonga laughed. Intense anger overwhelmed Lutris. He rushed the starfish and bit off its head then bit off each of its arms. The fireball dissipated, and the image of Wonga went limp.

"The conversation went bad anyway," Lutris said.

Dara tended the clamifore, removed the cylindrical object, and the clamifore began to regain its strength.

"No permanent damage to this clamifore," Dara said. "Thank you, Lutris. You must realize how difficult it is to thank an adversary."

"Is the link broken?" Stephen asked.

"Yes, it is," Dara said. "I shall destroy this projection device."

Dara placed the cylindrical object in a tube connected to the floor, and the object disappeared.

"Wonga cannot harm us here," Dara said. "The projection device has been destroyed."

"She cannot harm us at the present. But this news of unearthing Amicolli troubles me," Lutris said.

"Why? Are you afraid of this other sea otter? Is he a rival?" Stephen said.

"Amicolli is a *she*," Dara said.

"A girlfriend?" Claire said, breaking into tears. "But I thought...you and me...Lutris!"

"I have never met Amicolli," Lutris said. "She is much older than I, by a few thousand years. She was captured as a slave in ancient Egypt and then escaped. There are many legends about her, and not all agree. One says she will awaken and marry a great being. Another says she will join forces with me and rid the world of evil. Friends in my time said I was to marry her."

"Would you?" Claire said through tears.

"No, of course not," Lutris said, and he kissed Claire.

"But Amicolli is said to hold great power. Wonga wishes to wield that power," Dara said.

"Another of our legends says much the same, that one of great power will subdue her and command her to great things. I was told it would be for good," Lutris explained, "but now I see it can also be for evil."

There was a silence in the chamber, an uncomfortable silence. Dara and the clamifores were still nervous about Lutris's presence there, but he did help them, and so for the moment the tension was in check. Lutris was concerned about Wonga, Claire was concerned about a possible rival in Amicolli, and Stephen just wanted to get away from animals and any strange life forms, at least by his reckoning.

"Well, at least we know what happened to the others—Loran and Loa'neth and the picocians, I mean," Stephen said. "Strange how Wonga caught them."

"We knew of this," Dara said.

"You did?" Claire asked. "How?"

"Since the transformation of Loran and Loa'neth, we have been able to track their movements, sometimes even seeing what they see," Dara said. "When Sleego attacked, Loa'neth used her scepter, and we were able to see what happened. After Claire, Stephen, and Sleego fell out of the vehicle, underwater vines gathered and prepared at the lake's bottom as the vehicle descended. When the vehicle hit the bottom, the vines entangled the vehicle and pulled it into an underwater chamber. There your friends were taken away by sentries from Meyta Merco and then taken deeper into Sathiakia where they met Wonga. After a brief conversation, Wonga sent them into a gold mine as workers."

"And you just sat here and watched? What kind of things are you?" Claire asked.

"They're animals," Stephen said. "That's what animals do. Watch as others suffer and die."

Lutris walked over to Stephen, grabbed him by the neck, and lifted him.

"I could snap your neck for those words," Lutris said.

Stephen's face turned deep red as he struggled for air.

"Lutris, no!" Claire said.

"But I care for the living, not the dead," Lutris said, and he released Stephen, who fell to the floor and gasped for air.

"Don't trust him, Claire," Stephen gasped. "He'll do us all in."

"If I had wanted to do that, I would have done so long ago," Lutris said. "But our real problem is Wonga. She is a being of great power and will choke us all before the end. Should Wonga animate Amicolli to her will, Wonga will begin a march on this world that will include this island. You cannot escape. You have already made your own prison here."

"But we have been filtering evil," Dara said. "We've been keeping the world in check."

"For how much longer?" Lutris asked.

"And what about my friends? Loran, Loa'neth, Gliria, and Myoxi?" Claire asked. "We must help them."

"Yes, we must," Lutris said. "It would appear I am the only one left who has the power to stop Wonga. Dara and the clamifores are content to stay here and filter the ether. You and Stephen will follow me."

"No, I won't," Stephen said. "As soon as we get out of here, I'm going back to Millfork."

"No you're not," Claire said. "You're going with us to help our friends."

"I'm done with friends and animals. I want to sit back in Braegan's bar and sip some mead and eat some toasted bread," Stephen dreamed.

"The problem is mercury," Lutris said. "It's a powerful poison, and the one thing I'm not prepared to handle."

"How do you know that?" Claire asked.

"I sensed it when I bit the starfish," Lutris said.

"Sathiakia is filled with mercury," Dara said. "And arsenic, lead, and cadmium. It's known as MALC. A previous civilization has filled the soil with MALC from their refuse and unwanted devices."

"Amicolli," Lutris said. "She must be the answer."

"Let her rest in peace," Claire said, still a bit jealous of Amicolli. "Let her legend remain undisturbed."

"I wish I could, but Wonga will exhume Amicolli if I don't get there first," Lutris said.

"I don't want to lose you. I don't want you falling for another otter," Claire said.

"I promise that you are the only one in my life," Lutris said. "You took a piece of my heart the moment I first saw you."

"Lutris. You cannot stay here. The clamifores are growing restless," Dara said.

"Then I shall command them into my service," Lutris said.

"No," Dara said. "I forbid it."

"You both hate me and love me," Lutris said. "I can destroy any of you. But I won't. Not unless it is absolutely necessary. But I will bite at your shells and twist your tails, so to speak, to rouse you to action. You will not remain idle in this tomb. I command you. Arise!"

Half the clamifores extended appendages and began to walk toward Lutris.

"Lutris! Do not disturb my people!" Dara said.

"I've noticed that you aren't a clam, but are instead one of these little people Claire has told me about," Lutris said.

"Loa'neth said you were a picocian who died," Claire said.

"And these are not your people, but you command them as if they are," Lutris said. "Now I command them."

"Not all of them," Dara said. "Like any society, my people are ideologically bifurcated. You will take half from me, but the other half will stay."

Lutris stared hard at Dara. Then he looked at Claire.

"Don't press the issue," Claire said. "I feel a civil war will break out, clam against clam, if you try to take all clams with you."

"You are very wise," Lutris said. "Very well. There will be no civil war, but war I make against Wonga, and those who follow me shall be my army. To war!"

The clamifores in favor of Lutris joined him. Lutris touched the amulet around his neck, and several clamifores opened a passageway to the surface —not the one Loran had taken earlier, but a larger one. Lutris, Claire, Stephen, and the clamifores then left the chamber and climbed to the surface. Clamifores floated on Lake Meadowash, and the three stood on one and used it as the lead boat for travel south on the lake to Sathiakia.

Wonga's Gold Mine

"Loran," Loa'neth called with a slow, monotone voice. "The vines...they are pulling us. I...can't stop it."

"I feel numb," Loran replied.

"What can we do?" Gliria said with an equally slow and monotone voice.

Vines under direction of Wonga pulled the vehicle into an underwater tunnel. Stephen and Claire had escaped and were swimming to shore, but Loran, Loa'neth, Gliria, and Myoxi were drugged and could not get their muscles to move. It was as if they had been drained of energy. Fortunately, Loran and Loa'neth did not need to breathe, and Myoxi and Gliria had their two weeks of oxygen reserve, so none of the four would drown. But they had to wait for the conclusion of this capture.

The capture didn't take long. Vines pulled the vehicle to an underground transit passageway from Meyta Merco to Wonga's Lair. Several slaves from Meyta Merco transferred the four friends from the captured vehicle to a small train, and the slaves wasted no time in sending the train along those underground tracks fast to Wonga's Lair, which was deep in Sathiakia.

"My...scepter," Loa'neth said.

She looked around as quickly as the drug would allow, but she could not find it.

"*My scepter, my scepter*," the slaves mocked. "You have no need for a scepter where you're going. The queen will dispense with you soon enough."

The train picked up speed, incredible speed. Lights on the tunnel walls flashed by so quickly that Myoxi and Gliria thought they would be sick. For Loran, this was the worst part of his journey. He was completely powerless and out of control. He had hoped to find Lillianina and rescue her. Now he himself needed rescuing. And in the process, he had led Loa'neth, Gliria, and Myoxi into captivity.

"I've betrayed Lillianina, my friends, and myself. What good am I?" he whispered.

The train now exited the tunnel and traveled above ground. It passed an open-strip gold mine, where people of Meyta Merco attire worked to remove gold. It then passed another mine, full of old disused electronics equipment, and next to that mine was a foundry where the electronics were melted with gold brought in by carts from the neighboring gold mine, and fresh MALC discs the size of crackers were produced.

"They *make* MALC," Gliria said. "Like food. They make it like making food."

Beyond the foundry was a shiny castle built of MALC, with many windows on the side and on angled roofs, allowing maximum sunshine to enter. But with the smoke and stench from the foundry, there was less sunshine than one might desire.

The train entered the castle, and everything was a shiny variation of grey, yellow (from arsenic), blue (from cadmium), or black. There were many pools of liquid—some of water, but others of mercury. Then the train stopped, and the four friends were brought to their feet by the Meyta Merco slaves. The friends were walked down a long hallway, where at the end was an elder tree, with five large roots in the shape of a starfish. The elder tree had a head, but it was turned away. When the four finally reached the elder tree, it turned around and breathed a ball of flame at them. The four had recovered enough to duck from the flame, and when they stood, the elder tree spoke:

"Sooooo, you have decided to invade my kingdom, Loran Laculic of Laculic Manor. And you have brought three picocians. Loa'neth is Lord Zdannag's servant. I shall send word that he may fetch her, so that she may continue assisting him in doing my work. Myoxi and Gliria I have not met, but I know they are miners in Rainbear Mountain," the elder tree said.

"Are...are you Wonga?" Loran asked.

The elder tree now took great height and swayed all about, thrusting her head immediately before the four friends. She laughed and spoke.

"I am known by many names. Acromata, Bregget, Ecoala, Feshk, Tartana, Vancha, and Wonga."

"See here," Loran said. "Have you imprisoned my cousin Lillianina?"

Wonga laughed.

"I have," Wonga said.

"Then I demand for her immediate release! You have no right to—"

Wonga then extended a branch as if to shake the four's hands in friendship, but instead the branch split into four, picked up the four, and lifted them high in the air. The four friends were now being whipped along in the air while being strangled.

"I have every right," Wonga said. "I have been chosen by an ancient civilization, to take all that they gave and make it my own."

"You'll poison the planet," Loran struggled to say.

"Let us go," Gliria complained.

"One creature's poison is another's delight," Wonga said. "This world is always changing and always filled with the sway of winners and losers. Now it is my turn. But I will not turn the losers away. I shall make them a part of my kingdom, as I do with you four. Send them to the gold mine!"

Wonga flung them across the hall, and the four landed badly, hurting their bones and ligaments. They could barely walk, but that didn't matter. Wonga's servants ushered them back to the train where they were taken as slaves to work the gold mine.

"Loa'neth," Gliria said as the slave drivers directed the four into the gold mine.

"No talking," a slave driver said as he cracked his whip.

"Can you still read my thoughts?" Gliria thought.

"Yes," Loa'neth thought back.

"Over here," said the slave driver. "You—Loran and Loa'neth—you'll dig into the mine. Snee-snocs—you'll operate the separator. Now dig!"

Not realizing Loa'neth was also picocian didn't help matters. Using picks and shovels, Loran and Loa'neth dug up the earth and tossed it into a separator. Water flowed through the separator and removed non-metallic material. The remaining material was fed through another separator which heated the material and spun it in a centrifuge to separate the gold from other things. Then out poured gold into a large container, which when full was hauled away on a cart. And all along, dragonflies buzzed around their faces and irritated the four.

"Loa'neth," Gliria thought. "We are seeing fragments of burial boxes and otter hair in the separator."

"That could explain why Wonga thinks Amicolli is here," Loa'neth thought back. "This gold mine is an otter cemetery. Now tell me, Gliria. Is any of the fur spotted?"

"No," Gliria replied.

"Then this isn't a spotted otter graveyard. And Amicolli could be elsewhere," Loa'neth said. "Now if we could but figure out where."

Stephen Deserts

Lutris, Claire, and Stephen were standing on the lead clam of Lutris's army, now speeding along Lake Meadowash toward Sathiakia.

"This is all wrong," Stephen said. "You're now exploiting these clams to your own will. Are we your slaves too?"

"Stephen! We're on the way to help our friends. No one is making you do anything," Claire said.

"Then if I were to leave right now, you wouldn't follow me?" Stephen said.

"Stephen!" Claire said.

"You are free to do as you please," Lutris said. "It was thought you wished to help free your friends."

"If they can be caught, so can we. This is a suicide mission," Stephen said.

"We have to try," Claire said. "We must!"

"So he's brainwashed you, Claire. Well I'm not so easily duped. I'm leaving!" Stephen said, and with that he jumped off the clamifore and swam back toward Crow Pits Island.

Lutris's clamifore army swam past Stephen. He had to dodge quite a number of them, and he wasn't pleased that yet another animal was getting in his way. But the last clamifore passed him by, and now he had open water between him and the island. The currents were with him, and he was able to swim back within another ten minutes. When he reached the shore, he rested for a moment and then walked toward the dugout canoe.

"No paddle," Stephen said. "That Lutris must have dragged us here. Oh, how am I going to get back to the mainland? I'll have to find something I can use for a paddle."

Stephen looked around the island for a plank or tree he could shape for a paddle. At that moment, Dara walked up.

"You have returned," she said.

"Not for long. As soon as I make a paddle, I'm going back to Millfork," Stephen said.

"Your friends will be disappointed, but I do not blame you for fleeing. Lutris is going to war, and the major outcome is death," Dara said.

"Who says I'm fleeing? Are you saying I'm a coward?" Stephen asked.

"No. It takes great courage to know when to retreat," Dara said.

"But I haven't fought a battle. How can I retreat?" Stephen asked. "Don't answer that."

"You are welcome to stay here," Dara said. "We will be watching as the battle unfolds."

"With animals? And what do I care about the battle? Animals against animals. No, I'm through. If you can help me make a paddle, then I'd be grateful, and I'll leave you to your battle."

Dara suddenly descended into the sand as a pit opened up. Minutes later, she returned with a paddle.

"This is made of the same material as a clamifore shell. It is unbreakable and will float on water. May you reach your destination with safety and speed," Dara said.

Stephen looked at her dumbfounded.

"I've never been helped by an animal before. Seems I'm always fighting one. Maybe your kind on the island isn't so bad. Well, I'm not staying around to find out," he said.

"One more thing," Dara said. "Place this low on the tail of the canoe."

Dara handed him a small, half-clam shell, but it was flexible and was sticky on the inside.

"What is it?" Stephen said. "A tracking device?"

"It is a means of propulsion," Dara said. "It communicates with the paddle. Hold the paddle with both hands touching each other and point the paddle in the opposite direction you wish to go. The mini clamifore will push water that direction and thus send the canoe forward. When you wish it to stop, pull your hands apart. And if you wish to communicate with us on Crow Pits Island, yes, you may hold the paddle up and speak to it. But these are not for tracking you, Stephen. Best of luck."

Stephen placed the clam on the outside back of the canoe. He then pushed the dugout canoe into Lake Meadowash, jumped in, shoved off with the paddle (making sure his hands didn't touch while holding the paddle), and paddled away. When he felt he had reached a safe enough distance from shore, he pointed the paddle behind him and brought his hands together. The mini clamifore sent a jet of water behind the canoe, and the canoe moved forward rapidly. Stephen spent some effort learning how to steer the canoe with this new propulsion method, and he settled on holding the paddle in the water as a rudder and pointing it backward.

"Should I go to Slaffton?" he asked himself. "No, that's the wrong direction. I'll go north and dock in Millfork itself."

With the mini clamifore providing propulsion, Stephen made good speed.

"Here I am, now using an animal to work for me. I don't know if I should be thankful or disgusted. It's another example of an animal being used by another. Yeah, I guess Claire is right—we're all animals."

Stephen navigated the canoe toward the western shore so that he could approach and thus identify Millfork. He reached the shore quickly enough, and roads along the shore were filled with people marching south, carrying packs, shields, and spears as if going to war. He reached Lord Zdannag's dock, but the property had been ransacked and deserted.

"What's happening around here?" Stephen asked himself.

Stephen continued along the coastline, and he made the mistake of getting a little too close. A vine from the shore slithered into the water and attempted to capsize the canoe and drag it ashore. Stephen swatted at the vine with his paddle, and jets of water squirted all over from the clamifore, getting Stephen wet and pushing the canoe around in unexpected ways. Finally, Stephen had the idea of using the water jet as a weapon. He maneuvered the canoe's tail and pointed the paddle at the vine with his hands held together. The clamifore sent a burst of water at the vine, and the vine withdrew. The canoe was shoved around from the water jets, however, and Stephen had to lean against the canoe to counteract the jets so the canoe would not tip over.

"Whew! That was close!" Stephen said.

And so, Stephen directed the canoe farther out from shore. He continued northward toward Millfork, and all along the way he saw more people with more attack gear. It wasn't long before he reached Millfork. He directed the canoe into port, but the port was strangely abandoned, and there were no people around.

"It's like a ghost town," Stephen said.

Stephen tied the canoe to a post and walked along the dock until he reached shore. He saw movement ahead and made for it quickly to ask what was happening, but it was only a large paper bag caught on a post and blowing around in the wind.

"It's been abandoned too," Stephen said.

He made his way to Laculic Tavern and went inside. Empty, except for Morga who was sitting in the far corner at a table with Braegan.

"Morga, Braegan. Am I glad to see you two! I need a drink! Some mead would be fine, but even a beer would be welcome!" Stephen said.

"We're closed," Morga said.

"What?!" Stephen gasped.

"Everyone went south to fight the war, but before they left, they took all our food. We have nothing left," Morga said.

"But...I...you're still here?" Stephen stumbled.

"We're getting ready to leave for Buckner Falls," Braegan said. "We were just discussing it. Look, here's the map we have."

Braegan showed the map to Stephen. Stephen studied it and then returned it.

"It will be a difficult journey," Morga said. "The snow is melting and sliding down slopes. Anyone caught in such a slide will be buried alive."

"And anyone caught on top of the slide would be tossed into boulders below and splattered like—" Braegan started.

"No need to say more," Stephen said. "What am I going to do? I came up here to get away from those animals and from war."

"You're welcome to come with us to Buckner Falls," Braegan said. "Did you bring anything warm?"

"No, I didn't," Stephen said.

"Follow me," Braegan said. "I have some extra furs in back."

Stephen followed Braegan into a back room. Braegan handed a large fur coat to Stephen. Stephen tried it on, but it was too big, and he was completely buried in fur.

"I'm like some overgrown fur ball animal. I can't wear this, and I can't go to Buckner Falls," Stephen said.

"It will be dangerous to stay here," Morga said, now walking into the back room. "There's no food in Millfork, and the respectable folk are gone. I expect looting to start tonight."

"I don't care," Stephen said.

"Look, if you really are intent on staying, perhaps my brother's cabin will provide refuge. The north and west sides are against the mountain, the east is by the lake, so you would only have to defend the south side. Here is the key," Braegan said.

Stephen hesitated.

"Go on, take it," Morga said. "I'm sure Loran wouldn't mind. In fact, I know he'd appreciate it if you would look after it."

"If only you knew," Stephen said. "Loran is a captive of Wonga, a hideous tree/starfish/woman creature of Sathiakia."

Braegan and Morga exchanged glances.

"Can it be true?" Morga asked.

"There's only one way to find out," Braegan said. "We must go south to Sathiakia and fight."

"I wouldn't do that," Stephen said. "You'll be caught too."

"But what else is there to do?" Braegan said. "I can't go to Buckner Falls knowing my brother is in trouble. I might not see him again!"

Then Morga and Braegan rushed out the door with packs barely filled, leaving Stephen all alone.

"Wait!" Stephen said, chasing them down the road a little. "Don't leave!"

But they were gone.

"Now what?" Stephen asked himself. He then tossed Loran's cabin key in the air. "Go to Loran's cabin? What else is there?"

Stephen left Millfork and headed north. He traveled for a bit before reaching a sign pointing to Wretched Cave.

"Wretched Cave," he mused. "I remember hearing about that place. Never went. Was too scared as a child. But now I'm older. Well, I have nothing better to do. Might as well go. From what I've heard there are no animals, so that should be good."

And so, Stephen walked to the Wretched Cave, the place Loran, Myoxi, and Gliria had visited not long ago.

"Here it is," Stephen said. "I don't expect to find anything useful inside. Probably a bunch of silly lights and sounds of the wind."

But Stephen stopped before going in. Was he afraid? What held him back? Or perhaps he just didn't want to be disappointed one last time.

"Okay, time to go in," Stephen said.

Stephen walked into the Wretched Cave. He stared at the wall. Nothing.

"I'm here! Do your thing," Stephen yelled. "Hello? Show me your stuff!"

But the fungi did nothing.

"I don't know what people find so interesting about this cave. Just a bunch of nothing," Stephen said. "Let me guess. People get scared by ferocious animals from the past. Very well. Show me the worst animals that ever roamed! It won't matter. I'll hate them anyway."

Then the fungi echoed the sound of a grizzly bear. Now Stephen was in the ancient past, with a stream nearby and a snow-capped mountain in the distance. A grizzly bear caught a fish in its mouth, but on seeing Stephen, the bear dropped the fish and ran for Stephen.

"And that's supposed to scare me? It's all so fake," Stephen said.

The bear pawed at Stephen and gnashed its teeth, but Stephen was uninjured, of course, since this was only an illusion.

"That's why animals are extinct. They only thought of exploiting others," Stephen said.

The scene changed. Instead of seeing wild animals, Stephen saw Wonga's slaves in the gold mine.

"More exploitation," Stephen said.

The slaves continued digging, but then they reached a sarcophagus—one that Wonga had predicted would be Amicolli. Ropes and pulleys suspended from a crane lowered onto the sarcophagus, and workers hurried to get the ropes underneath. The crane began to lift the sarcophagus, but too early—ropes on one side slipped off, and one end of the sarcophagus fell and crushed three workers, who screeched briefly in pain before being splattered across the mine.

"How sickening. There is no limit to the barbarism of animals," Stephen said.

The crane lowered the sarcophagus, the ropes reattached, and the crane lifted it again then swung the sarcophagus through the air until it was just above the flat bed of a train. Close-by and watching were Loran, Loa'neth, Myoxi, and Gliria. Slave drivers forced the four friends into a train car behind the flat bed, and the full train started down a track and headed toward Wonga's Lair.

"This isn't Amicolli," Loa'neth thought to the other three, and somehow Stephen was also able to hear her thoughts.

"Then who is it? Or what is it?" Loran thought.

"Something else. Something made of MALC. Not animal at all," Loa'neth thought back.

"What could be buried in a sarcophagus that is metal and not animal?" Stephen wondered.

For the first time, Stephen was concerned. Or thrilled. Or frightened, or maybe all emotions at once. He wasn't sure if he should cheer this new find or be fearful of it. Lutris had spoken of Amicolli's find and capture as the end of all things, but what of this other find?

"This can't be real, can it?" Stephen said. "I mean, I'm still in the Wretched Cave. Is this what's really happening in Sathiakia?"

The sarcophagus entered Wonga's Lair, and she expectantly awaited its arrival. Loran, Loa'neth, Gliria, and Myoxi attended along with slave drivers and other slaves.

"Tartana my queen," the lead slave driver said. "We present the sarcophagus of the Sathiakia Gold Mine."

Wonga walked over to the sarcophagus with her five, thick roots. She stood atop the sarcophagus, and like a starfish attacking a clam, she pried open the sarcophagus to reveal a humanoid shape of metallic design.

"What are you?" she mused. "Totally made of MALC. Rise, then."

Wonga lifted the shape and placed it on the floor, feet first. It was now apparent that this was a robot or android of some form. She wrapped two of her roots around the robot and brought it to life.

"Wake now, my obedient servant, and speak your name and origin," she said.

"I am Mersladium, the ultimate creation of Craymar Industries," the robot said.

"Craymar," Wonga said. "I've heard that name before. It was an ancient corporation that was formed to put Dayla Industries out of business."

"It succeeded. I am the reason for its success," Mersladium said.

"I see, I see," Wonga said with excitement. "How is it you put Dayla Industries out of business?"

"I created an army of *merselats*—robots like myself. We took over design and production of complex product lines by improving the worker," Mersladium said.

"How exciting! Now I have brought you back to life, Mersladium, and for that you are in my debt," Wonga said.

"I am in your debt and in your service," Mersladium said.

"Good. I knew you would be helpful. I need an army. Humans on land are marching from the north, and a sea otter named Lutris is leading an army of clamifores on the lake," Wonga said. "I want you to make merselats—many merselats!"

"To make merselats, I shall need human donors," Mersladium said.

"I can help there," said the lead slave driver, who snapped his fingers and motioned forward new captives.

"I demand representation!" said the one of twenty captives ushered into Wonga's Lair.

"It's Captain Friscott," Gliria said.

"You worms!" the captain said, pointing to Gliria and Myoxi. "I knew you were behind all this!"

Wonga laughed.

"No, my good captain, these picocians have nothing to do with your capture. It is I who have sent for you. These waters belong to me, and anyone who sails in them is my property."

"People aren't property. Let us go," the captain protested, and he became enraged and swung his arms wildly, giving the guards much grief in restraining him.

"Start with the captain, Mersladium," Wonga said.

"No!" the captain screamed. "You can't do this!"

Mersladium took the sarcophagus and positioned it upright on the floor. He touched several buttons inside, and the sarcophagus grew in height and width and sported a doorway of plasma. Mersladium then jumped over to Captain Friscott in a single bound, reaching a great and ominous height.

"Magnificent!" Wonga said.

Mersladium pushed Captain Friscott along, with the captain screaming and pleading for his life. Loran, Loa'neth, Gliria, and Myoxi looked on in horror. Stephen continued to watch, not sure what to expect. Mersladium now had Captain Friscott by the arm, and the two were in front of the converted sarcophagus. Mersladium tossed Captain Friscott in through the plasma door, with one final scream from the captain, and then Mersladium strode in through the doorway. The sound of a billion clashing metal filings filled Wonga's Lair. Then Mersladium exited alone. He stood for a few moments then crossed his arms. A merselat robot exited the converted sarcophagus chamber. It was perhaps eighty-percent as tall as Mersladium, and instead of having Mersladium's yellow, black, and silver coloring, it had red, black, and silver coloring.

"This one has plenty of toxic metals in its body," Mersladium said. "That made the conversion process very easy. The iron, however, could not be eliminated, and it shows up as red."

Gliria covered her mouth to muffle a scream.

"Note the number on the upper chest. This unit is MT1, which stands for Merselat 1," Mersladium said.

Mersladium then threw additional members of Captain Friscott's crew into the chamber, and they too came out converted into merselat robots, and each had a sequential number such that there was an MT2, MT3, etc.

"Animals, animals, animals!" Stephen yelled. "Even the robots consume others like animals! Where does it end? Where does it end?"

Stephen then threw rocks at the fungi to disturb the scene. The view distorted as if being viewed under water, but it returned to a clear view showing Mersladium creating more merselat soldiers for Wonga's army.

"Enough already!" Stephen yelled.

Stephen threw all sorts of rocks, one at a time, at the scene. And it changed from showing Wonga's Lair to a bunch of young boys in a circle throwing rocks at a single boy in the middle.

"Eat worms, Robin! Eat worms!" taunted one boy.

"Sing like a bird!" taunted another.

"Fly away if you can!" taunted a third.

"ANIMALS!" Stephen yelled.

Stephen threw several rocks at a time to break up the scene. It changed to that of a delivery room, where Stephen's mother was giving birth to himself. She screamed in pain from the contractions, and the delivery bed was all bloody.

"Such a primitive act. Animals!" he yelled.

The doctor cut the umbilical cord and handed the newborn to a nurse, who cleaned it up and cut the newborn's foot for the blood test.

"Animals! Cutting and bleeding and pain," Stephen cried.

"Do you have a name?" the nurse asked.

"Yes. Robin Stephen Royer," Stephen's mother said, and the scene changed from the delivery room to a close-up of a robin singing, hopping, then looking for a worm, hopping again, looking for another worm, finding it, pulling it out of the ground, and slurping it.

"AAAAAARRRRRRRRR!!!" Stephen yelled, and he ran up to the fungi and kicked them like mad.

The fungi shot out sparks and flames and spat all sorts of hot goo on Stephen's legs.

"I'm getting out of here! I HATE ANIMALS FOREVER!" he screamed.

Stephen ran out of Wretched Cave and up Rainbear Mountain as fast as he could in hopes of never seeing an animal or human again. His legs were on fire, and he couldn't believe how quickly they ran. Up, up, up a mountain path he ran and climbed. The air cooled, and the terrain changed from dry boulders to snow and ice. He didn't care. The fire in his legs kept his whole body warm. The path became less smooth and more rocky, and Stephen had to jump more than run, but he kept going, and he was able to travel many paces this way. At one point he reached a little cliff, and he decided to stop and look out toward Lake Meadowash. Far in the distance, he could see the smoke of war.

"I'm going to make it," Stephen said. "I just have this one mountain to climb, and no more animals. No more animals!"

Stephen looked down at his legs. They were still covered in goo, but the material on his pants had dissolved away, and the skin on his legs was inflamed. His leg muscles twitched and jerked, discontent with being still.

"It will cool off in the snow," Stephen said. "I must get moving again."

Stephen climbed up rock after rock, but the snow grew deeper, and now instead of climbing rocks, he was scaling glaciers. The snow first came up to his calves, then his knees, and then his thighs. He was nearly at the top of the mountain when the air became too thin for him. He was disoriented and felt a little drunk, and now his lungs filled with fluid, making breathing all the more difficult.

"What's happening? What's wrong with me?" he asked. "My legs want to keep moving, but I have no power. And no matter how hard I breathe, I can't get enough air. My hands—I can't feel my hands."

His hands had now turned white and went rigid. The rigidity traveled up his arms until both arms were now frozen to his sides.

"Must...keep...going," he said.

But his progress was slowed. His legs still burned like fire, and they oozed, but the ooze froze partway down such that many icicles formed.

"I'm not just an animal," Stephen said with difficulty. "I'm...not...just...an animal."

He could hardly move his jaw, and that too was beginning to freeze. His eyes glazed over, making vision more difficult.

"Where am I? Must...find...shelter. Must..."

But everything looked the same to Stephen—white. The brilliant snow, combined with his blurred vision, washed out everything. He tried feeling his way around with his legs, but his raw sores made steps more difficult and more painful.

"I *am*...an animal. The mountain...has beaten me," he said.

He paused at a small cliff, the last one overlooking Lake Meadowash before crossing the summit and descending to the west toward Buckner Falls.

"Cannot...reach...the summit," Stephen struggled to say. "Cannot. Animal. Animal!"

It was no use. He had reached his last breath, and his legs would go no farther. He would die on this little cliff and remain there for all to see. He could not stay. With his last effort, he hobbled to the cliff's edge, looked up to the sky, said farewell, and slipped off.

A New Acquaintance

Stephen's fall carried him deep into a crevasse. It was dark, lonely, and deathly silent.

"Say goodbye to the animal," he said, and he fell unconscious.

Stephen's legs were wedged in between the two ice sheets, and the little bits of fungi goo melted the ice, which slowly lowered Stephen into the crevasse. The fluid in his lungs began to freeze, and his breathing became increasingly shallow. Death was only moments away. Moments away.

His descent slowed and was nearly stopped, but the goo reached something in the ice, something that was not water or plant. It was the single paw of a frozen animal. The goo loosened the ice, and the paw began to move a little. Then a little more, and a little more, like a chick breaking free of its egg. Stephen had nearly expired, but the goo had awakened and freed this animal. It touched Stephen and realized Stephen was not just a living being but one in great distress. It dug a little passage sideways through the crevasse and dragged Stephen with it, digging and digging until it reached a warm cave in the mountain, a hotspot that was free of the ice.

The animal found ancient bark and conifer needles in the cave, and it made a little bed for Stephen then placed Stephen on the bed. The animal reclined on the bed and extended its coat over Stephen to warm him.

Hours (or days?) later, Stephen awoke to the sounds of soft opera-like humming from a woman.

"Where am I?" he asked, not expecting an answer.

"You are in Rainbear Mountain," said the woman with a bit of a sing-song to her speech, as if she were from a Scandinavian country.

Stephen looked around. Several glass spheres on shelves glowed from electrical charge, providing light, but his vision was still recovering, and so he could only see near.

"I can't see you," he said. "Who...who are you?"

"Shhh," she said. "You're in need of nourishment. Here, try this."

Stephen looked, and he could see the woman walking toward him. She had long, thick, brown hair that traveled halfway down her body, yet she was tall and slender, as best as he could see. She wore a simple tunic and had sandals on her feet. She gave him a wooden cup with fluid inside. Stephen gulped the fluid.

"Slowly," she said. "Slowly."

"I...I'm just so thirsty," he said. "This is good. It's filling and sustaining."

"You lost a lot of blood," she said. "Your legs bled from that fungal infection. But I've cleaned up your legs and bandaged them."

"I'm like an animal with legs injured from a trap. An animal!" he said.

Suddenly, Stephen remembered his revulsion toward animals. In a panic, he stood up quickly and ran for the opening. But the woman caught Stephen and sat him down on a rock padded with moss. Her resolve surprised Stephen. She had five times the strength of any strongman he'd ever met.

"Shhh," she said. "Relax. Your bandages must need changing again for you to get restless legs so easily."

"Restless legs?" he asked.

"Yes. You kicked much in your sleep—always when your wounds needed cleaning. Now stay here. I'll be right back."

The woman walked away and resumed humming, and her hum grew to a moderate-volume, opera-like singing. Stephen remained sitting on the rock. Who was this woman? Was she from Buckner Falls? Or did she live in this cave? She certainly wasn't from Millfork or anywhere nearby. The woman returned with a bucket of water, a sponge bar, and clean wrappings. Stephen got a little nervous and kicked his legs.

"Relax. I won't bite," she laughed, though her laughter suggested in some instances she would.

"The wrapping is so tight that I can't even see where it starts or ends," Stephen said.

But the woman didn't find the beginning. Faster than Stephen could see, she sliced her fingernail along the length of one leg then the other, and both bandages came apart—all the while singing. In fact, when she wasn't speaking, she was singing.

"Wow!" Stephen said. "You...cut those bandages cleanly. But I didn't feel anything on my skin."

"I have great precision," she said.

She pulled his bandages away, dipped the sponge in the water, and cleansed his legs.

"There, doesn't that feel good?" she asked.

"It tingles a little," he said.

"That's a good sign. It means your nerves are returning to normal," she said. "So tell me, what brings you into the mountains like this? From what are you running?"

"How...how'dge you know?" he asked.

The woman laughed.

"You don't know who I am, do you?" she asked.

"No. I can hardly see you," Stephen said.

"Here then," she said.

The woman dipped the sponge in the water, wrung out the excess, and wiped Stephen's eyes closed. Then she took an eye-dropper bottle from a pocket and placed a drop in the corner of his right eye and a drop in the corner of his left. Stephen opened his eyes and blinked, and his vision improved markedly. He could see she was young and beautiful, with dark chestnut eyes and brown hair. He saw blond spots and highlights in her hair.

"Now do you know?" she laughed.

"You must be an angel, because no woman in this world could look as beautiful as you," Stephen said. "Are you? I don't even know your name."

"My name is Hydricetistelidalina Maculisarcolleenivorsa," she laughed. "Say that three times quickly."

"I cannot," Stephen said. "But when you say your name, my ears tickle."

She moved very close to Stephen and whispered her name in his ear. Stephen laughed.

"Stop it!" he laughed. "You're tickling me! You must have a nickname you can say without tickling me to death."

She paused.

"I do," she said. "But I don't think I want to tell you. I think I want to tickle you first!"

Now she tickled Stephen all over. He laughed, pulled away, and withdrew to the bed. She followed and tickled him more until she pinned him to the bed. Her long hair flowed over her body and onto his.

"Stephen?" she said.

"You know my name?" he asked.

"Yes. Do you know that when my long hair is covering us, we are the only two in the world?"

"It is very long," he said.

"I want to know something," she said. "What is it like to nuzzle?"

"You...you can't tell me you've never cozied up to someone," he said. "A beautiful woman like you?"

"I never tell a lie," she said. "No, I've never nuzzled anyone. Have you?"

"Well sure, lots of women," Stephen said.

Then she gazed into Stephen's eyes and pierced into his soul.

"No, not lots of women," Stephen confessed. "I...well, I've imagined nuzzling with lots of women."

"A-hah!" she laughed. "For that you get punishment!"

And she tickled Stephen again.

"I'm going to tickle you until you sing like a robin, Robin," she said.

Stephen went rigid with fear.

"Shh, don't be afraid. I'm not like that," she said. "You are named after an ancient bird—one that used to sing wonderful songs. Would you like to hear such a song?"

"How can I? The robin is extinct," Stephen said.

Then Hydricetistelidalina began whistling like a robin, and Stephen felt he was in a different time and place during springtime with flowers blooming and butterflies dancing in the air.

"I...didn't know...but how could you know? No modern human has heard a real robin, and no decent recordings have survived, not even the phonographs from Buckner Falls are much good. Wretched Cave maybe? But no, that sounds bland and fake."

"It's a mystery, at least until tomorrow morning," she said. "When I reveal my other name, you'll know."

"I'd like to know now," Stephen said.

"No. Right now, you are going to teach me how to nuzzle," she said.

"Me?" Stephen squirmed.

"Yes, or I'll start tickling you again," she laughed.

"Okay, okay. It goes something like this," he said.

Stephen pulled her head down and parted her hair as best he could. He then pressed his nose next to hers and the side of his forehead against hers. Her skin was soft and smooth.

"Let me try," she said.

She nuzzled him under his chin, on the side of his face, and around his ear. Stephen laughed.

"You're tickling me," he said.

"What about like this?" she said.

Hydricetistelidalina placed her nose next to Stephen's and her forehead directly on Stephen's. She stared into his eyes. Stephen stared back in her eyes, and he felt electrical energy surging from her forehead. Her long hair danced on ends in gentle waves, like a fresh breeze on daisies, and Stephen felt he was outside watching a clear brook flow on stones with banks of green grass and flowers in a time before people and animals soiled the earth.

"I...don't know what to say...I...you...are like fresh water on daisies. I've never known anything like it. I don't know what to call it...it's like having all the comfort one could ask and never being hungry again," Stephen said.

"You have a good heart, Stephen," she said.

"It's as if you never have need to eat, yet you are always full of energy," Stephen said. "It's hard to believe anyone can be like that. I wish I didn't have to eat. I wish I could just walk around and enjoy life without having to be a slave to animal needs."

Hydricetistelidalina smiled.

"You are perceptive. I am full of energy. I don't know if the world is ready for me. But perhaps you are," she said.

"Ready for what?" Stephen yawned.

"You are tired," she said.

"Just when I was getting to know you better, I'm chained to my animal need for sleep."

"You have a good night's sleep, and we'll talk more in the morning. I'll keep you company," she said.

Hydricetistelidalina reclined next to Stephen and tossed her long hair over him, creating a blanket to keep him warm and comfortable. Stephen quickly fell asleep.

Stephen awoke, and it was morning. He knew it was morning, because the glass spheres were dark and light bounced in from the opening of the cave. Hydricetistelidalina was singing around the corner and preoccupied. Stephen stood up and walked around the corner to find her, where he saw Hydricetistelidalina boiling several liquids over a wide and flat heating crystal.

"Good morning," she said, and she gave him a nuzzle. "Did you sleep well?"

"Very well," he said as he stretched. "In fact, I feel perfectly well all around."

"Good," she said. "Breakfast will be ready in a moment. Would you like some coffee?"

"Some what?"

"It's an ancient beverage that helps a person wake up in the morning," she said.

"Just being with you wakes me up quicker than anything," he said.

"I'm pleased," she replied. "This coffee is special, as it has chocolate."

"I don't know what that is either, but I will try it," he said.

Hydricetistelidalina poured the chocolate coffee into a wooden cup and gave it to Stephen. He drank it.

"It's like the king's drink," he said. "I'm amazed by the things you can make and do. I really think you're from another place."

"Or time," she said.

"Or time?" he asked.

"Breakfast is ready. Please sit," she said.

She served him breakfast in the form of another drink that was filling and sustaining. She sat with him at a little table with chairs.

"Again, very good food," he said. "Never have had this. Aren't you going to have some?"

"I only drink water," she said. "And only when I really need to."

"Then you don't eat or drink like other people," he said.

"No, I don't," she said.

"Are you...an angel?" he asked. "I know I've asked before. But are you?"

Hydricetistelidalina laughed.

"Of course not, silly. I'm from this world. I've just been sleeping for a long time," she said. "A very long time."

"Maybe that explains your beauty. The ravages of time and men haven't touched you," Stephen said.

Hydricetistelidalina smiled.

"Stephen?" she asked. "I...I never thought I would say this...but...I am growing fond of you. I hope you don't think unkindly of me."

"Me? You're the most incredible woman I've ever met. Ever," he said.

But Hydricetistelidalina's smile faded. Stephen moved close to her and gave her a hug.

"What's the matter?" he asked. "Are you a prisoner in this cave?"

"In a way. I'm just so happy right now. I don't want it to end," she said.

"It doesn't have to end. I'll make sure of that. We can stay here or leave here or go wherever you want," he said.

"We could go wherever, yes. I'm not really a prisoner here. I'm just afraid to go out there," Hydricetistelidalina said.

"You? Afraid? Why with the strength you have, nothing could attack you. You'd show anything and anyone a thing or three," Stephen bragged. "And you'd be my woman, and I'd be proud of you."

"Do you mean that? Really?" she asked.

"Yes, of course," he said.

"Because there's something I must tell you. I don't want to tell you, but I must. I told you I don't lie, and so far I have not. But I cannot continue like this until I tell you everything. I can sense your thoughts, Stephen, and I know how you might react. And it is that reaction that concerns me," she said.

"Shhh. Now what could you have done, hmm? Killed a man?" he asked.

"No," she replied.

"Stolen something? No, not you. Wait, you were married and...no, you never nuzzled with a man. Maybe it was an arranged marriage," he said.

"I will tell you my other name, and then you will know. Please be kind, Stephen. You were once taunted, so you know how it feels. Please be kind," she said.

"I'll be kind."

"My other name is...Amicolli," she said.

Stephen's jaw dropped. Amicolli? The spotted-neck otter? But that was an animal. Yet Claire said everyone was an animal. And Stephen said he hated animals.

"Lutris told us about Amicolli in ancient Egypt," Stephen finally said after a long pause, "that you were to be made a slave, but you escaped. Amicolli. I don't understand. Are you an? An?"

"A spotted-neck otter," she said. "Yes, an animal."

Then she pulled away from Stephen and changed shape into a spotted-neck otter. She was not the size of a conventional spotted-neck otter but in fact had the same mass in otter form as she did in humanoid form. She sat next to Stephen and stared at him. Her round button eyes and small ears were just too cute for Stephen, and she turned her head sideways and gave Stephen a loving gaze.

"Is this your...how long can you..." Stephen stumbled.

"Yes, this is my natural state. I can remain like this as long as I like. As for my humanoid form, well, I can maintain it for many days," Amicolli said, still in otter form. "But after a time, I must spend five thousand heartbeats in my natural state. I will change automatically if I stay in humanoid form too long. It's like when you stay awake too long—you just fall asleep."

"Your fur...may I touch it?" Stephen asked.

Amicolli laughed.

"You're just too cute. Of course you may touch it. In fact, you touched it for quite a while. When I first found you, I used my natural coat to keep you warm," Amicolli said.

"But where did you come from? How did you get here? How is it you don't eat? What are your plans?" Stephen asked.

Amicolli laughed.

"I am from the very ancient world," she said. "From ancient Egypt, as you were told. I lived along the Nile River, and quite happily. Then one day I was crossing the Nile at the first cataract when a rock falling from the sky struck me on the head. Part of the rock chipped off and went down my throat. I was dazed and floated down the Nile until I reached an Egyptian settlement where slaves were building a pyramid. Then slave drivers pulled me out of the water to send me working on the pyramid. It was then I realized I had taken humanoid form, and that the rock had changed me."

"I escaped the Egyptians," she continued. "My body was tired and reverted back to its natural otter shape, and so I swam away. I was scared and didn't know what to think. Would I die? I decided the best thing to do was to find the rock and then bring it to the wisest Greek people to learn my fate. I went back to the first cataract and found the rock. It was easy to find, because the sun had set and the rock was glowing, so I knew it had its own energy."

"I began swimming with the rock back down the Nile toward the Mediterranean when I reached Alexandria and came across a Greek ship preparing to depart. I then hitched a ride on the Greek ship back to Athens, where natural philosophers examined me and the rock. I told them my story, and they admitted the rock was not of this world, and so I was telling the truth. They were also amazed at my ability to change shape, and they immediately proclaimed me a goddess. However, there were others who thought I was an evil goddess sent to wreak havoc on Athena's realm. So with the help of a dolphin, I escaped. The dolphin took me west along the Mediterranean, into the Atlantic Ocean, and south along Africa until I reached the South Atlantic. I met his dolphin friends, and all was well, but then an orca attacked us. The dolphins fought back, and I decided to break up the rock and have each of us eat a little bit. The dolphins became powerful and were able to overpower the orca. The dolphins could now change shape like me, but the rock was too much for me, and I fell unconscious until a little while ago. How I got in this cave, I don't know, but I'm guessing the dolphins hid me until someday I would awake, which thanks to you I did. And I don't eat because the rock changed me. My cells are powered by thorium."

"Thorium power. I thought that was a myth. Stories tell of dolphins and whales in an ancient ocean who were powered by thorium. But the paleontologists in Buckner Falls never found such animals. Not even thorium itself has been found," Stephen said.

"Then they must have left," Amicolli said.

"Left?"

"The way I left Greece. They must have left this world. This planet. Stephen—humans, well, they are afraid of more powerful beings," Amicolli said.

"Well now there are other beings besides humans," Stephen said. "There are the little people called picocians, there are giant clams, and there's another animal...uh...otter like you. I mentioned him already. He's Lutris."

"Yes, you did mention him, but I don't know that name," Amicolli said.

"Really?" Stephen smiled with satisfaction. "Well, my cousin—her name is Claire—yes, Claire has fallen heads over heels in love with Lutris. And he fancies her too. Well the whole thing disgusts...disgusts..."

But Stephen's voice softened.

"I guess some animals are good," Stephen said.

"Only some?!" Amicolli said.

She changed back to humanoid shape, fuzzed up her hair with electrons, and tickled Stephen.

"Stop it!" Stephen laughed. "You're tickling me to death. If ever you were an animal..."

"If ever I were an animal," she tickled. "Very well. I'll treat you like an animal and tickle you until you apologize."

"I'm sorry! Sorry I'm so ticklish!" Stephen said.

Amicolli changed shape into a polar bear, stood tall, and growled. Stephen's hair stood on end, and he shrieked in fright. Amicolli changed back to humanoid form, and Stephen relaxed.

"Try to have some fun with animals," Amicolli said. "Don't fear them. Celebrate them."

"What's to celebrate? Attack and pain and death," Stephen said.

"Don't let yourself be trapped into thinking that all there is to animal life is attack, pain, and death. When you think such things, you become those things. Become more than the primitive animal. Become energy independent. Then things like attack, pain, and death fall swiftly behind," Amicolli said.

"But I have to eat. All humans have to eat. We're no better than animals. Claire was right. How can I become energy independent?" Stephen asked.

Amicolli touched Stephen gently on the face with her hand.

"Yes, that's true. I suppose the remaining people on this planet won't be free unless...unless..."

"Unless what?" Stephen asked.

Amicolli just smiled. She looked down briefly, looked up, then looked back at Stephen.

"I have a special gift," Amicolli said. "A Greek musician gave it to me. Would you like to see?"

Amicolli showed Stephen a small box. He opened it, and Greek music played.

"Isn't that clever?" she said. "The Greeks would dance to this music. I would like to dance with you now."

Stephen was stunned.

"You are full of surprises. Is this how I become energy independent?" he asked.

"In a way. I'd like to remember this moment, Robin Stephen Royer," Amicolli said.

"Is something about to happen?" Stephen asked.

But Amicolli would no longer speak. She took Stephen by the hand and danced with him. And while she did, she sang. Not words, really, just half-play sounds of nothingness, like an opera singer happy with life. Then she paused in her singing and whispered:

"The reason you still have primitive animal needs is because your body has the wrong metals."

Then Stephen pulled away and closed the music box.

"Wrong metals?" he asked. "Metals are bad. Look at what MALC does to people. Do you know about Mersladium and Wonga's new robot army? Made of MALC? Wrong metals? Wrong metals!"

"Those are wrong metals," she said.

Amicolli walked up to Stephen and touched his forehead.

"Yes," she said, reading his memories. "Wonga has control of a region named Sathiakia. She is creating an army of robots, made of mercury, arsenic, lead, and cadmium. Those are waste materials from an ancient human civilization. That civilization created creatures made of silicon and mixed them with MALC. The MALC robots nearly destroyed the people, but the people destroyed all the MALC robots, except one, which was buried deep in a gold mine. He is named Mersladium."

"You can read my thoughts too?" Stephen asked.

Amicolli smiled.

"An easy trick. I could teach you if...if..."

"If what?" Stephen asked.

"There's something else too. Lutris is leading an army of clamifores to fight her army," Amicolli said.

"You can read my thoughts," Stephen said. "Can you read the future?"

"Something has changed," she said. "I only realized it a moment ago. But...but..."

Amicolli paused again, and an expression of paralyzing fear gripped her face. Stephen was about to say something, but the expression passed quickly, and she sang half-nothing opera again.

"Then you know the future," he said.

"Yes," she said.

"And you have to do something," he said.

"Yes," she replied. "It's almost time. Another few moments, Stephen. Come. Dance with me one last time."

The War

"Convert these two next," Wonga said to Mersladium, pointing to Loran and Loa'neth.

"No! I won't allow it!" Gliria yelled.

Gliria ran toward Mersladium to attack him, but Mersladium simply swatted her aside. She landed against a statue and fell to the ground. It was

Myoxi's turn. He grabbed the trumpet that had fallen from Gliria and blew it toward Wonga, but Wonga lashed out a vine and swatted the trumpet aside.

"This is so boring," Wonga said. "You can't even entertain me. Go ahead, Mersladium."

Loran was taken first, and Loa'neth raised her scepter, but that too was swatted away by Wonga.

"Too boring, too boring," Wonga said.

Mersladium threw Loran into the chamber and then stepped in himself. But Mersladium stepped out of the chamber, coughing and choking. Loran walked out unchanged.

"He has no MALC at all in his body," Mersladium coughed. "There must be a minimum of contamination as a seed to convert humans to merselats."

"That can be solved quite easily," Wonga said. "Head slave driver—take the four *friends* to the MALC mine. Let them dig their own seeds of contamination!"

The head slave driver escorted the four out of Wonga's Lair and onto a train where they were taken to mine MALC. They were there for only a little while when another train arrived—a train full of merselats. It unloaded, and a group of existing human workers were taken back to Wonga's Lair for conversion into merselats.

"They're converting the people into robots," Loa'neth said.

"It's murder!" Gliria said. "Wonga is murdering people!"

"I want to stop it," Loran said. "But I can't. The power Dara gave us doesn't work here. Loa'neth and I don't need to eat, but that's it. What were we thinking, that we could just walk in here and solve all problems? So far we've created more problems."

"Look," Loa'neth said. "At the top of Wonga's castle. The window. Do you see?"

The other three looked up and saw the shape of a woman by the window.

"Lillianina," Loran said. "She looks helpless."

But then their gaze was disturbed. Several cracks of thunder echoed in the air. Boulders from the shore of Lake Meadowash landed on Wonga's castle. Lutris's army of clamifores had arrived, and they hurled these boulders from the shore. Mersladium then led his army of merselats to meet Lutris. It was a bitter fight. Clam fought MALC, and MALC fought clam. Calcium carbonate, mercury, arsenic, lead, and cadmium were all shed as clams where pulverized and merselats were shredded. Lutris gave his amulet to Claire, and she suddenly gained great fighting strength. She armored herself in calcium carbonate remains from killed clams, and she fought side-by-side with Lutris.

And in Rainbear Mountain, Amicolli's dance with Stephen ended. She knew this was her moment.

"It is time, Robin Stephen Royer. The last war on this planet has begun. And all life as you know it will end," Amicolli said. "I must leave this place now."

"Wherever you're going, I'm going too," Stephen said.

"I had hoped you'd say that," Amicolli said. "But stay close as we descend the mountain. It's still bitterly cold."

The two began descending Rainbear Mountain. Amicolli extended her long hair around Stephen, and that kept him warm.

"Time is short," she said. "Lutris's army of clamifores is sustaining heavy losses. Wonga and her MALC robots—the merselats—are winning. Hold on, Robin Stephen. We will fly with great haste."

Amicolli turned herself into a giant osprey, and she carried Stephen on her back with her back feathers covering him and keeping him warm.

"I wish we could just fly away like this," Stephen said.

"So do I," Amicolli said. "But my life is no longer my own."

"You've been saying things like that," Stephen said. "I have a horrible feeling that I'm losing you."

"All that you know—me included—will be lost. But if I am successful, you will gain something new," she said.

"And you?" Stephen asked.

But Amicolli would not answer. She simply flapped her wings and carried Stephen over to Crow Pits Island. Amicolli landed, and she changed to otter form.

"Why are we here?" Stephen asked.

But Amicolli did not answer.

"Dara!" Amicolli called. "I am Hydricetistelidalina Maculisarcolleenivorsa. I have come."

Dara appeared on the surface.

"Amicolli. Your arrival is met with great dread," Dara said. "Lutris has taken half my clamifores to fight Wonga. The other clamifores will not fight. You are too late if you are looking for an army."

"I will not fight," Amicolli said. "But I do require your remaining clamifores."

"You otters would see us destroyed!" Dara said.

"So this is it? Lutris and Claire commanded one army of clamifores, and you and I will command another?" Stephen asked. "Well, I guess Claire and I now have something in common."

"We are not going into battle," Amicolli said. "As I said, I will not fight."

"Then why do you need us?" Dara asked.

"We must dive deep," Amicolli said. "The only way to overcome ascending tyranny is to undermine it."

Dara and Stephen exchanged confused glances.

"You'll see," Amicolli said. "Stephen. For us, this is goodbye."

"What!? What are you saying?" he asked. "We just met. I thought...that we...no, this can't be goodbye!"

"It must be. As I said, all life must now change. Even me. But do not be sad or weep for me. Old metals will make you do that," Amicolli said.

"Then I don't want anything to do with *right* metals or independent energy if I can't be with you. Just when you come into my life, you decide to leave it. That's not fair," Stephen said.

Amicolli hugged him.

"I appreciate your sentimentality," she said. "You do have a good heart. But be strong. You will see happy days again."

"I don't want happy days. I want you," he cried.

Dara pulled Stephen away.

"I intend to undermine Wonga," Amicolli said to Dara. "Do you understand? I ask your clamifores for help in this."

"I understand," Dara said. "You are more gracious than I thought. And the stories of you uniting with greatness are true. I appreciate your sacrifice."

"Well I don't!" Stephen wailed.

Dara held onto Stephen and hugged him.

"It's the only way?" Dara asked.

"Unfortunately," Amicolli said. "Stand clear."

"No!" Stephen cried, but Dara held him from running toward Amicolli.

And so, while Lutris and his army battled Wonga and hers, Amicolli stood on the shoreline. She then sang in her loudest opera voice. The clamifores rose from underground and formed three overlapping circles that rotated within themselves and revolved as a threesome around Amicolli. In this way, the clamifores formed a drilling team, and they started to drill into the sand.

"Amicolli, no!" Stephen yelled.

The clamifores dug deep and quickly into the sand, and Amicolli followed them.

"AMICOLLI!" Stephen shouted one last time, then his voice failed and he said with a hoarse voice, "She's...gone."

With her clamifore mining team, Amicolli dug deep, very deep. And as she did so, lightning came down from the sky directly where Amicolli had descended. The wind picked up and blew debris all about.

"We must move away from here!" Dara yelled through the hostile winds.

"No," Stephen said. "Amicolli! No!"

"Stephen! Over here," Dara said.

"I don't want to go down to the chamber. I don't want to hide," he said.

"No, just around this rock cluster," Dara said. "We won't be hiding anymore. But I think Amicolli would want us safe at least. Give this to her as a final gift."

Dara led Stephen to the rock cluster, which was protected from lightning and debris. The wind did not buffet them quite as badly, and they were able to look south toward Sathiakia.

Lutris and army were finally overrun by Mersladium and the merselats. Wonga in her joy paraded onto the scene so as to personally quash Lutris and Claire. In the ordeal, the merselats at the MALC mine joined the regular fighting merselats, and this left Loran, Loa'neth, Gliria, and Myoxi unguarded. The four took a chance and rushed into Wonga's castle, where they found Lillianina in a trance. Gliria gave Lillianina something to bring her back to conscious thought.

"Loran, Loran," Lillianina said. "I've been in such a horrible situation. Wonga...she..."

"No time for that. We must leave here," he said. "We must fight Wonga."

"I am too weak. Fight for me," she said. "Fight, my dear cousin."

Loran paused for a moment then nodded in affirmation. The four left the castle and ran for the beach to help Lutris, leaving Lillianina behind.

"So, Lutris of the east Pacific sea otters, this is your end," Wonga said.

"A vicious monster such as you deserves no life," Lutris said. "You will be destroyed before the end, even if all life on this planet must perish."

"And you, young woman of Lutris," Wonga said to Claire. "Are you willing to give up your life for a common animal?"

"To destroy the likes of you, yes!" Claire said.

Then Claire made a rush toward Wonga in a suicidal attempt to inflict as much damage as possible. But Loran, Loa'neth, Gliria, and Myoxi also rushed toward Wonga to fight.

"ALL OF YOU WILL DIE!" Wonga said, and she lashed out.

Then it happened. Subatomic waves from the ether blasted upward from Amicolli's position deep in the ground. She had harnessed the electrons from the lightning and converted herself into pure energy. The energy disrupted the MALC and split it into lighter elements. Mercury and lead became gold and hydrogen, cadmium became silver and hydrogen, and arsenic became boron and oxygen. All MALC mines were vaporized, all merselats were vaporized, all heavy metals in the remaining people evaporated through their pores, and the metals that were in Wonga also vaporized, creating a massive mushroom cloud that ascended high in the air. All that remained of Wonga and her empire was a shadowy outline of her form in the sand.

Dara and Stephen watched from afar, and Stephen cried.

"She's converted herself into pure energy," Dara said. "She did it for all of us. You should be proud."

"I am," Stephen said. "But I am also heart broken."

But then the mushroom cloud coalesced and condensed, becoming heavier than air. It fell back to the ground in the form of boron, silver, and gold raindrops. The new metals and cleansing action of boron fell on all people and replaced their consumptive cells with a new type of fusion cell. It was the type that powered Lutris, and the type that powered the pilot whales of the Pacific Ocean in Debbie Dayla's time.

Lutris watched as his friends were converted. Claire acquired a new glow of eternal youth, the picocians Gliria and Myoxi acquired a similar glow, while Loran and Loa'neth, though already somewhat converted by Dara and the clamifores, came into their own as fully self-sufficient people. Dara herself was also fully energized, and Stephen was converted into eternal self-sustaining youth.

"It's over," Dara said to Stephen. "Amicolli has put a part of herself in all of us. And now I can leave this island and go wherever I wish. You are free too."

Stephen looked at Dara, and then suddenly from the sky fell what looked like a ghost or apparition of Amicolli.

"Stephen," Amicolli said. "I must go now. I wish you happiness until the end of time. Go with Dara and explore the universe. No other animal deserves more happiness."

"I will," Stephen said. "And thank you."

Then just before Amicolli left, her spirit leapt into Dara's body. Dara's body grew to human height, and her hair became long.

"Let me nuzzle you one last time," Amicolli's spirit said from within Dara's body.

And he did.

The Friends Depart

Dara kept her new height and extra hair.

"I've changed, Stephen," she said. "Part of Amicolli's spirit is still in me."

"Then I haven't lost her!" Stephen said. "Dara...if you would be so kind to accompany me to Sathiakia, I would be glad. I must find out what has happened to Claire and the others."

"Of course I'll accompany you," Dara said, and she kissed Stephen on the cheek.

Dara's clamifore friends returned from the deep. Dara communicated her intentions to the group, and they understood. They took a position in the water along the shore, and Dara led Stephen to the largest clamifore.

"Let's go to Sathiakia then," Dara said, and she instructed the clamifores to swim south.

On arrival, the two were shocked to see such a large number of empty clamifore shells.

"This is why I dreaded Lutris when he took half my people," Dara said, "and why I dreaded Amicolli when she arrived."

"But Amicolli returned what she took," Stephen said.

"I only wish Lutris could have done the same," Dara said.

"Did I hear my name?" Lutris said from a distance.

Lutris and Claire had been walking through the debris, looking for survivors.

"I'm sorry about everything," Lutris said. "Wonga gave us a hard fight and nearly beat us."

"But some power from below vaporized her and her army," Claire said, now walking up.

"It was Hydricetistelidalina Maculisarcolleenivorsa," Stephen said.

"Who?" Claire asked.

"Amicolli!" Lutris said. "But from where did she come? And to where did she go?"

"I found her in Rainbear Mountain," Stephen said, "or rather, she found me. There's lots to tell."

"We should find the others," Claire said, "so we can all get caught up on things. They were here for the battle but rushed off."

"Yes, we should find them," Lutris said.

"The others are in Wonga's castle," Dara said. "They are tending to Lillianina."

Stephen looked at Dara with surprise.

"How...do you know that?" Claire asked.

"Amicolli?" Lutris asked.

"Yes," Dara replied.

"Indeed. I look forward to our exchange of stories. I would change to an eagle and carry Claire to the castle, but I would not want to leave you two behind," Lutris bragged.

"That's a good idea. But I'll turn into an osprey instead. Then we can all fly up to the castle," Dara said.

Lutris looked at Dara with a deflated ego.

"Amicolli again?" Lutris asked.

"But of course," Dara said.

"But how?" Lutris asked.

Dara laughed.

"That's her way of saying that she'll tell you later," Stephen said, then he walked up to Dara and whispered in her ear, "You really are Amicolli, aren't you? That's something she would say."

Dara laughed again and nodded.

"Partly," Dara said. "Partly."

"You two have secrets," Claire grinned. "I wonder if those will be discussed."

"Oh, Claire!" Stephen said.

"Oh, Stephen!" Claire said.

Lutris turned into a giant eagle, Dara turned into a giant osprey, and Claire and Stephen climbed upon the backs of their respective rides.

"You've changed, my dear cousin," Claire said as Lutris and Dara took to the air. "You had this great hatred toward animals. Heck, you chided me for being with Lutris. Now look at you."

"Yes, look at me," Stephen said. "I'm flying on the back of an osprey. But the animals of old are gone, as are those primitive animal traits that I so hated. And there was Amicolli. And Dara."

"And Dara," Claire said. "I'm happy for you. I'm happy for us all."

The four landed on a balcony at the top of Wonga's castle. Dara and Lutris turned back into humanoid shape, and the four went inside. Standing around a bed were Loran, Loa'neth, Gliria, and Myoxi. In the bed was Lillianina.

"What happened?" Claire asked.

"Lillianina took ill after it rained gold and silver," Loa'neth said. "We have all tried to bring her back to health, but she has only declined."

"I don't understand," Stephen said. "People were supposed to be freed from pain and death. Why was Lillianina not spared?"

"Lillianina," Dara said as she walked over and touched her.

Lillianina opened her eyes.

"Amicolli," Lillianina said in a weak voice. "I guess I looked in the wrong place for you."

"Don't try to speak," Dara said.

"I thought I could turn MALC into something useful," Lillianina said. "It got out of control. Wonga...she was just a tree and starfish I meshed together. Out of control. Sorry. So sorry..."

"Rest easy, Lillianina," Dara said.

"Can you help her? Can you?!" Loran asked.

"Her bones absorbed too many bad metals, including radioactive ones. There was a bad reaction when I...when Amicolli changed the world," Dara said.

"Why does she call you Amicolli, Meorus?" Loa'neth asked.

"After the world conversion, part of Amicolli's spirit merged with mine. The rest left this planet for another place," Dara said.

"Then this was all for nothing!" Loran cried.

Loran knelt by Lillianina and hugged her.

"Don't give up now. Don't!" he said.

Stephen walked over and put a hand on Loran's shoulder. So did Loa'neth.

"I wish things didn't have to be this way," Myoxi said.

"It seems someone we love must die for the world to be right again," Gliria said.

"Not always," Myoxi said. "I love you, and you're still with me."

"Oh, I'm glad you're still with me," Gliria said, and the picocians hugged each other.

And so, Lillianina died.

"Couldn't she be brought back to life on Crow Pits Island?" Loran asked. "You remember, the way you helped bring Loa'neth back?"

"The island lost all its power," Dara said. "The conversion changed every-thing."

"Then there really is no hope?" Loa'neth asked.

"I'm sorry," Dara said. "I really am."

The friends took Lillianina far into the Sabina Salt Desert. Amazingly, the giant dolphin was still functional, and so they used that for transport. They reached a point so remote that no people would be sure where they were.

"This is good enough," Loran said. "I don't want anyone finding her."

"The way Mersladium was bur..." Myoxi started to whisper before he caught himself.

"What?!" Gliria said in surprise.

"Nothing," Myoxi backtracked.

"No, you said something about Mersladium," Gliria said.

"So what if I did? I meant nothing," Myoxi said.

"No, you were about to say that we are burying Lillianina the way Mer-sladium was once buried. Are you saying that people will dig up Lillianina someday and use her to build an army?" Gliria pressed. "That's disgusting!"

"They're at it again," Loran said.

"Dara," Loa'neth said. "We must protect Lillianina's tomb."

"Yes, of course," Dara said.

Then Dara sang, much like Amicolli had sung for Stephen. She touched the bare salt, and it became crystals of many colors, surrounding and protect-ing Lillianina's tomb, and finally making it disappear altogether.

"It's...gone!" Loran said.

"It is hidden from view," Dara said. "Dive deep, Lillianina. Dive deep!"

The sand parted, and an impression formed the same size as Lillianina's tomb. The depression then sank, and the salt filled in over it.

"No one will disturb her tomb," Dara said.

"Thank you," Loran said. "Well, I came to rescue Lillianina, but I failed. I'm really at a loss as to what to do with myself."

"Amicolli meant for us to set aside our preoccupations with greed, pain, and death and begin to explore the planet and the ways of the universe," Dara said.

"I don't even know what that means," Loran said.

"Let's return to Wonga's castle and clean that up," Dara said. "On the way back, we'll tell you our stories."

The group returned to Wonga's castle, and they shared what they knew about what happened.

"I would like to give this castle a new name," Claire said.

"I have the perfect name," Myoxi said. "Call it *Amichellori.*"

"Amiche-what?" Claire asked.

"Amichellori. Like *Amicolli*, *Michelle*, and *Lori* wrapped into one."

"Who are Michelle and Lori?" Gliria demanded to know.

"Just these two picocians I met on the other side of—ow!" Myoxi said, but Gliria interrupted him with a slap across the face.

"Meet this side of the mountain!" Gliria said, and she punched Myoxi.

"Break it up. Ooof!" Lutris said as he forced himself between the fighting Myoxi and Gliria duo, but he tripped in the commotion.

"Stop it, you two!" Claire said. "Amicolli sacrificed herself for us. Is this your thanks? You could show gratitude for this bay that she liberated. Why, this is her cove."

But Myoxi and Gliria continued fighting each other around Lutis. Claire raised her voice and yelled:

"IT'S AMI'S COVE!"

The fighting stopped, and all fell still and silent. Then Lutris broke the silence.

"Ami's Cove it is," Lutris said. "Claire and I will make our home here. We will honor Amicolli's request and make a place of enlightenment and learning in her name. We will study the world and the stars. We will discover music and oratory, and we will learn chemistry and physics. All will be welcome to stay and explore."

"Amicolli would be pleased," Dara said. "We will visit you often, but now we must say goodbye."

"So soon?" Claire said.

"Dara is right," Loran said. "I must return to Millfork and my home, if but for a little while."

"I will accompany you," Loa'neth said.

"I had hoped you would," Loran said.

"And don't forget us!" Myoxi said.

"Our paths are the same for a little while," Gliria said. "We will return to our own people, to see how they fared during the conversion."

"Yes, perhaps our people will spend more time in the light than in the mountain," Myoxi said.

"I trust you two will be instrumental in that effort," Dara said.

"What about you, Dara?" Stephen asked. "Are you going back to Crow Pits Island?"

"No," Dara said. "I have an errand with the folk in Buckner Falls. I need to update them on some interesting facts about ancient history."

"Then that's where I'm going," Stephen said.

Claire walked up to Stephen and hugged him.

"I will miss you, dear cousin," she said. "Visit us as often as you can."

"We will," Stephen said.

The friends exchanged hugs all around, and then Loran, Loa'neth, Gliria, Myoxi, Dara, and Stephen departed. They took the road back toward Millfork, and along the way they stopped at Slaffton. The town was no longer what it once was. All evidence of vine and plant had vaporized, and a steady stream of young people now walked northward toward Millfork.

"It happened everywhere," Loran said.

"Yes," Dara said. "Every living thing on this planet was vaporized or converted."

The friends continued on the path to Millfork. They reached Laculic Tavern, but it was boarded up. Braegan and Morga were nowhere to be found. Dara walked up to the tavern and touched it.

"They've moved on to Buckner Falls of all places," Dara said. "Many people have, but many people are staying in Millfork."

"We will stay," Loran said, and Loa'neth smiled.

"Now it's our turn to say goodbye," Gliria said.

Loa'neth and Loran knelt to hug Gliria and Myoxi.

"I shall miss you, my little picocians," Loran said. "It seems a long time since I first put you both to sleep with Ethaloid."

"And woke us up with Daylazine," Myoxi said.

"And took us to Beguiling Grotto," Gliria said.

"Yes," Loran said. "Beguiling Grotto."

Dara, Stephen, and the picocians headed to Buckner Falls, and Loran led Loa'neth back to his home.

"But first," Loran said, "I'd like to take one little side trip and show you what the picocians call the Beguiling Grotto. I call it the Wretched Cave. I used to go there to make myself feel better. But I don't suppose I'll need to do that again."

"Remember that I started off as a picocian and still have picocian tendencies," Loa'neth said. "It's still Beguiling Grotto to me."

"I wonder how the conversion changed the cave?" Loran asked. "Or if there are any fungi left after they attacked Stephen?"

The two reached Wretched Cave. Loa'neth paused.

"It *is* Beguiling Grotto," she said. "I never thought I'd go in here. But that was when I was a mere picocian."

"Let's go inside," Loran said.

The two went inside. It was very dark, but Loa'neth clapped her hands together, and they suddenly glowed.

"A new ability from the conversion," Loa'neth said.

"I wonder how many new abilities we'll discover?" Loran asked.

A single remaining fungus heard Loran's request, and it activated. It showed Lutris and Claire and many others building tables and chairs and musical devices. It showed Dara, Stephen, Gliria, and Myoxi in the mountain pass between Millfork and Buckner Falls. They had stopped for a moment, with Dara and Stephen playing "echo tag". Dara would sing a short burst, the echo would fly around, and Stephen would "catch" the echo by singing back at just the right time and timbre to cancel the sound wave.

"So we can just use our voices," Loran started.

"To discover the world," Loa'neth finished.

The scene ended. The one fungus glowed dimly. Loran and Loa'neth approached it.

"Before the conversion," Loran said, "there were many fungi, and they were not safe to touch. Now there is but one fungus left."

"Look," Loa'neth said. "This one is changing."

The fungus grew a covering. Indeed, it looked very much like a clam now. It detached itself from the wall and slid to the ground. Loa'neth walked over to the fungus clam and picked it up. She then sang softly to the clam, and it opened up. She sang a different tune, and it projected images.

"Amazing," Loran said. "By choosing how you sing to the fungus, you can see different parts of the world. You can zoom in close and see things with incredible detail, or pan out and see many things at once."

"I only wish there were more fungi," Loa'neth said.

"Perhaps we can learn how to make more," Loran said. "And we can give them as gifts to our friends."

"I like that idea," Loa'neth said. "We have all the time we can ask."

The fungus seemed to coo in Loa'neth's hand, as if absorbing energy from her.

"It likes me," Loa'neth said.

"It likes your energy," Loran said. "I could become jealous."

Loa'neth laughed.

"And here I thought all emotions had gone away. Being noble and all that, remember? Well then, let's return to your home before you lock horns with this fungus," she said.

The two left Wretched Cave and continued northward. After a time, they reached Laculic Manor—Loran's home.

"This is it. But it looks different," Loran said. "This house was built from wood. But the wood is fossilized. It's hard as stone. And all the pine shrubs are gone."

"Well? Aren't you going to carry me over the threshold of your front door?" Loa'neth asked.

"Oh, I'm dreadfully sorry. I've forgotten all manners," Loran said.

Loran attempted to open his front door, but it was jammed.

"That's odd," Loran said.

"Here, let me consult Giginufi," Loa'neth said.

"Gigi-what?" Loran asked.

"That's the name I've given this clam fungus," she said, pulling out the clam.

Loa'neth hummed softly to Giginufi, and it opened. She then hummed a little more, and it showed the door was wedged shut at the bottom.

"Wedged shut?" Loran asked. "But how? That could only be done from the inside. Wait, where's the wedge?"

"Here at this bottom corner," she pointed.

Loran looked around and found a slender stone. He then shoved it under the door to push the wedge out of the way. The wedge moved, and he was about to open the door when Loa'neth spoke.

"Wait, there's something going on inside!" Loa'neth warned.

Loran couldn't wait. He pushed open the door and then double-stopped himself at what to say. The house was filled with picocians engaged in a wild party, laughing, singing, running around, jumping on counter and table, swinging from hanging lights, tunneling under carpets, and spraying bottles of fluid all over. One such bottle (now empty) rolled to Loran's feet.

"Lucinasium," Loran read.

"What is it?" Loa'neth asked.

"They broke into my stores of Lucinasium. I used it to inhibit aggressive responses in oysters. Now these picocians are wrecking my home!"

Loa'neth watched as Loran ran about his home, yelling at the picocians to stop tearing up his place. But the picocians only chased around after him and mocked him, becoming all the more defiant and boisterous. They laughed at Loran. Laughed.

"Not a noble moment," Loa'neth laughed. "What would Dara say? Or Lutris?"

"I swear to you, you shall all face the fire of my oyster cookers if you don't vacate my home immediately! I'll get my Ethaloid gun and mow you all down into sleeping picocians!" Loran warned.

"Ethaloid, Ethaloid!" the picocians echoed. "We know all about your Ethaloid!"

Several picocians took bottles of Loran's Ethaloid, placed it in an applicator gun, and sprayed it around. Other picocians stumbled and lost balance, then they fell unconscious. Several other picocians took bottles of Loran's Daylazine and sprayed it. Those who fell asleep awoke and laughed.

"Stop it! You can't waste all my pharmaceuticals like that!" Loran barked.

"Loran has forgotten that he has been converted," Loa'neth said to herself. "He has no more need for pharmaceuticals. But why are these picocians reacting to pharmaceuticals? Didn't they get converted like the rest of us? Perhaps I should consult Giginufi."

Loa'neth hummed softly to Giginufi. Its outer shells opened, it glowed, and then it closed. Suddenly, all picocians disappeared as did the debris of drink and food and broken items. All was restored to its original place in Loran's home.

"What...what happened? Where did the picocians go?" Loran asked.

"They were never here," Loa'neth said. "It was all an illusion, created by Giginufi."

Loran stared at Loa'neth in shock. Then he let out a hearty laugh.

"We have much to learn about Giginufi and this new world of ours," he said.

"Yes, my love. We do indeed," Loa'neth laughed.

The two embraced and began their new lives together, enjoying the wonders of Giginufi. They visited the others quite frequently, sharing their knowledge of Giginufi, and the others were able to create their own versions of Giginufi, exploring the world of fact and possibility to the ends of time.

Save for Proper Buyer

I am a short man. I'm not proud of it, but it is the reality. I hate it. A hundred and fifty centimeters doesn't impress women and prevents other men from taking me seriously. I'm a boy to them.

My short stature has plagued me my entire life. I was the shortest in my elementary school when I started at age eight. Teachers promised I'd grow taller than everyone else when I became an adult, but that never happened. And when my male high school classmates attended mandatory military school, I was rejected, even though the law requires two years of service.

Rejected.

The only thing I was good at was English. I studied how to read the language, how to speak it, and how to write. I would call local girls of my own age on the telephone and pass myself off as a natural English speaker who was visiting from abroad. I even hid the squeak that so many of us local men have that gives away our racial identity. Not me. I sounded like a rich, English-speaking man.

The problem with these pranks was that I became too infatuated with them. I loved the false identities I portrayed, and the young women loved them too, so much so that they wanted to meet me—the *me* on the telephone. But the real me was not a man in their eyes, at least not face-to-face, and I always made up an excuse to break off the "relationship".

Life on the peninsula was otherwise miserable. Raw tonnages from barges dumped garbage from English-speaking countries onto our soil, and the majority populace spent long days sifting through the garbage for metals of all sorts: steel, stainless steel, aluminum, brass, and precious metals like copper, silver, gold, platinum, palladium, and rhodium. These metals are then sold to the scrapyard. There are many stories about people who got rich quickly from selling tons of gold and platinum to the scrapyard, and it is those stories that attract more people into salvage.

I'm destined for the salvage business, but I resent such a fate. People pick through garbage like vultures through poisoned meat. Yes, poisoned, because in order to get ahead of the next salvage person, one must smelt the garbage down to yield the precious slag, but that smelting results in black smoke that chokes my lungs and in deadly metals like lead and mercury that slip through my pores and sap strength from my soul.

Both of my parents smelt for precious metals. I hate it. Before I went to school, I was forced to dig through the deepest, filthiest garbage piles and find the best electronic circuit boards before the other children did. Being small, I could crawl into places others could not, and so I could retrieve the best finds for my parents. I did this all day, and at the end of the day, they put all that I had gathered into a blast furnace and separated the metals from the rest. Dinner and black smoke made me sick. I never slept well and was always tired.

School was at least a break from the salvage business, though only for a few hours of the day. I tried figuring out ways to stay longer at school to avoid the end-of-day smelting, but the teachers sent me home all too eagerly. There's no arguing with teachers of my country—they are highly respected and paid and are the final authority in all matters except politics and militarics.

So it was that I dreamt of a sudden growth spurt to add thirty or forty centimeters to my height. And lighter hair. Stronger muscles. Money and power. I needed those things, but I would never get them on the peninsula—not by poisoning myself with smelting for metals.

I graduated from high school. That was the worst moment in my life, because with no prospect of further education, I knew my temporary haven from salvage was now gone. High school graduation was in reality a rite of passage from the last freedoms of childhood into full bondage of adulthood.

The summer following my high school graduation marked a change in the salvage business. Hard times forced my parents to sell the blast furnace and move into a small apartment. Instead of bringing home my sifted spoils for my parents to smelt, I took my finds to a friend's furnace, a furnace that liquefied my metals quicker than my parents' could and without the fumes to scorch my lungs. This came at a price, in that my friend took a cut of my spoils, and so there was less to take home. Still, I managed to earn enough to buy dinner food on the way home for my parents and brother to eat.

Each day that I picked up dinner, I passed by a shop named, "Antique Imports." I thought nothing of it, except maybe that it was only for the rich people I'd never be, and so the summer turned over into autumn, and then I saw it—the first day of school for others, but instead of leaving the garbage pits behind so that I could attend class, I worked them, and no longer did I see people younger than I. All were older, and all looked sullen and beaten.

My fate.

After a week of this, I became numb to the world. This was it, this was the end, and day and night would pass as it had and always would without a forgotten flower being seen as anything other than a weed.

At the end of one particular work day in October, after unmemorable hours of sifting through garbage, I walked to the local store where I picked up food for dinner, but before I reached the store, I noticed that Antique Imports had a "Closed" sign on it. I thought little of it, except that maybe the owners went on holiday. But then the following day had the same "Closed" sign. Curious further, I left work early to see if I could catch the antique store open. Perhaps I'd go in and look at all the things. It was surely better than digging through garbage all day. Closed. What were the hours posted? None. I went back to my regular routine of gathering metal from salvage, smelting it in my friend's furnace, buying dinner, and bringing it home.

It was strange, and I suddenly felt as if a friend of whom I had never spoken to was now gone. Why did this antique store bother me so? I didn't know. A week of walking by, and the store was empty. Then one day, I took action. I went to the front door, expected it to be locked, and to my surprise it was not. In through the front I walked, and around the store I browsed, but only dust presented itself for sale, and I wasn't buying. But if an item of value presented itself, would I purchase it? With what? The little I earned from salvage and smelt was spent on supplies for family and friend. There had to be more. There had to be something beyond the daily grind that would spare my bones from wear and save my soul from the grave.

Thunk!

What was that? Something from below. I had to look, I had to satisfy my curiosity. Find a way to get down. But how? Look. No, nothing over here. In back. Look, there's a narrow door. A closet?

Thunk!

The sound was behind that door. I opened it. Stairs. Followed them down until...until...

"These crates go next," said an old man.

Incensed aroma of sweet grass, bearberry, and red willow wafted up the stairs. From the way the old man spoke, I could tell the incense was from a pipe and smoke. I crept and crouched down the stairs, enough to see a little and hear a lot.

"This one too?" a mover asked, pointing to a rectangular crate about the size of a child's coffin.

"No!" the old man said, which I could now see and confirm was smoking a pipe of the herbal threesome. "That one goes back to the island. No proper buyer here."

The island! I had always dreamed of escaping the peninsula and living on the island. The people, the food, the...everything!

"Who's there?" the old man asked after my day dreaming caused my waving hands to hit the wall.

I froze. Should I make my presence known?

"Come down here at once," the old man demanded.

Like a schoolchild caught, I walked down the stairs. There was not one but two movers. Both looked at me briefly before attempting to move the rectangular crate that was to go to the island.

"Ah-ow!" the other mover cried.

The box was dropped, first by the other mover and then by the first. Crashing to the ground, a side broke open and deployed the contents.

"It's a suit of armor," I gasped.

"No!" the first mover said. "It cannot be! But it is! The Anfractuous Armor! Run!"

The movers dashed up a trap door they had been using to load crates from the antique store's basement to a moving van. Into the van they hopped, and away in the van they sped.

"Superstitious fools!" the old man said, and he drew a long puff from his pipe.

"It's amazing!" I said, and I reached for the armor.

"Not for you," the old man said as he tripped my progress with an outstretched leg. "I save for proper buyer, but no buyer come. Now I send it back to island, but it scare movers away because of foolish superstition that it curse anyone it touches."

"If it is foolish, then why stop me? Maybe I want to buy it. Yes, I'll buy it. I have gold in my pocket. Here."

I pulled a gold slag from my pocket, still warm from my friend's blast furnace. A small part was for dinner and the other part for new clothes and tools, but now I was ready to part with the entire thing for...for...what did the mover call it?

"This gold slag for the Anfractuous Armor," I said.

The old man laughed.

"You don't know what you say," he said.

"Take the gold!" I said.

"This gold is corrupt and impure," he said. "And gold alone is not enough to purchase this artifact. The armor plates themselves are made of the strongest and lightest bismuth alloys. The price can only be paid one way."

"Name the price," I said.

"I cannot," he said.

"You just said—"

"I know what I say," he said. "The vest chooses its price."

"Vest? That's no vest. It's full armor," I said.

The old man laughed again.

"You really want this vest?" he asked.

"Armor," I corrected.

"As you say. Then touch it. But do not cry to me later of the consequence. I will take your gold slag, but the vest must choose you. There is no other way."

I touched the armor, and suddenly without warning, the hand, foot, arm, leg, and head coverings receded like a shriveled-up plant and exposed the ancient remains of a corpse. I shrieked in horror, but before my screams died down, the corpse dissolved in the air, and what was once an armor suit which exposed a corpse was now a small, thin, shiny vest.

"It's a magic vest!" I said. "With great power!"

"Power is never great or good," the old man said. "It preys on the mind and ensnares the body, until one day you will be that corpse and blow away in the wind!"

I shivered in fright for a moment, but then I looked hard at the old man. It was he who was old and beaten. His business failed, his youth had evaporated, and all he could do was smoke a pipe and try to scare a young person, me, into a submissive follower.

That would not happen.

"I've made my purchase!" I said. "Good day to you!"

I tried picking up the vest, but to my surprise, it stuck to the ground. I pulled and pulled, but it would not budge. It couldn't be a problem with being too heavy.

"There must be glue under the vest. I cannot lift it," I said.

"It has not chosen you. It is saved for proper buyer," he said.

"We went through this already. Give me the vest, or give back my gold."

The old man laughed. He puffed one last time on his pipe and blew smoke throughout the basement. The air became thick with his exhaust, and my vision failed me, but within seconds the air cleared and so did the basement. The vest's crate, the vest, and the old man were gone.

"I must have imagined it," I said to myself.

I reached into my pocket for the gold slag. Gone.

"No, I didn't. The gold is gone. And there's absolutely nothing here, no gold or anything."

I retraced my steps up to the main store and back to my friend's furnace, but the gold was gone, and so were my spirits. I dreaded the empty looks my family would give me when I would offer nothing but empty pockets and a mediocre story.

"I must borrow a little gold," I begged my friend.

"You just left here with the largest gold slag ever," he replied.

"I lost it," I said.

"How could you lose it?" he asked.

I told him the story. He laughed.

"That was a terrible lie," he said.

"It's true," I said.

My friend stared at me for a moment, then he broke out in a smile.

"Here," he said as he gave me a gold coin, "buy dinner for your family. But do not go into entertainment. No one will throw coins in your hat."

The sour rumbling in my stomach was not from hunger. I did something stupid, and worse, I admitted my stupidity to my friend. But at least I could save face with my family. I chose dinner carefully so as not to cost too much, and my family, though a little puzzled, did not dwell in thought on the type of food and simply ate it.

"You came home late," said my mother.

"Oh leave him alone," my father said. "He probably found a new friend to spend his money on. That's why we eat cheaply tonight."

My father winked at me. Surprised, my mouth hung open like a dog who'd had his prized bone stolen.

"What's her name? Where does she live? She'd better be at least our class or higher," my mother said.

"Everyone else is in class higher than us," my father said. "Let the boy have some space. Someday he'll want his own family."

"We are his family," my mother said.

That was close. My parents invented a story for me, so I didn't have to explain to them. But my younger brother, who was already taller than I, shot me a look of disbelief. I tried keeping quiet the rest of the evening, but he caught me alone while I was outside staring up at the stars.

"You don't have a girlfriend," my brother said. "I know you like a brother."

"Because I am your brother," I said. "And your older one at that."

"No one outside our family believes that," he said. "I'm thirty centimeters taller than you. So what really happened? Did you get mugged?"

"What!?"

"You have no gold for today. I know that look. You were mugged once before, and this was how you looked," he said.

"Forget it," I replied.

"Hey, I'm your brother. You don't have to let someone else beat you up. I have new friends. They'll help you. They'll protect you."

I didn't like the sound of these new friends.

"What kind of friends?" I asked.

"I belong to a club now," he said.

"You mean a gang?" I asked.

"We like to call it a club," he said. "I told them about you. They're willing to offer protection, for a small price."

"I knew it. Everyone wants the gold slag," I said.

"Not all of it," my brother said. "Only a little."

"That's stealing," I said.

"Stealing is when someone you don't know takes everything," my brother said. "This is protection. Better to keep most of your gold than risk losing it all."

"Little brother," I started to say, but my brother stretched his hands high in the air to exaggerate his stature. "Little brother! Stay away from gangs. They will only get you into crime. It will catch up with you."

"We don't do anything crazy like selling drugs," my brother said. "Anyway, think about what I said. You know where I live."

My brother went inside.

"Yes, I do know where you live. I know where we all live," I muttered.

I looked up to the stars and wondered if this was the way I'd spend the rest of my life, scavenging for metals during the day so that I could spend a few moments in the evening hoping for something better, something that wouldn't turn me into another zombie of the waking world.

I stood outside longer than usual, so much so that the evening wore on and grew late. I was tired. I didn't want to be tired, because it meant time for sleep, a sleep that would carry me into the next dreary morning of salvage drudgery.

Sleep overtook me. I don't remember what I dreamt, only that it was another dream of feeling trapped. I awoke early. I looked around my room. My younger brother was still asleep.

"Might as well get up for the day and go to the salvage yard," I thought to myself.

I dressed quietly, packed a small lunch, and slipped out the door into the alley. I took three paces away from the front door and turned back, as if half-expecting my father or mother to peer out a window to see me leaving early, but they didn't. However, something against the alley wall did catch my eye.

"No, it can't be," I whispered to myself.

It was. The Anfractuous Armor.

"I...I..." I stumbled to say.

I couldn't believe my eyes! How did it get there? There was no time to think. Several approaching voices from down the alley told me that if I didn't claim this prize, someone else would. I rushed over to the vest and knelt. The vest glistened and glittered in the early-morning light. For a split second I was afraid to touch it, but like a sudden jump into a river, I reached for the vest, grabbed it, and tucked it behind my back as I stood up against the alley wall. The voices down the alley were now closer. They glanced at me as they passed, and I nodded my head to them as a greeting. I watched them pass through the end of the alley and disappear around the corner, and as I did, a sense of relief overcame me. Whew!

But before I could pull the vest from behind my back, someone tapped me on the shoulder.

"What you got behind your back?" asked a thug with three of his thug buddies.

"Nothing," I said without thought.

"I think you got something you want to give us," he said.

"I left it here," another thug lied. "And he took it."

"Well?" the first thug said. "Give it back."

"I took nothing of yours," I said.

"I said, GIVE IT BACK!" the first thug said, and he stabbed me in the shoulder.

The knife blade broke off, with the pointed end deep in my shoulder. My shoulder stung, and I bled. I fell to my knees in pain, and as I put my hands to each side to steady myself, the vest fell from my grasp and slipped to the ground behind me.

"I see it," said the second thug. "You got my jacket."

"It's not a jacket, and it's not yours," I said.

The pain caused my body to heat up and go into a panic. I shook and perspired profusely. Something in my sweat stung my skin like acid. I felt an overwhelming urge to fight back, to throw away my life against these thugs to defend my pride. I would lose, and they'd take my life, but not my heart. That I would keep forever.

"Move aside!" said a thug, and he kicked me.

Strangely, I didn't feel the kick. Was it the adrenaline of the moment? I didn't know, but a new sense of fulfillment surrounded my chest, back, and sides and flowed into my arms and legs. I stood up, and the thug with my blood on his broken knife lunged at me, yet strangely I felt no desire to step aside. I stood my ground and was willing to take his attack, because a sense of warmth and fulfillment would protect me.

"Ow!" the thug said as his knife rebounded off my chest and cut into his hand.

"You slime!" said another thug.

The others joined in with their knives and fists, slashing and beating at my torso, arms, and legs, but their attacks were foiled. How? I did not know. One head-butted me, but his skull cracked. I know, I heard it. My head felt none of it, though. Finally, they pushed me aside. I fell down, and they leapt upon me, but I arighted myself by flipping onto my feet and in so doing was able to throw them across the alley. Bruised and bleeding, they limped away, bitter that they'd been beaten.

"I feel strange," I muttered. "They ran away. How did I survive that attack? I'd better check for wounds."

I unbuttoned my shirt and removed it, but instead of seeing my arms and chest, I saw the vest that moments ago was behind my back. It had become armor and had covered my arms and traveled down to my legs! But as I stood there and regained my composure from the fight, the armor withdrew from my limbs and shrank into a vest, gradually, until the vest which was once firm was now loose. I unzipped the front of the vest and removed it. My shoulder was completely healed, and the broken-off blade had seemed to disappear.

"Oo-lau-wa," I exclaimed in excitement as I put my shirt back on.

But my excitement was short-lived. I suddenly felt watched, and this feeling shifted into a growing fear that the vest would be snatched from my hands by some swooping scavenger bird. I looked up and cowered, expecting such a bird to swoop down, but it did not. My pulse quickened, and my skin perspired. I had to run somewhere and hide the vest to save it for some purpose that I knew it held for me.

"He left already," I heard my younger brother say as he approached the door to the apartment.

"He's going to steal it!" I cringed. "He'll see me, and that will be it!"

I broke into a run while holding the vest above my head, but suddenly and without warning, the vest slipped over my head and between my shirt and chest. But I was running the wrong way. Instead of running down the alley away from my family's front door, I ran toward it.

"What am I doing?" I asked myself. "I can't let him see me!"

I dove to the alley wall directly opposite my front door. There was nothing to hide behind—I was an easy sight for anyone in that alley by my front door. My younger brother exited our apartment, and I swear—he stared directly at me. I held my breath, but I was convinced the rapid thuds of my heart would give me away.

"I'll be home late," he yelled back to my parents. "I want to search a new garbage yard by the lighthouse."

"Don't be too late," my mother called back.

How could he not see me? I looked down at myself...at...where was I? My chest, my legs, even my arms—where did they go? Was I dreaming? No, this was real. I had become invisible. I walked out of the alley and along the side of the road. I was invisible. No one could see me.

"Ugh!" said someone while bumping into me.

That person looked around to see what he'd walked into, but he couldn't figure it out. Stunned, he walked away.

"So I may be invisible, but I'm not porous," I said.

"Who's there?" said an old woman.

"And people can hear me speak," I said.

"It's a ghost! This street is haunted! My life, my life!" she cried, and she ran off.

I couldn't just walk around like this. It was too easy for people to bump into me. Perhaps I could jump over people as they approached. Yes, that's what I'd do. When front, back, left, and right don't work, jump up. And I did. As I approached a person, I jumped. My first attempt didn't work out, and I landed on the person.

"I must get a running start," I said.

With the approach of the next person, I took three running steps and jumped. I had to twist my body to avoid hitting the person, and I knocked off that person's hat, but I did it. With the next person, I jumped again, and I went higher and cleared the person without touching any part of him. I did this again and again, needing fewer running steps and jumping higher until I could simply lift up on my tippy toes and send myself up many meters in the air.

"I...I can almost fly," I said. "I *can* fly!"

I jumped up to a ledge and stayed there. I looked down and watched people, carts, and trucks go by.

"No one can see me, absolutely no one," I said.

I jumped higher and higher until I reached the top of the building, and then I jumped from building to building until I reached the highest building in the area. I was high—high above the filthy haze below. The air was clear, the sky beautiful, and rays from the sunrise lit the clouds in colors of orange and pink. The view was peaceful, relaxing, and I didn't ever want the color-ful clouds to fade. The sun arose quickly, the clouds lost their special colors, and my invisibility left me. I became visible, my armor receded into the vest, and the vest fell off.

"Oh, this is bad!" I said with a sudden realization. "How will I get down? It's a long way."

I looked over the side of the roof with one hand holding onto the vest and another bracing myself against the edge. Just looking down made me dizzy. I pulled away from the edge and sat on the roof.

"This was stupid. This was really stupid. I'll have to find a way down. Maybe there are stairs somewhere. Maybe—"

I didn't have long to wonder. A gang burst through a stairwell door and ran around the side, followed by the police.

"Hey you, stay there," yelled one of the officers to me.

"He's not one of them," said another officer. "They went this way."

"All the same," said the first as he approached me.

The other police officers went after the gang. Two gangs already? This was too much. But I didn't engage the police before. Now what?

"What are you holding behind your back?" he asked.

It was happening again. I held the vest behind my back, just as I did while in the alley. I couldn't let this police officer take it. I had to learn more about the vest. Besides, he had no right to take it. But he would, and he'd find out, and where would that leave me? Back to that miserable job of metal salvage amongst filthy, sickening garbage.

"That's stolen property," the officer said. "Give it to me."

I backed up. There was nowhere to go, because the roof's ledge was behind me. I was scared. I shook with fright, though I shouldn't have. If only I had the vest on and were invisible, then he would never see me. But he did. I couldn't just give him the vest. It was worth more than me, worth more than life itself, and I'd give mine to keep it.

"You can't have it," I said.

The officer lunged at me, and I fell backward, over the edge, and down, down, down. Time slowed. My vision narrowed into a small point of light, I went deaf, and my sense of feeling deserted me. My body was nothing but a heart, one massive heart chirping at incredible speed. The sun was still, the air like water, and I was drowning, drowning in a wispy-thin sea of nothingness.

"Ah-roh-lor-a-gra-lerg!" I gurgled, as if I were underwater.

Wasn't I underwater? Wasn't this the end? Where was that vest? I could use it, I...I...

The vest slipped over my head all on its own and molded itself to my chest. It enwrapped and engulfed my body, forming armor and providing support in the form of oxygen, energy, and strength. With my heart still racing and adrenaline coursing through my body, I leveraged the vest to my will and landed on the ground with a large bounce, then a smaller bounce, and smaller, making a loud *thud* sound on the first bounce but gradually swaying the vest to soften its acoustics until I finally landed no louder than a feather floating freely to a field.

"Amazing," said an onlooker.

"Did you see?" said another.

"He is a super human," said a third.

A large group surrounded me like birds converging on fresh food. I felt constricted and began to panic.

"How did you do that?" one asked.

"Please, share with me your power!" said another.

"Help me, I need help with my cargo."

"Let me out of here!" I yelled.

I spun around and around with my arms flailing about, and I cleared enough space to fly out of there. As I did, a larger crowd gathered to witness my departure. Then a news helicopter arrived, and it flew around me and chased me like a hawk chasing a smaller bird. Was not the air even safe for me? Why wasn't the suit rendering me invisible? The helicopter came too close, and its metal blade caught my protected arm, causing the armor to rip and my arm to bleed. It pained me, and I brought my arm close to my body. Then the helicopter became disoriented and lost track of me.

"I'm invisible," I said.

I flew several kilometers away until I reached a grove of trees, and I perched there like the bird the helicopter thought I was.

"I am hungry," I said to myself. "What happened to my lunch? I must have lost it when I fell off the building."

The vest did not provide food or drink.

"I'm still invisible," I said to myself. "I can sneak some food from a nearby cafeteria."

I dropped to the ground and looked around, and I found myself on university grounds. There it was in front of my face, the University of Hammencase. I chose a path between tree and twig that led me into the open big. And still there were none who could see that I was about to eat for free. The walk was short and quick, and soon I had food to lick. And eat and drink. Students I walked in between, dressed in colors of blue and green. But food and drink were now aplenty, and I ate my fill in less than twenty—minutes that is, and for desert a strawberry fizz. Full as can be, I walked down a hallway to see and see, and then my balance was full of doubt, and oh my-my I just passed out.

"It cannot be removed," said a voice.

"And yet it is impervious to our cutting tools," said another.

I awoke in the university's lab with two people hovering over me.

"He's awakening," said the first voice.

"Who are you? Where am I?" I asked.

"My name is Doctor Julia Craymar, and you're at the University of Hammencase, in the 104 physics lab of the Wenniar building."

"Physics lab?" I asked.

"Yes. To test your vest. It's incredibly protective. Can you remove it?" Julia asked.

"I see. You wish to keep it for yourself," I said. "This method is more devious than what the thugs use on the street."

Julia laughed.

"Well I'm very curious about any vest made by Dayla Industries," Julia said. "I'll give you a hundred American dollars for it."

"This vest must be worth more than that," I said. "I was told this is the Anfractuous Armor, and that it is only meant for a proper buyer."

"And I can be that proper buyer," Julia said. "But why do you believe it is worth more?"

"Because of the things I can do. I can be protected from harm, I can fly, and I can become invisible," I said, but as I said those things, I realized it was a mistake to reveal such properties, because Doctor Craymar listened too eagerly.

"You're right. This vest is worth more than a hundred dollars or even a thousand dollars," Julia said. "But you did pass out. This vest is not for everyone. It might even cause you harm. Did you ever think of this?"

I sat up.

"I think I'll leave now," I said. "Perhaps we can meet again. But I have some things I'd like to do."

"Of course," Julia said as she patted me on the back.

"I'm actually surprised that you're letting me just walk out of here," I said. "I would think you would wish me to stay."

"Have a good day," she said.

And I left. I left campus and decided to use my vest to enter one of the most hostile sections of town—a section that also had the most valuable discarded electronic boards. What I did not know was that Julia's interest in me had not dissipated. After I left the physics lab, she called her father on her cellphone.

"Father? Julia here. I've found the stolen Dayla vest. Yes, it just walked onto campus, out here in the Pacific Rim. Can you believe it? Whoever thought that my overseas work would turn up a prize like this!"

"Did you get a chance to analyze it?" he asked.

"Yes. The vest consists of a special bismuth alloy," Julia said.

"That part we expected," her father said.

"But it seems altered in some fashion," Julia said. "Our intelligence on the vest says the bismuth should be in a low energy state. But my instruments recorded an unusually high energy state."

"How is that possible?" he asked.

"I don't know. I wasn't able to remove the vest from the subject," Julia said.

"And you just let him go?" he asked.

Julia laughed.

"I have a theory that the vest interacts with the tissue-stored metal," Julia said. "I scanned an accumulation of heavy metals in his body, most likely from a job of scavenging precious metals from circuit boards. That's a prevalent profession in these parts. I also scanned the remains of a broken knife in his shoulder that already had begun dissolving in his flesh which then exchanged subatomic particles with the vest."

"Then that could be the answer," Julia's father said. "Think of this, Julia. Americans don't have the level of heavy metal accumulation that is found in the Asian Pacific Rim. That's why the Dayla vest failed—it was tested on Americans."

"Then even if we acquire it, we can't use it without a toxin-filled subject," Julia said.

"Let's learn more about our subject," he said.

"I am," Julia said. "I've attached a tracking device to our subject's vest. We will learn all we need to know."

I entered the hostile section of town, where crime and greed go hand in deed. Already I was approached by a gang of thieves—they poked and prodded, and I wanted to heave. But I did not.

"Step aside," I said, but they laughed at me.

"Pay the fee—to walk out free," the leader said to me.

"No," say I.

"Then you die."

And the thugs attacked me, much like the others before. One knife stuck me good, then two, then four. The vest became armor, it went through detection, assimilated the knives and thus gave protection. My strength increased, to that of many men, and when I struck the gang, they became a blend—of fearful dogs and foolish frogs. Metaphorically, of course, but their emotion was real. They scattered and ran for more to steal, but not from me.

I was on my way to harvest the best precious metal in the city, not just the mere itty-bitty.

I walked into an electronics pile deep. All the metal surrounded me, like frost on a fir tree. I had never seen frost, but I had read about it, and I imagined I was that fir tree, seeking out with needles to flourish with metal and nourish my family.

But I didn't need to imagine. I had the sudden sensation I could smell metals, like the effect one has when chewing aluminum against silver fillings. It was an electrified salt smell, and each precious metal had its own slightly different scent charge. I was bold and sniffed for gold. And there it was, under a steel plate, an engineering device for focusing a special kind of radiation, for detecting micro-stress fractures. And the device had millions of little gold-plated fins. I grabbed the device and held it in my hand. I removed the outer covers and sifted my fingers through the gold-plated strands, and as I did, the gold slid onto my fingers and along my arms and into the vest, where it stored the gold like an egg in a nest. I went through more circuit boards and ran my fingers across them, and other metals now coursed through my fingers and into the vest, metals like silver, platinum, palladium, and rhodium. But what I didn't realize at the time was that the vest was also drawing mercury from the circuit boards.

My time spent soaking in metals was short, as the vest was very good with my new sport. Now all that remained was cashing my claim and bringing money home to my family's good name.

"You're loaded today," said my friend when I turned in my metal. "How did you get so much so quickly? And you have other precious metals as well."

"It's a secret," I said.

"C'mon. You found a new location, is that it?" he asked. "I didn't see you in the regular junk yard. So where is it?"

"Now, now, contain yourself. It's not for you," I said.

"It had better be, or else look for a new furnace," he said.

He gave me half of the melted metals, but the mercury did not come out of my vest. Like I said, my realization was not the best, and so the mercury became a silent pest. I exchanged the remelted bars for cash, bought food in a dash, and brought all home for an evening bash. My parents impressed, my brother depressed, that I had done so well and he so poorly.

"I'm still taller than you," he said sorely, "and I can beat you in anything. Anything."

His jealousy of which I did not wait, but instead I finished my plate, of dinner and then there was desert, which filled me fine but left him inert. To cheer the night and remove his blight, I struck instruments of tone and to cheer my brother lone. I sang words so ancient and dear, and so I record them now and here:

> *Vest itu a lito place,*
> *Trest itu na gibo sace.*
> *A hah bialopi,*
> *A sah sialogi,*
> *Sest itu ma tio slace.*

Other verses burst forth, and my parents joined in, but my brother could not concede my win. He decided instead to head for bed and hide his dread we would not tread. We were happy and full of cheer, and night grew old and morning near. My parents could not believe the time, of wonder and joy so full of rhyme. But morning came and time for work, and so I left with strength and torque.

I began my trip back to the place of gold and plenty, but I sensed I was followed from those not so friendly. I turned back from time to time to see who was up to such a crime. But no one. So on to hostile place I went, to earn my keep with time well spent. More boards to pick, more metals to click, and the day went as well as it did before. But the day grew old, and for gold it was time, to melt it down, but my friend would not get his half of mine.

"There you are," the friend said without notification.

"What are you doing here?" I asked.

"I followed you," he said. "To find out where you're getting your top metals."

"You found it. Are you satisfied?" I asked.

My friend looked around and rummaged through the devices.

"I don't understand. Where are the large finds of metals? I'd have to take apart all of these devices and pull out their circuit boards just to get a little metal."

"That's your problem," I said.

He could not see, that by simple touch I could absorb precious metals— much. He rummaged and sifted, but he was not gifted. He found only tin, and anger set in, so now he gave his ultimate warning.

"You'd better stop by the furnace soon, so that I can receive my cut. Or else," he said.

"You don't scare me," I said.

He left. And I decided I could melt the gold and other metals on my own, with heat from my vest, a furnace home-grown. But this I did away from junk yards. Instead, I went back to the store that had closed, the one from where the vest came. And there, in the still and quiet, the vest heated the stored metal. I pointed a finger at a table, and the vest emptied its stored metals onto that table—pure.

"I still have plenty of money from yesterday," I said to myself. "I'll take these home and give them to my parents for safe keeping."

And that's what I did. I went home with many precious metal bars and gave them to my parents, who put them in jars, and hid them in the wall, where they were stacked deep and tall. We had a dinner fine, drank expensive wine, and then it was time for song and dance. But my parents were tired from the night before, and they went to bed early and began to snore. So I and my brother were left alone, and he became busy on the phone, bragging to a new girl, no less, and promising to buy her a skirt and dress. But the night was too young for me, and so I went out and traveled the cit-y.

First I needed clothes from a tailor near, something bold and full of cheer. I found one ready to make, an outfit with class of nothing fake. And so I hired a taxicab, and had him drive around for seafood and crab. A tavern he found for me to see. I paid my fare and entered with glee, the tavern that is, where food was great, with dancing and music and chocolate cake! It was the cake that made me a friend, her name was Kara, and she was ten-plus-ten. She loved chocolate too, and so after dinner for two, we took a cab to a store of value, with the best chocolate candy through and through.

"I love this," Kara said. "I could eat it forever. The darker the chocolate, the more like heaven. It makes me alive. Really alive! Let's go for a drive on the beach."

And that's how we spent the evening. The night grew old, I was too bold, and dawn was around the corner. I dropped Kara off at her upper flat, and returned home to clean off the splat, of lipstick and food from dirty face, and mine for more metals at that special place.

But when I reached home, all was amiss. Amiss. Poetry left me. The place was ransacked. Trashed. Robbers had broken in and smashed the walls. The jars—gone. My parents and brother—dead. Dead!

"I...how could this happen? They were just here. Alive," I said.

I called the police, and they took my statement. I was promised an investigation, but...the promise felt empty. Empty. As was I. I walked along the streets to gather my thoughts, but as the shock wore off, deep hatred set in. I vowed I would get those robbers and make them pay. Make them pay!

"They want metal. I'll give them metal!" I vowed.

It was at this point that the mercury surfaced on the vest. I touched it, and I felt a new purpose and drive in my life—to seek out any and all murderers and deal with them—in my own manner. I used my nose to sniff out the metal trail the robbers created when they made off with the precious metals. I took a cab, yes another cab, and I hung my head out the window. Why didn't I use my vest to fly? I didn't know. Perhaps I felt I needed to be grounded, like a hound dog on the trail. I reached a business district with several warehouses. I paid the fare and let the taxi go. Gold. I could sniff it in the air, as I could with silver, platinum, and palladium. I was angry, and my anger made me invisible. The smell of metals went up, and I flew to an upper office balcony in one of the warehouses. I stood there and listened to a conversation inside.

"We should break each bar into three pieces," said one voice.

"Four pieces," said another that sounded familiar.

"Your girl doesn't count," said the first voice.

"I have a press that can break them," said a third voice.

"Then do it," said the first voice. "We need all the metal we can get."

"Then you shall have it!" I yelled as I became visible, burst through the window, and sprayed the three men with hot, toxic mercury.

"Who are...arggh!" one of them yelled, and he started running.

The other two just looked at me in disbelief, then they experienced involuntary muscle movements.

"You!" I said, recognizing my friend from the furnace. "And you," I said, recognizing the taxi driver.

"How did you find us?" the friend laughed.

The taxi driver laughed too. The first man didn't return. Now the friend and taxi driver cried, and they yelled and screamed at me. They threw things at me, but their muscles jerked uncontrollably, and they fell to the ground and lost strength until finally they stopped moving and their mouths foamed over.

"Good!" I said with glee.

I was surprisingly pleased with extracting my revenge, even though one was my friend. And yes, his was the familiar voice, and so he had a girl, and I kept that in the back of my mind should I need to continue my revenge. But

I needed to find the leader, and that was easy. He left a trail of mercury vapor. I followed him to another window and another balcony. I entered the balcony, expecting a confrontation, but instead I saw his prone body on the street below. He had jumped and killed himself.

"Oh!" gasped a female voice from a nearby room.

So, this was the woman who was in on the robbing and murdering of my family. Time for more revenge. The vest prepared itself for another few shots of mercury to fire. I left the balcony and went back into the office area, then I sensed that she was in a little office room close-by. The door to that room was closed, and the walls were solid, preventing me from seeing directly. But the vest gave me a sense of where she stood, and I also sensed that she influenced my friend to rob my family for the precious metals. Then in addition to the leader who had killed himself, this woman had also driven my former friend and the taxi driver to the crime they committed. I could see now how I was set up. The friend had the taxi driver pick me up and take me wherever to keep me out of the way, while the friend and the leader did the robbing and killing. The friend knew I had the metals and knew where I lived. It all made sense. And so it was time to exact my revenge on the last piece of the puzzle. I would not storm into the room. I would blast the mercury through the wall and impact her directly. The vest gave me her location, and this was becoming my new habit.

Blast!

She screamed, then cried, then laughed, then ran around the room in a frenzy. I didn't go in to face her—I could hear everything. I simply waited for her to die. And only after her death did I enter the room.

Kara!

I was struck with sudden shock and grief. How could this be Kara? The chocolate lover? Then it hit me—she was part of the ruse. She distracted me and kept me away all night. But it was all so real. She was all so real.

"Kara, Kara!" I yelled.

But froth covered her mouth, and her eyes were frozen open.

"I killed her," I said. "Dead. Oh, this wasn't revenge at all. It was a horrible mistake. Kara, Kara! How could you be mixed up in all this?"

My revenge turned sour. I was now miserable. Then I began to laugh hysterically.

"What a stupid thing for them to do," I continued to laugh.

I laughed my way out of the office building, onto a balcony, and through the air as I flew away. I flew to the ocean shoreline and stood there, listening to the waves. There was something wrong with me. I should not have laughed. I should not have sought revenge. But I did all those things. What would I do now? No family, no friend. I still had the vest, and I could get more metal, but then there would be other people wishing to rob and kill wherever I went.

"I must rid myself of this vest," I said.

I went back to the store from where the vest came, and I entered. It was empty for the moment, but then two Americans walked in.

"Mr. Tau?" one asked.

"Who are you? How did you know my name?" I asked. "I'm in a really bad mood."

"We've been watching you," the other said.

"And we'd like to make you happy," said the first. "We'd like to give you a job."

"I don't need a job," I said.

"It's not just a job," the other American said. "You'd have a prominent position in national security."

"As in working for your federal government?" I asked. "I hate federal governments."

"You wouldn't have to meet with any politicians, Mr. Tau. All you need do is find criminals, as you have just now. You wouldn't need to kill them or anything. Just find them," said the first.

"But if you would like to participate in their punishment, we can arrange for that too—any sort of thing you prefer. These are criminals that would not enter the court system, so whatever you do would be acceptable," said the other.

"No. I want nothing to do with the American government," I said. "You ship your garbage over here and create the salvage industry that we have, an industry that pollutes our land and water."

"We very much wish you to consider our offer," said the first.

"Consider it very seriously," said the second.

"No," I said.

"Then consider it as final. Since you won't go willingly, you are under arrest for the illegal possession and use of an American military vest," said the first.

"No!" I yelled.

I became invisible, ran out of the store, and flew around the city. I was now lost and disoriented—not geographically, but emotionally. What was left in my life? I spent three days circling the city. Three days. Mostly to see if

I could exhaust myself of the vest. The vest kept going, but I did not. I fell asleep, and the vest, directed by my disturbed dreams, took me out to sea and began drowning me. I suddenly awoke and found myself looking at sea water in all directions. I was completely lost, and now I was hungry and thirsty. There was no food, the salt water of the sea was undrinkable, and so I was convinced I would soon die.

But as luck would have it, a research vessel came across my position. It launched a small life boat, the boat picked me up, and I was taken aboard the vessel.

"Hello again," said Doctor Julia Craymar, then she turned to the captain and said, "False alarm. I know this gentleman."

"What are you doing out here?" I asked.

She laughed.

"That's my line," she said. "I teach oceanography, and I'm with my students on a field trip. You know, I didn't catch your name last time."

"My name is Tau," I said.

"Well, Tau, you must be thirsty and hungry. Come with me. We just finished our lunch, but there's plenty left over," Julia said.

"I'm not hungry," I said, suddenly losing my appetite.

"Oh," Julia said. "Well if you change your mind, the cook always keeps cold cuts in the fridge."

"I'll stand here by the railing and watch the ocean, if you don't mind," I said.

"That's fine," she said.

Then a student walked up with wet plastic garbage and showed the teacher.

"Yes," Julia said. "You'll note that sea garbage tends to collect together, like dust bunnies."

"This looks like simple garbage," the student said.

"You're correct. No debris from the crash," Julia said.

"Crash? What crash?" I asked.

"A small, private jet disappeared from the sky yesterday," Julia said. "It was last reported in this area. We were planning to go out anyway to study ocean garbage, and so we combined two field trips into one. Now we are looking for survivors. We thought you were a survivor from the plane until we brought you aboard. Which brings up the question again—what *are* you doing out here?"

"Looking for the lost," I said, and I activated my vest and flew above the research vessel.

"Look at him fly!" yelled one of the students.

"Jet pack?" another asked.

"No, there are no fuel tanks," Julia said.

I sniffed the air, and I could make out the scent of aircraft-grade aluminum. I flew through the air at top speed, quicker than I've ever gone. I could feel the air molecules pressing and buzzing against my nose, and a rumbling sound coned outward around my body. It wasn't long before I came across an oil slick, but otherwise no debris. And yet the smell of aluminum met the water. I plunged into the water and dove deep, amazed that I could survive the increasing water pressure and the lack of breathable atmosphere. The vest then was providing air and protection. I continued diving, and the light faded, but I was able to yell in the water and hear the echo, and this combined with sniffing the aluminum brought me to the submerged airplane. Its wings had broken off, but otherwise the body was intact. The nose had settled on a boulder, and the tail was lower. I dove to the tail, touched it, and the vest absorbed a bit of the aluminum frame and created an opening. But the opening was not some raw opening that would allow sea water in. No, the opening perfectly matched my body, and so I passed into the plane's body without the water slipping around my body and going into the aircraft.

Passing through the opening, I realized that the air inside was undisturbed by the sea water. I continued from tail to nose and found two passengers and one pilot—all unconscious, but breathing. I needed to bring these people to the surface. One at a time? Would they survive the trip up? The vest would protect me, but what would protect them? And how would I get them out?

A thought hit me...could I bring the craft to the surface? I touched the side of the craft, and the vest transmitted my thoughts into the frame. The craft began shedding the tail fin and extra weight, and the body in the tail shrank toward the cockpit. I moved the passengers into the cockpit as best as I could, and so all but the cockpit had been shed. The cockpit ascended.

"It's working," I said.

The cockpit bobbed on the surface, with the nose pointing upward like an Apollo space capsule. I touched the side one more time, and a bit of the side shot out and upward with heat and flame, forming a natural signal flare. The opening also allowed fresh air in yet was above the water line, so no water entered.

And the time came. Julia's research vessel saw the signal and cruised over to the cockpit. A crane swiveled over from the ship, lifted the cockpit, and brought it onto the deck. Julia and several students rushed to the cockpit.

"Hello in there," Julia called.

"There are three people in here in need of help," I said.

"Tau!" Julia exclaimed.

Technicians rushed over and broke out the windows, and then I helped move the pilot and two passengers out of the cockpit.

"It's Doctor Wilson and his assistant," Julia said to a technician.

"Wait," Doctor Wilson said as he regained semi-consciousness. "In the plane...you must retrieve it...experimental...or go super critical."

"Take them and the pilot to the medical bay," Julia said to a technician.

"That's it. No more," I said as I exited.

But the students circled around me in awe.

"What?" I asked.

"That was incredible," Julia said. "You left here and then we find you floating in the cockpit. I can't guess how this all happened. And the rest of the plane?"

"Still underwater. I made some minor changes to the body," I said.

"Minor!? This is a major miracle!" Julia said. "Tau. Do you realize the significance of what you just did? I mean besides saving three souls."

"I haven't thought about it. I just acted," I said.

"You're a natural born first responder," Julia said.

"Doctor Craymar," said one of the technicians. "These markings on the cockpit...this is the vitamin B12 shipment with a special cobalt isotope."

"The ocean pressure...Doctor Wilson is right. Tau, can you go back down and retrieve a metal cylinder in a special ice chest? If we don't..." Julia explained.

"Right away," I said.

I dove back down into the ocean, and again the students were amazed to see me leave. There was a new trail of aluminum scent to follow, and I followed it down to the bottom of the ocean. The body was now long and stretched as a result of when I first visited it and reduced the metal. I touched the body as before and entered as before, and I was pleased to find an air pocket still inside with normal atmospheric pressure. With the body now narrower, I had to crouch down while walking, and I did so toward the tail, where I found what looked like an ice chest, only this ice chest had several indicator lights and a display panel, indicating status.

"So, it's self powered," I said, "but it's on battery power, with about four hours left. It was using the plane's power. I'd better bring this connection cord with me. But how will I bring it to the surface without exposing it to the sea?"

Then I had an idea. I could wrap part of the plane's body around me and also the ice chest, similar to how I had pulled everyone into the cockpit and closed off that section. So I moved the chest to the side of the plane, and I touched the plane's wall. The vest reacted with the wall and caused the aluminum frame to wrap around the ice chest and me, and we ascended upward like an escape pod. But something strange happened. The ice chest glowed, and the vest tingled like it was full of electricity. My flesh boiled, and I cried out. The air grew bad with the smell of my skin. It heated up too quickly, and I thought I would surely die. I pushed the pod upward as quickly as possible, but just a few meters before reaching the surface, I'd had enough. I blasted the pod apart. The ice chest floated to the surface, and sea water cooled my limbs.

The crane swiveled over and fished the chest out of the water. I flew from the water to the deck, and then the students stood around me and gasped again. Julia walked over and looked at my arms. They had become cobalt red.

"What's wrong with me?" I asked.

"I'm not sure," Julia said, "but it appears your vest reacted with the cobalt in the ice chest."

"Get it out of me! Get it out!" I yelled.

"Fortunately, we have a lab on board. Follow me," Julia said.

I followed Julia, but I could hardly contain myself. I had a deep desire to destroy everything around me. Indeed, when I placed my now-metallic-red hand on a door handle, I crushed that handle.

"I'm going to go crazy. I can't stand myself!" I yelled.

"Shh," she said as we entered the lab. "First, let's remove the vest."

But the vest would not come off. It was fused into my metallic skin.

"Perhaps a tranquilizer," she said.

Julia filled a syringe and attempted to inject me with medication, but the needle bent.

"Your skin has completely metallicized," she said. "Only metal can react with it now."

"You must help me! Something! I'll kill myself! I swear!" I screamed.

"Jump into this vat," she said. "Hurry!"

I jumped into the vat. Julia pressed a few buttons, and the vat filled with mercury. The vest absorbed it, and I relaxed a little.

"How do you feel?" she asked.

"I'm not totally crazy now," I said. "But I'm still edgy."

"I'll cool it down," she said.

The mercury cooled, but then I felt even edgier.

"No! I'm going crazy again," I said.

"Higher temperature? That doesn't make sense. This would kill a man. But..." she said, and she hit a few buttons.

The mercury temperature went up.

"I feel a little better," I said. "Can you make it hotter?"

"If I do, the mercury will begin to evaporate. Plus, mercury is highly toxic to humans."

"I...don't feel very human right now. I need more of something," I said.

"Let's try this," she said.

Julia pressed another button, and liquid lead poured in.

"Ahhh, that feels good. Feels good. Feels...I can't stop repeating myself," I said.

"A little arsenic should cure that," she said. "Here."

She pressed a button, and I could think clearly again.

"Uh oh, the cobalt in you is becoming radioactive," she said.

"You mean you didn't get the cobalt out?" I asked.

"No, I couldn't. Not without...wait...maybe I can electroplate it...with some cadmium," she said.

Julia pressed yet another button. Liquid cadmium poured in, and it mixed with the other metals and me. Then she pressed a few more buttons, and several arcs of electricity shot from an iron sphere above me and into the vat and thus into me. I jerked several times from the first few shots, but after about eight or nine, I rather liked the electricity. The last elements of my humanity had left me, and as my new body took shape, I saw and heard an image of the old man from the shop, laughing with cruel delivery as to my fate.

"Show me your strength, Tau. Break out of the vat," she said.

With my two arms, I thrust against opposite inside parts of the vat, and I ripped it open. The metal that was once in the vat was gone—all had been absorbed by me—the new amalgam of vest, cobalt, mercury, arsenic, lead, and cadmium. I looked more machine than human, and my body had colors of yellow, black, and silver.

"I...am no longer Tau," I said. "I owe my new existence to you."

A cunning smile grew over Julia's face. She then stepped over to a satellite telephone and made a call.

"Father? Julia. Yes, I have the vest. And an even greater surprise for you —a new form of industrial servant—made primarily of MErcury, aRSenic, Lead, and cADmIUM. And I will name it from those four elements. Mersladium. I will hand him over to you. But not as a gift. You will need to reimburse me greatly for this one. Yes, I have saved this one for you, the proper buyer."

Return from Lagenora

Vorlac returned Roger to the trial arena, which was now well lit. Three chairs had been placed in the center, with one chair of heavy build and restraint capability. Vorlac placed Roger in the chair and secured the restraints. Vorlac turned to where he thought Sparfy should be, but Sparfy wasn't there.

"As command, all in order," Suproc said from the balcony.

"Wait," Roger said. "Prince Sparfiacus isn't here yet. We must wait."

Suproc Krivat raised his ears in pleasant surprise. Vorlac replied with a large grin.

"With delight, onward with the trial!" Suproc exclaimed.

The audience clicked, splashed, and cackled with pleasure. The lights dimmed except for a bright spotlight on Roger and a dim aura around Suproc. A fog of light coalesced into a holographic projection.

"As fact, evidence now on display by direct mandate of the sponge complexus," Suproc said.

"The walls are running the projection?" Roger muttered.

"Your silence, defendant," Vorlac said. "The complexus by right as the first citizens of Rhynchus. Their need in priority over cetacean and ray citizens, and certainly over you, human. No hope of your understanding."

A hush fell on the arena as soothing, undulating musical harmonies danced through the air from the sponge walls, directed by the complexus, with the harmonies imparting a feeling of serenity and respect for ancient Earth. The holograph displayed a mountain scene, high up, then gradually zoomed in on a waterfall, following the waterfall until it became a brook then emptying into a small mountain lake, clear and clean as the sunrise that twinkled across the ripples.

The scene was violently disturbed by the drilling platform and the SO-ZOD, which had now blasted through the ocean and breached through the Rhynchus outer wall. Sparfy, Tugan, Brela, Metavasi, Korlan, and Delfa— Sparfy's seadogs—were shown leaping from the water and into the air several times, sending out electro-acoustic waves that formed a toroid around the drilling platform. The toroid was known as a vonk wave, and it gradually built in height and enveloped the drilling platform. With a final command from Sparfy and his seadogs, Metavasi delivered an explosive to the SOZOD, just ahead of the vonk wave that collapsed on itself and the drilling platform, intensifying as it did, until it sent out both an electro-magnetic pulse and a compression wave. The combined effect caused electronics and power to fuse and ignite into a lightning blast that destroyed the SOZOD, shattered structures, and blasted the humans off the rig and into the ocean. The audience erupted in angered yells but switched to wild cheering when the humans were thrown into the ocean.

"As command, order," Suproc said.

"The drilling rig as shown in its final moments of attack," Vorlac said to the audience. "As witness to events next for review."

The scene showed debris floating on the ocean both from the drilling rig and from Rhynchus. The audience reacted in horror when it saw bits of the outer wall, dead sponge, dead electric ray, and dead dolphin floating on the water's surface. Korlan and Delfa tried swimming, but they were badly injured and spent part of their time floating lifelessly. Sparfy tended to Delfa while Brela tended to Korlan. Metavasi led a pack of dalli porpoises toward the AC Sniar, but the ship turned and sped away from the wreckage at top speed. It struggled to stay ahead of Metavasi and his pack, but it could not outrun him, and eventually Metavasi and pack reached the AC Sniar. The porpoises launched a vonk wave, and this destroyed external electrical equipment, with much flashing and sparking. However, items stored inside the carrier were safe, and the hull only suffered minor damage. Metavasi and pack generated two other vonk waves, or more like vonk clouds, one to each side of the aircraft carrier, and used those clouds to force the AC Sniar on a path of Metavasi's choosing, which was Gough Island. Metavasi and pack then forced the carrier to stay there until instructions of what to do with the carrier were received.

"Prince Metavasi as guard of the human aircraft carrier and in waters of Gathona, the ancient graveyard," Vorlac said.

Cheers from the audience, including chants of "Metavasi, Metavasi." Then other chants came in such as, "Dallis have it right," "Death to humans," and "Lagenora forever."

Sparfy then arrived.

"As command, order," Suproc said.

Meanwhile in Curatidoma, Debbie was now in her own tank that resembled a bed but had water instead of a mattress. She was among many other badly injured dolphins, porpoises, and electric rays who were also in their own tanks and were variously between humanoid and natural states. In the tank next to Debbie lay King Acus, and at his side (and uninjured) was Queen Sparla, who sat and held the king's fin. Brela tended to Debbie.

"He is dying," Sparla said. "Where's Prince Sparfiacus?"

"In the arena, defending Debbie's father and Debbie," Brela said. "This is Debbie. A spongiont united with her. She could become a fulltran."

"How can a human be a fulltran?" Sparla asked. "Will she transform into another shape? A dolphin?"

"I don't know," Brela said. "She might not transform at all, at least not at first. But her metabolism is rapidly changing. The thoriocyanobionts are attempting to merge with her cells, but her cells are rejecting them."

"Our kingdom has been discovered and attacked," Sparla said. "Citizens who should have lived forever are dying and have died. We cannot allow the humans to return word to their country of this event. More will come and attack."

"Sparfy will figure out something," Brela said.

"Soon my husband will be dead, and then it will be up to me to make things right," Sparla said.

She placed a hand on a sponge wall (to tap into the trial) and relayed its progress to those in Curatidoma:

"The trial is in progress. Metavasi is holding the human ship at Gathona. And now...now...they are showing the scene...where it all happened. This human girl next to me...she is being shown operating the controls of the human SOZOD machine. She is the prime killer!"

"I sense something different in her," Brela said. "She realized the SO-ZOD was doing harm. She tried to stop it. But her sister, Connie Dayla, was acting on a subliminal suggestion from a fulltran. This suggestion forced Connie to resume the drilling with the SOZOD and breach Rhynchus."

"Then this girl is not to blame," Sparla said. "Nor is her sister. But who planted the suggestion?"

"I don't know," Brela said. "Debbie could sense that there was a subliminal suggestion from a fulltran, but she couldn't identify from whom."

"It's possible Croius is behind this. We know he has been posing as a senator. Do we know his whereabouts during the attack?" Sparla asked.

"No," Brela said.

At that moment, Acus awoke.

"Sparla," Acus said.

"Shh," Sparla said.

"I am dying," he said. "I can feel the thorios poisoning me."

"Brela, the thoriocyanobionts are killing King Acus," Sparla said.

"I know," Brela said. "We don't have the ability to reverse the damage. He can't take on a new spongiont. The spongionts will reject him, as they have the other poisoned fulltrans."

"I...want to try," Debbie said.

"What is it you say, Debbie Dayla?" Sparla asked.

"I must touch the king's fin," Debbie said. "Something tells me I must."

"A human must not touch a royal fulltran," Sparla said.

"But she contains a spongiont, a first citizen," Brela said.

"Our laws conflict on this matter," Sparla said. "Is the girl trying to hurt or help the king?"

"She wishes no harm to good life forms," Brela said. "But she is a killer. I sense a past of killing humans and animals on land, using stored poison in her skin."

"What kind of poison?" Sparla asked.

"Monkshood," Brela said. "She might poison the king."

"I am already dead," King Acus said. "Allow the girl to touch me."

Sparla and Brela exchanged glances, and then Brela nodded yes.

"Very well," Sparla said. "Debbie Dayla, you may proceed."

Debbie sat up, put her legs over the side of her tank, and reached for Acus. She then touched his other fin (the one Sparla wasn't touching). And then Debbie began to hum. Her humming was pleasant and inebriating. In fact, the other medical attendants began humming in harmony with Debbie. Even Brela and Sparla began humming. Soon, the king's thoriocyanobionts repaired themselves and recovered the poison they had generated, thus restoring health to the king. Sensing this, Sparla transmitted this acoustic energy through the sponge complexus. The medical attendants then mimicked Sparla's behavior. They held a hand on the sponge wall and the other on the injured fulltran in question. Immediately, the fulltran being touched rejuvenated and healed its injuries. Many then who had not yet died were now recovering. Debbie stopped humming, and King Acus stood up, now transforming fully into humanoid shape.

"My dear Debbie Dayla, you truly are a holy now," he said. "We cannot allow you to perish under trial. You are now, for better or worse, a Lagenor."

"Then I ask of you one favor, Your Highness. Please spare my father from the death penalty as well," Debbie said.

"There is still the problem of what to do with the humans," Brela said.

"Agreed," Sparla continued. "They cannot return to their country and warn their kind of our existence."

"And only Debbie is a holy. The other human cannot stay," King Acus said.

"But please, don't kill us!" Debbie begged. "Just forget everything."

"We cannot forget what has happened," King Acus said.

"But can we make the humans forget?" Sparla asked Brela.

"I've been experimenting with such a method," Brela said. "A group of fulltran dolphins can make a single dolphin forget. A group of fulltran electric rays can do the same to a single ray. But we don't have a group of fulltran humans to make the other humans forget."

"But we have a human fulltran—me," Debbie said.

"You are not a real fulltran as you cannot change shape, though you have a spongiont, but you are not powerful enough even with the spongiont," Brela said to Debbie. "However, we can help you. I think with the help of the electric rays, it can be done."

"But will Debbie Dayla forget as well?" Sparla asked.

"No, she won't. And that's the flaw with this plan," Brela said.

"Then she must remain here," Acus said.

"Oh please don't make me stay here," Debbie said. "Let my father and me return to Georgia."

"But you will tell others," Brela said.

"And they will return and attack," Sparla said.

"No, I won't," Debbie said. "I'll keep it a secret."

"How can we be sure of this?" Sparla asked.

Sparla looked at Acus for an answer. So did Brela. And Debbie. And the rest of those in Curatidoma.

"I must confess I am at a loss here," Acus said.

Acus placed a hand on the sponge wall and tapped into the complexus. All that had just transpired in Curatidoma was now being transmitted to the trial court for the audience to sense. Acus received a response from Suproc that King Acus, Queen Sparla, Queen Brela, and Debbie should proceed to the trial arena for a final decision.

"It will be decided in the trial," Acus said. "Let's go."

The group then headed to the arena. Korlan and Delfa, however, were still critically injured, despite Debbie's help to all in need, and so those two remained behind. Debbie sat on one side of Roger, and Sparfy sat on the other.

"Your arrival as late," Suproc said. "The humans have their sentence. Death."

"Wait," Sparfy said. "The holies cannot be executed. Debbie carries a sponge symbiont. To kill her would kill the sponge. First citizens cannot be executed. To do so is a first order crime and would result in the execution of those performing the murder."

The audience argued with one another over the issue.

"Procedure as this. The Roger human will have death on the Debbie human. He then will have death on himself for the death of a first citizen," Suproc said.

"I would never kill my daughter," Roger said. "What kind of creatures are you to suggest such a thing?"

More rumblings in the audience.

"We propose to erase all memories from the humans," Sparfy said. "This includes humans on the AC Sniar. They will then be sent to their homeland."

"For return one day and for more destruction to Lagenora!" Vorlac yelled.

The audience erupted with hostilities. Some threatened to run onto the floor and launch attacks against Roger and Debbie. Guards struggled to restrain them. But then Debbie began to hum, and her music resonated throughout the arena and quieted the ruckus.

"There, you see?" Sparfy said. "Debbie has abilities helpful to our people. She cured many fulltrans in Curatidoma, including King Acus."

King Acus walked into the light, and the audience gasped.

"Your Majesty," Vorlac said. "Our pleasure has resonance throughout Rhynchus."

"I have wish for speech," the king said. "We dusky dolphins have pride in Rhynchus. But as terrible as the deeds by the humans, we have duty and responsibility for the truth."

"What truth?" Vorlac asked. "We have the truth before us. Eyes have the truth. This arena has the truth."

"Only a cloud of truth," the king said. "The evil behind our losses has origins with Croius of Aiadaka."

The audience roared to life again.

"Order!" Suproc commanded. "Has the king evidence of this new truth?"

"I will present it," Sparfy said.

Sparfy waved his hand, and a projection of Croius and Arcella appeared while they were scheming on the AC Sniar. The plan to send Connie over with the final suggestion was also shown.

"How has the prince this evidence?" Suproc asked. "The complexus has not. The duskies have not. But the prince has?"

"I have. With a link to Debbie Dayla. She has provided it," Sparfy said.

The audience erupted in protest.

"Objection, oh Suproc!" Vorlac said.

Suproc slammed his gavel in his podium several times to get his word in.

"Evidence out of order!" Suproc said. "Humans have not the credibility for reliable testimony."

"The testimony is intermingled with a first citizen," Sparfy said. "It is admissible."

More uproar.

"Don't you see?" Sparfy continued. "There is only one explanation. We have known that the orcas wish to war with us. Croius and his orcan friends manipulated the humans into assaulting Rhynchus Prime. Look at the projection. This is the real criminal!"

Sparfy waved his hand, and an image of Croius grew in size, frightening the audience and sending shivers through Vorlac and Sparfy too.

"Off with the display!" Suproc ordered.

Sparfy waved his hand to end the display, but the image of Croius would not go away.

"What is it, my son?" King Acus asked, now stepping alongside Sparfy.

"Something is interfering with my control of the display," Sparfy said.

"One of the Zigos?" King Acus asked.

"No. Another power that does not belong. Oh, it cannot be!" Sparfy exclaimed.

But it was. Croius jumped through the display and landed in the middle of the arena, followed by four orcan commandos. He quickly ran up to Debbie, threw a hood over her head, and whisked her away before anyone could do anything, and he disappeared as quickly as he appeared.

"My daughter!" Roger yelled. "You must save my daughter!"

"I will get her back," Sparfy said, and he left.

"We're with you," yelled Brela as she and Tugan ran with Sparfy.

"A first citizen with us no more, by hand of Croius and his four!" yelled Suproc Krivat. "The watch of our guard in failure. This failure under our king and prince. The Zigos have demand for vote of no confidence."

The audience quickly chatted amongst themselves and then voted.

"The vote has a result," Suproc said. "The House of Acus has no more claim to sovereignty. The House of Zigo now has rule. Acus and Sparla with new change of residence. The Zigo family as replacements in Royal Palace."

Queen Sparla and King Acus gasped. What am I saying? No longer may I call them Queen and King. How sad. Now they are simply Sparla and Acus. Two guards removed the former king and queen's crowns, and royal insignias were ripped from their clothing.

"In first decree," King Krivat said, "the human Roger Dayla will have transportation to the AC Sniar with the other humans by our guard runners, and the AC Sniar's hull will have collapse and submersion by duskies and friends, and so the humans will have proper punishment through death. As command, the word to Metavasi for completion of this order."

Sparla and Acus looked at Vorlac and Suproc Krivat as if they were enemy soldiers.

"Your freedoms have continuance," Vorlac said, "but your titles have not."

"Citizens, have ears for me!" Acus called.

But the audience had dispersed. Guards loyal to Acus now changed colors to signify their new allegiance to King Krivat. Roger was taken by a dusky dolphin fulltran guard. The guard formed a bubble around his own back and placed Roger there. The two left the arena, entered a portal pool, passed through the semipermeable seamount wall, and swam to Gathona.

"Sparla! Our kingdom is in mutiny!" Acus said.

"It is a dark day. The duskies have turned against us. How can we stay? I would ask Brela and Tugan to take us in," Sparla said.

"No. I will not leave our people. We will stay. And Sparfy may yet accomplish great things. Rhynchus is his kingdom to win back," Acus said. "And so is his future bride. We must do all we can to help."

The two traveled to Curatidoma amidst a frenzy of duskies running about and arming for battle.

"The orcas," Acus said. "So it has begun. If I were but a bit younger, I would join them in battle, even lead them."

"We are old, Acus. Too old," Sparla said.

"I cannot think that we are too old to be of use. I cannot let the time of my house pass in such dismal fashion," Acus said.

"But it has. An era has ended," Sparla said.

New duskies injured in battle were already arriving in Curatidoma. Acus and Sparla walked to the back, where Korlan and Adelfarina both remained in comas.

"Why did I order her to help disarm the human weapon?" Acus said. "It was a foolish thing to do."

"It was all in fun," Sparla said.

"A king should know the difference between fun and battle," Acus said sternly, mostly to himself. "A king would know the difference."

"Times were different," Sparla said.

"It shouldn't matter. Carelessness in times of fun leads to tragedy in times of pain," Acus said.

At that moment, Korlan awoke.

"Korlan!" Sparla remarked.

"My body has strange feelings," Korlan said slowly and with great strain.

"Rest easy, Korlan," Acus said.

"The human attack," Korlan said. "With us success?"

"The humans have been stopped, yes," Sparla said.

"But we...have...alert," Korlan said. "King Acus...your crown. Queen Sparla...your crown...where? I must bewith dream."

"Shhh," Sparla said. "Rest, Korlan, rest."

"I...must have words with...the royal tailor...about his lack of care with your attire. I will...I will..."

Korlan fell back asleep.

"I don't know how Korlan will take the news," Acus said. "He has been so loyal to my house. Yet he is a Zigo."

"The news would tear him apart," Sparla said. "It's good you did not tell him in his condition."

Acus turned his attention back to Delfa.

"Adelfarina," Acus said. "Wake up. Adelfarina."

But she did not wake.

"Sparfy, your forgiveness," Acus said. "No order should I have made."

Sparfy and his seadogs swam at top speed toward Aiadaka. In his company was a group of dalli porpoises loyal to Brela and Tugan. But Sparfy and group could not keep up with the Sara Vossy, the craft Croius used to carry Debbie Dayla.

"We can't catch Croius," Tugan said.

"The human craft is incredibly fast," Brela said.

"But Aiadaka does not move," Sparfy said. "We will reach the seamount and launch our rescue effort."

"Sparfy—another pod of orcas," Tugan said.

"We'll go around," Sparfy said.

"They are becoming more numerous," Brela said.

"Part of Croius's plan to convert voitran orcas to fulltran," Sparfy said.

"It is as if he is preparing for war," Brela said.

"I feel as if war has already started," Sparfy said. "I hope I'm wrong."

Then Tugan and Brela stopped.

"What is it?" Sparfy said, circling back to them.

"A lone dalli porpoise is gaining on us," Brela said. "At high speed, too."

The three waited, and up swam the visitor.

"Litivito!" Brela said.

Litivito reached the group, and he was exhausted. He gulped water and expelled it as steam to help cool his overheated thorium cells.

"I...Meta...vasi...the..." Litivito struggled between gulps and expulsions.

"One moment," Brela said. "Catch your energy."

Brela placed her fin on Litivito and transferred energy.

"You must have been exceeding your available energy stores to be putting out steam like that," Brela said. "We don't normally get that hot."

"These aren't normal times," Litivito said. "I had to swim beyond what my thorium cells could provide to catch you. I have ill news about Rhynchus and the AC Sniar. Suproc Krivat has succeeded King Acus to the throne through a no-confidence vote."

"Then I am no longer a prince," Sparfy said.

"You are to us!" Tugan said.

"King Krivat has new orders for Sparfiacus. You are to abort your rescue attempt and swim directly to Gathona, where you will supervise the crushing of the AC Sniar and the deaths of the humans," Litivito said.

"Litivito, you are one of our subjects and not of Rhynchus," Tugan said.

"I swam ahead of the official messenger to warn Prince Sparfiacus," Litivito said. "But you are right, I claim no power or authority. And I want to help, if I can."

"Thank you for the warning, Litivito. Please swim to Gathona and tell Metavasi to do everything in his power to keep the AC Sniar afloat. Save the humans—for now," Tugan said.

"It will not be easy. Only a few of us dallis are there as it is. King Krivat is planning to send an army of duskies to ensure compliance," Litivito said. "Come to think of it, Prince Sparfiacus, I believe he is going to send an army with his messenger to ensure *your* compliance."

"Tugan, Brela, I—"

"We can't let you go into Aiadaka alone," Brela said.

"She's right," Tugan said.

"I must," Sparfy said. "Once I refuse to swim to Gathona, I'll be an outlaw. But your path is clear. You must protect the AC Sniar from Krivat and his minions."

"What about the minions he is sending to take you?" Brela asked.

"Perhaps you could give me some interference. Slow them down enough so I can complete the journey to Aiadaka unfettered. I would be grateful."

"Sparfy, no!" Brela said.

"There's no other way. I'm sorry," Sparfy said.

"So are we. It's bad enough having Croius and his orcas as enemies. But I never thought I'd see the day when we dallis had to fight our dusky brothers," Tugan said.

"You will succeed. You are dalli," Sparfy laughed.

"Only in name," Tugan said. "Saying goodbye to our alliance is a bitter parting."

"As is saying goodbye to you, Prince Sparfiacus," Brela said. "Well, be off then. Do take care."

"We'll do what we can about helping Delfa recover," Tugan said.

"Shh," Brela said. "Oh, too late."

"Adelfarina," Sparfy lamented. "How I wish she were well and with me. Goodbyes are bitter indeed. I must go now, before I lose my composure in front of my seadogs and my friends."

Sparfy then swam alone toward Aiadaka. King Tugan, Queen Brela, Litivito, and the other dalli porpoises first swam back toward Rhynchus and managed to delay the dusky dolphins sent by King Krivat to escort Sparfy to Gathona. The duskies were only held back for a time, and then they moved on toward Sparfy. The dallis swam for Gathona to help Metavasi.

Sparfy increased his speed, and his cells overheated. He panted to rid his body of excess heat, and hot steam from water in his tissues exited his blowhole. He swam like this for hours, and fatigue set in.

"Get hold of yourself, Sparfy. You'll only drive yourself mad. No, I can't slow. Curse that Croius. This Debbie human has powers no one yet understands. If he learns to harness those powers, the orcas will overrun us all. And here I am, a lone dusky dolphin in the South Atlantic. The task is upon me to stop this. Me alone. Just a terrible burden. I wish Delfa were here. Delfa, speak to me. Help me through this."

"Sparfy..." echoed a whispering voice from behind toward Rhynchus.

Sparfy began swimming on his back toward Aiadaka so he could look back toward the voice.

"Delfa?" he called back.

Then an image of Delfa appeared just over the horizon, ascending in the air like the moon. The distance and proximity to the horizon gave Sparfy the impression that a huge ghost of Delfa was rising.

"I'm dying, Sparfy," she whispered.

"No. I don't believe it," he said.

"You're dying too," she continued.

"We're immortal!" Sparfy struggled to say in his saddened and exhausted emotional state. "We'll live forever. You and I. We'll live forever."

"The world is changing. It is not forever. Nor are we. My spirit is failing. It's time for goodbye," she whispered. "For goodbye."

"No," he said. "I cannot bear to bury you at Gathona!"

"I won't go to Gathona," she whispered. "I will go supercritical. The duskies will need to bury me in the deep before my body explodes."

Sparfy now choked on his words and could not speak. He tried to say, "not fair," but he was just a blubbering wreck.

"Sparfy. I'll love you always," Delfa whispered.

Her image faded, and the last echoes of her voice subsided to the sound of jet engines. Sparfy turned over in time to see himself face-to-face with the Sara Vossy, now barely hovering over the waterline. Orcan guards encircled him and dragged the exhausted dusky onto the aircraft. The Sara Vossy took off and headed for Gathona.

"Prince Sparfiacus," Croius said. "What a surprise to find you out here all alone. Where is your royal escort?"

"I..." Sparfy tried to say.

"He's exhausted," Arcella said. "I'll give him a thorium charge."

Sparfy pined at the opportunity. Arcella brought a thoriocyano sponge near Sparfy, and then she snatched it away before he could touch it with his weakly outstretched hand. Croius laughed.

"Please, help me," Sparfy begged.

An orca walked up to Arcella, said something in her ear, and walked away.

"Croius, word is that the Zigos now rule Rhynchus," Arcella said. "Oh, and this about Sparfy's betrothed."

Arcella whispered in Croius's ear.

"Then Sparfiacus is no longer a prince," Croius chuckled. "Well, well, well, the mighty have fallen. No more Royal Palace, no seadogs, and no real prospects. What were you doing in these waters anyway? What did you hope to accomplish?"

"I..." Sparfy stumbled.

"Fool! Did you think you could play the hero and save your precious dusky dolphins from the new order?" Croius asked. "You've lost everything, Sparfiacus—your kingdom, your beloved Adelfarina, the humans on the AC Sniar, and one other human. This Debbie Dayla. We have yet to convert her completely to our will, but we are making progress."

"No," Sparfy said under his breath.

"Wouldn't it be wonderful if we could convert Sparfy into a spy for us?" Arcella suggested. "Or even a slave of sorts. He could tow my sea chariot."

"Duskies make the worst of slaves," Croius said. "They are too stubborn for their own good. No, we'll extract his thoriocyanobionts for our orca conversion program. And after we deal with the dallis and duskies on Gathona, we'll leave Sparfiacus's body to dry on a South American beach, where the locals can use him for swine fodder. He can then be the Prince of Swine."

Two orcan guards walked Sparfy toward a chair where they prepared to strap him down. But not wishing to go down so easily, he emitted a powerful vonk wave. The wave interfered with the Sara Vossy's navigation, and the craft began to nosedive toward the Atlantic. Sparfy and the others on board were tossed about, and an orcan guard struggled against the forces to reach Sparfy, where he punched Sparfy in the face. Sparfy was stunned a bit, and the vonk wave dissipated, allowing the Sara Vossy to regain control and altitude. But Sparfy recovered and sent out another vonk wave. Again the Sara Vossy took toward the Atlantic. Now three guards went after Sparfy. Each tried suppressing Sparfy, but he used vonk waves to fight them off. The aircraft steadied between shots but went into a nosedive each time he used vonk waves against the guards.

"Stop this madness!" Croius said.

"If I go down, you go down with me!" Sparfy shouted.

"Does your price include Debbie Dayla?" Croius asked. "Or did you forget she was here?"

"What!?" Sparfy recoiled.

"She's on this aircraft. She'll die too. Is that part of your grand scheme?" Croius barked.

In his exhausted state, Sparfy had forgotten that simple fact. Yes, he had originally traveled toward Aiadaka in hopes of rescuing Debbie, who he knew was on the Sara Vossy. How could he miss that fact now? Sparfy sent a soft vonk wave through the aircraft's hull to inquire. The wave returned. Debbie was being held in the back of the Sara Vossy. Realizing he couldn't decide Debbie's fate in this manner, he abated his attack. The Sara Vossy smoothed, and the guards got in a few extra punches to ensure Sparfy's compliance.

"That's enough," Croius said. "Take him to the back and show him our prize."

The guards took him away.

"I underestimated his ability to use vonk waves by himself," Croius admitted to Arcella. "I always thought he could only perform them in concert with his seadogs. I must set up a dynamic dampening shield to suppress any future outbreaks."

Croius tapped a few buttons on a console.

"Just a little more," he said. "There. Protected."

"You're brilliant!" Arcella said. "But perhaps we could extract that knowledge from his brain. You know, how to harness vonk waves."

"It may be worth a shot. It will mean we won't have to wait for another SOZOD to be built. We could use Debbie and this ship to create vonk waves and attack any cetacean kingdom we desire," Croius grinned. "I've always been the master at *blocking* vonk waves—"

"Or Sparfy and his seadogs would have overrun Aiadaka years ago," Arcella said. "A pity you couldn't block them for the original SOZOD attack."

"He wasn't supposed to know about the original SOZOD. But no matter. His vonk wave technology will be used to overrun Lagenora. Rather a fitting end. A fitting end indeed," Croius gloated.

Sparfy was taken to the back of the Sara Vossy. He heard bubbling and electric sparks surging. He passed through a doorway, and inside a water tank stood Debbie Dayla. She was barely recognizable. Her body from the neck down was submerged in water and had taken on the shape of an intertwined mass of spongy tentacles, like a plant with its roots in the water. Her face was recognizable, but a fine-meshed array of Medusa-like tentacles covered her head on the top, sides, and back. At times the tentacles, actively probing, would cover her face, and at other times they would recede and allow a last bit of her humanity to shine through.

"Debbie Dayla?" Sparfy called.

Debbie hummed softly.

"Debbie, is that you?" Sparfy called. "Debbie, you've been captured by Croius. Can you break free? Think, Debbie. Try to get control."

"She cannot think for herself. She never could," Croius said as he walked in.

Arcella walked in too.

"The thoriocyanostigon device is ready to assimilate Sparfiacus," Arcella said.

"She can be trained," Sparfy said about Debbie. "All humans can."

Unaware of the conversation so far, Arcella looked at Croius.

"You see, Arcella, dusky dolphins think that with a little training, humans who follow can learn to lead. But why spend the effort only to be disappointed when the humans fail? Better to lead them directly and save the trouble," Croius explained. "And now, Sparfiacus, your time has come. Say goodbye to Debbie Dayla. This is your end and hers."

Then Arcella laughed. She sang a victory song, and the guards joined in. It was a horrible moment for Sparfy. Debbie didn't even respond to the ruckus. Where was the hope now? Sparfy tried sending one last vonk wave to Debbie, but the tank repelled it and focused it back on Sparfy, knocking him to the ground. Croius, Arcella, and the guards laughed at the incident.

"A fighter to the end. Good for you," Croius mocked. "Arcella, have the thoriocyanostigon chair moved into this room, so that Sparfiacus may appreciate the superior orcan method at work."

Arcella left briefly and returned with two guards and the chair. The guards strapped Sparfy into the chair and attached suction plates to his head and legs, suction plates attached to hoses which attached to the base of the chair. The chair's base was rectangular and as wide as the seat, as it contained the main thoriocyanostigon device itself.

"Back to the control room," Croius said.

Croius, Arcella, and the orcan guards exited for the control room, leaving Sparfy alone with Debbie. The thoriocyanostigon device stirred into action, and Sparfy could feel the thoriocyanobionts being pulled from his body. The effect was very much like when a human loses blood, as he felt the life force leaving him. He became incredibly hungry, and he breathed heavily as his tissues began to self-consume themselves to survive.

"Debbie," Sparfy called weakly. "Debbie Dayla."

But Debbie did not respond. Sparfy extended his senses to listen for any faint whisper she might return, but instead of hearing Debbie, he heard Croius interacting with his crew.

"How far to Gathona?" Croius asked.

"Only a few more moments," replied a crewmember.

"Sir," said another crewmember, "an army of dusky dolphins ahead. They are heading for Gathona. Another army of dalli porpoises will meet them."

"Interesting development," Croius said. "Two armies to deal with at Gathona. That should make for a fascinating test. Slow speed to subsonic. We do not wish to disturb our brethren kin."

"You're so thoughtful, Croius," Arcella said.

"Only for the moment," Croius replied. "We will perform the first test on them. Prepare for a SOVONK wave."

With his extended senses still working (though not for much longer), Sparfy realized what has happening. Croius was using elements of SOZOD control technology with the vonk waves his own people had invented to make a hybrid SOVONK weapon.

"Debbie," Sparfy called again. "Croius is going to kill my people. He will use you to kill. Can you stop him?"

Debbie did not reply.

"It is like before, but instead of humans and Debbie drilling into Rhynchus, the orcas and Debbie are drilling into duskies and dallis," Sparfy said to himself.

Then Debbie's body was thrust upward in the tank, and she convulsed. Sparfy sensed a thick beam of light traveling downward from the Sara Vossy into the ocean water. The beam was followed by a carousel of SOVONK waves that traveled helically and counterclockwise around themselves and the light beam. Dusky after dusky were pulled from the water and tossed like fish from a barrel.

"Debbie, stop this madness!" Sparfy begged.

Next, the beam and SOVONK waves moved on to the dalli porpoises. Tugan and Brela, seeing the disturbance, called for their dalli kin to swim from the carousel of destruction. But Croius had the Sara Vossy pilot move the aircraft to pursue the dallis, and so the king and queen had to take drastic measures.

"Dive deep!" Brela called.

"Dive deep!" Tugan also called.

"They are submerging into the deep," the SOVONK controller said to Croius.

"Quickly. Adjust parameters on the SOVONK to cut into the water," Croius called.

"Making adjustments," the SOVONK controller said. "The water is a heavier medium and is causing increased refraction. The SOVONK waves are breaking down. But I believe I can compensate by altering the focus."

"It's pursuing us, Tugan," Brela said.

Tugan called on his dallis to create underwater vortices by swimming abeam and then crossing paths in arcs, all the while twirling their bodies. The water was churned up, and the SOVONK waves broke down even farther, but not before dallis were hit and injured, sending those injured to the top where the more powerful sections of the SOVONK waves destroyed them.

"Keep it up! Dive deep and twirl. All the way down!" Brela called.

That was the last Sparfy heard from Brela or Tugan or anyone else in the water. His senses faded, and even now he had lost perception of Croius and his crew. All that remained was his weak link with Debbie.

"Debbie...you...must..." Sparfy tried.

Sparfy slipped into unconsciousness. He found himself no longer on the Sara Vossy, but as a spirit floating above the land. And below him was Debbie Dayla. It was late at night, and she was wandering the streets alone. A drunk driver crossed the street's dividing line and traveled into oncoming traffic. Traffic veered around the drunk, but still the drunk continued. The drunk then drove onto the sidewalk and struck Debbie. She landed on the hood and blocked the drunk's vision. The drunk then plowed into a light pole and stopped. Debbie's body continued forward but was stopped by the pole, so she remained somewhat on the hood. Angered by Debbie's supposed interference, the drunk staggered out of his vehicle to the front, yanked Debbie off the hood, and proceeded to kick the life out of her.

Debbie sang several musical notes. She pulled on the drunk's lower leg and caused him to fall. She jumped to her feet, motioned her arms to the sky, and then summoned the winds onto the drunk, lifting him into the air but in prone position. The drunk cursed and swung at Debbie, but she was out of reach. Then from on high she called down the lightning. But instead of a long bolt, she pulled down a lightning ball. The ball struck the drunk and encircled him. The electrical energy permeated his pores and set fire to the alcohol, engulfing the drunk in flames. He screamed in agony, and as he did,

Debbie sent the drunk back into his vehicle. The fire had by now destroyed the nerves in his limbs, and so he was paralyzed and could not run, but instead he lay there and endured the last pain he would know. The fire carried into the vehicle and set the plastic grains afire. It wasn't long before the heat and pressure carried to the fuel tank and caused its rupture, finishing the drunk with a massive fireball.

Debbie walked away from this, pulled a leaf of monkshood from a pocket, and nibbled it. Then the scene changed. Sparfy was in Corleopus, when he was young and swimming back from his party with the bottlenose dolphins. Delfa was hiding Sparfy's inebriated condition from her people, and she was trying to talk sense into him.

"Sparfy, life is such a precious thing. Don't throw it away on senselessness," she said. "We often take too many things for granted. I guess immortality does that to a dolphin. But I must warn you. The mortals do not see the world the way we do. They think of nothing but the taking of life and property. There are exceptions, and only for brief moments, but otherwise each waking day is focused on the death of others. Do not become subservient to such desires or the beast of desires."

Then a ghostly image of Debbie came into Sparfy's view, but only visible to Sparfy. Delfa did not understand why Sparfy reacted the way he did.

"The killer!" he stated. "She slays the beast of desires!"

"You're hallucinating," Delfa said. "Shhh. Drink this and rest here."

Delfa gave Sparfy a special drink to block the alcohol's effects. The scene changed, and Sparfy briefly regained consciousness. Debbie had just stopped convulsing, and now she was breathing heavily as if having just completed a marathon.

"Her cells have not been fully converted," Sparfy said. "She will die of exhaustion. Debbie...Debbie!"

But Sparfy's weak call was overshadowed by Croius's new command to the pilot.

"Move on to the AC Sniar. We will demonstrate the new orcan power to the *homo sapiens*."

Sparfy faded in and out of consciousness. As Debbie's body was called upon to create SOVONK waves, Sparfy sensed how these waves tore holes into the AC Sniar, wrecking ship, equipment, and crew. Then Sparfy was elsewhere, in a past war where bombs were dropped and torpedoes were launched into ships. Explosions jarred his ears and burning alkanes seared his tongue. He had no nose nor sense of smell, but he could taste the effects of death and destruction. Then the scene changed to a time when Debbie was younger. She was swimming in the family pool with sister Connie and Connie's friends Vicia and Ramona. All four then played a game to see who could hold their breaths the longest underwater.

The scene changed again, and Sparfy was back in the Atlantic defending Rhynchus from the effects of Debbie and the SOZOD. He could now see that two human casualties were known very well to Debbie.

"Debbie," Sparfy strained to say. "The son of your father's friend, Doctor Kukovich, is dead. Brian Kukovich, Debbie. He's dead. And your sister. Connie Dayla. She's dead. The SOZOD, Debbie, it killed her. It did."

A tear dropped from Debbie's eye.

"It wasn't your fault, Debbie," Sparfy said.

"I...killed...Connie," Debbie whispered. "I killed...my sister. There is only one thing left to do. One thing."

"Debbie, hold on," Sparfy said. "Fight Croius. Fight."

"No," Debbie said slowly. "I am now the beast of human desire. I must kill all desire, even my own. This all ends now. I dive deep."

With a sudden jerking motion of her body, she flipped herself into an inverted position. Her head was now forced against the bottom of the tank. She choked on the water. The SOVONK waves stopped, and Croius and guards rushed to find out what went wrong.

"She's trying to kill herself," Croius said. "Aright her body. Now!"

But the guards could not aright her. The tentacles that she used as legs gripped the upper part of the tank like death, and they could not be redirected.

"She's dying!" Arcella yelled.

"She has not been fully converted to our control, nor can her skills be fully emulated by the computer," said the SOVONK controller. "She must be kept alive."

"Pump oxygen into the water. Force her to breathe air," Croius ordered.

Debbie faded into unconsciousness. And now she was in a different place and time. She was a trilobite, diving deep into an early Cambrian ocean. She dove deeper and deeper to escape the greatest narcotic ever produced—oxygen. Oxygen, the great liberator of energy and enslaver of free will, produced by cyanobacteria and consumed by animals, creating life forms that consume other life forms instead of living in symbiosis with the deep wisdom of the earth.

"Make her breathe the oxygen," Croius said. "Force her."

But no! Debbie dove the deepest of all, beyond the time of oxygen and through the upper layers of the oceanic microbial mat, entering a place rich in sulfur and devoid of oxygen. Time went in reverse, before cyanobacteria created the Oxygen Catastrophe, and she entered such a time when life fed from the sulfur and grew in cellular knowledge and wisdom, exchanging cell components and information strands to the benefit of all life.

"Kill them all now!" Croius barked.

"NOOOOOOO!" Debbie roared.

She burst forth from the tank and slung all tentacles in all directions and sprayed sulfuric acid at all in range. The acid burned like fire and sent the orcas running for the nearest exit where they bailed out of the Sara Vossy and escaped into the sea. Arcella led the way, but Croius lingered behind, and he made one last attempt to contain Debbie, but she shot another spray of sulfuric acid and caught him in the eye. He screamed in pain and jumped out the aircraft. Sparfy was spared from most of the spray, but some burned his flesh, particularly his legs. The Sara Vossy stopped attacking the AC Sniar, but now the craft was badly out of control and heading for Gathona in what would be a horrible crash. Debbie sprayed acid like a surgeon to free Sparfy, and then she used the last bit to burn off the tentacles and restore her own limbs and body. She rushed to the front of the craft to steady out the descent, but the craft was going too quickly, and its thrusters could not guarantee a smooth landing.

"We're ditching!" Debbie called to Sparfy.

She threw on a parachute jacket, picked up Sparfy, and jumped out the hatch. She immediately pulled the chute open, and the two descended onto the side of a mountain on Gathona. The Sara Vossy crashed, not completely disintegrating, but crashing nonetheless with enough force to kill anyone either aboard or in its path. The orcas, however, had ditched over sea, and so they swam away—having reverted to their natural states as they dropped through the air.

Debbie and Sparfy landed on a rocky point, and Debbie hit the side of her head on a boulder. Her face became bruised and swollen, as if someone had punched her savagely.

"Live in harmony with the earth," Debbie whispered quietly. "Rid my body of the excesses in oxygen desire."

"It's over, Debbie," Sparfy said. "You're safe."

"Life is just beginning. All over again," Debbie smiled.

She blinked her swollen eyes and kissed Sparfy on the nose.

Brela and Tugan saw what had happened and climbed the mountain quickly.

"Prince Sparfiacus," Tugan said.

Sparfy was weak and also bruised.

"You don't have to call me Prince," Sparfy managed to say.

"You'll always be a prince," Brela said. "But come now. We must bring you both to lower ground."

Brela carried Sparfy, and Tugan carried Debbie.

"I could almost fall half asleep," Sparfy whispered.

"Should I sing you a lullaby?" Brela asked. "I haven't sung one since Metavasi was a baby. But I'll care for you like my own, until you are on your flukes again."

"I may not have flukes if I ever change back to dusky form. My legs are badly burned with acid," he said.

"We'll cure you in Phocayna's medical center," Brela said. "I have a special medicine for just such a thing."

As the four descended, the U.S. Navy arrived with an amphibious supersonic jet plane known as the Craymar CC-33, similar to the F2Y Sea Dart, but larger and with the ability to carry cargo or many people. It featured retractable skis that had excellent stability in high waves. Designed by Craymar Industries, it was an especially low point for the Daylas, as Craymar was a competitor.

"Debbie," Brela said. "Your people are here. They'll take you home. And now we must leave here and take Sparfy with us."

"Is he going home too?" Debbie asked.

"Not yet," Brela said. "He must recuperate for a time with us. But some day when you are looking east at the Atlantic, one of us will visit and bring news."

"I hope it is you, Sparfy," Debbie said.

"Goodbye," Tugan and Brela said.

Sparfy waved, and the three were gone.

The seaplane launched several rescue boats, some of which helped rescue those trapped in the AC Sniar and others floating nearby in the water. The dallis had done what they could to help those who had survived the SOVONK blast, but now they were gone so as to keep their identity a secret. Other rescue boats landed on Gough Island. One such boat carried someone Debbie had met before.

"Debbie?" the woman said.

"I'm so glad to see you, Ramona," Debbie cried, and the two hugged.

"Let's go home," Ramona said.

Readjusting to life in Brunswick was not easy. There were many funerals to attend, including that of Connie Dayla. Julie was a complete mental wreck and had to be sedated the entire service. Roger was found sneaking sips of whiskey from a bottle he kept inside his suit coat. It was a habit he only recently acquired, and it would stay with him the rest of his life. He often spoke of how proud he was of his daughters, and he carried on as if Connie were alive, always explaining that she was out on a date, and how young people are always on the go and never around. The sedatives were not enough for Julie Dayla, and she went mad. Roger and Debbie were forced to commit her to the Dayla Institution for the Neurologically Impaired.

Vicia was too overcome with grief to stay in Brunswick, and she moved to Kentucky. She started a horse farm and never looked back.

Debbie stayed in Brunswick with her father, but his condition deteriorated rapidly. He lost all interest in running Dayla Industries, preferring instead to lock himself in his observatory and sleep the day away while staring at the heavens at night. Debbie then took over all operations at Dayla Industries and had to learn the business from scratch. The business lost millions the first year, and the stock value fell through the floor.

Then one Saturday evening as the sun was setting in the west, Debbie sat by a fire while roasting a southern brand hotdog. Ramona kept her company, and the two had been discussing Ramona's new adventures as a Georgia State Patrol officer.

"You're holding up incredibly well, considering what you've been through," Ramona said. "No signs of post-traumatic stress at all."

"Thank you," Debbie said.

"You know, it's people like you who make this country great. I can't tell you how many people I've already come across who've given up on life. They fall into crime or drugs or some other bad thing. Their lives don't go for much longer."

"I plan to be around for quite a while," Debbie said. "I feel there's a lot yet I need to do."

"That's the spirit!" Ramona said.

Ramona suddenly looked out at the water and moved her head back and forth.

"Did you hear something?" she asked.

"Just the waves and the gulls," Debbie said.

"Hmm. I thought I heard something else. Must be the police training I've had. Always be aware of your surroundings," Ramona said.

"It's a good thing to do," Debbie said. "I used to trust everyone else around me. Now I'm the one people look up to at work. We're struggling to get the business back in the black, but we'll get there."

"Good for you!" Ramona said. "And speaking of awareness, I guess I fell into trusting that time would not get away from me, but it has. My shift starts in ten minutes!"

"You'd better get going then," Debbie said. "The state would be at a loss without the services of Trooper Bronc."

"Thank you," Ramona said. "We'll see you soon."

"See ya later," Debbie replied.

Ramona Bronc left. Then a few minutes later, a stirring in the ocean caught Debbie's attention.

"So Ramona wasn't imagining things," Debbie said. "Who's out there?"

Debbie took a step toward the water. She instinctively pulled a monkshood flower with leaf from her pocket and hid it behind her back, in preparation for the worst. She still could not control her rage side. A shape took humanoid form as it walked from the water.

"Come into the light," Debbie said with suspicion. "I'm cooking hotdogs. Don't they smell good?"

"Dolphins can't smell, Miss Dayla," the voice said.

The humanoid walked into the light, and it was Sparfy.

"Sparfy!" Debbie said as she dropped the monkshood, ran up to him, and hugged him. "You're healed and everything. Even the scarring on your legs."

"Queen Brela does excellent work," Sparfy replied.

"I missed you," she said. "And I'm sorry for all the trouble I caused. How's everyone? Did you get your kingdom back?"

"The dalli porpoises are just fine," Sparfy said. "King Tugan and Queen Brela have healed many who were injured by last year's battles and a few more from new battles this year."

"Oh no. What happened?" Debbie asked.

"War with the orcas," Sparfy said. "The dallis are holding the southern front."

"And the duskies? Your people?" Debbie asked.

"The Zigos and followers have allied themselves with the orcas. Others are quietly loyal to my family and resist the orcas," he said.

"Oh no, the duskies are in civil war," Debbie said.

"I'm afraid so. My parents have fled Rhynchus and are hiding in one of the other seamounts. I would tell you which one, but I promised to tell no one."

"That's okay. Don't tell me. It's safer that way. So that means you never got your kingdom back. I'm really sorry," Debbie said.

"It's a problem that's been brewing for a long time. You only accelerated things," he said.

Sparfy paced up and down the beach, in and out of the firelight.

"There's something else too, isn't there?" Debbie asked. "Come into the light. Let me read your thoughts."

Sparfy stood in the light, and Debbie pressed her temple next to his. The spongiont was still present in her head, and it made a mental connection with Sparfy.

"Adelfarina," Debbie said.

"My parents took her with them when they fled," Sparfy said.

"You love her, don't you?" Debbie asked.

But Sparfy could only cry.

"She was everything to you. But her injuries...that I caused. I really ruined your life, didn't I?" Debbie asked.

"Apologizing is a bad habit," Sparfy said. "We should not live in the sorries or sorrows of the past. She almost went supercritical a year ago, but Queen Brela found a way to stabilize Delfa. But no means to help Delfa's recovery could be found. Delfa's body has put up a good fight, but the process cannot be stopped. I want you to be with me when we bury her at sea."

"I learned that dolphins of your kind are supposed to be buried in Gathona," Debbie said.

"She will not be buried there. She cannot be," Sparfy said. "I cannot explain any more than that. Will you accompany me?"

"Yes," Debbie said.

Debbie transferred duties at Dayla Industries to an assistant, and she flew down to a northeast section of Lagenora in her newly purchased CC-33 from Craymar.

"It's a competitor plane," Debbie said sheepishly to Sparfy. "I'm just studying it."

"You don't have to explain," he said. "Let's make an agreement. No dwelling on regrets. Deal?"

"It's a deal," Debbie said with a hug.

The plane stopped in what seemed to be an isolated section of the South Atlantic, but suddenly a number of dolphins and porpoises surfaced. There were Acus and Sparla, King Tugan and Queen Brela, Prince Metavasi and his friend Litivito, Chusacuta and Circigi, and others. Then in the back of the group, two striped dolphins approached with a casket. The two were the king and queen of Corleopus—Delfa's parents.

"Sparfiacus," the queen said. "I am Queen Tharia of Corleopus."

"And I am King Adelfo," the king said.

"We know how fond you are of Princess Adelfarina," Queen Tharia said. "You would be married, in happier times."

"I am so deeply sorry for her passing," Sparfy said. "She was the entire ocean to me."

"She once told us that if anything should happen, she wanted you to be the one to perform the deep dive," King Adelfo said.

"Yes," Sparfy said. "It is the least I can do for her and for you."

"Do not be a hero, Prince Sparfiacus. If you are not strong enough for the dive, we have many striped dolphin volunteers who would perform the service," Queen Tharia said.

"No, I must. As my friends have taught me, we are redeemed through our deep dives. Especially one good friend," Sparfy said, and he touched Debbie's hand.

"Very well. Let it begin," King Adelfo said.

The cetaceans lightly slapped the water, not in haphazard fashion, but softly and in rhythm like percussion instruments. Then they varied the pitch of their slaps so that one thought the dolphins were playing drum sets. They began to hum, and Debbie fell into enchantment. Sparfy changed to his dusky dolphin form, and he towed the casket out from the group. He spy-hopped above the waterline, as if he were pulling in an especially large amount of air. Then he dove. The casket followed him down into the water. He dove deeper and deeper and deeper. The water pressure was incredible, and even his thoriocyanobionts could barely keep his tissues from rupturing. And he dove deeper still. He reached the bottom, and he planted the casket deep into the mud, below an ancient layer of microbial mat and into a layer where the wisdom of Earth's sulfur preceded the oxygen consumers from above. Then he ascended as quickly as he dared, fearing the rapid ascent would cause him to explode. Fatigued from the extreme pressures, he broke through the water's surface, and the stress forced him to expel bodily tissues and fluids from his lungs.

The dolphins became quiet. The ocean grew still, and Debbie wondered what the dolphins would do next.

"Is he—" Debbie started to say.

"Shh," Queen Tharia said.

Sparfy swam back to the Craymar CC-33, and he stood next to Debbie. Then he pointed over to the spot where he had taken Delfa down. A great shock wave carried upward from a deep ocean nuclear explosion, and a blast of water shot upward in that spot where Sparfy had been pointing. The water at first was a beam of spray, but then the middle of the spray formed the shape of a striped dolphin, that of Delfa, and it ascended into the heavens at rocket speed, never to return to Earth.

Debbie looked up in awe and felt completely at peace.

"She's beautiful," Debbie said, and she cried.

The funeral service ended, and all parted ways except for Sparfy, who lingered with Debbie. Sparfy's parents and Delfa's parents were the last to say their goodbyes to Debbie and Sparfy.

"They said goodbye as if you're not going with them," Debbie said.

"I can't," Sparfy said. "I'm an outlaw wherever I go in Lagenora. Only a few select friends will keep secret my location. I cannot stay here."

"Duskies and orcas?" Debbie asked.

"Not all duskies and not all orcas," Sparfy said. "Only those few who have become dutiful to Croius and his master Aiatethis, the great squid creature who has turned our wonderful Lagenora into a fight of dolphin against dolphin. A few bad dolphins spoil the ocean, as Delfa used to say. But she is gone now, and so is my heart. I ask to be your friend, and that I may live out my life in the Atlantic near your home. I promise I will cause no trouble."

"Oh, I'd be happy to have you stay with me!" Debbie said with tears of joy, and she gave him the biggest hug.

"I also promised to keep an eye on you, since you do know about us. Some fear that you will attack them, while I fear that some will attack you. I wish neither to transpire," Sparfy said.

"Then we best get back to Brunswick immediately, Sparfy my friend," Debbie said.

There was a young girl named Debbie Dayla who had a special dusky dolphin friend named Sparfy. She never married a human nor had a human family, but she experienced many interesting adventures with Sparfy, and the two lived beyond the length of their days.

Sense of Place

My name is Erebellasia, I'm twenty-one, and I'm blind. I live in a cave connected to a stick and mud hut lived in by my mother, Cuperia, and this hut is part of our village named Skulava.

I shouldn't say I live in a cave. I hide in a cave. And I hide because of my blindness. If my neighbors discovered my visual inability, I would surely be killed.

I am told that life in Skulava is simple and based on one word—equality. "Equality" means living as equally as possible with the local surroundings. I know that doesn't make much sense to you. I've spent my life trying to understand it from stories my mother tells me. But what it means for our people is this—we are to live no better than the animals around us, and no worse. That means we make simple houses, hunt a little (but only for ourselves with a hunted portion going to the elders), and make simple clothing. No farming is allowed (the animals don't do it). That means no planting crops and no farm animals. But gathering nuts is allowed (since squirrels gather nuts). Someone once made the argument that planting seeds should be allowed since squirrels bury nuts, but the argument was overruled. Squirrels "store" their food by burying it, so the people are allowed to store extra food.

I know, I hear the questions already. What's this about elder portions, how can I hunt with my blindness, how can I go out if people are going to kill me, and what about progress and a better life?

Progress is a crime in our community. We are taught that progress is a selfish desire for power over others, a desire that corrupts the spirit within and forever banishes a person from the equality of the community. The punishment for the crime of progress is death. Our community tells us that a person driven by progress has killed the spirit within, and so the death of the physical body is only a matter of time. The community simply accelerates this external death, a *mercy* killing so to speak.

My mother has taught me everything I know about the community, of which I have had no contact. As I said, I'm blind, and they'd kill me. Not that I search for equality. On the contrary, I represent anti-equality to them, and that's just as bad a crime as progress, because I can't perform and act as "equally" as they do.

So it is I'm at the mercy of my mother. When she realized I couldn't see, she dug a secret tunnel from the hut to a small cave in the mountain and placed me and my crib in the cave. She then told the community that she poisoned me, and she held a funeral for me using the remains of another dead baby that she acquired from an unprepared mother. Before you judge my mother, you must understand that she would have been considered a heretic had she openly announced her decision to keep me despite my blindness.

Now to answer the other questions. I can't hunt, as that means leaving the cave and exposing myself. I can't take that risk. But if I could leave, I would be a competent hunter, even though I am blind. You see, I have taught myself to see, in a manner of speaking. I can click my tongue against the roof of my mouth or clack two rocks together and gain a quick glimpse of my surroundings. I've also trained my ears to locate the source of even the quietest sounds. So I could listen for my prey and click to zero in on it. But I know I won't get the chance to hunt, not while living in a cave.

I can, however, farm—even though it is forbidden. Not that I can till a field (I don't have that much land in the cave), but I do grow special reeds and food crops from seedlings in my cave. There is a small opening at the top of the cave, and whenever it rains, the water collects outside the cave and pours in through the opening. I use that water for drinking and cooking, as it is the cleanest water available, and I collect the surplus for days when there is no rain. There is a mountain stream that flows through that I use for crop irrigation, but I'll get to that in a moment. As for the opening in the top, I also use it as a vent to remove fumes from fire and to help pull in fresh air. The opening also helps me know when a day has passed, as the high sun of the day shines a small dot of light on the cave floor for a hundred heartbeats before disappearing. I can feel it.

The light from the sun is not enough for plants to grow, and so I've created artificial light with a collection of glow tubes. Each tube has a glowing wire inside that is fed by some strange tingling power from a pair of metal lines. I'm not sure how it works, but I've connected one metal line to a post in a cold part of the cave, and another metal line to a post in a warm part of the cave, and those lines then connect to both ends of the wire in the glow tubes. I showed the setup to my mother (Cuperia, remember?), and she was both impressed and fearful, because she knew that now if I were discovered, I would also be accused of the great crime of progress. It didn't matter to me because I would already be killed for being blind, but somehow my achievement made my mother worry all the more.

There's also running water in the cave. Comes from the mountain and trickles down in a little waterfall. The water is warm and nearly pure, and I use it for cleaning, bathing, and for irrigating the crops.

About the elders. They live high up on the mountain. Once a week, they travel down to Skulava and accept their portion from each person in the village. They stay for the night, eat dinner with us, sleep, and then return to the mountain the next day. In return, the elders make all laws and major decisions in the community. I'm not sure how this furthers the idea of equality. Their response is that each person on acquiring age and wisdom (if approved) will join the elders, and so equality over the years is maintained, though not necessarily for all at the same time. In truth, only the young men go up to the mountain. Some aren't seen again until they are older, while others act as sentries or cart pullers when they accompany the elders to Skulava, from what I'm told.

So you may have guessed that there are no men in Skulava, which then leads to the question of this—who is my father? Cuperia has never answered that question directly. She deflects it by saying that most children in the village have an elder as a father, from the elders' once-a-week visit for food and perpetuation of the population. When I first learned of this elder perpetuation of the population, my perception of "equality" went from euphemism to pejorative.

Cuperia visits me daily. You see, my cave is my home, and I often fix breakfast for us two of eggs, (you didn't know I raised chickens in the cave, did you? Cuperia helped me start them), legume bacon, toast (I make flour out of wheat, too), nuts, and coffee (again, Cuperia gave me starter plants).

It was during breakfast one morning when Cuperia and I had the following conversation:

"You are twenty-one, Eren," she said, calling me by my nickname.

"I've been twenty-one for three months now, Cuperia," I said.

I always call my mother by her first name. I never call her "mother" or "mommy" as I have heard of others doing.

"I know, I know. It pains me to think you will spend the rest of your life in this cave, not experiencing the world outside, not interacting with other people," she said.

"You gave me life. Isn't that enough?"

"Not for this...this cave is a prison," she said.

"It's my home," I said.

"Eren, I've been thinking," Cuperia said. "One night when all is dark and no one is watching, we should leave the community and find a people who will accept us for who we are, not for what we cannot be."

"Where would we go?" I asked.

"There are other villages besides Skulava," Cuperia said. "Some folk in these villages farm crops. Some have sheep and goats. These folk have real farms, Eren, where they make and trade new things. It can be a whole new beginning for us."

"But what about all my experiments and inventions?" I asked.

"We'll bring what we can. They'll love you, with everything you can create. One village in particular is willing to give you all the help you need with supplies and assistants. It's many thousands of paces away, but they have all sorts of museums and people named scientists. The town is Farthar Falls. They have a wonder waterfall that crashes into a beautiful fjord. Oh, Eren. The people, the people! And you'll make friends, lots of friends."

"I knew it!" I said. "You're trying to push other people onto me."

Cuperia laughed.

"No, my daughter," she said. "I'm not doing anything of the sort. I only suggest we escape this oppressive land of equality, where everyone is pushed down to the same, miserable level. And we should do so before...before..."

"Before what?" I asked.

Cuperia smiled and hugged me.

"Thank you for breakfast. Eren, I have a gift for you."

"I wondered about the box," I said.

"Your echolocation is good. Open it," Cuperia said.

Cuperia slid the box over to me.

"It's a large box," I said. "I can't wait to find out what's inside."

I opened the box and touched the contents. Inside I found tubes of all sorts. Straight tubes, angled tubes, bendable tubes, expanding and collapsing tubes, and a set of earmuffs with much smaller tubes. The larger tubes were as thick as my arms, and there was one last piece that resembled a funnel.

"What is it?" I asked.

"It's a *sonopicon*," Cuperia said. "An invention from Farthar Falls. You assemble it and push it through the hole in the ceiling. There are strings you can use to adjust the funnel shape and direction, and there's a stand here to hold the entire contraption. The stand lets you turn the tubes without turning the stand. You can sit or stand next to the device."

"It's a listening device!" I said with excitement.

"That's right!" Cuperia said.

"Wait a moment," I said with new suspicion. "This is your way of getting me to explore outside of my home."

"I've checked the hole from the outside. You may elevate the tube your own height plus half without it being seen," Cuperia said.

"And changing the topic," I said.

"Yes, I want you to learn more about Skulava," Cuperia said. "I'm not asking you to like it. Fact is, I don't like it myself. But you know that. I want us to leave. Maybe once you hear what people say, you'll understand why leaving is so important. We...well, just listen."

"I'll try," I said.

The sound of someone knocking on Cuperia's front door echoed through the hut and into the cave.

"Cuperia!?" shouted a voice through the slats. "It's Elder Zatto. I wish to speak with you."

Cuperia briefly placed a finger over my lips to keep me from speaking. She rushed from the cave into the hut, closed the secret door, and opened the front door. I crept to the secret door and listened.

"Welcome, Elder Zatto. Do walk in," Cuperia said. "I am surprised by your visit. It is not yet the end of the week."

Elder Zatto walked into Cuperia's hut, along with two other people.

"Would you like something to drink?" Cuperia asked.

"Cuperia," Elder Zatto said, ignoring her offer for drink, "what were you just doing?"

"I don't understand," she said.

"Before you opened your door," the elder said. "What were you doing?"

"Why, nothing at all," she said.

"Then why does your breath smell of food, and yet when I look around your hut, I see none at all?" Elder Zatto said.

"I ate breakfast a little while ago," Cuperia said. "Leftovers from yesterday. Surely my breakfast is not what brings you to my home?"

"No, it is not," the elder said.

"And I pay my portion of earned goods to the elders," Cuperia said.

"Yes, that's true too," the elder said.

"Then? How might I help you?" she asked.

"You might help me, but you might not," Elder Zatto said. "There's strange talk about you, Cuperia."

"There's always strange talk about me," she said. "Ever since I put my less-than-equal baby to rest there's been talk. I keep my life as equal as possible."

"So you say," Elder Zatto said. "But talk is stranger by the moment. Folk say you plan to leave Skulava."

"Absurd. Why would I leave?" Cuperia said.

"That's what I'm here to find out," Elder Zatto said.

"You see me here as I am," she said. "What else is there?"

"There's Inasherry, for one," Elder Zatto said.

"What about her?" Cuperia asked.

"What do you know about Inasherry leaving Skulava?" Elder Zatto said.

"If Inasherry or anyone would leave our community, she would invite the death penalty. Everyone knows that," Cuperia said.

"You know the community laws well," Elder Zatto said.

"Thank you."

"An *exequi* is issued against anyone for violating the greatest laws of Skulava," Elder Zatto said. "I believe it's time we issue one against Inasherry. There have been recent sightings of her on the road between Plateauville and Farthar Falls."

"I don't even know what those are," Cuperia said.

"I think you do. I think you know a lot about those two villages," Elder Zatto said. "I'm having additional sentries posted on our borders, and I think I'll send a few abroad."

"Well I hope they don't starve," Cuperia said. "We're making some extra-specially wonderful pheasant stew and nut pie."

"I'm sure you *would* want them here for the end of week—so your operatives can travel the roads unwatched!" Elder Zatto said.

"How dare you!" Cuperia replied.

"The sentries will be given their food," Elder Zatto said. "But they *won't* be leaving watch of the roads—or our borders. Good day!"

The two others left with Elder Zatto. I heard Cuperia pace in the hut. She looked out the window. Then she considered seeing me in the cave. She changed her mind twice, paced a little more, and left the hut.

I spent the morning assembling the tubes and placing them in the stand. I pulled several strings, and the telescoping tube sections lengthened, sending the tube through the hole in the ceiling and a little above.

"Now I turn the tube like this," I said to myself.

I heard birds singing in trees, with leaves flapping in the wind.

"Such a beautiful sound," I said. "How is it people can be other than appreciative of life around them? I know not. But I could listen to these all day and night."

I turned the tube and pointed it more toward the village center. Then I adjusted the elevation downward. Nothing. How strange. I pointed the tube away from the village, and when it was pointed in the opposite direction, I could hear people speaking. Strange again, but I listened.

"Lady Spenwick," said a young woman out of breath, and she ran up to someone. "Lady Spenwick!"

"Yes, Tuina."

"We are running low on food in Mother's Hall," Tuina said. "Biaba has gone in search of pheasant."

"I've told her many times not to do that," Lady Spenwick said. "We are the greater equals, and it's up to the lesser equals to provide for us. That means Cuperia and her kind. Where is Cuperia now?"

"She...there she is," Tuina said.

"Cuperia!" Lady Spenwick said. "Over here!"

I didn't like the way Lady Spenwick yelled at Cuperia. That made me mad. I wanted to yell out the sonopicon, but I didn't.

"Yes, Lady Spenwick," Cuperia said.

"Your group of lesser equals is behind on its food payment," Lady Spenwick said.

"Yes, I am sorry. Food is scarce this time of year. We have been gathering all we can for the elders' visit this end of week," Cuperia said.

"And what about the greater equals? We are hungry now. We must eat," Lady Spenwick said. "We are the mothers of Skulava."

"Yes, you are," Cuperia said. "Mothers must eat for two."

"Or more," Lady Spenwick said. "As leader of the greater equals and this town, I've been very lenient with you and the lesser equals, Cuperia. You have been exempt from the elders' perpetuation of population program for two years. Should we make an exception this end of week?"

"No. I will have the lesser equals work twice as hard," Cuperia said.

"You can start by going after Biaba and sending her back to Mother's Hall. She went hunting for food in desperation," Lady Spenwick said.

"I will. I will," Cuperia said.

I took apart the tube and then yelled in rage. How could Cuperia stoop that low?! How?! I wanted to rush out of the cave, out of Cuperia's hut, up to Lady Spenwick, and strangle her. And I hated Tuina. I'd put her on a leash and drag her around Skulava with that high, squeaky voice of hers.

I spent the rest of the day tending to my crops and inventions. Cuperia must have been out working late, because she did not visit me in the evening. And so I fell asleep.

The next day, Cuperia visited me for breakfast.

"I assembled the sonopicon yesterday," I said. "I pushed it through the hole in the ceiling and listened to the outside."

"But the sonopicon is all in pieces," Cuperia said.

"I got mad," I said. "The things I heard...not like the birds and trees... Lady Spenwick...and why do you take orders from her...and strange how the sonopicon hears from the opposite direction."

"One moment, please. Let's start at the beginning. I'll explain things, but one at a time."

Cuperia explained that the reason the sonopicon had to be turned away from the village was because a section of mountain rock blocked a direct line to the village, and what I heard was an echo off the mountain. She said the mountain face acted like a giant ear and reflected sound to the sonopicon.

"As for Lady Spenwick," Cuperia explained, "she runs the village operations. She is a proxy for the elders when they are away. And yes, the village is split in two. The greater equals live in Mother's Hall, and the lesser equals like me live in surrounding huts. We lesser equals have a different name for the greater equals. We call them *pullbacks* because they pull us back from progress. The lesser equals—us—well...we call ourselves *forthers*. Because we are going forth with progress—in secret, mind you. And yes, we provide food and service for the pullbacks so we forthers don't have to endure the elders' perpetuation of population program. Now Eren, I wish you'd take better care of the sonopicon. Inasherry traveled a great distance to find it. She would be disappointed if she knew—"

"Who's Inasherry? She must be a forther," I said.

"She is. The best," Cuperia said, and she paused a moment.

"Cuperia. You're crying," I said.

"Like I said, she's the best. I think you're old enough now to know more. I had worried that you might be found and forced to tell things, and I kept things from you to protect you. But silly me, if you're found, they'll kill you first for being blind and non-equal and won't worry about asking questions."

"Let's not think of such things," I suggested.

"Of course," she said with a hug and kiss. "These things I've given you— you like them, don't you?"

"Yes, of course."

"And yet none of them are from Skulava," Cuperia said. "One person from our group leaves Skulava to acquire things. That person is Inasherry. I went with her once when I was much younger. We went to Farthar Falls."

"That's how you know about Farthar Falls," I said.

"Yes. Belsl was with us too."

"Who?"

"Doctor Belsl. Well, she wasn't a doctor back then. She is now. She's working on a plan...well...I'll get to that. Back to Farthar Falls. The three of us snuck out of Skulava for three days," Cuperia said.

"And no one noticed?" I asked.

"We pretended we were sick and had others vouch for us staying in our huts. We had the time of our lives. It was a wonderful, wonderful time. But it was dangerous. I could never do that again. As it is, when Inasherry goes out, I put on a disguise periodically and pretend that I am she. But the elders are suspicious. And so this cannot go on for much longer. Fortunately, things are changing, Eren. We forthers are preparing to make a move—either on the others in Skulava, or to Farthar Falls—permanently. Whatever happens, you must be prepared for change."

"What do you mean by making a move on the others?" I asked.

Cuperia opened her mouth to speak but then closed it.

"Some people cannot see beyond their own vision," Cuperia said. "The pullbacks do not and will not see that the elders are manipulating them."

"But aren't the pullbacks manipulating the forthers? By making you give them food and do work for them?" I asked.

"It may seem that way, but things are temporary. That will end soon. Very soon. And then things will become ugly, Eren. Belsl wants to save as many pullbacks as possible. But I fear the time is too late for them. I want us to leave before that time comes."

"What time?" I asked.

"You'll know when it happens. Put your sonopicon back together and listen. You'll know. And one more thing—I don't know where I'll be when things happen. You must be prepared to leave your cave, my hut, and Skulava. Make for the east. Others will see you and will help, if it comes to that. You'll know when you meet them. You'll know."

"You're scaring me," I said.

"Which is why I've waited this long to tell you these things. You'll understand more in time," Cuperia said.

Someone knocked on the front door again.

"Time to go," she said with a kiss.

Cuperia returned to the hut, closing the secret door behind her. She answered the front door, and in walked four people.

"You visit me again, Elder Zatto," Cuperia said.

"Cuperia, you'll be interested in knowing that an exequi was issued against Inasherry late yesterday. And earlier this morning, the exequi expired."

"I don't understand," Cuperia said. "An exequi stays in effect until the named person is dead. The elders never reverse an exequi. Did they reverse the—"

"No, they did not," Elder Zatto said.

"Then Inasherry is—"

"Yes. She is dead. We caught her just outside our borders, trying to sneak back into Skulava. She was interrogated briefly before final judgment was performed," Elder Zatto explained. "But she said something rather interesting before she died. Would you care to guess what she said?"

"I can't imagine," Cuperia said. "How could I?"

"She said that killing her will do no good. That the lesser equals will take her place," Elder Zatto said. "What do you have to say to that? Do you plan to take her place? Do you plan to leave our borders? Inasherry was caught coming back from Plateauville. Is that where you will go, Cuperia?"

"What is a plateau?" Cuperia asked.

"You tell me," Elder Zatto said. "There's Inasherry's word, suggesting that you plan or others plan to leave."

"How can I? I haven't left the community at all. If there are people beyond our borders, how would I know?" Cuperia asked.

"Don't play games with me," Elder Zatto said. "I would never visit you without cause. You are hiding something, Cuperia. Perhaps you intend to leave our community against the law you know so well. Or perhaps you know plans about others leaving the community. There are many possibilities. But do not seek them. Please! I ask that you seek counsel with an elder immediately. If not me now, then another. But make haste! Secrets breed desire, desire breeds progress, and progress breeds inequality and the desire to be god-like. Do you seek to be god-like?"

"No. I am plain and equal," Cuperia said.

"All the same," Elder Zatto said, "I'm posting three sentries by your side, one at a time, and in equal shifts to fill the day."

"I don't understand," Cuperia said. "What do you want of me?"

"Simply go about your daily routine," Elder Zatto said. "That will prove or disprove your innocence. The sentries will report what they see."

"Am I to spend my remaining days under guard?" Cuperia asked.

"That depends on you," Elder Zatto said. "You may travel where you will within the community of course, but a sentry will always be with you."

Cuperia was about to say something else, but she stopped herself short.

"Good day to you, then," Elder Zatto said, and he left with two sentries while the third remained behind.

I did not see Cuperia after that visit from Elder Zatto, and there was a problem. I could not produce my own supply of salt. Other things I had: food, water, and air, but not salt. I had only enough stored for a month. Cuperia knew this, but what could she do? She was under heavy guard.

A month passed, and still there was no visit from Cuperia. To pass the time, I listened to village doings with the sonopicon. Yes, I reassembled it. I heard Lady Spenwick shouting orders all month, without any sense of courtesy. Tuina kept fawning over her own appearance in her squeaky voice, and Biaba pushed people around with orders. Guessing from discussion, I would say Tuina was obsessively self starved, and Biaba was happily heavy-set. But they were Lady Spenwick's left- and right-hand people, and she gave them free rein to make the lives of the forthers miserable. How? By destroying things and making forthers build things again, or being picky with food and wasting it.

I learned about two new forthers—Solina and Cherabina. Solina is the feisty one, and I can tell she would like nothing better than to throw a few punches at Tuina's and Biaba's faces. Cherabina is very quiet and sullen. By listening to the way people expressed their condolences to her, I learned she is Inasherry's daughter.

Belsl didn't come out. The pullbacks never spoke of her, but I did hear whispers about Belsl being almost done with the new invention. What new invention? It must have been very much a secret, because no one spoke of it. Secrets were punishable by death, so all forthers would be killed if found out.

I was able to listen in on Inasherry's funeral. It was...well...it became political. Lady Spenwick used Inasherry's death as an example of what happens to those who do not follow the ways of equal living. There was no equal living. The elders used the pullbacks, the pullbacks used the forthers, and the forthers were about to strike back. But how? With this new invention? I could only wonder.

The funeral made me sad, and it was difficult to spend my entire day listening to village ramblings. To help pass the time, I sat with the chickens for their daily ritual with the *efferfont*. Oh, that thing. Yes, I forgot to explain it. The efferfont is a visual device about the size of a pitcher of water, maybe a little taller and a little narrower. Cuperia says it looks like a water fountain, but no water comes from the device. Somehow the efferfont plays tricks with the light, because one can pass an object like a hand through the visual image of the fountain. A fountain noise also comes from the efferfont. The chickens like watching it, but I could never understand why. Cuperia says everyone in Skulava has an efferfont and is required to look at it at least once a day. She said there's a large efferfont in the middle of Skulava that people must also look at for at least a hundred heartbeats a day.

I was getting desperate, to the point where I was willing to go into the hut in search of salt. I would have to be careful and time it such that Cuperia was out on business. That would draw the sentry away, but how could I be sure no one would see me through a window? What if one entered through the front door suddenly and caught me?

It was decided, then. I would go into Cuperia's hut when she next left. I sat by the secret door to her hut and listened. And waited. And listened and waited. I fell asleep by the secret door. Nothing deep, just a light nap. I dreamed of what the world might be like, crowded with strange creatures fighting for a little space with one another. I was caught in that crowded world, unable to move or breathe, and all along there was a heavy stench engulfing me, a stench that poisoned the life out of me and pulled me down to my knees and onto the ground, onto the ground...

I awoke with a start from a tapping noise. I was still sitting next to the secret door. The tapping was at first distant, like the tapping one does on a wall when looking for a hollow area. The tapping grew closer, and I knew I was in trouble. Cuperia never tapped like that. This was obviously someone who was looking for the secret door.

The tapping was too close. Soon I would be discovered. My imagination overcame me, and it produced the following interpretation: the sentries, who had been following Cuperia night and day, discovered nothing, and so while she was out with a sentry in tow, another sentry was now searching her home.

My only chance was to secure the secret door as best I could, but that would make noise, and surely the searcher would hear me. It was a risk I had to take. I propped metal bars against the secret door to hold it shut, and only just in time. The tapping reached the secret door, and I could hear the door move a little from the tapping. I held another metal post in hand, preparing to defend myself. But strangely, the tapping stopped. I heard a heavy scuffing sound and the front door to the hut opening and closing.

It seemed only a few moments had passed before another person entered, but I wasn't sure. The thought of almost being captured sent me into shock, and I sat in a stunned position for an unknown period of time. The second person had a horribly nasal sound to her breathing, and she broke into Cuperia's food locker and began eating. It could have been Biaba. I don't know. But she left, and I pulled out of my shock in time to hear a third person enter the hut. This third person did not tap but instead poured something grainy into a jar. Then I heard the sloshing of the grainy material in the jar getting closer to the secret door. A light knock sounded on the secret door, and I heard a soft voice:

"Erebellasia, I have salt for you," said a soft, female voice.

What should I do? Was this a trap?

"Cuperia sent me to give you salt. We know you are getting low," she said. "Hurry, before she returns with the sentry."

This person knew my name. If this were a trap, the sentry would surely burst through and take me away. I decided to trust this person and take the salt. I removed the metal posts from the door and unlatched it. In crawled a young woman with a salt jar. She was a little shorter than I, but she was limber and agile.

"My name is Chrba," she said. "I live across the way from Cuperia's hut. I'm...so glad to meet you at last. I've heard so much about you. To think that I'm meeting the legend."

I giggled. I couldn't help myself.

"Don't make fun of me," Chrba said as she walked around the cave. "I've had a hard time lately with family issues, but I've decided it's time I take action. I didn't believe Cuperia about your inventions. Now that I see them, I'm awestruck. Just plain awestruck."

"Well thank you," I said.

"I can't stay long. Cuperia led the sentry to market with her. I must be gone before they return," Chrba said. "And I'm expected at a one-month memorial service for my mother. She was killed last month."

"I'm so sorry," I said. "Wait. There was an elder here last month — Elder Zatto. He said a woman had been killed on our borders. Her name was Inasherry. And there was a funeral. Inasherry, she —"

Chrba began to cry.

"Do you have a sister named Cherabina?" I asked.

There was dead silence while Chrba restrained her tears and dried her face.

"I *am* Cherabina."

I opened my mouth several times to say something, but my throat welled up, and I could barely get out another, "I'm sorry."

"Chrba is my nickname," she said. "I didn't mean to bring my troubles in here. Life is more important than death, and I brought you salt for life. It took me a little while to find the secret door."

"Were you tapping on the wall a little while ago?" I asked.

Chrba paused for a moment.

"No, I wasn't," she said. "Did the person make a metal-rattling sound, like a sentry's armor clanging together?"

"No, but I heard a pa-click-i-ty foot scuffling," I said.

"That had to be Lady Spenwick," Chrba said. "Oh no, that's bad. She's now snooping in Cuperia's hut. Can't she keep her nose out of things for once?"

"It's not so bad. She didn't find me," I said.

"But Lady Spenwick might have seen me enter Cuperia's hut," Chrba said. "I shouldn't stay long."

"Maybe and maybe not. After she left, Biaba entered and ate my mother's food," I said.

"She's been doing that a lot lately," Chrba said. "I'll be glad when this whole thing with the elders and the pullbacks is over."

"So something *is* going to happen," I said. "Tell me what you know."

"Maybe when we have more time, when Cuperia's hut isn't being ransacked by the pullbacks. I should go now," Chrba said. "I'll return with more salt when it's safe. Until then."

"Wait," I said. "Let me touch your face."

Chrba remained motionless. I placed my hands on her head and felt her soft curls. Then I drew my fingers down to her ears, to her temples and forehead, over her eyes, her nose, down her cheeks, and across her chin.

"You have a beautiful face," I said.

"You do too, Erebellasia," Chrba said.

"Call me *Eren*. My mother calls me that," I said.

"*Erebellasia* is a beautiful name. But I will call you *Eren*. And now I must leave," Chrba said.

"I hope to meet you again, Chrba."

"Goodbye," Chrba whispered.

She crawled through the secret door, passed through Cuperia's hut, and was gone. My fingers trembled for the next ten thousand heartbeats with the memory of another person fresh in my mind. Curls. She had curls. I had never touched curls before. My own hair is straight, as is Cuperia's. Then suddenly I wondered what it might be like to have curly hair. Would it tangle? Could I invent something to make it curl?

Then I thought about Chrba's skin. It was very smooth. I touched my face, and although it was smoother than Cuperia's, it was not as smooth as Chrba's. I had to invent something to make my skin smooth, like Chrba. And curl my hair. Imagine the surprise when Cuperia sees me with curly hair and touches my soft face!

Cuperia. Would my mother ever visit me again? Why couldn't those sentries go away? I thought hard about what Cuperia said—living in a cave, the isolation, and the problems with our community. For the first time, I truly wanted to leave the cave. I couldn't bear to just exist without having conversation with Cuperia. And now I understood what she meant about making friends. Chrba was different, and I cherished that difference. How many others could I meet? What new things might I experience? I suddenly wanted to learn about people, about why they do the things they do, including why they say we are all equal when in fact we are not.

Cuperia never returned from the market. A week passed, and another. Cuperia was definitely gone, and there were no visits from Chrba. Two more times did Lady Spenwick tap inside Cuperia's hut, searching for what I hoped would not be found. And it wasn't. Biaba did not return, and so I guessed she had eaten all remaining food in the hut. Then one day to my delight, Chrba knocked softly on the secret door.

"Eren. It's me, Chrba. I have salt for you, and news too."

I opened the secret door, and in crawled Chrba. She closed the door behind her.

"What did you do to your hair?" Chrba asked. "It's...bright green! And curly! And your face is...orange!"

"I wanted to make my hair curly, so I invented a lotion and applied it," I said. "I don't know what green is. Does it look natural?"

"No," Chrba replied.

"And my face is smooth," I said. "I made another lotion just for my face."

"It doesn't look natural either," Chrba said. "But I can help you. I have a friend who dyes hair, adds curls, and can remove that orange from your skin. Her name is Belsl. She's a *forther* like you."

"Doctor Belsl. Cuperia told me about her. And about the forthers," I said.

"Then you know that a forther is someone who's willing to go forth and make progress toward a goal of improving life for people. We don't say *progressor* because of the evil connection with *progress*."

"For some reason I've never thought of myself as a forther. Maybe because my mother just told me about forthers a little while ago. Or maybe because I'm not out there in the village with the other forthers," I said.

"Here is more salt," Chrba said.

"Thank you," I replied as I took the salt and placed it next to a collection of empty jars. "I don't suppose you can help me fill these empty salt jars?"

"Perhaps. But I have other things to tell you," Chrba said. "First, Cuperia has been taken away by the elders."

"I knew there was something wrong," I said. "Why did they take her?"

"They suspect she is up to something. They couldn't prove anything, but they held her overnight, and I guess they have a way of telling if a Skulava woman has been staring at her efferfont, because they know that someone has been staring at hers but also know it could not be her," Chrba said.

"That's because it's in here. The chickens stare at it," I said.

Chrba laughed.

"So that's how she did it," Chrba said.

"Why are the elders so determined to have people stare at this thing?" I asked.

"It makes people calm. Too calm. They don't ask questions when they should. They simply do as they're told," Chrba said. "We forthers have a way of dealing with that. Belsl taught us. One simply taps the tongue against the room of one's mouth while breathing in and out. The tapping is quiet to those around but vibrates the skull ever so slightly, and this is done in cadence with a rhythm and beat that we have learned defeats the efferfont."

"That's like my method of echolocation, only quieter!" I said.

"I've never thought of it that way, but yes. Belsl pioneers many things like that. She's blind like you," Chrba said.

"Now I understand," I said. "She simply modified her method of echolocation for this purpose."

"Well, it gives us the ability to resist the efferfont," Chrba said. "There were only three people who could resist the efferfont before we learned the technique—Cuperia, Inasherry, and Belsl. Being blind helped Belsl, but she is blind no more."

"No more? How did that come about? And was she born blind? How—"

"Wait!" Chrba said. "I'll try to answer. Many years ago, the elders came down one weekend as they usually do. Belsl was very young at the time—Belsl is a doctor, as you may know, but she wasn't then. Well, they chose Belsl for their perpetuation of population plan. Cuperia may have told you, or you can guess. And Belsl did too. She gave the elder a good fight to keep him from fathering a child with her. The fight was brutal. The elder beat her up badly, and her eyes were damaged. So she became blind."

"That's horrible," I said.

"Inasherry and Cuperia took turns caring for Belsl. But now here's the interesting part—since Belsl couldn't see, she couldn't see her efferfont. And she realized it wasn't our place to be 'equal'. In fact, it was our place to be free and above this mode of subservience that the elders had pushed upon us," Chrba explained.

"Go on," I said.

"Inasherry and Cuperia then revealed to Belsl that they each had been able to resist the efferfont, but they were too afraid to tell anyone, lest they be turned over to the elders for heresy. All those years that your mother could have told my mother or vice versa. They both had pretended to be like all the other *equal* Skulavians," Chrba said.

"Well the elders must have figured out that Belsl couldn't stare at her efferfont anymore," I said.

"They did. And they issued an exequi against her, but before the elders could take Belsl away, Cuperia and Inasherry hid her in a cave just east of Skulava. Belsl made that cave into a secret facility, which we call the Auberge. There are secret passages leading into and out of the Auberge, and both Cuperia and Inasherry used them to get in and out of Skulava. Your mother did not travel as much outside of Skulava as my mother did. The elders became suspicious of my mother and had sightings of her outside of Skulava when she made one of her many runs to other villages, and so the exequi was issued against her. But to answer a question you haven't asked yet—most of your goods in here are from my mother."

"I didn't ask because Cuperia already told me. But I am thankful," I said.

"Inasherry would go to other villages and bring back goods to the Auberge. Your mother then smuggled those items from the Auberge into Skulava. And there were things not just for you, but for others too. I have some of those things. So does Solina."

"Tell me about Solina. I've heard of her. But who is she?" I asked.

"Another forther. She also happens to be Belsl's daughter," Chrba said.

"But you said—"

"Solina, you, and me are the only young women in Skulava with fathers who are not and have never been elders," Chrba said.

"I knew it!" I exclaimed.

"Shhhh!" Chrba cautioned. "Not so loud."

"Cuperia would never tell me. But who is my father? Who is yours? And Solina's?"

"Your father's name is Lanceri. He's a carpenter and blacksmith," Chrba said. "My father's name is Beugo, and he's a trader. Solina's father is Lord Trancelo, a banker. And the three live in Farthar Falls."

"I wish Cuperia would have told me! How I've wondered about my father!" I said.

"She had many things to worry about, and protecting you was one of them," Chrba said. "After the exequi was placed on Belsl, Cuperia knew that having a blind child would lead to the same. Also, if somehow the elders found you and questioned you, you could honestly deny any knowledge of our fathers. But after my mother...her...she was not questioned long before she was killed. So protecting you from knowledge is no protection at all."

"Yeah, Cuperia told me the same," I said. "Is that why things are different now?"

"In part. Let me continue. Inasherry was always on the road to other villages, leaving Cuperia in the Auberge to look after Belsl and baby Solina— yes, Belsl had Solina not long after moving into the Auberge. Belsl was looking for a way to restore her vision, and Cuperia found an alien device in the deep tunnels while helping Belsl excavate. It had strange markings on it, but one word that could be read was—AYMA."

"Ayma. What does it mean?" I asked.

"No one knows. But it was Belsl who learned its secrets. It took twenty years, but she figured it out. Being blind, her sense of hearing and touch improved, and she learned to communicate with the device by shaking her voice."

"Huh?"

"You know, like a yodel or some such. Different vibrations caused different things to happen. In fact, Belsl received images from the device, and so she learned how to use it as a fabricator. Well, that was the beginning of the Auberge's change from simple caves to the well-sculpted facility it is today. Inasherry traveled afar to bring back any special raw materials needed, and Belsl fabricated all sorts of tools from the Ayma device, but it soon became clear that Belsl, Cuperia, and Inasherry could not do all the work alone. So Cuperia taught others how to resist the efferfont. But she had to be clever and pick only those who she knew would become good forthers."

"I hope she didn't try teaching Tuina or Biaba," I said.

"Oh no," Chrba laughed. "Now as far as how things are different—my mother's death sparked a deep need for action among the forthers. There was already discontent with the elders, and the Ayma has been giving us whatever tools we need to put an end to their regime, but always the debate went on as far as how to end it and when. Solina wants to end it by force. Belsl wants a peaceful solution where all can live as true equals. No one likes that word anymore, though."

"Equals?"

"Right," Chrba continued. "Because no one believes it possible. Inasherry, before she passed, suggested that we forthers all move to Farthar Falls and leave the pullbacks here."

"Why leave the pullbacks here?" I asked.

"Because they load us down with their paralyzing dependencies on living no better than a wild animal," Chrba said. "But Cuperia didn't like the idea of leaving the pullbacks behind because it means they would still suffer. And now we come to the important part."

"What important part?" I asked.

"The elders are descending from the mountain this evening, as they do once a week. They have decided that since Inasherry is dead, I am now available for their perpetuation of population plan. Strangely, Lady Spenwick has approved, even though I'm not a greater equal and don't live in Mother's Hall."

"That's horrible!" I said. "What are you going to do? Run away?"

"The elders would issue an exequi against me, if I did," Chrba said.

"You can't let them...let them...take your dignity from you," I said.

"I have debated the issue extensively," Chrba said.

"I can't believe Belsl and the forthers would allow this to happen," I said. "Stay here with me. No one need know."

Chrba smiled.

"I'd love to, but it's too late," Chrba said.

"What do you mean?" I asked.

"You aren't the first one to know," Chrba said. "In fact, neither am I. When I asked Belsl about your hair, it was she who told me about the elders' plan. Yes, she doesn't want it to happen. But she doesn't want violence. She's really torn about this situation. For once she's using the Ayma to make armor and other defensive weapons. And then there's Solina's solution."

"I'm afraid to ask," I said.

"She gave me this little bottle. See?"

I took the bottle and read the label.

"andronide — for stopping him when he goes too far," I read.

"It's poison," Chrba said. "It kills only men. And only when they come in contact with the poison."

"I've never heard of something so atrocious," I said. "You...she really gave you that bottle? And you're going to use it?"

"What else can I do?" Chrba cried.

"It's wrong to kill others," I said.

"But it's wrong to allow others to do wrong," Chrba said. "I can't let them hurt me."

"And how is this progress? Or going forth? What will this accomplish?" I asked. "You gave me all this hope of a bright future with these other forthers, and I learn one of the forthers resorts to killing like the law of equality dictates. I'm disgusted, Chrba. Completely disgusted."

"I've never used andronide," Chrba said.

"And that makes it acceptable? But to kill! Why would Solina give you such a thing? Why, Chrba, why?"

"You want to know why? Really know why? They killed my mother! Isn't that enough?"

"No," I said.

"What if they killed Cuperia? What would you do?" Chrba asked.

I couldn't reply.

"That's what I thought!"

"But if you use that and an elder dies, they'll issue an exequi against you for murder. What about that?" I asked.

"Andronide is insidious. It has a delayed effect of six days or so. When the elder is eating, he will suddenly choke on his food and die," Chrba said. "So you see, I'm not really killing him outright. It will be his great appetite for food that kills him."

"Doesn't make it right," I said.

"Again, what would you do? Or what would you have me do? Hide here? Can everyone in Skulava hide in here?" Chrba asked.

"I'll make the space, if I have to," I said.

"Even you can't dig that quickly," Chrba said.

"Please. Don't," I said. "If you won't stay in here, let's leave Skulava. We'll find Cuperia and start a new life in another village, like Farthar Falls."

"The Auberge is safe for a little while, but the roads are watched, now that Inasherry is dead," Chrba said. "And everyone wants Cuperia free, but there are too many sentries. I think the only answer will come from Solina. Outright attack. Doesn't help that there's a food shortage."

"Wait, what did you just say? What's this about a food shortage?" I asked.

Chrba held silent for a moment.

"I can hear your heart rate increasing. And your breathing is labored. Something is going to happen, isn't it? Tell me!" I demanded.

"I didn't want to tell you about the food shortage, because I thought it would frighten you," Chrba said.

"Is something bad going to happen?" I asked.

"Many bad things could happen, Eren. You're now more in danger than ever before," Chrba said.

"How? Does the community want me to supply them with food?" I asked.

"The community isn't like that. We forthers will work together, of course, but the others—the pullbacks—have not stored food like they should. They waste food, in fact, and that's the reason for the shortage."

"They could learn to store food. I myself cannot depend on a steady supply of food, so I store as much extra as I can," I said.

"The pullbacks aren't like that. They are a me-me-me society. This will be their first experience with starvation. And starved people revert to the most brutal, barbaric savages. They will fight for and steal any food they can find to survive. That is the wild animal world, and that is what we forthers are fighting to avoid," Chrba explained.

"They will steal. So does that mean they will try stealing my food?" I asked. "As in my crops, my chickens and—"

"The pullbacks would erupt in a frenzy over their discovery of your food stores," Chrba explained. "And they'd destroy your inventions, Eren. All that you've created, they'd destroy."

Suddenly, we heard a soft knock.

"Erebellasia, Cherabina, it's me, Solina. The elders are due to arrive soon."

"I have to go now," Chrba said.

"I hope your use of andronide does not come to pass," I said.

Chrba hugged me and left with Solina.

Each moment spent in my cave was one spent in agony, not knowing if Chrba would go ahead with her plan to poison the elder or not. Listening through the sonopicon revealed nothing, as Skulava was unusually quiet. Again I wanted to leave the cave, leave Cuperia's hut, and explore Skulava to find out what was happening. But who would see me? And how could I be safe? So, I remained in the cave, but I could not just stay there and do nothing. I put the chickens in front of the efferfont. I pretended that I could see and that I needed to tap the roof of my mouth in cadence to block the efferfont.

Then a sound came from the sonopicon. Something was happening in the village. I put the efferfont away and rushed over to the sonopicon and listened. I was ready to burst with excitement and wished someone were with me to share the excitement, but I bit my lip to quell my speech. I didn't dare speak out loud for fear that the tube would carry my voice into the outside. But I did hear all sorts of sounds. A large fire was built. Women prepared meats and placed them on sticks above the fire. Other women moved tables and chairs together and still more placed other collected foods on the tables. This all was going on outside, but already I could hear that there was less food than normal, and there was anxiety on how to explain this to the elders.

Then I heard music. Well not quite music. More like instruments being tuned and tested and played in partial mismatched harmonies.

"They are descending the mountain," Biaba said.

"I see them," said Tuina. "They will be here soon."

I heard a horn blown from up the mountain. It was distant and echoed, but then it grew closer, and just before it arrived in Skulava, I also heard squeaking and wood hitting rock, more like rolling on rocks, and I wondered if these were the carts Cuperia had once described to me. They had to be, because I heard several elders giving orders to young men pulling the carts.

"They are here!" Lady Spenwick shouted. "Take your places."

I could not tell what that meant, but the chaotic running about ceased, and the air was mostly silent except for the crackling of fire and the unloading of carts. Then based on confidence and heaviness of footstep, I surmised that the young men who had pulled the carts now stood guard encircling Skulava. The elders were seated at the tables, and they immediately remarked at how there was less food than normal. Some even accused the lesser equals of holding back and threatened to have Skulava turned upside down if more food were not placed on the tables.

The air was silent again. But then forther women brought more food to the tables, and I could tell that this was more than just their portion, this was almost all the food they had left.

"And now let us have dancing while we eat," an elder said, and I recognized the voice as that of Elder Zatto's.

Light dancing music began, and from the lightness of footfall, I could tell it was women who were dancing. They danced in a circle of sorts around the tables, more like footsteps, but they stopped and started and stopped. My guess was that they lifted their arms at times, because I could hear the rustling of their clothing.

"We should not limit ourselves to the greater equals, Elder Gavak," Elder Zatto said.

"Oh? Have you lowered your standards, Elder Zatto?" the other elder said, who I guessed was Elder Gavak.

"The greater equals are clean and tidy, yes. But the lesser equals are wild and feisty. They are full of energy, energy I never realized could exist with such women," Elder Zatto said.

"And how could you know that?" Elder Gavak asked.

"I had the best one last week, Elder Gavak," Elder Zatto said. "See that one over there? Her name is Solina."

"Yes," said Elder Gavak. "You always get first choice."

"Because I am the eldest and thus the leader," Elder Zatto laughed. "But you are the second eldest, and so I suggest you take Solina tonight. You will understand that sometimes one must review one's sense of place with these women. I will choose another lesser equal—Cherabina."

"I think it unfair that you always have first choice," Elder Gavak said. "I challenge you to a contest. The victor gets the spoils."

Elder Zatto laughed.

"And what is this contest?" Elder Zatto asked.

"From the spoils shall the spoils be chosen," Elder Gavak said, holding up a wishbone from a stolen chicken.

"The stolen chicken?" Elder Zatto asked.

"The women here are required to steal one from a neighboring village," Elder Gavak said.

"It would not be *equal* of them to raise chickens of their own," Elder Zatto said. "And if we should catch that woman leaving Skulava for the other village, she would receive an exequi."

The two laughed, and a shiver shook through my shoulders.

"Here then is a wishbone from the stolen chicken," Elder Gavak said. "To the greater equal."

"To the greater equal," Elder Zatto said.

I can only imagine that the two played some sort of pulling contest with the wishbone, because after a moment or so, the wishbone broke.

"To the victor the spoils," Elder Zatto said. "I congratulate you."

"I thank you," Elder Gavak said.

"Bring forth Cherabina!" Elder Zatto called.

The music stopped, as did the dancing, and slow drum music thumped. I could not see where Cherabina was or what she was doing, but from the gawking and calls, I guessed she was being paraded along the top of the tables until she reached the end where Elders Zatto and Gavak sat.

"You are mine tonight, dove," Elder Gavak said.

Elder Zatto took a big bite of chicken, spat out the bones, and snickered.

"Give Elder Gavak hut number four," Elder Zatto yelled.

"That's Inasherry's hut," yelled a woman.

"Not anymore!" Lady Spenwick replied.

"Chrba, no!" I gasped.

Then all went quiet.

"Who said that?" Elder Gavak insisted.

"It came from over there," yelled Elder Zatto. "Next to Cuperia's hut."

"Someone has skipped the festival," said another elder.

"Impossible," said Zatto. "I know every woman in Skulava. And all are here."

"Then we have an interloper," said the other elder.

"I will find that interloper," Elder Gavak said. "If man, he shall pave the road with his blood. And if woman, I shall save Cherabina for next week."

The elders laughed. Elder Zatto took a particularly large bite of chicken. Elder Gavak with his heavy breathing walked toward Cuperia's hut, along with three sentries.

"Stop," Chrba said from the tables. "STOP!"

"You know something about Cuperia's hut?" Elder Zatto said.

Chrba held silent, but her plea did arrest Elder Gavak's progress.

"Well?" Elder Zatto insisted. "Speak, Cherabina! What is it you fear? Who is in Cuperia's hut?"

"Cuperia!" Chrba said back.

The elders laughed.

"Cuperia is locked up," an elder said.

"This is exactly the problem with Skulava today," Elder Zatto ranted between bites. "The youth of this village can think of nothing better to do than tell lies. Why? I'll tell you why! Because we wait too long for initiation. Twenty years of age? That's too long. They're old and corrupt. Beginning next week, girls of age fourteen shall be selected, and from both greater and lesser equals. All those older who are not yet initiated shall be so with the help of all elders. That will put an end to contempt. That will end their need for...for..."

But Elder Zatto choked. At first the other elders laughed. But Elder Zatto's emergency was real. I could only speculate that Solina's poison had been used on Elder Zatto, and it was now taking effect.

"We need help here!" Elder Gavak said. "We need a doctor!"

"Elder Balco is vacationing in Plateauville," said another elder.

"Then get one of the women," Elder Gavak said.

"I will help him," Solina said.

"You? You can help him?" Elder Gavak said.

"Yes, I will help him," Solina said.

Solina spat on him, and Elder Zatto died right there. I know, because all sounds stopped from him. Skulava became silent for several heartbeats as rage built up. And then everything exploded.

"Get her!" Elder Gavak shouted to the sentries.

I heard Solina making, "yai-yai-yai," sounds and running away into some hut. Elder Gavak and many heavy-footed sentries followed her toward the hut. But then Solina burst from the hut yelling, "Shoot them all! Shoot them all!"

I heard twangs and sounds of smooth, straight twigs flying through the air. Many men screamed in pain and fell to the ground. Many more charged the women and attacked with their swords. It was mayhem and chaos, and for the first time in my entire life, I wished I were deaf. I could no longer stand there and listen through the tube. I jumped away from the sonopicon and prepared to die. No one could survive such an onslaught. If a chance sentry didn't discover me and kill me, the grief of listening to the event would overcome me and crush my spirits. I ripped small strips of cloth, rolled them, shoved them into my ears, and curled up in a ball in a corner.

"Erebellasia? Erebellasia! It's me, Solina. Can you hear me? Erebellasia!"

I didn't want to hear anything. But someone opened the secret door, entered the cave, and pulled the strips of cloth from my ears.

"Eren? It's Chrba."

"Chrba," I said, and I gave her a big hug.

"I'm not hurt at all. I gave the andronide back to Solina. No need," Chrba said.

"I'm so glad," I said.

"We are in the eye of the hurricane," Solina said. "Reinforcements are on the way and will be here any moment!"

I heard Solina's voice from the secret door opening. She had wide shoulders and could not climb through the doorway. She waved her hands frantically for Chrba and me to follow her. Now you may wonder how I could know that she waved her hands. I could tell because as her hands passed in front of her, her speech sounded slightly different.

"Let's go, Eren," Chrba said as she released her embrace and led me by the hand.

Chrba and I crawled through the secret door into Cuperia's hut. It was the first time I had been in Cuperia's hut since I was a very small baby (when Cuperia first learned I was blind).

"Your hair and face, they—" Solina started.

"We'll cover her up," Chrba said. "Eren, throw this on."

I slipped my arms into a jacket with a hood that covered my hair and all but shrouded my face. The jacket smelled like Cuperia.

"My mother's jacket," I said.

"We'll take her to the Auberge," Solina said.

"How do we get there?" I asked.

"Just stay with us, and you'll be fine," Chrba said.

We made for the hut's front door and squirmed our way out just as three pullbacks pushed past us and entered Cuperia's hut. The noises around me were jumbled and chaotic, making sight through tongue clicking difficult. I had guessed that the elders and the other men were dead or driven back by the forthers, and the pullbacks did nothing during that fight, but now that the fight was over, they scavenged the village for any extra food and supplies they could find. Cuperia's hut was one such target.

"Watch out!" someone said as I was rushed past several collapsing huts.

Voices shouted that there was no food in this hut or that, and the pullbacks ran chaotically and mindlessly throughout Skulava. With Chrba holding my left arm and Solina holding my right, we fought seemingly upstream against the flood of these pullbacks. Several times the stampede forced me to the ground, and each time Chrba and Solina pulled me upright.

This was my first feel of the community while in the open air, and my attempts to visualize the surroundings of huts and hills were still thwarted by the yelling and screaming people, and so I gave up my attempts at echolocation.

"Be careful where you step," Chrba yelled in my ear. "We're going to leave the common way and enter a grove of trees."

"You mean it gets worse?" I asked. "I can barely stay on my feet now."

"That's from the people around us," Chrba said. "That will change soon."

Chrba was right. The ground suddenly went downhill. The number of arms flailing around us faded inversely proportional to the number of shrub branches lashing us. We were nearly clear of the flailing arms when someone shouted, "it's a blind one," and smacked a club into my back, with its thorny surface driving splinters deep into my spine. A sharp fire burned into my back and jerked my legs out from under me, sending me face first into the ground with an exposed tree root ready to make chopped stew out of my face.

"Yowwwwwww!" I screamed.

"Baaarrrrrgh!" Solina yelled as she charged the offender and others away.

"We won't make it to the Auberge at this rate!" said Chrba.

"Steady her, careful, she can't walk fully...wait, let me help," said a new voice. "We'll take her through the emergency entrance."

"Belsl!" Chrba said with delight.

"I don't want to die," I said, with the feeling of fire coursing up and down my back and legs.

"Don't worry," said Belsl. "Solina is dealing with the pullbacks."

I touched my face, and it was wet.

"Hold this to your face," Belsl said as she passed me a cloth. "It'll slow the bleeding."

The cloth took up the blood from my nose and forehead.

"Are...are my eyes injured?" I asked Chrba.

"No," she replied. "Fortunately not."

"Good, then I won't go blind from injury," I said in my state of shock.

I could sense Chrba and Belsl turn and look at me in astonishment.

"Gallows humor," Belsl said. "Don't worry, we are almost there."

My sheltered and quiet life in the cave did not prepare me for all this excitement, and with my legs twitching and the blood pouring from my face, I was at wit's end. Just when I was ready to collapse and give up completely, Chrba placed my free hand on the trunk of a large spruce tree. The trunk was immense. It had to be, because I felt no curvature as I imagined I might.

"We are here," Belsl said. "Follow me down the steps."

Belsl led me through an opening in the spruce tree! We were now inside the tree! But how?! I had no time to think. We descended spiral steps until we reached a small passageway, then what seemed a long ways along the passageway we went until we reached a doorway. We passed through the doorway, went up another flight of steps, through a short hallway, and into a room where Belsl, Chrba, and someone else helped me to a reclining bed while Solina watched the doorway.

"Where am I?" I asked.

"The Auberge," Chrba said. "We wouldn't have made it had it not been for Belsl."

"And the emergency entrance," Solina said.

"Chrba, Nance, easy now. Lower her on her left side. Don't let any pressure go on her back," Belsl said. "Good. Chrba, you hold her from rolling. Nance, let's clean her face and repair her injuries."

So the new person's name was Nance. She seemed like a nurse of sorts the way she assisted Belsl in everything. I could tell the difference between Belsl's touch and Nance's. Belsl had a firm and determined touch while Nance had a soft and more yielding touch.

"Apply *tassa nelumacaine* to her face," Belsl said.

Nance doused a sponge from the top of a bottle and placed the sponge on my face. The liquid stung my face at first but then made it numb.

"Good. The bleeding has stopped," Belsl said. "Do you feel that?"

"Feel what?" I asked.

"Good. Your face has been anesthetized," Belsl said.

"That means the pain is gone for the moment," Nance said.

"Hand me the *trystypion*," Belsl said.

Nance handed a three-pronged rod-like device to Belsl.

"Hold her head steady," Belsl said to Nance.

I felt Nance's soft hands holding my head but could only hear and guess that Belsl was now repairing lacerations and puncture wounds on my face. I heard Chrba's nervous breathing a short distance away and wanted to reassure her, but I thought it better to concentrate on being still.

"Her face is completely healed," Chrba said as Belsl finished with the trystypion.

"It only looks healed because the surface cells are rejoined. However, much healing must continue underneath. The trystypion mends flesh by gluing it together. The glue will dissolve and be replaced with living tissue," Belsl explained, though I think Chrba already knew this.

"Look, the orange is gone from her face, too," Chrba said.

"Yes, besides closing bleeders and numbing tissue, tassa nelumacaine restores original skin color. Were you trying to fashion some sort of skin lotion?" Belsl asked.

"*Yesh*," I said, when in fact I tried saying, "yes," but my face was still numb from the medication.

"Well, we have lotions you may try that don't change the color of your skin," Belsl said.

"What about her green hair?" Chrba asked.

"We could strip it out, but that would leave Erebellasia's hair thin and brittle," Belsl said.

Suddenly, my legs twitched violently for fifteen heartbeats.

"But as Erebellasia's spine is telling us, there's another matter more important," Belsl said. "Reposition Erebellasia so her back faces up, but make sure her face does not touch the bed. Lift her like this, yes, so her face is beyond the head of the bed. Good. Erebellasia, look down and think of pleasant things."

"I can only think of my mother, Cuperia, and the meals we would share together," I said.

"Good. Think about that," Belsl said. "Roll her shirt, gently."

"There's no blood," Nance said.

"The wounds are deep," Belsl said. "We cannot cut the spikes out without damaging her spinal cord."

"Each puncture point is red and inflamed," Nance said. "And the inflammation points are expanding in circular patterns."

"This is too quick to be infection. Must be a natural poison," Belsl said. "Prepare a five-drop dose of *zanvelox* in a syradermic needle."

Nance froze.

"Nance!" Belsl said. "Now!"

"Zanvelox!?" Nance questioned with a trembling fear.

"Yes!"

Nance grabbed a syradermic needle and the bottle of zanvelox. She inserted the needle into the bottle and drew the medication into the syradermic chamber, but in her nervousness and fright, the needle fell to the floor, and the bottle bounced off her recoiling arms and dumped its contents onto my back. Now my back burned worse than the thorny spines. I jumped to my feet, ran all about the room, and tried to go into the hallway, but Solina held me back. My skin burned like fire and poured with perspiration.

"Someone help me!" I yelled, and my vocal cords trembled when I spoke.

Chrba screamed in fright. I heard a loud but low buzzing sound from down the hallway. It was so loud that people went rushing around in terror.

"It's the Ayma," said one.

"It's out of control," said another.

Belsl came up to me, injected something into my arm with a syradermic needle, and I passed out. When I awoke, I was back in the treatment room and lying on a bed.

"She was only out for a few hundred heartbeats," Nance said.

"Yes. Fortunately the sedative worked," Belsl said.

"What did you use?" Chrba asked.

"It had to be *ethaloia*," Nance said.

"Yes," Belsl said. "The only drug that can safely reverse zanvelox. But the thorns are gone and Erebellasia is back to normal."

"But..." Chrba started. "That sound. It was horrible. Like some machine tearing itself apart."

"That horrible sound was from the Ayma," Belsl said.

"Eren interacted with it. She must have," Solina said.

"Telecommunication?" Chrba asked.

"I...don't understand," I said.

"Nance, the Ayma. Bring it here," Belsl said.

"Right away," Nance said, and she left.

"Erebellasia," Belsl said. "You are blind."

"Yes."

"But you are able to *see* us," she said.

"By clicking, yes," I said.

"And when your voice shook, the vibrations carried through the air, and the Ayma reacted, much as solid objects react from your clicking by sending back an echo of the click," Belsl explained.

Nance wheeled the Ayma into the room.

"Erebellasia, this is the Ayma," Belsl said. "I have spent much of my life learning how to use it. It responds to sound vibrations. But so far, I am the only one who can control it, thanks to this."

Belsl lifted her shirt to reveal her abdomen.

"A control belt!" Chrba said.

"It also allows me to see," Belsl said. "And as it turns out, I have another control belt stored in the Ayma. Let me pull it out."

Belsl removed a belt from the Ayma.

"I've been waiting a long time for this, Erebellasia," Belsl said. "I'd like for you to put the belt on. It will help you with the Ayma, and it should give you vision as well."

"You've been waiting to give this to Eren?" Solina asked in jealousy.

I put the belt on, and I felt a connection with the Ayma.

"I feel tingles around my abdomen," I said.

"Why don't I get a control belt, your own daughter?" Solina asked.

"It is tailored for the blind," Belsl said. "Solina—Cuperia and Inasherry have each tried to communicate with the Ayma, and both have failed. There is something about being sighted that interferes with this connection."

"But you've never let me try," Solina said.

"Erebellasia, try a voice tremor," Belsl said.

I tried shaking my voice with a yodel or other such thing.

"Nothing happened," Chrba said.

"But something happened," I said. "I could see a bit better. I mean, I could see through things. Like those jars behind the cupboard wall. I could see those jars."

"Try again," Belsl said.

Again, I yodeled and shook my voice.

"Hmm," Belsl said. "Something is different."

"I don't want that stuff on my back again," I said. "I just can't."

"No, we won't put more zanvelox on your back," Belsl said. "You must learn to do everything with the control belt."

"Chrba was screaming before," Solina said. "That's what's missing now."

"I can't just scream like that. I'll burn out my throat," Chrba said.

"Perhaps you don't have to," Belsl said. "Try shaking your voice at the same time as Erebellasia."

I shook my voice again. Then Chrba did hers. Belsl made adjustments to the Ayma with one hand and gestured to Chrba with the other.

"Lower, Chrba. Higher, Erebellasia. Now swap. Do alternating chords. Chase each other. There, you have it," Belsl said.

Suddenly, I could see items in the room with great clarity. I focused my attention on the far-table items. First one ink feather began to move. Then a piece of paper. A jar and a chair lifted. Chrba became frightened and screamed. The control was lost, the items momentarily scattered, and then nothing moved.

"This is amazing," Nance said. "If Erebellasia and Chrba could—"

"Please," I said. "If you're going to call Cherabina by her nickname, then you'd better call me by my nickname. I'm *Eren*."

"Very well, Eren," Belsl said. "Nance was about to say that we could use you two for combat."

"Well I wasn't going to put it that way!" Nance said.

"But that's what it comes down to, doesn't it?" Solina asked. "I mean, that's what life is about. The elders fight us, we fight back, and the winner gets the spoils."

"I could never fight like that," I said.

"Nor could I," Chrba said.

"What else is there?" Solina asked.

"There's exploration for one," Belsl said. "And discovery. And invention."

"Yes!" I exclaimed. "I love inventions. I made lots of things in my cave by my mother's hut. Cuperia! Where is she? I must find her."

"We don't know where she is," Belsl said. "The elders took her away."

"I must sound selfish," I said.

"Not really," Belsl said. "Most of us in the Auberge have lost family in some way. This has led us to various forms of life-long searches for meaning and purpose. Occasionally we are distracted by things like battles and riots in the village and such."

"Then I'd like to explore. I'd like to find my mother. I know it's selfish. But if she's still alive, then I really don't belong here anyway," I said. "Chrba, I hope you'll help me."

"Be happy to," Chrba said.

"And you too, Belsl," I said.

"I don't think you'll need me," she said.

"But we were lost without you," I said.

"I helped you get your start, yes. But you know the basics. Simply work with each other and let the control belt soak up the experience. The rest will follow," Belsl said.

Suddenly, Nance picked up a device and held it to her ear.

"Other casualties," Nance said. "They're flooding in now."

"Please excuse us," Belsl said. "Stay and rest as long as you like."

With that, Belsl and Nance were gone, leaving just Chrba, Solina, and me.

"I know you want to find your mother, Erebellasia," Solina said.

"Please, call me *Eren*," I said.

"But this riot will do us in if we're not careful. I say we practice self defense and all that sort of thing," Solina continued. "My mother is right. Your control belt will absorb the experience, making it easy for anyone—I mean you—to use. No point in running off into the wild only to get attacked by the elders or trampled by the pullbacks."

"I hate the idea of fighting," I said.

"It's not fighting," Solina postured. "It's defending."

"It's fighting," Chrba said. "And we're no better than those who fight if we fight ourselves. We need to understand our surroundings. We need to know first."

"Defending is protecting against known attackers," Solina said.

"But how can they be known attackers if we don't know about them?" Chrba asked. "We must explore first."

"Then we'll get killed," Solina said.

"Enough then," I said. "We seem to be caught between knowledge and warfare. Well I don't know anything about defense, so we'll have to explore first."

"We can explore defense," Solina said.

Chrba sighed.

"Well Chrba, let's try moving the objects in the room again," I said.

"I'm ready," Chrba said.

I shook my voice, and Chrba shook hers. I could sense the objects, but they didn't move.

"You have to change how you shake your voice," Chrba said, breaking away from shaking her voice.

"Well we can't if you talk," I said.

"Or if you talk," Chrba said.

"I didn't start," I said.

"I'll do the talking," Solina said. "Now you two try shaking your voices again. I'll work with the Ayma and tell you what you need to do when."

And that's how we learned to move things. Solina was our conductor and told us how to modify our yodeling or voice shaking. We moved objects individually and then orchestrated them in numbers to form shapes like a shield or bat.

"But how can you tell us what to do?" I asked. "I can sense if things are moving or not."

"Each object glows with two different colors," Solina said. "When there's too much orange, your voice is too powerful. When there's less orange and too much violet, Chrba's voice is too powerful. But when the colors balance, then the object moves."

"So Chrba can make the objects glow too?" I asked.

"Not really," Solina said. "As soon as you stop shaking your voice, all colors fail."

"So I can move things, but what I really need is a way to see great distances," I said. "I see through the cupboard door when I shake my voice. I wish I could see through the wall and hundreds of paces in the distance to find Cuperia."

"I'm thinking that even if you could, we would want you to tell us what you see," Chrba said.

"Yes, at least so I can conduct your yodeling," Solina said.

"You mean redirect us into defense or combat," Chrba said.

"Well someone needs to," Solina said.

"Since when?" Chrba asked.

"Since this riot!" Solina said.

"We're not dealing with riot," Chrba said.

"We'll have to," Solina said.

"No," Chrba said.

"Yes."

"That's enough," I said. "We're going to try something different."

Both Chrba and Solina gave me funny expressions.

"In the spirit of exploration," I said.

"Yes, that I can go along with," Chrba said. "Exploration."

"Chrba, stand on my left. Solina, on my right," I said.

"You act as if you know what you're doing," Solina said.

"I don't. But we must start somewhere," I said.

"Well I think Chrba and you should do more voice shaking," Solina said. "We could try different chords and patterns."

"We've done that," Chrba said.

"You're just agreeing with Eren to disagree with me," Solina said.

"When have I ever done that?" Chrba asked.

"Never, until we got together with Eren," Solina said.

"Don't be talking badly about my Eren," Chrba said.

"Ladies, please!" I said. "I have the power. So let's try it my way."

"I like that," Solina said. "Nice, strong, leader type."

Chrba was going to say something, but she bit her lip, and I was able to sense her doing so. I guessed she was going to complain about the strong leader type image, as it had military connotations, but then I also sensed that secretly she would like to see me as a strong leader type, and so I was flattered. And I think she knew, because I could feel myself blush. I knew the feeling even though I could not see myself blush, because my mother told me when I blushed. But from what Cuperia said, sighted people couldn't see themselves blush either.

"Let's all face the same direction," I said, now that the others stood where I asked. "Shake your voices out there in front of us."

Chrba did as before, and Solina's voice sounded amazingly like an opera singer.

"Now I'll shake my voice," I said.

And I shook my voice. Jars shattered and chairs broke.

"Stop, stop!" I said.

"It's not working," Solina said. "Maybe if I—"

"Let Eren direct," Chrba said.

And I blushed again.

"Do like before, but this time I'll be silent," I said.

Chrba shook her voice, and Solina did her opera voice work. I sensed a very subtle change in what I could sense. Their voices provided echolocation, but their echoes touched me, and then I sensed echo images of objects inside the cupboards.

"Stop," I said.

"Anything?" Chrba asked.

"I did sense something different," I said. "Chrba, Solina—face me."

And so Chrba faced my left side, and Solina faced my right.

"Now shake your voices again," I said.

They did. Now I could see through the cupboards and into the next room. Belsl and Nance were treating injuries for a half-dozen patients. I lifted my arms to my sides, and immediately I lost vision into the next room. I lifted my arms completely above my head, and my vision of the next room returned. I stretched my arms ahead of me, and it diminished. I swung my arms back slowly, and as I did, the vision increased, to the point that when I touched Chrba and Solina, my vision extended several rooms away. I moved my arms over their heads and touched them on their backs. Again, my vision extended, and so I wrapped my arms around them and pulled them toward me in a group hug.

Now I could see very well. I realized that their vibrations needed to transmit through my body for me to see. I turned their bodies to face in front, and I could see many hundreds of paces ahead. But they weren't pointing perfectly in front. I had them pointing at slight angles, and in this way I could control how far ahead I could see. Yes, see. A blind person with distance vision. It was incredible.

"What do you see?" Solina sang.

"This building, what everyone calls the Auberge...I can see it from the outside. It looks like a little mountain," I said.

"It *is* a little mountain," Chrba sang.

"And there's a moat around it. There are new elders, and a great number of men in armor with swords on the outside of the moat, and the drawbridge is raised. But the water is low. Too low. Several men are climbing down into the moat. It's only knee deep. They'll get across and invade the Auberge," I said.

"We have the knowledge," Chrba said.

"And now we must have the defense," Solina said.

"But there are so many," I said.

"Lift objects to block them, or simply push them back," Solina said.

"Flood the moat," Chrba said.

I looked around but only saw a dried-up river bed feeding into the moat.

"The river bed is dried up," I said.

"More knowledge," Chrba said.

"But useless," Solina said.

"More men are descending into the moat," I said.

"If you can't find water above ground, look below. Dive deep!" Chrba said.

I looked deep into the ground and found the water table. Scanning around, I realized there was a maze of natural channels in the rock that led to a single high point, which was blocked from entering the bottom of the moat by a flat stone. I concentrated on moving the stone, but the leverage required to do so caused my body to fall forward. I braced myself against

Chrba and Solina, and then I leaned backward. Then interspersing my own voice with Chrba and Solina's, I was able to move the stone ever so slightly. The water at first trickled upward into the moat, but as more water flowed, the flat rock became more dislodged, and suddenly I had created an aquifer that raised the water level in the moat.

"Now they're swimming," I said. "Some are swimming to our side of the moat."

"Block them!" Solina said.

"I...how?" I asked.

Then I felt a surge of power from Solina, and my vision regressed from bright color vision to dim black-and-white. I saw a coiled-up rope in a shed slip through a crack below the shed's door, shoot out into the air, and act as a long clothes line. This line flew to the moat and pulled the rioters back into the water.

"What's happening?" Chrba asked.

"I...didn't do that!" I said.

"Do what?" Chrba asked.

"Pull the rioters back with a rope," Solina said.

"You did that?" I asked.

"With your help, Eren," Solina said.

"But what if people were hurt? They could have been choked by the rope," I said.

"There was no time for such thoughts," Solina said. "I had to act, and I did. Now you will see that the rioters are swimming back to the outer edges of the moat and are leaving. See? I was helpful."

"I'm not sure how you saw that," I said.

"Nor am I. I can't see a thing," Chrba said.

"But I can. I took the vision from Eren," Solina explained.

"That's why my vision went from color to black and white," I said.

"Now we're ready!" Solina said. "We can drive back these men with great speed. We can take over the village. We can even launch an attack on the elders in the mountains and free ourselves from their tyranny!"

That's the last I heard before I passed out.

When I awoke, Chrba and Belsl were looking over me. I was resting in bed—still in the Auberge.

"Eren?" Chrba called.

"I'm awake," I said. "What happened?"

"Solina...overpowered you. She stole your control belt and then used a *vaculuxion* device to siphon your essential energies—essential energies that you used to drive the control belt. You lost strength and slipped into a coma," Belsl said.

"I tried to stop her, but she attacked me too," Chrba said. "I was dazed. I tried to get up, but I couldn't."

"It's not your fault," I said.

"It is my fault," Chrba said. "I was wrong to trust Solina."

"No one knew," I said.

"I knew enough," Chrba said. "I never told you how the elders were overpowered so quickly."

"She and her fighting group used arrows. I heard them from the cave," I said.

"But they were tipped with poison," Chrba said. "And not the slow-acting andronide. She used the quicker and more powerful *androtolynite*—a poison and microexplosive in one."

"You're a forther too, aren't you Belsl?" I asked.

"I am, but not that kind," Belsl said. "I had hoped for more peaceful methods. But hope doesn't work too well in this world, Eren. I suppose if I can save one more life, then my hope is satisfied for the day."

"And you saved Eren's life again," Chrba said. "For which I am thankful."

"Yes, after five days in a coma," Belsl said.

"I was beginning to lose hope," Chrba said.

"As was I," Belsl said.

"Five days?" I asked.

"Yes, five days," Chrba said. "Belsl tried to bring you out of the coma several times, but you didn't stir."

"Yes, without the Ayma, bringing you out of the coma became more difficult," Belsl said.

"What do you mean? Where's the Ayma?" I asked.

"Solina stole it," Chrba said. "She and a new group of super forthers took the belt and the Ayma and almost all the armor and weapons. They've formed their own fighting group."

"Each new power that comes along bifurcates humanity," Belsl said. "I wish it weren't true, but unfortunately...unfortunately..."

Belsl turned away.

"I've failed," she said.

I got up out of bed and hugged Belsl.

"No, you haven't," I said.

"We still love you, Belsl," Chrba said. "Even if Nance deserted you."

"Another failure," Belsl said. "She joined Solina in Solina's new cause. My own daughter, Solina. How I wish things were different."

"I wish you could have awakened me sooner," I said. "Maybe I could have helped."

"I'm sorry," Belsl said. "I tried many things—*pneuminaira*, *daylazina*, and *zakanazia*. But these did not work. In desperation, I used some experimental *jayladopa*, and that brought you to consciousness. But you could just as easily slip back into a coma. The jayladopa effect is only temporary. Much depends on you."

"I want to stay awake," I said. "I feel badly that I've caused all this trouble."

"Don't blame yourself for something others did," Chrba said.

"She's right," Belsl said. "I must come to terms with this and say that Solina is to blame."

"But it does bring to light one important thing—there are those who can handle power responsibly, and those who cannot. And power attracts all kinds," Chrba said.

"So I've discovered," I said. "I only want to find my mother. But other things get in the way."

"I think it would be best if we could sneak you out of the Auberge, away from the fighting. You need rest, away from these stressors," Belsl said.

"I wish Chrba to accompany me," I said.

"Chrba? Are you up to the task?" Belsl asked.

"I am!" Chrba said. "I think we should try for the plateau. You'll get to know all the sheep herders. Sheep are pleasant animals. You'll find no trouble there. Belsl, is the deep channel still open?"

"Wait. You may try for the plateau, but do not expect all to be well. Word is the elders have taken it over," Belsl said. "Now I said I don't know where Cuperia is. That is true. But I do know she is locked up. Most likely she is either at the top of Elder Mountain, or she is in Plateauville. And as to your question, Chrba, the deep channel was open until it flooded with water five days ago."

"That was me, wasn't it?" I asked.

"Yes, I'm afraid so," Belsl said.

"Well how did Solina leave the Auberge?" I asked.

"She fought her way out," Chrba said. "No. You're not fighting your way out."

"Well, isn't the way clear? I mean, she *did* fight her way through the men, didn't she?" I asked.

"She did," Belsl said. "And the crowd has thinned. But still there are the strays."

"Well, we must try," I said. "We made it in here, and so we can leave here."

"I must warn you that you could slip back into a coma. Jayladopa is unpredictable and has been known to leave people in a catatonic state in a few heartbeats," Belsl said.

"Then I'll have to take a chance and trust Chrba will awaken me," I said.

"It may not be enough," Belsl said. "Also, the jayladopa is only good for one dose. Whatever method Chrba uses to awaken you must be something other than medicinal. I would give you a dose of straight *jayla* to take with you, but that drug is for people on their way out of this world."

"We want to stay in this world, thank you much indeed," Chrba said.

"I should be fine," I said.

"Here, let me give this to you," Belsl said as she removed her own control belt and placed it in my hand.

"But...this is yours," I said.

"With the Ayma gone, it's useless to me," Belsl said. "But should you come across the Ayma, it may prove useful."

"Thank you," I said.

"Also, there's something else about which I should warn you," Belsl said.

"Is it about Eren? Or me?" Chrba asked.

"No, but—"

"Then we must deal with it when we must," Chrba said.

"Good and well," Belsl said. "Best of success then."

Chrba and I decided to leave through the main entrance. We went out into the open air, and immediately I noticed an odd scent.

"Do you smell that?" I asked.

"No," Chrba said.

Amazingly, there were no men around. Where did they go? Solina must have really driven them back for them to be gone. As it was, Chrba led the way, but I clicked my tongue to the roof of my mouth for my own vision. We crossed the moat and I followed Chrba, and she headed east toward the plateau. The scent grew stronger, and I didn't like it.

"Whatever the smell is, it's getting stronger," I said. "Over that rise I'd say we'll discover something horrible."

"I smell it now, too," she said. "I wonder if this is what Belsl wanted to tell us. But I don't understand how—"

We walked over the rise. Chrba stopped short and screamed. She turned around and ran at top speed back to the Auberge.

"Chrba! Chrba!" I called, but she was too frightened to reply and too distant to hear.

"I've smelled this before," I said, suddenly remembering my little domestic farm I had in the cave. "When an animal was no more, it was...this."

I knelt down, reached out with my hand, and touched the remains of a dead person.

"Death," I said. "These people had life. But now that is gone. They have nothing. Such a waste. Such a waste."

So that was the secret. Life is everything. Death is nothing. I have nothing unless I have life. And my life—any life—is more meaningful than death.

"Chrba!" I called as I walked back to the Auberge. "I have a new idea."

I found Chrba huddled in a room drinking a light beverage and chatting with Belsl.

"The bodies! Did you see all the bodies?" Chrba said to Belsl. "They... didn't even look human. But I knew they had to be. They were...they...something had already begun to eat them."

"Chrba," I said. "I'm here."

"Eren! You didn't become afraid? But you couldn't see them," Chrba said.

"I could smell them, and I touched one. I knew what was before me," I said. "Chrba, I realize now I can't limit myself to finding my mother. I hope I find her, yes, but there are more important things we must do first."

"You mean that *you* must do first. I can't go back out to that," Chrba said.

"Yes you can. You are alive and more powerful. They cannot hurt you. The fighting has ended," I said.

Chrba shook her head.

"No. It won't end," she said, still frightened.

I put my hands on each side of Chrba's head and looked her in the eyes, at least that's how she saw me. I couldn't really see her, of course.

"Chrba. I'm blind. Some people pity me. But I do not. I learn to work around it. You can learn to work around this too," I said.

"I can't," she said.

"Yes you can. Just a little bit at a time. And I'll help you," I said.

I felt tears roll down from Chrba's eyes.

"I...I'll try," she said.

We hugged.

"I hope the sky you are right," she said. "But if you're not going to look for your mother, then what?"

"I'm going to just look," I said. "It's what we wanted to do in the beginning, before Solina suggested that defense and fighting are more important."

"Eren is right," Belsl said. "The time for fighting has ended."

"And I want to know what caused the fighting, I mean what *really* caused it," I said. "I don't want the fighting to happen again."

"The elders," Chrba said.

"But how did that all happen, I mean, how is it we have elders at all? Why don't people all live and work together?" I asked.

"That is a very good question," Belsl said. "The elders have been around as long as anyone can remember, and more. But staying here won't give you that answer."

"Then let's go now, Chrba," I said.

"I...I want to go, but...but..." Chrba waffled.

"I have an idea. I'll blindfold you," I said.

"I don't want to be trite," Belsl said, "but—"

"You're going to say the blind leading the blind. I don't think so. I think this is an excellent idea, as long as we don't get separated. I don't know how I could get around, though," Chrba said.

"I could teach you how to echolocate," I said. "In fact, we should start that first."

Belsl passed me a blindfold.

"Good. Here goes," I said.

I tied the blindfold around Chrba's eyes.

"There. Nice and dark?" I asked.

"Yes. I feel so helpless," she said.

"Belsl, do you have a thimble and a jar lid?" I asked.

"Here, will these do?" Belsl asked.

Belsl retrieved a jar lid and thimble from a drawer.

"Take these," I said. "Now place the thimble on your first finger, and hold the lid between your thumb and other fingers. Tap the thimble on the jar lid."

"There," Chrba said. "Now what?"

"You must concentrate and listen. Hold the lid above your head and tap it. Now below. To the left side and right."

"I don't understand," Chrba said. "The tapping doesn't do anything."

"Stand over here in the middle of the room," I said. "The tapping will make more sense now. As before, tap the lid above your head."

"There. Something is odd. I feel like I'm caught in something," Chrba said.

"Good! You're hearing the echo," I said.

"I know what an echo sounds like, and this isn't an echo," Chrba said.

"It is, you just don't know it yet," I said. "Now tap the lid about once per heartbeat and walk slowly toward this wall. I'll lead you."

Chrba did so.

"Wow, that's like a zing I can hear from the far wall," Chrba said.

"As you get closer to this wall, it will have more of a dead or solid sound, while the far wall is more alive with a zing sound, as you've noticed," I said.

"Let me walk around," Chrba said. "Oops. I walked into this chair."

"You won't be able to see objects like a chair yet," I said. "I'm not sure how long it will take for you to see objects smaller than a wall. Days? Weeks?"

"Could be longer," Belsl said.

"Oh, I was hoping only a few minutes!" Chrba said.

I laughed.

"Being in the dark isn't funny!" Chrba said.

"I'm sorry. It seems funny to me. Maybe because I don't think of sight as something I'm missing. You might adapt quickly. It depends on your willingness to learn. And one more thing—don't remove your blindfold. If you open your eyes and look, you'll lose your echolocation ability and the sense of place in your surroundings. Sight is like that—it steals everything from you."

"How can you say that if you're blind?" Chrba said.

"It's because I'm blind that I can say it. I *see* better without sight," I said.

"Like sense of place?" Chrba asked.

"Yes. Sense of place," I said. "Now stand in one place and tap the lid again. Tell me if you notice anything."

I passed a book in front of Chrba.

"Something changed. The zings disappeared for a moment," Chrba said.

"Let's try that again," I said.

Again I moved the book around in front of her.

"Something's blocking the zings, but only for a moment," Chrba said. "Are you standing in front of me? Or holding something in front of me?"

"Very good. Yes, I'm holding a book in front. Keep tapping," I said.

Now I walked in front of her, then I moved the book in front of her without standing in front, and I repeated—walked in front and passed the book in front.

"I get two different zing patterns. One is like a little zing surrounded by a big zing, and the other is just a big zing being blocked by something tall," Chrba said.

"That's incredible," Belsl said. "No one learns to echolocate that fast. Actual blind people can take years in some cases. And Chrba has picked up the basics in no more than five thousand heartbeats."

"You were meant to be blind," I said. "I mean...that's not what I mean."

Now Chrba laughed.

"I guess I have talents I never realized," Chrba continued to laugh.

"Yes! That's exactly what I mean. Think about all the hidden talents we have yet to discover. But the problem is just that—they are hidden. And outside forces keep them hidden. We must remove those outside forces and bring forth the hidden gifts," I said.

"I understand now! Incredible! What's next?" Chrba asked.

"You're ready! Let's go outside!" I said.

"Wait," Belsl said. "One more thing."

She handed Chrba a smelling salt on a stretchy string for holding under Chrba's nose.

"Would you like one too, Eren?" Belsl asked.

"I don't think I'll need one, but I'll take one just in case," I said.

Belsl gave me a smelling salt, and I placed it in my pocket.

"Now you're ready," Belsl said.

I led Chrba outside, and she tapped on the lid to navigate.

"The hallway has a hollow feel to it," Chrba said. "But noise from other people disturbs the zings."

"It does. We'll be outside soon," I said.

And we were.

"Let's cross the moat," I said.

"I can sense the drawbridge," Chrba said. "And the water carries the zings along in a special way from the far bank. Otherwise, it's strangely quiet around here, but I sense people are moving, at least, there are zingless shapes moving around."

"Those are people. They are moving the dead away," I said. "Only a few dead in these parts. Most are over the rise where you took one look and ran away."

"I know. So we're going back to that rise, aren't we?" Chrba asked.

"We must. You must overcome your dread of death," I said.

We walked up the rise and stood at the top.

"The smell is still there," Chrba said. "But I sense more moving shapes."

"The dead are being moved, a few at a time," I said.

"Such a sad thing. But I'm not afraid. I'm rather subdued. I feel we should say words of meaning or sing softly as we would do at a funeral."

"There's a small hill just past this first group of dead. I'd like to climb that hill and take a look at the countryside," I said.

"I will follow," Chrba said.

As we walked past the dead, I clicked my tongue and Chrba tapped the lid. Then something quite interesting happened. We alternated our clicks with each other. Then we clicked in harmony. Slow, rhythmic, and steady with syncopation. I could sense that the living were appreciative of our clicking, as if we were giving our own last blessing of the dead. Some even clicked back in response, and those few became a few more and a few more until when we reached the end of the dead, many of the living were clicking in a great choir saying the last farewell.

"That never would have happened had I used my own eyes and simply walked through. Well, meaning that if I had the courage to walk through. More like I would have been extremely nervous and rigid," Chrba said.

"But our walk wasn't nervous and rigid. It was soothing and healing," I said. "Now we have that hill to climb."

"I can hear it...or I can sense it," Chrba said.

"Yes, it's sense of place, not hearing of place," I reminded Chrba.

"The hill is not just a simple hill. The zings are singing like birds," Chrba said.

"Funny, I sense that too. I've never had a sensation like this. There are hard parts and flexible parts buried under a thin layer of soil," I said. "I wonder if we even need to climb to the top of the hill. Maybe we should explore the hill itself."

As we approached the hill, the control belt gave me funny sensations.

"There's something unusual about this hill," I said.

"How?" Chrba asked.

"I'm not sure. Let's climb to the top."

We climbed the hill and reached the top.

"The feeling is very strong," I said. "Like with the Ayma."

"Could it be we have found the Ayma? That Solina is hiding in this hill?" Chrba asked.

"If she is, she has the best camouflage ever invented," I said. "Let's do a test like we did at the Auberge. Shake your voice, and I'll shake mine. I'll try sensing the hill and not moving things about."

We shook our voices, and they echoed around the rocks, racing around like a flock of birds with their beaks on fire, looking for puddles of water to cool themselves, but only finding rocks and shrubs and other dry assortments.

"There's some sort of machine in the hill!" I said. "Do you see it?"

"No, I don't. But I see a group of crazy birds flying all about!" Chrba said. "How is this possible?"

"You must be picking up my visual energies," I said. "The birds aren't real. They are side effects of our voices trembling."

"Well they seem very real. They're coming this way!" Chrba warned. "Drop low!"

We fell to our knees, and we felt the imaginary birds zing past our hair.

"That was close," she said.

"I'll try to stop them," I said, and I stopped shaking my voice, but the image of the machine became more clear, and I could see that it was a flat disk large enough to stand on, but only two hands high.

"The birds are getting stronger!" Chrba said. "They're making another pass."

"Drop low!" I said, but the imaginary birds came by and nicked us in our arms and faces.

"Ow!" Chrba said.

"I'm bleeding!" I noticed.

"So am I!" Chrba said. "Eren! You must get rid of these birds. They'll attack us and maybe kill us!"

"I know!"

"Send them somewhere!" Chrba said. "Send them in the hill!"

"Where though?" I asked.

"Anywhere! Do it now! Hurry!"

I shook my voice in a sideways manner. The birds grouped, dove toward the hill, burrowed into it, and then they exploded! A plume of dirt shot outward and blasted us on our backs. I landed on a shrub, but Chrba landed on a rock.

"Ow, ow, ow!" she said.

"You'll be fine," I said, helping Chrba to her feet. "Try to walk it off."

I helped Chrba to her feet, and without thinking, I began to shake my voice. Ghostly hands came from nowhere and massaged Chrba's back.

"Thank you," she said.

"I didn't really touch you," I said. "I just felt like...I guess it was like those imaginary birds."

"Well, thank you imaginary hands," Chrba said. "I sense exploits from an explosion nearby."

"Yes. Let's explore the explosion exploits," I said.

We walked down the hill a little and found a new cave entrance. The dirt and dust were still circling in the air. I tore a bit of cloth from my tunic and tied it around my mouth to keep out the particulates. Chrba did the same.

"We must be careful not to disturb anything loose. We don't want to be trapped inside this hill," I said.

The cave reached an end, and a bit of hard, flat material was exposed.

"Strange," I said. "This isn't the device I imagined."

"And yet this is something. It's not a natural part of the hill," Chrba said. "I wonder if there's a door."

"Let's find it through our senses," I said.

Chrba shook her voice, and I was about to shake mine, but an image formed in my mind immediately, and I could see that we were in fact at a door.

"It's here," I said. "We only need move a little dirt like this...and here it is."

"I'm simply dying to see what this door looks like," Chrba said.

"Not yet," I said. "Let's go inside and explore. I'm afraid that if you remove your blindfold too soon, we will lose out on learning important information."

We walked inside a room the size of a living room. The air was stale but breathable, if but for a little while.

"I'll prop the door open to let fresh air in and to make sure we aren't trapped inside," Chrba said.

"Good idea," I said. "Now the device is in this room. It's by a small table... over here, yes. Come here, Chrba, and sit. There are three chairs, but we only need two. The device is on the floor. I will need your help to activate it."

We both sat at the table, with me next to the device. I touched the device to sense for an activation button but could not find anything.

"We may have to shake our voices," I said.

"Wait," Chrba said. "There's a headset on this side shelf. Here."

I put the headset on, and I could sense an electrical connection with the device on the floor.

"The device feels alive!" I said.

Then Chrba and I sensed the device growing several hands in height, and a voice projected from the device.

"This is Debbie Dayla. If you are playing this video, it means this bio-propagation device has survived."

"Biopropagation device?" Chrba said. "I wonder what that means? Can it make plants grow?"

"The Bioprog is a repository of DNA samples taken from animals and plants around the globe. It is a Noah's Ark library, and the hope is that someday when Earth becomes more hospitable, someone of good conscious will use the Bioprog to bring life back to the planet. That is, if anyone is left on Earth. But DNA may not mean much to you, if you are in the very distant future as I hope. You might not even understand my language."

"We understand," Chrba said.

Then Chrba took the headset from me and put it on.

"This is the only Bioprog left in existence. Craymar Industries has destroyed all others," Debbie said.

"Why did you take the headset from me?" I asked.

"I wanted to know if wearing the headset allowed me to see the image of Debbie," Chrba said. "I wanted to know if you could see her at all being blind and all that."

"It doesn't and I can't," I said. "See her at all?"

"Well, um, yes, uh, hmm," Chrba said apologetically. "Here, take it back."

Chrba placed the headset back on my head.

"Craymar Industries has become too powerful and has threatened all that is beautiful that Dayla Industries has created. I can no longer live on Earth. Sparfy and I will soon leave for Bruxima 5. I am taking very few things with me and am hiding all other important things deep in the ocean floor."

"She's adorable," Chrba said.

"Chrba! You removed your blindfold!" I said as I removed the headset. "That's what you meant by *see her at all*!"

"I couldn't help it. She said something about video, and I had to see. When she speaks, I can see her on this square on the device. And this room is beautiful! There are all kinds of paintings of Debbie and water and swimming creatures. And there are books with pictures. More swimming creatures and in caverns. Here's a book showing buildings. Wow. And strange-looking self-powered carts. Why, it's like a whole new experience, a whole new world. We've got to learn everything about Debbie."

"Debbie Dayla," I said. "And I'm guessing Sparfy is in some paintings and pictures."

"As I was saying, we've got to learn everything about this Debbie Dayla, and we should learn about this Bioprog, too. I wonder if we could make beasts of burden. Maybe even servants. Think of it, Eren. We could have servants do whatever we need. That would give us the freedom and power to do anything we want. Anything!"

"Anything?" I repeated. "Like Solina's anything? Power for warfare? To set up a master ruler like the elders do to us? I'm tired of the push from on high. 'Pushing agenda puts people agin ya,' as my mother used to say, and I'm against anything pushed as agenda. Should we decide to use this device to create servants and enforce power over others, we would be guilty of pushing agenda, not to mention the questionable ethics of creating servants to begin with. It screams slavery no matter how you look at it."

"I'm sorry, Eren. I'm just so excited about the Bioprog. We *could* learn a lot from it. Maybe it could even cure your blindness," Chrba said.

"We need to learn about our surroundings," I said. "How many more of these devices are buried in hills or mountains? There's the Ayma, this Bioprog, and who knows what else? Maybe the elders have a device in their mountain. Maybe they've been using it against us for years without our knowledge. I need to find out."

"It's just that...well...I want to learn more about the Bioprog. What else does Debbie Dayla say?" Chrba asked.

"Let's see," I said. "In truth, you don't want to listen as much as you want to see. I warned you what would happen if you removed your blindfold. Still, I have my blindness undisturbed, so perhaps this isn't such a bad thing. Here. Take the headset. I'm going to explore the device using Belsl's control belt."

Chrba placed the headset on her head, and Debbie's voice and image continued to describe the Bioprog. The Bioprog, in addition to storing a large library of DNA samples, contained a vast amount of raw materials for producing organic things, and it contained a built-in thorium power source.

"How can this hold so much stuff?" Chrba asked. "It's way too small to hold much of anything."

Debbie explained that the heart of the device was a mass compressor that stored the DNA library, the vast amounts of materials, and the thorium reactor. The Bioprog could also produce essential materials for life, such as basic food, water, and medicine.

"This really is the greatest device ever created," Chrba said. "I'd even say it's better than the Ayma."

Chrba's interest was now so great that she all but worshiped the Bioprog, and that worried me, because nothing is forever, and the laws of the universe say power received quickly leaves just as quickly and is diminished. I didn't want Chrba to be diminished beyond her control. I wanted her to be around as my friend for many years to come.

"Well the first thing we need to do is remove the Bioprog from this hill," Chrba said. "Ugh, I can't lift it."

My hand had been on the wall of the Bioprog, and I had learned much of the device's internal workings just by sensing their places. Yes, Debbie had made provisions for moving the Bioprog, but there were locks in place to prevent those with impure hearts from moving it, and this prevented Chrba from lifting it. Yet I was able to collapse the device, unlatch its locks, and then lift it with ease. This device wasn't supernatural or anything—a symbiotic link between the operator and the Bioprog was required. This link allowed the operator to control the Bioprog, but then the Bioprog had the power to monitor the operator's body in the utmost detail. Apparently, those with impure hearts create detectable chemicals that appear in the blood stream and differ from those more considerate.

"How is it you can lift it, but I cannot?" Chrba asked as I made the device expand.

"I unlocked it," I said.

"I must figure out that trick—how to lock and unlock. Could come in handy. Debbie says there are multiple videos with educational material on using the Bioprog."

"Those videos may be helpful, but they are lacking key bits of information," I said.

"How do you know, and why would they be lacking?" Chrba asked. "I wish I could lift this thing."

"The videos are designed as a first defense against those who would abuse the power of the Bioprog," I said. "And I know because I've been in direct contact with the device."

"But Debbie is so real and authentic. And I've tried a few things. So far the things she's told me and the things I've tried are true and work," Chrba said. "Look. I can make what they called a steak burger. See? And here's beer to drink with it. Try it."

I sampled the steak burger and the beer. Both I spat out immediately.

"Yes, I do *see*," I said. "I can *see* how heavy it is."

"But you've raised chickens. This is a different kind of meat. And this beer—"

"Is all just too much for me. It's enough to make me switch to eating plants and nothing else," I said. "But then again, the Bioprog has a secret that you won't learn from Debbie's videos. You'll notice on watching that Debbie never eats nor drinks."

"So?"

"So," I continued. "She didn't need to, at least not in the end. Her body was converted to a life without consuming other life. That's the answer, Chrba, to all this fighting and killing. Why do people fight anyway? To consume. Whether it's to take our food or our space or to push agenda and consume our freedom, that's what consumers do. Debbie tried to convert her world, but they didn't want it. It's a paradox, if you think about. Debbie was pushing an agenda of non-agenda through non-consumption. I don't think people have changed much since then. I could be wrong, and maybe I should try to be sure, but my guess is they'll reject a long life without food over a short life with food."

"I...how can a person live without food?" Chrba asked. "Everyone must eat."

"Do the plants eat?" I asked. "But they are forms of life."

"Debbie is a plant? Was a plant? No. She could move and talk," Chrba said.

"But think if we could be like the plants and draw energy from the sun," I said, "then we—"

"I don't think there'd be a way to get that much energy from the sun," Chrba said.

"But there could be other sources of energy," I said. "Debbie found it. I wish I could. And you could too."

"Sounds scary. Like it would kill us. Let's just take this device and make our own village of exotic plants and animals. We're young and have plenty of time to think about living forever," Chrba said.

I smiled.

"I'm debating whether to take the Bioprog with us or leave it here," I said.

"We can't leave it here," Chrba said. "How then could we use it? Besides, someone could steal it."

"I could lock it back to the floor, and we could cover up the entrance," I said.

"We could also take it back to the Auberge and lock it there. Or we could find a new place and lock it there. No one need steal it," Chrba said. "Look, I'll make a backpack for you to use—completely organic."

Using the headset, Chrba spoke, and the Bioprog produced a backpack.

"You make a compelling argument," I said. "And with a backpack, it would be very easy to carry the Bioprog back. I could compress the Bioprog enough to where the backpack would hold it. Like this."

I took the device, compressed it, and placed it in the backpack.

"Still, a tool of power like this draws the unwanted," I said. "I'm not sure how we'll evade detection."

"I'll help you there," said a voice at the doorway.

"Elder Gavak!" Chrba yelled. "I thought you were killed!"

Elder Gavak laughed and entered the room with four sentries behind.

"Grab them and that device!" he ordered.

There was no time to pull the Bioprog out of the backpack and secure it to the floor. I had barely enough time to instruct the Bioprog to go into self lockdown when one sentry held me and the other grabbed the backpack. The backpack was handed to Elder Gavak. Then the sentries dragged us outside and placed us on a wagon. Elder Gavak sat with us, but the device was placed in a wagon behind us. Elder Gavak gave a whistle, and men pulled both wagons forward.

"I don't understand," I said. "This device was hidden in that hill for years. But how did you find it and us?"

"Thank Solina for that," Elder Gavak said.

"She would never betray us," Chrba stated.

"Not in the way you think," Elder Gavak said. "But we were scouting for a device taken from the Auberge."

"What device?" Chrba feigned.

"My dear, you know very well what *device*," Elder Gavak said. "My friend, Elder Ecton, has a way with *devices*. He had noticed a new diota-wave *device* in the Skulava vicinity. Word is your friend Solina took this *device* from the Auberge. We did not know it existed before."

"Yes," Elder Ecton said. "The Auberge has a shielding that prevents us from probing it. We suspected there was activity between the women in Skulava and the Auberge, but we could not prove it."

"But your Solina and her friends made that quite known," Elder Gavak said. "We were tracking her device but then received a new signal from the hill you were in."

"It too has a diota-wave signature," Elder Ecton said. "All of these tools of power give off diota waves. See?"

Elder Ecton showed Chrba and me a flat hand-held display showing two waves diverging and converging in the shape of a two-handled vase.

"Technology? Is that plain and equal?" I asked.

"No it is not. But someone must watch over you Skulavians," Elder Gavak said. "And a good thing too. It's clear that you and Chrba are NOT plain and equal. You seek progress. And so must those in the Auberge! This is exactly what we have preached against. And what has it gotten you? What? Nothing but trouble and death! Exequis will be issued against you both."

"You can't just kill us!" Chrba said. "You'd have to kill yourselves too for not being plain and equal."

"Those who set the rules are the first to break them," I said. "That's something my mother told me."

"She did not invent it," Elder Gavak said. "It's an ancient saying. We know many such sayings. If you were a man, I would take you to our great device of knowledge and power. You would learn much about the ancient world and why it perished. You see, only men are responsible enough to deal with power. Women go crazy with power. It is why they must remain plain and equal, for their own sake."

Chrba spat at Elder Gavak, and he laughed.

"Exactly!" Elder Gavak said. "You make my point very well, Chrba. My words to you are knowledge. Knowledge is power, but you cannot handle my words, and so you cannot handle power. That is the nature of a woman."

Chrba was about to spit at Elder Gavak again when I stopped her.

"A-hah! You do have some control after all," Elder Gavak said to me.

"Your word games don't impress us," I said.

"Oh but they are not games," he said.

"Yeah they are. If you have so much power, how is it you couldn't stop Solina from killing Elder Zatto?" Chrba squawked.

"Chrba!" I said.

"So! Solina worked some devilry to kill the chief elder! And we all thought he choked to death. Now I see I have underestimated Solina and her army this entire time. How did she do it? Delayed poison?"

Chrba shuddered a little at the mention of poison.

"Yes, it was. And thank you for answering in the affirmative. Your body language gives you away," Elder Gavak said.

"I wouldn't put too much faith in your eyesight," I said. "It gives you the worst of vision."

Elder Gavak waived his hand in front of my face.

"You're blind. But it cannot be. The only girl your age who would be blind is dead," Elder Gavak said.

"She's not dead! Erebellasia is alive and well," Chrba blurted.

Elder Gavak laughed.

"Erebellasia! Er-e-be-llaaaaa-sia!" Elder Gavak mocked.

"So what happens now?" I asked.

"I told you already. We will take you back to the mountains to fulfill the exequi," Elder Gavak said.

"Such a waste! All of this is a waste!" Chrba said. "What good can come of this?"

"One cannot let progress get in the way of equality," Elder Gavak said.

"So true," Elder Ecton said. "But we should not kill them just yet."

"Why not?!" Elder Gavak barked.

"They may know something about the device in the other wagon. We may need their help to unlock its secrets, as Solina appears to have done with her device," Elder Ecton said.

"We don't need this daughter of the traitor Inasherry and the blind daughter of a wanna-be traitor Cuperia to aid your studies," Elder Gavak said. "If you're so worried about cracking the device, remove yourself from this royal wagon and ride with the cargo!"

Elder Ecton held silent and didn't move.

"Well?!" Elder Gavak asked.

But Elder Ecton said nothing. Elder Gavak instructed the driver to stop the royal wagon, and the cargo wagon that followed also stopped.

"Get out," Elder Gavak said to Elder Ecton.

"I...would rather stay here," Elder Ecton said.

"WE GO NOWHERE UNTIL YOU LEAVE THE ROYAL WAGON!" Elder Gavak roared.

Elder Ecton got up slowly, jumped down from the royal wagon, and walked to the cargo wagon. He climbed aboard it slowly and disappeared from view.

"Move on," Elder Gavak instructed the driver.

The men began pulling the royal wagon, and the cargo wagon was pulled along too.

"There, you see? Civility," Elder Gavak said to Chrba and me.

The ride to the mountain was slow. Elder Gavak went into one of his many sermons about the equality of women. Chrba stared outside at the passing landscape, and I...well, I could not stare anywhere. I concentrated on connecting with the Bioprog, but I needed to touch it to unlock it, and that was impossible at the moment. Then I thought about what was said about diota waves and these "tools of power". Was that how one communicated with them? Could I use the control belt for much the same? I hummed ever-so-quietly to myself in hopes of activating the control belt. The belt tingled a little, and I felt a faint connection with the Bioprog, but instead of being able to tell it to attack or make creatures for defense, I slipped into a daydream...

"We should see if we can navigate it," Chrba said in my daydream.

We were in some sort of aircraft, a device I could not have imagined by myself. But there we were, and on the wall in large letters was the name Sara Vossy.

"We can explore and look for Cuperia and see what else is happening. Let's go to what is called the cockpit," Chrba said.

And we did just that. Chrba sat in the pilot's chair and I in the co-pilot's chair.

"I bet I could learn all these buttons if I had enough time with that headset," Chrba said.

"No need. I know all we need to know," I said.

I pressed several buttons, and the energy section powered up into an activated state. A mass compressor released fuel into the thrusters, and the Sara Vossy blasted dirt and debris away from the aircraft. My control belt tingled but otherwise did nothing else.

"Strange," I said. "I should feel a connection with the Sara Vossy."

"Your belt is over your tunic," Chrba said. "Perhaps the belt must touch your skin."

I placed the belt under my tunic and around my waist. I tightened it so that my skin would have good contact with the belt.

"Interesting," I said. "I can feel it getting warmer. And warmer. Oh, it's getting tighter on me."

"Remove it," Chrba said.

"I can't," I said. "It's stuck. And still it's getting tighter. I'm having trouble breathing."

"You have to remove it! It will kill you. Oh why do you have to trust these devices? Everything manufactured is evil!" Chrba said.

The belt grew wider. It flexed and reshaped my middle, becoming a dynamic corset.

"Oo, oo, oo," I said, trying to breathe with the added pressure on my abdomen.

"Your eyes are about to burst out of your head!" Chrba said. "And your tunic! It's shrinking around your body—skin tight!"

"I feel like everything is about to burst!" I said. "This belt is incredibly hot, and it has shrunken my tunic. Wait, it's not squeezing any more than it was."

"You mean it's releasing the pressure?" Chrba asked.

"No, the pressure is still there, but the pressure is not rising," I said. "Let me breathe. In, out, in out."

I coughed to see if I still could. I could.

"Are you going to make it? I mean, that belt thing isn't going to kill you, is it?" Chrba asked.

"I don't think so. It certainly has more blood pumping to my head. Well, maybe that was the intent. I can think much more clearly," I said. "Link is complete. Time to get the Sara Vossy moving."

I sent the directive to the Sara Vossy, and it lifted vertically.

"We're going up!" Chrba exclaimed. "You did it! We can go anywhere!"

"I must concentrate," I said, "or this could be a one-way trip to our end!"

The Sara Vossy lifted higher and higher. We ascended above the cloud deck, and the blue sky became darker and darker until it was all black. I could not see this with my own eyes, but my connection with the Sara Vossy gave me this information.

"Eren!" Chrba yelled. "It's too high! And I feel so heavy! I...can't move! Eren! Help! We're too far away from the ground! Oh, we'll be lost forever! We...we..."

The rate of acceleration pulled the blood from Chrba's brain and forced her to pass out, but the belt had kept the blood flowing to my brain, and so I was able to stay awake. But I had to do something quickly, or else Chrba would die. I concentrated as hard as I could.

The Sara Vossy stopped ascending, and Chrba awoke suddenly, convulsing and shaking uncontrollably.

"Easy, Chrba," I said.

I placed a hand on her, and she stopped shaking.

"Where are we?" she asked. "I feel very light. Look, I can jump with little effort. And the stars are so brilliant."

"I'll turn the Sara Vossy," I said, and I did.

"What's that blue and white circle?" Chrba asked.

"That's where we live," I said.

"Oh! It's much smaller up here. And it looks so fragile, like a great giant could pick it up and crush it in her hand," Chrba said.

"Let's hope that doesn't happen," I said. "We should go back down now."

"Please! I'm getting dizzy or something. My sinuses are all plugged up," Chrba said.

I concentrated, and the Sara Vossy approached our planet, which grew larger in the window. But then our speed picked up, and forces pushed Chrba and me back in our seats.

"I feel like we're falling backward!" Chrba yelled. "Too fast! I feel like... like...passing out."

"Hold on, Chrba. I'll try to slow us down," I said.

I focused on the controls, but the Sara Vossy continued flying toward the ground. The clouds grew quickly, and we were upon them.

"We're going to die!" Chrba yelled.

"I don't know why the link is failing," I said. "I told it to slow down. I want it to. I need it to. I need...no, I don't need. Let the Sara Vossy and our world be soft and beautiful like a butterfly on a spring day."

The Sara Vossy slowed and floated its way back to the ground, or at least it seemed that way. We landed on a plateau, and I realized we had not just landed on any plateau, it was *the* plateau—the one where the Plateauians lived. Chrba and I exited the craft, and we were surprised that no one rushed over in excitement to the Sara Vossy. In fact, the people continued about their business of herding sheep and hauling grain.

"I feel invisible," Chrba said. "It's like no one can see us."

"They can't be all blind," I said. "I hear no clicking."

"What about you?" Chrba asked. "I don't hear you clicking."

"The belt continues to give me sensory perception of place," I said. "And you still have your blindfold off, because I hear no clicking of the lid and thimble."

"Can't help it," Chrba said. "Ever since I saw the Sara Vossy, I couldn't keep my eyes closed."

"Except for when you passed out," I said.

"Except for that," Chrba said. "Well, perhaps we can find someone in charge."

"The belt tells me my mother is here," I said. "We should find her first."

We walked amongst the villagers, completely unnoticed, with me leading the way.

"That belt is a handy thing," Chrba said. "Maybe we could make another one using the Sara Vossy."

"You were telling me to be rid of it a moment ago, that it would kill me," I laughed.

"Well now that I see it won't, I don't see a problem," Chrba said.

"We don't know the long-term effects," I said. "It may yet kill me. One never knows with these tools of power."

"I guess I've never thought of a belt as a tool of power. The Sara Vossy seems more like a tool of power than the belt."

"But the belt controls the Sara Vossy, so it in a sense is a tool of power," I said.

"And you hinted that the Sara Vossy controls you back, so it may consider you a tool of power," Chrba said.

"I've never thought of it like that," I said.

"So where is your mother?" Chrba asked.

"She's in the market building," I said. "Let's go inside."

We went inside, and I was surprised to find a relatively quiet marketplace. Where was the shouting and general chaos? Instead, people proceeded orderly from shop to shop and communicated barely above a whisper.

"It's so quiet that I could click my way around if need be," I said.

"Like the living dead almost," Chrba said. "Where is your mother?"

"At the shop near the very end," I said.

We walked through the marketplace, and I clicked my tongue against the roof of my mouth—not because I needed to, but because I wanted to know if I could use clicking to see in such a quiet place—and I could.

"I wish our old village had such a nice marketplace," Chrba said. "But I suppose the riot has destroyed what little marketplace we had to begin with."

We reached the next-to-last shop, and the belt told me that the woman wrapping goods in a package for a customer was my mother.

"We must have missed her," Chrba said. "I don't see Cuperia anywhere."

"She's here," I said. "Surely you see her by now."

"There are only these customers and shop folk. This one woman is dressed in heavy clothing. It's a wonder it doesn't drag her to the ground," Chrba said.

"That's my mother. That's Cuperia!" I said.

I walked over to Cuperia and touched her. As Chrba had described, Cuperia was heavily covered in clothing such that only her eyes were visible to others.

"Cuperia!" I said in a loud voice.

Others turned toward my direction in surprise and dismay—that much I could sense.

"Please, do not raise your voice," Cuperia said. "You are not from around here. Please, take a look at these goods and make a fair offer."

"Don't you remember me? Your own daughter? I'm Eren," I said.

"Eren?" Cuperia asked, not seeming to remember.

"Erebellasia!" I said.

"I...you look familiar," Cuperia said.

"And I'm Chrba," Chrba said. "Do you remember me? My full name is Cherabina."

"Cherabina and Erebellasia—no, I don't remember you two," Cuperia said.

"You must remember our hut," I said. "And the cave you hid me in? Because I'm blind? And the elders wanted me killed."

"And here are the elders!" said Elder Gavak.

"How did you get here?" Chrba demanded.

Elder Gavak laughed. Five sentries followed him up.

"My sentries have been searching the countryside for you, Cherabina, and here you deliver yourself and Cuperia's daughter to the very place I wish you to be," Elder Gavak said.

"No one is being delivered," I said.

Elder Gavak laughed again.

"You see," Elder Gavak started, but he waved his hand in front of my eyes. "No, you *don't* see. You're still blind. It does not matter. The exequi against you is still in effect. But there's time. You need not be executed right away. I have plans for you and Cherabina in my new domain. There was too much freedom in Skulava. Despite our best efforts to train the women to remain equal, still there were some who would not conform. But here, all women conform, thanks to this. It's called *calemear*. It will make you as *calm* as a *clam*."

He held something in his hand, a vial of fluid.

"Let's get out of here!" Chrba yelled.

Chrba fought and flailed away, but the sentries held her. I stood my place, sensing the contents of the vial.

"You do not fear us as Chrba does?" Elder Gavak said.

"The vial contains an ionic mixture of cadmium, lead, mercury, and arsenic," I said, using the belt to sense the contents and purpose of the vial. "You use it to...poison the women's minds!"

"What!?" Chrba reacted.

"It's toxic! It will give them brain damage!" I said.

"That's unethical!" Chrba yelled.

"Who says so?" Elder Gavak said. "You Cherabina? The one with blood on her hands for being in league with murderers and thieves? And you, daughter of Cuperia, you're just a stupid, blind woman. What do you know about anything? A woman doesn't have a mind as it is. There's nothing to damage or poison."

The sentries laughed. And all along, Cuperia stood there and did not react.

"You poisoned her too!" I said. "With calemear!"

"Eren! Do something!" Chrba yelled.

"Eren!" Elder Gavak said with glee. "So that is your name!"

"Her full name...is...Erebellasia," said a voice.

The voice was Cuperia's!

"Mother! You remember!" I said.

"I only remember things. I do not have feelings for them," Cuperia said.

"I'm going to give you one warning," I said. "Withdraw all men from this village, or I will do it for you!"

Where did that come from? I surprised myself by saying such a thing. However, Elder Gavak and the sentries laughed.

"You? A blind girl?" Elder Gavak chuckled. "Well, you've given us a good laugh for the moment. Time to begin your first treatment. More sentries for Eren!"

Four more sentries entered the area, and they held me. I don't know what I was thinking making that threat. What could I do? Now I had regrets for not listening more to Solina. Knowledge is fine, but now I needed help.

"I am a statue. You cannot change me. I am invisible. You cannot see me," I said.

I then thought about the Sara Vossy and the journey Chrba and I took high above the ground, that moment of sheer terror followed by fantastic freedom. And then I saw what I needed to see. Tiny particles so incredibly small that they were beyond the vision of any device devised by humans. But I could see them. They were incredibly fast, so fast that light was a turtle by comparison. And they alternated between forming spheres of influence around larger particles, and shooting around to find other larger particles around which they formed spheres of influence. They were like electrons, but on a smaller scale—they formed the bits of innards that made up electrons, protons, and neutrons. I didn't even know those terms by myself—this knowledge had all come from the Sara Vossy through the belt. But it was the speed of these tiny particles that gave the illusion that they had a sense of place and form. It was like a grinding tool with a broken cut-off wheel. Spinning at incredibly high revolutions per heartbeat, the little bit of broken wheel gave the sense of a full, solid wheel.

That was what these elders and their men were. They were little points of nothing that only gave the sense of large power and strength by keeping one step ahead of their victims. They had suppressed knowledge and free thought from the women in Skulava, and this was how they kept that one step ahead and gave the sense of being a full circle of the grinding wheel when they were in fact just a broken-off piece of stone.

But the Skulavian control had failed, and that was their ultimate destiny wherever they went. It was just a matter of time, and their time had to be slowed so that others could catch up and see the evil of their ways. I would slow them down. I would do it now.

And therein lay the problem. The jayladopa had worn off. My mind slowed, and I could hardly stay awake—all before Elder Gavak had administered the calemear.

"Eren, fight it!" Chrba urged. "Stay awake!"

It was too much drowsiness to fight. Elder Gavak placed the syradermic needle full of calemear in my arm. I felt a pinch. A pinch...

"Eren, are you well?" Chrba asked.

We were back in the wagon, and she was pinching me in the arm. The wagon had stopped, and it soon became clear we had arrived at the Elders' little village in the mountains.

"Don't worry," Elder Gavak said. "We won't keep you long. Your execution will be quick and merciful."

"To kill for such petty things makes you yourself petty," I said.

Elder Gavak did not like that, and he punched me in the jaw.

"That will shut you up for a bit," he said.

His sentries pulled Chrba and me from the wagon and paraded us around the mountain village. Men of all ages cheered and jeered.

"This is your court and your trial," Elder Gavak said. "And all find you guilty of progress. You will understand what it is like to pay the ultimate penalty for your treason."

Sentries tied us up to a post in the center of the little village. I heard liquids being poured around us, and I smelled animal oils.

"They're going to burn us alive," Chrba said. "They're all savage animals. The sentries take pleasure in doing their job. I can tell. Looks like Elder Ecton has taken the Bioprog to a side hut. Oh Eren, how I wish Solina were here to bust through their ranks and give them all broken teeth."

"Interesting that she has not," I said. "She was intent on fighting the elders."

"She may be planning a way to break through the front gate," Chrba said. "There's a barrier that we passed through. I can't explain exactly what it was. It was like a wall made of slushy ice and water, but it held its shape, yet little ripples flowed around this strange barrier, like ponds had been turned on their sides and then fashioned into walls."

"That's not natural," I said.

"No, it's not," Chrba said.

"They must have a device for controlling that," I said. "If only I could get this control belt to search for that device."

"Please hurry," Chrba said.

"If only I had more time," I said.

"Gavak," called an old woman from the distance.

"Who's that?" I asked.

"I've never seen her before," Chrba said. "She's not from Skulava."

"Gavak, aren't you forgetting something?" she called.

"Yes, Mother," Gavak said.

"That's twice now you've forgotten," she said as she walked toward us. "I told you after Inasherry's punishment that there would be no executions until I had a chance to meet with the accused."

"She's your mother?" I asked. "I didn't think any women lived up here."

"She is Kuianka, beloved and honored by all in these parts. You will not speak to her without being spoken to first," Elder Gavak said.

Kuianka laughed.

"So this is Cuperia's daughter, Erebellasia. Also known as Eren. And Inasherry's daughter, Cherabina. You see, Gavak, you have neglected another detail. Since Cuperia's daughter is alive and well, she is guilty of harboring an illegal child of Skulava. Sentries! Bring out Cuperia and tie her to the same stake as her daughter!"

The sentries pulled out someone from a prison hut, I speculated. Her gag was removed, and she began shouting.

"You are the most despicable woman ever to set foot on land," Cuperia said. "To think that killing these girls will accomplish anything is foolhardy. What measure of equality will it bring? You have what you want, me. Yes, I kept Erebellasia a secret so that she may have life. You condemn others from your contempt, and the equality of this mantra is that others condemn you just as much."

"Hah!" Kuianka said.

"It is true!" Cuperia said. "What you do to others will be done to you! This is your equality!"

"Put the gag back on," Gavak said.

"Are you afraid to hear the truth?" Cuperia asked.

"There is no truth, only deception," I caught myself saying.

Cuperia was surprised but also saddened. Grief welled up in her, and she was speechless. As she was being tied up, she did her best to touch my hand with hers.

"If only there were more time, we could entertain such philosophical discussions," Kuianka said. "Alas, time itself is guilty of progress, and we must allay that. But I will say this—things are out of balance, and that balance must be restored. That is the equality under test. And it begins here. You three are part of Solina and her kind, the lesser equals. You have murdered many elders including my beloved eldest son, Elder Zatto. And so you can especially appreciate this, Cuperia. Your group took my son, and so I take your daughter. Equality is met. Case closed."

I focused on my belt, and I established a weak link with the Bioprog. Elder Ecton was attempting to understand its workings, but the device kept shocking him.

"Give me the torch, Gavak. It's time," Kuianka said.

Elder Gavak passed a torch to Kuianka. Kuianka waved the flames about in a ritualistic fashion.

"Ironic, isn't it? I mean, here Elder Gavak was talking about how women can't handle power, and this Kuianka woman has the power over the elders," Chrba said.

"You said that, Gavak?" Kuianka said.

"I, uh, was just making a point," Elder Gavak said nervously.

"I'll deal with you later," she said. "Now to set these criminals afire!"

"Chrba, now is not the time for ironies," Cuperia said.

"Start humming softly," I said. "Both of you. Follow my lead."

And they did. Cuperia and Chrba hummed musical notes one might do when celebrating a spring day or fresh fruit after a harsh winter. And I hummed with them. Then I clicked in rhythm to our humming. The Bioprog activated lightly, and it produced a visual display of Cuperia, Chrba, and me, rising above the fire that was about to be set upon us. Elder Ecton came rushing out of his hut with the Bioprog, crazed with terror, and he threw the Bioprog in the middle of the little village, not far from me.

"What is the meaning of this, Ecton?" Kuianka asked.

Elder Ecton fell to his knees and quivered.

"Speak now or I'll set the fire to you!" Kuianka ordered.

"It's...it's..." Elder Ecton stuttered.

"Bring it here, Gavak," Kuianka ordered.

Elder Gavak picked up the Bioprog and brought it over.

"It seems you have managed this last bit of trickery before final punishment," Kuianka said. "A holographic projection? For what purpose?"

"It's bedeviled!" Elder Ecton said. "I cannot master it...it will bring our doom!"

"That little thing? Nothing is as powerful as the Sara Vossy!" Kuianka bragged.

The Sara Vossy! So the aircraft wasn't just a dream. It must really exist. But where? And did Kuianka somehow derive power from it? Or perhaps Elder Ecton did.

"I have mastery over the biopropagation device," I shouted. "Should you kill me, the device will seek revenge on all those here!"

The men grew quiet. Some muffled gasps. Others whispered.

"Is that a challenge?" Kuianka asked. "You are hardly in a position to bargain. But I will defer your execution on this stipulation—you unlock access to this biopropagation device, teach Elder Ecton and Elder Gavak how to use it, and I will grant you a stay for two days. You will have time to spend with your friend and your mother to seek proper closure. That will bring true equality to your life."

"I am not responsible for your actions or your purported deals," I said. "I will grant *you* a two-day stay of revenge if you turn over control of the Sara Vossy to us three."

"What!?" Kuianka exploded. "How dare you. How dare you! You impudent blind cave rat. Do you think by toying with me you can bluff your way with this blind folly? Ecton—throw your bedeviled device in with the three. Let them all burn!"

But Ecton would not move.

"Ecton? Should we add you to the list?!" Kuianka shouted. "Very well. Sentries, tie Elder Ecton to the stake with the women. Let the fire equal out all things."

The sentries tied Elder Ecton to our stake.

"You kill your own elders?" I said. "People, hear me! Your enemy is not progress or equality or other such free words. It is the enslaving words of this woman you call Kuianka. Why throw your lives away for these mere sounds? Seek instead the sounds of music. Music has no bonds of murder."

But the sentries and other elders were paralyzed with fear. Elder Ecton was now secured to the stake, the Bioprog was tossed in at our feet, and Kuianka threw the torch at us. But as she did, I made new contact with the Bioprog, and out flapped a white-collared kite (the bird not the toy). It quickly expanded to the size of one of us, and it caught the torch in its beak and flew about the village terrorizing the sentries and elders. The elders ran for shelter while sentries attempted to fend off the kite, but it extended its claws and picked up the sentries' weapons and tossed them aside. Then it threw the torch at a particularly large hut, and it caught fire. Sentries hurried to put it out, but the kite fended them off and instead dismantled the other huts to feed this new flame.

"It's incredible!" Chrba shouted. "Such a beautiful bird capable of great destruction. But I'm scared, Eren. Scared!"

"Eren, we are not safe here," Cuperia said. "The bird is tossing logs and things all about. We're liable to be hit!"

"Don't worry, Cuperia! I'll save Eren's bird the trouble and end your lives right now," Kuianka said. "Behold!"

The side of the mountain collapsed, creating a cloud of dirt. The kite backed away from what emerged from the mountain—the Sara Vossy. It was Debbie Dayla's clone of the American Space Shuttle, and it now hovered in the air.

"You have made one critical mistake, Eren. There is strength in numbers. Always has been and always will," Kuianka said.

A hatch opened on the side of the Sara Vossy, and a flood of rats poured out. The kite flew down and attempted to toss the rats aside, but there were so many of them. The rats encircled us four, building a wall upon themselves. I instructed the kite to hover and wait, and it did.

"Very wise, Eren. Your bird would only be caught in the massacre and be destroyed itself. So can you produce more birds? Isn't that the solution? Fight numbers with numbers?" Kuianka asked.

"I cannot win in a fight of numbers against numbers," I said.

"Of course not. Say goodbye then. The numbers always win," Kuianka said.

"The numbers may win but they are self consuming. All rats go hungry," I said.

I hummed a tune, and the Bioprog released waves to force the cells in the rats' bodies to release all stores of energy. The rats chased one another around the circle at increasing speed until they became a blur of light, and they—being consumptors of equal speed—consumed one another at equal rate until the equality of their existence formed a slurry-type cylindrical solid about us that released massive amounts of heat outward, leaving a crystal-clear cylinder of ice.

The heat blasted Kuianka and the others in the little village, setting them afire. Kuianka commanded the Sara Vossy to land so that she could escape and cure her third-degree burns. She rushed to the landing aircraft ahead of elders and sentries who ran to the Sara Vossy for the same aid. But the rule of equality was exchanged for the fight of survival, and only Kuianka and Elder Gavak made it to the Sara Vossy. The hatch closed, the Sara Vossy departed, and the others died of their burns.

All became quiet. The kite flapped dirt on all fires and put them out. Despite the oil around us, no fire reached us. The kite perched on top of the ice cylinder, tapped it, and a crack set through the fragile structure and shattered it instantly. Then the kite broke our bonds and set us free. Elder Ecton had survived with us, but he was now in mental shock and could not make sense of things.

"It's over," Chrba said.

"At least for now," I said.

"Kuianka will start a new regime," Cuperia said. "Those kind always do."

"And the cycle will start again," I said.

"But at least we don't have to be part of it," Chrba said.

"No, we don't," I said.

"Maybe we can rebuild Skulava," Chrba said. "The Bioprog can—"

"Can be a tool of success or massive failure," I said.

"If we realize that large numbers are self consuming but small numbers are self sustaining, there's a chance," Cuperia said.

"It will be difficult," I said. "Solina has her army, and she will want numbers."

"I've heard about her army," Cuperia said. "And about how Elder Zatto died. I also learned about the Sara Vossy, how a woman named Debbie Dayla hid it for fear the large numbers of corrupt people would rise again and use it as a tool of mass enslavement."

"Also known as mass equality," I said.

The kite perched on my shoulder and rubbed his beak on the side of my face.

"Then I think I'll follow the lead of someone who taught me well and keep the Bioprog a secret. Only us three should know, and the kite too. Let's explore what we can do with it," I said.

"I wonder who taught you?" Chrba grinned, hinting about Cuperia.

"I can't imagine," Cuperia laughed.

"What about Elder Ecton?" Chrba asked. "He knows about the Bioprog."

"He doesn't even know his own name," Cuperia said.

"Should we take him into our care?" I asked. "See if he can be rehabilitated? But I think my kite friend here is not just a bird, either."

"You are right," the kite said as he flapped from my shoulder and changed into humanoid form.

"You can change shapes?" Chrba asked. "You're a man now?"

"My name is Chusigi. I'm the son of Chusacuta and Circigi," the man said.

We all stood there in silence.

"I'm a seal," he said. "My parents were dolphins and could change shape too."

"You are a seal with dolphin parents? That's a story I'd like to hear! But your parents were dolphins like Sparfy, right?" I said. "That was Debbie Dayla's friend."

"That's right," Chusigi said. "I decided to stay on this planet, but to survive the wars, I asked Debbie to hide me in the biopropagation device. My parents had already left for Bruxima 5. It was my hope that this day would come."

"What is your hope?" Cuperia said.

"To see this planet become full of life again. To see something of beauty arise from the wars," Chusigi said.

I could feel Chusigi looking at me. Couldn't see him, just sensed his gaze.

"Maybe he could help create things of beauty," Chrba said.

"I think he's already found it," Cuperia said, and I blushed.

The four of us started our walk down the mountain, with a fresh sun to our backs. In the distance we could see the ruins of Skulava with Solina's army chasing the last of the stray sentries. Smoke arose from the ruins, and I knew we would have much work to do. Chusigi changed back into a kite, and he flew up very high and looked down, scouting a safe path but also protecting us from surprise. I was tired but happy, because I had Cuperia, Chrba, and my new beloved Chusigi.

Echoing through the mountain, as if a last sound before the close of the day, a grasp for sense of place gave us laugh for slumber.

"Ecton is here...wait for me!"

Suflessence

"Your body will not last much longer, Bedora," said Doctor Otot.

"What?!" Bedora responded with surprise. "What are you talking about? I feel fine. This physical is supposed to be routine. My blood pressure is good, my cholesterol is low, I exercise and eat right—what did I do wrong?"

"Nothing, from what I can see," the doctor replied. "But you have cancer, and it is spreading rapidly. You have only three days left. Maybe."

"Maybe? That's all I have left in life is a maybe? Maybe?!?"

"I am sorry. Really. But there is nothing we can do," Doctor Otot said.

The doctor left the examination room, and the nurse escorted Bedora through the hallway maze until she reached the exit. The receptionist asked for her copayment, but the first moments of her finality set in, and she decided she didn't need to pay for things any more. What was the worst society could do now, jail her? Sentence her to death?

"I'm already dead. There's nothing left for me," Bedora thought.

"Stop, stop!" the receptionist yelled.

Bedora didn't care. There was nothing that anyone could do to her that was worse than the death sentence the doctor had prescribed. She exited the clinic and was half-tempted to rush in front of a car on the crossing street, but she didn't.

"There she is. Get her!" the receptionist shouted to a security guard, who had burst forth from the clinic building.

Bedora ran across the street and into the parking structure where her car awaited. She jumped in and started the engine. But then another thought of death hit her—why did she need to drive anymore? What was the point? Bedora exited the car with the engine running and opened her purse.

"Do I need a driver's license or money or a grocery card or health insurance card anymore?" she asked herself.

No, she didn't. She dumped the purse and cards all on the ground and left them there, by the car, which was still running, and she proceeded from the parking structure down a distant flight of stairs and wandered the city. Bedora looked back and saw the flashing lights of a law enforcement vehicle bouncing around the inside of that parking structure.

"They are looking for me, at least the old me who was still alive," Bedora said. "But that doesn't matter now. The old me is gone. This is all I have left, this little walk through the city."

She walked through a residential neighborhood where it was quiet and dark. The sun had already set, and she could see people gathering for dinner in their respective homes.

"Food, what good is it now?" Bedora asked. "What good are houses or sidewalks or buildings or any kind of civilized structures?"

These questions and more filled her mind. House after house she passed. What was the point of it all? To work, eat, and sleep only to die at some unknown time?

"I suppose all of us know that we'll die, but we conveniently bury that thought under the common day-to-day desires," she said to herself. "Those desires will be gone from me soon. Very soon."

Houses changed to small shops, and as she passed one after another, wondering why people went to all the effort of running a store when death would take them anyway, her cellphone rang.

"I still have this thing? Get rid of it!"

Bedora threw it into an alley between stores, where it continued to ring.

"Hey you!" called a voice from the alley.

Why should Bedora listen? She was a nobody now, a non-participant in the society of the living, or so she thought.

"I'm calling you, and I expect you to answer!" the voice insisted.

Two youths emerged from the alley, one with something in her right pocket pointed at Bedora.

"This way," the first youth motioned, and Bedora realized the youth had a gun.

Bedora laughed.

"You think this is funny?" the youth said, and now she pulled out her gun in plain sight and pointed it at Bedora.

But a sudden sense of freedom overcame Bedora. Here she had been a slave to working for money to buy food, pay for a home, and pay homage to the various insurance industries, and this self-serving gun-youth believed herself to have real power over her environment.

"You're absurd. This is the absolutely last comment on humanity—from a punk with a gun," Bedora said.

"I have the power. I'm in control," the gun-youth said with a growing anger in her voice. "Give me everything you got, or I'll take your life."

"Take what you think you can take, but you'll find nothing. You're only one amongst billions in this world, and you have no more power over your fate or mine than anyone else," Bedora said. "So make your play. Shoot me."

"I'm serious!" she said.

The gun-youth's hand wavered a little. She motioned for her friend to search Bedora. Bedora stood there but felt detached, as if she were watching a bad movie.

"She's got nothing," the friend said.

"I don't believe it. She's obviously high on drugs. Where are your drugs, old lady?" the gun-youth asked.

But Bedora laughed again. The friend kicked Bedora behind the knee, and she fell. The youths continued to kick Bedora.

"Give me everything you got. Right now!" the gun-youth yelled.

There was no point in staying on the ground. Bedora stood up boldly, grabbed the pistol from the gun-youth's hand, and threw it down the alley (in the same direction as the thrown cellphone).

"You shouldn't have done that!" the gun-youth yelled.

The gun-youth pulled a second pistol from inside her waistband and shot Bedora three times in the chest. Bedora fell to the ground and bled. The youths yelled briefly before disappearing down the alley, where the gun-youth retrieved her first pistol. She was about to return and continue shooting, but a shopkeeper rushed out with her shotgun and fired it into the alley. The youths ran down the alley and disappeared.

"I'll call an ambulance," the shopkeeper said, and she dialed 911 on her cellphone.

"Don't bother. Let me die here," Bedora said.

The shopkeeper ignored Bedora's words and instead worked on controlling her bleeding until help could arrive. And help arrived. An ambulance hauled Bedora away and returned her to the very clinic where the doctor had given her the fatal news.

"You're going to be fine," a voice told Bedora as she was wheeled into an emergency operating room of the clinic.

Bedora looked up and saw her doctor! Doctor Otot was accompanied by several other medical folk. One placed a needle in Bedora's arm and administered something for pain, another stuck another needle in the other arm and fed blood into Bedora, others prepped Bedora's wounds, and Doctor Otot wasted no time in cutting Bedora open, removing the bullet fragments, and sewing tissues together.

"There," Doctor Otot said. "You'll make a full recovery."

"And what is that? What is a full recovery?" Bedora asked, but the doctor was already on the way out, and other medical personnel were transferring Bedora from the operating table to a wheelchair.

"What a strange life I have," Bedora said. "I have three days to live, and they stitch me up like I'll live another fifty years."

Bedora was wheeled to the receptionist's desk, yes, the very one where she decided not to pay. Only there was a police officer waiting.

"Spend the rest of my three days in jail?" Bedora mused. "Doesn't seem right."

But that's what happened. Shortly after Bedora indicated she was unable to pay, the officer arrested her and took her to jail. Bedora half-listened to the charges of failing to pay, car abandonment, running from the law, etc.

"It doesn't matter," Bedora said. "I'll die in three days."

The police clerk ignored Bedora and instead stated that Bedora would stay in jail all weekend and be up for court on Wednesday. And so Bedora was escorted to a shared prison. Lo and behold, there were the two youths who assaulted Bedora. Shortly after Bedora was locked up and left to these thugs, they assaulted her again, and Bedora fell unconscious.

"Ending my life in jail at the hands of two, young, naïve, selfish girls," Bedora thought, "will be the final nail of pathos in my coffin."

"You are lucky to be in my care again," Doctor Otot said as Bedora awoke in a recovery room. "Otherwise you'd be dead."

The doctor showed Bedora a bloodied bed spring that had been straightened on one end and shaped into a needle-like weapon.

"This is insanity. I'm either in here being patched up or out there being attacked so that I can be in here again," Bedora said.

Doctor Otot turned to a nurse and said, "The midazolam."

The nurse passed a small injection-spray bottle to the doctor. Doctor Otot inserted it into each of Bedora's nostrils and sprayed. Despite Bedora's complaints, she lost ability to express them vocally. Doctor Otot left the room with a smile, as did the nurse, and Bedora was alone. She wanted to speak, but she couldn't. The drug shut her up and kept her locked in this new vicious mental cycle of street compulsion and clinical seizure.

Bedora sat in a wheelchair, in an office-cubicle-sized area, with three walls and a curtain. The curtain was her privacy "door", and she wheeled toward the curtain and edged it open. A nurse appeared out of nowhere, pushed her back toward the far wall, and closed the curtain emphatically.

"Stay in here! Doctor's orders!" she barked.

Bedora wanted to stand up and speak her mind, but the midazolam chained her last bit of humanity to the chair. All she could do was stare at shadows on her curtain as other folk walked by.

"The third room on the left, Professor Wykepper," said the nurse down the way to an inquiring visitor.

Like every other person who had walked past, the visitor's shadow also passed across Bedora's curtain. Yes, the curtain wasn't very thick, giving Bedora some ability to observe when people walked by. Bedora heard the visitor enter the recovery room just past Bedora's room, and the visitor spoke to a woman.

"Curiami. I am Professor Wykepper. I know you even if you do not know me. You must leave here at once."

"I have not been released, Professor," Curiami said. "This Doctor Otot is very insistent that I wait until told otherwise."

"Your time and place is no longer bound to the ones who consume meat," Professor Wykepper said. "An unstable loss of *suflessence* has begun with you. It cannot be reversed. If we do not modulate it quickly, all that was once of conventional energy and respiration will dissolve away."

"How much time?" Curiami asked. "How much time before...before..."

"Before it's too late? We have perhaps an hour. Arrangements are already being made in the archarbor," Professor Wykepper said. "Curiami, a great many people will benefit from your transformation. They are there, now, and they await your help."

"Well how shall I leave here? Will we just walk out?" she asked. "Won't people notice?"

"People only notice those who eat the same meat that they do. Your time of eating meat is rapidly waning. They will notice you with the same small mind that they give a fluff of fur floating in the wind," Professor Wykepper explained. "Let's go, Curiami. You will see."

Professor Wykepper left Curiami's room and returned past Bedora's curtain. Bedora saw Wykepper's shadow, but not Curiami's, despite hearing her footsteps outside Bedora's room. Confused, Bedora wheeled herself to the "door" and peered beyond the curtain and down the aisle. She saw

Wykepper walking but saw no one else. Yet Wykepper held her arm to her side as if escorting another person, and she paused when she reached the end of the aisle.

"All done, Professor Wykepper?" the nurse asked.

"Yes, and I have a friend with me," Wykepper said, but the nurse saw no one.

"Of course," the nurse said to be agreeable. "Thank you for visiting."

Professor Wykepper turned a corner and escorted Curiami, but Curiami stopped suddenly and turned back. Bedora knew this, because instead of just seeing the professor, she saw a shape standing next to Wykepper, a shape resembling a white, conically pleated dress with interspersed sequences in between the pleats, like stars of the night or something, and it was the same height as the professor, but it moved as if controlled by a human.

"I see something, at least, I, well, what am I seeing?" Bedora asked.

"There is someone else," Curiami said. "Someone else does not belong here. This change...what did you call it? Suflessence? Someone else has it."

"Go then," Wykepper said.

Curiami returned toward Bedora. Bedora slunk back into her recovery room. The sedative was wearing off, faster than it should have, and her nerves began to ratchet up with tension.

"You know I am here," Curiami said.

Bedora was afraid. Of what? She wasn't sure. But Curiami opened the curtain anyway. Bedora looked, and the sequences glowed then swirled around her, leaving twinkling trails around her dress.

"My name is Curiami," she said. "And you are Bedora."

"How did you know? Did the nurse tell you?" Bedora asked.

"No. I didn't know until just a moment ago," she said.

"From suflessence?" Bedora asked.

"Yes," she said. "It fluctuates in you as it does in me—the last glowing embers of a campfire late in the night before dawn snuffs it out."

"What do you mean?" Bedora asked.

"You're dying," she said.

"I already know," Bedora said.

"Not that kind of dying," she said. "Your physical body is dying, yes, but another part of you is dying too."

Wykepper appeared in the doorway. She held her left hand close to Bedora and looked at what appeared to be a wristwatch on Wykepper's left wrist. But the wristwatch had a crystalline face and emitted swirling, glowing patterns when close to Bedora and a different pattern for Curiami.

"You see it, don't you?" Curiami asked.

"Yes. She has unstable suflessence, too," Wykepper said. "But hers is even weaker. She has maybe five minutes, ten at the most. I'm sorry, but we are too late."

"No, no, no!" Bedora cried. "I don't want to be too late. Help me! Please, help me!"

"We must help her," Curiami said to Professor Wykepper.

"We can't," Wykepper said. "If only we had discovered her sooner."

"How is it you were able to detect the suflessence in me but not in Bedora?" Curiami asked the professor.

"I don't know," Wykepper said. "It's a terrible puzzle—one that we won't have time to solve."

"But I have time," Curiami said. "You have some ability to harness this power, is that right?"

"Somewhat," Wykepper said. "But my tools are limited here."

"Well, we can wait no longer. You must transfer some of my suflessence to Bedora," Curiami said.

"You might not have enough to survive," Wykepper said. "If you lose too much, you will permanently devessitate."

Curiami paused only long enough to take a deep breath and gather her strength.

"If I am to help others," Curiami said, "I must begin now."

Wykepper, after a pause of her own, nodded in agreement.

"Very well. Hold onto each other," Wykepper said. "I will act as arbiter. Are you ready?"

"Yes," Curiami said.

"Yes," Bedora said.

Professor Wykepper placed her left hand on Bedora's head and her right hand on Curiami's shoulder. The professor hummed something, and then Curiami hummed in harmony. Suddenly, Bedora stood up as if pulled by a powerful force.

"I am ready," Bedora said.

But Curiami collapsed onto the floor. The sparkling sequences quiesced, and her form withered and paled.

"It was too much!" Professor Wykepper said.

Bedora knelt by Curiami and placed a hand on Curiami's shoulder.

"I had given up on the world just a moment ago. Now I want more than anything to live. And I want you to live too," Bedora said. "Come back with me. Come back!"

Swirls and eddies chased around Bedora, but they stayed with Bedora.

"It's not working," Bedora said.

"Focus your suflessence," Wykepper said. "Imagine your arms as if they formed a great megaphone."

Bedora spread her straight arms as if speaking to the world and then gradually bent them until they were cupped outward toward Curiami. Bedora then cupped her hands and moved them toward Curiami until they touched Curiami's head. The sparkling swirls and eddies now flowed from Bedora's hands and rejuvenated Curiami. Curiami took a sudden gasp of air, and Wykepper broke the link between the two.

"I...I couldn't let go," Bedora said. "How did you know?"

"I know, I know," Wykepper said. "Another moment more, and you would be permanently devessitated."

"Do we have enough time?" Bedora asked. "Enough time for the...whatever you called that place?"

"I hope so. We will go to the archarbor now," Wykepper said. "There we will modulate and reignite your suflessence as well as Curiami's. But we must hurry!"

Bedora helped Curiami to her feet, and the three exited the clinic without anyone noticing.

"You see, already you have changed markedly," Wykepper said to Bedora. "Your suflessence causes those who eat meat to ignore you."

"I don't understand all that," Bedora said.

"You will soon. I will explain much to you, but only after we reach the archarbor and you proceed through transuflessiation," Wykepper said.

Bedora and Wykepper helped Curiami into Wykepper's mode of transportation—a short, low-riding vehicle that was dome-shaped like a mid-20th century bus but low in height like a limousine, and it was powered by hydrogen-fueled steam.

"Oh this?" Wykepper said in reply to Bedora's silent question about the vehicle. "I call it the *boosmosine*. Or *boosmo* for short."

The boosmo chug-a-chugged along the road like an old-style locomotive. Its steam flowed in through the front windows, mixed with the suflessence from Bedora and Curiami, and exited the back window, creating a ghosting trail of vapor, some of which curled around the back corners and some of which trailed behind the bus, creating an obscurity that allowed the boosmo to pass unnoticed. The three arrived at the archarbor—a structure where two half-domes merged together, with one dome meeting above the seam of the other. A lot next to the archarbor was full of parked cars, and so Bedora knew there had to be many people inside.

"Help me carry Curiami in through the side entrance," Professor Wykepper said.

With Bedora under one shoulder and Wykepper under the other, the two helped Curiami walk from the boosmo to the side entrance. Wykepper opened the door, and the three entered, one at a time, though it was somewhat awkward.

"We need help here," Bedora said. "Call for an assistant."

"I have no assistant," Wykepper said. "It's just me."

With Wykepper leading the way, the two helped Curiami inside the archarbor to a place on the floor resembling a water fountain as one might find in a park, and it was directly below where the two domes met. One dome had a smaller radius than the other, and so this meant the meeting point was about one third of the way along the total length of the building. Arch supports ran from the floor up the dome walls and met at the top, while other supports ran helically and in different directions.

"Help Curiami sit," Wykepper said to Bedora.

Bedora and Wykepper helped Curiami sit on a marble bench that encircled the fountain. The bench had a corresponding table encircling the fountain, and so one could in theory sit and eat as if at the dinner table at the fountain, but Curiami was not there to eat. Her arms broke her fall only barely as she collapsed on the table.

"We have only moments left," Wykepper said.

The bench and table were open in three places around the fountain, and Wykepper walked through one of those openings toward the center of the fountain. Bedora followed closely behind. She held out her hand to what she thought was water spraying out of the fountain, but her hand did not get wet.

"It's not water," Wykepper said as she arranged crystalline stones in a pyramid configuration near the base of the fountain. "It's suflessence."

"I thought suflessence was in me and in Curiami," Bedora said.

"Like water, suflessence is both in you and around you. But unlike water, suflessence is very rare and much more precious," Wykepper explained.

Wykepper dropped one crystal into the fountain stream and then quickly rushed Bedora away, saying, "Hurry with me behind that wall."

"But Curiami. We can't leave—"

"No time for talk," Wykepper said.

The two rushed back through the opening of table and bench and then through an opening to a transparent wall encircling the bench, table, and fountain. Twinkling and swirling drops like water ushered upward from the fountain, but as stated earlier, these drops were not water. Then Bedora looked up and saw a light streaming from a point where the arches met.

"That's the *arbor accommodus remodulator*," Wykepper said.

"The what?" Bedora asked.

"Just call it the *arbodulus*," Wykepper explained. "It searches for unbridled suflessence, accumulates it, and restreams it into a modulated form. Look!"

Bedora saw that Curiami was now standing up. Curiami stepped onto the bench and then the table. The beam of light moved around her and the fountain as if tracking an oversized shared electron between the fountain and Curiami.

"Curiami is now going through transuflessiation," Wykepper said. "The natural suflessence inside of her is regenerating and changing her form."

"She looks the same to me, except for the brighter swirls around her," Bedora said.

"It is not how you see her, it's how others see her, and how she interacts with those others," Wykepper said. "But that's something...something new."

"What do you mean by *something new*? What about the other people you've studied who have this, you know, this suflessence?"

"Curiami is the first," Wykepper said. "I proved the existence of suflessence, at least on paper, and I built the archarbor building to focus the natural suflessence around us, but never did I detect it in people until a couple of days ago when I detected the first amounts in the clinic. That was when I first visited a sleeping Curiami and learned she was dying. The clinic cat, who only visits those who are dying, was already sleeping at the foot of her bed. This imitation wristwatch is linked to the arbodulus, and I used it to confirm Curiami's initial suflessence, and I also determined that the clinic cat has a similar detector in her olfactory glands. Had I realized this earlier, I might have saved myself thirty years of research in developing such a detector—I merely had to find the right cat!"

The light from the arbodulus stopped, and the extra fountain activity subsided and returned to normal flow.

"There. It is done," Wykepper said. "Now Curiami must recover in an arbochaise."

Bedora followed Wykepper to a side room, and the two pushed a *chaise longue* with legs on wheels and having two raised ends (like a *récamier*) but with the foot end shorter than the head, having armrests, and having a sloping middle for underknee support. They pushed until they reached the waterfall bench, and then they helped Curiami to the arbochaise and wheeled her only a very short ways to the head of many rows of pews, as if the archarbor were a church, but there was no altar and no stage. If one didn't know better, the fountain might be considered the central object of "worship", but in fact the fountain was only used for transuflessiation, and so far only used for that action this one time, and so its existence was often overlooked as no more than a curiosity or decoration.

"Now people will visit with Curiami as she recovers, and we will see how much she can help them," Wykepper said.

Bedora was about to ask what that all meant, but she felt very faint and collapsed onto the floor.

"Your strength is dissipating quickly, Bedora. We must get you to the fountain now!"

Wykepper helped Bedora to her feet and escorted her as quickly as possible to the fountain. Bedora was only semi-conscious. Was this death? She was sure of it. Her body felt numb, and she was at peace and ready to accept the final end, but Wykepper didn't want Bedora to pass away so easily, nor did Wykepper wish to let another opportunity at transuflessiation go to waste.

"It really doesn't matter anymore," Bedora said with a hazy voice as Wykepper ushered her to the fountain bench and helped her sit.

Bedora was running out of time. Knowing this, Wykepper then rushed to the fountain base and placed three more crystals from her pocket onto the other existing crystals and rearranged them. She then pulled one more crystal from her pocket and placed it in the fountain. The fountain rose to life much like before. Bedora felt a little strength return, and she began to stand, but the fountain suddenly sputtered and collapsed upon itself. Bedora did much the same on the bench and table.

"Grace becurse me!" Wykepper uttered.

Wykepper rushed to a side room and re-emerged within a few seconds holding two crystalline stones, one in each hand, and despite huffing heavily from exhaustion, she placed those crystalline stones onto the fountain and pulled herself back just before the fountain erupted in a furious frenzy. Deep oranges and reds mixed with black, and haze pushed upward from the fountain, the result of pleasant suflessence mixing with noxious agriecorsteck.

"I put too much in!" Wykepper said.

But Wykepper was too tired. The sprint for the crystals and the power of the fountain's shock waves kept Wykepper in place and prevented her from suppressing its effects on Bedora. Bedora remained motionless at first, and smoke escaped the pores of her skin. She was being consumed. And then, as if yanked on the strings of a puppet master, Bedora sprang to her feet and danced on the bench and table in the herky-jerky manner of that puppet on strings.

The needful people gasped and backed away from the violent fountain. It let out a roar and boom that pounded hearts and rattled bones. Bedora had lost all control of her body, and her skin turned dark red from the suflessi-agrieco radiation.

"I...must...stop...this..." Wykepper struggled to say, but the fountain's power retained its grip on her. "If I could but throw this suppressor crystal into the fountain, I...I..."

A hand touched Wykepper's, took the crystal, and walked toward the fountain.

"Curiami, no!" Wykepper pleaded.

But Wykepper was powerless to stop Curiami, who now had walked from the fountain wall to the gap between benches, between table, and to the fountain itself, where she placed the crystal in the fountain's base. The fountain engulfed the crystal and collapsed. Curiami was pulled atop the fountain's base and collapsed, and Bedora collapsed on a fountain table.

A heavy silence pressed downward from above. Curiami and Bedora were prone and unmoving, the crowd stood motionless in shock, and Wykepper struggled to clear her mind from the stupor the fountain had forced upon her. She managed to pull herself to her feet and take two steps toward the fountain, but then the arbodulus activated. It broadcast its rays onto Curiami and attempted to rejuvenate her, but Curiami did not move. The arbodulus then broadcast its rays onto Bedora. Bedora shivered, as if she were cold. She awoke, stood up, and reached up for some sort of imaginary coat, but the coat became real, having become fashioned by the waves and motions of Bedora's hands. It was a coat made of suflessence fibers that one who didn't know better would call strands of energy, but in fact the fibers were the transuflessed remnants of wood fibers, released from their storage in the archarbor's supporting joists. Bedora's skin changed into something resembling flexible, suede leather. This new skin gave her the appearance of wearing suede clothing, as her natural body had changed. Though her head, shoulders, and arms remained much the same form, her waist on down changed into a permanent sort of sealed dress concaving at the bottom, like the trunk of a tree where it meets the ground. Yet Bedora was able to move about through some sort of hovercraft-like ability as the bottom of her "trunk" expelled suflessence as propulsion. She could then glide around, and she did—she glided around the fountain's outside wall and around the archarbor.

But the immediacy of the situation brought Bedora back to the fountain, where Curiami's body was strewn. Wykepper walked to Curiami's body too, but Wykepper was at a loss for what to do next. Bedora lifted Curiami's body and returned it to the arbochaise.

"She is still alive," Bedora said. "But she lives by full suflessence now."

"And you?" Wykepper said. "I thought you were lost."

"I'm different from Curiami, somehow. I've lost my legs—that you can see. But there's another difference, though I can't seem to figure out what," Bedora explained.

"I would like you to rest on your own arbochaise, right next to Curiami," Wykepper said. "It is time for the people to learn what help they may receive from you two, if any."

"I don't know if I can help," Bedora explained. "I don't know what I would do for people."

"If you have any gifts, you will learn to use them," Wykepper said. "It's the one thing I am sure of."

Wykepper rolled out another arbochaise and placed it next to Curiami.

"Rest here," Wykepper said. "The people will come. Do not say much, but try to sense the ills of others."

"I will try," Bedora said.

Bedora, with her ability to defy gravity, floated her body into a relaxed sitting/lying-back position on her arbochaise. Wykepper disappeared into a side room, re-emerged with a harp, and began to play music. The people lined up and approached Curiami's arbochaise first. One by one, people paused and looked down on Curiami with such sadness and misery that one would think the people were paying last respects to a deceased person in a casket.

"She's not dead," Bedora said to each passerby. "She can help you. Just touch her."

But the people ignored Bedora. They simply paused at Curiami's arbochaise, whispered something soft like a prayer, and moved along, eventually returning to each one of their seats.

"She's not dead! She's not!" Bedora begged.

The last of the people passed the arbochaises.

"I don't understand. No one was helped at all," Bedora said. "In fact, some people are crying. And there's a woman in a chair just on the other side of my arbochaise. She weeps but on the inside. She will not openly express her sorrow. In a moment, it will consume her. If I stand up...if I...I can't even stand up. I don't have legs. Well, if I arise to the floor, I could reach out to her and touch her."

Bedora did just that. She arose from the arbochaise, glided over to the back of the chair where the inside-weeping-woman stood, and Bedora began to reach for the woman, but the woman suddenly became faint and collapsed. The woman's daughter, standing to the left, knelt down to assist her mother, but the mother remained collapsed. Bedora then made the effort, reached out for the woman, and touched her shoulder. Immediately, the woman felt strength return, and she stood up, much to the delight of her daughter who quickly whispered, "Thank you," to Bedora.

"There's nothing else for us here," the woman said. "Your Aunt Curiami has passed."

The general consensus of the people was that Wykepper's experiment had failed. None had received the hope for which they had sought. Not even Curiami's sister, the collapsed woman (who Bedora had helped) realized that she had received special help beyond the normal sustenance derived from a meat-eating culture. Little by little, the people left the archarbor, leaving just Bedora, Wykepper, and Curiami. Bedora's attention had been so fixed on watching the people leave that she didn't see Curiami stand up from her arbochaise and approach Bedora.

"Don't worry about them," Curiami said.

Bedora turned suddenly and was surprised to see Curiami with a healthy complexion and youthful pose.

"Curiami! I thought you were very ill. And the people, and your sister— they all treated you as if you were dead," Bedora said.

"In a way, I am," Curiami said. "But so are you."

"No I'm not," Bedora said. "I helped your sister, and your daughter thanked me."

"But did you notice how everyone ignored you?" Curiami asked.

"Yeah, that was strange. And something else was strange. With all those people in pain, why didn't you stand up and help console them?" Bedora asked.

"I couldn't," Curiami said. "Whenever a meat-eating person is in my presence, I become too weak to do much of anything."

"It explains a lot," Wykepper said, now approaching the two. "As a vegetarian, I do not cause Curiami to grow weak. But you, Bedora. You have discovered your gift, at least the beginnings of it. I saw how you helped Curiami's sister, Dralla. She's also a vegetarian. Had she been a meat-eater, you would not have been able to help her."

"I don't understand," Bedora said.

"We can prove your abilities when next we see a meat-eater, but from what I can tell during your transuflessiation, you absorbed fibers from the archarbor. Plant fibers. Your power comes in helping those with plant components," Wykepper said. "Wait, something is happening with the arbodulus."

Indeed, the arbodulus broadcast rays, and Bedora found herself in another place and time.

Bedora was now standing in the middle of a great garden of extravagant flowering plants, shrubs, and trees. And they were all being tended by big cats—cats standing on two legs! They wore clothing spun from fur and wore straw hats—also made of fur. They tended to these plants by pruning and watering and fertilizing. Then a call came from a great hall, and the big cats broke for lunch. Bedora floated along the ground and followed them into the hall. The big cats were now in a cafeteria line. Each took a plate and utensils and placed various vegetarian foods upon their plates. Not one leaf nor other plant part used for daily living was on these plates—only the stored foodstuffs of plants were to be found. Fruits, seeds, and nuts—these were the foodstuffs of the big cats. And the most prized food, that of the taurine apple, contained essential organic acids in its skin that was necessary for good health and clean teeth. The sight of these big cats eating such apples was a shock to Bedora, but her surprise was interrupted by a great horn sounding outside. All big cats rushed outside and cornered an arriving group of rabbits. The rabbits had invaded to consume all leaves from the great gardens of the big cats.

Bedora was afraid, and she tried to protect the rabbits. But to her relief, the big cats did not eat the rabbits. Instead, the big cats escorted the rabbits to a building of great architectural design, the design resembling that of the ancient Greeks. It was the Hall of Judgment, and inside were columns of columns, with stone steps along the sides large enough for an audience to sit. The big cats herded the rabbits to the far end, where a bonsai tree stood. The tree was the height of Bedora, and it hovered in its pot, which resembled a cone not much different from Bedora's. Its leaves were of many colors, like a permanent autumn ensemble, and its branches and trunk were thick and well formed.

"Bring the accused," the bonsai tree said.

The big cats herded the rabbits forward, and again Bedora was surprised. The rabbits stood on their hind legs, and they wielded their front legs like arms. Then one particular rabbit removed a set of glasses from a hidden pocket (Bedora now noticed clothing taking shape on these rabbits), and the rabbit placed the glasses over her eyes.

"I am Lepsus, attorney at law. I wish to represent my kind as their defense counselor," the rabbit said.

The big cats laughed.

"These rabbits were caught defiling the sacred parts of a plant's body," one big cat said.

The other big cats murmured in agreement.

"Nasty pigs," said one big cat.

"They're so destructive," said another.

"They like to destroy but not restore that which is above all else," said the first big cat.

"We are hungry and were forced into these lands," said Lepsus. "Big cats from our homeland have devoured our kind. We have nowhere else to go."

"Did you not think to first consult us before you assaulted my kin?" the bonsai tree said.

"They are not the kind to think," blurted another big cat.

"Numbers do not think," said a third big cat.

"Creation of all that is beautiful is an act of time and planning," said the bonsai tree. "But your kind has not such comprehension."

"We're willing to try," said Lepsus. "Give us the opportunity to help."

"Let us execute them the old fashioned way, oh great Tree of Ages," said the first big cat. "Let us consume them."

"No!" the bonsai tree said. "Meat is full of poison—metals and carcinogens and all evil that has accumulated in that rabbit. You would become no better than the rabbit and what it ingested. Here then I make judgment. The rabbits shall be placed on probation and taught to cultivate the fields. Let one moon cycle complete. Bring them back to the Hall of Judgment, and their deeds shall choose their fate. But before they are sent to the fields, let them attend the passing of Leothi, the great lioness."

"Outrageous," said one big cat.

"An injustice to Leothi," said another.

"No rabbit would pay respects to a cat," said a third.

"Exercise tolerance and restraint," the bonsai tree said. "For all creatures must be given a chance to show merit."

There was much grumbling amongst the big cats, but they acquiesced. The place changed, and Bedora was now on a mountain ledge overlooking a sunset. A great lioness was carried in a clear casket by six big cats—three on each side. There were many shrubs overlooking the sunset—shrubs with needles instead of leaves, and all shaped loosely after a big cat. The procession reached an empty spot on the ledge and then halted. From nowhere, the bonsai tree appeared, floated in its clay pot, and spoke:

"From the beginning of this age, the greatest of the Felidae have moved on to a world of peace and eternal bonds with the sunset. Let Leothi now join this sunset."

Bedora watched as the bonsai tree touched the casket with an extended branch. The winds picked up, and coniferous needles surrounded the casket. The casket opened, the needles surrounded Leothi, and they lifted her from the casket into the air. Then Leothi was transformed from the remains of animal tissue to a new coniferous shrub. The winds placed the new Leothi onto the mountain ledge, and roots took hold.

Bedora felt a sense of completion and satisfaction from this event, and suflessence filled the air. All who attended absorbed the suflessence, including Bedora, and she wanted to join Leothi's side and become a coniferous shrub, extending branch and bark to the sunset and anchor into the wisdom of the ages of the mountain ledge.

At length, the big cats left, and they took the rabbits with them (who had been surprisingly well behaved). Bedora dwelled, however, as did the bonsai tree.

"It is not yet your time," the bonsai tree said to Bedora.

"You can see me?" Bedora asked.

"Yes. I have known of your presence since you first arrived. Curiami visited before you, and of course she will again, but now it is your turn to help," the bonsai tree said.

"I don't understand," Bedora said.

"Humans also have a mountain ledge of their own where they will anchor deep and enjoy the eternal sunset," the bonsai tree said. "There have been many great people, but there are many more, and so more suflessence mediums are needed for those people. You are needed for this purpose. When their corporeal time is at an end, the swirls and eddies of suflessence will transfer from you to them, and they will join the place of their kind."

"How will I know what to do?" Bedora asked.

"The time and place are chosen," the bonsai tree said. "You will be taken to the place of need, and a cat will be there and act as liaison. Suflessence will do the rest. The cat knows."

The time and place changed again. Bedora was now in the same hospital where Doctor Otot had treated her. She hovered behind the resident cat as it walked to its next destination, a young girl who suffered from critical injuries after a truck had struck her while bicycling. The girl's mother sat at the girl's side and held her hand. The cat jumped onto the end of the bed and curled up. Bedora felt suflessence leave her own body, pass through the cat, and permeate the girl's body. The time and place changed back to a special ledge for little girls. The cat was there along with Bedora, Curiami, Wykepper, and the bonsai tree. The girl was transformed into a coniferous shrub, where she could be liberated from her broken body and enjoy the wisdom of the mountain with eternal light from the setting sun.

For Thy Service

It was late. The final episode of a prominent medical drama had long since finished broadcasting. The television was now off, my wife was asleep, and I was beginning to drift into light unconsciousness. But as is my habit for falling asleep, I had a first dream that I was in a hospital being poked by several needles. A few minutes later, I awoke myself to find my cat kneading his claws against my arm. I shooed him away, got up, took an allergy pill to help me breathe, and I returned to bed where I slipped into conflicted sleep.

"Armich," Metoni, my bunk mate said from below. "Wake up. It's almost time for work. The energy ingestion bar will open soon."

"Work," I said with dread hanging down my eyelids.

"Get on down from there," he said, and he whipped his sock at my face. "If you're not on the line after ingestion period ends, you'll be extrasent to the lower levels, and me along with you. We are assigned—"

"Working pairs, I know, you don't have to remind me like you do every morning," I said.

"I have to remind you, Armich. I must, because you are so difficult to motivate," Metoni said.

"I'm motivated if the right thing motivates me," I said.

"And that is?" Metoni asked.

"I'll tell you when I find out," I said.

"You're a dreamer, Armich," Metoni said.

"I am," I said, and I realized that this was all a dream, because my real name is K Gerard Martin, not Armich. But I was too tired to awake and hope for another dream, so this one had to do.

"Get up!" Metoni insisted, and now he had placed a leather glove inside his sock to increase the force of impact on each swipe he landed on my head.

"Let me sleep, will you? I'm dead tired," I said.

"Can't sleep now," Metoni said. "The energy ingestion bar will open soon. The guard...he...I hear him now."

Our bunk was one of many in an all-male chamber. A guard opened the door and made an announcement.

"Run now and carve your energy or starve!" the guard shouted.

My fellow chamber mates dashed for the door, but they bounced off one another in their excitement and traded blows to scramble through the door before the other. In doing so, several bed pans and items of hygiene were knocked to the ground, creating terrific crashes and clattering. I blinked, and instead of seeing people knocking over things, I, K Gerard Martin, was briefly awake, aware that my cats were chasing each other and knocking various items over.

"Open your eyes and climb out of bed, or we'll begin working without energy," Metoni said.

I blinked, and I was back in the chamber. I crawled out of bed and followed Metoni (along with my chamber mates) to the energy ingestion bar. The bar was a tall, dome-shaped room, and at the center was a black sphere, as tall as a house, with ropes dangling over and along its sides. Already, chamber mates climbed the ropes and sliced the best portions from the top of the black sphere. They placed the slices directly over their faces, and their pale, white bodies turned bronze from top to toe as the energy slices from the sphere diffused into their flesh.

This sphere contained our energy, the sustenance that fueled our cells and kept our bodies going. As I said, the best energy portions are at the top of the sphere, and by the time Metoni and I were able to work our way in to the sphere, there was little left but the hard, lower crust, which by itself would not diffuse into our flesh.

"We'll have to mix it with gear tar," Metoni said.

"I hate gear tar," I said.

"I know, Armich, that's why we must be first when the guard opens the door in the morning. If we are fast enough, we can get a good slice before the energy sphere is gone," Metoni said.

We each grabbed what was left of the sphere and placed those remains in our packs. Pale and weak, we were forced to follow our chamber mates to the main productory. Here again, there was a mad rush for privileged work stations. Those who had energized with juicy sphere matter had the best speed, and they chose supervisory pedestals. The next quickest chose lead platform conductors, the next chose machine operator positions, and the last (including Metoni and me) wandered around in vain, looking for an open operator station, but all were taken, meaning we were stuck doing portery.

Carry raw metal. Carry gears. Carry hydraulic arms, compressor fluid, cleaning brushes, caustic cleaning powder, and so on. It wasn't until after a good part of the day had passed that we were instructed to carry gear tar, and we had to make the best of things with carrying the gear tar and sneaking some tar to mix with sphere crumbs to energize our bodies.

The sphere crumbs had little energy, and the gear tar soaked with the crumbs into our flesh. My gut felt wretched, like vile worms were swimming around in circles in an effort to make my gut explode. I wanted so desperately to remove the bitterness from my body, but slavery to service blocked all efforts for relief. While this all sounds bad, things were worse on the lower levels where we would go for days without energy slices and would have to barter and steal for the very necessities of daily continuance—all with hot-tempered people who clubbed and punched and beat whenever things didn't go their way (which was often). At least now I didn't have to worry about sliced skin or broken bones. But still, it had been a thousand sleep cycles since we were promoted to this level, and I was restless for an improvement. Anything.

The work day grew on. I was tired and wanted to sleep, but Foreman Gorah (not one of my chamber mates) called Metoni and me over and into his private office.

"You two have delivered your portings on time and consistently without flaw or failure in all the time I have watched you," Gorah said. "I need a pair to make a special delivery. The goods to be ported are not machine parts, rather, they are special and are to be delivered to highly guarded parts of the complex. I will not order you to do this job, but I see potential in you Metoni, and I know you are easily qualified, Armich. Together, I know I can trust you both to make this special delivery without diversion or delay. And, you must keep secret the contents of the cargo."

Metoni grinned from ear to ear. I could practically hear his thoughts. Indeed, he looked me in the eye and all but said, "This is the chance of a lifetime! We must take this assignment! And there will be more! I know there will!"

"To sweeten the deal," Foreman Gorah continued, "you will be given special energy slices afforded only to elite workers. That means no more gear tar."

"How did you know?" I asked.

Foreman Gorah laughed.

"Don't worry," the foreman said. "There's plenty of gear tar, and you can take all you like. But just because we let you steal gear tar, don't expect to steal anything else and get away with it. If you steal anything from special portings, I'll super-extrasent you both to the lowest of levels, where you can fight the sewage snakes for your daily energy."

"Yes, sir," we both replied.

"Good. But first, you'll need to change into clean uniforms. Tibbit will show you," Gorah said.

Gorah whistled twice, and a short man walked in.

"Tibbit, Armich and Metoni have accepted. Clean them up and brief them on their roles," Gorah said.

"For thy service," Tibbit said to the foreman in acknowledgment.

Tibbit led us to a pair of archways, just tall enough for a man to walk through.

"Take off your shoes and pass through the arches, one by one," Tibbit said.

I passed through the first arch, and waves of invisible ant-like pulses pelted my body, sending all dirt, sweat, and dead cells to the floor and down the drainage grate below. I looked at Tibbit, and he motioned me to enter the second archway. As I did, I heard Metoni enter the first archway accompanied by the same slopping sound of dead cells, sweat, and dirt falling to the floor and flowing down the grate. The second archway transformed my raggedy clothing into a smartly pressed white and black uniform with blue highlights. But what about shoes?

"Leave your shoes behind," Tibbit said, seeming to read my mind. "You will wear black boots now. The archway cannot replicate boots yet, so you must find a pair that fits."

Metoni now passed through the second archway, and he too was fitted in a well-groomed blue-highlighted black and white uniform, and a hat. I touched the top of my head and realized that I too wore a hat.

"This way please," Tibbit said.

We followed Tibbit down a hallway that grew increasingly narrow, first with many doors, then with a few, and finally with a single door at the very end. He opened the door and ushered us inside. Expecting a small room, we were surprised to find a large, bright, clean and well-furnished room with many drawing tables, rolls of drawings, lighting fixtures above, to the side, and below, and to our astonishment the most amazing thing was the people...or...what were they? Creatures who crafted lines on paper to make the drawings. Each had six arms and four legs, a slender body, and what looked like a head with a ring around the top third and a bubbly liquid circling inside the ring.

These had to be robots or some sort of artificial forms resembling life. They had no mouths and no ears, certainly nothing that suggested they could speak. They were slightly shorter than me when on all four legs, but they could stand on two legs and exceed my height. At first I thought they had skin, but on further study they seemed to have more of a rose-colored marble surface with streaks and patches of white and black for an outer layer.

Tibbit chirped like a bird, or so it seemed, and a leader of the creatures chirped back at five times the speed and then brought forth a rolled-up drawing. Tibbit unrolled the drawing and was about to explain our mission, but our jaws kept their dropped poses, and Tibbit was not one to ignore the obvious.

"You've never seen a *taniculat*, have you?" Tibbit asked.

"I...no," I replied.

"They are highly intelligent and don't take kindly to too many humans," Tibbit said. "You will do well to behave and have the utmost respect for them. They design everything in the complex."

"Everything?" I asked.

"Yes, everything. You don't think a human could design hypersonic showers or hyperbolic conversion planes, do you?" Tibbit asked.

"Is that what those arches were?" I asked.

The taniculats chirped and squealed in squelching cacophonies such that the conflicting dissonance racked Metoni's and my nerves worse than a thousand bone shards serrating our skulls. Tibbit chirped something to them and then turned to us.

"This way," Tibbit said abruptly, and he led us to a side room with the drawing.

The room we entered was small, with only a single table, a window, and an overhead light. The light was already on, and a curtain was drawn from the window, but Tibbit immediately closed the curtain over the window to create privacy.

"We are safe in here," Tibbit said. "No one in the main design room can hear us. Taniculats are easily offended by lesser beings like ourselves."

"Who says so?" Metoni said. "How can we be inferior to any kind of life form?"

"It's a bitter glob of tar to chew on, I know," Tibbit said. "After I first learned of the taniculats, it took me several weeks to get over the fact that I am part of an inferior life form. But I learned it's best to praise them with my servitude. I learned their language, as best as a human can, and I always finish my conversations with the phrase, *For thy service.*"

"All I heard was you chirping," I said.

"That's how it sounds to you, but to them it's their language," Tibbit said. "Their language is mathematical and based on combinations of sonic frequencies. It can sound like music to a trained ear. But that is not why you two are here. Look at this drawing."

I looked.

"It's a floor plan," I said. "We are here. This is where we sleep."

"We get our energy slices from here," Metoni said. "And we've spent many a wakeful cycle working machines and delivering supplies in this area."

"Gorah was right," Tibbit said. "You two *can* read maps."

"There's writing here. Words," Metoni said. "And numbers. There are measurements and names for each room, chamber, aisleway, and stairwell."

"I can read them too," I said.

"Gorah suspected you two had learned how to read," Tibbit said. "What does this say, Armich?"

"*The Royal Corridor*," I said.

"It connects our complex with another," Metoni said. "I didn't know this other complex, the Royal Complex, existed."

"And that is a secret you must keep, under penalty of death, or worse," Tibbit said.

"What's worse than death?" Metoni asked.

"The taniculats have devised archways of torture that you do not wish to experience," Tibbit said. "But on to more pleasant things. Your mission is to deliver a flat of archways to the Royal Complex. When you arrive, you will be greeted by a royal servant who will show you where to install the arches."

"I don't know anything about installing arches," I said.

"That will be solved quite easily with evertraining," Tibbit said. "Follow me."

Tibbit rolled up the drawing and led us from the small room to the main design room. The taniculats had settled back into work. Tibbit chirped something, handed the drawing to the lead taniculat, and chirped his farewell phrase again, "For thy service."

Tibbit led us back down the hallway, but only a short ways. We passed through another doorway and into a library of archways, row after row of archways, archways with names labeled at the top, names like *history 1*, *history 2*, etc., *mathematics 1, 2, 3*, etc., *biology 1*, etc., *physics* etc., and so on. There were also archways for fictional stories, simulated worlds, and further.

"Remmen," Tibbit called.

A middle-aged man with a gray-speckled beard and medium-length wavy hair approached.

"How may I perform for thy service?" the man asked.

"This is Armich and Metoni. Armich and Metoni, this is Remmen. He is the Master Librarian, keeper of the knowledge archways."

Remmen made a double-circle underhanded gesture with his right hand to bid us welcome. We had not seen that kind of gesture before, so we emulated his gesture to return the welcome.

"Remmen, Armich and Metoni must be trained in the ways of archway installation for the Royal Complex," Tibbit said.

"Royal Complex archway installation," Remmen mused.

"Follow Remmen," Tibbit said. "Return here when you finish."

Remmen mumbled something about four rows left, two right, no, one back, another this way, a few more that way, no, wrong aisle, upstairs.

"Are you looking for the right archway?" Metoni asked.

"No, my beverage," he said. "There it is."

Remmen reached for and grabbed a corked bottle, removed the cork, and took a swig. He breathed a sigh of satisfaction from the liquid.

"What about the archway of knowledge, the one that will teach us how to install archways in the Royal Complex?" Metoni asked.

"I'm getting to that," Remmen said. "I must stop the wheels in my mind and focus. A man cannot accomplish a deed unless he applies brakes to all assaults of external stimuli upon his consciousness. He may then reach into his side consciousness for the very bit of knowledge he has stuffed away, safe from theft."

I looked at Metoni, and he at me. We were confused and unable to make sense of Remmen.

"Yes, yes, the archway of royal training, with setting three-eight-two, special chapter on archway installation. This way, please," Remmen said.

We were following Remmen past a number of archways of various colors and strange decorations when he stopped at a black and dark-red colored archway.

"This is Cherry-Charry Archway," Remmen said.

I was about to step into the archway, but Remmen stopped me.

"Wait. Do not enter the archway as you are, a mind filled with petty little things of today and yesterday," Remmen said. "Go instead with a blank mind, with one indifferent to perceived injustices, passions of desire, or hopes of happiness. Enter with a stunned sense of emptiness."

Remmen retrieved a hooked baton from under his robe and lightly knocked the backside of the hook against my forehead and Metoni's. Then Remmen pushed me into the archway.

The light from the library faded, and I felt as if I had no eyes, for vision in the traditional sense was lost upon me. Instead, I became part of movement, of wheels spinning, of levers lifting, of wedges dividing, pulleys lifting, and steam compressing. I was action and form and time without distraction, rather, I was the toroid of space-time where speed of dimension drives shape and force, direction and boundary, barrier, harmony and frequency until millions upon billions of interconnecting segments of field shapes came together into my human body and gave me the essence of archway balance, form, motivation, energy source, and performance. I shrank from a universe of size and back into a single dot, then two dots, dots that became eyes where darkness lifted into the light of the surrounding library.

"You are ready," Remmen said.

I walked out from under the archway, and Metoni entered. He had hardly stood there a heartbeat when Remmen said to him, "You are ready."

"Was that long enough?" I asked. "I stood under that archway for quite a while."

"You each stood for the same count of moments," Remmen said. "You are ready for Royal Archway installation."

Remmen led us back to the library's main entrance, where Tibbit and now Gorah were waiting.

"They are ready for thy service," Tibbit said to Gorah.

"Good," Gorah said. "Tibbit, I want you to take over my foreman duties until I return."

"For thy service," Tibbit said, and he left.

"Come then," Gorah said, and he led them from the library, down the hall, through another doorway, and down a ramp which led to a cargo vehicle skinned in obsidian and quartz. The vehicle shone like a rainbow that shifted position and color depending on lighting and one's angle of perspective when looking at it.

Two guards stood—one on each side of the front side door. Two other guards stood in back as workers loaded padded archways into the vehicle.

"The *vattertram* is ready," Gorah said. "Get in."

Metoni led, I followed, and Gorah also followed with the two guards following up the rear. The last guard closed the vattertram's door behind us, leaving the other two guards outside.

"Metoni, you navigate," Gorah said. "Armich, you co-navigate and operate the *dialogiar*. I'll monitor and rate performance."

Metoni strapped himself into the front left seat, and I strapped myself into the front right. Gorah sat behind Metoni while the guards sat farther back with the cargo. Metoni actuated the controls, and I spoke into the dialogiar, a communication device like a two-way radio, but using some sort of subatomic frequency that could pass through most objects—steel, rock, and planetary matter, unlike radio waves that can be distorted and blocked by such.

"This is Shollernat One. Preparing for launch," I said.

"Shollernat One, proceed," said a voice over a speaker.

The vattertram levitated a human leg's length into the air and glided forward along the open area until it entered a tunnel.

"Shollernat One now entering Priva Tunnel Two," I said in the dialogiar.

Priva Tunnel Two is a privileged tunnel used for special cargo runs to the Royal Complex.

"Confirmed, Shollernat One. Advise on reaching the Royal Compl... (static)...princess will confirm...(static)...return," the speaker voice said.

"Repeat message, Base Control," I said. "Your signal is breaking up."

"...(static)...the archways... (static)...escaped...(static)..."

"Check the *squaliapitar*," Gorah said. "There should be no deviance from zero."

"Set at zero," I said. "There should be no signal problems."

"You were trained for such a situation," Gorah said. "Analysis, Armich."

"Most likely the dialogiar's signal is being dispersed by anto-ionic regression waves," I said. "Which means we are about to be under attack."

Metoni hit several buttons quickly and warned us, "Brace for quick-stop!"

The vattertram stopped abruptly. The guards drew small weapons, but only for invaders should they board the vattertram.

"Armich, ready your silotron," Metoni said. "I shall do the same."

Metoni and I activated aiming scopes, peered into the scopes, and watched. The path ahead was clear, but only for a moment. Something small was thrown from the tunnel's side and landed forty paces in front of the vattertram. It came to a rest for a single heartbeat of time and then exploded. There was no damage to the vattertram, but the vehicle shuddered from the shock waves.

"They have explosives," Metoni said.

"How many, Armich? Do you have a count?" Gorah asked. "Scan for subverter cyano-infrared signatures."

"Three humans," I said after reading my scanner.

"They are subverters, not humans," Gorah corrected. "Locations?"

"One is twenty-three arctos left of center by one elevat by forty-three paces, another is thirty arctos right of center by one elevat by thirty-nine paces, and the third is one arcto right of center by eighty-eight elevats by fifteen paces!" I said, realizing the third was nearly directly overhead.

"I have them too, Foreman Gorah," Metoni said.

"Fire," Gorah said.

Metoni fired his silotron, as did I. Metoni's silotron disrupted a machine gun with shield into powdered metal and then agitated the cells of the human standing behind the former shield until those cells burst into spontaneous combustion. The human screeched briefly before falling into a powdery ball of flame.

I fired my silotron too, and the human in my target was also hiding behind a machine gun with shield. As with Metoni's silotron blast, the machine gun and shield shattered into powder from my silotron's blast, but the human in my sights moved at the last moment, requiring me to fire a second and third time. He tried hiding around a bend in the rock, but that's the nice thing about silotrons—their blast can go around corners without loss of energy. The human erupted in a powderball of flame, he screeched, and died.

"One left," I said. "He is ninety elevats and descending."

"Armich, are you ready?" Gorah said.

"Yes," I said.

"Proceed," Gorah ordered.

I stood up from my seat, moved past Metoni and Gorah, grabbed a portable silotron, and climbed a service ladder to the vattertram's ceiling. I opened the inner hatch, ascended, and closed the inner hatch below me. The outer hatch above was all that protected me from the third subverter.

"Remember," Gorah said through an earpiece, "if you force him to the front or back, Metoni can silotron him. And stay clear of the blast."

"I will," I said.

I pulled a portable cyano-infrared viewer over my eyes. The world turned into reds and blues, the same colors used in old-time three-dimensional movies, only the images before me did not have the double-exposure look of a raw three-dimensional movie frame. The reds showed unobstructed heat, while the blues showed obstructed heat. In this way, I could see the third subverter and his movement, even through the vattertram's ceiling and roof. The subverter descended quickly from a rope and landed atop the vattertram's roof. There was no time to waste. I thrust the outer hatch upward and jumped atop the vattertram's roof in time to catch the subverter planting an explosive device on the roof.

I shot at the subverter with my portable silotron. He moved out of the way, and only a slice of the beam nicked him, but nicked him it did, and it dissolved and burned his left arm. He shrieked. He didn't remain motionless but instead took quick action and kicked the silotron from my hand.

"The explosive has a twenty-heartbeat fuse," Gorah radioed into my earpiece. "I'm sending help."

"No," I said, "this one is mine."

The sudden gush of fluid coursing and expanding my flesh gave me a delusional sense of power and ultimate authority. I dove at the subverter, snapped his neck, and while holding his body in one hand, I dragged the body to the explosive and prepared to shove the explosive in his mouth.

A faint voice from far ahead yelled, "Armich, no!" I peered ahead and thought I saw the face of a young woman darting away, but the moment darted with her departure. I finished shoving the explosive in the subverter's mouth and threw his body with explosive far ahead of the vattertram, where Metoni's waiting silotron blast detonated the explosive and incinerated the subverter's body—all in time for the guards to see. They acknowledged my deed with a tip of their hats. One exited the vattertram, retrieved my silotron, and tossed it to me. I caught it and thanked him. We then returned to the vattertram, where I took my seat next to Metoni.

"Well done, well done," Gorah said. "You'll be interested to know that Metoni called in to Base Control with request for identification of those subverters."

"Shollernat One, this is Base Control. Identities of subverters are former factory workers from Chamber Forty-Five," a voice said over the speaker.

"Chamber Forty-Five, wow!" Metoni said. "We used to sleep in Chamber Forty-Five."

"Their names were Sellan, Tabiun, and Forlatt," the voice said.

"Base Control, Shollernat One. We acknowledge," I said into the dialogiar. "Preparing to resume delivery."

"Shollernat One, we show the rest of the way is clear. New information: we have secured a fourth subverter and taken her prisoner," said the speaker voice.

"Then there *was* another subverter," I said.

"You said there were three," Metoni said.

"When I was on the vattertram's roof, I thought I saw and heard a woman far ahead," I said.

Gorah reviewed recordings from several instruments.

"Confirmed," Gorah said. "There was a fourth subverter. She doesn't show up on our cyano-infrared scanner, but a subsonic phasic raster scan shows a record of her. I'll feed this information to Base Control."

A few heartbeats passed of silence, and then the speaker voice said, "Shollernat, Base Control. Foreman Gorah's data matches the subverter we caught. Your diversion allowed us to catch her. Well done. Proceed to the Royal Complex at maximum speed."

"Base Control, Shollernat. We acknowledge," I said.

Metoni pressed a few buttons, and the vattertram lurched forward and into high speed.

"What diversion?" I asked.

"Your fight with the third subverter on the roof, that's what diversion," Metoni said. "I didn't think you were such a good fighter."

"I didn't either," I said.

"Remmen's archways have fully trained you two in ways you will not understand until the time comes," Gorah said. "Your training is indeficient."

I wasn't sure what Gorah meant, but it worried me. The way I acted on the vattertram's roof...it...scared me. I felt like someone took control of my body and puffed it out like a deranged demon, unwilling to let me stop until the mission at hand was complete, no matter what pain or suffering it caused others. What had that archway done to me? I thought it had only trained me to install royal archways, but apparently it had done more, and there was no way I could find out these hidden agendas until the situation forced my body into mandate.

As a reward for our service, we were moved out of the shared bedroom chamber and received a room for just the two of us, with better beds and our own bathroom. By dinner time, we were allowed to get our energy slices from a different room not used by the common workers, and instead of gear tar as a filler, we had honey. Honey! But how was it made and from where did it come? Metoni didn't care, he simply enjoyed the new comforts.

"This is what I'm talking about," Metoni said. "We're moving up now. Don't ruin anything."

The following day was another delivery (military supplies to an outpost) based on following another map, but again the vattertram was besieged by subverters. Our silotrons made quick work of those subverters, and we only lost a couple hundred heartbeats of time.

"Your efficiency is improving," Gorah said at the end of the day. "I am pleased."

By the end of the week, we were anticipating subverters and dealing with them before they had time to react, resulting in no delays to our deliveries. Gorah was shocked that we had managed to do so well.

"No one has been able to predict subverters in advance," Gorah said. "This is beyond your training. We must know more about how you do this so that we may teach the others."

"Simple," Metoni said. "We found this book while dealing with one of the subverters."

Metoni passed the book to Gorah.

"Yes, I've seen this type of book before. But it is written in code. No one can break it, not even the taniculats," Gorah said.

"That would be Armich here who broke it," Metoni said.

"Indeed! Please explain," Gorah said.

"The book is less language and more geometry. These symbols form a kind of angular grammar that changes and means different things depending on the angle of the sun or moon overhead," I said.

"And yet the taniculats are experts with mathematics but cannot translate the subverter code. Impressive, Armich. But how can these subverters know what angle the sun is at? No one can see it, except for those in the Royal Complex," Gorah said. "For that matter, how can you see it?"

"I can't," I said, "but based on time of day, I can deduce the angle of the sun. I only needed to synchronize the writings of our first encounter with the subverters to decode the rest."

"Then I know what your next mission will be. Remmen has many such confiscated code books in the library. You will report to him and decode those books," Gorah said. "Meanwhile, Metoni will carry on with the vatter-tram by himself for now. I will accompany him from time to time until I can find a replacement. Hmm. Not many have such talent for reading maps. It may take some time."

Gorah led me to the library.

"Remmen, Armich has cracked the subverters' code book. Have him translate all such works in the library," Gorah said, and he left me there with Remmen.

Remmen led me to a back room with piled books, magazines, and dust.

"This is our temporary room," Remmen said. "We repair binders and shrink magazines into book form. Sit at this table."

I sat at a table. Remmen gave me blank paper, a feather pen, a bottle of ink, and a subverter book.

"Before you write anything, open this book and tell me what it says," Remmen said.

I opened the book.

"This looks like a worship book or a collection of poetry. No, a worship book written like poetry," I said. "These people worship the sun, moon, and stars. Anything that radiates light naturally. Now they speak of fire and creatures that glow in the dark, both flying in the air and swimming in the water."

Remmen walked away, kept his back to me, and then turned toward me.

"Who else knows how to do this?" he asked.

"Just me. I tried showing Metoni, but he didn't understand," I said.

Remmen then walked over to the door, closed it, and locked it.

"What are you doing?" I asked. "Are you going to torture me?"

"No," Remmen said. "I wish to conduct a simple test first. I should have done this sooner, but...who would have thought that...hmm...no, not me."

"What say you? I don't understand," I said.

Remmen removed a handful of square cards from a cupboard and showed them to me.

"I'm going to show you a number of pictures. I want you to use your thumb to indicate in what direction the action is going," Remmen said. "Use your left thumb to point in that direction."

"Sounds simple enough," I said.

Remmen showed me several cards. One was a man running. Another man threw a spear. A hose shooting water. And others. Each time, I rotated my hand to point my thumb in that direction.

"Now these two," he said, and he flipped two cards in quick succession.

The first card showed a one-point perspective picture with people running off into the distance. Because of the awkward angle, I simply bent my thumb forward to point away from me instead of trying to turn my hand so that my thumb pointed away. I could have done that, but bending the thumb was easier and almost comical. I laughed. The second picture showed the same one-point perspective but with the people running toward me. I then bent my thumb toward me. Toward me.

Remmen put the cards away.

"Don't do that again," he said.

"Do what again?" I asked.

Then Remmen became cold and distant. He tossed a book at me.

"Open it and decode," he said.

I opened the book, but I could not make sense of the symbols.

"I...can't," I said. "I don't recognize this."

"So much for your abilities," Remmen said. "No more decoding."

Remmen called Gorah up on a transcommunication device attached to the wall.

"Only one book. The easiest one. No, he couldn't. He is of no use here," Remmen said.

Tibbit came by and took me back to the vattertram, where Metoni met with me.

"So how did it go?" Metoni asked.

"Not well," I said as the vattertram took us toward the prison section. "I could read one subverter book, but not another. And Remmen got mad at me. He's very strange."

"They say he's moody," Metoni said. "Is chatty and friendly one moment then quiet and cold the next."

"Yes, that's what happened. He became quiet and cold," I said.

"I wouldn't worry about it," Metoni said. "Besides, it's not like he's a subverter spying on us. Have you noticed that the subverters we deal with have an unusual ability to bend their limbs? Why I'd say they are contortionists. If it weren't for our weapons, the subverters would surely use some contorted strangle hold on us to choke us or contort their bodies to escape. That's why we can't use something simple like rope to tie them up. We must stun them or kill them."

Then an odd feeling hit me, like I wasn't who I thought I was.

"How flexible are you?" I asked.

"Oh, about like the average guy, I guess," Metoni laughed.

"What about with your fingers?" I asked. "How much can you move them?"

"They wiggle just fine," he said.

I reached out, grabbed his thumb, and tried bending it backward. He hollered in pain.

"What do you think you're doing?" he yelled. "That hurts!"

"Metoni," I said, releasing his thumb. "We're friends, right?"

"We were until a moment ago. I'm still smarting," he said. "What's wrong with you?"

"Remmen had me take a strange test," I said.

"Oh? What sort of test?" Metoni asked.

"He showed me pictures, and I pointed my thumb in different directions, like this," I said, and I showed him how I pointed my thumb up, down, left, and right.

"So?"

"Then he showed me people running away, so I bent my thumb like this. He next showed me people running toward me, and I bent my thumb back like this."

Metoni quickly straightened my thumb.

"Don't ever do that again," Metoni said. "Do you hear? Never!"

"You're acting like Remmen now—getting all mad at me and everything," I said.

"Stand up," he said. "Stand up!"

I stood up.

"Can you touch your toes without bending your knees?" he asked.

"I've never tried," I said.

"Wait. We're passing an observed zone. Good, done. We're in a tunnel. Try it now, but do it quickly," Metoni said.

I touched my toes easily.

"Don't ever do that again either," Metoni said.

"Tell me what's going on!" I demanded.

"You want to know," he said. "Is that it? Do you? Do you know what will happen when I tell you? Oh, tunnels of abyss, this is the worst thing that has ever happened to me. The absolute worst thing! And just when we were moving up in the world! Total dismal failure. Of the worst kind! And I know about you! What do I do? What do I do?"

"Tell me what's got you all worked up!" I said. "That's what you do!"

"But wait. Remmen knows. So why are you here? Unless...he doesn't want you to...then he must...I don't believe it. I just don't believe it."

"I wish you'd stop not believing and help me start believing. What in gear tar are you talking about?" I asked.

"I can't tell you. Not here. Not now. But how can we solve this problem? Things are complicated. I need time to think. Wait, we can go to Remmen. He can explain."

"Good, because you're not doing a bit of good with your riddles and mysteries," I said.

"Just keep quiet about everything. Don't tell anyone. And stay stiff as a board," Metoni said.

I had given up on Metoni. What was to tell? I had no clue. And this stiff-as-a-board thing was just plain nonsense. At least at the time it seemed so. We made our delivery to the Royal Complex. Servants had nearly finished unloading when a beautiful woman approached Metoni.

"You must be Metoni," she said. "I'm Princess Gella. You're too cute to be doing this kind of work without refreshments. Why don't you accompany me to the Royal Diner. And bring your friend...I'm sorry, I didn't catch his name."

"I'm Armich," I said.

"Oh, you're the one decoding subverter books," Princess Gella said.

Metoni was paralyzed with awe that Princess Gella asked him for refreshments. He could say nothing.

"I think Metoni likes you," I said to Princess Gella while jabbing Metoni in the shoulder.

But as I jabbed him in the shoulder, my thumb bent backward. Metoni felt this and instinctively turned a little and placed his hand over my thumb.

"I'd really love to have refreshments," Metoni said. "But we have a schedule to keep."

"Oh, work and schedule. I so much desire to dine with you. I could order you to stay," she said.

"I could not refuse an order," Metoni said. "But...I..."

"Armich, Metoni, where are you with that delivery?" blared Gorah's voice over the dialogiar.

"Metoni is busy getting married to me, and Armich is the best man," Princess Gella called back on the dialogiar.

"Princess Gella?" Gorah called back.

Princess Gella laughed in the dialogiar.

"Your delivery men are being perfect gentlemen," the princess called back. "I am conversing with them."

"Oh, yes Your Highness. For thy service at any time," Gorah called. "Armich and Metoni, carry on."

"They will," the princess called back, then she turned to us. "Oh the drudgery of work. I will not toy with you any longer. But it was fun watching you both get into trouble. You both blush the deepest of red. Well then, until we meet again."

The princess walked away and left us. Metoni took no action to get the vattertram moving, so I pressed a button and we were off.

"Princess Gella! She likes me, Armich. She likes me! And what was that trick you pulled by bending your thumb? Were you trying to get us imprisoned?" Metoni asked.

"You still haven't explained what's troubling you so much by my simple body movements," I said.

"If you were one of us, there wouldn't be an issue!" he blurted before realizing his mistake.

"One of *us*? Of what are you accusing me? I'm a man like you. Speak, Metoni!" I commanded.

"I give in then. You are a subverter. *That* is the problem!" Metoni said.

I laughed.

"Don't laugh. You'll just delude yourself all the more," Metoni said.

"And you think Remmen believes the same thing? But what makes you think so?" I asked.

"Angles! You can move in angles. Contortions, remember?"

Then it hit me. The entire subverter culture was based on the geometry of angles. But I was no thug. I was like Metoni and all the others in this underground factory. Or was I? There was the woman's voice who called my name. How did she know me? And why did she sound familiar? Like family? I'd never known my family, that is, if I ever had one. I'd been in this slave-based factory my entire life.

"But what about Remmen?" I asked. "Remmen and his subverter books? I could read one, but not the other."

"Ask yourself this," Metoni said. "Did the second book look like the first?"

"No, not really. It looked very different," I said.

"Probably a fake," Metoni said, "to throw everyone off the trail that you're a subverter. Which means Remmen is protecting you, which also means Remmen is sympathetic to subverters."

"Then he may know much more than he lets on. He may even know... Metoni, I wonder if Remmen knows a way out," I said.

"It's not safe in the open world. Everyone knows that," Metoni said.

"We've been told that. But what if that's a lie? To keep us from trying to escape this factory subservitude?" I asked.

"If it were safe outside, the royal family would live out there. But they don't. They live underground like us," Metoni said.

"Maybe they do that to perpetuate the myth that the outside is unlivable. I think they are part of this entire bifurcated society that forces lower social groups to serve upper groups. And the subverters are fighting against that."

"Then why are the subverters here? Why don't they just leave and live outside, if it's so safe and wonderful?" Metoni asked.

"Maybe they can't find a way. But I bet Remmen knows. And if he knows, we could find out. Metoni, does it really matter if I'm a subverter? I just want to live a free life. You do too, although you don't speak of it openly. But I can see it in your eyes. You don't like working down here."

"I don't. But it's better to live in the upper class down here than struggle to survive as a free person, if such a thing is possible," Metoni said.

"You don't really believe that, do you?" I pressed. "Well?"

"What do you want me to do, Armich?"

"There's this, too," I added. "You're nervous that I may be a subverter."

"You *are* a subverter," Metoni said.

"Very well. I am. How long can we hold out given that fact? It's only a matter of time before others find out. I'll be executed. And you'll be executed for association."

"I know, I know!" he said.

"Then we have nothing to lose by looking for a means of escape. If we die on the outside, it will be no worse than dying down here," I said.

"Except I had a chance down here. A real chance! And it's all gone. Gone!" Metoni moaned.

The vattertram arrived at its point of origin. Gorah had been alerted to a subverter attack in the east, and so we were sent to help out another vattertram under attack. We went there at top speed, but by the time we arrived, the occupants of the other vattertram had been taken. We didn't know if they were killed or what.

"Looks like they gave a good fight," Metoni said. "But they were dragged away. There are trails of blood."

"And another book," I said. "Must have fallen out in the fight."

"It's not one of ours," Metoni said. "Can you read it?"

"Yes. It's written in the subvertian language of angles," I said. "Some sort of religious planning book. Has a full list of names and family trees, and their relation of service to the whole."

"Something tells me that you'll find your name in there but not mine," Metoni said.

I flipped through the pages.

"I...am in here," I said with shock. "It's really true. I'm not one of you. But somehow deep down I knew it the entire time. I guess it took this long to unbury the truth."

"But you aren't savage like the other subverters," Metoni said. "I'm glad you're not savage. Perhaps we can use that."

"Now you're talking," I said. "And as for this book..."

"What will you do with it? Will you give it to Gorah?" Metoni asked.

"No, I think this one I'll keep secret. I'll use it as a conversation piece with Remmen."

We finished up our duties and ate dinner. With dinner complete, Metoni asked about Remmen.

"Let's go see him," I said.

We went to the library and rang for Remmen. But Remmen was not there.

"He's left for the day," said an assistant.

"I thought he lived here," I said.

"No," the assistant said.

"Could you tell him Metoni and Armich were here?" I asked.

"I...could tell him that," she said.

"What is your name?" Metoni asked.

"Ashley," she said. "I heard you saw the princess today. Is she pretty?"

"Not as pretty as you," Metoni flirted.

"Oh not again," I murmured.

"Oh, thank you," Ashley said, and she bent her hand back at extreme angle.

She was a subverter! One of my people! How did Metoni not notice? But Metoni was falling for her, as he had with Princess Gella, so he didn't notice. But now I wondered if she were hiding something.

"Ashley," I said. "I found another book from the subverters. I can read it, too."

I pulled out the book, and the color in her face faded quickly.

"There are names in here of all the subverters," I said. "In fact, I think that you are...right here."

Ashley started to run away, but Metoni grabbed her hand.

"You're a subverter?" Metoni asked. "A beautiful girl like you?"

"Oh please don't turn me in. Please!" Ashley pleaded.

"Do not worry," I said. "I'm a subverter too. That's how I can read this book. Look—my name is here."

Ashley looked down at the book and then looked up.

"Remmen told me about you. He knows. He didn't think you figured it out. One of those books he showed you—"

"Was a fake. I know," I said. "To throw me off the trail. He was afraid for my safety."

"You are both in great danger," Ashley said. "I am too, but not as much as you two. Gorah is planning to send you two deep into subverter territory. And I happen to know the subverters have heavily armed themselves. You will not come out alive."

"Then it's over. We must see Remmen and leave now. Is he hiding in back?"

"No, he really is out," Ashley said.

"Can you help us?" Metoni asked.

Ashley stood there and looked at me, then at Metoni, at me, and back at Metoni.

"I...I can try. But it must be now. Oh, this is so unexpected. And it will be the end of your life as you now know it. Everything will change. I wish you all the luck. Metoni, you're not a subverter, so things will be more difficult. Armich, you must be willing to help Metoni."

"I'll do all that I can," I said.

Ashley looked around to see if we were being watched, and after a moment, she ushered us into the very room where Remmen had tested my thumb flexibility. Ashley closed the door behind us, locked it, and then tapped three times, paused, tapped twice, paused, and then tapped three times on a tall cabinet. The cabinet moved aside, revealing a dimly-lit passageway.

"Into the tunnel," Ashley said.

We went inside, and Ashley tapped two-three-two to close the cabinet.

"Your fate lies at the end of this tunnel," Ashley said.

"That sounds rather scary," Metoni said.

We reached the end of the tunnel, and a large room with bright lights greeted us.

"This is—" Ashley started to say.

But before Ashley could complete her statement, a man turned around and punched Metoni and me in the face. I fell unconscious. I then awoke as K Gerard Martin and realized my cat had just run across the bed and used my face as a launching pad. I went into the bathroom and looked at the freshly-bleeding scratches caused by my cat. Should the cat be declawed? I cleaned up the wound and went back to sleep.

The dream resumed, and I awoke as Armich. Metoni had been placing smelling salts under my nose.

"Get that away from me. It's awful," I said.

"I had to wake you," Metoni said. "Things may not work out with the subverters."

"Your face is swollen. Come to think of it, so is mine," I said.

"The subverters don't take kindly to us," Metoni said. "Ashley is trying to convince them that we're friendly. But the subverters seem to think we're murderers."

"We did kill a number of them. But the subverters we killed looked nothing like the ones down here. We killed savage creatures, more like wild animals than human. But those down here look like us," I said.

I took to my feet. Ashley led the subverters into the room where I had been recovering, and I feared for my life. Though looking like ordinary humans, they were tall and strong, and a fire of resolve burned in their eyes that could not be quenched.

"This *is* Armich," said one. "Killer. Traitor to us all!"

"Borrak, he didn't know," Ashley said.

"And his friend spy, Metoni. Not one of us at all," said another.

"They will help us, Sarrio," Ashley continued.

"How?" Borrak asked. "By betraying us? They know too much as it is. I say we end things now. Here."

"Armich is talented," Ashley said. "He can read the ancient books. Look."

Ashley passed me a book.

"Read it, Armich," she said.

I opened the book. It was filled with many geometric shapes—drawings of buildings and architecture beyond what I had ever imagined.

"It's beautiful," I said. "It's what mathematics should have been. Here. Here's a passage. 'The water as has, in mind and thought, comes from within, and fades it not. When one is one with one of heart, our heart is thought and shards are not. From time our time when ours is not, comes time and place where ours is space. From one to some our place not none, our place divine in space and time.'"

I stopped. I wasn't sure what it meant, but it sounded interesting to me. Ashley, Borrak, Sarrio, and the others had their heads bowed and had spoken the words with me.

"Now do you believe?" Ashley asked.

There was silence for a moment.

"Let him prove himself," Sarrio said. "He can atone for his murders by freeing the prisoner."

"Yes, have him set Nola free. Then we will be convinced," Borrak said.

"And to ensure he doesn't talk, we'll cut out his tongue," Sarrio said.

"Wait! No!" I protested.

"Metoni's too," Sarrio said.

"Not mine too!" Metoni protested.

"It is the only way," Borrak said. "I have a tool for just such a purpose."

Borrak approached with a pair of clamping snips that seemed more appropriate for snipping off hoof material than a tongue.

"Wait," I said. "The book speaks of such things for enforcing silence, but there are temporary methods. A drug injected buccally will do. I can make it."

"You just keep reading the book. Ashley will make it," Sarrio said. "And the drug will be tested on Metoni first. If he survives, it will be tested on you and then one of us."

Metoni looked frightened.

"Agreed," I said.

"Armich, no!" Metoni said. "This drug...it...I mean...won't it hurt?"

With Ashley watching, I pointed to a passage in a subverter book.

"That's just the thing," she said. "It won't hurt. The drug causes numbness."

"We won't be able to move our tongues either," I said, "which would make for difficult speech."

"As intended," Borrak said.

"The formula is very geometric," Ashley said as I explained the procedure.

Ashley collected several mushrooms and fungi, crushed them in a glass jar, poured a little fluid in the jar, and then placed the jar on a burner. She alternated between pouring a blue fluid in the jar and an orange fluid in the jar. After doing this for five minutes, she removed the jar and poured the fluid into a funnel with filter paper. A powder collected on the funnel paper. She took the powder, placed it in another jar, placed a pink fluid in the jar, and heated it. Another five minutes, and she removed the jar from the heat and poured the contents into funnel paper, creating another powder. She rinsed this new powder with fresh water and then mixed the powder with salt water in a dispensing bottle.

"This should be it," Ashley said. "You first, Metoni."

But Metoni shook in fear.

"I'll go first," I said.

Ashley took a syradermic needle, filled it with the drug, and then injected it inside my cheeks—first the left side, and then the right. I felt a crushing feeling on the sides of my face, as if I were being gripped or clamped. I was surprised, because all feeling was supposed to fade. Then all went black.

I awoke as K Gerard Martin and realized my cat was sleeping on my head. He had one paw on one cheek and another paw on the other. He kneaded both paws, causing claws to needle my face. I moved my cat aside, turned over, and fell back asleep.

"You had a reaction and passed out," Ashley said. "But you are awake now."

I wanted to say that a cat had my tongue, but I couldn't speak.

"Good, you can't speak. Metoni, your turn," Ashley said.

But Metoni lost all resolve and rushed out of the room in sheer panic. I chased after him and tried shouting, but I sounded like a dumb brute. Borrak and Sarrio initially gave chase, but Metoni exited the tunnel and burst into the library—with Gorah, Tibbit, and two other men looking around for us.

"Metoni! You're late! What's this all about?" Gorah barked.

But Metoni was speechless.

"Armich! Explain!" Gorah barked.

I could not speak with a paralyzed tongue. I blacked out and was awakened as K Gerard Martin to my cats running around and chasing each other by climbing high places and jumping down and outward as far as possible like torpedoes on a mission to bomb the other cat. Their jumping escapades included jumping on the bed, but I swatted them by whipping up the blanket a little bit. They scattered to another room, and I fell asleep.

Gorah shoved me.

"Speak," he said.

I awoke as K Gerard Martin.

"Oh sorry, I thought you were one of the cats," the wife said after pushing me in the shoulder.

I rolled over to my other side, and Gorah was waiting for me. But I had an idea. I jumped up on a library table, grabbed a tapestry from the wall, and whipped it over the heads of Gorah and Tibbit. I then jumped up and kicked the other men in the room to disable them.

I was pushed again.

"Stop kicking your feet," the wife said.

The dream was too much, and I went to the living room couch to continue it. I fell back into slumber and immediately led the way for Metoni. There was an alarm with rumbling and flashing as the community had been alerted of the trouble. We fought our way through folk. Several men fired silotrons. They missed me, but one shot nicked Metoni in the leg. His stride failed, and he fell. I helped him up, and we continued running. I then approached a door and opened it. Water blew in my face. The flashing and rumbling was incredibly intense.

"Close that door!" a voice said.

I awoke as K Gerard Martin. I had the back door open. Rain blew in from an electrical storm, and the wife, who had already woken up from her alarm clock, was now telling me to close the door. I returned to the main bed and fell back asleep.

"There's a secret door over here," Metoni said. "But it's not in the wall. It's in this overhang. Armich—move that box over here. I'll place this one there. Good. Climb up, and I'll follow."

I climbed first, opened the door, and pulled Metoni up with me. Then I kicked the boxes below and closed the door behind me. Immediately, I realized there were stairs that went up. The stairs circled around in spiral fashion, so I knew we were in some sort of cylinder or silo. We ascended the stairs, higher and higher, and as we did, the circumference shortened, meaning the circle was tighter. We ascended what felt like a conic pyramid, and every so often, powerful golden light peered in through cracks in the wall. It was a light I'd never seen before, and it felt strangely attractive, like some primitive drive had been awakened.

"Hurry, Metoni, we're almost at the top," I said, suddenly getting my tongue movement back.

"You can speak!" Metoni said. "I thought..."

"I woke up and fell back into this world," I said. "I think that reset everything."

"I don't understand, but it doesn't matter," Metoni said. "Armich, go ahead."

"No," I said. "I'll wait here for you to catch up."

"Just blaze the way," Metoni continued. "I won't be far behind."

"And spoil the excitement for us both? We go together. That's the deal," I said.

"Armich," Metoni called. "My leg is hurt badly. That silotron really got to me. Go by yourself. I'll stay here."

"You must go on," I said. "We're almost at the top."

"You should reach the top first. You deserve it."

"No, I won't leave you," I said. "You're my friend."

"Being with a friend won't help me run quicker," he said. "But it does make my heart feel better. Sadly, my leg is swelling. It won't move."

"Then I'll help you. Throw an arm over my shoulder," I said.

With Metoni's arm, I helped him up the stairs. I was surprised at how light he felt, but I was motivated. No longer did I wish to remain in the service of either complex. Plain and simple, I wanted a life, a life outside with the sunshine and with anyone else who would join us. There would be others later, but only once we had escaped the complexes and established a steady life on the outside.

"We are nearly at the top," I said.

The steps narrowed, the walls grew closer, and we spiraled up the last little bit. Golden light poured down from the upper steps, and we had to stop just before ascending the last bit to let our eyes adjust.

"It's so bright," Metoni said. "Everything...so...white and bright."

"Give your eyes a hundred heartbeats to adjust," I said. "That's what the book says."

"It's so amazing that a book made by the subverters can tell us things we never knew existed," Metoni said.

"If the book is true, we'll see strange life that we never knew existed," I said. "Flying things called *birds* that land in motionless life forms called *trees*."

"I can't imagine a life form not being able to move," Metoni said.

"It does a little, but not like us. It has no bones, and not even a brain," I said.

"Incredible," Metoni said. "I bet Remmen knew of such things. I wish he were here to see this."

"As do I," I said. "Perhaps we can help him escape, once we establish ourselves."

We reached the top. To our surprise, there was no way out into the open. There were windows, yes, and we could see very clearly a grove of trees with birds flying about. One such bird perched close to the window, and I reached to touch it, as if the bird would let us out. The bird only looked back with curiosity.

"We can't get out," Metoni said.

"Let's break a window," I said.

"With what?" Metoni asked. "There's nothing here we can use."

"Our shoes. They'll have to do," I said.

We beat upon the windows in hopes of shattering them, but they did not break. Two light beams shined up in the window. From something outside? I tried yelling, but I doubted anyone could hear me.

I awoke as K Gerard Martin and realized I was now in the stand-up attic, holding one of the cats. My wife was leaving for work, and her headlights had shone onto the window. A shoe was in my hand—not something I had worn to bed, but part of an excess collection of shoes stored in the attic.

"This dream is getting out of control," I said to myself.

I returned to bed but glanced at the clock and realized I only had half an hour left before getting up for the day, so I knew I had to hurry if I were to salvage the rest of this dream.

"There!" said Tibbit.

Metoni and I were caught and brought down the spiral staircase, back into the factory area, and dragged into the lower levels where dripping hot gear tar choked off the breathable air.

"You have betrayed us all," Gorah said. "I gave you free rein to climb the social ladder. You would have earned rewards for your efforts and the respect of the princess. But instead you will be condemned to work the rest of your days in the lowest levels. You will eat and sleep down here as well, never ascending a single level, and never seeing another person again. Let the gear tar determine your fate."

We were in real crisis. How could I escape the factory? Was this how the dream would end? Worse, I could barely breathe. I knew that the waking K Gerard Martin's body had run out of asthma medication and was suffering from same. To awaken now to take medication would end any chance of completing the dream. I had to stay asleep and suffer through suffocation.

"Armich," Metoni said. "I can't stay here much longer. The gear tar is too much."

"We must look for a way out," I said. "I seem to recall something from the subverter's book that I saw. The prison is not far away. The gear tar flows into a channel. Perhaps we can follow it."

"We'll die. The tar is too hot," Metoni said.

"No choice. We're almost out of time," I said.

We crawled through the channel. As it turned out, there was a narrow ledge slightly above the flow of gear tar, and so we could crawl along that. But the gear tar was hot and sticky, and fumes stuck on our flesh and filled our lungs.

"Armich," called a female voice.

"It's her," I said. "The subverter from the tunnel. The one who was caught. She's my cousin. I saw it in the subverter book. I—"

But I choked on my words. Breathing became too difficult to speak much more.

"Over here," she said.

Metoni and I found a small opening leading to a prison cell but blocked with vertical bars.

"My name is Nola," she said. "I'm your cousin, Armich. Please help me. I will perish down here."

"As will we all," Metoni said.

I tried pulling out the bars, but I was too short of breath.

"Let me try," said Metoni, and he pulled out the bars easily.

"I don't understand how you could—"

"No time for wheezy comments," Metoni said. "And I know how we can get out. Look in Nola's prison cell. There are four coffins."

"They hold people who have died in my cell. They will be sent to the incinerator soon," Nola said.

"Armich—where does the gear tar tunnel lead?" Metoni asked.

"To a gear elevator that lifts the gear tar up," I said. "Wait! That's an interesting idea."

"Remove the people from the coffins, Nola. We're riding the gear elevator inside these things," Metoni said.

Nola removed the people and passed the coffins through the opening one at a time.

"But when we get to the top of the elevator, the gear tar will flow down. We'll be crushed," I said. "I can already feel my chest crushing down on me."

"No, we won't," Metoni said. "There's an overflow valve. The first coffin will be crushed and jam the gear elevator, forcing the overflow valve open. It's a positive relief system, so the rest of us will be thrown clear."

"Or crushed if the relief valve doesn't open," I said. "Oh, my lungs are all but done. I can't continue down here."

"Then let's move now, before we are all lost," Metoni said.

Nola pushed the last coffin through the opening, and we now had the coffins all lined up on the ledge. Then Metoni helped Nola through the opening, and she dropped right into Metoni's arms.

"I hope I can hold you in my arms again soon," he said.

"So do I," she said.

"As you said, Metoni, let's move now," I said.

Metoni and Nola paused, with their eyes exchanging thought and feeling. Then Metoni broke the embrace and helped secure Nola in the third coffin. Next, he secured me in the second coffin.

"Take this laser cutter. You may need it," he said. "Also, pack these items in your coffin."

"A pry bar and shovel. But where did you find them?" I asked.

"No time to explain. Oh, one more thing. If anything goes wrong with the first coffin, I hope you don't mind being the guinea pig," Metoni said.

"Not appreciated," I replied.

"Don't worry. I'll open your coffin first on the surface," he said. "But if I don't, you have these tools."

There was no time to fight over coffins. Once I was secured, Metoni launched the first coffin, me in the second, and Nola in the third. He quickly launched the fourth coffin and secured himself inside. We traveled along, and I could hear the first coffin enter the gear elevator. Then my coffin entered, and I began to ascend. Nola was next, and her coffin also ascended without issue. Metoni made it too. But breathing became incredibly difficult, and in desperation I pressed on my abdomen to force fluid out of my lungs.

Then it happened. The first coffin became lodged in the gear works, and the hydraulic pressure built beyond safe limits. An alarm went off and beeped at regular intervals, and the pressure blasted my coffin, Nola's, and Metoni's through the relief valve and up to the planet's surface.

I now realized the alarm was also my alarm clock, and a brief double-blink showed that I was right, and though I had reached freedom in my dream, I was not satisfied as to its conclusion, and so I closed my eyelids and held them down hard. In so doing, I was able to ignore the alarm clock a little longer.

I reentered the dream and was still in the coffin. Surely I was on the surface, but Metoni had not freed me as he had promised. Did something go wrong? I couldn't wait. I found the pry bar that Metoni had given me. It was tucked in the coffin's inner side. I positioned it between the lid and side, and I pried. And pried. The lid lifted a little, but not much. I pried again, and dirt fell into the coffin. So I wasn't on the surface. I was still in the ground, but how far below? A sudden dread filled me—as the dirt filled the coffin—that I wouldn't get free, and my time would end in solitude, surrounded by the very dirt I'd slaved to be free of.

No, I won't stay buried. I must...just...wait...could I find the shovel in my coffin? Where did I put it? Near my feet. Strange it would be there. But I need to resolve the dream quickly. Move the shovel up with my feet. Hurry. Slide it along a little at a time. Little bit more. Please...yes, got it with my hand. The shovel. Dig a little, put the dirt in the coffin, but don't get trapped. No, don't get trapped. Dig a little more, a little more. There's light, and I hear something. Something moving. I think air pressure is causing things to move. It's wind.

I pushed through the dirt and swam my way to the top, and I stopped. Again, the light from the sun was too bright, and I waited two dozen heartbeats for my eyes to adjust. And they did. I pulled myself atop the planet's surface and looked. I was on a flat, open area, but in the distance I could see those non-moving things called *trees*, and further in the distance I could see those large, pyramids of rock called *mountains*.

"Nola!" I called. "Metoni!"

Near my coffin grave, I saw movement in freshly-dug soil. A few fingertips poked through, and I knew it was Metoni.

"You're almost through!" I said.

I dug with my hands as quickly as I could to free Metoni. In a moment, I pulled him to the planet's surface and helped brush the dirt from him.

"We made it!" I yelled. "Yippie-hoo-ray!"

"Don't celebrate yet!" he said. "We have to find Nola!"

He retrieved a human-detection device from a pocket, held it in front of him, and pivoted in a circle. The device beeped, and he followed it, and I followed him, a good few footsteps from our graves.

"Just a few paces more," Metoni said, and suddenly he stopped.

"What is it?"

"I don't understand," Metoni said. "It says she's here."

"But there's nothing here but these boulders," I said. "How can she be here?"

"Armich, the device doesn't lie. She's here!" Metoni said. "Quickly, help me move the boulders aside."

Our first attempt failed. And our second.

"We need leverage," I said.

"Try the shovels," Metoni said.

The shovels broke.

"The pry bars," Metoni said. "Try them."

Not strong enough.

"Perhaps a branch or log," I said.

"What's a branch?" he asked.

"It's a limb from a tree," I said. "We have limbs that we call arms and legs. On a tree, a limb is known as a *branch*. It's like an arm, but there are no elbows, wrists, or fingers. Find a branch, preferably a straight one, and bring it back."

Metoni ran for the grove of trees and noticed that not only were some branches attached, but some were on the planet's surface, unattached. He grabbed one of those and brought it back.

"Good," I said. "I dug a hole while you were away. Place the branch in the hole, Metoni, and we'll lift the boulder."

We did just that, but as we put our weight on the branch, it broke.

"Where did you find this branch?" I asked.

"In that grove of trees on the planet's surface," he said.

"Then it wasn't attached to a tree?" I asked.

"No," he replied.

"The book says that an old branch like this gets weak after it becomes dismembered from a tree," I said. "We need a fresh branch."

"Fresh?"

"Yes, Metoni," I said. "That means newly cut from a tree."

"But won't that hurt?" he asked. "I mean, when Foreman Gorah cut the arm off a traitor, the traitor screamed in pain."

"Don't worry," I said. "The book says that trees don't feel pain. Go ahead, cut a branch. Here, use this."

I gave him a cutting laser. But he fumbled it and dropped it.

"I can't leave Nola," he said. "I shook with fear the first time I looked for a branch. Here, you take the cutting laser and cut a branch."

I took it, ran to the grove, and cut a fresh limb. The tree quivered a little after it lost its branch, and sap oozed out of its wound. I felt badly for the tree, but Nola's life was at risk, so this had to be done. I brought the branch back to Metoni, and like before, we pushed the branch under the boulder and lifted. The boulder lifted, we shoved the branch under a little more, lifted, and finally, yes finally, we moved the boulder aside. We dug with our hands only a short ways and reached the top of the coffin. We pried the lid open, and there was Nola. An expression of fright melted into relief when her eyes met Metoni's.

"I'm so glad you helped me!" she said as Metoni pulled her up to the planet's surface.

They hugged and kissed and hugged again.

"We made it!" Nola said. "We're free!"

Metoni yelled again in celebration, and I too let out a holler.

"I don't know what I would have done," Nola said. "I can't understand why my coffin lid wouldn't move."

"A boulder pressed down on your coffin," Metoni said.

He pointed to the boulder.

"How did you move it?" she said in amazement.

"With leverage," Metoni said. "Using this branch."

Metoni showed the freshly cut branch to Nola.

"Is it alive?" she asked.

"Not for long," I said. "I had to cut it down from a tree."

"But it looks like it's still alive. Maybe we can give it back to its tree," Nola said.

"Is that possible?" Metoni asked me.

"I don't know," I replied. "The book never mentioned reattaching a limb to a tree. The book says how to do it with human limbs. I guess we can use the laser to bond the outer cells together, but I've never worked with this kind of life form before."

It was decided that we would try. I carried the branch back to the grove of trees, with Metoni walking on my left holding his detection device and Nola strolling next to him.

"I'm getting very odd readings on my device," Metoni said.

"What sort of readings?" Nola asked.

"It doesn't make sense," Metoni said. "It says there are other people here. Living people."

"I don't see anyone," I said.

"I don't either," Nola said.

"But they are here, nonetheless," Metoni said.

"Are they below the planet's surface?" I asked.

"No," Metoni said.

"Are they hiding?" Nola asked.

"No," Metoni said. "They are in the open air. They are a little above us. If I had to guess, I'd say they are in the trees."

"You mean there are people standing on tree branches, waiting to attack us?" I asked.

"Or they could be hanging," Metoni said.

"Metoni, I'm frightened," Nola said, and she moved close to him.

"Stay calm," he said. "Armich will reattach the branch, and we'll leave soon enough."

I led our little group to the tree where I'd cut the branch.

"This is it," I said, but when I looked at the place where the branch had been, the open wound was no more.

"I don't understand," Nola said. "Where did you cut this from?"

"It was this tree," I said. "I swear it was."

"You are right," Metoni said. "The DNA from this branch matches this tree. But the tree has changed."

"How?" I asked.

"It has sprouted new branches, see?" Metoni said. "But they are not like the other branches. The new ones...see how they move? Like vines, or tentacles. They...good mountain of fire...they are...after us!"

Metoni was right. The open wound had sprouted three tentacular vines that descended quickly like snakes. We turned to run, but then the cut branch suddenly turned into mush and exploded, sending debris onto all three of us. Green mush diffused into our skin, and our skin tone changed to green.

"Look at us!" I yelled.

Nola screamed.

"Those energy spheres...they were made from these trees!" Metoni yelled as he fought off a tentacular vine from the tree.

"Why don't I feel stronger?" I yelled back, with my own vine to fight off. "I feel weaker."

"Someone in the complex processed a tree and converted it into an energy sphere," Metoni said. "We're dealing with a raw tree!"

"Metoni, help!" Nola screamed.

Metoni and I turned to look, and the vine lifted Nola into the air.

"Nola!" Metoni yelled. "Armich, help!"

I lifted the laser to cut the vine holding her, but my vine knocked it from my grasp and onto the planet's surface.

"Fight with all your strength," Metoni yelled as his vine sapped him of all energy. "Fight...fight..."

His voice failed, and he went lifeless. Then the vine lifted him in the air and diffused his flesh into its cells. The vine solidified into a branch and bore a cone at its end, a cone with a facial imprint of Metoni.

Horrified, I fought my vine and climbed it to reach Nola. Nola screamed, but her voice also failed, and her vine diffused her flesh into its cells, causing it to solidify and form a branch with a cone at the end bearing the imprint of Nola's face.

"Nola!" I yelled.

My vine rolled up and split into three pieces. The sides split into two each, and now those side pieces were four and pinned my four appendages against the base vine. The middle split of the three rolled up the length of the vine and rolled along my right side, making a scratching sound and wearing away at my flesh like rough sandpaper. I yelled as the vine stripped layers of my skin away, and it continued rolling upward along my gut and to my head, where it stripped layers of my face away. The torture was unbearable. It was only a matter of seconds before the vine would diffuse my flesh into its cells and place my imprint on a cone. Seconds, seconds, seconds, and four thorns from the rolled-up vine now pierced my gut.

I blinked and blinked again. I opened my eyes, and now instead of seeing a vine, two eyes stared back—two eyes that were attached to a furry creature with pointed ears.

It was my cat licking my face, letting me know the alarm was going off. I pushed him aside and disabled the clock's alarm. Then I looked at the time—seven-fifteen in the morning. The cat ran off and chased the other cat around the house. I got up, took an asthma pill, and gave my cat some attention—happy that I was no longer in service to the complex nor in new service to a tree. But I'm still in service to my cat.

Glossary

'Busa *(real)*
A nickname for Suzuki's Hayabusa motorcycle.

7th Avenue *(real)*
A north-south street that runs within a few blocks of Lake Michigan in Kenosha, Wisconsin.

999-000-0100 *(fiction)*
Telephone number for Save-a-Save Service Station in *The Aimless and the Atlantic*.

999-ANY-TIPS *(fiction)*
Police hotline for reporting crime tips in *The Aimless and the Atlantic*.

AC Sniar *(fiction)*
Robert Sniar's aircraft carrier. Is in South Atlantic during SOZOD drilling.

acquiesce *(real)*
To give in to another person's demands.

Acromata *(fiction)*
One of several names given to Wonga in *Between the Lake and Mountain*.

Adam and Eve *(religion)*
Biblical first humans on Earth. Matt in *Trechopagia* says moss has been around since Adam and Eve, suggesting moss is ancient.

Adapto-transicon *(fiction)*
A device created by Dayla Industries useful for analyzing other devices. It contains a special crystal that can only be created in micro-gravity or less environments.

adrenaline *(real)*
A neurochemical stimulant often released in the bloodstream as part of a fight or flight response in people and animals resulting in a number of physiological changes including increased heart rate, blood pressure, sense of strength, and mental activity.

agriecorsteck *(fiction)*
An ethereal accelerant used by Professor Wykepper in *Suflessence* to reactivate the fountain. It mixes with other crystals and can generate a great deal of ethereal material in a short time, much like throwing kerosene on a weak fire.

Aiadaka *(fiction)*
A kingdom consisting of several seamounts in the South Atlantic where orcas live. One such seamount is the Zenker Seamount.

Aiadaks *(fiction)*
The orcan citizens of Aiadaka.

Aiatethis *(fiction)*
A mega squid creature ruling Aiadaka in Sparfy's time and later in Gathona in the distant future.

Aita *(fiction)*
The main seamount in the Aiadaka kingdom.

Aleut *(real)*
A people native to the Aleutian Islands and vicinity, who for a time interacted with Russian fur traders, particularly in sea otters.

Alexandria *(real)*
A great city both in modern and ancient times, located in Egypt and on the Mediterranean Sea.

Alford Park Drive *(real)*
A road along Lake Michigan and Carthage College in Kenosha, Wisconsin.

Alice Bachproon *(fiction)*
Computer scientist and employee of Farrencamp Digital. She has a crush on Major Kyler Bohr.

Aliotra *(fiction)*
A planet where the aliotrotes live. Aliotra is four hundred light years from Earth.

aliotrote *(fiction)*
Alien creatures who consume mercury but hate iron. Aliotrotes invade Earth in *Mirini and the Aliotrotes*.

aliotrotic *(fiction)*
Having to do with the aliotrotes.

alkaloid *(real)*
Medicinal chemical based on nitrogen and derived from a life form, typically from plants, with a wide range of effects. People have extracted alkaloids from plants since prehistoric times and have used alkaloids to treat a wide array of ailments. Alkaloids can also be deadly.

alkane *(real)*
A hydrocarbon. Alkanes are collections of hydrogen and carbon, are inflammable, and are typically used as fuel or as solvents. Common alkanes include methane, butane, and straight gasoline (without additives).

Allegheny Front *(real)*
A south-east facing escarpment two to three miles wide on the eastern border of the Allegheny Mountains.

Allen Beacon Dofer *(fiction)*
A main character in *The Duchess of Darby* who starts off as a journalist but is fired and makes his way into the life of Duchess Devanna. He is 13th Knight of Barley.

Alpha Tech *(fiction)*
Lead technician for Baroness Vasha in the story *The Duchess of Darby*.

Alpine Audi *(fiction)*
Audi dealer in Brunswick, Georgia, located next to Bnatta BMW.

amalgam *(real)*
An alloy based on mercury and one or more metals.

Ambiothargic *(fiction)*
A made-up word combining the meanings of "ambi" for "both/around", and "lethargic" for lack of energy. "Ambiothargic" is used to describe the feelings of both Debbie and Roger Dayla in the beginning of *Debbie's Trial* of being surrounded by a duality of conditions giving them a sense of weakness as if from disease.

Amelia Earhart *(real)*
Famous American pilot of the 1920s and 1930s who disappeared over the Pacific Ocean while flying around the world.

Ami's Cove *(fiction)*
New name of Wonga's castle in *Between the Lake and Mountain*, given by Claire in honor of Amicolli.

Amicolli *(fiction)*
A spotted-neck otter from the Nile River in the times of ancient Egypt. Her full name is Hydricetistelidalina Maculisarcolleenivorsa. She can change shape from otter to humanoid and back and helped the first dolphins of the Mediterranean/Atlantic Ocean change shape. She became dormant for thousands of years until she reawakened in *Between the Lake and Mountain*.

amino acids *(real)*
The building blocks of life. Amino acids are composed primarily of hydrogen, carbon, nitrogen, and oxygen and are used to create protein chains which in turn are used to build a vast array of biological components.

amnesia *(real)*
A loss of memory, either a temporary loss or permanent.

amoeba *(real)*
An amoeba in common language typically means a single-cell protozoan in the amoebozoa phylum. There is also an Amoeba genus farther down the line from the amoebozoa phylum, but that usage is not represented in this work of fiction. The name "Arcella" is taken from the genus Arcella under the amoebozoan phylum, and so Arcella is not an Amoeba in the strict taxonomic sense, but it is an amoeba in the general/common-language sense of amoebozoan.

ampule *(real)*
A sealed glass container with a fluid. It is commonly used to hold a single-use medication that can be drawn into a syringe for injection into a person or animal.

AMRAAM *(real)*
An air-to-air missile originating from the United States, typically fired from an aircraft.

anchovy *(real)*
A small and common salt-water fish found in oceans around the world. Anchovies provide a valuable food source for predatory fish, birds, and marine mammals. Anchovies are also eaten by humans, especially in pizza.

android *(almost real)*
An artificial life form designed to resemble a human.

andronide *(fiction)*
A slow-action poison that kills only men in *Sense of Place*. Andronide kills the victim after a week from first contact.

androtolynite *(fiction)*
A fast-acting poison and microexplosive that only kills men in *Sense of Place*.

anemically *(real)*
Weak, suffering from anemia (a blood condition of reduced red blood cells causing a pale skin and reduced energy).

anesthetized *(real)*
Made insensitive to pain or touch.

anfractuous *(fiction)*
Without fracture. Solid. Without defect.

Anfractuous Armor *(fiction)*
A vest of power in *Save For Proper Buyer* that gives special powers to the wearer such as protection, invisibility, and the ability to fly. The vest can change into armor and back.

ANG *(real)*
Air National Guard.

Anglo *(real)*
An ethnicity of Anglo-Saxon origins, a people who migrated to and lived in England since the 5th century. "Anglo" is often used to denote people of fair skin and European background.

anthropogenic *(real)*
Created or caused by humans.

anthropological *(real)*
Of the science of humans and their way of life, typically historical.

antibiotic *(real)*
Chemical produced by a microorganism to slow or stop growth of another microorganism. Jack Highbower is given antibiotics to treat his Rocky Mountain spotted fever infection.

Anti-blinner League *(fiction)*
A group of people on Gathona who discuss strategy and make plans against the blinners in *The Blinners of Gathona*.

antidote *(real)*
A medicine to counteract a poison. Loran believes he has been poisoned by a sunderag and that he needs an antidote as a cure.

Antique Imports *(fiction)*
A store in *Save for Proper Buyer* that sells antiques and special products, including the Anfractuous Armor that the narrator acquires.

anto-ionic regression wave *(fiction)*
A jamming wave to disrupt communications, created by subverters in *For Thy Service* just before they attack.

APB *(real)*
Law enforcement abbreviation for All Points Bulletin, a broadcast from one law enforcement group to another with information, typically about a wanted person.

apeponic *(fiction)*
Afflicted or one who is afflicted with *apeponisis*.

apeponisis *(fiction)*
Condition in toothed cetaceans where one cannot echolocate due to a damaged or missing melon. Comes from Greek *a-* "without" + *pepóni* "melon" + *-sis* "condition".

Apollo *(real)*
American space program of the 1960s and 1970s that carried people to the Moon and back.

Appalachian Mountains, Appalachians *(real)*
A mountain range in eastern North American from Maine and Canada down to Alabama and Georgia.

Appanakahi, Leiolaki, Reekaiya *(fiction)*
Commands that Loa'neth uses to pull a cage containing Stephen and Claire from a tar pit in *Between the Lake and Mountain*.

apparition *(real)*
A ghost or such image, typically of a person.

Applied Transformation 101 *(fiction)*
A course taught in cetacean school on transforming one's shape into other life forms and back. Circigi admits to Chusacuta in *The Blinners of Gathona* that he barely passed the course with a grade of D.

Arabia *(real)*
The Arabian Peninsula.

aragonite *(real)*
A crystalized form of calcium carbonate.

arbochaise *(fiction)*
A long chair (*chaise longue*) with a wheel on each of the four legs. Each end is raised so as to support a reclining person's head and feet, with the head end being higher than the foot end so that one's head is a bit higher than one's feet. The middle portion toward the foot has a small "hill" so that a reclining person's knees may bend and be supported.

arbodulus *(fiction)*
See *arbor accommodus remodulator*.

arbor accommodus remodulator *(fiction)*
Also known as the arbodulus, a device invented by Professor Wykepper that sits atop two intersecting arches. It searches for unbridled suflessence, accumulates it, and restreams it into a modulated form.

Arbreezias *(fiction)*
A lead blinner and close friend of Darlina in *The Blinners of Gathona*.

Arcella *(fiction)*
Assistant and close friend of Senator Croius from the Debbie Dayla stories.

archarbor *(fiction)*
A building with two half-domes merged together, used by Professor Wykepper in *Suflessence* to control the use and transfer of suflessence.

archeological *(real)*
Of or having to do with archeology.

archeologist *(real)*
One who studies archeology.

archeology *(real)*
The study of human activities in the past.

archray *(fiction)*
The top-ranking electric ray of a seamount in Lagenora.

Archray Diplobus *(fiction)*
Archray of Corleopus and a former teacher of Korlan's.

arcto *(fiction)*
An angular unit of measure for azimuth, corresponding to one degree.

Armich *(fiction)*
A main character in *For Thy Service* who also represents the author as he dreams.

Arrival *(fiction)*
A process used by Master of Slaffton whereby people are converted into plant-like slaves in *Between the Lake and Mountain*.

Ashley *(fiction)*
A library assistant to Remmen in *For Thy Service*.

Asmondo Arliaco *(fiction)*
An assassin and traitor of Bruxima 4. Asmondo changes shape to deceive his victims.

asthma *(real)*
A physical condition of animals where the lung passageways constrict and fill with fluid, making breathing difficult. In *For Thy Service*, the author runs out of asthma medication and experiences difficulty breathing, coinciding with his dream where he is working in the lower levels with the gear tar, making breathing difficult.

Athena *(religion)*
Patroness goddess of Athens and daughter of Zeus in ancient Greece.

Athens *(real)*
In *Between the Lake and Mountain*, Athens refers to the ancient city of Greece.

Atlantic mackerel *(real)*
A schooling fish in the North Atlantic Ocean, heavily consumed by cetaceans.

Atlantic torpedo ray *(real)*
A large electric ray of the Atlantic Ocean. Korlan of the Debbie Dayla stories is an Atlantic torpedo ray.

Atlantic white-sided dolphin *(real)*
A dolphin inhabiting the North Atlantic Ocean with stripes along the length of its body. Chusacuta is an Atlantic white-sided dolphin.

atrophy *(real)*
A condition where a muscle or other fleshy organ of an animal withers and loses strength or ability to function.

attenuate *(real)*
To thin, taper, or reduce in strength. Debbie Dayla speaks of the SOZOD beam already being attenuated in reply to Vicia's request to focus it. In this meaning, the beam is tapered.

Auberge *(real/fiction)*
An auberge is an inn. In *Sense of Place*, the Auberge is a secret place of knowledge and research run by Doctor Belsl, and is considered by the Skulava progressor women as a place of hospitality, like an inn.

autocanary *(fiction)*
A device in *Between the Lake and Mountain* that checks if the environment is fit for humanoid existence. It is an inanimate form of a canary, a bird once used to test for breathable air in mining conditions.

avionics *(real)*
The electronics used in an aircraft.

axon *(real)*
A nerve fiber that carries electrical impulses.

Ayma *(fiction)*
A device created by Craymar Industries to convert raw materials into usable tools. It is found by Cuperia in *Sense of Place* in a cave that becomes the Auberge. The letters "AYMA" are the only readable letters found on the device. In fact, those letters are what's left of the word CRAYMAR, which was written on the device.

Baby 'Busa *(fiction)*
The name Kakuda gives his motorcycle in *The Duchess of Darby*.

Baliotrotes *(fiction)*
Mercury-based robots created by Mirini's grandfather, Silano, to help fight the iron wars on Bruxima 4, in *Mirini and the Aliotrotes*.

Barnaby Nith Barcloff *(fiction)*
Owner and Chief Editor of Darby Magazine, and for a time the boss of Allen Dofer, in *The Duchess of Darby*.

Baroness Vasha *(fiction)*
Royal woman in *The Duchess of Darby* who is in line to the throne after Duchess Devanna and whose sole focus is to discredit Duchess Devanna to effect her own ascension to the throne.

Barry *(fiction)*
Former boyfriend of Jack Highbower's mother in *Trechopagia* who "promised the world".

Baruben *(fiction)*
Gliria's suggested name for a future son she might have in honor of her grandfather, in *Between the Lake and Mountain*.

Base Control *(fiction)*
Communication control center in *For Thy Service* that Armich speaks with while traveling in the vattertram.

bearberry *(real)*
A low-growing plant with berries bears like to eat. The leaves can be used for medicinal purposes. The narrator in *Save for Proper Buyer* smells a combination of sweet grass, bearberry, and red willow from the basement of Antique Imports.

Bedora *(fiction)*
Main character in *Suflessence* who is told she only has a few days to live.

Beguiling Grotto *(fiction)*
The picocian name for Wretched Cave in *Between the Lake and Mountain*.

Betty *(fiction)*
One of the blind folk in *The Blinners of Gathona*, who with Nolan offers help to Circigi in his quest to rescue Chusacuta.

Beugo *(fiction)*
Chrba's father, a trader in Farthar Falls.

Biaba *(fiction)*
One of Lady Spenwick's assistants in Mother's Hall, from *Sense of Place*.

bifurcated *(real)*
Split or forked.

Bill *(fiction)*
One of several young men at a party held shortly after Connie Dayla's graduation from Varcher University.

Bimmer *(real)*
Nickname for a BMW automobile.

Bioprog *(fiction)*
Short for Biopropagation device. A repository of DNA samples created by Dayla Industries so that Earth's many life forms would survive centuries of ecological devastation. In *Sense of Place*, Eren and Chrba discover the device in a room hidden inside a hill.

biotoxicacity *(fiction)*
The act of disrupting the ecological balance of a community by introducing foreign life, much like introducing a biotoxin. In *Between the Lake and Mountain*, the Master of Slaffton accuses the visitors of biotoxicacity.

Black Hawk *(real/fiction)*
One of the last surviving Nicoleño people on San Nicolas Island off the coast of California. Black Hawk's interaction with Lutris in *Between the Lake and Mountain* is fictional.

Blackbird Five, Seven, Nine, Ten *(fiction)*
Air National Guard aircraft pursuing tumbling satellite Scythoc Three across the United States in *Mirini and the Aliotrotes*.

Blackpier *(fiction)*
A city in *Between the Lake and Mountain* where plant-burning is illegal.

Bleam *(fiction)*
Call sign for Kyler Bohr in *Mirini and the Aliotrotes*.

bleeder *(real)*
A severed blood vessel.

blinner *(fiction)*
A blinner is a person who is in service to Aiatethis. Most blinners are blind and use special head gear for vision. Those who use this head gear are known as "helmetbanders".

Bnatta *(fiction)*
Owner of Bnatta BMW. Mr. Bnatta has sold many BMWs to Roger Dayla and also provided the BMW for Connie Dayla's birthday present.

bonsai *(real/fiction)*
A Japanese art where miniature trees are grown. In *Suflessence*, the bonsai tree is a leader of a group of vegetarian cats.

Boosbaby *(fiction)*
The personalized name of Kakuda Mori's Hayabusa motorcycle, from *The Duchess of Darby*.

boosmo *(fiction)*
A nickname for "boosmosine".

boosmosine *(fiction)*
A cross between a bus and a limousine owned by Professor Wykepper in *Suflessence*.

borax *(real)*
A compound of sodium and boron, and a salt of boric acid. Borax historically has been used as a laundry detergent. Borax has other uses, one of which is a component of glass.

boric acid *(real)*
A compound of boron, hydrogen, and oxygen often used in insecticides and herbicides. Boric acid is useful for enhancing the properties of glass and fiberglass.

Borrak *(fiction)*
One of several subverters Ashley knows in *For Thy Service*.

bottlenose dolphin *(real)*
A common and well-known grey dolphin with a wide ocean range. Bottlenose dolphins are friendly to people and are found in marine parks.

Braegan Laculic *(fiction)*
Loran's brother in *Between the Lake and Mountain*. Runs Laculic Tavern with his wife, Morga.

braille *(real)*
A written script using a pattern of bumps to indicate characters instead of ink-based printing. Braille is used by blind people to read. In *The Blinners of Gathona*, Darlina claims to read braille books at home.

breeberry *(fiction)*
A berry distantly related to barley and useful in producing ale as used in *Between the Lake and Mountain*.

Bregget *(fiction)*
One of several aliases for Wonga in *Between the Lake and Mountain*.

Brenda *(fiction)*
Wife of Jack Highbower in *Trechopagia*.

Brian Kukovich *(fiction)*
Son of Doctor Anton Kukovich. Plays bass guitar in the music group Ramona and the Smackadeliacs.

Brunswick *(real)*
City in Georgia on the coast of the Atlantic Ocean. Home to Debbie Dayla and her family.

Brunswick 500 *(fiction)*
A five-hundred mile automobile race in *The Aimless and the Atlantic*.

Brunswick Crab Co-op *(fiction)*
Seafood store next to Alpine Audi in Brunswick, Georgia, where Connie Dayla crashes a stolen Audi.

Brunswick Ogres *(fiction)*
College football team of which Jayvogg Hochenstock is a quarterback.

Bruxi *(fiction)*
A citizen of Bruxima 4, from *Mirini and the Aliotrotes*.

Bruxima 4 *(fiction)*
Home planet of Mirini from *Mirini and the Aliotrotes*.

Bruxima 5 *(fiction)*
Future home of Earth's cetaceans, and a neighboring planet of Bruxima 4.

Bu *(fiction)*
Nickname for WBU channel 48 in *The Aimless and the Atlantic*.

Buckner Fair *(fiction)*
Also known as the Buckner Falls Paleo Fair. A store that sells fossils and other relics of the past in *Between the Lake and Mountain*.

Buckner Falls *(fiction)*
A city on the west side of Rainbear Mountain in *Between the Lake and Mountain*.

Buran *(real)*
Soviet spacecraft modeled after the American space shuttle.

cacophony *(real)*
Mixture of uncoordinated sounds, often annoying the listener.

calcium carbonate *(real)*
Compound of calcium, carbon, and oxygen. Calcium carbonate is an ingredient in shells such as egg shells and sea shells and is common throughout marine life.

calemear *(fiction)*
"Calemear" is a combination of the words cadmium, lead, mercury, and arsenic and is a mixture of those four elements. "Calemear" is referenced in *Sense of Place*.

Cambrian *(real)*
First geological period of the Paleozoic Era, the Cambrian period (approximately 542 – 488 million years ago) was known for the rapid development of life, often known as the Cambrian explosion. Microbial mats, which were common on the seabed at the beginning of the Cambrian period, were all but destroyed at the end of the period by burrowing animals. In *Return from Lagenora*, Debbie Dayla dives in the Cambrian sea into and below a microbial mat and back in time before the Oxygen Catastrophe (about 2.4 billion years ago).

Captain Friscott *(fiction)*
Merchant captain in *Between the Lake and Mountain* who hates picocians but who is also converted into a merselat.

Captain Pat Wallace *(fiction)*
Leader of the Sea Herder movement to disrupt whaling ships in *Mirini and the Aliotrotes*.

carbonyl *(real)*
A group of organic compounds containing a carbon atom bonded twice to an oxygen atom. Carbonyls produce fruity aromas in smokehouses.

carcinogen *(real)*
A cancer-causing agent.

cardinal *(real)*
In *Mirini and the Aliotrotes*, "cardinal" means one of the four compass directions: north, east, south, or west.

cardio *(real)*
Related to the heart.

Carthage College *(real)*
A four-year college on the north side of Kenosha, Wisconsin.

cartography *(real)*
The study and making of maps.

cataract *(real)*
In *Between the Lake and Mountain*, Amicolli refers to the first cataract of the Nile River. A cataract in this sense means the rapid-flowing first cataract portion of the Nile where rocks protrude from the shallow riverbed.

catatonic *(real)*
Having lack of movement and limited thinking ability. Doctor Belsl warns Eren that jayladopa could leave Eren in a catatonic state, meaning Eren would be unable to move or think, like being in a deep daze.

Cathy Crepp *(fiction)*
Employee at Darby Magazine in *The Duchess of Darby*. Co-worker of Allen Dofer while he worked there.

cauldron *(real)*
A large, round pot with handles and often with legs that sits over a fire and is used for boiling.

caustic *(real)*
Able to destroy tissue or another material. Corrosive. Also means a harsh or scathing social interaction.

cauterize *(real)*
To burn tissue with a hot brand historically or with a modern device, often as part of a medical procedure to destroy bad tissue or seal ruptured blood vessels.

CC-33, Craymar CC-33 *(fiction)*
A supersonic amphibious jet plane created by Craymar Industries. The CC-33 is similar to the F2Y Sea Dart but much larger and can carry cargo or many people.

Cenozoic Era *(real)*
A span of time in Earth's history in the study of geochronology from 66 million years ago to modern times. This book was written in the Cenozoic Era, and as of this writing, the era is still in progress. In *Trechopagia*, Jack Highbower refers to the DNA of moss being left over from the Cenozoic Era. Moss evolution predates the Cenozoic Era, and so the reference time-wise would seem to be erroneous. However, the reference is to the time when Jack lived in Kenosha, circa 2011, and so the reference to the Cenozoic Era is accurate.

Central Records *(fiction)*
A repository of information, like a library, located in Kmina, a seamount kingdom in Lagenora. Circigi is an obituary recorder for Central Records in Kmina.

central tethis *(fiction)*
A hub where neural activity of the blinners and the sighted of Gathona converges. It is located in a chamber where Aiatethis resides, and it is Aiatethis who controls the central tethis.

CEO *(real)*
CEO stands for Chief Executive Officer, a title used in business to indicate the leader of a company. Roger Dayla was for many years the leader of Dayla Industries until the SOZOD incident in the South Atlantic unbalanced him.

Cetacea *(real)*
A taxonomic order that includes whales, dolphins, and porpoises.

Cetacea of the Dead *(fiction)*
Another name for Gathona, an island where most fulltran Lagenor cetacean citizens are buried.

cetacean *(real)*
An animal in the Cetacea order, meaning a whale, dolphin, or porpoise.

chaise longue *(real)*
From French. A long chair, often with a back half-way along its length, though some forms do not.

Chamber Forty-Five *(fiction)*
A chamber where Armich and Metoni once slept, in *For Thy Service*.

Charla Grayto *(fiction)*
General Grayto's daughter in *Mirini and the Aliotrotes*. She is Asmondo Arliaco's target.

charlock *(real)*
A wild mustard plant. It is considered a weed in most places where it grows.

charlock salt *(fiction)*
A special herbicide salt that kills charlock but leaves other plants unharmed. Charlock salt is mined by picocians.

Chawbree *(fiction)*
Professor Monfri's assistant in *The Aimless and the Atlantic*.

chelation *(real)*
In this book, "chelation" refers to "chelation therapy", a process where heavy metals are removed from the body.

Cherabina *(fiction)*
See *Chrba*.

Cherry-Charry Archway *(fiction)*
An archway of knowledge, maintained by Remmen in the library as told in *For Thy Service*.

Chief Physician *(real/fiction)*
A title indicating the top leading doctor in a group or society. Queen Brela is the top doctor in the Kingdom of Phocayna and directs the style of treatment among her doctors.

Chief Scientist *(real/fiction)*
Another title indicating the top scientist in a group or society. Vorlac is Chief Scientist in Rhynchus.

Chrba *(fiction)*
Daughter of Inasherry and friend of Eren in *Sense of Place*.

Chusacuta *(fiction)*
An Atlantic white-sided fulltran dolphin in *The Duchess of Darby* and *The Blinners of Gathona*. Chusacuta is the leading fertility scientist of Lagenora.

Chusigi *(fiction)*
Adopted son of Chusacuta and Circigi. He makes an appearance in *The Blinners of Gathona* and *Sense of Place*.

Circigi Cento *(fiction)*
An hourglass fulltran dolphin from Kmina. He is deeply attracted to Chusacuta.

Claire Stackhart *(fiction)*
Young woman in *Between the Lake and Mountain* who falls in love with Lutris, a Pacific sea otter. She is cousin to Stephen Royer.

CLAM *(fiction)*
In *Between the Lake and Mountain*, George Snake reverses words, and "CLAM" is a reverse of "MALC".

clamifore *(fiction)*
Large clam creatures living in a chamber below Crow Pits Island in *Between the Lake and Mountain*.

Clamiforia *(fiction)*
The name of the clamifore kingdom in *Between the Lake and Mountain*.

Clamiforia Celebration Day *(fiction)*
A day of celebration as declared by Master of Slaffton in *Between the Lake and Mountain*.

Clan Acus *(fiction)*
A line of dusky dolphins with King Acus as its current chief.

Clan Zigo *(fiction)*
A powerful family of electric rays of which Korlan, Vorlac, and Krivat are members.

Colonel John Von Brock *(fiction)*
Pilot in the Georgia Air National Guard in *Mirini and the Aliotrotes*. Interacts with Major Kyler Bohr, at times like a friend, at other times not.

combersoni *(fiction)*
The Lagenoran term for Commerson's dolphins.

Command Center *(fiction)*
An underground aeronautical control center located in South Dakota, charged with monitoring aircraft and other objects both in Earth orbit and in Earth's atmosphere.

Commerson's dolphin *(real)*
A black and white dolphin native to the southern tip of South America and to the Kerguelen Islands in the Indian Ocean.

commonwealth *(real)*
A commonwealth is a political unit, often on a larger scale than a city or county. It can be a state such as the Commonwealth of Virginia, or a country.

Commonwealth of Darby *(fiction)*
The country of Darby. See *Darby*.

complexus *(fiction)*
See *sponge complexus*.

Conclusion *(fiction)*
A process on Crow Pits Island in *Between the Lake and Mountain* where organisms become part of the underground clamifore community.

Concorde *(real)*
Supersonic passenger aircraft operated by Britain and France from 1976 to 2003.

Connie Dayla *(fiction)*
Constance Leeann Dayla, also known as Connie Dayla, is the daughter of Roger and Julie Dayla and the older sister of Debbie Dayla.

co-op *(real)*
A cooperative business run by the people who buy/sell its products and services. In *Trechopagia*, Jack Highbower makes a deal with a co-op owned

by Mortgage Bank Brothers to buy the methane from his Cyclozyme. In *The Aimless and the Atlantic*, Connie Dayla crashes into Brunswick Crab Co-op.

Corleopus *(fiction)*
Corleopus is a kingdom ruled by King Adelfo and Queen Tharia. It is located close to the Crawford Seamount in the South Atlantic and inhabited mainly by striped dolphins. Princess Adelfarina is from Corleopus.

cortexicon *(fiction)*
A device in *Mirini and the Aliotrotes* used by the blinners to extract knowledge from and control a brain.

Count Fenton of Farr *(fiction)*
One of several royal men and potential future husband of Duchess Devanna in *The Duchess of Darby*.

County Hospital *(fiction)*
A hospital serving the Brunswick area in *The Aimless and the Atlantic*.

Coyla *(fiction)*
A small coal- and clay-mining town in the Appalachians, somewhere in the Pennsylvania/West Virginia area. It is the hometown of Jack Highbower in *Trechopagia*. "Coyla" is a mixture of the words "coal" and "clay".

CPR *(real)*
Cardiopulmonary resuscitation. The act of assisting another person who has stopped breathing and has a stopped heart by breathing air into the victim's lungs and performing compressions on the chest to force the heart to pump. The goal of CPR is to restore a minimum level of blood and oxygen flow in the victim's body to prevent death until the victim can be resuscitated with more advanced medical techniques.

Craymar Industries *(fiction)*
Competitor to Dayla Industries. Craymar uses unethical methods to achieve its success and at times is able to provide superior products to what Dayla Industries can provide.

crevasse *(real)*
A wide and deep crack in a glacier.

Crow Pits Island *(fiction)*
An island in Lake Meadowash in *Between the Lake and Mountain*. Under the surface is a community of clamifores and undead.

CT scan *(real)*
Computerized tomography scan uses multiple X-ray angles to achieve a three-dimensional view of an object, often of the human body.

cufflet *(real)*
A garment wider than a bracelet but shorter than a sleeve that is worn on the arm typically over the wrist and forearm.

Cuperia *(real)*
Eren's mother in *Sense of Place*.

Curatidoma *(fiction)*
"House of cure." Curatidoma is the name of the main medical center in Rhynchus.

Curiami *(fiction)*
A woman in *Suflessence* who is about to die but is helped by the main character, Bedora, and by Professor Wykepper.

cuttleberry *(fiction)*
A mixed derivative of cuttlebone and elderberries created by Morga in *Between the Lake and Mountain*.

cuttlebone *(real)*
An internal shell of a cuttlefish, composed of aragonite, and often used as a dietary supplement for caged birds.

cuttlefish *(real)*
An invertebrate marine animal that lives in shallow waters.

cyano- *(real/fiction)*
In this book, "cyano-" refers to shades of blue (or blue-green) such as found in cyan. Armich uses a cyano-infrared viewer, which allows him to see subverters in shades of blue (cyano part) and red (infrared part).

cyanobacteria *(real)*
A form of bacteria capable of photosynthesis.

Cyclozyme *(fiction)*
In this book, a Cyclozyme is a machine that uses cylinders and enzymes in a cycle process to convert farm crops into methane. Jack Highbower invests in a Cyclozyme in *Trechopagia* at enormous cost.

cynalla, cynalli *(fiction)*
A cynalla is the distance a dalli porpoise can swim in one cynor (in 14.4 minutes), a distance of about 13.2 kilometers or 8.16 miles. The cynalla is a unit of measure used by the cetaceans of Lagenora.

cynor *(fiction)*
A unit of time equal to 14.4 minutes, used by the cetaceans of Lagenora.

Dall's porpoise *(real)*
A fast-swimming cetacean with its primary habitat in the North Pacific Ocean. In the Debbie Dayla stories, the Kingdom of Phocayna in the South Atlantic Ocean contains such porpoises. This is a special exception to the rule that Dall's porpoises are only found in the Pacific Ocean.

dalli porpoise *(fiction)*
A fictional name for Dall's porpoise. In the Debbie Dayla stories, the dalli porpoises inhabit Phocayna in the South Atlantic.

Dalliana *(fiction)*
One of many female dalli porpoises with whom Prince Metavasi socializes.

Dana Farrencamp *(fiction)*
Owner and Chief Executive Officer of Farrencamp Digital, a company located in Victoria, British Columbia.

Dara *(fiction)*
A picocian in *Between the Lake and Mountain* who at one time works for George Snake, then escapes with Loran and company, and merges first with Meorus and next with Amicolli.

Darby *(fiction)*
The Commonwealth of Darby, or Darby, is an unmapped island in the North Atlantic Ocean, not far from England. It is largely forgotten by the world except for royal folk in England, who know of Darby but prefer not to speak of its existence so as to protect the island's heritage from outside influence. Darby is the home of Queen Cythia, Duchess Devanna, Baroness Vasha, Allen Dofer, Mr. Barcloff, Cathy Crepp, Kakuda Mori, and many others.

Darby Bakery *(fiction)*
A bakery in Darby which produces the finest desserts and often supplies such baked goods to the royals.

Darby Dolphinarium *(fiction)*
An aquarium in Darby that holds many species of dolphin.

Darby Grand Prix *(fiction)*
A once-a-year automotive racing event held in the Commonwealth of Darby.

Darby Magazine *(fiction)*
A periodical magazine company in *The Duchess of Darby* where Allen Dofer works and is fired. Chief editor is Mr. Barcloff.

Darby TV3 *(fiction)*
A television station in the Commonwealth of Darby that covers news stories.

Darlina *(fiction)*
The town alchemist in *The Blinners of Gathona*. She purportedly can see for very brief periods of time and strikes up a relationship with Circigi, only to turn against him in the end.

Darmon *(fiction)*
The bouncer at Laculic Tavern in *Between the Lake and Mountain*.

DAYCON *(fiction)*
See *Dayla Control*.

Dayla *(fiction)*
The last name of several people in this book, primarily Debbie Dayla and her family.

Dayla Control, Dayla Central Control *(fiction)*
A spacecraft coordination control room much like NASA's Houston Control, but oriented more toward Dayla spacecraft. Also known as DAYCON.

Dayla diamond computer *(fiction)*
A computer with integrated circuits based on diamond carbon instead of silicon. Dayla diamond computers run much more quickly than traditional silicon computers.

Dayla Earth High Orbit spacecraft, DEHO *(fiction)*
A spacecraft built by Dayla Industries capable of attaining a geo-sync orbit or higher (altitude greater than 22,000 miles).

Dayla Earth Sub-Orbit spacecraft, DESO *(fiction)*
A spacecraft built by Dayla Industries that cannot attain Earth orbit but can attain sub-orbital flight and uses such for rapid transportation from one place to another.

Dayla Industries *(fiction)*
A company founded by Roger Dayla that produces all sorts of high-quality devices from garbage cans to spacecraft.

Dayla Industries Hangar *(fiction)*
A place where aircraft are stored for Dayla Industries in the Debbie Dayla stories.

Dayla Institution for the Neurologically Impaired *(fiction)*
An institution founded by Roger Dayla to advance mental health treatment for people in the Brunswick area.

Dayla Malf Machine *(fiction)*
An aircraft built by Dayla Industries that can simulate weightlessness, similar to NASA's reduced gravity aircraft (vomit comet).

Dayla Spacecraft Assembly Building *(fiction)*
A tall building capable of holding a variety of spacecraft. The building is used to prepare such craft for spaceflight.

Dayla vest *(fiction)*
An experimental vest created by Dayla Industries that finds its way to the Pacific Rim and is used by Tau in *Save for Proper Buyer*.

daylazina *(fiction)*
A variation of Daylazine that acts as a stimulant in the human body. It is referenced in *Sense of Place*.

Daylazine *(fiction)*
A stimulant discovered by Lillianina in *Between the Lake and Mountain* and used by Loran Laculic.

Debbie Dayla *(fiction)*
Full name is Debra Jo Dayla. Main character in the Debbie Dayla stories such as *The Aimless and the Atlantic*, *Debbie's Trial*, and *Return from Lagenora*. She is the second daughter of Roger and Julie Dayla. Debbie has strange powers and has been known to kill people and animals, though this killing is an involuntary response to perceived evil. She strikes up a friendship with Prince Sparfiacus of Rhynchus.

Deep Lab 3 *(fiction)*
A lab at Farrencamp Digital positioned deep underground so as to be protected from outside forces such as invasion. Alice and Kyler enter Deep Lab 3 when aliotrotes invade the Victoria area.

DEHO *(fiction)*
See *Dayla Earth High Orbit spacecraft*.

Delfa *(fiction)*
See *Princess Adelfarina*.

Department of Energy *(real)*
A branch of the United States federal government that concerns itself with energy policy.

DESO *(fiction)*
See *Dayla Earth Sub-Orbit spacecraft*.

devessitate *(real/fiction)*
"Devessitate" in this book means to diminish (one's life-force) to the point of being unresponsive. The word comes from the Latin word *devexitas*, which means downward slope.

Devie Cede Nim *(fiction)*
The supposed magic words written on Myoxi's map that is actually "mine deceived" spelled backward.

devitiate *(real/fiction)*
To corrupt or spoil. In *Mirini and the Aliotrotes*, it means to corrupt one's cells by means of a device for absorption by an aliotrote.

devitiator *(fiction)*
A cellular corruption device that converts a person's body to a form usable by aliotrotes.

DF-23, Dayla DF-23 *(fiction)*
An experimental aircraft built by Dayla Industries and based on the Northrop/McDonnell Douglas YF-23.

dialogiar *(fiction)*
A communications device built into the vattertram in *For Thy Service*.

diota wave *(fiction)*
A wave form resembling a double-handled vase, referenced in *Sense of Place*.

Director of Science and Medicine *(fiction)*
The government head of all science and medical groups, appointed by Queen Cythia in *The Duchess of Darby*. The Director of Science and Medicine helps form policy to ensure all scientists and medical people follow safe and proper procedures, and the director also can use resources to do research and to publish books.

DNA *(real)*
"DNA" stands for "deoxyribonucleic acid" and is a molecule used to hold genetic information. DNA is referenced in *Trechopagia*, *The Duchess of Darby*, *Mirini and the Aliotrotes*, *Sense of Place*, and *For Thy Service*.

Doctor Anton Kukovich *(fiction)*
Lead scientist and engineer at Dayla Industries. Father of Brian Kukovich.

Doctor Belsl *(fiction)*
Runs the Auberge in *Sense of Place*. Doctor Belsl became blind from an elder's attack and so has devoted her ensuing life to help others. She learned how to use the Ayma device. Mother of Solina.

Doctor Cephaligi *(fiction)*
A doctor of medicine in Gaviceti 5. Doctor Cephaligi specializes in animals outside of cetaceans, including humans.

Doctor Dictionary *(fiction)*
An uncomplimentary name given to Von Brock by Kyler in *Mirini and the Aliotrotes*.

Doctor Hochenstock *(fiction)*
Geologist who helped Robert Sniar with his oil drilling operation but quit over the issue of drilling into the R.S.A. Seamount. Adoptive parent of Jayvogg.

Doctor Julia Craymar *(fiction)*
Professor at the University of Hammencase in *Save for Proper Buyer*. Her father founded Craymar Industries.

Doctor Otot *(fiction)*
A doctor of medicine in *Suflessence* who does everything she can to keep Bedora alive.

Doctor Von Brock *(fiction)*
See *Colonel John Von Brock*.

Doctor Wilson *(fiction)*
A passenger in a crashed plane who is rescued by Tau in *Save for Proper Buyer*.

dolphinarium *(real)*
An aquarium for dolphins.

dolphinic *(fiction)*
Of or relating to dolphins.

Donovan *(fiction)*
Van driver for Sueann's catering service in *The Duchess of Darby*.

Dralla *(fiction)*
Curiami's sister in *Suflessence*.

Drayk Nasher *(fiction)*
One of several lucky journalists who wins an invitation to Duchess Devanna's birthday party in *The Duchess of Darby*.

Drojiap *(fiction)*
A Norwegian royal family of which Allen Dofer has relations.

Duchess Devanna *(fiction)*
Queen Cythia's niece and first in line to the throne in *The Duchess of Darby*, a story in which Duchess Devanna seeks a husband through a birthday party.

Duke Arthur of Cantaloofa *(fiction)*
One of several royal men and potential future husband of Duchess Devanna in *The Duchess of Darby*.

duo-phasic polaric wavelength *(fiction)*
A special wavelength that allows a laser beam to penetrate water.

dusky *(fiction)*
A nickname used in this book for a dusky dolphin.

dusky dolphin *(real)*
A dolphin with light and dark colorations found in the southern hemisphere. The habitat location around Tristan da Cunha was the inspiration for the South Atlantic seamounts as the location for the fictitious Lagenora region.

Earthquatic *(real/fiction)*
The word "earthquatic" can be found in rare usage, though not officially listed in any dictionary. In this book, it means an earthen-like aquatic environment, meaning the inside of the seamounts having an air atmosphere though surrounded by water.

echolocation *(real)*
A process of locating objects by using sound waves, typically by emitting high-pitched sound waves.

echolocator *(fiction)*
A device used by a blinner to echolocate and thus navigate using sound waves.

eckelberry *(fiction)*
A berry used by Loran in *Between the Lake and Mountain* to make Pneuminair, a drug that helps people breathe.

Ecoala *(fiction)*
One of several names given to Wonga, an evil creature in *Between the Lake and Mountain*.

Ediom *(fiction)*
Mirini's father and leader of the resistance on Bruxima 4 in *Mirini and the Aliotrotes*.

efferfont *(fiction)*
A device resembling a water fountain but with no water, used in *Sense of Place* to control the women of Skulava.

Eicor Mountain *(fiction)*
A mountain in *The Duchess of Darby*.

Eicor Mountain Resort *(fiction)*
A resort owned by the Royal Family in *The Duchess of Darby* on Eicor Mountain.

Ekans Egroeg *(fiction)*
"George Snake" spelled backward, as noted by Loran in *Between the Lake and Mountain*.

Elbart Academy *(fiction)*
Debbie's high school, founded by Julie Elbart's grandfather. Ramona's mother is the principal.

eldebrecken *(fiction)*
A plant similar to seaweed in *Between the Lake and Mountain* that feeds on a variety of chemical waste products. The plant tends to entangle itself around other objects including passing boats. Loran and company run into eldebrecken when boating to Slaffton.

Elder Balco *(fiction)*
An elder in *Sense of Place* who is also the chief doctor of the elder village.

Elder Ecton *(fiction)*
One of the elders in *Sense of Place*. Elder Ecton is the device expert and can make or repair all sorts of mechanical and electronic devices.

Elder Gavak *(fiction)*
Younger brother of Elder Zatto and son of Kuianka in *Sense of Place*.

Elder Mountain *(fiction)*
The mountain where the elders in *Sense of Place* live.

elder tree *(real)*
A flowering plant that lives in warmer parts of world. The tree puts out a berry that, when ripe, is edible. However, the unripe berry and the rest of the tree are poisonous.

Elder Zatto *(fiction)*
Older brother of Elder Gavak and first son of Kuianka in *Sense of Place*. Elder Zatto dies from poison administered by Solina, resulting in a war between the forthers of Skulava and the elders.

elderberry *(real)*
Another name for an elder tree or the name of the berry from an elder tree.

elderhag *(fiction)*
An evil creature that is part woman, part elder tree.

electroaudio *(fiction)*
Sound with electrical qualities. Debbie Dayla is said to have electroaudio qualities in her voice, meaning she is able to control electrical devices with sound.

elevat *(fiction)*
An angular measurement of altitude, equivalent to degrees of angular elevation.

EMP *(real)*
Electromagnetic pulse, often in reference to a strong electromagnetic pulse capable of damaging electronic equipment.

EMT *(real)*
"Emergency medical technician" is a person who is part of an ambulance crew and administers first treatment to a person in need of medical assistance and helps keep the person stabilized until a hospital is reached.

Enpriosol *(fiction)*
A drug for sobering up in *Between the Lake and Mountain*.

epidermal *(real)*
Of or relating to skin.

epinephrine *(real)*
Another name for adrenaline, a stimulant released by the adrenal glands during a fight or flight response.

Erebellasia, Eren *(fiction)*
A main character in *Sense of Place*. Erebellasia, daughter of Cuperia, is blind and lives in a cave in Skulava. Her nickname is Eren.

ESP *(paranormal)*
Extra sensory perception, the ability to sense things without using one of the five natural senses.

Eta *(fiction)*
A South Atlantic seamount in the Aiadaka group, inhabited by Orcas in the various Debbie Dayla stories.

ethaloia *(fiction)*
A drug in *Sense of Place* that puts a person to sleep. It is similar to Ethaloid in *Between the Lake and Mountain*.

Ethaloid *(fiction)*
A drug used to put people to sleep in *Between the Lake and Mountain*.

ether *(archaic physics)*
In this book, "ether" refers to the 19th-century physics term for ether, meaning a medium for conducting electromagnetic or gravitational forces.

ethereal salt *(fiction)*
A substance that helps people keep control that is gradually lost after consuming something, which is then picked up and consumed by clamifores in *Between the Lake and Mountain*.

ethos *(real)*
A belief or ideal.

EVA *(real)*
Extra-vehicular activity, also known as a spacewalk, the act of working in space with only a spacesuit as protection.

Evan *(fiction)*
One of Jayvogg's friends in *The Aimless and the Atlantic* who befriends Debbie Dayla at a party.

evertraining *(fiction)*
The process of learning in *For Thy Service* where one walks through an archway of knowledge.

exequi *(fiction)*
An execution edict issued by an elder in *Sense of Place*.

extortician *(fiction)*
A technician in *Mirini and the Aliotrotes* who maintains the osmozicons. "Extortician" comes from the word "extort" which means to obtain by force. An extortician obtains needed materials from humanoid life to sustain the aliotrotes.

extrasent *(fiction)*
A form of punishment in *For Thy Service* where a worker is sent to the lower levels for an extra long time.

extrication *(real)*
The process of removing one thing from another, often when the first thing is trapped in the second.

F-22 *(real)*
Air Force fighter jet used by John Von Brock to reach Brunswick during the invasion of the aliotrotes.

F2Y Sea Dart *(real)*
A supersonic Navy fighter jet that could land on and take off from water using skis.

F-35B *(real)*
A supersonic, stealthy fighter aircraft for the U.S. Marines that can take off and land vertically.

fab *(real)*
A shortened form of the word "fabrication", used in *Mirini and the Aliotrotes*.

Farmer Picocioli *(fiction)*
A picocian in *Between the Lake and Mountain* who learned how to make plants glow in the dark.

Farthar Falls *(fiction)*
A town in *Sense of Place* where people live by more advanced social dynamics than Skulava.

Felidae *(real)*
The taxonomic family for all cats, including the big cats such as lions and tigers, and the small cats such as the house cat and black-footed cat.

Fellanina *(fiction)*
One of Metavasi's female dalli porpoise companions mentioned in *The Blinners of Gathona*.

FEMA *(real)*
Federal Emergency Management Agency, an agency of the U.S. government that manages disaster relief.

ferrocrystallus *(fiction)*
A crystalline material based on iron released by pilot whales in *Mirini and the Aliotrotes*.

ferrosiberry *(fiction)*
Berries from the ferrosinia plant found on Bruxima 4 with a high iron content.

ferrosinia *(fiction)*
A plant on Bruxima 4 that stores iron and is used as a staple crop for the people of Bruxima 4 in *Mirini and the Aliotrotes*.

ferroxicate *(fiction)*
Super-hard crystalized iron found on Bruxima 4 as discussed in *Mirini and the Aliotrotes*.

ferrum *(fiction)*
Another name for iron on Bruxima 4 in *Mirini and the Aliotrotes*.

Feshk *(fiction)*
One of several names given to Wonga, an evil creature in *Between the Lake and Mountain*.

First Darby Cathedral *(fiction)*
The top-level church in Darby, used by all members of royalty.

First Guard of Slaffton *(fiction)*
Top-ranking guard in Slaffton who reports directly to the Master of Slaffton in *Between the Lake and Mountain*.

fissionic *(fiction)*
Capable of undergoing nuclear fission such that energy is released, usually in reference to elements heavier than iron.

flexy glass *(fiction)*
A flexible glass based on regular glass and boron trioxide, and used by Circigi as a protective layer in *The Blinners of Gathona*.

Foreman Gorah *(fiction)*
A foreman in *For Thy Service* who directs the work of Armich and Metoni.

Forlatt *(fiction)*
One of three subverters killed by Armich and Metoni while traveling in a vattertram in *For Thy Service*.

Forsyth *(real)*
A city in Georgia where the Georgia Public Safety Training Center is located. Ramona Bronc goes there to become a Georgia State Trooper.

Fox Three *(real)*
Code spoken by Air Force pilots to indicate the launch of an active radar-guided air-to-air missile.

fulltran *(fiction)*
An animal life form capable of changing shape to resemble another animal life form, specifically the cetacean citizens of Lagenora in the South Atlantic in the Debbie Dayla stories, though it has been discovered there are fulltrans in the Pacific as well.

fusionic *(fiction)*
Capable of undergoing nuclear fusion such that energy is released, usually in reference to elements lighter than iron.

Garadon *(fiction)*
A dalli porpoise Phocayna guard assigned to protect Chusacuta and Circigi on their trip to Gathona in *The Blinners of Gathona*.

Garwood Harvington *(fiction)*
The Daylas' butler in *The Aimless and the Atlantic*.

Garwoot *(fiction)*
A nickname for Garwood, given to him by Connie Dayla.

Gathona *(fiction)*
The cetacean island of the dead in Lagenora. "Gathona" is the cetacean name for Gough Island.

Gaviceti *(fiction)*
A group of five seamounts where fulltran cetaceans live in the North Pacific, as mentioned in *Mirini and the Aliotrotes*. General Byan's orcan citizens live in Gaviceti 2 while Prime Minister Barecki lives in Gaviceti 5.

Geiger counter *(real)*
An instrument used to measure ionizing radiation.

General Byan *(fiction)*
A Pacific orca of Gaviceti 2 who is introduced in *Mirini and the Aliotrotes*.

General Delivery *(real)*
A form of mail delivery where one does not have a residential address. The recipient then must go to the post office to pick up the mail with only a name for mail identification. Lillianina receives mail in Sathiakia under General Delivery in *Between the Lake and Mountain*.

General Grayto *(fiction)*
A General on Bruxima 4. He has a daughter named Charla who is targeted for assassination in *Mirini and the Aliotrotes*.

Genory the Great *(fiction)*
Superhero of the Atlantic white-sided dolphins. Chusacuta mentions him in *The Blinners of Gathona*.

George Snake *(fiction)*
Also known as Lord Zdannag, the owner of a mansion in *Between the Lake and Mountain*. George makes money by deceiving people. He sells a fake treasure map to Myoxi and Gliria.

Georgia Air National Guard *(real)*
The air force militia of the State of Georgia, United States.

Georgia State Patrol *(real)*
State-level law enforcement for Georgia, United States.

geo-sync orbit *(real)*
Also known as geosynchronous orbit, an orbit by a satellite around Earth such that the time spent to travel once around Earth matches an Earth day, giving the appearance from the ground that the satellite is stationary. The altitude necessary for a geo-sync orbit is (depending on source) between 22,200 and 22,300 miles above sea level.

g-force *(real)*
A measure of acceleration that gives the sense of heaviness equivalent to the gravity exerted on a body resting on Earth at sea level. While g-force is a result of acceleration (or deceleration), people often use g-force to mean a force of any kind equaling that of Earth's gravity at sea level.

Giginufi *(fiction)*
A clam-fungus adopted by Loa'neth in *Between the Lake and Mountain* capable of providing information and projecting illusion.

Gliria *(fiction)*
A picocian and Myoxi's wife in *Between the Lake and Mountain*. At one point she is called "Gliria the Herald" or "Herald Gliria".

Global Research Analysis Center *(fiction)*
A room at Farrencamp Digital in *Mirini and the Aliotrotes* where Alice Bachproon and Tara Farrencamp do research on global detection and analysis.

G-LOC *(real)*
A loss of consciousness from excessive g-force.

Gough Island *(real)*
An island in the South Atlantic. In the Debbie Dayla stories, Gough Island is also known as "Gathona", a graveyard for cetaceans.

Grandma *(fiction)*
The narrator's grandmother in *Trechopagia*.

Grandpa *(fiction)*
The narrator's grandfather in *Trechopagia*.

Green Economy *(real)*
An economy that focuses on renewable resources without negatively impacting the environment. For example, electricity-producing windmills are part of the Green Economy. "Green Economy" is referenced in *Trechopagia*.

Greenpeace *(real)*
An organization that focuses on environmental issues.

Grim Reaper *(mythology)*
A personification of death, often of a hooded skeleton with a scythe.

Gs *(real)*
An abbreviation used in this book for g-like forces. A person feels one G when on Earth at sea level. Two Gs would give a person the sense of feeling twice as heavy as normal.

guaiacol *(real)*
An organic compound found in wood smoke that can add flavor to food.

Hall of Discussion *(fiction)*
A large room in Rhynchus where King Acus and Queen Sparla hear cases presented to them in the various Debbie Dayla stories.

Hall of Judgment *(fiction)*
A courtroom where the big cats bring the accused to a bonsai tree for judgment in *Suflessence*.

Harrier *(real)*
A military aircraft capable of vertical takeoff and landing. In this book, "Harrier" refers to the AV-8B model.

Hayabusa *(real)*
A speedy, sporty motorcycle produced by Suzuki.

Haymar *(fiction)*
A Command Center coordinator in *Mirini and the Aliotrotes*.

Heaven *(religion)*
A place of eternal paradise for the soul after one dies.

Heimlich maneuver *(real)*
A form of medical assistance to relieve choking whereby one person forces air out of the lungs of another to remove a lodged object.

helmetband person, helmetbander *(fiction)*
A person in *The Blinners of Gathona* who is normally blind but wears a helmet band that permits a form of vision. Most such persons have joined a militia that maintains control of Gough Island and as such are blinners.

Herbert *(fiction)*
Jack Highbower's father in *Trechopagia*.

Herpenda *(fiction)*
A skunk in *Trechopagia* with whom Nytar, the narrator, falls in love.

Hibbing *(real)*
A city in Minnesota with the Hull-Rust-Mahoning Iron Mine, one of the largest iron mines in the world.

Highway L *(real)*
A highway in Kenosha County, Wisconsin.

hippopotamid *(real)*
A mammal of the taxonomic Hippopotamidae family. The hippopotamus is a member of this family. The hippopotamid and cetaceans have a common ancestor, which explains Queen Pollyenpa's mention of the hippopotamid as brothers in *The Blinners of Gathona*.

Hochenstock Geology International *(fiction)*
A corporation specializing in the exploration and location of natural resources such as precious metals, minerals, and fossil fuels, as mentioned in the Debbie Dayla stories.

holies *(fiction)*
Special sponge life forms that live in the Lagenoran seamounts of the South Atlantic in the Debbie Dayla stories. These sponges can form symbiotic unions with cetaceans and thus give the cetaceans the ability to transform shape and subsist without need to eat. The holies are to be protected from harm. They are also known as first citizens, as their rights come before all others.

hominid *(real)*
A taxonomic great ape, being chimpanzee, gorilla, human, or orangutan.

homo sapien *(real)*
The taxonomic name for a human being.

House of Acus *(fiction)*
The family of King Acus (Clan Acus), his ancestors who ruled, his son Sparfiacus, and close relatives who are in line to the throne.

House of Lies *(fiction)*
Loa'neth's name for George Snake's estate in *Between the Lake and Mountain*. George Snake was known for deceiving people, thus the name "House of Lies" for his estate.

House of Zigo *(fiction)*
The family of Zigo, or Clan Zigo, who have ruling or potential ruling power. Korlan, Vorlac, and Krivat are members of Clan Zigo.

Houston *(real)*
NASA's mission control in Houston is often referred to as "Houston" in radio communications between it and spacecraft.

hoy *(fiction)*
A gender-neutral third-person singular subjective/objective pronoun used by the people of Gathona in *The Blinners of Gathona*, instead of referring to a person as "it". Compare to: *he, she, him, her, it.*

hoy's *(fiction)*
A gender-neutral third-person singular possessive pronoun used in *The Blinners of Gathona*. Compare to: *his, hers, its.*

hoyself *(fiction)*
A gender-neutral third-person singular reflexive pronoun used in *The Blinners of Gathona*. Compare to: *herself, himself, itself.*

Hughward *(fiction)*
Loran's mail delivery person in *Between the Lake and Mountain*.

Hull-Rust-Mahoning Mine *(real)*
An iron mine in Hibbing, Minnesota. Mirini recommends that Debbie and Von Brock divert to this mine in *Mirini and the Aliotrotes*.

hydrargyria *(real)*
Another name for mercury poisoning.

hydrargyrum *(real)*
Another name for elemental mercury.

Hydricetistelidalina Maculisarcolleenivorsa *(fiction)*
Amicolli's full name in *Between the Lake and Mountain*.

hydronium *(real)*
A molecule consisting of three hydrogen atoms to one oxygen atom that is naturally occurring in water.

hyperdermaferriosis *(fiction)*
A skin disease of Pacific fulltran cetaceans similar to dermatitis in humans, causing excess scales of iron to form.

hypoglycemic *(real)*
Of or having a medical condition of hypoglycemia, meaning a low blood sugar level.

ID *(real)*
Identification card. A card with a person's name and often a photograph used to identify that person and possibly the person's age. This can be an automobile driver's license, but can also be other forms of identification such as a school ID.

Inaccessible Island *(real)*
An island in the South Atlantic close to Tristan da Cunha and part of the Lagenora in the Debbie Dayla stories.

Inasherry *(fiction)*
Chrba's mother in *Sense of Place*. Inasherry would bring goods from other villages back to Skulava for the forthers.

incandescence *(real)*
Emission of light from a hot object. Early light bulbs generated light through incandescence because the filament generated heat and thus light. Compare with luminescence, which is the emission of light but without the heat of incandescence.

indeficient *(real)*
Not deficient.

Interstate *(real)*
"Interstate" refers to the Interstate Highway System, a freeway network in the United States.

iridescent *(real)*
Showing many colors that change when viewed from different angles.

iron oxide *(real)*
Another name for "rust".

Ithaca High School *(real)*
A high school in New York state which at one time had a skunk as a mascot. In *Trechopagia*, Jack Highbower's own high school team plays Ithaca High School in a fictitious "Skunk Bowl" football game.

IV *(real)*
Intravenous. An IV needle is an intravenous needle, used to administer drugs or draw blood.

Japanese Research ship *(real)*
Ocean-faring Japanese ships with the word "Research" painted on the side that clandestinely hunt whales.

jayla *(fiction)*
A chemical catalyst and stimulant as referenced by Belsl in *Sense of Place*. By itself it acts as a short-lasting stimulant, but when mixed with another drug, jayla is less a stimulant and instead causes the other drug to stay in the bloodstream longer than usual.

jayladopa *(fiction)*
A chemical similar to but longer lasting than levodopa that is converted into dopamine, epinephrine, and norepinephrine.

Jayvogg Hochenstock *(fiction)*
A character in the Debbie Dayla stories who has dishonorable intentions. Debbie reveals that Jayvogg is a super model, spokesman for Royal Yacht Clothing, and a star quarterback and punter for the Brunswick Ogres. Vicia believes Jayvogg to have killed a woman. Jayvogg acts under Senator Croius's direction.

Jekyll Island *(real)*
An island off the coast of Georgia near Brunswick.

Jekyll Island Reformatory *(fiction)*
A juvenile detention center in the Debbie Dayla stories.

John Mark "Jack" Highbower *(fiction)*
Main character and narrator in *Trechopagia*.

jon boat *(real)*
A flat-bottomed boat useful for fishing or hunting. The construction works best in calm waters.

Joshua "Josh" Jones *(fiction)*
One of two men Debbie Dayla kills while being attacked in Jayvogg's apartment in *The Aimless and the Atlantic*.

Juana Maria *(real)*
A Native American woman who lived on San Nicolas Island in the 1800s. She was the last surviving member of her tribe, the Nicoleño tribe. She meets Lutris in *Between the Lake and Mountain*.

Julie Elbart Dayla *(fiction)*
Roger Dayla's wife and the mother of Connie and Debbie Dayla.

Julietta Mercrei *(fiction)*
Baroness Vasha's personal assistant in *The Duchess of Darby*.

Kakuda Mori *(fiction)*
Allen's friend in *The Duchess of Darby* who is caught up in scandal with Duchess Devanna and four royal men.

Kara *(fiction)*
A love interest of the narrator, Tau, in *Save for Proper Buyer*.

Kazhak *(fiction)*
An aliotrote in *Mirini and the Aliotrotes* who reports to Savien and is in charge of rejuvenating other aliotrotes at the expense of killing humans in osmozicon devices.

Kellington Catering Service *(fiction)*
Catering service owned and operated by Sueann Kellington in *The Duchess of Darby*.

Kelofuge *(fiction)*
A laughing gas used by Loran in *Between the Lake and Mountain*.

Kennedy Drive *(real)*
A road in Kenosha that travels along the shore of Lake Michigan.

Kenosha *(real)*
Both a city and a county in Wisconsin, United States.

Kenosha Medical Center *(real)*
A medical facility in downtown Kenosha.

Kieulor *(fiction)*
Mirini's husband-to-be on Bruxima 4 in *Mirini and the Aliotrotes*.

King Acus *(fiction)*
Acus, also known as King Acus, is a fulltran dusky dolphin and ruler of Rhynchus at the beginning of *The Aimless and the Atlantic*. He is Sparla's husband and Sparfy's father.

King Adelfo *(fiction)*
A striped dolphin and King of Corleopus. King Adelfo is married to Queen Tharia and is the father of Princess Adelfarina.

King Talenopi *(fiction)*
A peroni dolphin and benevolent ruler of Aiadaka in ancient times before the orcas took over in the Debbie Dayla stories.

King Tugan *(fiction)*
King of Phocayna in the Debbie Dayla stories. Tugan is a dalli porpoise and the father of Metavasi. He is also married to Queen Brela.

Kingdom of Kush *(real)*
Ancient kingdom south of Egypt that eventually took over Egypt.

Kingdom of Phocayna *(fiction)*
A community of dalli fulltran porpoises living in the Yakhont Seamount in the South Atlantic.

Kingdom of Rhynchus *(fiction)*
A community of dusky fulltran dolphins living in the R.S.A. Seamount in the South Atlantic.

Kinnabarics *(fiction)*
A medical department specializing in aliotrote and other mercury-based life forms. Kazhak tells an aliotrote to report to Kinnabarics for reassessment of its lifespan in *Mirini and the Aliotrotes*. "Kinnabarics" is formed from the Greek word "kinnabari" for cinnabar (mercury sulfide) and "-ics" for an area of study.

Kita *(fiction)*
One of several seamounts in the Aiadaka kingdom in the Debbie Dayla stories.

Kiyomi *(fiction)*
Camerawoman for Darby Magazine.

Kmina *(fiction)*
A seamount in the South Atlantic populated by hourglass dolphins in the Debbie Dayla stories. Kmina is the home of Circigi.

Kminadoma *(fiction)*
The Kmina medical center in the Debbie Dayla stories.

Kminian *(fiction)*
A citizen of Kmina in the Debbie Dayla stories.

Kona Shred *(real)*
Connie Dayla had a 20-inch Kona Shred, a bicycle for children five to eight years of age.

Korlan *(fiction)*
A fulltran Atlantic torpedo ray and a good friend of Sparfy in the Debbie Dayla stories.

Krypto Silvo *(fiction)*
A project in the Debbie Dayla stories to convert elemental mercury to krypton and ruthenium through nuclear fission.

Kuianka *(fiction)*
Head matriarch of the elder village in *Sense of Place*.

kylalac *(fiction)*
A male plant-creature living in Slaffton in *Between the Lake and Mountain*.

Laculic Manor *(fiction)*
Loran Laculic's home in *Between the Lake and Mountain*.

Laculic Tavern *(fiction)*
A tavern run by Braegan Laculic and his wife, Morga, in Millfork in *Between the Lake and Mountain*.

Laculor *(fiction)*
A name Myoxi wishes to give to a future son, after Loran, in *Between the Lake and Mountain*.

Lady Spenwick *(fiction)*
Leader of the greater equals, the town of Skulava, and of Mother's Hall in *Sense of Place*.

Lagenor *(fiction)*
A citizen of Lagenora in the Debbie Dayla stories.

Lagenora *(fiction)*
A region in the South Atlantic with several seamounts where multiple species of fulltran cetaceans and rays live in the Debbie Dayla stories.

Lagenoran *(fiction)*
Of or pertaining to Lagenora or the citizens of Lagenora.

Lagenorian *(fiction)*
The language spoken by the Lagenors in the Debbie Dayla stories. Lagenorian includes all slang words and unofficial words, whereas Lagenorian Standard excludes those slang and unofficial words.

Lake Meadowash *(fiction)*
A large lake to the east of Loran's property in *Between the Lake and Mountain*.

Lake Michigan *(real)*
A large lake to the east of the author's property (as of this writing) in Kenosha, Wisconsin.

Lanceri *(fiction)*
Erebellasia's father in *Sense of Place*. Lanceri is a carpenter and blacksmith.

Last Stand *(fiction)*
A reference to a great fight between dolphins and humans in *The Blinners of Gathona*.

Leiolaki *(fiction)*
A command Loa'neth uses in *Between the Lake and Mountain* in an effort to save Stephen and Claire from a tar pit.

Leothi *(fiction)*
A great lioness who passed away in *Suflessence*.

Lepsus *(fiction)*
A rabbit attorney who offers her services to defend fellow rabbits who are caught eating plants in *Suflessence*.

Ligrino *(fiction)*
A pilot whale in *Mirini and the Aliotrotes* who begins a relationship with Mirini. Ligrino has hyperdermaferriosis that Mirini is able to minimize.

Lillianina *(fiction)*
Loran's cousin in *Between the Lake and Mountain* who is captured by and forced to work for Wonga against her will.

Litivito *(fiction)*
A dalli porpoise and one of Metavasi's friends in the Debbie Dayla stories.

Loa'neth *(fiction)*
A picocian who leaves George Snake's mansion to travel with Loran and his company. Her full name is Loaninafaliracalineth.

Loran Laculic *(fiction)*
A main character in *Between the Lake and Mountain*. Loran goes on a journey to find his cousin, Lillianina, and meets several people along the way. At one point he is called "King Loran of Clamiforia".

Lord Trancelo *(fiction)*
Solina's father in *Sense of Place*.

Lord Zdannag *(fiction)*
See *George Snake*.

Lozox *(fiction)*
A lozenge that produces oxygen and thus helps a person breathe in a bad atmosphere in *Between the Lake and Mountain*.

Lucinasium *(fiction)*
A drug that inhibits aggression and higher cognitive thinking in animals and in so doing creates a relaxed and overly festive mood.

Luta *(fiction)*
One of several seamounts in the Aiadaka kingdom in the Debbie Dayla stories.

Lutris *(fiction)*
A Pacific sea otter in *Between the Lake and Mountain* who falls in love with Claire.

Mach *(real)*
An object's speed using the speed of sound as a measure. Mach 1 is at the speed of sound, Mach 2 is at twice the speed of sound, etc.

magelectrometer *(fiction)*
A device that senses power sources. It is used by Gliria in *Between the Lake and Mountain*.

magno-hydraulic suspension tube *(fiction)*
A tube in *Mirini and the Aliotrotes* for people to stand in that fills with a special fluid and allows for special communication between the user and the outside world.

Mail Steward *(fiction)*
A person who delivers mail in *Between the Lake and Mountain*.

Major Kyler Huehigh Bohr *(fiction)*
A pilot and main character in *Mirini and the Aliotrotes* who develops strong feelings for Mirini.

MALC *(fiction)*
An acronym for Mercury, Arsenic, Lead, Cadmium in *Between the Lake and Mountain*.

maloople *(fiction)*
A monetary unit of measure in *Between the Lake and Mountain*.

Mara Brilla *(fiction)*
The name of the boat Loa'neth, Loran, Myoxi, and Gliria take on their journey to Slaffton in *Between the Lake and Mountain*.

Marchese Antonio of Gravati *(fiction)*
One of four royal men invited to Duchess Devanna's birthday party as a prospective husband in *The Duchess of Darby*.

Mariana Trench *(real)*
A trench in the west Pacific Ocean. The Mariana Trench is the deepest part of the ocean.

mass compressor *(fiction)*
A device capable of compressing mass from normal state to a much smaller state without causing a fusion reaction. A mass compressor works by flattening electron orbits.

Master *(fiction)*
Arbreezias refers to Aiatethis as "Master" in *The Blinners of Gathona*.

Master of Slaffton *(fiction)*
Ruler of Slaffton in *Between the Lake and Mountain*. The Master is married to Supreme Queffil Stilillick.

Master One *(fiction)*
A boat docked in Slaffton in *Between the Lake and Mountain* that belongs to the Master of Slaffton.

Matt *(fiction)*
The narrator's older brother in *Trechopagia*.

McNish Seamount *(real)*
A seamount in the South Atlantic known as Persipi by the Lagenors and populated by pygmy killer whales in the Debbie Dayla stories.

Medusa *(mythology)*
A female creature in Greek mythology with snakes on her head, capable of turning a person to stone who gazes upon her.

melon *(real)*
A focal pad on the head of toothed cetaceans that aids in echolocation. The pad helps focus the clicks that are sent out into the water.

Meorus *(fiction)*
A clamifore being that transfers its consciousness into the picocian body of Dara in *Between the Lake and Mountain*.

Mercalli Dream *(fiction)*
A boat on Bruxima 4 that takes Kyler to an office complex when Kyler relives a memory from Mirini's cufflet in *Mirini and the Aliotrotes*.

merselat *(fiction)*
Robots under control of Mersladium in *Between the Lake and Mountain*.

Mersladium *(fiction)*
A robot created when Doctor Julia Craymar of Craymar Industries converts Tau from human to machine by infusing him in a mixture of toxic metals.

metlurometer *(fiction)*
A device used by Gliria in *Between the Lake and Mountain* to detect metal types on objects.

Metoni *(fiction)*
Armich's friend in *For Thy Service* who helps Armich escape to the surface.

Meyta Merco *(fiction)*
A village on the inside edge of Sathiakia in *Between the Lake and Mountain* where people live in the trees. Loran and company meet Sleego in Meyta Merco.

Mianna *(fiction)*
Ediom's wife and Mirini's mother in *Mirini and the Aliotrotes*.

midazolam *(real)*
A drug that causes sedation or sleep.

mike *(real)*
Another name for microphone.

militarics *(fiction)*
The theory and practice of creating and maintaining a military in Tau's country in *Save for Proper Buyer*.

milkweed *(real)*
A plant with a number of historic uses but poisonous.

Millfork *(fiction)*
A town just south of Loran's home in *Between the Lake and Mountain*.

Millfork Fire Department *(fiction)*
A fire department that Loran applied to for a job but was rejected, serving the Millfork area in *Between the Lake and Mountain*.

Millfork Trading Mart *(fiction)*
A place of business and trade in Millfork in *Between the Lake and Mountain*.

Ministry *(fiction)*
A governmental group in charge of daily operations for the Commonwealth of Darby in *The Duchess of Darby*.

Mirini Baliotra *(fiction)*
A woman from Bruxima 4 who is one of the last survivors of her planet. Mirini is a main character in *Mirini and the Aliotrotes*.

Miss Chi *(fiction)*
Owner of Seaside Sushi restaurant in *The Aimless and the Atlantic*.

Mission Control *(real)*
In this book, "Mission Control" refers to NASA's Mission Control Center in Houston, Texas.

mitochondria *(real)*
Cell components that produce energy.

Mitothoriac *(fiction)*
A Dayla Industries chamber device capable of reorganizing cellular structure, specializing in mitochondria transformation as referenced in *Between the Lake and Mountain*.

mittamat *(fiction)*
A rubber-like mat invented by the fulltrans of Lagenora that partially sinks into and thus adheres to a selected surface that permits easy vertical climbing and up-over-edge climbing.

Mockenboose Bank *(fiction)*
A cutthroat bank that owns many foreclosed houses including the one in which the narrator lives in *Trechopagia*. Its logo is that of a *mockingbird* taunting the customer by lifting its tail feathers and displaying its *caboose*.

Mohs scale *(real)*
A simple hardness scale from one to ten with ten being the hardest (diamond).

monkshood *(real)*
A highly toxic plant with a flower resembling a monk's hood.

Morga *(fiction)*
Braegan's wife and Loran's sister-in-law in *Between the Lake and Mountain*.

Morse code *(real)*
A code that uses combinations of short pulses ("dots") and long pulses ("dashes") to represent letters and numbers for communication, especially in situations where conveying regular speech is not possible.

Mortgage Bank Brothers *(fiction)*
A bank that financed high-risk agricultural technologies, including the Cyclozyme, in *Trechopagia*.

Mortidoma *(fiction)*
A morgue in Rhynchus to prepare the dead for their final resting place at Gathona in the Debbie Dayla stories.

Mother's Hall *(fiction)*
A residence of women in Skulava in *Sense of Place* headed by Lady Spenwick. These women are knowns as "pullbacks", and they are served by another group of Skulava women known as "forthers".

Mount Everest *(real)*
The tallest mountain on Earth.

Mr. Boulder *(fiction)*
After a SOZOD experimental test at Dayla Industries, Debbie refers to the test target as "Mr. Boulder".

MRI *(real)*
Magnetic resonance imaging. In this book, an MRI refers to the process of scanning a person's body using a magnetic resonance imaging device.

MS Unapluto *(fiction)*
A ship owned by Pat Wallace's Sea Herder organization that is used to deter other ships from illegal whaling in *Mirini and the Aliotrotes*. "MS" stands for "Motor Ship".

MT1, MT2, MT3, etc. *(fiction)*
Designation numbers for merselats in Mersladium's robot army in *Between the Lake and Mountain*.

myoglobin *(real)*
A protein in muscle tissues capable of storing oxygen. Animals who hold their breath under water have a high concentration of myoglobin to permit sustained underwater activity.

Myoxi *(fiction)*
A picocian and Gliria's husband in *Between the Lake and Mountain*. At one point he is referred to as "Myoxi the Jester".

Nance *(fiction)*
A nurse and assistant to Doctor Belsl in *Sense of Place*.

nargiometer *(fiction)*
A device capable of detecting organic material in *Between the Lake and Mountain*.

NASA *(real)*
National Aeronautics and Space Administration, the federal agency responsible for exploring Earth's atmosphere, its nature, and outer space.

neesp *(fiction)*
A unit of time equal to 0.0864 seconds in the Debbie Dayla stories and used by the fulltran cetaceans.

nelumacaine *(fiction)*
A topical anesthetic that is often mixed with other drugs. *In Sense of Place*, Doctor Belsl uses a compound named "tassa nelumacaine" to numb pain and heal injury.

neuroanalyzer *(fiction)*
A device in *Mirini and the Aliotrotes* used to interface with Kyler's brain at Farrencamp Digital.

nialla, nialli *(fiction)*
The distance a dalli porpoise can swim in one neesp, about 132 centimeters, as used by cetaceans in Lagenora. *Nialli* is the plural form.

Nick Fye *(fiction)*
The keyboardist in Ramona's band in the Debbie Dayla stories.

Nicoleño *(real)*
A Native American tribe who lived on San Nicolas Island in the 1800s. In *Between the Lake and Mountain*, a Pacific sea otter named Lutris meets with the Nicoleño.

Nightingale Island *(real)*
One of three islands in the northwest corner of Lagenora in the South Atlantic.

Nile *(real)*
In this book, "the Nile" refers to the Nile River in Egypt.

Noah's Ark *(religion)*
A boat in the Hebrew Book of Genesis which carries a pair each of the world's most important animals to survive a flood that will ravage the earth. Debbie Dayla speaks of the Bioprog as a Noah's Ark, meaning the Bioprog stores essential life codes to survive a period of desolate time.

Nobel Prize *(real)*
There are several Nobel Prizes given out each year for excellence in one field or another. In *The Aimless and the Atlantic*, it's made known that Doctor Kukovich won one of the Nobel Prizes.

Nola *(fiction)*
Armich's cousin in *For Thy Service* who escapes with Armich and Metoni.

Nolan *(fiction)*
One of several blind people on Gathona in *The Blinners of Gathona* who gives aid to Circigi.

nucleolumino array *(fiction)*
A collection of devices that will cause nuclear-based life forms to glow in the dark in *The Blinners of Gathona*.

Nurse Yetaria *(fiction)*
A fulltran pilot whale who tends to Kyler's injuries in *Mirini and the Aliotrotes*.

Nytar *(fiction)*
The narrator's name as a skunk in *Trechopagia*.

Old Sturleo Lighthouse *(fiction)*
A lighthouse on Bruxima 4 in *Mirini and the Aliotrotes* where Kyler finds Mirini.

Ordovician *(real)*
A geological period in Earth's history almost 500 million years ago when marine life flourished and land-based life was just beginning. In *Trechopagia*, the narrator travels back to the Ordovician period.

organelle *(real)*
A component of a biological cell. The fulltran cetaceans of Lagenora have thorium organelles that provide energy.

osmoze *(fiction)*
To deflate a person into nothing but skin in a device known as an osmozicon in *Mirini and the Aliotrotes*.

osmozicon *(fiction)*
A tall, tube-like device that a human stands in that extracts components useful for an aliotrote in *Mirini and the Aliotrotes*.

outlanders *(fiction)*
People from outside of Slaffton in *Between the Lake and Mountain*. First Guard refers to Loran and his group as outlanders.

oxiometer *(fiction)*
In this book, an oxiometer is a device to measure oxygen levels, as used by Gliria in *Between the Lake and Mountain*.

Oxygen Catastrophe *(real)*
A time approximately 2.4 billion years ago when a surplus of oxygen accumulated in Earth's atmosphere from cyanobacteria, resulting in a mass extinction event.

oysterphane *(fiction)*
A clear plastic sheet similar to cellophane but made from oysters.

Palace Security *(fiction)*
A security force that patrols the Royal Palace in *The Duchess of Darby*.

paleontologist *(real)*
One who studies ancient life forms.

Paschal candle *(real)*
A large, white candle used by various Christian faiths and is lit during services during the Easter season and special occasions.

patoosh *(fiction)*
An expression of distaste spoken by Mirini to Kyler in *Mirini and the Aliotrotes*.

PCP *(real)*
Also known as phencyclidine or "angel dust". PCP is a drug that acts as an anesthetic and hallucinogenic.

pectoral fin *(real)*
A front side fin in cetaceans that is used to turn and stop. A pectoral fin is analogous to the arm in humans.

pejorative *(real)*
A word or phrase with a negative or belittling meaning.

pelapine *(fiction)*
An herbicide effective against charlock plants in *Between the Lake and Mountain*.

pepona *(fiction)*
The cetacean name for the *melon*, an organ used in echolocation.

peroni dolphin *(fiction)*
The Lagenoran name for a southern right whale dolphin in the Debbie Dayla stories.

Persipi *(fiction)*
The Lagenoran name for the McNish Seamount. The pygmy false killer whales live in Persipi.

pharmapetty *(fiction)*
A life-form that feeds off chemical runoff in *Between the Lake and Mountain*.

phenol *(real)*
A group of organic chemicals with a variety of uses such as making plastics or drugs. Guaiacol is a phenolic compound that adds flavor to smoked meat.

Phira *(fiction)*
The lowest seamount of the Aiadaka kingdom in the Debbie Dayla stories.

Phocayna *(fiction)*
The Lagenoran name for the Yakhont Seamount. Phocayna is where the dalli porpoises live.

physiology *(real)*
The study of what makes a life-form function.

picocian *(fiction)*
A small human-like creature in *Between the Lake and Mountain*. Picocians have good skills with tools and stonework.

picosneezey *(fiction)*
A name of disaffection for a picocian. Myoxi refers to Gliria as a picosneezey woman.

Pike River *(real)*
A river that flows into Lake Michigan on the north side of Kenosha, Wisconsin.

plastican *(fiction)*
A material used by Lagenors to entomb the dead and to prevent radiation leakage. It is mentioned in *The Blinners of Gathona*.

Plateauian *(fiction)*
A resident of Plateauville in *Sense of Place*.

Plateauville *(fiction)*
A village near Skulava in *Sense of Place*.

ploca *(fiction)*
A Lagenoran unit of time measurement, equaling 8.64 seconds.

plocalla, plocalli *(fiction)*
A Lagenoran unit of distance measurement, about 132 meters, or the distance a dalli porpoise can swim in one ploca.

Pneuminair *(fiction)*
A drug used by Loran in *Between the Lake and Mountain* to wake the picocians. It is similar to smelling salts in that it stimulates the respiratory tract to action. It also clears the sinuses, throat, and lungs of congestion.

pneuminaira *(fiction)*
A drug used by Belsl in *Sense of Place* that is similar to Pneuminair.

polyoplenican *(fiction)*
A Dayla Industries product that is flexible like plastic but with a Mohs hardness of 9.5.

porpoising *(real)*
Leaping clear of the water while swimming.

porpoiso-dolpho *(fiction)*
A name spoken to another cetacean while perturbed. Circigi uses this name with Queen Pollyenpa when he is upset with her method to get his attention.

Prime Kylalac *(fiction)*
The top male plant in Slaffton in *Between the Lake and Mountain*.

Prime Minister Barecki *(fiction)*
Leader of a Pacific seamount named Gaviceti 5 in *Mirini and the Aliotrotes*. Barecki is a pilot whale.

Prince Metavasi *(fiction)*
Dalli porpoise and son of King Tugan and Queen Brela. Metavasi is the quickest swimmer of all those in Lagenora. He lives in Phocayna.

Prince Sparfiacus *(fiction)*
Also known as "Sparfy", son of King Acus and Queen Sparla. Is from Rhynchus and strikes up a special friendship with Debbie Dayla. Sparfy is a dusky dolphin.

Princess Adelfarina, Delfa *(fiction)*
A striped dolphin and princess from Corleopus. Daughter of Queen Tharia and King Adelfo. A very close friend of Prince Sparfiacus. Goes by the nickname of Delfa.

Princess Gella *(fiction)*
A princess in *For Thy Service* that Metoni has a crush on.

Priva Tunnel Two *(fiction)*
A privileged tunnel used for special cargo runs to the Royal Complex in *For Thy Service*. Armich and Metoni enter this tunnel with their vattertram.

productory *(fiction)*
An area in *For Thy Service* where factory work is performed.

Professor Monfri *(fiction)*
A professor at Varcher University in *The Aimless and the Atlantic*.

Professor Wykepper *(fiction)*
Brings Curiami and Bedora from a hospital to a special building where the group can explore suflessence in *Suflessence*.

Psychozyme *(fiction)*
Brenda's disparaging name for the Cyclozyme in *Trechopagia*.

pullback *(fiction)*
A women in Skulava who enjoys being subservient to the elders' rule in *Sense of Place*.

Queen Brela *(fiction)*
Queen of Phocayna and wife of King Tugan. She has a son named Metavasi.

Queen Pollyenpa *(fiction)*
A peroni fulltran dolphin who lived in ancient times. Circigi and Chusacuta meet her in *The Blinners of Gathona*.

Queen Pyamara *(fiction)*
Queen of the Persipi pygmy false killer whales in the Debbie Dayla stories.

Queen Sparla *(fiction)*
Queen of the dusky dolphins in Rhynchus, wife of King Acus, and mother of Prince Sparfiacus in the Debbie Dayla stories.

Queen Tharia *(fiction)*
Queen of Corleopus and mother of Princess Delfa.

queffil *(fiction)*
A female plant-creature living in Slaffton in *Between the Lake and Mountain*.

R.S.A. Seamount *(real)*
A seamount in the South Atlantic. The fictional dusky dolphin realm of Rhynchus is located in the R.S.A. Seamount in the Debbie Dayla stories.

radiinox *(fiction)*
A special emulsion of stainless steel and radioactive elements used at Farrencamp Digital in *Mirini and the Aliotrotes*.

Raian *(fiction)*
Ediom's and Mianna's son in *Mirini and the Aliotrotes*.

Rainbear Mountain *(fiction)*
The mountain to the west of Loran's home and to the west of Millfork in *Between the Lake and Mountain*.

Ramona and the Smackadeliacs *(fiction)*
A music group led by Ramona Bronc in the Debbie Dayla stories.

Ramona Beckusa Bronc *(fiction)*
Connie's friend and later Debbie's friend in the Debbie Dayla stories. Ramona's father is the local sheriff while her mother is principal of Elbart Academy.

récamier *(real)*
A couch with a high headrest, low backrest, and usually no back.

red-tailed boa *(real)*
A boa constrictor snake of South America. Kyler refers to flying with a red-tailed boa in *Mirini and the Aliotrotes*, a reference to both the snake and Alice with her streak of red in her hair.

REM *(real)*
Rapid eye movement, a level of sleep where one dreams.

Remmen *(fiction)*
A librarian and subverter in *For Thy Service*.

Rhyncho *(fiction)*
A citizen of Rhynchus in the Debbie Dayla stories.

Rhynchus *(fiction)*
A seamount also known as the R.S.A. Seamount and home of the dusky dolphins in the Debbie Dayla stories.

Rhynchus Prime *(fiction)*
The capital of Rhynchus where the Royal Palace is located. At one time, King Acus and Queen Sparla rule there.

Rick Lefter *(fiction)*
One of Jayvogg's friends in *The Aimless and the Atlantic* who is killed by Debbie Dayla.

rigor mortis *(real)*
A stiffening of the body shortly after death.

robbershaft *(fiction)*
To exploit or plunder a region on an epic scale such that resources are heavily depleted, often to the detriment of the native inhabitants, resulting in their conquest, loss of culture, or death.

Robert Sniar *(fiction)*
Vicia Sniar's father and owner of Sniar Oil.

Robin Stephen Royer *(fiction)*
Born Robin Stephen Roastbranch. His father died when he was six months old. His mother remarried, and he was adopted and took the new name of Royer. Goes by the name of "Stephen". His cousin is Claire. Both Stephen and Claire are in *Between the Lake and Mountain*.

Rocky Mountains *(real)*
A mountain range in western North America.

Roger Dayla *(fiction)*
Founder of Dayla Industries. Debbie and Connie's father.

Rosa *(fiction)*
A secretary for the heavy-set man on Bruxima 4 in Kyler's memory experience.

Royal Archway *(fiction)*
An archway that Armich and Metoni are supposed to deliver and install in *For Thy Service*.

Royal Complex *(fiction)*
Where the royal people live in *For Thy Service*.

Royal Corridor *(fiction)*
A corridor connecting Armich's and Metoni's living area with the Royal Complex in *For Thy Service*.

Royal Courtyard *(fiction)*
Sparfy finds Delfa speaking with Queen Sparla in the Royal Courtyard of Rhynchus in *The Aimless and the Atlantic*. This courtyard is decorated with statues, cultivations, and other things of art.

Royal Diner *(fiction)*
A place where royal people eat. Princess Gella invites Metoni to the Royal Diner in *For Thy Service*.

Royal Palace *(fiction)*
Royal people typically live in a Royal Palace. Such a place is referenced in *The Aimless and the Atlantic* and *The Duchess of Darby*.

Royal Yacht Clothing *(fiction)*
A high-end clothing brand in the Debbie Dayla stories for which Jayvogg is a spokesperson.

Rumormill *(fiction)*
Vicia Sniar's television segment in the Debbie Dayla stories.

Sabina Salt Desert *(fiction)*
A desert west of Lake Meadowash and south of Rainbear Mountain in *Between the Lake and Mountain*.

sallerite *(fiction)*
Ethereal salts stored in salt crystals, as mentioned in *Between the Lake and Mountain*.

San Nicolas Island *(real)*
The place where Lutris meets the Nicoleño in *Between the Lake and Mountain*.

Sara Vossy *(fiction)*
A supersonic aircraft created by Dayla Industries, resembling the Space Shuttle but stretched out.

sarcophagus *(real)*
A coffin made of stone.

Sarrio *(fiction)*
A subverter in *For Thy Service*.

Sassi Bryer *(fiction)*
Plays drums in the music group Ramona and the Smackadeliacs in *The Aimless and the Atlantic*.

Sathiakia *(fiction)*
A region to the south of Lake Meadowash where the evil creature Wonga dwells in *Between the Lake and Mountain*.

Sathiakia Slaughter *(fiction)*
A mass murder of three hundred picocians when one refused to work in a slave camp in *Between the Lake and Mountain*.

Save-A-Save *(fiction)*
A gasoline station that Connie wants Garwood to buy in *The Aimless and the Atlantic* so she can command the attendant.

Savien Pavanko *(fiction)*
Leader of the aliotrotes in *Mirini and the Aliotrotes*.

scion *(real)*
A descendant, often an heir to a wealthy family. In *Trechopagia*, the word "scions" is used to mean a blowfly's descendants.

Scott Braylo *(fiction)*
An alias that Kyler must assume while reliving a memory from Asmondo Arliaco on Bruxima 4 as referenced in *Mirini and the Aliotrotes*.

Scythoc Three *(fiction)*
A falling satellite in *Mirini and the Aliotrotes* that Mirini uses to land on Earth.

Sea Herder *(fiction)*
An environmental group chartered to protect cetaceans from illegal whaling ships, as mentioned in *Mirini and the Aliotrotes*.

seamount *(real)*
An underwater mountain. Seamounts exist primarily in the ocean and are formed by volcanoes. If a seamount grows tall enough, it becomes an island.

Seaside Student Apartments *(fiction)*
Location of a party that Debbie Dayla attends and where she meets Jayvogg and his group in *The Aimless and the Atlantic*.

Seaside Sushi *(fiction)*
Japanese restaurant where Debbie Dayla often goes to eat after finishing one of her rage episodes. She finds herself there in *The Aimless and the Atlantic*.

Sellan *(fiction)*
One of three subverters killed by Armich and Metoni while traveling in a vattertram in *For Thy Service*.

Senator Croius *(fiction)*
A fulltran orca from the South Atlantic and a U.S. Senator from the State of Georgia. Croius is evil and looks for opportunities to expand his control over others. He is subservient to Aiatethis.

sentience *(real)*
Awareness of one's surroundings through the senses, leading to perceptive thought.

shellioster *(fiction)*
A lightweight, flexible material that is strong and heat resistant. Loran seeks to make such a material in *Between the Lake and Mountain.*

Sheridan Road *(real)*
A road that runs through Kenosha, Wisconsin and at times is close to Lake Michigan.

Sheriff Bronc *(fiction)*
Sheriff of Glynn County, Georgia in the Debbie Dayla stories. Father of Ramona Bronc.

sholiff *(fiction)*
A law enforcement officer in *Between the Lake and Mountain.*

Sholiff Grant, Head Sholiff Grant *(fiction)*
The head sholiff of Blackpier in *Between the Lake and Mountain.*

Sholiff Gregg *(fiction)*
A sholiff in Blackpier and subordinate to Sholiff Grant in *Between the Lake and Mountain.*

Shollernat One *(fiction)*
The name of the vattertram in *For Thy Service.*

Shuffleblood *(fiction)*
A game played by Asmondo Arliaco, Kyler, and Mirini where the contestants fight to overpower the others with hydraulic pressure by pumping blood into a manifold in *Mirini and the Aliotrotes.*

Silano Baliotra *(fiction)*
Mirini's grandfather and a rebel on Bruxima 4 in *Mirini and the Aliotrotes*.

Silicon Valley *(real)*
Nickname for a region in the San Francisco area where many high-tech companies are located.

silotron *(fiction)*
A hand-held weapon used in *For Thy Service* against subverters that causes living cells to burst into spontaneous combustion.

simian *(real)*
A monkey or ape, including humans.

singleton *(real)*
One thing of a kind.

Skulava *(fiction)*
A village in *Sense of Place* where Erebellasia lives and where the society is divided into two groups of women—the privileged women who have children, and the working women.

Skulavian *(fiction)*
A resident of Skulava in *Sense of Place*. Also an adjective for something of or to do with Skulava.

Skunk Bowl *(fiction)*
A high-school football game where Ithaca High School plays against Coyla High School in *Trechopagia*. Both teams in such a contest feature a skunk as a mascot.

Slaffton *(fiction)*
A port town on Lake Meadowash in *Between the Lake and Mountain* that at one time is ruled by a Master and Supreme Queffil Stilillick.

Sleego *(fiction)*
A resident of Meyta Merco and one who Loran and Loa'neth use as a guide for a short time in *Between the Lake and Mountain*.

SLR *(real)*
Single lens reflex, often in reference to a type of still-photo camera. For film photography, SLR cameras give the best quality and control of the photo taken.

smarf *(fiction)*
To worry about, as used by Ramona in the Debbie Dayla stories.

smarvey *(fiction)*
Marvelous. Used by Ramona in the Debbie Dayla stories.

smave *(fiction)*
To wave or motion one's arms, as used by Ramona in the Debbie Dayla stories.

smoiky *(fiction)*
Wonky or off-balance. A word invented by Ramona in the Debbie Dayla stories.

smonderful *(fiction)*
Ramona's way of saying "wonderful" in the Debbie Dayla stories.

smonko *(fiction)*
Animated, with the energy of a bronco horse. Another word invented by Ramona.

smonna *(fiction)*
Smoother than smooth, like velvet. A word invented by Ramona in the Debbie Dayla stories.

smooging *(fiction)*
Throwing up. A word invented by Ramona in the Debbie Dayla stories.

smoolavator *(fiction)*
Something elevating to how one feels. A word invented by Ramona in the Debbie Dayla stories.

smoove *(fiction)*
Smooth. A word invented by Ramona.

smoovey *(fiction)*
Groovy, excellent, "cool". A word invented by Ramona.

smriendly *(fiction)*
Friendly. A Ramona Bronc word.

smullible *(fiction)*
Gullible. A Ramona Bronc word.

smunking *(fiction)*
Very. A Ramona Bronc word.

snapport *(fiction)*
Support. A Ramona Bronc word.

snealy *(fiction)*
Pushy. A Ramona Bronc word.

snee-snoc *(fiction)*
A derogatory word for a picocian in *Between the Lake and Mountain*.

Sniar Central Airport *(fiction)*
Airport in Brunswick, Georgia, owned by Robert Sniar and used for his commercial ventures.

Sniar Oil, Sniar Oilfield Service *(fiction)*
A company owned by Robert Sniar in the Debbie Dayla stories that drills for crude oil and other natural resources.

snickety *(fiction)*
Quickly. A Ramona Bronc word.

snight *(fiction)*
Night. A Ramona Bronc word.

snonk *(fiction)*
A person with a stuffy, rigid personality. A Ramona Bronc word.

snonkadiliac *(fiction)*
A person suffering from snonkadiliosis. A Ramona Bronc word.

snonkadiliosis *(fiction)*
A make-believe mental disorder where a person is excessively stubborn, rigid, or overly conservative. A Ramona Bronc word.

snonky *(fiction)*
Stubborn. A Ramona Bronc word.

sodium acetate *(real)*
An ingredient along with stainless steel used in an emulsion by Mirini and others to help defeat the aliotrotes.

Solina *(fiction)*
Doctor Belsl's daughter and leader of a rebellion in *Sense of Place.*

Sonic Zonaton Device *(fiction)*
See *SOZOD.*

sonography *(real)*
The study and practice of using sound to form images. "Sonography" is commonly used to mean "ultrasonography" for the purpose of using ultrasonic waves for medical imaging.

sonopicon *(fiction)*
A tubular device somewhat resembling a periscope that allows a person to visualize the surroundings using sound. Erebellasia uses such a device in *Sense of Place.*

Soomadeen *(fiction)*
A skin-restoration lotion, as mentioned in *Between the Lake and Mountain.*

sourfran weed *(fiction)*
An alkaloid weed with a sour taste and pharmacological properties when mixed with other plants. As such, it is used as an ingredient in drug preparations in *Between the Lake and Mountain.*

SOVONK *(fiction)*
A hybrid weapon that uses SOZOD control technology with vonk waves in the Debbie Dayla stories.

SOZOD *(fiction)*
A sonic zonaton device that can be used to drill through various materials in the Debbie Dayla stories.

sozzed *(fiction)*
To be disrupted/destroyed by a SOZOD. The word was used by Debbie Dayla in *The Aimless and the Atlantic*.

Space Shuttle *(fiction)*
An American spacecraft with wings capable of landing as a glider plane.

spongiont *(fiction)*
A sponge symbiont in Lagenora in the Debbie Dayla stories.

squaliapitar *(fiction)*
A radio-reception enhancement circuit used in vattertram radios as mentioned in *For Thy Service*.

squelching *(real)*
In this book, "squelching" refers to the sound the taniculats make. Their "squelching cacophonies" refers to both a sucking and abrupt type of sound.

SRB *(real)*
Solid rocket booster. In launching spacecraft, a solid rocket is attached to the main rocket and provides the extra thrust need to attain orbit or beyond. Solid rocket boosters, once lit, cannot easily be extinguished.

stalactite *(real)*
A cave formation that "holds on tight" to the ceiling.

stalagmite *(real)*
A cave formation that "pushes up with all its might" from the floor.

Stone Age *(real)*
A prehistoric period in human history marked by the use of stone tools. The narrator in *Trechopagia* makes a passing reference to the stone ages meaning that Brenda's family is not one of progress.

subverter *(fiction)*
A rebel group in *For Thy Service*.

subvertian *(fiction)*
Of or having to do with a subverter in *For Thy Service*.

Sueann Kellington *(fiction)*
Owner and operator of Kellington Catering Service in *The Duchess of Darby*.

suflessence *(fiction)*
A paranormal energy that all life forms possess as mentioned in *Suflessence*.

suflessi-agrieco *(fiction)*
Adjective. Anything related to the mixture of suflessence and agriecorsteck. Bedora is burned from suflessi-agrieco radiation.

Sugar Flowers *(fiction)*
A college quarterback that Connie Dayla dates briefly as revealed in *Between the Lake and Mountain*.

Sulfaurium *(fiction)*
A chelation agent that removes mercury from the affected patient's body as mentioned in *Between the Lake and Mountain*.

sunderag *(fiction)*
A vine in *Between the Lake and Mountain* that infects people, causing such people to do the vine's bidding. It is a variant of the sundew plant.

sundew *(real)*
A carnivorous plant of the genus Drosera.

Superdaco *(fiction)*
A superhero dalli porpoise of Phocayna in the Debbie Dayla stories.

Superpyco *(fiction)*
A superhero of the pygmy killer whales of Persipi in the Debbie Dayla stories.

Supreme Queffil Stilillick *(fiction)*
The top-ranking female plant creature living in Slaffton in *Between the Lake and Mountain*. She is wedded to the Master of Slaffton.

Suproc *(fiction)*
The lead judge in Rhynchus in the Debbie Dayla stories.

Suproc Krivat, King Krivat *(fiction)*
King of Rhynchus after King Acus loses his crown. King Krivat was Suproc Krivat and presided over Debbie's and Roger's trial.

Swenett *(real)*
Ancient city which in modern times is known as Aswan. Swenett was the location of the first cataract of the Nile and is mentioned in *Between the Lake and Mountain*.

symbiont *(real)*
An organism living as a part of another.

symbiosis *(real)*
A beneficial arrangement between two organisms living together.

symbiotic *(real)*
Of or having to do with symbiosis.

syncopation *(real)*
An unexpected variety of rhythms in music.

syradermic *(fiction)*
Similar to a hypodermic needle. Used for administering drugs under the skin. Referenced in *Sense of Place* and *For Thy Service*.

Tabiun *(fiction)*
One of three subverters killed by Armich and Metoni while the two traveled in a vattertram in *For Thy Service*.

taniculat *(fiction)*
A highly intelligent life form who designs things in *For Thy Service*.

Tara Farrencamp *(fiction)*
Dana Farrencamp's daughter and an excellent engineer at Farrencamp Digital in *Mirini and the Aliotrotes*.

Tartana *(fiction)*
One of Wonga's names in *Between the Lake and Mountain*.

tassa nelumacaine *(fiction)*
Numbs pain and heals tissue in *Sense of Place*.

Tau *(fiction)*
The main character in *Save for Proper Buyer* who finds a magic vest but whose life changes for the worse.

taurine apple *(fiction)*
An apple in *Suflessence* with taurine that the big cats eat to maintain good health.

telly *(real)*
British slang for television.

The Dallas Sunrise *(fiction)*
A newspaper based in Dallas, Texas. In *The Duchess of Darby*, a journalist from *The Dallas Sunrise* is permitted to cover Duchess Devanna's birthday party.

The Darby Globe *(fiction)*
A newspaper in Darby that receives an invitation to Duchess Devanna's birthday party.

The Four Leaf Clover *(fiction)*
A restaurant in *The Aimless and the Atlantic* where the Daylas enjoy dining.

thoriocyanobiont, thorio *(fiction)*
A symbiont sponge-type life form based on thorium and cyanobacteria.

thoriocyanostigon *(fiction)*
A device for removing cyanobionts from a cetacean's body. Croius uses such a device on Sparfy in *Return from Lagenora.*

thorisponitis *(fiction)*
An infection of the thorium sponge organelles as mentioned in *The Blinners of Gathona.*

Tibbit *(fiction)*
Armich's and Metoni's instructional guide in *For Thy Service.*

tilefish *(real)*
A fish known to contain mercury, and thus people are warned against its consumption.

Today's Snitchline *(fiction)*
A television program segment hosted by Vicia Sniar in *The Aimless and the Atlantic.*

Tom Collins *(real)*
An alcoholic beverage.

transicon *(fiction)*
A short name for Adapto-transicon, a Dayla Industries device.

transicrystal creator device *(fiction)*
A device created by Dayla Industries that is used to create a crystal for the Adapto-transicon.

transuflessiation *(fiction)*
A process whereby suflessence is regenerated inside a person and changes that person's form.

Tree of Ages *(fiction)*
A bonsai tree in *Suflessence* that is worshiped and respected by a group of large cats.

Trey *(fiction)*
Baroness Vasha's head butler in *The Duchess of Darby.*

Trial Arena *(fiction)*
A place where Debbie and Roger Dayla are put on trial by the citizens of Rhynchus for the SOZOD attack.

trilobite *(real)*
A marine arthropod that lived millions of years ago in ancient seas.

Tristan da Cunha *(real)*
An island in the South Atlantic. In the Debbie Dayla stories, this island forms the northwest corner of Lagenora.

tritium *(real)*
A radioactive isotope of hydrogen often used for illuminating points of light on devices such as on watch dials.

trote *(fiction)*
A nickname for aliotrote, as used in *Mirini and the Aliotrotes*.

TRUST *(fiction)*
Von Brock's definition for "TRUST" is "Try Reality, U Stupid Trustaholic" in *Mirini and the Aliotrotes*.

trystypion *(fiction)*
A three-pronged rod device used for medical treatment in *Sense of Place*.

Tuina *(fiction)*
One of Lady Spenwick's assistants in Mother's Hall, from *Sense of Place*.

Tursiopus *(fiction)*
Home of the bottlenose dolphins in Lagenora in the Debbie Dayla stories. Tursiopus is a collection of three islands: Astrala, Truncata, and Aduna. These correspond to the real-world islands of Inaccessible Island, Nightingale Island, and Tristan da Cunha respectively.

TV *(real)*
Short for television.

TV3 *(fiction)*
A television station in the Commonwealth of Darby in *The Duchess of Darby*.

uniont *(fiction)*
A life-form chosen by a thoriocyano sponge to enter into a symbiotic relationship. Cetaceans living in Lagenora with thoriocyanobionts are unionts.

UV *(real)*
Short for ultraviolet light.

V8, V10, V12 *(real)*
These refer to the number of cylinders and the configuration of the cylinders into two lines resembling the letter V in an internal combustion engine.

vaculuxion *(fiction)*
A device in *Sense of Place* used to pull essential energies from a person.

Vance Hall *(fiction)*
A fraternity in Brunswick where Sugar Flowers lives as revealed in *Between the Lake and Mountain*.

Vancha *(fiction)*
One of Wonga's names in *Between the Lake and Mountain*.

Varcher University *(fiction)*
Where Connie Dayla receives a bachelor's degree in *The Aimless and the Atlantic*.

vattertram *(fiction)*
A transportation vehicle in *For Thy Service*.

Velo Scorpion (HP) *(real)*
A recumbent tricycle given to Connie Dayla as a tenth-birthday present.

Vetch *(fiction)*
A fictitious name used by Vicia Sniar while posing as an Audi salesperson.

Vicia Sniar *(fiction)*
Connie's friend and daughter of Robert Sniar in the Debbie Dayla stories.

Viscount Darro of Breyton *(fiction)*
One of four royal men invited to Duchess Devanna's birthday party as a prospective husband in *The Duchess of Darby*.

visicort *(fiction)*
An implant in *The Blinners of Gathona* that taps into a person's memory so that it can be televised for others to watch.

voitran *(fiction)*
Natural cetaceans without any thoriocyanobionts in their cells. Voitrans live and die a natural life and do not have the extended life of the halftrans and the fulltrans. While natural cetaceans really exist, their association with thorium-based cetaceans and thus their classification as voitrans is fictitious.

vonk *(fiction)*
A wave emitted by dolphins and porpoises of Lagenora that can be used as a moving barrier to block or destroy things.

Vorlac *(fiction)*
An attorney in Rhynchus and of Clan Zigo.

waiyo *(fiction)*
A word hummed by porpoises in *The Blinners of Gathona* to help Chusacuta and Circigi return home.

Walter Elbart *(fiction)*
Grandfather of Julie Elbart and founder of Elbart Academy.

waxy wheat *(fiction)*
A special type of wheat that produces wax in *Between the Lake and Mountain*.

WBU Channel 48 *(fiction)*
A television station Vicia Sniar works for in *The Aimless and the Atlantic*.

Weather-Sat Dayla 5 *(fiction)*
A satellite orbiting Earth in *Mirini and the Aliotrotes* that Kyler and Mirini visit in hopes of converting the satellite into a tool to defeat the aliotrotes.

Wenniar *(fiction)*
A science building on the University of Hammencase campus in *Save for Proper Buyer*.

wight *(mythology)*
A form of undead creature capable of taking life from the living.

Wiley *(fiction)*
One of Sueann's workers in *The Duchess of Darby*.

Wilfred *(fiction)*
Queen Cythia's butler in *The Duchess of Darby*.

Wonga *(fiction)*
An evil creature that is part woman, part elder tree in *Between the Lake and Mountain*.

Wonga's Lair *(fiction)*
The residential chamber where Wonga dwells in Sathiakia, in *Between the Lake and Mountain*.

Wretched Cave *(fiction)*
A cave in *Between the Lake and Mountain* that responds to the emotions of those inside of it through the use of illusion.

Yakhont Seamount *(real)*
A seamount in the South Atlantic. The fictional dalli porpoise kingdom of Phocayna is located in Yakhont Seamount in the Debbie Dayla stories.

Yamaha YZ125 *(real)*
A motocross motorcycle produced by Yamaha. Connie Dayla owns such a device in *The Aimless and the Atlantic*.

YF-23 *(real)*
A prototype fighter plane developed by Northrop.

yow *(fiction)*
You. A word used by the inhabitants of Gathona in the distant future in *The Blinners of Gathona*.

yower *(fiction)*
Your. A word used by the inhabitants of Gathona in the distant future in *The Blinners of Gathona*.

zakanazia *(fiction)*
A powerful stimulant in *Sense of Place* that Belsl uses in an attempt to bring Erebellasia to consciousness.

zanvelox *(fiction)*
A general-purpose antidote used by Belsl in *Sense of Place*.

Zdannag Hall *(fiction)*
George Snake's residence in *Between the Lake and Mountain*.

Zellapuvia *(fiction)*
One of many female dalli porpoises that Metavasi enjoys entertaining in the Debbie Dayla stories.

Zenker Seamount *(fiction)*
A seamount in the South Atlantic known as Aita in the Debbie Dayla stories.

zonaton *(fiction)*
A particle that is between an electromagnetic and sound wave. Such particles cause matter to liquefy and harden in the Debbie Dayla stories.